"John Toland brings to his first novel, *Goas of War*, the same gifts for meticulous research and narrative drive that have made him a Pulitzer Prize-winning historian of World War II. Skillfully weaving fact and fiction, he spins out an old-fashioned saga telling the stories of two families connected by marriage—one family American, the other Japanese—from the days before Pearl Harbor through the atom bomb dropped on Hiroshima and Nagasaki . . . an absorbing piece of work."

—*Newsday*

"You have to find out what happens, who survives what tragedy and how, and if the families are ever reunited . . . Toland does have a story to tell."

—*Los Angeles Times*

"Exhibiting the sweep, scrupulous attention to detail, broad humanity and balanced perspective that won renown for *But Not in Shame, The Rising Sun* and others of Toland's historical studies of World War II . . . this is a highly accomplished novel."

—*Publishers Weekly*

"Historical fiction of high quality."

—*Library Journal*

GODS OF WAR

GODS
OF
WAR

JOHN TOLAND

TOR

A TOM DOHERTY ASSOCIATES BOOK

GODS OF WAR

Reprinted by arrangement with Doubleday & Company, Inc.

First Tor printing: November 1986

A TOR Book

Published by Tom Doherty Associates, Inc.
49 West 24 Street
New York, N.Y. 10010

ISBN: 0-812-58900-9
CAN. ED.: 0-812-58901-7

Library of Congress Catalog Card Number: 84-10171

Printed in the United States of America

0 9 8 7 6 5 4 3 2 1

TO THE MATSUMURA FAMILY

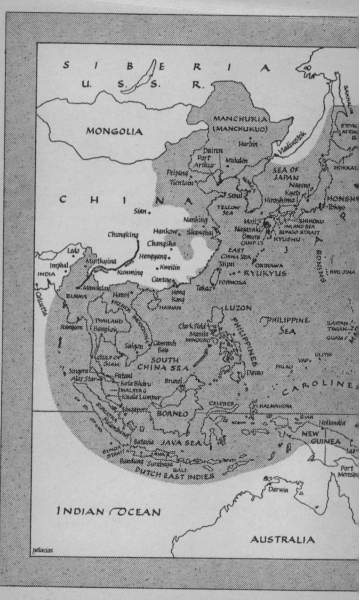

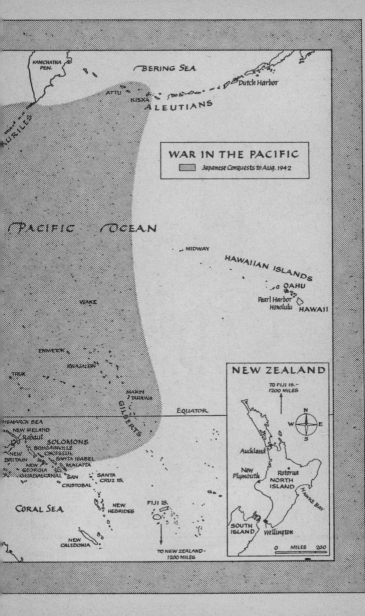

KAMCHATKA PEN.

BERING SEA

Dutch Harbor

ATTU
KISKA
ALEUTIANS

KURILES

WAR IN THE PACIFIC
Japanese Conquests to Aug. 1942

PACIFIC OCEAN

MIDWAY

HAWAIIAN ISLANDS

OAHU

WAKE

Pearl Harbor
Honolulu
HAWAII

ENIWETOK

KWAJALEIN

TRUK

MAKIN
TARAWA

GILBERTS

EQUATOR

NEW ZEALAND

TO FIJI IS.—
1200 MILES

N
W   E
S

BISMARCK SEA
NEW IRELAND
Rabaul
SOLOMONS
BOUGAINVILLE
NEW CHOISEUL
BRITAIN SANTA ISABEL
NEW MALAITA
GEORGIA
GUADALCANAL SAN
CRISTOBAL
SANTA
CRUZ IS.

Auckland

New
Plymouth

Rotorua
NORTH
ISLAND

HAWKE BAY

CORAL SEA

NEW
HEBRIDES

FIJI IS.

NEW
CALEDONIA

TO NEW ZEALAND—
1200 MILES

SOUTH
ISLAND

Wellington

0   MILES   200

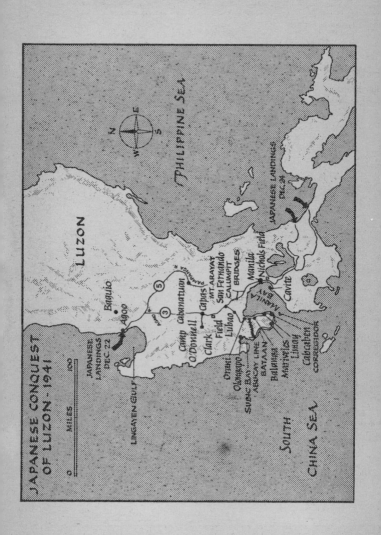

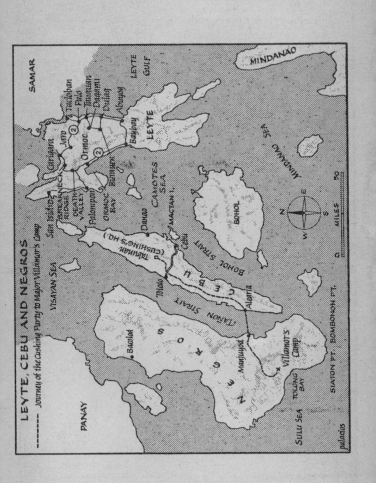

LEYTE, CEBU AND NEGROS
------ Journey of the Cushing Party to Major Villamor's Camp

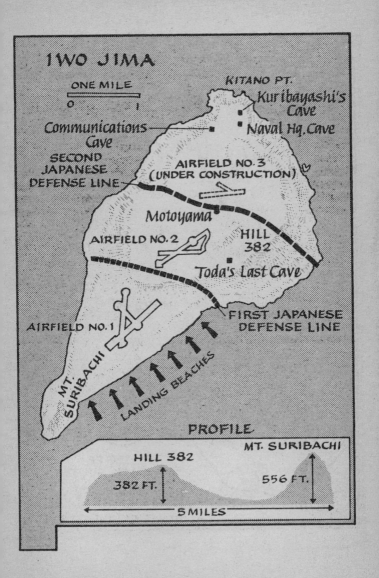

NEW IRELAND

BISMARCK ARCHIPELAGO

Rabaul
NEW BRITAIN

SOLOMON ISLANDS

0 MILES 200

S O L O M O N S

PACIFIC OCEAN

BOUGAINVILLE

CHOISEUL

SHORTLAND

VELLA LAVELLA

NEW GEORGIA

THE SLOT

SANTA ISABEL
FLORIDA
MALAITA
Tulagi

Solomon Sea

N
W   E
S

SAVO
CAPE ESPERANCE

GUADALCANAL

SAN CRISTOBAL

Japanese Attempts to Retake Guadalcanal 1942

0 MILES 10

IRON BOTTOM SOUND

Kokumbona
PT. CRUZ
MATANIKO R.
LUNGA PT.
Henderson Field
ILU R.
TENARU R.
KOLI PT.
Taivu PT.
Tasimboko

LUNGA R.

MT. AUSTEN

BLOODY RIDGE

THREE ATTACK ROUTES

←·—·— Ichiki , (Aug. 21)
←——— Kawaguchi , (Sept. 13-14)
←------ Maruyama , (Oct. 25-26)

Contents

Foreword

Over the past years I have devoted much of my professional life to studying and writing the history of the relationship between the United States and Japan before and during World War II. But even the most scrupulously researched history can be only an approximation of the truth. And that is why I have turned to fiction, the fittest stage for humanity. You will meet invented people, you will read conversations I did not hear and scenes that I did not witness. Despite that, I believe that the story you are about to read is as real as, if not more real than, formal history.

There are also numerous historical personages in this book, and the military units are authentic. Much of the action centers around the 1st Battalion, 6th Marines. I chose this outfit not only because of its outstanding history prior to World War II but because its performance in the Pacific typified, in my opinion, the U.S. Marine Corps. It was a true band of brothers in battle, and remained so in peace. I know of no battalion commander in any army who was more respected or loved than its leader, Lieutenant Colonel (later Lieutenant General) William K. Jones. All the characters in this unit in the following pages, however, are fictional and any resemblance to real persons is coincidental.

The prisoners of war, with a few noted exceptions, are also fictional but the prison camps are factual, excluding Camp 13 in Kyushu which is a compilation of four camps in Japan.

Principal Characters

Father Thomas O'Malley
Private Popov
the Angel
the One-Armed Bandit
Mr. Wada
Lieutenant Wakasugi
Major Susumu "Gentleman Jim" Watanabe
Lieutenant Fred Wilkins
Benny Williams

OTHERS

Father Joseph "Jumping Joe" Callahan
Third Lieutenant Mateo Domingo
Colonel Henry A. "Heavy Hand Hank" Evans
Jack Finn
Hinemoa Finn, his daughter
Shimpei Fujita
Lieutenant Fukuda
Michiko Goto
Hajime Goto, her son
Tamiko Goto, her daughter
Corporal Akira Isobe
Hiroko Kato
Jun Kato, her cousin
Miss Kuroki
Lieutenant Edwin MacDowell
Hideo Maeda
Father Joseph "Big Joe" O'Brian
Major Ricardo Paraguya
The Pocatello Kid
Molly Pritchard
Sergeant Merwin Redd
Socorro
Tomohiko Yabe

HISTORICAL

General Korechika Anami
Father William Cummings, M.M.
Colonel James Cushing
Major Harry Fenton
Vice Admiral Shigeru Fukudome
Professor Kiyoshi Hiraizumi
Major Kenji Hatanaka
Emperor Hirohito of Japan
Secretary of State Cordell Hull
Brigadier General Albert Jones
Corporal Kiyoshi Kamiko
Marquis Koichi Kido

Prime Minister Kuniaki Koiso
Prime Minister Prince Fumimaro Konoye
Saburo Kurusu
General Douglas MacArthur
General George C. Marshall
Rear Admiral Miller ("Skipper Min")
Admiral Osamu Nagano
Katsuo Okazaki
Ernie Pyle
President Manuel Quezon
President Franklin D. Roosevelt
Major General Lemuel C. Shepherd, Jr.
Robert Sherrod
Admiral Shigetaro Shimada
General Holland "Howlin' Mad" Smith
Secretary of War Henry L. Stimson
Field Marshal Gen Sugiyama
Prime Minister Kantaro Suzuki
Lieutenant Colonel Masahiko Takeshita
Hidenari Terasaki
Foreign Minister Shigenori Togo
Prime Minister Hideki Tojo
Colonel Masanobu Tsuji
Captain Tsuneyoshi
General Yoshijiro Umezu
Major Jesus (Jess) Villamor
Lieutenant General Jonathan "Skinny" Wainwright
Lieutenant General Tomoyuki Yamashita
Admiral Mitsumasa Yonai
Shigeru Yoshida

The Gods of War feed on the vanities of men.

Frank McGlynn, *When East Met West*

PART ONE

The Lowering Clouds

CHAPTER ONE

1.

Tokyo. February 25, 1936.

Early that afternoon Tokyo was shrouded by clouds. The city lay under a foot-deep blanket of snow and it was predicted more would fall that evening. Not in fifty-four years had the capital seen such snow. There was little traffic and life seemed to be at a standstill. But beneath the tranquil exterior a plot was brewing that threatened to turn the streets into chaos.

Just outside the ancient stone walls of the spacious Imperial Palace grounds revolt was being plotted at the barracks of the 1st Division by a group of young officers disillusioned by abject poverty and corruption in government and business. The authorities had been warned that these young idealists were to assassinate advisers of the Emperor that very day. Although such violence was not uncommon, the *Kempeitai*, the military police organization, was not too concerned. As a precaution, however, they had already put several suspects under surveillance and provided bodyguards for prominent public officials.

Two cabinet ministers about to set out for the Tokyo Kaikan Building near the Imperial Hotel were grumbling about the embarrassment it would cause. They were bound for a wedding reception, an international social event celebrating the union of two well-known families— one Japanese and one American.

Christian services were already being held a few miles away in Aoyama. Only the families and close friends were present as the bride was escorted up the aisle by her father, the eminent professor of oriental history, Frank McGlynn. Floss, tall and slender, was dressed in the same wedding gown worn by her mother Clara thirty years earlier in the same simple little church. Presiding at that ceremony had been Clara's father, a prominent missionary, Robert Dalrymple, who had objected in vain to the marriage of his daughter to a penniless graduate student in Japan on a year's fellowship from Harvard.

A year later Floss was born, and the headstrong McGlynn had been forced to become an instructor at Aoyama, a college run by the Methodists. In the next seven years he had not only become an associate professor but had published a history of the Meiji Restoration which, to his father-in-law's surprise, brought renown and an offer to teach at his alma mater. He was an immediate success at Harvard. Except for a few victims of his sharp Irish wit, the students worshipped him. Soon after their arrival in Cambridge a son was born. Willard was a bright, happy baby, and to the delight of his father he turned into a bright, happy boy. By 1920 McGlynn had written two more books about Asia to become recognized as one of the nation's leading Japanologists. Clara was one reason for his success. Until meeting her he had doubted he would ever marry, since he could only abide a mate who was his equal. She had been that, a descendant of strong Scottish women, and he had come to depend on her taste, judgment, and grit. That Christmas Eve she gave birth to twins, a boy and a girl. Two days later she died.

McGlynn was stricken. His wit turned to irascibility and, like so many other Irishmen, he took to drink. By mutual agreement he left Harvard, and it had taken Floss to keep the family together. Only fourteen, she became the mother of Mark and Maggie. The only position McGlynn could get was back at Aoyama College. He pulled himself together, became a full professor and wrote two more books, one a highly successful biography of the first American ambassador to Japan which won a Pulitzer Prize in 1931. This brought an offer of a chair in modern history at Williams College. The twins, after years in strict Japanese schools, rose to the top of the freshman class at Williamstown High School, and their father flourished. His lectures were rarely cut and the hall was inevitably crowded with auditors; it was with reluctance that in 1935 the administration agreed to give him a year's leave without pay to research another book in Japan. And so, except for Will, a senior at Harvard, the family had moved back to Tokyo that fall. The twins were now in their last year of high school with Maggie already accepted as a freshman that fall at Bennington and Mark at Harvard. Only then had Floss felt free to marry Tadashi Toda. They had been waiting for five years, deeply in love but not yet lovers. McGlynn had marveled that Tadashi had chosen Floss, for he could have had almost anyone. But time had been kind to Floss. Today she actually looked bonny—thanks, thought her father, to the fact that she had inherited Clara's good bone structure.

As Floss neared the altar her eyes met Tadashi's. Unlike so many Japanese, he managed to look distinguished in tails. He was tall and

20

slender like his father, who watched with pride from the first row. Akira Toda had been brought into Christianity by Clara's father, and had become a close friend of McGlynn's. The strife and misunderstandings between their countries over the years had only strengthened their ties, for each saw the limitations of his own government. On Toda's right sat his wife, Emi, slight and willowy but with an air of authority. She had been a *moga*, a modern girl. On the eve of her arranged marriage in Nagasaki to a banker's son she had refused to go through with the wedding. Hustled off to Tokyo to lessen the family disgrace she had proceeded to embrace Christianity, and since, often to her husband's regret, had embraced social reforms and other unpopular causes.

Like the church itself the ceremony was simple; the only hitch—a minor one at that—came when the groom's younger brother Shogo, spruce in his uniform as a first lieutenant in the Imperial Army, reached into the wrong pocket for the ring.

2.

The wedding party moved in limousines and taxis to the Tokyo Kaikan for the Japanese-style reception. Mark and Maggie rode with their father, who was still angry with his younger son. Just before leaving for church the professor had learned that Mark had turned down the bid from Harvard. Instead he was going to Williams. For years their relationship had been stormy. Mark was a born rebel, impatient and impetuous—his father's son. He was too proud to explain why he had chosen Williams. He did not want to follow Will, who was graduating at the head of his class, was the intercollegiate squash singles champion and a member of the best clubs.

At the Tokyo Kaikan the guests were seated at a score of round tables. Besides relatives, former teachers of the couple, classmates, family friends, and professional associates, there were many notables in addition to the two cabinet ministers. Seated near the head table were officials of the Foreign Ministry, superiors and colleagues of Tadashi who was an assistant to the chief of the American Bureau. After graduating from Tokyo Imperial University, Tadashi had spent three years at the embassy in Washington, then a year at Amherst College studying English and English literature, followed by the welcome assignment to Tokyo. It was Tadashi's dream to return eventually to Washington in a responsible position to help promote good relations with the nation he had grown to love. His love for Floss as well as for America presented difficulties that caused his father grave concern. Marrying an American in these parlous days was not the path to promotion. It had taken help from influential friends of the Toda family in the Foreign Ministry such as Saburo Kurusu, married to an American, and Shigenori Togo, married to a German, to get permission to wed Floss. But the presence of so many important people today was encouraging.

Floss and Tadashi were flanked by their go-betweens, former Ambassador to England Hatano and his wife, close friends of the Todas. Floss had changed into a stylish burgundy satin dress and Tadashi into a dark blue suit he had bought in London. They were, thought McGlynn, about the most striking couple he had seen.

The ceremony began with Ambassador Hatano's congratulations to the bride and groom—he had known them both for years—first in Japanese and then more briefly in English. The gentle but seasoned diplomat followed this with sage advice on marriage. "As an old hand I can testify that life in the foreign service also has many problems. You will face many tests overseas in these critical times, but fortunately you both come from good stock and together will be able to withstand these trials." He looked fondly at the couple. "These are times to try men's souls. We must not compromise our ideals or change our goals. Yet we must proceed with judgment and caution."

Floss knew their old friend was referring to Tadashi's open opposition to those in the Ministry favoring closer ties with Hitler as well as to those militarists who were demanding seizure of North China. Yet dear Tadashi, unlike her feisty father, was not suited for conflict. He was gentle, compassionate, idealistic. These were the traits she had found so appealing, and her maternal instincts, brought forth by being second mother to the twins, had become centered on Tadashi.

As the guests ate and drank, the ambassador called upon the most prestigious guests to congratulate the couple, and their closest friends to relate significant anecdotes. Although McGlynn felt the ceremony was a thinly disguised public display of moral support for the bride and groom, he was moved by the genuine words of praise and affection from Floss's teachers and friends, as well as the statement of Tadashi's superior that the marriage solemnized the warm friendship between two great countries. This was followed by eloquent affirmation in fluent Japanese from the American embassy counselor Eugene Dooman which brought a spontaneous feeling of fellowship throughout the hall.

Even McGlynn, who abhorred sentiment, felt a lump in his throat. It was a joyous occasion despite the underlying understandable disapproval of some of the celebrants to such a mixed marriage.

As the guests were leaving, the chief of the American Bureau took Toda aside. Tadashi, he said, was being sent to a foreign embassy.

"Washington?"

"No."

Toda was apprehensive. "London?"

"I'm sorry. Mexico."

Toda felt as if he had been struck. Punishment for marrying an American had been quick in coming.

As soon as the couple set off in a limousine for their honeymoon at a hot springs resort, Toda took McGlynn aside. Ordinarily the two families would not meet after such a ceremony, but something had come up that should be discussed. The Todas lived in Azabu, a historical area graced by old temples, shops, and residences built long ago by feudal lords. Their rambling home, one of the oldest in Azabu, had a landscaped garden, wooden gate doors, and stepping stones inside leading to the entrance hall.

While Maggie and Mark played Parcheesi with the two youngest Todas—Ko, fourteen, and his seven-year-old sister, Sumiko—Toda took McGlynn to his study. He told about the assignment of Tadashi to Mexico. Both men agreed that it was a form of punishment but nothing could be done. Then Toda confessed that what worried him even more was Shogo. "You must have noticed he wasn't at the reception. He said he had some duty or other to perform, but he is a poor liar."

McGlynn knew his old friend had been distressed by Shogo's refusal to accept his grandfather's offer to go into the family silk business. Instead he had entered the army. Four years earlier, after the assassination of Prime Minister Inukai by radical officers, nine young men had asked to take the place of the assassins on trial and, to show their good faith, enclosed their own nine little fingers pickled in a jar of alcohol. One of those fingers had belonged to Shogo, then a cadet.

"He's a good boy motivated by lofty purposes. Just like his mother! But lately he's got mixed up with a very dangerous group at his barracks." They were convinced that the senior statesmen, those closest to the throne, powerful financiers and bureaucrats, were attempting gradually to corrupt the government and the army for their own selfish

23

interests. "I don't seem to be able to handle the boy. He doesn't realize that I'm only asking him to do what is best for him."

"And what is that?"

"Stay away from those dangerous radicals. It's only common sense."

"I've been trying to cram common sense into Mark for years. I'm afraid, old friend, that you and I are both facing a hopeless situation."

"Why can't he be like Tadashi?"

"Why," said McGlynn wryly, "can't Mark be like Will?"

3.

Shogo and fourteen hundred other rebellious officers and men of the elite troops charged with defense of the Palace grounds were making final preparations for revolt. Just before dawn, attack groups would strike simultaneously at six Tokyo targets. They were about to try to redress the social injustices in Japan through force—assassination—convinced that tradition legitimized such criminal action.

While intricate preparations for these attacks proceeded, pleasure-seekers roamed the darkening streets in search of entertainment in the Ginza, originally a vast swampland noted as duck-hunting grounds but now the romantic symbol of the outside world to young Japanese—a fairyland of neon lights, boutiques, coffee shops, Western-style dance halls side by side with traditional shops and restaurants. A few miles away, in the Akasaka section, the old Japan also anticipated a night of pleasure. Geishas looking like something out of antiquity were pulled in rickshas through the narrow, willow-lined streets. Here lights were muted, and the traditional red lanterns carried by the police gave off a soft, nostalgic glow against the snow.

There was little thought of peril at the official residence of Prime Minister Okada. He was hosting a banquet celebrating the recent victory of his party in the general election of the House of Representatives. Two other men marked for assassination were also enjoying a party several blocks away at the American Embassy. Ambassador Grew was giving a dinner for thirty-six in honor of the replaced prime minister, Viscount Saito, who had just been named Lord Keeper of the Privy Seal. Another guest was Kantaro Suzuki, Grand Chamberlain to the Emperor. The highlight of the evening was the private showing of *Naughty Marietta* starring Jeanette MacDonald and Nelson Eddy. The aged Saito had never attended a sound movie before and Grew expected him to take a nap. But he was so enraptured he stayed to the very end of the show. Scattered flakes of snow drifted down gently as the Saito car finally drove off at half past eleven.

It was not until four o'clock in the morning of February 26 that the rebel leaders routed out their enlisted men, most of whom imagined they were going out on another night maneuver. Snow was now falling steadily in huge flakes as the groups headed for their various destinations in Tokyo.

Another unit, led by Shogo, piled into cars and headed out of the city to kill Count Nobuaki Makino, former Privy Seal and counselor to the Emperor. Finding him registered at a resort hotel in the mountains, they set the building on fire. The count's granddaughter, Kazuko, helped him escape out the rear and when the rebels began firing she stepped in front of the old man, spreading out her kimono sleeves.

Shogo was so impressed by the girl's courage that he ran forward and held out his arms to stop the fusillade. "Success!" he cried. "Now let's get the devil out of here." Several protested that they should finish the job but Shogo managed to induce them to leave.

The violence in Tokyo was incredibly bloody, but after killing seven people the rebels surrendered peacefully the next day. To most foreigners the mutiny was no more than another ultranationalist bloodbath, few realizing its significance. Frank McGlynn did, guessing that this would lead to expansion into China—and possible conflict with the United States.

McGlynn was correct. The mutiny was over but not the causes of discontent, and like a stone tossed into a millpond, its ripples soon began spreading eastward across the Pacific.

CHAPTER TWO

1.

Washington, D.C. July 26, 1941.

It was a sultry Saturday afternoon but the streets of the capital were alive with bustling pedestrians and impatient cab drivers. Everyone seemed bound on a mission of pressing import. The urgency of the widening war in Europe seemed at last to have reached Washington. Although there was not an American uniform in sight as Professor McGlynn descended from a taxi outside the White House, he guessed that many of the purposeful men carrying bulging briefcases were in the service.

A year earlier Roosevelt had asked him to take an indefinite leave from Williams and join his vaunted Brain Trust as adviser on Asia, but he feared conflict over policy with the President's other advisers. McGlynn compromised by agreeing to give occasional counsel, and this was the third time in a year that he had answered the summons. He had left Williamstown annoyed to be leaving his work again but flattered that he might by some wild chance help turn the course of history.

So far the President had taken his advice to continue serious negotiations with the Japanese and not be cozened by Secretary of War Stimson, Secretary of the Interior Ickes, and the China lobby to "get tough with the Japs." Some new crisis must have risen and he guessed it probably had something to do with the sudden invasion of Russia by Hitler the preceding month. An informant in Tokyo had written him that this had resulted in a great battle between the army, which wanted to attack Siberia, and the navy, which wanted to drive south for oil and other resources. It looked as if the former was going to have its way.

The President greeted his old classmate warmly, stretching his arm across the table, grinning broadly. "Understand you just reached three score years. Congratulations! With your Irish temper it's a wonder." For several minutes he recalled their carefree days in Cambridge, reminding McGlynn that he himself would not be sixty for a year, then gently chaffed the professor on his latest book which propounded the theory that America shared the blame with Japan for their growing differences. Critics who had highly praised his other books predicted it was the end of his career.

"I'm not defending Japan," he said. "She is almost solely responsible for bringing herself to the edge of war with us. But her aggression in Manchuria and China has been the inevitable result of Britain's efforts —and ours—to eliminate Japan as an economic rival." Added to this were the Depression, her population explosion, and the necessity to find new resources and markets to continue as a first-rate power, and finally the threat of Communism from both Russia and Mao Tse-tung.

"Don't tell me you're beginning to see Reds under every bed, Frank?"

"When they're there, Mr. President." He leaned forward. "What puzzles me is why so many of your advisers cry Yellow Peril and yet have little apprehension about Japan as a military foe. The intelligence reports you're getting of the low efficiency of Japanese pilots are simply preposterous. Nor are the Japanese ships and planes second-rate. I saw a cartoon the other day showing little buck-toothed Japanese soldiers and sailors as bunglers more to be laughed at than feared. Please don't underrate them, Mr. President. I'm afraid that a sense of racial superiority is subconsciously tempting Mr. Stimson and Mr. Hull to put pressure on you to drive the Japanese to the limit of their forbearance."

"Read this." Roosevelt passed to him the translation of an intercepted cable from the Japanese Foreign Minister to his ambassador in Vichy. The Japanese Army was pushing into Indochina on July 24 no matter what the Vichy Government decided to do. Roosevelt plucked the message from the frowning McGlynn. "You never saw this, of course." He put a new cigarette in his long holder. "The day before the deadline Vichy agreed to the peaceful entry of the Japanese troops." He extended another message, this from the Japanese ambassador in Vichy to the Foreign Minister. "When Hull saw this he stormed in here cussing."

McGlynn read: "The reason why the French so readily accepted the Japanese demands was that they saw how resolute was our determination and how swift our will. In short, they had no choice but to yield." McGlynn slowly, silently handed back the message.

"Hull wants me to impose a new embargo on Japan. One with real teeth. Old Stimson thinks we should order all Japanese assets in America frozen."

McGlynn clenched his fists. "Mr. President, do you know what that means?"

"Yes. All trade with America will cease."

"But, sir, America is the major source of their imports!"

"I'm well aware of that, Frank."

"It's practically a declaration of war."

"I wouldn't go that far."

"The Japanese will certainly take it that way. Try to see it through their eyes. They came into Indochina by negotiation with Vichy France. I know you don't approve of Vichy, but it's a country we recognize and the Japanese have international law on their side."

"It was a takeover. You're beginning to sound like their lawyer, Frank."

"I hope I sound like an historian. This freezing will be taken in Tokyo as the last step in the encirclement of their empire by the ABCD* powers. A denial to Japan of her rightful place as leader of Asia and a challenge to her very existence."

"I hope they see it as a lesson to those who dare to aggress."

"Please think of the consequence, Mr. President. This move will pull the rug from under our friends in Tokyo. And we have many good and powerful friends. The Emperor's chief adviser, Marquis Kido, is a man of peace. So is the Emperor himself. Prime Minister Konoye wants peace. He's a damned fool in some respects, but I'm sure Ambassador Grew has told you how helpful he and many other prominent Japanese have been in trying to bring about a reasonable agreement between our two countries."

Roosevelt chuckled. "Frank, you're a breath of fresh air!"

"Sometimes I think you regard me as a purveyor of hot air."

"You've given me much to chew on," said the President soberly, "and I am very grateful you took your valuable time to give me another history lesson." They shook hands. "Say, that boy of yours, Will, has turned out to be a real help to George Marshall. I think he may turn out to be smarter than you."

"I hope so."

"I also had a little visit from your younger son. He reminds me of you, Frank."

McGlynn was puzzled. Roosevelt was amused. "I only saw him from a distance. He was out front picketing with the American Peace Mobilization."

McGlynn could feel himself redden with embarrassment.

* American, British, Chinese, Dutch

"Don't take it seriously, Frank. Better Red than a young Republican."
His grin was infectious. "And thank you again," he said seriously. "Everything you've told me today makes very good sense, but the realities of politics unfortunately govern our poor world. Even though I don't always take your advice, I want you to know that I do consider it. I assure you I have not yet made up my mind. I repeat, you've given me a lot to chew on. I thank you."

As McGlynn left the White House he thought: Poor Franklin—a cut above all the others here in Washington, but destined to remain a political animal. How could the leader of a nation rich in resources and land and free from fear of attack understand the position of Japan, a tiny, crowded island empire with very few natural resources, fearful of attack from their ruthless neighbor, the Soviet Union? Roosevelt knew that America had contributed to the atmosphere of hate and distrust by excluding the Japanese from immigration, yet could not see that this was flaunting a racial and color prejudice that justifiably infuriated the proud Japanese. Franklin was being misled by his fear of Hitler and his love of England to go along completely with Churchill. And that old rascal would never let democracy pass through the Suez Canal.

There was only one chance in a hundred that his classmate would listen to long-range reason rather than pragmatism regarding the embargo. He swore, then had to smile. There was an endearing quality about Franklin. McGlynn recalled the fall day in 1932 when Governor Roosevelt had passed through Williamstown during his presidential campaign against Hoover. The governor of Massachusetts, Ely, an alumnus of Williams, had urged Roosevelt to speak to the students from his open car. It had stopped on the hill near the chapel. McGlynn and young Mark had been close to the car, and both noticed the fury on Ely's face once the students, almost to a man Republican, booed and refused to let Roosevelt speak. He only smiled good-naturedly as if to say, "just what I expected from a country club college." Somehow this little action had raised Franklin in his esteem more than any of his exuberant speeches. Infuriated at the unfairness, McGlynn had dragged Mark to the next corner where some hundred workers from the factory on the river had gathered. As the car slowly passed, Franklin took off his soon-to-be famous fedora and smiled. It was an embracing smile and the look of adoration on each worker's face as well as the heartfelt ovation that followed remained indelible images. This was a Roosevelt he had never known at Cambridge and the one he still supported despite their numerous differences.

McGlynn flagged a taxi and in ten minutes was at the apartment of Floss and Tadashi, several blocks from the Japanese Embassy on Massachusetts Avenue. Despite the problems of the last five years, her face showed no strain. She was blessed with the same serenity Clara had possessed. After two frustrating years in Mexico dealing with trade arrangements, Tadashi had been sent farther down the ladder to Havana as a minor vice-consul, a post that appeared to be a dead end to his hopes. Then early in 1941 had come the surprising news that he was returning to Washington. His elation was dampened to learn on arrival that he had been brought there only because of his fluent command of English. As he was one of Ambassador Nomura's principal interpreters, it was his primary task to familiarize himself with all documents—both American and Japanese—dealing with the negotiations between Japan and America. Nomura, an admiral, rarely asked for his advice, relying instead on his own long acquaintance with the President. "I am a friend of Japan," Roosevelt, on greeting him to his post as ambassador, had said. "You are a friend of America who knows our country well. And so we can talk frankly." Unfortunately Nomura's talk was almost exclusively with Secretary of State Hull, a stubborn Tennessean convinced that the Japanese could not be trusted.

Tadashi had tried to warn the ambassador that Hull's show of personal friendship was only a façade and that he was completely under the influence of the pro-Chinese advisers on his staff. By now it was obvious to Tadashi that the negotiations were deteriorating. He recalled his grandfather, the silk trader, telling him of the black ships that had carried the red barbarians of America uninvited to the sacred land of Nippon. The old man would sing a song in his faded voice:

> They came from a land of darkness,
> Giants with hooked noses like mountain imps;
> Giants with rough hair, loose and red.
> They stole a promise from our sacred master
> And danced with joy as they sailed away
> To the distant land of darkness.

The Americans kept coming back, explained the grandfather, but they never understood the sacred land, and the people of the sacred land learned from the red barbarians only things that made them discontent. The ships were still sailing back and forth, thought Tadashi, but the two lands were farther apart than ever. A few like himself had learned that there were no major differences. But the red barbarians and the children of the gods had not yet found this out.

In his heart Tadashi felt war was inevitable. What would happen to Floss and their five-year-old son, Masao? He kept telling Floss there was really nothing to worry about; it was inconceivable that there could be a collision between their two countries. But she knew better. She pretended to believe his words of optimism and appeared to be as buoyant and cheerful as ever.

After dinner Will arrived, apologizing for not being able to come earlier. His gawky Jimmy Stewart walk was deceptive, as his opponents on the squash court had learned to their dismay. Deceptive also was his slow, almost countrified speech, as his opponents in debates had also learned. After graduation from Harvard Law School near the top of his class he had clerked for Supreme Court Justice Frankfurter. Last year Frankfurter had suggested that he accept a commission in the army to serve on General George Marshall's staff. Reasoning that war was inevitable, Will had complied. He was an admirer of Roosevelt, convinced that the New Deal was the wave of the future. And if there was anything he truly believed in, it was being on the winning team. One must play the game fairly and lose or win gracefully. But it was far better to win than to lose and Will had almost always done that. Still, he had been genuinely modest after winning the national squash championship, and he eventually made a good friend of the man he beat. Will had tried to teach this lesson to Mark. They had always been close, but Mark was never one to listen to practical advice. At Williams he had refused to join a fraternity and seemed to make a career out of hanging around every oddball on the campus. He seemed almost compulsively to choose the hardest road.

Will greeted his father warmly. "Understand you were in the Oval Office again today." He was proud of McGlynn's friendship with the President, but could not understand why he had refused to become one of his regular advisers like Harry Hopkins. How could he choose to remain in a small college when he could walk the corridors of power?

Will guessed from his father's grunting answer that he had not been able to dissuade FDR from invoking the embargo. His own shop had been in an uproar all day making contingency plans. Both Marshall and his opposite number in the navy, Admiral Stark, had been advising the President to do nothing drastic since they were not yet ready for war in the Pacific. Both again urged concentration on Hitler. The general had shown Will a warning from the War Plans Division of the navy that such an embargo would probably result in an early Japanese attack on Malaya for oil; and possibly involve the United States in early war in the Pacific.

As usual the talk in Tadashi's presence was guarded. There was no mention of the growing danger of war. The main topic was Mark. He had always been unpredictable and pigheaded, complained McGlynn. At Williams he had insisted on working and living on campus in the poor boys' dorm. After his sophomore year he announced he was going to hitchhike to California and he didn't return until the day before school began. The next summer he again refused to go to the family cottage on Squam Lake. Instead he rode freight trains, sending back a series of blank postcards addressed to Floss indicating where he was. At Williams he made so much money as an entrepreneur—running special trains to New York, establishing a typing agency, and managing the student bookstore—that a Standard Oil scout had offered him an excellent position after graduation. Instead he had spent the summer again riding freight trains and then left for New York City to join the Communist Party. Presently he was selling Singer sewing machines in the daytime and helping organize street rallies at night. What particularly irked McGlynn was that Maggie had followed her twin to New York to become a cub reporter on the *Herald Tribune*.

Floss couldn't keep from smiling at McGlynn's complaint that Mark seemed doomed to obey every impulse.

"What's so funny?" he asked.

Floss wanted to say, "Just like his father." So many of the professor's problems had come from his own need to obey that impulse. He and Mark were so much alike. Both had quick tempers but never held a grudge. Both were rebellious and opinionated, and impatient. Both were inveterate defenders of the underdog, impatient and impulsive. Papa, born a Catholic, had quit parochial school in the seventh grade when a nun beat him unjustly on the hand with a metal ruler. He had stubbornly insisted on attending a public school and later had infuriated his father by refusing to go to Notre Dame. Instead he left Sioux Falls, South Dakota, for the most effete school in the effete East.

Tadashi listened to McGlynn without comment, thinking of his own disagreements with his father. Perhaps he should not have ignored his wise counsel not to marry Floss. The jangling phone brought him back to reality. He answered it and paled. There was a report, he announced, that the President had just ordered all Japanese assets in America frozen. He excused himself and hurriedly left for the embassy.

On the cab ride to his hotel McGlynn silently cursed the fools who had persuaded the President to make such a blunder. The two countries he loved were set on destruction. Both Roosevelt and the Emperor wanted peace, but each was shackled by the restrictions of his own culture and political system. Even the Japanese militarists were not culprits, but men caught up in a feudal system. Nor were Stimson, Hull, and Ickes villains, even though they had committed a fatal mistake by driving their opponents into a corner, giving them little alternative to capitulation but war.

The villain was the times, and McGlynn feared for his children. What a terrible fate for Floss! And both Maggie and Mark were so filled with energy that they would somehow get themselves dangerously involved. Possibly only sensible Will would survive; he would be safe with Marshall in Washington.

His thoughts turned to Japan. The Todas and his other friends were doomed. How could little Nippon stand against a mighty force like America? She would be crushed and her people, civilians as well as military, were fated to suffer unimaginable hardships and tragedies.

While Floss waited for the return of Tadashi she wondered what would become of them all if war broke out. Would they be interned for the duration? If so, it would be hardest on Tadashi since he would blame himself for their predicament.

2.

Back in New York, Mark and Maggie heard the news at Sunday breakfast. They shared the bottom floor of a tiny cottage on West 143rd Street near Riverside Drive. Both realized it meant a long step toward war. Maggie couldn't help thinking that although war was terrible, it would give her the chance to realize her great ambition. Since McGlynn had taken her to Europe two summers ago and introduced her to Sigrid Schulz, she knew she would not be happy until she too became a foreign correspondent. Just watching Sigrid, barely five feet tall, stand up to the Nazi press representatives had inspired Maggie to emulate her. And war would mean openings in both Europe and Asia.

Mark was confused and dejected. Before Hitler's invasion of Russia his real life had started at dusk. No place in the world had been as exciting as New York City in the progressive fight for peace. For Mark had not only been involved in neighborhood American Peace Mobilization street rallies, but had also served as a delegate to a nationwide left-wing peace symposium and attended major rallies in Madison Square Garden and other large halls. At these meetings he met many interesting young radicals but never realized his hope of finding a beautiful communist girl. The best he could date was a dynamic union organizer known as Red Rosa. He was infatuated by her animal vitality but his passion cooled when she passed on crabs. Being a gentleman, Mark could not give the real reason he had dropped her so abruptly, and was reproached by his comrades.

He had become a Communist since it was the only party that was genuinely for the underdog. It was also the only party that fought anti-Semitism and Jim Crow and came out for peace. But after the invasion of Russia in June, when the party turned the APM instantly into a war group, Mark had protested. He still believed in peace, and how could you call it an imperialist war on Saturday and a democratic war on Sunday? It had taken a persuasive official from downtown to bring Mark back into line and he had spent a few weeks selling *The Daily Worker* at the I.R.T. yards as the subway employees left work late in the afternoon. He enjoyed the challenge at first and soon had half a dozen regular customers, a remarkable feat that brought him back into favor. Even so, he chafed under party discipline and his main interest in life became a new romance with an attractive Jewish girl named Miriam he had picked up at the Thalia movie theater. Twice a week he brought her to the little cottage on 143rd Street. Maggie did not approve, since the girl worked at a cookie factory, but obligingly made sure to be out of the house whenever Mark was entertaining.

"I'm going out," said Mark and set off for another of his long tours of Washington Heights. He was disgusted with the party, bored with selling sewing machines, and beginning to regret he had become so infatuated with Miriam. She was a sweet, good-natured girl and he had been intrigued by her stories of the perils of working in a cookie factory, such as avoiding the amorous clutches of the older women. But she was now talking about marriage.

CHAPTER THREE

1.

Tokyo. July 28, 1941.

The New York *Times* on Sunday characterized the embargo as "the most drastic blow short of war," but as McGlynn had foreseen, Nippon's leaders took it as a challenge to Japan's very existence. In Tokyo it was Monday, the twenty-eighth. Still in a state of shock, Naval Chief of Staff Nagano first assured the Emperor that he wanted to avoid war and this could be done by revoking the Tripartite Pact which the navy had always maintained was a stumbling block to peace with America. Then he warned that their oil stock would last only two years and concluded, "Under such circumstances, we had better take the initiative. We will win."

The Emperor was an unlikely-looking monarch, slouching around the Palace in baggy trousers with tie askew, dreamingly peering through glasses as thick as portholes. He was so oblivious to his appearance that occasionally his Western-style jacket would be fastened with the wrong button in the wrong hole. But looks were deceiving. He was shrewd enough to see that Nagano made poor sense. In his brief counsel he had put in a word for peace, cleared the navy of responsibility for any diplomatic disaster, prophesied an oil famine, suggested a desperate attack, and predicted victory. The insignificant, round-shouldered monarch, who looked and acted like a village mayor, still had some of the qualifications of a great man. He was free of pride or ambition, desiring only what was best for his people.

"Will you win a great victory?" he asked. "Like the Battle of Tsushima?" He was referring to the crushing defeat of the Russian fleet in 1905.

"I am sorry but that will not be possible."

"Then," said His Majesty grimly, "the war will be a desperate one."

Akira Toda was in his office at the Nippon Steel Building checking the feasibility of setting up a combined mine and steel mill in Central

China. After graduating from the Tokyo College of Foreign Languages, where his father had sent him to prepare him to take over the family silk-trading firm, he had spent a boring year with the firm before getting reluctant permission to seek more compatible work.

He was interrupted by a phone call from a college classmate, Tomohiko Yabe. Both had been prize pupils of their English teacher, a descendant of Lord Tennyson, and had consequently met many important Westerners. Tomohiko now was second secretary to Marquis Kido, the Lord Privy Seal and the Emperor's chief adviser. "I must see you at once," he said in English as if he feared the telephone call might be intercepted by the *Tokko,* the Special Secret Service Police.

Toda was so puzzled by the concern in his friend's voice he agreed to meet him in Hibiya Park. Half an hour later Yabe was telling him of the embargo. It was shocking news to Toda, who had been too busy to read any papers. He was thoughtful, making the curious sucking noise through his teeth which most foreigners thought was hissing, then said, "Stupid, stupid!"

"The Privy Seal is most concerned," said Yabe. "He asked me to inquire cautiously of a few close friends with Western connections. Might it be a good idea to arrange a private meeting between Prime Minister Konoye and the President?"

Toda had learned from McGlynn of Roosevelt's predilection for unique actions. "I think it might appeal to the President. Of course, Stimson and Hull and others would strongly oppose, but perhaps there is one chance in ten of success. We should try it anyway, otherwise . . ." He never finished the sentence but his friend knew what he meant and hurried off to pass on this information to Kido.

Toda wandered through the park. The chances of peaceful negotiation seemed small. He knew the Privy Seal vigorously opposed Japan's rising militarism and the growing sense of desperation in high places that were leading Japan toward war with the United States. The Emperor also was a man of peace, but rash American actions like the embargo were only provoking the militarists and making war inevitable.

He knew that Japan would not have a chance against America's overwhelming industrial power. What future would there be for his three sons? All had inherited their mother's rather alarming sense of independence and idealism. Their oldest son had married an American, well knowing it would impede his career as a diplomat. Ko, the youngest, was studying law at Tokyo Imperial University but spent most of his time painting and openly criticizing militarism. Emi had nagged until he had finally agreed to send the boy to Paris during the long vacation. But the middle son, Shogo, was still his greatest concern. Fortunately he had not been arrested after the abortive 1936 mutiny, but Shogo had since become a devout follower of Colonel Masanobu Tsuji, whose brilliant maverick spirit inspired fanatic devotion among younger radical officers. They revered him as Japan's "God of Operations," the hope of the Orient. He dreamed of making Asia one great brotherhood, an Asia for the Asians. And that could be attained only by driving all Westerners out of the continent by force.

War Minister Tojo had seen the genius in Tsuji but also the madman, and had exiled him to Formosa; and Shogo, one of his assistants, had willingly followed him.

2.

At the Imperial Household Building, located near the Imperial Palace, Yabe was reporting his findings to the Privy Seal. Despite the long odds, Marquis Kido decided to attempt to arrange the meeting of the two heads of state. Preferring to stay in the background, Kido passed on the task of approaching Konoye to Yabe.

The latter had met Konoye on many formal occasions, but this would be their first personal meeting and he wondered how he would accomplish his task. A prince by birth and a socialist by inclination, Konoye had such a variety of interests that he could empathize with those of conflicting political beliefs. Consequently each imagined Konoye to be in agreement. It took him long to reach any decision. Yet once he did so it was well nigh impossible to change his mind.

Yabe also was aware that Konoye gave the appearance of being democratic, in line with the socialist leanings, and treated all alike with courtesy. But his innermost self remained aristocratic. Didn't he come from the Fujiwaras, just as good a family as the Emperor's?

Konoye greeted Yabe cordially. First they talked of America, for Yabe's friendship with foreigners was well known. Then Konoye asked how the Privy Seal's golf game was progressing—he was known as "Kido the Clock" for his precise swing—and smiled appreciatively when Yabe replied, "Same as usual." With some embarrassment Yabe changed the subject by bringing up Kido's suggestion. The prince acted as if he had not heard.

Afterward Yabe reported his failure to Kido, but he only smiled and said, "Wait." Several days later Konoye summoned the heads of the army and navy, announcing that he proposed to meet privately with Roosevelt to settle once and for all the question of China. "If the talks are carried out with broad-mindedness, I am sure we can reach agreement. I promise you I'll be neither too hasty nor anxious to come to terms, nor will I assume a supercilious manner or act submissively."

Both War Minister Tojo and the navy minister were impressed, but refused to commit themselves before consulting their colleagues. The idea was received enthusiastically by the navy but Tojo found disagreement in his ranks. He wrote Konoye that although it was feared the summit meeting would weaken Japan's current policy, the army would go along with the meeting provided the prince promised to lead the war against America if Roosevelt refused to understand Japan's position.

Next morning Konoye advised the Emperor of his intentions. His Majesty, briefed by Kido, acted as if he knew nothing. "You had better see Roosevelt at once," he said. The proposal was received politely in Washington but with little enthusiasm. Were the Americans merely playing for time? Each day's delay meant consumption of twelve thousand tons of precious oil.

This feeling of desperation overshadowed the session of the liaison conference which started at eleven on the morning of September 3. This was an informal meeting of the prime minister, foreign minister, war minister, and navy minister with the army and navy chiefs. "With each day we will get weaker and weaker until finally we won't be able to stand on our feet," protested Naval Chief of Staff Nagano. "Although I feel sure that right now we have a chance to win the war, I'm afraid this chance will vanish with the passage of time." There was no way to check the enemy's queen—their industrial potential—and the initial victory had to be decisive. "Our only chance is to strike first!"

The army chief of staff sprang to his feet and shocked the civil members by proposing a dangerous new element—a deadline. "We must try to achieve our diplomatic objectives by October 10. If this fails we must dash forward. Things cannot be allowed to drag out."

Prince Konoye did not object and after seven hours of discussion it was agreed that they would negotiate sincerely for peace until October 10—and then wage war against America, Britain, and the Netherlands.

Operational plans for war had already been completed. There would be simultaneous attacks at Pearl Harbor, Hong Kong, Malaya, and the Philippines. Curiously, the navy had not informed General Tojo of the planned attack on Pearl Harbor until that moment.

It was in Konoye's nature to delay, and he did not return to the office of the Lord Privy Seal for two days. Then he finally revealed that he had to request an imperial conference to make the recent decision official. It was scheduled to take place the next morning. Twenty minutes before it was to start, the Emperor sent for Kido. "Can Japan win a war against America?" he asked. The Privy Seal was dubious. "What about negotiations in Washington?"

Kido's answer was to advise the Emperor to remain silent at the meeting. "But once the discussion ends, Your Majesty should break precedent." Kido paused, for what he was about to propose went against everything the Emperor had been taught: He should cease to reign and momentarily rule. That is, he must take direct personal action. "Instruct the chiefs of staff to cooperate with the government in negotiating successfully." Only such a dramatic break in tradition, Kido explained, could reverse the potential disaster of the deadline policy.

At exactly ten o'clock the military and civilian leaders of Japan filed somberly into the conference room, each man aware that the fate of Nippon was at stake. The military was convinced that war was inevitable, and a few of the civilians agreed. Those opposed knew there was little chance to turn the tide but had promised Kido to protest. The Emperor sat on his throne implacable as a statue.

After the military explained that war must be waged unless Japan's minimum needs were met, privy council president Hara, a staunch civilian supporter of Kido, asked the supreme command, "Will the emphasis be placed on diplomacy or belligerency?"

There was an embarrassed silence. His Majesty stared at the conferees and then did what none of his ancestors had ever done. He spoke out in his loud, high-pitched voice, "Why don't you answer?"

He had abandoned his passive role as Emperor who reigns but does not rule. His listeners were stunned to hear his voice. After a long, painful moment the navy minister rose. "We will start war preparations, but of course we will also exert every effort to negotiate." He sat down and there was a long pause as the members waited for one of the chiefs of staff to speak. But both men sat as if paralyzed.

"I am sorry the supreme command has nothing to say," said the Emperor. Taking a piece of paper from his pocket, he read:

> "All the seas, everywhere,
>   Are brothers one to another
> Why then do the winds and waves of strife
>   Rage so violently through the world?"

The listeners, military and civilian alike, sat awed. They knew this was a poem written by his grandfather. No one could speak in the face of such censure. The members could scarcely breathe. "I make it a rule to read this poem from time to time to remind me of Emperor Meiji's love of peace. How do you feel about all of this?"

At last the naval chief of staff forced himself to stand. Head bowed, he mumbled an apology for not replying. The army chief of staff also rose. He floundered an explanation. "However, I'm overawed to hear His Majesty tell us directly that His Majesty regrets our silence." He assured the Emperor that the supreme command would certainly give first consideration to diplomacy, not war.

The Emperor had done his utmost and now was compelled to approve with his seal the decision to commence hostilities unless the negotiations were concluded by October 10. The decision was made, but Hirohito's displeasure left a sense of doubt even among the military. And the civilians inwardly felt a surge of hope, a last chance to win peace.

3.

In Formosa, Tsuji had been assigned the apparently useless project of gathering data on tropical warfare in Southeast Asia. Instead of feeling sorry for himself he had thrown all his considerable energies into creation of a brilliant operation to take Malaya.

Through his own resources he discovered that the island of Singapore, connected to the tip of the Malay Peninsula by a causeway eleven hundred yards long, was an impregnable fortress from the sea. But there were almost no defenses in the rear and it was from this direction that Tsuji planned his attack.

He had assigned Shogo and another officer to act as secret agents and explore all of Southeast Asia for firsthand information. Shogo, with fanaticism equal to Tsuji's, studied the languages and geography of Burma, Thailand, and Malaya. Already he had spent so much time in the last country that he was familiar with its history, people, and terrain. Posing as an agronomist, Shogo spent weeks in Malaya. He bribed local officials who let him photograph key beach areas as well as the strategic strait between the tip of Malaya and Singapore Island. Scores of talks with natives, many of high rank, uncovered the strengths and weaknesses of the British defenses and convinced him that Malaya could be taken only by unorthodox methods.

Armed with this information, Tsuji had then secretly conducted maneuvers on Hainan, a large island in the Gulf of Tonkin. Here he tested new concepts of landing operations. Formerly it had been considered suicidal to send men and horses in transports to the tropics. Tsuji had insisted it was only a matter of training, discipline, and spirit, and he kept horses and men in the sweltering holds of ships for a week with almost no water. The men had been so inspired by Tsuji that they made a successful beach landing under bad conditions.

In the meantime, friends at army headquarters had persuaded Tojo to utilize Tsuji's remarkable operational talents. He and Shogo were recalled to Tokyo and ordered to plan an operation to seize Malaya. They arrived to find many of the general staff officers urging an attack on the Russians. Hitler was obviously going to crush the Soviets on the western front.

At dinner the following night an argument broke out at the officers' mess. Tsuji heatedly argued for going south. "Japan will be staking her national destiny if she goes to war, so why aid Hitler in his fight with Russia? If Germany wins and seizes Russia and Siberia east of Lake Baikal, what gain will there be for Japan or for Asia? Hitler is just another red barbarian from the West." All the whites had to be thrown out of Asia.

Shogo felt a thrill of pride just to be sitting next to Tsuji. Officers from other tables had crowded around to hear what he had to say, and Shogo could see on many faces the eager light of converts. "For the past century or more," continued Tsuji, raising his voice so everyone could hear, "Britain has ruled ten times as many of the peoples of Asia as has Russia. Singapore is the key to Southeast Asia. Its seizure will emancipate the oppressed peoples of Asia and will also exert a powerful influence to bring about the settlement of the China Incident." He stood up. "No war with Russia!" he exclaimed. "Attack to the south!"

That night before retiring Tsuji confessed to Shogo that he detested most of the older headquarters officers. "They are only working for their medals. They spend too much time going to parties and playing

41

with geishas." Once, in a fit of moral indignation, Tsuji had burned down a geisha house filled with fellow officers. "I know they hate me because I have the nerve to speak out as I did tonight. Even so I think the supreme command will agree with me."

He was right. Within a few days it was decided to risk Japan's diminishing oil supply on a single operation to the south. In late September Tsuji and Shogo flew to Saigon to draw up the final operational plan. For this Tsuji would need exact information about the tides of the beaches he had finally chosen for the invasion. He also needed a study of the terrain from the landing area to the Singapore causeway. As insurance, Tsuji dispatched two men, Shogo and a bright staff officer named Asaeda. Previously Shogo had been disguised as a carelessly dressed, myopic scientist. Now he was a ragged peasant and passed without notice in the towns of Singora and Patani. Within two days he knew everything about the beaches and he headed south on foot toward Singapore.

In little more than two weeks Shogo and Asaeda were back in Saigon sitting cross-legged on mats in the operations room explaining on a spread-out map what the situation was. There would be a northeast monsoon the middle of November and seas three meters high would break against the beaches. There would be some losses. At the same time few Thai troops defended the area and there were no barbed wire entanglements or pillboxes. The roads to Singapore were not good; trucks would find rough going.

On hearing this last, Tsuji said, "Bicycles." There was a silence, and his staff wondered if he was joking. "Bicycles," he repeated. "It will catch the British by surprise." His enthusiasm was catching. Those higher up were dubious but the commanding general liked the idea, particularly after Tsuji assured him that most of the bicycles could be commandeered from the natives.

Tsuji increased the tempo of work as he and his staff sweated out the operational details of the campaign. He worked with almost no sleep and would eat only when Shogo shoved food at him. The colonel was obsessed with the conviction that whether Japan would win or lose the war depended solely on him, and his fanaticism spread to his subordinates. The number of those suffering from night blindness and nervous prostration increased. It seemed impossible to finish in time.

Sitting on his mat one night, Tsuji vowed to the gods that he would abstain from wine and tobacco until the task was finished. Shogo found him in what seemed like a trance. But Tsuji turned and said, "I am abandoning worldly passions, lust and appetite. Even life and death. My whole mind is concentrated on gaining the victory." He stared ahead, his shaven head shining with sweat. "We will win," he chanted. "We will win."

4.

Tokyo. October 17, 1941.

The announcement by Secretary of State Hull in early October that the proposed meeting between the President and Konoye would have to be postponed hastened the latter's resignation as prime minister. On the seventeenth the *jushin*, the seven ex-premiers, selected Tojo as his replacement. The general was at his modest little home, wondering what would become of him. He knew that His Majesty would be unhappy for his leading role in the fall of Konoye. Where would they now assign him? To some minor post in China? His wife called him to the phone. It was the Grand Chamberlain, who said without explanation, "Come to the Palace at once." Tojo hurriedly stuffed into his briefcase papers that might support his position.

He sat tensely in the staff car that took him to the Palace grounds and by the time he entered the Palace he was sure his career was over. He felt a sense of awe as he was silently led from the waiting room to the presence of His Majesty, and he at first doubted his ears upon hearing the Emperor order him to form a cabinet. "We believe that the nation is facing an extremely grave situation. Bear in mind that the army and navy should, at this time, work in even closer cooperation. We will later summon the navy minister to tell him the same."

Tojo's throat was dry but he finally managed to request time to consider and backed out to the waiting room. What should he do? To be premier was a great honor but could he serve His Majesty and the nation well in such a position? While he was still struggling for an answer Kido joined him. The Privy Seal had engineered Tojo's selection and had already advised His Majesty to ask Tojo to reconsider the September 6 decision for war. Such an extraordinary act by the Emperor could force the most powerful military men in the nation to think in terms of peace. Kido was counting on Tojo's reverence for His Majesty to follow this request.

"With regard to the decision on our *kokutai* [national essence]," he said, "it is the Emperor's wish that you make an exhaustive study of domestic and foreign conditions—without regard to the decision of the September 6 imperial conference. I convey this to you as an order of the Emperor."

Tojo stared at Kido in astonishment. This was unprecedented in Japan's long history. Never before had an Emperor rescinded a decision of the imperial conference.

"You are ordered," said Kido, a small but imposing figure, "to go back to blank paper. You must start with a clean slate and negotiate in all sincerity with America for peace."

Tojo was still dazed. He could not fully comprehend what had happened to him in the past few minutes. He was stuck for words at first but finally managed to say, "I accept the responsibility thrust upon me by the Emperor." He left the Palace hardly knowing what he was doing, and asked to be driven to Yasukuni Shrine where Japan's war dead were sanctified.

The purpose of the shrine was to comfort the souls of fallen soldiers. It being the autumn festival, *Reitaisai*, many family members were on hand to pay their respect to relatives who had died in war by presenting rice, sake, fish, cakes, vegetables and dry food. Tojo's car entered the shrine grounds and stopped at the Hall of Arrival. He walked in, signed the guest book and was led by a priest to the *Temizusha*, the little temple of purifying water, to rinse his mouth and wash his hands. Then Tojo was escorted to the Hall of Worship where the priest expelled evil spirits by waving the branch of a sacred tree.

They marched solemnly, silently, up the stone steps of the Main Hall. At the top was a table on which lay the *tamagushi*, a ceremonial cone. The priest handed it to Tojo who set it on another table facing the altar where the gods were enshrined. Tojo bowed twice, clapped his hands twice and bowed again. "I face a completely new life," he told himself. "From this moment I shall think as a civilian, not as a soldier. Mine shall be a national, not a military cabinet. Above all, I shall follow scrupulously the wishes of the Emperor."

The ceremony over, Tojo and the priest returned to the Hall of Arrival where they sipped green tea. Later, on the drive back to his residence, Tojo felt unwonted tears surging to his eyes and vowed to live by this motto: "To have the Emperor as the mirror of my judgment." Every action he planned, every decision he made he would take to the Emperor. If His Majesty's mirror was clear, Tojo would then proceed. But if it was clouded even slightly, he would reconsider.

5.

Five days later Toda's middle son was jammed into an unmarked, un-armed twin-engine plane with Tsuji. They had left Saigon at dawn on an espionage mission. Tsuji wanted Shogo to point out to him the beaches they were to storm. Both men were wearing air force uniforms in case they were forced to land in British territory. By now they had crossed the Gulf of Siam and before them the eastern coast of Malaya grew clearer. Shogo pointed to the left. "Kota Bharu!" he shouted through cupped hands. This was the northernmost town of British Malaya. Shogo then pointed to the right at two smaller coastal towns. "Patani and Singora!"

"Down! Get lower!" Tsuji told their pilot through the speaking tube. The plane dropped until they could distinguish the waves on the beaches of Singora. "Good!" shouted Tsuji. His eyes glistened. It was just as he had imagined, and he could picture his troops splashing to the shore. As they approached a pitifully small airport, they could clearly make out rubber plantations on both sides of the main road. Tsuji aimed his camera, snapped several pictures. "One battalion!" he shouted against the wind to Shogo. He knew that Tsuji meant a single good battalion could grab the airfield and use it as a base of operations.

They climbed and veered toward the west coast of Malaya. Rain spattered against the fuselage, then became a downpour so heavy that Tsuji asked the pilot to drop lower. Suddenly, at 6,500 feet, through the haze, appeared a large airfield.

"Alor Star!" said Shogo. This was a British base.

They headed south and to Tsuji's surprise came upon two more equally impressive airdromes. He ordered the pilot to head north again. In half an hour they found two more large British bases. Shogo was as stunned as Tsuji. All but one of those bases were new to him. Either they had been recently built or he had missed them. In any case, he felt humiliated.

The pilot reported that they were running low on fuel. "End the reconnaissance," said Tsuji regretfully. They turned back toward Saigon. After they came to a smooth landing the pilot cut his motor and turned around with a big grin. "Ten minutes' fuel left, sir."

"I saw all I wanted to see," said Tsuji. "Now I know we will win."

As they walked off, Shogo expected a dressing-down but Tsuji said, "We can't use Singora as a base." Their own planes would be immediately wiped out by attacks from the new British airfields. "We must seize Alor Star and Kota Bharu at any sacrifice. And soon after we land."

The two drove in their staff car to the office of the new commander of the 25th Army without changing uniforms. Tokyo had decreed that General Yamashita, a forceful man, should take charge of the battle. After reporting their findings, Tsuji went to the large map of Malaya. "We must devise new operations for simultaneous landings at Singora, Patani, and Kota Bharu." The troops at the first two beaches, he said, would seize the strategic bridge over the Perak River and occupy the Alor Star airdrome. "The others must take Kota Bharu and its air base without delay and then push down the east coast toward Singapore."

Yamashita and his staff asked a few questions before unanimously approving Tsuji's plan. A few days later the drastic revisions were ratified by Imperial Headquarters.

6.

To the dismay of his comrades in arms, Tojo kept his vow and took over the premiership as a civilian, holding off the disgruntled military while the diplomats continued negotiations in Washington. On the last day of October he insisted that they consider three possible courses: to avoid war; declare war at once; or continue negotiations but be ready to wage war if necessary. "Personally," he said, "I hope that diplomacy will bring peace."

The crucial liaison conference that followed the next day in the Imperial Courtroom opened acrimoniously. Chief of Staff Sugiyama and the other military men were disgusted. Tojo was sounding more like a civilian than a general! But the new prime minister did not bow under pressure and, after an exhausting and bitter debate that lasted until long past midnight, the army and navy agreed to send a final proposal to America. Foreign Minister Togo—often confused with Tojo by Americans even though his name was pronounced Tohngo—had already drawn up two. Proposal A, a watered-down version of previous offers, agreed to withdraw all Japanese troops from China once the communist threat ended. Proposal B was to be used only if the first was turned down. In it Japan promised to make no more aggressive moves south;

and once peace was restored in China or a general peace was established in the Pacific, Japan would immediately move all troops in southern Indochina to the north. In return, America was to sell Japan one million tons of gasoline.

On the morning of the fourth of November, thirteen men filed solemnly into the room set up for the imperial conference. At last the fourteenth man, the Emperor, appeared, and the ceremony proceeded according to custom. After explaining that the decision of September 6 had been reconsidered, Prime Minister Tojo said, "As a result, we have concluded that we must be prepared to go to war with the time for military action set tentatively at December 1. At the same time we shall be doing our best to solve the problem by diplomacy."

His Majesty remained silent according to custom as Admiral Nagano said, "Our battle plans must remain secret since the fate of Nippon depends on a decisive victory in the first moments of the war."

Despite the brave talk there was a sense of doom in the large room, and this was accentuated when the foreign minister was asked what chances of success might come from Proposal A or B. "There are only two weeks left to negotiate. Therefore, I think the chances of success are small." He promised to do his best. "But I regret to say I see little hope of success, perhaps a ten percent chance."

"Forty percent!" exclaimed Tojo optimistically, yet moments later he too sounded the warning of a prolonged war. "I can see no end to our troubles. How many years and months will our people be able to bear it?" Despite the "forty percent" chance so recently vowed, Tojo soberly said he also feared that they would have to go to war. "I am afraid we would become a third-class nation in two or three years if we just sat tight." He vowed not to make this a racial war. "Do you have anything more to say? If not, I take it the proposals have been approved in their original form."

There was silence. As in every imperial conference but the last one, the Emperor said nothing. Kido had advised him that there was no second trump card to play. The decision lay in Washington.

CHAPTER FOUR

1.

Washington, D.C. November 15, 1941.

At the White House it was, ironically, the two military chiefs who were urging the President to do nothing at all that might force a crisis. Both Marshall and Stark had been unhappy with the embargo and were jointly arguing that it was the defeat of Hitler that had to be their main objective. They urged the President to send no ultimatum to Tokyo. "At least," added Marshall, "not for three or four more months. By then we should have strengthened the Philippines and Singapore sufficiently to resist any attacks."

Roosevelt thanked them. "I'll keep my war dogs on the leash," he said with a smile. Later in the day he called in Secretary of War Stimson. "Colonel," he said, "we must find a way to give us further time to build up the Philippines."

"I'll work on it with old Hull," he promised.

That afternoon Admiral Nomura brought a special envoy to meet Hull. Saburo Kurusu had been sent by the Foreign Ministry to assist in the negotiations. One glance at the diminutive, bespectacled man with the neat mustache was enough for the Secretary of State to conclude that he could not be trusted. The President, on the other hand, greeted the newcomer affably, having been informed by McGlynn that he was genuinely for peace. Roosevelt, in fact, was so impressed by Proposal B, presented by Kurusu and Nomura three days later, that, despite Hull's protest that it was nothing more than a damned ultimatum, he jotted down in pencil a counterproposal offering a six-month truce and cancellation of the oil embargo if Japan sent no more troops to Indochina. Then had come reports of a Japanese invasion force heading south, and the aroused Roosevelt reversed himself and empowered Hull to send a harsh reply to Tokyo.

On the afternoon of November 26 the Secretary of State sent for Nomura and Kurusu. Hull handed them the new offer drafted the night before. Kurusu was dismayed. It looked more like an ultimatum than a proposal.

Nomura couldn't even talk. The terms were harsher than an American proposal submitted in June. Finally Kurusu said politely in English, "Can't we informally discuss this proposal before sending it to Tokyo?"

Tight-lipped, Hull said, "It's as far as we can go. . . ."

Dejected, Kurusu said, "Then your note just about means the end."

Two days later Kurusu secretly summoned Tadashi Toda and Hidenari Terasaki, one of the First Secretaries, to his office. After closing the door the special envoy took them to the far end of the room. "We all have something in common," he said with a little smile. "American wives." He lowered his voice to a whisper. "I called you two here since I have a great favor to ask. What I am going to propose is contrary to my instructions from the Ministry and the government." Tadashi felt a surge of hope. Kurusu was a far abler diplomat than Nomura and must have a new plan. "The only way to prevent war," he said, "is to ask the President to send a private cable to the Emperor."

Tadashi could not hide his enthusiasm. *"Meian desu ne!"* (Great idea!)

"I suggested this to the Ministry when I forwarded Hull's answer but they rejected the idea. Therefore, Ambassador Nomura and I cannot take up the matter officially. It must be done by a third person. And he must insist that the President's cable be delivered directly to the Emperor and not through the Ministry or Premier Tojo." He surveyed the two listeners. "What I want you to do is work on Roosevelt through a third person. It is a very difficult task but you two have many influential American acquaintances. I think everything will go smoothly."

"It's an excellent idea," said Terasaki. "As a matter of fact, I was thinking of something similar."

"I must warn you both that if this were to leak out you could be treated as traitors."

"So be it," said Tadashi grimly.

"It could mean your death and death for your families too," said Kurusu.

Tadashi hesitated. How could he jeopardize his family? But he found himself nodding in agreement.

"Diplomats are supposed to be prepared to risk death for the mother country," said Terasaki.

That night Tadashi tossed and turned until he wakened Floss.

"Aren't you feeling well?" she asked.

"I'll be all right," he said. He forced himself to lie quietly. He decided that if he were found out he would not let Floss and Masao return to Japan with him.

2.

Tokyo. December 1, 1941.

A new patriotic song was being broadcast by radio station JOAK:

> Siren, siren, air raid, air raid!
> What is that to us?
> Preparations are well done.
> Neighborhood associations are solid,
> Determination for defense is firm,
> Enemy planes are only mosquitoes or dragonflies.
> We will win, we must win.
> What of air raid?
> We know no defeat.
> Come to this land to be shot down.

This expressed the indignation and determination of civilian as well as military leaders upon reading Hull's peremptory reply to Proposal B. The American demands were outrageous, an ultimatum. It was enough that Japan had offered to withdraw troops from Indochina at once. Now Hull wanted all troops withdrawn immediately from China. An impossibility. Manchuria had been won by sweat and blood and its loss would mean economic disaster. No nation with any honor would submit.

The tragedy was that if the President's original proposal had been sent, it would probably have been accepted. Tojo had already prepared an offer with new compromises since he had vowed to carry out the Emperor's wishes and avoid a war. A war that need not have been fought now seemed inevitable.

The Malay attack force, already discovered by the Americans, was well on its way south. Still unknown was that the Pearl Harbor Carrier Striking Force—six mighty carriers holding 360 planes—was headed for Hawaii. But its commander had orders to turn back in case of a last-minute peace arrangement. Zero hour for war was December 8, which would be December 7 in Hawaii. And so on the first of that month the Emperor was forced to take the last formal step to war at an imperial conference. "Matters have reached a point," announced Tojo in clipped tones, "where Japan must begin war with the United States, Great Britain, and the Netherlands to preserve the nation."

The Emperor remained passive and silent on his dais as Tojo detailed the long, tedious history of the Washington negotiations. "We tremble with awe in the presence of His Majesty," he said in conclusion. "If His Majesty decides on war, we will all do our best to repay our obligations to him by bringing the government and the military closer than ever together, resolving that a united nation will go on to victory, making every effort to achieve our national purposes and thereby putting at ease His Majesty's mind."

The members bowed to the Emperor. Without expression and without uttering a word, he left the room. A few minutes later he was delivered documents to be signed proposing war. In private he pondered, then he summoned Kido and said, "Hull's demands are too humiliating." The Emperor had done everything in his power to prevent war by defying tradition and training. He reluctantly affixed his seal to the historic papers. The decision for war was formally sanctioned.

At two o'clock that afternoon Field Marshal Sugiyama sent a cable of two words to the commander of the Southern Army: HINODE YAMAGATA. This was the code for the date of commencing operations, December 8. Admiral Yamamoto sent a slightly longer cable to the Pearl Harbor Striking Force: NIITAKAYAMA NOBORE 1208. It meant: "Attack as planned on December 8."

3.

In New York it was a few minutes before midnight, November 30. That morning Mark had quit his job selling sewing machines and spent most of the day wandering aimlessly around the neighborhood. He had eaten dinner alone since Maggie was on an assignment in New Haven. He was engrossed in Dostoevski's *The Possessed*. The weird gang of radicals reminded him of some of his comrades, particularly the brainwashers downtown. They could justify anything, even murder, if the goal was lofty. He marveled how he could have been fooled by them so long.

The phone jangled. It had been ringing all evening and again he ignored it. It must be Manny, the leader of his group, wanting to know why he had missed three meetings in a row. He felt strangely guilty. Leaving the party was like a divorce and it was difficult adjusting to the realization that something he had believed in with all his heart was suddenly meaningless, even abhorrent.

The ringing finally stopped but a few minutes later resumed. Manny was an obstinate character. Or perhaps it was Miriam. He had broken the last two dates with lame alibis and he hated the idea of giving another. She was such a sweet girl and the hurt in her voice put him to shame. But he could no longer pretend he still loved her. The thought of marriage—of being tied down in a little apartment with her—was depressing.

Perhaps he should get out of the city and its problems. Hitting the road had always been a good way to clear his mind. Riding freight trains was about the last adventure in America. He got along well with his fellow bindle stiffs. They were straightforward, uncomplicated, and they stuck by you. There was more action in a single day, scrounging food, avoiding railroad detectives, and finding shelter for the night, than in months of ordinary life. And he had found more kindness and understanding among the poor than among the affluent. He smiled wryly. It was this same feeling for the dispossessed that had propelled him into the party. But their concern for the underdog, he was now convinced, was not genuine. The poor were only tools.

There was a hubbub at the front door. As the door opened he heard Maggie protesting good-naturedly, "No! Arnold, please!" Mark guessed she had been fending off that bright young reporter. She must have persuaded him to drive her to New Haven. He heard her laugh and the slam of the door.

"I got it!" she said. Her impish face was bright with excitement. She had been sent to Yale to try to interview a young instructor under fire for his radical exhortations in and out of the classroom. "Arnold offered to go with me. They were classmates at CCNY."

"I see you got rid of him with your usual dispatch!"

"Would you like him for a brother-in-law?" She affectionately ruffled Mark's hair. "This is no time for romance. There's going to be a war before you know it and I've got to hustle up more credits so I can get overseas."

The phone sounded. She hurried to it. "Mark," she called. "It's *Miriam* again." She winced at her brother's choice of girl friends. But the Cookie Queen was at least better than La Rosa of the Crabs. She listened with amusement to Mark's excuses. Thank God. Now they wouldn't be overwhelmed by the bags of rejected cookies Miriam always brought.

Moments after Mark shamefacedly hung up the receiver there was another call. Again Maggie answered. "It's Manny," she said.

"Tell him I've gone to Alaska."

"He says there's a very important policy meeting downtown tomorrow."

Mark slowly came to the phone. "Manny, I'm too busy." He listened patiently to a long plea. "I'm sorry, Manny, but I'm through. You know damned well what's bugging me. I can't stick it any longer." He hung up.

Maggie was worried. She was used to Mark's ups and downs but usually a depression was quickly succeeded by a new enthusiasm. He had been in the dumps ever since the invasion of Russia. Last week he had disappeared, phoning after a day to say he was in the Bowery. He had come back a few days later smelling vile from sleeping on the floor at the Salvation Army and with his beautiful hair hacked off at a barber's college.

Maggie felt that she alone realized that Mark's eccentric actions such as riding freight trains or becoming a communist were not a revolt against Papa but a search for something that kept eluding his grasp. She knew because she was a twin and felt similar stirrings. Being a girl, she had not had Mark's opportunities for adventure nor had her own displays of independence irked Papa. There must be some chemical reaction between the two.

The professor had only been pleased when she told him, after meeting Sigrid Schulz, that she wanted above all to be a foreign correspondent. If it had been Mark, probably a bitter argument would have erupted. But Papa had persuaded a good friend, an executive of the *Herald Tribune*, to put her on the payroll at twenty-five dollars a week. Her first good stories had come from assignments which the city editor had imagined were routine, such as an interview with Mike Quill of the National Maritime Union who unexpectedly gave her an inside story on the union's political intentions.

Mark couldn't get to sleep. By four o'clock in the morning he had convinced himself that he had to get out of the city. Never had he been on the bum in cold weather and now he could experience what real bindle stiffs had to endure. It would also give him a chance to see the Pocatello Kid, his closest friend on the road. Recently Poky had written that, incredibly, he now had a permanent address in Seattle. He had it made at last.

After quietly packing his knapsack Mark wrote a note to Maggie apologizing for having been such a drag lately. He enclosed a check for $250 to cover his share of house expenses. He then scribbled a card to Poky saying he'd be in Seattle in a week or so. Finally he forced himself to write Miriam apologizing for leaving so suddenly. He tried to think of a kind way to say their romance was over. He told her it was not because of another girl and let it go at that. He was disgusted with himself and cursed his prick for bringing either the pain of being rejected or the shame of rejecting.

He put on his sheepskin over a heavy sweater, clapped on a stocking cap. At the corner he mailed the letters, then took the subway to the Holland Tunnel. Soon he was in a truck bound for Pennsylvania. As they plunged into the tunnel he recalled that Gorky, a tramp in his youth, after becoming a successful author had gone back on the road on a sentimental journey. Well, he was neither successful nor sentimental. But it would be nice seeing old Poky again. Next to his father, Poky was the person Mark most admired.

The following morning Tadashi and Terasaki decided that the best go-between was a prominent Methodist missionary, Dr. E. Stanley Jones. Through Terasaki's wife a meeting was set up at a restaurant, the Purple Iris. To the conspirators' delight Jones agreed immediately to act as intermediary with the President.

That evening Tadashi was about to tell Floss of his dangerous involvement but convinced himself that he should wait until the Reverend Jones saw Roosevelt.

CHAPTER FIVE

1.

Washington, D.C. December 3, 1941.

An intercepted warning from Tokyo to Hitler that war might "come quicker than anyone dreams," alerted official Washington. The only question was: When? The growing tension was palpable that morning at both the Munitions and Navy buildings; and one wag, a former accountant, calculated that 1,776 rumors, all of them false, would be passed from floor to floor and wing to wing before the day was finished.

Will was summoned by Marshall. "We're sending you on a trip, Captain," he said abruptly. "You are going to Manila. Ostensibly you will be there to expedite shipment of supplies to General MacArthur. In fact you are to determine how reliable his reports to us have been." He gathered up papers. "Here are your travel orders. The President and I have reason to question some of General MacArthur's figures. We want you to dig and find out *exactly* what is going on out there and whom we can trust. You will keep us informed regularly by special code."

Will, still at a loss, picked up the travel orders.

"There's a staff car waiting outside. You are to report to the President, then pack and get out to Bolling by noon. You'll be flown to Hamilton and from there to Hickam Field." Marshall extended his hand. "Have a good trip, young man, and get back to us safely."

The interview with Roosevelt was brief. He repeated what Marshall had said, stressed the importance of the mission, and wished him a hearty farewell. "I'll let your father know that you are going to be away for a spell on a personal mission for me." He smiled broadly. "I'll make it very mysterious. Do you think it will annoy him?"

"Knowing my father, sir, I'm sure it will."

"Do him good. Safe journey."

A few minutes after noon a medium bomber headed west with Will aboard. Although he knew he was heading into danger, it pleased as well as excited him. At last he was doing something of consequence. And it probably would mean a promotion.

That afternoon Mark leaped off a Union Pacific freight in Ogden, Utah. He was almost frozen, for he had been riding in a gondola filled with gravel. His face was pocked from hot cinders that had swirled into the open car inside the series of tunnels dug through this section of the Rockies. Because of the cold he was still not accustomed to the hardships of the road. As he trudged toward the Western Pacific yards, memories flooded back. Here in Ogden he had first met Poky. They had been arrested for trespassing on railroad property and had spent several days preparing the arena for the local Fourth of July rodeo. Later Poky had taught him the techniques of riding freights. He could still see him leaping gracefully onto a fast-moving train only a step ahead of an angry railroad detective, and then on top of a refrigerator car thumbing his nose antically like Till Eulenspiegel. He was probably the greatest living rider. He had gone through the Moffat Tunnel, held down the Mae West (the banana express from New Orleans to Chicago), and ridden the blind baggage of the Twentieth Century Limited.

Mark's father could never understand why he kept riding freights. How could he explain that he felt more at home in the lower depths of America where each day was filled with adventure? There were the wind and the rain to combat as well as the beating sun and the yard bulls. Hunger became so common that every meager meal was a banquet. This was life in the raw and excited some inner need in him. He saw how men and boys bore pain with a joke. He saw what fear looked like as well as hope. He saw courage and comradeship. And in women and girls he saw gallantry and faith in the face of hunger, cold, and despair.

Was he romanticizing this life? Had his journeys on the road merely been escapes from reality and not reality itself? It was an unsettling thought.

2.

Although Dr. Jones had agreed to see the President as soon as possible, Roosevelt was in Warm Springs, Georgia, and it was not until December 3 that Jones was ushered through a secret entrance of the White House to avoid reporters. The President readily promised to send the cable.

Jones cautioned him to dispatch it not through the Foreign Ministry but directly to the Emperor, otherwise it would never reach him.

"I'm thinking out loud," Roosevelt mused. "I can't go down to the cable office and say I want to send a cable from the President of the United States to the Emperor of Japan. But I could send it to Grew."

As Jones was leaving, he asked the President never to mention Mr. Terasaki who had approached him with the idea.

"His secret is safe," Roosevelt promised.

That afternoon Tadashi, Terasaki, and Kurusu quietly celebrated at a nearby café. When Tadashi arrived home that evening, Floss noticed that he was flushed with nervous excitement. After Masao was put to bed she asked her husband what was troubling him. "For the past few days you have been so jumpy."

Almost guiltily he finally told her of the cable. "Today Reverend Jones saw the President and he has agreed to send it."

Elated, she hugged him, then held him at arm's length. "Why didn't you tell me about this before?"

"I didn't want to worry you," he said guiltily. "I may be accused of treason if they find out."

"But you said the President promised not to reveal Terasaki's involvement."

"So many things could go wrong. I shouldn't have gotten involved in the first place."

"I would have told you to do it. I'm proud of you."

He would not be consoled. "I was wrong. Don't you see that I risked your life and Masao's as well as my own?"

She kissed him. "You silly man, let's go to bed."

3.

Two days later Shogo was sweating in the hold of the army transport *Ryujo-maru* anchored off the island of Hainan. He was supervising the loading of troops and supplies. The last man came aboard long after midnight, and Shogo went topside to join Colonel Tsuji who was studying papers in the dim light of a lamp. At dawn their convoy, twenty ships in all, would set sail. Tsuji turned off the light and they bedded down for a few hours sleep.

They were awakened by the movement of the ship and Tsuji led the way to the bridge as the convoy silently headed south toward the Malay Peninsula. On the right the southernmost coast of China was receding. Their transport carried no armament; externally it resembled a carrier. A ghost ship, thought Shogo. The clumsy vessel began to roll and pitch. Thank God they didn't have to stay below.

As the two watched Hainan getting smaller, Tsuji had visions of his old mother, and then of his wife and children. A deep red sun was slowly rising in the east as the moon, looking like a tray, vanished in the west. There was silence except for the reassuring deep throb of the engines. "The die is cast," Tsuji said. The destiny of their nation would be determined by their actions. "Japan's fate," he said more to himself than to Shogo, "is the fate of East Asia."

The moon was high as Will, carrying a parachute over his shoulder and hoisting a heavy flight bag, climbed into a Flying Fortress. The California night was brilliant with stars. A crewman told him to stow his gear on a pile of supplies and make a bunk for himself. At last the big plane was under way, its four motors roaring as if they were going to explode. "We should get to Hickam a little after dawn," said the crewman.

It seemed minutes later that Will was awakened by a rude shake. "Hey, the skipper thought you might want to come up front and see something."

Will carefully made his way forward. It was already dawn. The plane slowly swung around and Will could see Diamond Head. The pilot pointed ahead. "Hickam." Nearby was a thrilling sight. Scores of huge ships at anchor. "Pearl Harbor," said the pilot. He made the whistling sound of a falling bomb. "Boom! What a piece of cake!"

At Hickam Field Will made himself as inconspicuous as possible in the ready room, avoiding conversation by pretending to be asleep. After several hours he was at last put aboard another Flying Fortress, this one, unlike the first, ready for action. The machine guns had been cleaned of their Cosmoline packing and the ammunition prepared. "We may run into some trouble before we get to Wake," the bombardier told Will.

The long, dull trip to that tiny atoll was relieved by the sighting of a carrier and twelve or so other ships heading east. "Must be the *Enterprise*," remarked the copilot. "They were supposed to drop off some Grumman Wildcats and their pilots at Wake." Will wondered aloud how the copilot would know such top secret stuff and was rewarded with a laugh from those within hearing. "Everybody knows just about everything."

Someone shouted that they had passed the international dateline and had lost a day. It was now December 6. Soon they could see a tiny island. "Wake," said someone. "The asshole of the Pacific. Two and a half square miles of coral rubble. Anyone want to buy it for a bottle of beer?" There were no takers.

In the three-hour layover Will borrowed a jeep to tour the little island. The blue water was beautiful but the island itself was a barren piece of junk. He was glad when they took off—destination Guam. At least there were trees on it and some people, including girls, observed a gunner. "Ugly, but girls."

Time had passed without incident aboard the *Ryujo-maru*. But at noon on December 7, Tokyo time—Japanese ships kept Tokyo time whatever their position—word came that an enemy patrol plane had just been shot down. Had the pilot been able to send out a warning? Later that afternoon, to everyone's relief, fog and dense clouds closed in over the convoy in Thailand Bay.

Will was at the Guam Air Corps officers' club. It was pleasantly warm and there was plenty of Filipino beer. The most interesting thing Will learned was that the governor of the island was a navy captain named McMillin. "The navy always manages to get the cushiest jobs," someone complained. The pilot advised Will to hit the sack early, since they were taking off for Clark Field at first light.

In Hawaii it was early evening, December 6, and neither Admiral Kimmel nor his army counterpart, General Short, had any suspicion that six Japanese carriers were racing full steam at twenty-four knots toward the launching point, two hundred miles north of Pearl Harbor. They would be in position at dawn.

Mark was huddled in a crowded jerry-built diner at the edge of the Stockton, California, yards. He was wolfing down a heaping plate of "thousand-mile beans," guaranteed to last any bindle stiff through a thousand-mile ride. In several hours he would catch a freight bound for Seattle and Poky.

At 8 P.M. Washington time, Tadashi received word that Roosevelt had finally sent the cable to the Emperor. It had been delayed by Hull, who had argued that such an appeal should only be a last-minute resort. Tadashi phoned the embassy to inform Kurusu and was told he was dining at the estate of former Ambassador Belin in Georgetown. It took fifteen minutes to get hold of the special envoy, who returned to the dinner table to inform the company of the cable. "A clever move," said Kurusu as if he had known nothing of the matter, "since the Emperor can give neither a flat 'no' or even 'yes.' It's certainly going to cause headaches in Tokyo and more thinking."

The cable had reached Tokyo at noon but was automatically held up ten hours by a recent general directive, and it was not until ten-thirty in the evening that Ambassador Grew received it, despite its TRIPLE PRIORITY stamp. At fifteen minutes past midnight Grew finally arrived at Foreign Minister Togo's official residence, decoded message in hand.

Togo phoned the Privy Seal at his home. "Under such unusual circumstances," said Kido, "His Majesty can be roused even in the dead of night." Togo drove to the Prime Minister Tojo's official residence. "Does the message contain any concessions?" asked Tojo hopefully.

"No."

Tojo looked at his watch. In a few hours bombs would be falling on Pearl Harbor. "Well, then, nothing can be done, can it?"

Nothing at all could be done.

PART TWO

"For a Wasted Hope and Sure Defeat"

CHAPTER SIX

1.

At sea off Hawaii. December 7, 1941.

The men on the Japanese carrier force *Kido Butai* were at general quarters. At 3:30 A.M. the pilots and crews were routed from their bunks. They donned clean *mawashi* (loincloths) and thousand-stitch belts. Wives, mothers, or sisters had stood on street corners to ask passersby for a stitch and so each belt contained a thousand prayers for good luck and a good fight. Fingernail clippings and locks of hair had already been put in last letters for their families.

An hour before first light the force commander sent out four search planes to make sure the American fleet was still at Pearl Harbor and not Lahaina. Soon the six carriers would be at the launching point, two hundred miles north of the target.

Far to the west a great convoy was closing in on the Malay Peninsula in three sections. The main force, fourteen ships, was bound for Singora. Shogo Toda was with this group. To its left, three ships neared the village of Patani. Tsuji would lead this contingent and attempt a coup worthy of an adventure movie. It had been inspired by a dream which visualized the takeover of neutral Thailand by a thousand Japanese in Thai uniforms. After landing at Singora they would corral bar and dance girls as a cover. Buses could be commandeered and, under Tsuji's leadership, all would drive to the Malay border as a huge, rowdy party. The men, carrying Thai flags and Union Jacks, would wave them merrily while shouting out a few apt words of English taught them by the irrepressible Tsuji: "Japanese soldier is frightful!" and "Hurrah for the British!" The border guards, Tsuji assured his superiors, would be so confused by the boisterous "balls-up" (it had taken him some time to explain this British slang) that they would let the Japanese cross into Malaya.

Tsuji had no control at all over the third landing, the one at Kota Bharu. Its three transports reached their destination first. At midnight they dropped anchor just off the city. An hour and fifteen minutes later their naval escort began bombing the coast. The war in the Pacific had started by mistake, since it was only 5:45 A.M. in Hawaii. It was not the fault of the Japanese commanders in Malaya for this was the scheduled time. But so many pilots in *Kido Butai* had complained of taking off in pitch dark to attack Pearl Harbor that their departure had been delayed.

The first light of day was just glimmering east of *Kido Butai* as pilots and flight crews strapped themselves into their planes. To the south were patches of clouds and long, heavy swells rolled the six carriers up to fifteen degrees. In training, maneuvers were usually canceled once swells exceeded five degrees.

There was momentary confusion after the Z flag, an exact copy of the one Admiral Togo had used at Tsushima, was raised above the flagship, *Akagi*. It meant "On this one battle rests the fate of the nation. Let every man do his utmost." Several staff officers protested, for in the intervening years the Z flag had become an ordinary tactical signal.

Nearby, the sailors on another carrier, *Kaga*, became so excited by the sight of the Z flag that they hoisted their own, only to see *Akagi*'s flag flutter down. Moments later a Zero roared down the flagship's runway. Other Zeros were leaving the other carriers as if catapulted into the air. Within half an hour a huge, brilliant sun rose to the left. One young torpedo pilot, Mori by name, had never before seen a sunrise from the air. Up ahead the planes were etched in black silhouette against the red. It was such a romantic, startling sight that Mori could hardly believe he was heading for Japan's most crucial battle. To other pilots it was a sacred sight, marking as it did the dawn of a new era.

As Tsuji's feet hit the sand at Singora he was relieved to find that Shogo's report had been accurate. The footing was solid. But his dream plan was jinxed from the beginning. Their contact at the beach, a major posing as a consulate clerk, was not at his position. There were no café or dance girls or buses in sight. Now Tsuji's only interest was to join the other sections and help them break into Malaya in a more orthodox fashion.

At Kota Bharu those men who had reached the beach were met with such heavy fire from pillboxes that they had to back into the water and keep their heads out of sight. British planes were swooping down on the three transports while shore batteries flung shells at the helpless vessels. Two caught fire but the last of the landing parties leaped to safety and,

64

kept afloat by life jackets, slowly trudged toward the beach. Fighter planes began strafing launches, but the dogged invaders finally managed to dig shallow foxholes in the beach. They lobbed grenades into the loopholes of the pillboxes and the enemy's front line.

At Patani, Shogo's group was finding a different difficulty. It seemed at first as though they would have no trouble. Their launches reached the five-foot water level without casualties. But when Shogo leaped overboard, weighted down by full field equipment, he found himself sinking in mud. It was a horrible feeling, for he had expected a firm bottom. But the beautiful white sand he had seen from the shore did not extend into the water at low tide! The man next to him, carrying a machine gun, was struggling wildly to keep his head above water. Shogo tried to help but only sank deeper. He struggled free and finally could breathe. But the machine gunner had vanished. So had the gunner ahead of him. Shogo plunged forward, pulling his feet out of the sucking mud with the strength of desperation. Each step was torture and it became every man for himself. It took the survivors almost an hour to reach white sand. Once there they were raked by Thai fire. Shogo frantically dug into the sand for protection. He prayed that his colonel was having better luck.

2.

It was almost noon before Mark finally reached Seattle's refuge both for bindle stiffs and home guards, those who stayed in one city. This was Mark's favorite skid row. He liked its location near the docks as well as the constant surge of life within its perimeters. Every evening was like a show with Sally's band playing, union speakers haranguing, and a collection of nuts and zealots preaching salvation, damnation, social security, fascism or communism.

He located Poky's building in the western edge of skid row. The paint had long since worn off. It was dilapidated and leaned to one side like a cripple. Someone on the first floor told him Poky lived on the floor above. "But he ain't there. He's up at the main stem—not that it'll do him much good on a Sunday."

Mark knew this meant Poky was panhandling. He never had been good at it, since he was always embarrassed to ask for money. And why should he panhandle now? Then Mark heard a grating noise and glimpsed half a man propelling himself down the incline by hand on boards fastened to roller skates. There was a narrow platform attached to the front of the boards. Two small American flags on either side were flapping. The Pocatello Kid adeptly brought the wagon to a screeching halt with two rubber-tipped stubs of wood. He was grinning.

Mark had to fight to keep from showing shock at the sight of his legless friend. They shook hands with Mark struggling to hide his pity. Poky's face was the same—a little lined, but still radiant. He smiled sheepishly. "Now the town bulls can't grab me for panhandling." He jiggled a tin cup partially filled with coins. "Pretty good for a Sunday. I got a license." He indicated a card thumbtacked to the rack, which also contained a well-secured can filled with new pencils.

"Come on up and see my place," he said proudly. With his long, strong arms he maneuvered himself adroitly into the building. After parking his wagon in the hallway, he backed up the stairs. He was proud of his almost barren room. He showed Mark how he could cook and go to the bathroom, then in a matter-of-fact way told of his accident. He had been riding the Big Goat, the Great Northern. As they were coming into the Seattle yards, Poky had slipped while leaping from one boxcar to another.

One of his most prized possessions was a battered radio, mended in a dozen places. He turned it on and Mark admired its tone. All at once an excited announcer broke in to announce shakily that the Japanese had just bombed American warships in a place called Pearl Harbor. Mark could not believe what he was hearing. His first thoughts were for Floss. What would happen to her little family? Then he was angry. A sneak attack! How could the Japanese have been so stupid?

Maggie had just finished writing a short piece on the influx of German-Jewish refugees in Washington Heights. The city editor would probably cut it to ribbons or toss it in the wastebasket. As she switched from WQXR to get the Rodzinski concert on CBS an announcer interrupted to tell about Pearl Harbor. She also thought first of Floss, then of Mark. Yesterday she had received a laconic card from Cheyenne, Wyoming, saying he was on his way to Seattle. Would he be fool enough to rush down tomorrow morning and enlist? Yes. She felt a thrill. This was her chance to become a foreign correspondent. Maybe Papa had an influential friend.

McGlynn was not surprised, only very sad. All that he had predicted was stark reality. Tadashi would probably be interned, but what about Floss and the boy? And what about the poor Todas in Tokyo?

Floss was playing a Japanese card game with Masao and knew nothing until Tadashi phoned. "It's happened!" he said in dismay. "How could they have done such a stupid thing?"

"Done what?"

"Pearl Harbor! Our carrier planes bombed it!"

"What on earth are you talking about?"

"It's the end of Japan. War!"

She managed to get control of herself and tried to calm him.

Everything at the embassy was in an uproar, he said. "They'll be cutting off all our phones any minute. I love you, darling. You and Masao be brave."

"We'll be fine. Things will work out, but we must stay together."

"I doubt that we can," he said. "Good-bye."

"We'll soon be together again."

He said nothing and hung up.

3.

The Japanese people first learned about the attack at 7 A.M. December 8, when an NHK announcer said, "We now present you urgent news." Hostilities had begun against the American and British forces in the Pacific at dawn.

Toda and his wife were alone at the breakfast table. "A grave situation," he said grimly, although the bad news came as no real surprise. Would they intern Tadashi for the duration? For once Emi was speechless. Instinctively her hands had gone to her mouth. Shogo! They knew only that he was somewhere in the south. He was so impetuous and courageous!

Martial music blared out of the radio. It was a recording of "Umi Yukaba":

> Across the sea, corpses in the water;
> Across the mountain, corpses in the field.
> I shall die only for the Emperor,
> I shall never look back.

"What will become of Shogo?" she helplessly uttered, holding back tears.

"What's going on?" It was bleary-eyed Ko in a *nemaki*.

"War with America and Britain," said Toda.

"No!" That meant the end of his trip to Paris! He had secretly planned to stay in Europe and study painting, knowing that his mother would somehow help him. He was dejected; then, noticing his mother's anguished face, he tried to comfort her.

Sumiko had left early that morning to prepare for a test. She now attended a Christian school located in the suburbs. She was in a cheerful mood as she stepped out of the subway at Shibuya Station, for it was a special day—her thirteenth birthday. Mother would prepare a special dinner with red bean rice as she always did on occasions for celebration. As she started for the train station a voice called for attention from one of the numerous loudspeakers the government had placed in the Tokyo streets.

News of the attack blasted out. People stopped in their tracks, startled. Martial music blared, and many began clapping as if it were a baseball game. The dark, oppressive clouds that had hung over the country for months had suddenly cleared. Sumiko could feel a sense of restrained enthusiasm in the crowd, although she herself was distressed. The Todas would have to fight the McGlynns. And Japan did not have a chance of winning. A friend had been sending the family *Life* magazine, and anyone thumbing through its ads of all sorts of vehicles and equipment and pictorial stories of American industrial power would know how impossible it would be for little Japan, scarcely the size of California, to challenge such a giant. How often her father had remarked what a tragedy it would be! She felt helpless and worried, but hurried on to school. She had to pass that English test.

Older citizens were already converging on the Palace to pray for victory, not with jubilation but with solemnity. In the plaza news vendors with "extras" trotted by, the bells around their wrists jingling so loudly that they could be heard in Number Three East Reception Hall of the Imperial Palace. Here the Privy Council was in session, drafting an imperial rescript.

Just before noon the Emperor put his seal on the rescript and war was officially declared. He added one line expressing his personal regret that the empire had been brought to war with Britain and America. He also toned down the closing phrase, "raising and enhancing thereby the glory of the Imperial Way within and outside our homeland," to "preserving thereby the glory of our empire."

Some two thousand miles to the south, Will's B-17 was approaching Manila. No one aboard had any idea that America was at war, since radio reception had been so bad. "We should make it to Clark Field by noon," said the pilot. Head winds delayed them, and half an hour after their estimated time of arrival Will, now up forward with the pilots, noticed a dramatic conelike mountain ahead jutting out of a great plain.

"Mount Arayat," said the pilot. "According to the Flips, that dent in the cone is where Noah's ark landed." He swung the big plane to the left. Ahead, Will could make out Clark Field with many planes parked neatly. There were at least fifteen huge ones, probably Flying Fortresses. The pilot told him to get back and buckle up; they were going to land.

As Will climbed down to the tarmac he felt a wave of heat from the sun. While an enlisted man began piling their luggage and parachutes into a jeep, Will walked the kinks out of his long legs. A distant rumble grew louder and the enlisted man exclaimed, "Here comes our navy."

Will and the pilot turned to see twenty or thirty planes coming in from the north. "Navy, hell!" shouted the latter. "Those are goddam Jap bombers!" He pushed Will into the front of the jeep, then began throwing out all the luggage. The rest of the crew piled pell-mell into the jeep and it rocketed toward the flight line. There came a sound like rushing freight trains as they skidded to a stop. The hangar in front of them exploded. "Take cover! Bandits!" shouted someone and everyone scrambled for some sort of safety. By now the air-raid siren was wailing. Will stumbled. Something fell on top of him. Water dripped on his face. But it was red. The man on top of him was bleeding profusely. He had no head. Will screamed, unaware that not a sound came from his mouth. He stood upright like a statue until someone grabbed him and practically flung him into a shallow ditch. Will was still so confused, he tried to rise.

"Down, you jerk!" his savior, a little PFC, shouted. "Zeros coming in!"

Will flattened just as bullets from a strafer squealed by. He felt his heart beating as if it would come out of his chest. He tried to thank the PFC but his tongue seemed stuck. He heard air rush past, turned to see a dud bomb sticking in the ditch. "Get the hell out of here!" shouted the PFC, who clambered up and threw himself into a deeper ditch.

Will followed and leaped on top of him. "Excuse me," he said.

"Never mind," said the little PFC. "That's just one more body a bullet has to go through to get at me."

The uneven beat of the raider planes faded away and the survivors slowly climbed out of slit trenches. Parts of bodies littered the field. By some freak, one man was blown up like a balloon by an explosive bullet. To Will he looked almost transparent. A truck swung by, blood dripping out of the sides. It was filled with wounded heading for the Fort Stotsenburg hospital. Other wounded were walking dazedly as if in a trance.

Billows of smoke came from hangars and buildings. Will could see scores of the neatly lined-up planes burning fiercely out on the flight line. In seconds all that was left were molten skeletons giving off a frightening crackle as if crying out in agony. Then Will realized he was hearing the cries of wounded men and he himself was covered with a dead man's blood.

CHAPTER SEVEN

1.

Seattle. December 7, 1941.

Mark and Poky sat up until long past midnight talking of old times. After they turned in, Mark could not get to sleep even though the blankets on the floor made it the best kip since leaving New York. His mind was a mélange of thoughts about the war—and Poky. As soon as Mark finally fell asleep he visualized Poky leaping like a wraith from car to car, then suddenly slipping and falling out of sight between two boxcars. He saw Poky sitting at the side of the tracks holding two bloody legs and smiling. "I've got it made," he said. "Made, made." Mark awoke, heart beating, forehead sweating. And he couldn't, or perhaps wouldn't, go to sleep again. He tried to think of everything but Poky, who was snoring softly a few feet away. He thought of dear Floss, who was far more than a sister. He still had nightmares of the awful rumbling of the great Tokyo earthquake and the house bursting into fire. He would never forget his relief as Floss snatched him from the devouring flames. Would she now have to return to Japan? He thought of his father, who must be depressed because Roosevelt hadn't listened to him, and then of the Todas. They must be concerned about Shogo, who was probably already in battle.

As for himself, there was only one thing to do—enlist first thing in the morning. How could the Japanese have been so stupid and so deceitful? He didn't want to have to fight against old friends, but he'd always detested the Nazis. He'd go into the Marines and ask to fight in Europe.

He hailed morning with a light heart, springing from bed with that elasticity of spirit which is happily the lot of the young—or the world would never be stocked with the old. He felt he was heading for a new experience. He quietly got dressed and softly left the room, spurred by the excitement of adventures to come. Skid Row was deserted but he found an open newsstand up the hill. Nearby was an all-night diner and over a breakfast of hot cereal, toasted English muffins, and coffee he read about the war. It didn't seem possible.

Poky insisted on showing him the way to the Marine enlistment office and as Mark disappeared inside his friend began shaking his tin cup and cheerfully greeting passersby, all of whom had a common look of concern. It was the same all over the country. For the first time in years the United States was truly united. Rich and poor, Republicans and Democrats and even Communists were, for the most part, thinking of their country rather than themselves. People on the streets were exchanging glances with a new commonality and awareness. The bitter wrangles between the interventionists and the America Firsters now had no meaning. A few were gloating over future profits and a few foreign-born were more concerned for their mother countries than America. But these were the rare exceptions. Practically all of America's 130,000,000 citizens had accepted total war. Mark was no exception. Like millions of other young men, he felt a surge of patriotism and was eager to get into the fight. He had chosen the Marines because they were always the first to fight. His experiences as a bindle stiff were similar to battle and he figured this would give him a head start.

The Marine recruiting sergeant was tall, slim. His trim blue trousers had red stripes running down each leg. He had the hips of an eighteen-year-old but his hair was turning gray. He walked briskly up to Mark. His left hand was black and upon closer inspection as the sergeant fingerprinted him Mark realized it was artificial, made of some rubber substance. Mark had always thought you had to be a perfect physical specimen to be a Marine and wondered how this man had been accepted.

The sergeant escorted Mark to the adjoining navy recruiting office. He was given a physical and answered such embarrassing questions as, "When was your last sexual intercourse?" Mark noticed that the three youngsters ahead of him had answered this question with a manly, "Last night," although it was probable they all were virgins.

"Pipe down!" said the sergeant just before 10 A.M. "The President is going to talk." He turned on the radio and moments later they were thrilled, as were most Americans, to hear the familiar voice say, "Yesterday, December 7, 1941—a date which will live in infamy—the United States of America was suddenly and deliberately attacked by the naval and air forces of the Empire of Japan . . ."

After the physical the sergeant led Mark outside for lunch. Mark had left all his money with Poky. The sergeant grinned. "Son, it's on the Corps." They went to a small restaurant where the sergeant ordered a meal as well as a box lunch for Mark's trip to boot camp in San Diego.

While they ate the sergeant told about his own service in Nicaragua and the China Station, pride showing in every word he spoke. The three gold chevrons on his blue blouse, he explained, indicated his rank. And the two gold stripes on his lower sleeve were hash marks, each stripe representing four years' service. He also had a Purple Heart, which meant he had been wounded, as well as four ribbons, one for China, one for Nicaragua and one for good conduct. Mark wondered what the fourth ribbon—blue with seven stars—was for, and after the sergeant left to get an application blank his rugged-looking assistant said, "M.H., son." This was the Medal of Honor, the highest award a Marine could receive. "He got it in Nicaragua fighting Sandino. He grabbed a live hand grenade. He saved his squad and lost his hand. The Marine Corps takes care of its own."

Mark felt humble. For the first time he realized he was entering a special fraternity.

The one-handed sergeant read Mark's completed application, and while impressed that he was a Phi Beta Kappa, was concerned by the listing of a dozen jail sentences and that Mark once belonged to the Communist Party. After Mark explained that he had quit the party in disgust and the sentences were for riding freight trains or trespassing, the sergeant handed him a new application. "This time don't mention any of that crap."

With some reluctance Mark asked if he could possibly be sent to Europe. He had not mentioned he could speak Japanese fluently for fear he'd be used in the Pacific as an interpreter.

"Just tell them at boot camp." The famous 6th Marines were already training in Iceland and would undoubtedly be the first Americans to fight the Nazis.

Mark and the other recruits were marched into another room where a stern man sat behind a highly polished desk. Behind were two flags. On the right were the Stars and Stripes, on the left the colors of the Marine Corps. This Marine had a chestful of medals and wore silver-gold anchors and globes on his collar. On each shoulder was a silver oak leaf, indicating he was a lieutenant colonel.

"Do any of you men have any reservations?" he asked. No one spoke. "You are joining a family and are expected to be a Marine first. Please raise your right hands and repeat after me the oath of the Corps."

As they were marched out of the office, Mark felt a swell of pride. He was a Marine.

Floss had been awakened that morning by a stern-faced young FBI agent in a neat business suit. He informed her that Tadashi was being confined with other officials at the Japanese Embassy. She could shop and take walks but only under FBI supervision. Feeling against the Japanese was running high, he explained, and Mr. Hoover's measures were not so much to restrict as to protect.

"Can Masao go to kindergarten?"

"That wouldn't be wise," he said and she did not protest.

All three did go shopping and later Masao was allowed to play in a nearby park. He ran up to Floss in consternation. "Mama, look!" One of the cherry trees donated by Japan to Washington had been hacked to pieces. "Who did it?"

"Some foolish person," Floss said. She turned to their escort. "When can I see my husband?"

"I don't know, ma'am."

"Can't I phone him?"

He was genuinely sympathetic. "I'm sorry, ma'am. You must be patient."

Her father was writing Roosevelt that the spirit of Pan-Asianism preached by the Japanese and ridiculed by American experts as crude propaganda did indeed run throughout the Orient. "Down deep all Asians feel that the white man is, or could be, their common enemy. Even those who are our allies, like the Filipinos and Chinese, covertly watch our treatment of our own Negroes and Orientals." He warned that there was a growing underground colored solidarity throughout the world. "Most whites are either unaware or oblivious that there could come a radically different alignment of peoples according to race and color. Believe me, Mr. President, the Asiatics know it. Now is the time to act and rid ourselves of the burden of racial prejudice. Otherwise we will lose the war at home. Please forgive my frankness, but I am deeply concerned by the cries of a prejudiced group to imprison our Japanese citizens on the West Coast."

His son Will had already reported to MacArthur's headquarters in Manila at Number 1 Victoria Street in the walled city section, bought a summer uniform, found quarters at a BOQ, and paid a courtesy call to Cavite Naval Base. Will was still shaken by the bombings and strafings but relieved that he was by no means the only one still on edge. He soon found a Harvard man, a lieutenant commander, and by evening was a welcome guest at the officers' club. The talk mainly was of the colossal snafu by MacArthur to allow Clark Field to be caught napping hours after Pearl Harbor. The heart of the air force, including most of the bombers, had been wiped out.

"I understand," said one of the naval officers, "that the fly-boys've got a new slogan, 'Damn the torpedoes and head for the hills!' "

Will kept quiet. He could have mentioned the near panic at Clark Field that had lasted through the night, but he was too busy making mental notes for his first report to Marshall. The following morning, the tenth, Will returned to army headquarters to inform MacArthur's chief of staff, General Sutherland, that he had been empowered by General Marshall to assure MacArthur that everything possible would definitely be shipped to him. Sutherland, with a little smile that could have been ironical, replied that they had just received a radiogram from Marshall assuring General MacArthur that he had the complete confidence of the War Department.

While Will was lunching with several army officers at the Manila Hotel near the bay they heard the roar of approaching planes. All rushed outside in time to see bombers with rising suns on the wings pass overhead. Someone counted twenty-five, another twenty-seven. Bombs began to tumble down. Smoke rose from the suburbs. "Nichols!" shouted someone. They were hitting the fighter base. Then came a high-pitched whine as a mass of Zeros streaked overhead to strafe Nichols Field.

The church bells of Manila began ringing. Moments later another group of bombers approached from the north. "They're going to hit us!" shouted Will. As the group scattered for shelter the planes swerved right and began dropping bombs on ships in Manila Bay.

A third large group was coming in across Corregidor Island in a great V. In awe Will watched these planes pass over Cavite without any attack, then suddenly wheel back and unload over the naval base. The 3-inch antiaircraft guns from Cavite opened fire, but their bursts were far below the high-flying bombers. Fires were raging throughout the naval base and Will prayed they wouldn't reach the ammunition dump. Just then the wind shifted. Flames leaped high but fortunately there was no great explosion.

Late that afternoon Will sent his first report using his little code book. He told briefly of the bombings and the estimated damage and repeated what he had learned about the Clark Field debacle. General Brereton, commander of MacArthur's air force, had wanted to bomb Takao Harbor in Formosa with his Flying Fortresses once he learned about Pearl Harbor, but MacArthur had refused—they couldn't make the first overt act. After filing the report at the army message center, Will was downcast. Everything in this war seemed to be going wrong.

The next morning there was excitement in Manila over a great battle during the night at Lingayen Gulf. The thunder of land batteries had been heard for miles. The Japanese had tried to land in force but the 21st Division of the Philippine Army had sunk most of the landing craft; the bay was clogged with floating bodies; the beaches were strewn with Japanese dead.

Will got little information at MacArthur's headquarters, Number 1 Victoria Street, but that evening learned that Carl Mydans of *Life* had taken a trip down to Lingayen Gulf where he found no wreckage and not a single body on the beaches, except sunbathing soldiers. It was a hoax, revealed Mydans, even though many tons of shells had been fired. But Manila morning papers headlined eyewitness stories of the sensational victory which was confirmed by MacArthur's press chief, Major Diller. He handed out a release with details of the victory. The other reporters rushed off to file their stories but Will noticed that Mydans was taking Diller aside and overheard him protest, "Pic, I've just been to Lingayen and there's no battle there."

Diller pointed to the communiqué he'd just read aloud. "It says so here."

No one except Will paid any attention to Mydans. Headquarters was already in a state of euphoria over another great victory and the creation of America's first major hero, Captain Colin Kelly. He had given his life in the sinking of the Japanese battleship *Haruna*.

Those at Japanese naval headquarters in Tokyo were jeering at MacArthur's two communiqués. There had not been a single Japanese warship at Lingayen Gulf and the *Haruna* was fifteen hundred miles away in the Gulf of Siam at the moment Kelly supposedly destroyed it. The ship hit by one of Kelly's bombs had been a large transport that had been damaged only slightly.

2.

Several days later Floss received a phone call that Tadashi would be brought to the apartment shortly but would have to return to the embassy in the morning. The official voice said she herself would have the option of returning with him. She hung up, her decision already made. But when Tadashi arrived, exhausted and depressed, he pointed out that this meant she and Masao would also have to accompany him back to Japan.

"Of course," she said calmly.

He took both her hands. "You don't understand. Japan is going to be crushed."

"I know it."

"Life there will soon become miserable to all Japanese. Imagine how unbearable it will be for an enemy."

"I'm not an enemy!"

"You know what I mean. Our neighbors in Tokyo will detest you."

"We must be with you, Tadashi."

"They will jeer at Masao for being half American."

She set her chin. "Masao and I can take care of ourselves."

"But what if they discover I was involved in the cable to the Emperor? You could be imprisoned."

"If, if! What if a meteor hit us tomorrow? We are going with you and that's that." He started to protest again. "My great-grandmother helped settle South Dakota and she had nine children. I have only one."

The argument ended, but that night Tadashi could not sleep. He awakened Floss. "You could stay with your father in Williamstown."

"That would be worse than Tokyo." She kissed him, turned over, and went back to sleep.

The situation in the Philippines grew more desperate every day. On December 21 an American submarine confirmed the presence of a great convoy approaching Lingayen Gulf. At 2 A.M. the first of 43,110 Japanese began going over the sides of the lead transport. Their commander, Lieutenant General Masaharu Homma, anxiously waited for some retaliation from the shore. The only noise was the banging of landing craft against the sides of the transport. The only enemy was the high seas.

In Manila, MacArthur was radioing Marshall for air and naval support. Couldn't Kimmel's Pacific Fleet bring fighter planes within range of the Philippines? "Can I expect anything along that line?" This was impossible. The Pacific Fleet after Pearl Harbor was in a state of disarray, nor could it, under the best of conditions, have been risked on such a foolhardy mission.

Within a few days Homma's troops had overrun two green Philippine divisions which had been trying desperately to hold off well-armed Japanese troops and tanks with rifles and old-fashioned, water-cooled machine guns that kept jamming. With only pitiful remnants of a navy or air force, MacArthur could not possibly hold the enemy at the beaches as planned. His troops would have to consider falling back on War Plan Orange-3. This was the old operation designed primarily to defend Manila Bay. Those ground troops now holding off the Japanese would slowly withdraw to Bataan Peninsula, where they could hold out for at least six months. And by that time surely the U.S. Navy could come to the rescue with supplies and reinforcements.

Next morning came more bad news. Overnight twenty-four more Japanese transports had landed in Lamon Bay, sixty air miles southeast of Manila. "Now we're caught from two sides," gloomily announced Will's breakfast companion, an army lieutenant. "I hear the chief is going to order Parker to withdraw his two divisions from south Luzon and head for Bataan." This meant, he said, that the battle in the south was over before it began. Two hours later this prediction came true and before noon MacArthur's staff was hastily convened. As they dejectedly left the room, the lieutenant sighted Will. "Sutherland told us that headquarters is moving over to Corregidor tonight." This was the small island fortress in the mouth of Manila Bay. "We can take field equipment and one suitcase or a bedroll. Happy days!"

The conversation was ended by the growing rumble of planes. Someone shouted, "Air raid!" A siren shrieked. Will rushed outside in time to see a bomb hit the Marsman Building, home of navy headquarters. Soon the entire port area was in flames. Several blocks away a trolley car was pitched into a building, with its tracks curled up grotesquely behind. Clouds of dust from pulverized cement and stone began to mix with black billows of smoke to hang a deathly pall over the entire area.

Will tried to send out another report to Marshall but the message center was too busy preparing for evacuation. He decided to walk to the embassy and try there. The streets were jammed with army trucks and commandeered squat Philippine buses filled with dispirited soldiers and supplies. The long lines of traffic moved slowly in the hot sun. Everything was headed north—to Bataan. He found the embassy in disorder too. People were darting around distractedly, each one apparently on some vital mission. No one had the time to give him more than a moment and he left in disgust. On the boulevard he recognized an Air Corps acquaintance in a jeep. En route to Fort McKinley, now air headquarters, he offered Will a ride. They found this installation in a state of shock. No one knew what was going on. A disgruntled captain buttonholed Will and began to curse the high brass. "They're bugging out and leaving us with our asses bare to the wind. The rest of us are supposed to leave in a transport. Fat chance!" But he rushed off to pack just in case.

Will and his Air Corps friend drove back to Victoria Street. A staff officer took Will aside to advise him confidentially to be at the docks before dark. They were taking a little steamer over to Corregidor. Will decided to go since he could send a message to Washington from there. At the dock area he finally located the steamer he was to board, the *Don Esteban*. After an hour others began to arrive with suitcases or bedrolls and Will realized he had left all his gear at Victoria Street. Finally General MacArthur arrived and the ship headed across the bay toward the little polliwog-shaped island called Corregidor, only thirty miles away. Soon it was dark. The air was balmy and the moon was shining. Will sat with the others on the decks. Men talked in hushed voices. Behind, they could see flames rise from Cavite's oil dumps. Someone, thought Will, was at last doing something constructive.

"Merry Christmas!" said a voice in the dark.

In the morning, after sending his message, Will examined the island. He learned it was called "The Rock." An apt name, he thought, for it had been designed by nature for defense. Standing on the top of the main body of the polliwog, he could see Manila. Smoke still rose from some parts. Turning to the left, he looked down at the tail end of the polliwog and saw it was at sea level. There was a little airstrip. Only three air miles to the north he could make out the southernmost shores of the tip end of Bataan Peninsula. Beyond rose several impressive cone-shaped mountains. Probably extinct volcanoes, he guessed.

Atop Corregidor, more than five hundred feet above the water, there was a cool breeze but they were probably sweating down at sea level. He could see why MacArthur had come here. Whoever owned this small island, sticking as it did in the bay's throat like a bone, controlled Manila Bay. He walked down a sharply curving highway until he came upon a series of huge, well-camouflaged guns sitting in cement emplacements dug in rock. At the bottom of the road he found the docks where the landing had been the night before. He walked a few hundred yards on level ground to a huge hump of solid rock. A soldier told him this was Malinta Hill. Will could see a large entrance to a tunnel and learned that it had many laterals, ingeniously constructed so that ten thousand people could live in its dank catacombs without fear of bombs or shells. Offices were being set up inside the tunnel.

He was told that the general lived in a little cottage half a mile beyond the other end of the tunnel. MacArthur was there that Christmas morning, contemplating the problem. He had no air or sea support. It was humiliating.

3.

Christmas at the Japanese Embassy on Massachusetts Avenue was subdued. The children were delighted to find a huge Christmas tree alight in the lower hall. But their parents were thinking of the hard days to come for Japan and themselves. The Todas had a private celebration in their little room. Masao opened his presents with the expectation and joy of millions of other children in the country. "I love Christmas," he said.

Two days later they were told to pack. They were going to a hotel in Hot Springs, Virginia. Here they would be interned until an exchange for American diplomats in Japan could be arranged. The ambassador and a few high officials would be driving to the train station, but the rest were to go in buses. A crowd outside the embassy gates was shouting at those lining up to enter the buses. The Japanese men took off their hats and bowed low to the embassy before entering the vehicles. This brought new jeers. As Floss hurried Masao to their bus, several in the crowd saw she was not Japanese and shouted insults.

It was worse when they got off at Union Station. The crowd there was even more vociferous. Photographers' flashbulbs exploded on all sides. Plainclothesmen pushed aside the crowd, and at last they boarded the train. As it headed south, Floss was soothed by the clacking of the wheels and the motion of the train. Tadashi was silent. They were on the first leg of their long journey to the homeland. But how would they be received? What lay ahead of them?

Malaya. December 29, 1941.

Tadashi's brother Shogo was celebrating another victory with Colonel
Tsuji. They had taken the strategic town of Ipoh with almost no casualties and were approaching Kuala Lumpur, capital of the Federated
Malay States. Tsuji now had full confidence in their strategy. Everything was going as planned and for the past few days he had been
expending his energies on an equally important matter: the political
and moral indoctrination of carefully selected young officers. He and
Shogo had been going from one frontline unit to another, and whenever there was a respite in the evening he would gather those who had
earlier shown a longing for a return to the old virtues and talk to them of
the past over whisky captured from the British. Tsuji would always have
Shogo find an isolated place such as in a secluded part of a rubber
plantation. Then in the light of a small campfire Tsuji would relate the
long history of Western depredations in Asia; of British, Dutch and
Portuguese arrogance; of the self-righteous condemnation of Japan's
buildup of Manchuria by Americans who had themselves wiped out the
Indians. He told how the ABCD powers had been formed to stem
Japan's rise as an industrial power and so encircled her, stopping the
flow of fuel. Shogo had heard all this many times but he never failed to
be roused by Tsuji's passionate logic.

Shogo would have been sickened and disillusioned if he had known
that his chief was also holding secret meetings with key officers who
shared the fanatical conviction that the seizure of Malaya was only the
first step in the freeing of all Asia. As each country was freed, Tsuji
preached, the next task was to punish those treacherous natives who
had conspired with the red barbarians. They too must be wiped out as a
moral lesson. That was the only way Asia could truly be returned to the
Asians. Tsuji told these selected adherents how their forefathers had
cleansed Nagasaki of the spreading corruption of Christianity, and related how the Japanese converts in that city as well as the Portuguese
priests had been burned, crucified, and subjected to the water torture.
"Ruthless cruelty!" he exclaimed. "We must steel ourselves to act as our
forefathers did!" In the flicker of the fire, his face distorted by vengeance, he seemed like a god to listeners inflamed with ardor to join his
crusade.

By the end of December, Tsuji was worn out mentally as well as physically. Shogo urged him to get more rest, but the closer they came to Singapore the more intense he became. His face grew haggard and his intense eyes seemed to be burning. He was short-tempered, critical of the slightest mistake, and insisted on staying up front so he could push attack units to the edge of their endurance.

Bataan. December 31, 1941.

The hastily organized flight to Bataan developed into a nightmare as seemingly endless lines of military vehicles poured into the peninsula from north and south. There were few military police at the base of Bataan and traffic was continually snarled. Out of eagerness of the military to reach safety there were numerous wrecks and tie-ups. Adding to the chaos were thousands of terrified civilian refugees fleeing from Homma's rapidly advancing troops. They came in oxcarts, *carte-las,* and decrepit cars. No one tried to stop them although the original WPO-3 plan called for the evacuation of all Filipinos living on the peninsula. With no idea what was going on, the villagers had stared incredulously at the constant parade of trucks, cars and guns roaring past their barrios on the dirt roads, coating their bamboo houses with thick layers of dust.

There was nothing more for Will to learn at Corregidor and he received permission to ride over to Manila in a navy launch. Late that afternoon he found the city in even greater panic. The main streets were jammed with trucks and guns of the South Luzon Force heading up toward Bataan.

Civilians were scampering around carrying loads on their backs or in little carts. Some were following the troops; others were going in the opposite direction, which was beginning to look much safer. Will made his way afoot to 1 Victoria Street where he had left his flight bag. He gasped to find the headquarters building cavernously empty—no furniture, no files; even light fixtures were gone. Nothing remained except scattered mounds of paper and refuse. He went into the men's room. It too had been stripped by scavengers. There were no fixtures at the sinks. Toilet seats were gone. He tried to flush the urinal but no water emerged. He started upstairs to the operations room, though he was positive his belongings had disappeared with everything else of value.

The offices were bare except for useless junk and paper. To his amazement there was his blue flight bag, standing fat and safe. Now he could shave with his own razor and cream! And get a fresh change of underwear.

It was already dark and Will decided it would be safer to sleep in the abandoned building. As he made a bed of paper, he recalled stories Mark had told of sleeping in boxcars on wrapping paper. He had never thought much about it before, but as he twisted and turned uncomfortably he wondered what madness had driven Mark to willingly seek such torture. He lasted until several hours past midnight before leaving the ghostly building. It was pitch dark outside. There was not a sound in the old Walled City district. It was as if he were the last man on earth. Then he heard the distant sound of trucks and hurried toward the bay. A few blacked-out vehicles were heading north. As he approached the boulevard a line of cars and trucks approached. More South Luzon troops, he guessed. He waved to a truck. It kept going but a filthy, battered staff car drew up. The back door opened.

"Climb in, son," said someone.

Will joined two officers in the back seat.

"Don't know why anyone in their senses would want to come along," said the man next to him cheerfully. He introduced himself. "Jones. I'm in charge of this outfit." Will had heard of the brigadier general who had recently been put in charge of the South Luzon force. He had been described as a crusty Welshman, a West Pointer who knew how to get his own way.

They were bound for a small town about twenty miles north. "Just got word that I'm supposed to get up there and stop the Japs. With what?" He grunted in disgust. He said nothing for some time, then turned to a companion on the left. "Something must have happened to Skinny," he said. "He wasn't supposed to be coming down to Bataan for a week." "Skinny," Will knew, was General Wainwright, commander of all troops in North Luzon.

An hour later their driver located Jones's new command post in a schoolhouse. The first light of day revealed a typical small Filipino town. Jones examined maps laid out on a large table. The remnants of two Philippine divisions were streaming down toward them just ahead of Homma. The first elements of these battle refugees were reported a few miles north. "Use any of them you can," Jones instructed. He ordered a battalion of his own placed astride the road just to the north.

It seemed to Will that Jones had an impossible task, but the general maneuvered his few troops so expertly that by nightfall the oncoming Japanese were stopped. Fascinated, Will watched the general slowly wind down after the hectic day. "Nothing now to do but wait and hope," said Jones. "Come on outside and enjoy the air." They went into the darkness. The town seemed deserted. There was no noise of battle. The bright moon lighted up a fountain and Jones headed for it. The picture of complete serenity, he lay on his back on flagstones and, supporting his head with his arms, peered up at the brilliant sky. Will sat beside him, hands locked over knees. The evening was fragrant with the exotic scent of frangipani. They could hear the distant rumble and rattle of trucks and buses coming from Manila and heading for Bataan. "Our people," said Jones quietly. "Will they all make it?" A moment later the general sat up and grinned. "Do you think Georgie Marshall would have enjoyed a day like this?"

"I think so, sir."

At his little cottage on Corregidor, MacArthur was reading a radio-gram from Marshall: Why didn't President Quezon come to America and set up a government in exile? MacArthur pondered a few minutes and then penciled an answer. Any evacuation of the Philippine president would be too dangerous. Moreover his departure "would be fol-lowed by the collapse of will to fight by the Filipinos." Most of MacAr-thur's army were Filipinos. "In view of their effort," he scribbled, "the United States must move strongly to their support or withdraw in shame from the Orient." Was this too strong? No, nothing was too strong if it could get some action from the Munitions Building.

He walked up a rise to get a view of Manila. The city was dark except for flames. Fort McKinley must still be burning. Also Nichols and Niel-son fields and Cavite. And the brightest flames were probably from the Pandacan oil fields. What a waste! But nothing could be left for the Japanese. The enemy were at the gates of the once beautiful city. He wondered if the Manila Hotel had been bombed. Was the luxurious seven-room penthouse suite given him by the Philippine Government still intact?

As MacArthur slowly returned to his cottage he was consoled by reports indicating that he had fooled Homma, and many of his troops would probably escape into Bataan. It had been humiliating to order a retreat but it meant that the fight would go on. Until Washington finally sent help.

After accompanying General Jones into Bataan, Will was sent farther back to the headquarters of Skinny Wainwright, who would command one of the two corps set up to defend the peninsula. From Corregidor, MacArthur would command both corps. By January 7, fifteen thousand Americans and forty-five thousand Filipinos were prepared to withstand the first Japanese assaults. MacArthur was supposed to hold out for six months, an almost impossible task since only ten thousand of the Filipinos were professional soldiers of the elite Philippine Division. The rest were almost totally untrained.

Fortunately most of Bataan was covered with mountains and thick jungles with defense positions that could be hidden from air observation. The peninsula, fifteen miles wide and thirty miles long, boasted only two roads. The main highway led down the flat, swampy east coast; the second, a narrow cobblestone road, cut across Bataan like a belt through the valley between two large extinct volcanoes.

It was some seven or eight miles north of this cobblestone road that MacArthur planned to establish his main battle position. It was a strategic location since it used Mount Natib as its centerpiece. This volcano was so rugged and steep that it was an impassable defense. Only to its right and left would troops have to be emplaced.

Wainwright was to hold the left side, and Will was heartened to find that within forty-eight hours the exhausted, downhearted troops he had watched trudge into their positions had regained their fighting spirit. Food and rest had worked wonders, and for the first time he felt some optimism. He borrowed a jeep and went down the cobblestone road to visit the right flank commanded by Major General Parker.

By the time Will got back to Wainwright's headquarters on the other side of the peninsula it was dark. There were no gloomy faces at dinner. They all were determined to stay a long time. Wainwright sat down across from Will. "Gentlemen," he said, "we are going to have a visitor tomorrow morning. General MacArthur is coming over to see us." He turned to a major. "He wants every general officer to be on hand."

For the first time in a week Will slept until shaken awake. At breakfast Wainwright suggested he join the I Corps generals. "I'm sure Douglas will be happy to see that you're still among the living." The little group of generals proceeded to a clearing near the western end of the cobblestone road. Before long a convoy of four cars appeared from the direction of Parker's lines. MacArthur stepped out of a Ford and walked briskly up to Wainwright. "Jonathan," he said cordially. "I'm glad to see you back safely from the north. The execution of your withdrawal and of your mission covering the withdrawal of the South Luzon Force was as fine as anything in history."

It sounded to Will like a speech and he half expected MacArthur to pin a decoration on Wainwright. He noticed a quizzical look on the latter's face as if wondering whether he deserved quite that much praise.

"Where are your 155 mm. guns?"

"Let's go over and see them," said Wainwright.

"I don't want to *see* them," said MacArthur. "I want to *hear* them."

That was a good line, thought Will, and should be in a movie.

MacArthur walked along the line of waiting I Corps generals and talked briefly to each one. Upon noticing Will in the background he came over to shake his hand. "Glad to see you alive, young man," he said. Then he turned to address the group. He told of his optimism and enthusiasm about the way things were going.

Enlisted men watching the scene could not hear what MacArthur said but they were making snide remarks about his jaunty jacket, his smartly pressed pants and necktie. "Skinny," remarked one man, "looks like he just crawled out of a foxhole." Wainwright and his officers were in wrinkled khakis stained with dirt, sweat, and blood. "Dugout Doug's gang," said another, "look like they're going to a dance."

MacArthur was pleased with everything he saw and heard. As he was about to leave in the afternoon, he asked Will if he'd like to come back to Corregidor. Will accepted. Marshall should know what the situation was on Bataan. He felt a bit like a deserter as he watched the Bataan coast become smaller, but soon after entering Malinta Tunnel he knew he had made the right decision. Trouble was brewing in high places. President Quezon was becoming disenchanted with Washington's failure to send aid. "I hear he's about to blow his top," a navy commander told Will, "but apparently Mac knows nothing about it."

Disquieting reports soon came from Bataan. Wainwright's defense positions across the middle of the peninsula, the Abucay Line, were holding, but pressure was increasing. Then on January 24 it was learned that a Japanese regiment had done the impossible—it had climbed over Mount Natib with small mountain guns and was now behind the American lines. Rumors of the breakthrough spread along the Abucay Line. The defenders fought back desperately, but it was evident by afternoon that their position was hopeless. At dusk the retreat began and soon the trail to the rear was jammed with those in buses and on foot. Since there was no moonlight, infiltrating Japanese—about the same height as the

Filipinos—could easily have joined the sad parade moving south unnoticed. Yet there was no hysteria in the disciplined confusion. The chief prayer was that no shells would fall on the trail.

At Corregidor, MacArthur was writing a radiogram to Marshall. He had lost about 35 percent of his entire force and was retiring to a line behind the Pilar-Bagac Highway—the cobblestone road. "I have personally selected and prepared this position and it is strong." The next twenty-four hours could determine the future of Bataan and USAFFE.

4.

Malaya. January 31, 1942.

Tsuji was going from unit to unit driving the troops forward by inspiration, not threats. He and Shogo exposed themselves to enemy fire as if they were immune to bullets. This roused the men to deeds of derring-do. Everything seemed to work for Tsuji now. His mind was clear and he gave birth to operational tactics that brought quick success.

He had a new slogan, "Speed, speed, speed!" Although the Japanese were outnumbered two to one, he kept urging local commanders never to consolidate a gain, regroup, or wait for supplies. Yamashita was wise enough to give Tsuji his head. The invaders surged down the main roads of Malaya on thousands of bicycles. Nothing stopped them. At destroyed bridges they would wade across rivers holding their bicycles aloft. In deeper water they crossed on log bridges supported on the shoulders of rugged engineers.

On learning that bicycle tires were being blown by the intense heat, Tsuji sent word to ride down the paved highways on the rims. The clatter would sound like tanks and terrify the defenders. Perhaps the only man not at all surprised by the accelerating Japanese advance was Tsuji. Success had never surprised the "God of Operations," only failure.

By the end of January the surviving British forces were backed up to the tip end of the peninsula. By midnight of the thirty-first most of the troops had crossed the seventy-foot-wide causeway that connected the peninsula with the island of Singapore. Just after dawn, to a skirl of bagpipes, the remnants of the Argyll Battalion marched briskly onto the bridge—ninety men. Bringing up the rear was their commander, the last man off Malaya. Demolition squads laid charges on the causeway. At

8 A.M. there was a dull roar and, when the smoke drifted away, onlookers could see water rushing through a wide gap. "Fortress Singapore" was safely cut off from the Japs. The island extended twenty-six miles from east to west, fourteen miles from north to south. The bulk of the population was clustered in the city in the extreme south. There were a few scattered towns but the rest of the island was covered with rubber plantations and jungle growth. General Percival had decided to make his stand on the beaches. On paper he was favored. The Japanese had only thirty thousand troops (he had thought there were twice as many) and he had eighty-five thousand men. Of these, fifteen thousand were noncombatants and many of the others were poorly trained and armed. But the Japs would surely suffer disastrous casualties in any attempt to storm across Johore Strait.

For his headquarters Yamashita selected the Green Palace, a tall brick and tile building overlooking the causeway leading across Johore Strait. The command post was set up in the top of a five-story observation tower, giving the Japanese a strategic vista of the north coast of Singapore island. When one officer protested that this would make them sitting targets, Tsuji said, "The British would never have enough imagination to think we were foolhardy enough to do this."

Yamashita laughed. "I'm sure it also must run against British policy to bombard such a fine building."

Inspired by the view, Tsuji sat up all that night, kept awake by pots of tea brewed by Shogo, devising a plan that would throw the stolid British completely off balance. He guessed they would put their cards on a beach defense. Therefore, the plan should not only be unorthodox, but would have to be pushed despite casualties. In the first two days lay victory or an overwhelming defeat. Shogo agreed.

After many calculations Tsuji made his decision. "We will launch the main attack with two divisions to the right of the causeway. At night."

Early in the morning Tsuji revealed his plan. Yamashita nodded approval. "Success," said Tsuji, "will depend on complete secrecy." All inhabitants within a dozen miles of the strait were to be evacuated while the two attack divisions moved stealthily into position.

Yamashita summoned forty division commanders and senior officers to a nearby rubber plantation. As Tsuji and Shogo watched, the general read out the attack orders. His face was flushed. *Kikumasamune*, ceremonial wine, was poured into each man's canteen cap. A traditional toast was drunk: "It is a good place to die and we shall conquer."

5.

Will, chafing for action, was just boarding a navy launch at Corregidor. He was bound for Bataan where the new defense line had been set up. It was again divided into two commands, with Wainwright holding the western half of the peninsula and Parker the eastern.

Will disembarked at the tip end of Bataan at the town of Mariveles. A sailor in a battered car was waiting for him and he was driven up the east coast road. He was heartened to find that the survivors of the Abucay Line debacle were rested and in shape to fight. Then he was driven back to Mariveles and up the western side of the peninsula. Wainwright was conferring with several officers. He was even gaunter than before but his eyes were quick and piercing. He looked up with a smile. "Glad to see you again, Captain. Come over for a chat in the trailer as soon as you're settled."

The next morning Will drove forward with the general and his aide. At the front they inspected several company command posts and talked with squad leaders and privates. On the way back, shells began to fall on both sides of the trail. The car jerked to a stop and everybody jumped into foxholes—all, that is, except Wainwright. He sat on a row of sandbags talking to an infantry captain.

From his foxhole Will watched in wonder as the general kept on conversing as if he were in the Munitions Building. After the barrage Will said, "Don't you think that was a little foolish, sir, risking your life that way?"

The general smiled crookedly. "Will," he drawled, "what have we to offer these troops? More food? More ammunition? We can't give these poor devils anything but morale. That's why I come up front every day."

For more than a week Will toured both sides of the peninsula talking with enlisted men as well as officers, both American and Filipino. One of the most informative and interesting was Captain Jess Villamor, the sole Filipino ace. They met on a hot morning at the only airstrip on Bataan, near Mariveles. A bare piece of land scraped off the hogback of a small hill, it could only launch fighters and observation planes. Villamor had just volunteered to get aerial photographs of the region southeast of Cavite. The brass on "The Rock" needed this information, he explained, since cleverly concealed Japanese guns in that location were punishing Corregidor.

"Sounds suicidal," said Will.

Villamor smiled wryly. "I thought they'd give me a fast plane. But I found out you can't operate an aerial camera from a P-40. There's the one I'm going up in." He pointed to an old training plane sitting forlornly at one end of the airstrip. "A Stearman PT-11," he said. "It has no fighting altitude, maybe a few thousand feet. No armament. Top speed perhaps eighty-two miles an hour."

Will was appalled. "You'll be a sitting duck against a Zero."

"Well, the entire Air Force is going to escort me." Six P-40's, the last American fighters in the Philippines, began revving motors. "Hope I see you later, Captain," said Villamor and trotted toward his forlorn plane.

Will had heard some Americans make derisive remarks about Filipinos in battle. He wished they could have watched Villamor's little plane lumber down the runway and slowly climb toward its escort. Will joined a group watching the disappearing planes. They scanned the empty sky for what seemed like an eternity. Finally over the treetops to the southeast Will saw P-40's winging in low with throttled engines hovering protectively above a slow-moving plane. Someone said, "My God, they're throwing away fighting altitude." Suddenly there was a high, piercing scream as six fighter planes dived from above. "Zeros!" exclaimed the air intelligence officer. The flat rattle of guns broke out. The little group cringed as if the bullets were meant for them. A grounded pilot shook his fists and shouted curses.

Will could see one Zero detach itself from the others and swoop down on Villamor's Stearman. One burst would tear it apart. Villamor came in to the strip at top speed followed by the streaking Zero. As the Stearman's wheels lightly touched the ground, spurts of dirt kicked up on one side. Another Zero streaked down like a hawk. As it neared the Stearman, Villamor abruptly turned and these bullets also missed. "He'll ground-loop!" someone said. But Villamor somehow managed to hold the little trainer steady. Another marauder swept down and fired. Pieces of Villamor's right wing hurtled past the cockpit. The plane swerved in the other direction and just as the right wing began flapping another burst tore into the left wing. The plane was making for a revetment. There was a screech of wheels. The Stearman jerked to a stop in a cloud of dust—just inside the revetment. The cameraman leaped from the plane carrying the film, followed by Villamor. Pursued by another Zero, they raced for cover in a clump of bamboo trees.

Moments later the action was all above the airfield. Zeros and P-40's turned and dived, banked and climbed in a spectacular air battle. It was a wild free-for-all with individual dogfights. Will gaped. It was like something from the First World War. He could hear the chattering of long and short bursts as the P-40's, under every inch of manifold pressure, threw themselves all over the sky. He wanted to shout out to the heavier P-40's not to climb! He saw one on the way up quickly overtaken by a Zero as tiny, it seemed, as a butterfly. There was a quick burst and the P-40 flamed up and plunged downward. But other P-40's were diving on their smaller foes. There were two simultaneous bursts of flame and the two Zeros spun down together, almost as if their descent had been choreographed.

At last it was over and Villamor was reporting to his superiors.

"We did well today," Villamor confided to Will. "I hear Stone bought it but we knocked down four of them." Now that they were learning how to deal with the Zero it was too late, he added bitterly. Most of their comrades had been shot down because they had tried to climb on the lighter Zeros.

That afternoon Will got a ride to a Filipino division in Parker's corps. He had learned that the son of one of Quezon's closest friends wanted to speak to him. It took him two hours to locate Third Lieutenant Mateo Domingo, a small, wiry, intense young man who had left law school to join the army. For fifteen minutes he poured out complaints. "The Americans keep goddamning this blasted country for the war, the mosquitoes, and the lousy rations!" His men resented the Yanks' arrogant manner. "And they all think you people are getting better food. Besides, whose war is this? We're giving everything we've got and we're being left on the vine to rot."

Will finally got a chance to ask what he could do.

"You can come with me to Corregidor where I can tell President Quezon of the situation." As Will started to protest, Domingo quickly said, "I have permission from General Lim. You can confirm to the President what I say."

"What do you mean *I'll* confirm you?"

Domingo, almost a foot shorter, looked up with candid eyes. "Some of our people met you and they think you sympathize with us."

"Certainly I sympathize but—"

"All we ask is that you tell the truth—as you see it."

Will agreed reluctantly wondering how he could avoid antagonizing MacArthur. He felt uneasy all during the tedious trip to Mariveles, but as they boarded a small fishing boat and set off at dusk, the excitement of the adventure took over. There was no moon and Corregidor loomed only as a mysterious bulk. The water became choppy as they approached the island. Domingo started to strip.

"What's the matter?" asked Will.

"The fisherman won't take us much farther. He's afraid some trigger-happy American on guard will fire at us." Will reluctantly stripped and then covered himself with heavy oil as Domingo had already done. He watched in amazement as his small companion tied a bag on his back. "Life preserver," he explained. "It's filled with Ping-Pong balls. That's one thing the Americans gave us plenty of."

"Ping-Pong balls!"

He handed Will a similar bag. "We couldn't get any real life preservers," he said, then added somewhat apologetically, "Sorry, but I don't swim very well."

Will was speechless. The man must be mad. He tossed the bag aside. It would only be a hindrance. By now the little boat was rocking violently. He guessed there were strong currents ahead. The boat stopped and the fisherman waved for them to jump out. Will looked ahead. They must be almost a mile away. He himself was a strong swimmer; he had once swum ten miles across Squam Lake. Holding his knotted clothing in one hand, he dived into water that was surprisingly cold. He turned to see his companion clumsily clambering overboard, almost tipping over the fishing boat.

Domingo was proceeding slowly with an ineffective dog paddle. A large wave tipped him over and he began gasping for breath. In a few strokes Will was at his side. An hour later they ran into a heavy crosscurrent. Once more Domingo was in trouble and Will had to drag him fifty yards into calmer water. The little man was mad, thought Will, but he had guts. Domingo tried to say thank you, swallowed water and again had to be helped. Finally they could hear the lapping of water on a beach. "Quiet," said Will in Domingo's ear. Slowly, making as little splash as possible, they swam until their feet touched sand. Domingo pointed triumphantly ahead. They were near the mouth of Malinta Tunnel. No one was in sight. They wrung out their clothes and donned them. Domingo was so exhausted that Will had to help him as they entered the tunnel and made directly for the Quezon family quarters. A few minutes later they came upon two young women in the lighted corridor. "Nini!" said Domingo. "Baby!" These were the President's two daughters. Neither recognized Domingo at first. "You've lost so much weight!" one said and opened the door to their father's room.

"Papa! Look who swam to Corregidor. Mateo Domingo!"

Domingo saluted, then kissed Quezon's hand in respect to an elder. He introduced Will. The President told them both to sit down. "How thin you are, Mateo. How is it on Bataan?"

Domingo's exhaustion vanished. "We are doing fine, Excellency." Then he told of the growing dissension between the American and Filipino soldiers.

"You have to know the Americano to understand him," said the President calmly. "He is gruff and rough but it's just his way." He turned to Will. "I hope you are not offended."

"Not at all, sir."

"But, Excellency," protested Domingo, "why is it that they have better rations than we do? Why don't we get the same? We eat only salmon and sardines. One can per thirty men, twice a day."

"What?" Quezon was astounded and indignant.

"Isn't that so, Captain?" Domingo turned to Will.

"Yes, sir," he admitted.

"One can of salmon for thirty, two *gantas* of rice and two cans of condensed milk for breakfast."

Quezon turned to the embarrassed Will. He had to nod his head in affirmation. If MacArthur learned what he was doing!

"Puñeta!" cried Quezon angrily. "I did not know that."

Just then MacArthur walked into the room. Will's heart fell, but he came to attention as did Domingo.

"General," said Quezon, "this is Mateo Domingo, the son of Rigoberto, one of my cabinet members."

MacArthur shook Domingo's hand.

"I thought you were on Bataan, McGlynn," said the general, but didn't extend a hand.

Quezon's breath was coming in gasps. Domingo helped him into a chair. "Mateo," said Quezon, breathing heavily, "I want you to tell the general what you just told me."

While Mateo was doing so, Will noticed several officers behind MacArthur shifting uncomfortably. One caught Will's eye and gave him a hard look.

Quezon turned to the general. "I want you to improve the rations."

"We certainly shall, Excellency." MacArthur shook Domingo's hand again. "You did a fine and courageous service, young man." He glanced at Will.

"I came over to send a report to Washington, sir," he said.

MacArthur's face was impassive. "Next time, Captain, why not use the facilities on Bataan? We've run a cable over there, you know."

"Thank you, sir."

As soon as MacArthur and his officers left, the ailing Quezon put an arm around Domingo and said wistfully, "If I were only forty years younger, I'd be with you. Tell your comrades on Bataan that my thoughts are always with them."

Singapore. February 12, 1942.

Tsuji's plan to storm the island of Singapore had taken the British by surprise and the inspired Japanese assault troops, outnumbered more than two to one, plunged relentlessly toward the city of Singapore. In three days advance troops were approaching the racetrack at the edge of the city, but ammunition was dangerously low and there were no more reserves. There was talk of pulling back but Tsuji suggested they try and bluff the British commander, General Percival, with a demand of surrender.

A few hours later a Japanese reconnaissance plane dropped a tube marked by red and white streamers on the outskirts of the beleaguered city. It called upon the British to surrender to save the lives not only of troops but of civilians. For more than two days there was no answer. "If they hold out another twenty-four hours," Shogo glumly prophesied on the morning of February 15, they'll beat us." A field phone rang. An aide called out excitedly, "Sir, a report from the front. The British are sending out a flag of truce."

That afternoon Tsuji and Shogo watched as the surrender party dismounted in front of the Ford factory near a suburban village. "We did bluff them," he said in an undertone to Shogo. "We'd have been beaten if we'd had to fight it out within the city."

At 7:50 P.M. the truce was finally signed. Forty minutes later, as agreed, the roar of battle abruptly ceased. Singapore, the City of the Lion, one of the most famous fortresses in the world, was Nipponese. The British, lords of the Orient for so many years, had been crushed by orientals.

That night Tsuji told Shogo to keep order at their new command post. He secretly met with his radical followers. "We have proved to our Asian brothers that the white man can be defeated!" he said, eyes aglow. Then he began to rant about the treacherous Chinese who had been working for the British. "Did you see the way they glared stonily at us as we passed? They are worse than the red barbarians. They must be taught a lesson."

CHAPTER EIGHT

1.

San Diego, California. December 9, 1941.

When Mark reached San Diego, he and the other recruits tumbled out of the train and began asking questions of a tall, lean and mean-looking Marine sergeant standing on the platform. "Fall in!" he roared. "You idiots keep your yaps shut until I tell you to open them!" Underneath the brim of his pith helmet glared two little eyes and there was instant quiet. "On the double into that vee-hicle!" He jerked a thumb at a truck.

Mark climbed into the rear, wondering whether the sergeant was putting on an act or was as surly as he looked. The recruits were quiet, apprehensive, after their rude welcome to the Marine Corps. They rubbernecked at the palm trees and the picturesque Spanish architecture. Most of them had never been this far south, and it was a thrill to be only a dozen miles from the Mexican border. They stared at Marines returning to the base from liberty, and Mark felt a surge of excitement as he sighted the gate to the recruit depot. A Marine sentry was checking traffic. For Mark it was like that magic moment of entering a skid row for the first time and wondering what adventures lay ahead.

The trucks passed under a Spanish stucco arch onto a huge asphalt drill field. Two-story stucco barracks extended along one side of the field. Opposite were rows of tents and Quonset huts on wooden decks. The tents held eight recruits; the Quonset huts sixteen.

What fascinated Mark was the activity on the vast drill field; numerous platoons of young men rigidly marching to the singsong cadence of the drill instructors. Occasionally the pattern would be broken by a platoon standing stiffly at attention while a hands-on-hips drill instructor berated a hapless recruit, their two faces only inches apart.

The trucks pulled up in front of the Quonset hut area. The sergeant shouted, "Out!" without turning around. In a minute the group was standing apprehensively around him. He swept them with another glare. "Some of you shitheads are chewing gum. Get rid of it!" One man started to throw his away. "Not on the deck, shithead. It's your gum. Swallow it!"

After he told them they wouldn't be formed into platoons for a few days, Mark asked, "Where's the men's room?"

"Jeez Coo-rist, shithead, the head's over there. Talk like a Marine, Joe College."

"May I be excused?" said Mark.

The sergeant pursed his lips. "May I be eggscused! Go, before you wet your pants." Then he added as Mark started off, "And while you're there clean it up. Every single crapper."

In the next few days the Quonsets filled up. Single bunks were changed into doubles as young men from states west of the Mississippi began pouring in. They were all sizes and shapes and nationalities. They came from farms, factories, colleges, gas stations, and high schools. Mark was the oldest. Most were eighteen and entered wide-eyed, full of hopes and apprehensions. By this time Mark had learned a new language, as fascinating to him as the language of freight riders. Many terms had a naval basis: topside was up; below, down; port, left side; starboard, right side; deck, floor; overhead, ceiling; bulkhead, wall; ladder, stairs; scuttlebutt, gossip; boondocks, swamps and marsh or any back country; and boondockers, shoes worn in such terrain.

"You are *not* civilians," a tough D.I. instructed them. "And you will talk like Marines." He began counting on his fingers. "This is a rifle, *not* a gun. These are scivvies, *not* underwear. This is Joe, *not* coffee. This is moo for your coffee, *not* cream. This is shit-on-a-shingle, *not* ground hamburger on toast. This is foreskins on toast, *not* chipped beef."

A smart aleck interrupted. "Sergeant, I'm going to write my ma and dad a letter. Do you have any special words for them?"

"No," said the sergeant curtly, "but I've got a special word for 'Your ass is dragging.' That word is: 'Take ten laps around the parade ground, double time.'"

They were herded through clothing issue, receiving pith helmets, khaki shirts, ties, trousers, shorts and T-shirts, sox and rough leather high shoes. Next they drew their web gear: cartridge belt, bayonet with scabbard, first-aid packet, canteen and pack. Everything was stowed in a seabag. Finally came the rifle, the first that many, including Mark, had ever handled. Then in hectic, rapid sequence they were receiving inoculations, getting their heads shorn, and drawing mattress, sheets, blanket, mattress cover, pillow and cases.

At last they were formed into platoons and Mark's group inwardly groaned to discover their sergeant was the mean lanky one. He surveyed them. "You people got tough shit," he drawled. "You got me. You're lucky, though. You're assigned to a hut with a screen door instead of them fuckin' tents over on the sand. Shit! The mosquitoes are so big around here they can fuck a turkey standing flat-footed!"

He assigned them to bunks. "Up, Joe College!" he ordered Mark, pointing to an upper bunk. His mate below was a rosy-cheeked young farmer from Iowa named Marvin Owens. He confessed he had never been out of that state before. Mark had seen hundreds like him on the road and felt fortunate he had not been saddled with some loudmouth.

After they were settled the sergeant ordered them to line up. "Mah name is Redd with two d's and call me sir! Ah come from Mississippi and Ah'm proud of it. Y'all are boots, shitheads, and Ah don't want any damn-Yankee back talk. Ah don't want to hear a word from any motherfucker unless Ah ask for it. Here we call any talk in ranks, any smirk or move, grab-assing! And grab-assing means trouble! Get it! Now answer as your name is called." He finally hollered, "Owens!" Marvin was so nervous he could barely speak. "Ah can't hear you, shithead! Speak up!"

Marvin blushed furiously. "I'm not a shithead."

"You are a shithead, *sir!*" Redd poked Marvin's chest with a swagger stick and when the young man pulled away, kicked him sharply in the shin. Marvin cried out in pain. "Ah told you no grab-assing!" He kicked Marvin in the other shin.

Mark, standing next to Marvin, moved in protest toward Redd. Redd grabbed a handful of Mark's shirt. "That's also grab-assing, Joe College. Now take your best toothbrush and clean every crapper in the head. And this time do a better job of it! Move, before Ah get real mad!" He turned to the others and said with a sickening smile, "Ah want you men to know Ah love my mommy, Ah love my daddy, Ah love my little brother, and Ah love my baby sister. Ah'm really a nice guy"—he hardened his voice—"even if some of you shitheads think that a crow shit on a rock and Ah was hatched by the sun."

The next few weeks became a relentless grind of close-order drill, double-timing to class, bayonet practice, dog-trotting around the obstacle course, and simply standing at strict attention for an hour at a time. In between these exercises Redd would muster the platoon in front of the platoon hut for inspection and egg them to grab-ass and reap punishment. Once Redd walked up to Mark, stared at him, and in a piercing voice said, "You want to fuck my wife?"

"No, sir!"

"Oh, she's not good enough for you, Joe College? Let's see you do a hundred push-ups!"

The next day Redd asked Mark the same question.

"Yes, sir!" he said.

"Take that shit-eating grin off your face, McGlynn, you're a mother-fucker!" Redd ordered him to march around the parade ground that night with rifle and a heavy bag of sand.

Next morning Redd repeated the question. This time Mark remained silent. "What's the matter, Joe College, too chicken to express yourself? What the hell kind of Marine do we have here? See that flagpole over there? Do two laps around yelling, 'Ah'm a shithead from Yamasul' And you better do it fast." Mark did double time to the flagpole and back.

The other D.I.'s would use similar tactics to teach the men self-control but they were merely hard, not mean. While ragging the men one would say, "You're as useless as tits to a bull." At first several would laugh, but after a few weeks no one blinked an eye when the same sergeant said, "You're as useless as a bump on a nun's cunt."

The platoon corporal, Benz, was also a disciplinarian but with a crude sense of humor that helped break the monotony. After waking every-one in the hut with a blaring recording of "The Star-Spangled Banner," Benz would shout, "Hit the deck! Drop your cocks and grab your sox!" Then, while they were dressing he would deliver the morning lecture: "Is that as fast as you guys can go? Is this what your mom had to put up with every morning you got out of bed?" The next day he made every-one stand naked, mattresses rolled under the left arm. The majority would have erections as rigid as ramrods. And Benz would shout loud enough to be heard a hundred yards, "There'll be no hard-ons in my platoon!"

After three weeks of this regimentation Redd announced that they were going to see a movie that night. The boots couldn't believe their luck and in the dark they marched without rifles to the theater. They filed in and sat down. For a moment Mark almost forgot where he was. He looked around at his comrades: a bunch of scalped eagles, afraid to breathe too loud, afraid to talk, afraid to take a crap. He had been in jails but nothing as bad as this. They were like convicts in the Big House. He wondered if he could make it until he got into a real fighting outfit. The good thing was that he was not alone. Everyone looked like a scalded cat. And he remembered what he had read in the Marine pamphlet at

the recruiting office: "We will remove the last trace of individuality."
They were doing it in hopes it would save their lives in battle.

At last the platoon drew green blouses, trousers, and the same natty
fair-weather leather belts the D.I.'s wore. At last they looked like real
Marines. By this time the struggle between Redd and Mark had reached
a new level. Someone defecated in Redd's footlocker. He blew his
whistle, assembled them in a circle, and dumped the excrement in
Mark's hand.

"Pass it," he said and it went around the circle several times before it
was all gone. Then Redd stuck his nose a few inches from Mark's. "Did
you do this, shithead?"

"No, sir."

"Do you know who did it?"

Mark hesitated a split second since he knew. "Yes, sir."

"Well, who is it?" Mark was silent. "I said, 'Who the hell was it?' "
When Mark remained silent, Redd jabbed him cruelly in the stomach
with his swagger stick. As Mark bent over in pain, Redd kicked him in
the ankle. "Okay, smart-ass. You drill all night with your pack full of
rocks."

The climax of their confrontation came during the first jujitsu class.
The instructor, an ex-professional wrestler, demonstrated the art of
disarming and surprising an enemy and then called for a volunteer to
pretend to be a Japanese. He pointed at Mark. "You." Mark had attended judo classes in Japan and stepped forward warily. He would let
the instructor throw him.

"Let me show them," said Redd taking the instructor's place. Redd,
taller and heavier, edged toward Mark and suddenly made a quick
move. Instead of backing away, Mark darted forward and flopped Redd
to the sand. Only the training of weeks kept the platoon from cheering.

Redd, furious, scrambled to his feet. "I slipped," he said. "We'll try
again." This time as he approached Mark he threw a handful of sand in
his face. Mark dropped to hands and knees, rolled over and came to a
crouch. Although half blinded by sand he could see Redd lunge at him.
He flung a handful of sand in the sergeant's face, tripped him up with a
leg.

"That was quick thinking, son," the ex-wrestler told Mark as he
helped Redd to his feet. "You're sure doing a good job with your platoon, Redd."

Mark spent the rest of the afternoon running the drill field with rifle
and full pack. Fortunately for him, the next day the platoon was sent out

to the rifle range for a three-week small-arms course. It was like a vacation to Mark. The instructors, hard-boiled experts, were patient. All the boots were in good spirits. They had learned hard lessons the past two months and had endured the cruelties of Redd. They knew how to handle a bayonet, and could jog through the obstacle course without gasping for breath. They had learned how to dig gun emplacements and foxholes. At rifle drill their piece no longer felt like a dead weight, and they already had more than half an inch of hair. They were beginning to feel like real Marines.

Here at the rifle range they had a chance to add something to their $20.80 a month. Anyone qualifying as expert would get an extra five dollars; as sharpshooter, three dollars. More important, what they learned in the coming days could save their lives. All the instructors were tough but helpful, and Mark would never forget the wise words of his instructor: "Treat your rifle like your sweetheart. When you're in bed with her do you jerk her tit or do you gently squeeze it? So gently squeeze the trigger, don't jerk it! Take a breath and hold it and then squeeze her nice and gentle."

At first Mark was awkward in the prone position. "Don't stick up your tail like a Dago whoore," advised the instructor and pushed Mark to the ground. "Flat, like that." This went on relentlessly, endlessly day after day. Finally the platoon shot for record. Four boots got expert. Mark was one of them.

The platoon left the range elated and cocky. Everyone had qualified and there was only one week left for exams. Mark passed with high grades and was advised to apply for one of the specialist schools. But he surprised them by requesting assignment to the 6th Marine Regiment, which was just returning from Iceland. He assumed this outfit would be the first sent back to fight Hitler.

The platoon needed no prompting by Redd and Corporal Benz to prepare properly for the final parade. Since return from the range Redd had glared at Mark several times but had made no attempt to harass him. At last came the whistle for the final assembly. Redd and the D.I.'s went up and down the ranks inspecting each man, adjusting field scarves and caps. In their neat green uniforms they marched sharply and proudly down the big parade ground. They were United States Marines and would be for the rest of their lives. Mark never thought he would share such an emotion, but as the band played "The Marine Hymn" he felt a big lump in his throat. The insults, hardship and humiliation showered on him by the D.I.'s meant nothing for he realized this had been preparation for battle. But Redd, marching ahead, stiff as a ramrod, was something else. He was rotten.

There were shrieks of joy in the barracks as the platoon stowed away gear and prepared to leave the hellhole. Then came a harsh, "Hear this!" It was Redd. "I got a few last words. You're a pretty good bunch except for a few foul balls. Remember what I taught you and you may live. Anyway, good luck."

A few men came up and shook his hand but the rest just stared at him. Then Corporal Benz took over. "I've got your assignments, fellows." Most of them were assigned to a guard company. A few were to go to specialist schools, and one man to the range as a rifle instructor. "Mc-Glynn, you and Owens will join the 6th Marines." When Benz finished there were cheers and everyone wanted to pump his hand. Redd turned on his heel and marched out.

2.

Mark and Marvin carried their seabags to a barracks on the base where they were assigned to a casual company to wait several weeks for the arrival of the 6th Marine Regiment at nearby Camp Elliott. During boot camp Mark had only had time to send postcards but now he could write long letters to Maggie, Poky, Will, and Floss. He sent a shorter letter to his father who, he felt, would not be interested in the details of his boot training.

There was little to do except pick up cigarette butts and police the area. At first it was difficult to get used to the freedom and leisure time. Mark and Marvin would walk stiffly around the base expecting to be stopped any moment with a raucous, "Hear this!" But no one paid any attention to them. For a week they remained on the base, going to the movies, visiting friends in nearby tent areas, reading and writing letters. While buying an ornate pillow at the post exchange for Floss, Mark was told that Maggie was at the Grand Hotel. In half an hour he found her in the crowded, smoky lobby. She rushed to him and kissed him. "My God, your hair!" She ruffled the inch-long bristle. "You're so tan—and different." He was leaner, harder, meaner-looking. She hugged him, then noticed the gaudy pillow under his arm. "What is that thing?"

It was a mélange of loud colors—red, blue, green, orange—with a big bulldog, the Marine mascot, in the center. The dog's collar bore the inscription "Full of fight." He grinned. "It's for Floss."

She burst out laughing and read aloud the verse printed under the bulldog:

MOTHER OF MINE

I always think of Mother, no matter where I roam;
I always think of Mother, although I'm far from home;
Friends and many others, often prove untrue.
But never does a Mother—for her heart is always true.

"Do you think Floss will like it?" he asked.

"Like it! She'll love it!"

As they walked arm in arm down the street, Maggie asked if he planned to go to officer candidate school. He laughed. "Me, a brass hat? Don't be ridiculous. I just want to get into the fight, not make a career in the Marines."

It was just like him, thought Maggie. She explained that the Todas were interned at a hotel in Hot Springs. They were all being sent back to Japan. Both agreed that Floss would keep the family afloat in Tokyo with her buoyant spirit and courage.

Maggie told Mark what she was doing on the West Coast. She now was a roving reporter for *Inside,* a weekly Washington newsletter run by Max Steiner, an old friend of their father. He had nominated himself as the successor to Lincoln Steffens and other muckrakers and kept his readers amused, incensed, and enlightened with the most embarrassing tales of misdeeds and foibles committed by those who trod the corridors of power.

"You'd love Max. He can't be bought or scared off. And he wears a suit that hasn't been pressed since Roosevelt became President. He sent me out here to check on the internment of nisei in California."

Mark was astounded, for he had read nothing about it. "But most of them are American citizens! What the hell kind of democracy is that?"

"It's my first big story." She was bubbling with excitement. "They're opening the first concentration camp in a few days at a place called Manzanar. I'll be there!"

He was worried. "It could be rough. Don't shoot off your mouth."

"Look who's talking! It's the family curse."

They passed three boots whose hair was just beginning to grow back. "They look like convicts," said Maggie. "Cocky convicts."

"So were we all," said Mark.

A few days later Mark and Marvin learned that elements of the 6th Marines were arriving at a railroad siding outside of Miramar. They rushed by taxi, arriving just as men in winter uniforms and fur hats began slowly clambering out. They were carrying 1903 Springfield rifles. They wore polar bear patches and the shoulder fourragère awarded their predecessors by the French for heroism at Belleau Wood. They were unshaven, tired, and hot. With the commands "Sling arms" and "Left face" they marched off toward Camp Elliott in route step. Soon they began to perspire in the sun and their feet dragged. An army unit approached from the opposite direction. There was no command but the Marines snapped to attention as one man and proudly sailed by the dogfaces, who gaped to see such a sight in Southern California.

"Wow!" said Marvin.

"Like Napoleon's Old Guard," said Mark. These were older and tougher than the Marines at the base.

"Do you think we can make it with guys like that?"

"Why not?" said Mark. He felt a tingling of anticipation.

Time had passed slowly for the Todas in Hot Springs. The Homestead Hotel was comfortable and there were concerts in the lobby every afternoon. The guards were thoughtful and did their utmost to make things pleasant. The internees were allowed to read the New York *Times* and magazines and books that were not political. But it was still a prison and Floss had difficulty in keeping up Tadashi's spirits. The new rumors that came almost every day upset him. First they were led to believe they were leaving in a week from San Francisco; then came news they would go in two weeks from New Orleans.

Masao made friends and enjoyed tobogganing on a nearby hill. But Tadashi either paced endlessly or sat in their room staring out the window. And so Floss did not tell him she was two months pregnant.

CHAPTER NINE

1.

Corregidor. March 1942.

Will had not gone back to Bataan with Lieutenant Domingo but stayed on in Malinta Tunnel to find out discreetly what Quezon and MacArthur intended doing. Marshall had to know. For almost two weeks Will's queries brought little more than rumors. Then one afternoon a navy liaison officer led him in a conspiratorial manner to a dingy room far from MacArthur's office. He closed the door carefully and showed Will the copy of a document signed by Quezon on January 3. It was labeled, "Executive Order No. 1." The navy lieutenant had got the paper from an army clerk for two bottles of whiskey.

"My God!" exclaimed Will. "I can't believe this!" In recognition of outstanding service to the Commonwealth of the Philippines, MacArthur and three of his officers were "hereby granted recompense and reward, however inadequate, for distinguished service rendered between November 15, 1935, and December 30, 1941 . . ."

Will was appalled at MacArthur's reward. "Five hundred thousand American dollars!" Lesser amounts were granted to MacArthur's chief of staff, his deputy chief of staff, and his aide. "They couldn't take the money!"

"They damned well are going to," said the lieutenant.

"But it's against all regulations to accept any sort of gift."

"Wait'll you see this!" He held out a radiogram. It was from MacArthur to the War Department telling of Quezon's desire to transfer $640,000 from the Chase Manhattan Bank, which held the Filipino funds, to MacArthur and his three subordinates.

"That's the end of MacArthur!" said Will.

"Not by a damned sight. Word just came in today from Washington that MacArthur's half a million dollars has been safely deposited to his credit at the Chemical National Bank and Trust Company, New York."

Will's astonishment turned to anger. "I can't believe the War Department would okay this."

"They did. For some damned fool reason." The lieutenant laughed humorlessly. "Now we can understand why Mac refused to counter-mand Quezon's order preventing critical rice and sugar supplies from being removed from the provinces. And why bombing schedules were delayed when Quezon demanded it. But you haven't heard anything. You know, of course, how Mac has kept nixing Washington's request to bring Quezon to America. Too hazardous to attempt, he kept saying. Guess what's happening tomorrow. Quezon is leaving The Rock tomor-row on the *Swordfish*. Navy got the order an hour after Mac learned his money was at the Chemical Bank. Coincidence? Ha-ha. My mama al-ways told me that money talked."

Will felt drained. There must be some mistake. Yet he knew it was no mistake. Perhaps there was some complex reason for all this. Of one thing he felt certain: George Marshall would never have taken a penny. There must have been a good reason he and the President had gone along on this disgraceful business. But the public would never, never know. Perhaps it was best they didn't.

He wrote a final report to Marshall, left it at the message center and requested permission to return to Bataan. The air of Malinta Tunnel was too stifling. It didn't make sense, but he longed to be with the poor devils who were fighting.

He arrived after dark. There were a few far-off rumbles but the peninsula seemed quite peaceful. But next day at Wainwright's head-quarters Will learned that morale was low. The main complaint was lack of food. Front-line units were getting only a third of a ration a day. The men looked like walking skeletons. At a skimpy lunch Wainwright told Will that most of the carabaos, water buffalo, had been eaten. "Horse meat is not so bad, Captain." There were still 250 cavalry horses and almost fifty mules. One of the horses was his own prize jumper, Joseph Conrad. Wainwright got up from the table and turned to the supply officer. "You will begin by killing the horses at once, Major. Kill Joseph Conrad first." Before the general turned away, Will saw that his eyes were filled with tears.

Will visited several units that afternoon. Some men were lying beside their foxholes, stricken with malaria. Why weren't they being tended? he asked. "Sir," explained a sad-eyed aide, "the base hospitals are full. So are the collecting stations and the field stations and the aid stations! Where the hell do you want me to take them?"

The foxholes were filled with men weakened by hunger, malaria, dysentery, beri-beri, scurvy, and dengue. How long could they hold out? Matters were made worse by the official reports from Corregidor that vast supplies of food, planes, ammunition, and reinforcements would soon arrive. Until recently everybody had believed that the fabulous "mile-long convoy" was approaching. Some had even swallowed fantastic rumors that the convoy was bringing an entire cavalry division of Negro soldiers who would gallop to Bataan on snow-white horses.

But today even the most naïve knew nothing was coming. Foxhole poets were writing sarcastic poems about Roosevelt and "Dugout Doug," and their comrades were complaining that the men in the rear, the service troops, were getting far more food and steel helmets than the fighters. There was truth in these charges. Only one out of four up front had a blanket. At least twenty thousand were without shoes. There were also rumors that the people on Corregidor were living on the fat of the land, that they had plenty of liquor and more cigarettes than they could ever smoke.

There was consternation on Bataan a few weeks later when word came that MacArthur had left Corregidor in a PT boat. He was en route to Mindanao and then would fly from Del Monte airfield to Australia. The men felt that they were being abandoned. "Dugout Doug" was leaving the sinking ship. A week later Wainwright got a phone call from Corregidor. It was General Beebe, MacArthur's deputy, who was supposed to carry out orders from Australia.

"I've got a good piece of news for you, General," said Beebe. There was so much static, Wainwright couldn't understand. "A wire has just come in from the War Department promoting you . . ."

"Yes, yes. Go ahead," said Wainwright.

". . . promoting you to lieutenant general. The troops in the Philippines are to be called hereafter the United States Army Forces in the Philippines and you're designated as commander-in-chief. Can you come over first thing in the morning? I'll send a crash boat for you."

"I'll be on the dock at Mariveles at eight o'clock."

Early in the morning Wainwright turned over command of the Luzon Force to Major General Edward King. The third stars for Wainwright were cut from a tin can and pinned onto his shirt. "A soldier could wish for a little more ceremony when he gets another star," he said and bade farewell to his officers and Will. He was eager to get to The Rock and take over command. "Lee marched on Gettysburg with less men than I have here," he said. "We're not licked by a damn sight."

On the front lines the men were passing around a poem written by Lieutenant Henry G. Lee. Bataan, he wrote, had been

> . . . saved for another day
> Saved for hunger and wounds and heat
> For slow exhaustion and grim retreat
> For a wasted hope and sure defeat . . .

2.

The Japanese all-out attack that everyone feared finally came on Good Friday, April 3. The objective, a rugged jungle-covered hill called Mount Samat, was protected by General Lim's 41st Division. While Will was up front talking with Lieutenant Domingo that morning a shell burst on the ridge fifty yards ahead. Fragments rained down as Will and Domingo dove into a dugout. "This is it," said Domingo, assuming this was a preparation barrage. But nothing happened. The Japanese artillery was only registering. An hour later they began firing for effect and shells came so thick and fast they seemed to Will to be exploding on top of each other. The two men huddled in the tiny dugout. The incredible noise, the dust and smoke and shock were almost unbearable. Will heard a whistling noise and a crunch followed by a deep thud. A bomb had buried itself nearby and exploded underground. Then came the drone of planes. More bombs exploded. Finally men began creeping out of foxholes. Their eyes were glazed and they walked as if in a dream. Officers shouted to get back to cover. More planes! Will looked up to see clusters of sticks falling haphazardly. Dry leaves and bamboo burst into flames.

"Incendiaries!" someone shouted.

Another flight came over, dropping more incendiaries. A wind from Manila Bay sprang up, spreading the flames. All at once Will saw they were surrounded by flames. The heat was blasting. Flames leaped higher. The foxholes erupted with men looking for safety. There was a concerted rush for the second line of defense. But cover had been blasted away and it looked to Will like pictures he had seen of No Man's Land in the Great War.

Adding to the terror was a second bombardment. Shells shrieked, exploding on all sides. A strong gust whipped the fire over the barren stretch to the lush jungle growth beyond. Will saw scores of human torches screaming, writhing, falling. The survivors darted up the slope like frenzied animals. Will looked around in vain for Domingo, then with his long legs led the pack. His lungs burned but he forced himself to keep moving. Through the smoke he saw green jungle and he made for it. At last he could take a deep breath. This was a mistake, for he swallowed something and began to choke. He hacked until his throat cleared.

A captain staggered up to him. "We're licked!" He waved his arms frantically. "My men were roasted alive!" His eyes were crazy with terror, his hair rumpled, his uniform scorched. Others caught his panic. A Filipino major drew his .45 and stuck it at the captain's head. "Shut up, damn you!"

"Kill me! Go ahead, kill me! But we're beaten!"

The major slapped his face and prepared to launch a second blow when the captain said, "Sorry, sir."

"So am I," said the major, who motioned to Will. The two of them led the captain to a clearing. Then the major took out two carefully wrapped cigarettes. He offered one to the captain and the other to Will, who automatically took it though he didn't smoke. "The Japs will probably send in tanks. Help me set up a line of defense." The tanks came an hour later, bursting through the pitiful defenses and tearing a hole three miles wide in front of Mount Samat. Will and a few others escaped by climbing the slope. All that night this small group groped through thick jungle growth. At dawn they came upon retreating artillerymen whose guns had been destroyed by the bombardment. "We're heading north," an American lieutenant told Will. "Then we're going to turn east and make for the coast highway."

There was no trail and their progress was slow and painful in the beating sun. There was little food and only a few men had canteens. Will was lucky to get two mouthfuls of water from a sergeant. That night someone found a small stream and the men flung themselves at the water, soon turning it into a mudhole.

Easter Sunday dawned bright and clear. Within an hour the heat was oppressive. Behind could be heard the sounds of battle. A few miles to the rear Japanese were storming up Mount Samat and before noon the Rising Sun was planted at the crest. Now the Japanese had a commanding view of the shattered American lines.

That night Will's group came to a small clearing. The sky was brilliant. "The Southern Cross," said someone. It was a startling sight, incredibly beautiful. The next morning dawned hot. Within an hour they finally came upon a trail crowded with men fleeing the oncoming Japanese. The sick and wounded kept dropping out of line, groaning in agony and fear. Their comrades were too weak to carry them and they knew they had to be left to their fate. Every so often rifle shots in the north caused panic and men behind pushed frenziedly against those ahead.

Will lost all sense of time. At last they could see the east road, crowded with humanity moving slowly south like a mass of sheep. There was a feeble cheer and the pace quickened. But relief at reaching this goal soon turned to terror as Japanese planes dived on the retreaters, bombing and strafing. Men scattered into the jungle, leaving behind hundreds of dead comrades.

Officers shouted and threatened in order to get the troops back on the road. Some came back at pistol point but most were scrambling out of sight. Will continued along the road, and soon the thinned river of humanity was again filled by new groups pouring out of the jungle like spring freshets.

Then came another bombing and strafing. Once more the men fled into the jungle and this time fewer could be persuaded to return. Will stayed on the road. Behind he could hear the imperious honking of truck horns as half a dozen vehicles packed with men appeared. An American corporal in the rear of the first truck shouted, "All hell's broke loose! Japs are just down the road!" The corporal leaned over and offered a hand to Will. He grabbed it and was swung aboard. Other marchers tried to follow but were kicked off.

Terrified civilians milled around the streets of Cabcaben. Horns blaring, the truck convoy pushed through the crowd. On the other side of town the road turned sharply right. They went past the Bataan airfield where Will had witnessed Villamor's gallant flight. The winding road to the summit was narrow and progress was maddeningly slow. Finally they reached the top. Will saw a great white cross of sheets in a field and learned it marked the hodgepodge General Hospital No. 1 area. It was after dusk and Will had no stomach to go down the steep, zigzag stretch ahead in the dark. He thanked the driver and jumped out, then curled up outside the hospital and soon was asleep.

The next morning—another hot, clear day—Japanese bombers began circling above the white cross. A priest with thin face and partially gray hair introduced himself to Will as Father William Cummings. He had left his parish against his superior's order to become an army chaplain.

Will was impressed. "Aren't you the one who said there were no atheists in foxholes?" Father Cummings nodded. Will smiled. "I guess you could have said the same for agnostics."

The enemy planes dipped lower and Cummings hurried into the orthopedic ward of the hospital, followed by Will. He heard an uncanny whistling noise, then a frightening roar. A bomb had landed on an ammunition truck on the road nearby. Shrapnel, pebbles, and earth rattled on the tin roof. Will watched as nurses and corpsmen hastily cut traction ropes so the wounded men could roll out of bed. Father Cummings, eyeglasses askew, raised his arms and authoritatively asked everyone to repeat the Lord's Prayer.

After a succession of explosions, someone shouted that the mess area was hit. So were the doctors' and nurses' quarters! There came a banshee shriek of tearing tin and wood. Iron beds doubled, breaking jaggedly like matchsticks. Patients began screaming. Will feared open panic would break out and the patients would flee outside where they would be cut down. Father Cummings scrambled onto a nurse's desk. He prayed so loudly he could be heard above the roar of planes. His demanding presence brought calm. Will himself experienced a strange feeling of comfort as if his fate were now out of his hands. A nurse next to him wept in relief. Others were crying.

The sound of planes lessened. The priest awkwardly climbed down from the desk. "Someone take over," he said quietly. "I'm wounded."

Will was told he could do nothing and so returned to the road where another truck convoy was slowly passing. Patients banged on the trucks shouting, "Take us!" but they were all full and the drivers ignored the piteous cries. Will jogged down the steep hill and after an hour came upon the convoy, which had stopped for repairs. A driver called to him. "Captain, don't you remember me? I'm Grimes, General Jones's driver." He beckoned and Will wedged his way into the cab. Once the convoy moved again, gaining speed as the road abruptly dipped down in a series of zigzags, Will wished he was walking. It didn't seem possible to survive the perilous ride but at last the convoy safely reached Mariveles, the last town on Bataan. Mobs of disorganized troops from countless units clustered along both sides of the road. Everyone was trying to get to the docks where a few boats were loading passengers for Corregidor.

A brigadier general stopped Will's truck. "You can't go to Corregidor!" he shouted.

"What about them boats?" asked Grimes.

"Not for the likes of us," said the one-star general with a crooked smile. "Come on, move back," he said wearily. "We've all had it. We're waiting here for the Japs to kill us or capture us."

Will hopped to the ground. He could see vessels in the bay being towed out to be capsized, then heard the rushing noise of shells passing overhead. They exploded among hundreds of bancas and rafts heading for the dubious safety of The Rock. Will could hear the faint cries of the drowning. He helped Grimes and the general to herd the soldiers of the truck convoy off the dock. Only a few men protested and these soon saw the uselessness of trying to get into one of the escape boats. Darkness fell rapidly, as if a curtain had dropped. Will and Corporal Grimes climbed to a hill overlooking Mariveles and lay down to sleep under a clump of mango trees. Will was wakened by Grimes, who was shaking. "It's freezing," he said, and buttoned his shirt collar. Will felt his forehead. "You've got a fever."

The corporal swore. "Oh crap, malaria!"

Down below there was an angry glare. Fires were burning in Mariveles, reddening the sky. Then came deep, dull thuds. "Someone is blowing up ammunition," guessed Grimes. The sky lit up fantastically with bursting shells, colored lights, and pillars of rainbows as tons of explosives and ammunition erupted like a volcano. Grimes' teeth chattered and Will covered him with his own tattered blanket.

The ground began to shake. They could hear a man nearby crying out in terror, "It's the end of the world!"

Will had experienced many earthquakes in Japan and this reminded him of the 1923 earthquake. "Let's get out of here!" He dragged Grimes from under the mango trees, which were swaying and dancing perilously. Abruptly the earth stilled but diminishing explosions continued. It was the end of Bataan.

Will helped Grimes down to Mariveles. Grass shacks were ablaze. Men milled around in terror. An authoritative voice shouted, "Get rid of Jap souvenirs! Pass the word!" Someone wanted to know why and Will explained that soon they would be captured. Men began burning personal papers and company records. A private threw an American flag on the fire and a Filipino hit him. As the flag caught fire one man wept. Will found it hard to hold back his own tears.

Dawn revealed wreckage and a mass of beaten, filthy men. Acrid smoke still rose from the ruins. Dust from the road mixed with the fumes into a noxious white powder. To the south Will could now see the great extinct volcano, Mount Bataan. It was as if it had erupted the night before and buried the whole tip end of the peninsula.

Then he saw an angry swirl of dust down the road. Strange-looking tanks resembling monsters pushed toward them. Japanese soldiers appeared from the brush, advancing menacingly with bayoneted rifles. The turret of the first tank opened and a Japanese officer hoisted himself out. He began shouting, *"Michi ni dero!"*

"Move onto the road!" translated Will. "Move out and bring all your stuff." He helped Grimes to his feet.

"I can't make it," he said.

"You've got to," said Will and supported him for a few yards.

But Grimes pulled away. "Let me down."

A Japanese soldier prodded the prostrate Grimes with the butt of his rifle. Will stood between them and protested. *"Yamete kudasai!"*

The soldier shot Grimes in the head and turned as if to bayonet Will in the chest but was stopped by a sharp command from the Japanese officer, who helped Will to his feet. "I graduated from USC in '35," he said. He climbed the tank and this time addressed the prisoners in English. "The Imperial Japanese Army will take good care of you. You will get good food and treatment. Excuse the actions of a few ignorant soldiers. We will abide by the Geneva Pact."

An hour later Will, still stunned at the sudden death of Grimes, was trudging back up the zigzag hill toward Hospital No. 1. The ditches were littered with burned trucks, broken-down self-propelled mounts, rifles, and equipment. The prisoners were stopped by oncoming Japanese infantrymen who rapidly stripped the prisoners of blankets, watches, jewelry, razor blades, food, and even toothbrushes. Rings were particularly sought and one American officer who could not remove his wedding band had the finger chopped off.

It was almost noon by the time Will's group reached the top of the hill and Hospital No. 1. The Rising Sun flew over the main building. Will noticed that Japanese guards from a tank unit were patrolling the area and preventing other Japanese units from molesting or looting the patients. Perhaps the Japanese *were* going to observe the Geneva Convention. At a bend in the road almost everyone turned to see scarred Corregidor for the last time. Several men sighed and one said, "The last citadel." But everyone knew its days were numbered. It was already wreathed in smoke and dust from bombs and shells.

The march continued down the dusty road. Near the bottom they came upon a harrowing sight. Thousands of wounded Filipinos from Hospital No. 2 were streaming from a side road to join the march south. They had heard a rumor that the Japanese were freeing all Filipinos and, despite pleas from doctors, had been seized by mass hysteria. Those with critical belly wounds staggered in their wake.

Will's throat ached from dust by the time he once more passed the Bataan airfield and the road turned sharply north toward Cabcaben. Near town was a stream, and the guards allowed the prisoners to drink and wash themselves and their clothes. An hour passed and still their guards rested nearby, smoking cigarettes and ignoring them. For the first time the prisoners had a feeling of relief and even gaiety. Suddenly they were shocked to silence by an ominous series of roars. Shells from big Japanese guns emplaced to the rear began flying over their heads toward Corregidor. Seconds later large puffs of smoke appeared on "The Rock" as the shells exploded.

The men looked at each other uneasily. Will heard a sound like milk trucks going over a cobbled road—the rattling of hundreds of bottles in wire cases. "Mortar shells from 'The Rock'!" said a lieutenant and scrambled for cover. Will and the others leaped into a ditch just as the ground around them exploded in geysers. Rubble rained on top of Will but it was only dirt and brush.

Guards blew whistles and routed the prisoners from the ditch, kicking those who reacted slowly and shouting until their charges broke into a dogtrot. The pace was slowed as they entered Cabcaben, now a smoldering ruin without a sign of life except for half a dozen skinny dogs sniffing among corpses. The guards threw stones at the dogs and hastily began to reorganize the marching groups.

Will was in the first section that started north up the east road of Bataan. On the left was towering Mount Bataan, the peaks of its time-eroded crater wreathed in clouds. On the right were the blue-green waters of Manila Harbor. In peaceful times this was a scene of breathtaking beauty. But today the once colorful foliage was laden with dust and the road itself was a continuous, swirling cloud as Japanese artillery, tanks, and trucks rumbled toward the marchers. Some of the infantrymen in trucks jeered and pointed fingers at the prisoners. Others swung at the marching men with long bamboo poles, attempting to knock off caps and helmets. Late in the afternoon a tank battalion heading toward the prisoners stopped so the men could throw rocks at the marchers. They were followed by a straggling line of Japanese infantrymen on foot. They lent their canteens to the thirsty marchers and their officers saluted Will. There seemed to be no rhyme nor reason to the contradictory actions of the Japanese. "What the hell kind of people are they?" an enlisted man asked Will.

"Not like us," he said. He knew that the Japanese soldiers received brutal treatment in training and were accustomed to receiving slaps, kicks, and clubbings from their noncoms. He also knew the Japanese had been taught to regard surrender as an utter disgrace. Aware of all this, even Will could not fathom the inconsistencies.

At dusk the exhausted group was finally stopped near a barrio consisting of a handful of nipa huts and two ramshackle stores. Guards led them to two artesian wells, each with a spigot. At first the men swallowed water from the tap but a Japanese officer began lecturing them in English that this was not only unsanitary but selfish and wasteful. They were to fill canteens only and do it in an orderly manner or there would be no more water. This speech was approved by most of the men and a few were tempted to applaud. The prisoners were marched to a camp next to a cane field where they bedded down for the night.

Will was awakened by the sun. His whole body seemed to ache and he wondered if he had malaria. Guards were forming units and sending them down the coast road, but Will's group didn't start until midmorning and by then men on all sides of him were dropping to the ground from the heat of the sweltering sun. The road was even dustier on this second day. Will's group of several hundred men soon became scattered. The guards tried to keep the prisoners in close formation but within half a mile the weak ones began falling out. Others, parched by sun and dust, stopped to scoop water out of ditches. Will's tongue was thick with dust but he would not touch the ditch water. He was determined to survive.

The march stopped after an hour and the afternoon was spent sitting in a field enclosed by a barbed-wire fence near an abandoned barrio facing the sun. It was worse than walking, and several men began babbling like children. They had been promised food that day but there was none. It was a sultry night and there were so many men in the enclosure that it was difficult to turn over. Hordes of mosquitoes added to the misery. Even so, Will finally got to sleep.

3.

Bataan. April 11, 1942.

Although the brutalities of the first two days were unplanned, the situation changed with the arrival of Colonel Tsuji who had instigated the murder of five thousand Chinese in Singapore for "promoting British colonialism."

The excuse for Tsuji's presence was to witness the last stages of the final Japanese offensive which had been planned in Tokyo. Tsuji had left the operational details to Shogo while he spent most of his time convincing key officers on General Homma's staff that this was a racial war and that *all* prisoners in the Philippines should be put to death. The Americans deserved it for being white colonialists, the Filipinos for betraying their fellow Asians.

Tsuji was so successful that orders written up without Homma's permission had been dispatched the previous night to almost every major unit on Bataan. Several commanders, doubting that the instructions had come from Imperial Headquarters, refused to act without a written order. Others took the verbal command on faith and so the atrocities took on a more official aspect during Will's third day of marching. On the trip toward Balanga he saw a dozen men bayoneted or shot for lagging behind. One exhausted Filipino was thrown into a ditch for burial. The water revived him and he struggled to his feet. A guard kicked him back into his grave and ordered Will and another American to shovel dirt over him. When Will hesitated he was jabbed in the back with a bayonet. Once the job was finished a hand rose eerily from the soil. Will moved forward and had to be prodded again to get back to the road.

Just as they reached the cross-island cobblestone road where thousands of prisoners were pouring from the west side of the peninsula, a torrent of rain descended. At first the drenching felt wonderful and the prisoners luxuriated in the cooling downpour, holding up their arms as the rain beat down their parched throats and showered their sweating bodies. But soon everyone felt chilled. The road became a quagmire and shoes encrusted with mud seemed like lead.

The sun came out as rapidly as it had vanished. Its rays were welcomed until wet clothing steamed, causing more misery. They slogged in the mud past what had once been the Abucay Line and by late afternoon approached the town of Balanga, the capital of Bataan Province. Large groups of prisoners were quartered on both sides of the badly damaged town. Will could already smell the ghastly stink of human waste and dead bodies of those groups which had already passed through.

The tens of thousands that now poured into Balanga were broken up into units and placed in a variety of enclosures. Some were fenced in by barbed wire, others were in open yards. They were crowded into the courtyards of old buildings made by the Spaniards and into the town jail.

For the first time there was a semblance of order and a concerted effort to feed the marchers. Even so, some groups were moved in and out so fast there was only time for water. Will's group, crowded into a bullpen, were lucky enough to get a meal—a single rice ball and a piece of rock salt. A man near Will ate so voraciously that he vomited. Will ate slowly with relish, even though the rice was already sour and his lips were blistered. Despite the overpowering stink, Will slept well for the first time since the Good Friday attack.

Early the next morning they marched out of Balanga. A few Filipinos watched silently. One man winked at Will and surreptitiously made a V sign with his fingers. A woman held out a leafful of rice to him but a guard sent it flying with his bayonet and slapped the woman. An hour later they reached a clearing without any shade. The marchers were ordered to sit down and face the rising sun. Some of those slow in taking off hats and caps had them knocked off. The sun beat down mercilessly. Will wiped the sweat from his face and neck. As he was taking a swallow from his canteen a guard pricked him in the thigh with a bayonet.

An officer called for attention in English. "In Nippon we have order and discipline. I am teaching you order and discipline."

Back in Balanga, Colonel Tsuji was inspecting the assembly stations. He was disgusted with the condition of the prisoners. "Can you imagine Japanese soldiers deteriorating into animals?" he remarked to Shogo. "They have no discipline, no pride."

"But sir," said Shogo, who was just as appalled, "isn't it our responsibility to provide sanitary conditions?" There seemed to be little organization.

"These cowards surrendered so fast that General Homma was caught unprepared." Besides, they all had lost their manhood by surrendering and deserved no better treatment.

Shogo also had no respect for any man who surrendered but still felt pity. He had long since renounced Christianity but retained its principles of humanity.

Tsuji told him to patrol the last half of the march from Balanga to San Fernando where those who survived would be carried in boxcars to a prison camp in the north. He himself, he said, would head south to inspect. His real purpose was to make sure the verbal instructions to punish Filipinos as well as Americans were carried out.

A few minutes later Shogo was driven past a large group of bareheaded prisoners squatting in the sun learning discipline like Japanese recruits. Tsuji would approve but Shogo felt compassion at the sad sight. He still fervently believed all Westerners had to be driven out of Asia, but not like this. He was concerned that Tsuji, the man he respected above all others, appeared to be blind to the unnecessary cruelties being perpetrated.

Will's group sat cross-legged for more than two hours in the broiling sun. Those who fainted were kicked to consciousness. Finally the officer ordered the men to put on hats and stand at attention. Getting erect was a painful prospect, particularly among the older men after their cramped position. Although Will had been only slightly wounded by the bayonet jab, he had to be helped to his feet by a corporal.

"Come on, Captain," urged the corporal, "you can make it." He supported Will for a few yards.

"I'm okay now," he said, and hobbled forward.

It was another day of hell and during the eleven miles to the town of Orani two Filipinos were shot as they tried to escape through a cane field. Three other prisoners, an American captain and two Filipino enlisted men, were bayoneted when they became too weak to stay in line. The ditches were lined with bloating corpses from previous groups.

Will had imagined no town could ever rival the stench of Balanga but as they approached, in the dying daylight, the distant buildings of Orani he became aware of an even more disgusting smell, a gaseous stink. Like Balanga, it was a ghost town. Most of the buildings were destroyed. The prisoners were herded off the road into what looked like a cattle stockade; the ground was littered with feces crawling with maggots. This, thought Will, must have been what it was like at Andersonville. Hundreds had dysentery. Some of these could reach the straddle trench but most befouled themselves and their neighbors. Darkness brought another menace—swarms of vicious mosquitoes. The night air was oppressive and the hours dragged slowly.

At sunrise *lugao*, a rice mush, was served to the prisoners. "It tastes like paste," one man protested but the others gobbled it down. This morning brought no sun treatment but the prisoners were kept moving at a killing pace. Will overheard one guard tell another that their commander wanted to reach the next main station, Lubao, before dark. That was sixteen miles away. Will's thigh throbbed and he had to force himself to keep moving. As the sun climbed, its rays became unbearable. More men dropped out and were kicked into the ditches to die.

By midmorning they had reached the base of Bataan. They crossed a bridge and turned northeast. Will groaned to see the straight, flat stretch ahead. There was no sign of shade.

For two days Will hadn't been able to urinate and he was in agony. At last he was able to get out a few drops. They burned as if a hot iron had been shoved up his penis, but brought unspeakable relief. He could never have imagined he could be grateful for such searing pain.

At noon they reached a barrio that boasted an artesian well. Will stumbled against a scrawny private ahead of him. The private turned. "Hang on to my belt, Captain," he said. Will did and managed to keep moving for another hour. Then both legs felt numb, useless. The private said, "Hang on!" and dragged Will forward.

Several hundred yards ahead Will could see a few nipa huts and a clump of trees. It glimmered like an oasis. He had to reach it. He stumbled to the road. The private lifted him up and supported him. "You can do it! Just a little farther."

But Will couldn't move. He began to lose consciousness. As if in a nightmare he glimpsed an officer who was saying something in Japanese. Will's ears rang and he felt himself melting to the ground in slow motion. The face of the Japanese officer became bigger. The man looked like Shogo. Will tried to say his name but nothing came from his mouth. His last memory was a sharp report like a pistol shot and he knew he was going to die.

4.

Will felt cool water on his forehead and cheeks. Someone was tenderly washing his face. He opened his eyes to glimpse a kindly face.

"I'm Father O'Malley. We've been worried about you." Will tried to get up but was gently restrained. "Take it easy." The priest—he was middle-aged and wore captain's bars—spoon-fed Will water from a rusty tin can.

Will could make out a strange ceiling. Was he in some sort of arena? He was confused. Why wasn't he dead?

"A Japanese officer brought you here yesterday," said the priest.

Will remembered the face staring at him. "What did he look like?"

"Like most Japs." The priest spooned more water into Will. "You're in San Fernando, my son, the end of the line. You'll ride the rest of the way in a train."

"The Japanese officer? I thought he shot me." Could it really have been Shogo or was it a hallucination?

"He wouldn't leave until I assured him I would take care of you."

Will sat up. For a minute his head buzzed. Then it cleared. He looked around. This was a large cockpit arena jammed with prisoners. One of them exclaimed, "McGlynn!" It was Lieutenant Domingo, as thin as a rail, his face like a death mask.

"I just saw my father," he said in a low voice. "The Japs took me to a barracks to see him. He was with a colonel of the *Kempeitai*, who said my father was one of the leaders of the new Laurel government and offered to let me go home with him. I told him I could not desert my comrades and so here I am." He came closer and whispered, "But Papa is no collaborator, Will. He told me that President Quezon had ordered Laurel and him to pretend to collaborate with the Japanese. You believe it, don't you?" he pleaded. "Papa could never be a collaborator."

"I believe you," said Will, who did not.

"He told me that he and the others were working with General Homma to release all the Filipinos from prison camp. And I said, 'Hurry, Papa, we are dying like flies.' "

The next morning Will and Domingo were among those marched to the nearby railroad station. The street was lined with civilians. Many defied guards to run out and give the prisoners jars of water and baskets of food. The people moaned in open sympathy for the battered men of Bataan as they were loaded into small boxcars. Will and Domingo were shoved into a wooden car with more than a hundred others. There was room only to stand and once the doors were slammed shut, the heat became intense. There was little space overhead for the thick air to circulate and those in the rear soon were gasping. They made matters worse by shouting, "Open the door!" Several became hysterical and thrashed around. There was a crash as an engine backed into the line of boxcars. A guard opened one door and at last there was a breath of air. Without any discussion those suffering in the rear were brought near the door to breathe the sweet, fresh air. Will felt a lump in his throat for those who had voluntarily moved to the rear. What a decent creature man could be.

As the train rattled northward toward Clark Field, men voluntarily rotated in the jammed car. With each hour the air became more fetid. Those with dysentery could not control themselves. About every hour the train stopped at a station and their guard let those who had to relieve themselves get out. At each stop civilians would surround the train with gifts of tomatoes, rice, fried meats, sugarcane, candy, and water in bottles. Will's guard was lenient and just watched in silence. Other guards drove the people back but they would toss food over the guards' heads to the starving men. By some sort of local telegraphy word of the train's progress was relayed and the crowds grew larger at each successive stop.

After almost three hours the train approached Angeles and the men at the door passed the word back that they might be let off here since Clark Field was only a mile away. But the train didn't even slow down. It continued for another hour to Capas, where their guard jumped to the ground and motioned impatiently for the prisoners to get out. Domingo helped Will descend. Many of the cars had remained locked and when these were opened men burst out like apples spilling from a burst bag. They breathed in the fresh air as if it were a treasure. The multitude of civilians combed the debouching prisoners for relatives or friends and every so often loud screams of joy and sobbing would erupt. Two friends hugged Domingo and they chattered a minute before guards broke up the reunions.

"We're going to Camp O'Donnell," Domingo told Will. This was a partially completed installation for the Filipino army. "It's only about six miles from here."

The prisoners started up a dusty, shadeless road. The fresh air was like elixir and the men were happy to be in the open. With Domingo's help Will found himself growing stronger. He felt buoyed by the warm surge of friendliness shown by the people all the way from San Fernando.

The guards urged the men on but without prodding or beating. Those who fell exhausted were left by the side of the road with assurances that a truck would pick them up. No one was shot and eventually trucks did appear to gather up the weak ones.

After the first mile Will felt strong enough to walk without help. Life surged back into his body. The worst was over and he had come through. At the top of a rise he could make out a maze of tumbledown buildings spread out on a vast, dry, rolling plain that boasted only a few straggly trees. This must be Camp O'Donnell! As they drew nearer it was obvious that most of the barracks were unfinished. Some didn't have roofs and others consisted only of a bamboo framework topped by a grass roof. It looked like a poorly planned housing project, long abandoned for lack of funds and running to ruin.

The camp was surrounded by a high barbed-wire fence punctuated every so often by wooden sentry towers. Armed guards peered out at the approaching army of haggard, filthy prisoners. Will looked back at the world outside the barbed wire. Nothing was living except for clumps of tall cogon grass, motionless in the hot, still air. As Will stepped through the narrow gateway flanked by towers spiked with machine guns, he recalled Dante's warning to those entering hell: "All hope abandon, ye who enter here!"

He followed the crowd across a parched, dessicated parade ground. His group was counted and searched for weapons. Any objects appealing to a guard were confiscated. A noncom shouted an order and the prisoners were marched up a rise to a building flying the Japanese flag.

After the men had waited for an hour in the boiling sun, an officer emerged from the building. This was the camp commandant, Captain Tsuneyoshi. Small and bowlegged, he strutted importantly, sword clanking, up to a platform which he climbed as if he were General Tojo. He glared around a moment and then began to speak in a strident scream, stopping abruptly every so often for a plump little Filipino standing next to him to interpret.

"The captain say you are his enemies!" said the Filipino timidly. "The captain say you are his now. You should be grateful to the great Imperial Japanese Army for sparing your lives!" Tsuneyoshi continued his shouting, waving his arms vehemently. "The captain say you be treated as enemy captives, not as honorable prisoners of war." The interpreter was sweating. "The captain he say Nippon has captured Javver, Sumatter, and New Guinyah. The captain he say we soon have Austrayler and New Zealyer. The captain say you do not act like soldiers. You got no discipline. You do not stand at attention when the captain talk."

The translator glanced around nervously and said, almost meekly, "The captain say you going to have trouble from him."

The more ferocious Tsuneyoshi became, the more timid became the Filipino. Shaking a fist menacingly, the captain condemned Theodore Roosevelt for his interference in the Russo-Japanese negotiations in 1905. "The captain say you forget America. You now work hard to rebuild the New Philippines in the New World Order of Asia for the Asiatics. No more cursed Anglo-American imperialism."

The prisoners longed for water and shade, but there was no respite.

"Captain say you go twenty feet from barbed wire, sentry shoot you dead," concluded the interpreter almost apologetically.

The captain spun on his heel and stormed off. The prisoners were then divided into groups of officers and enlisted men according to rank. Will, separated from Domingo, was taken to a dilapidated shack at the north end of the compound with fifteen other American officers. What everyone wanted most of all was water. There were two pipes next to a row of shacks but nothing came out of the faucets. The pump engine was not working. Several hours later a detail was allowed to bring water from a river which ran through the jungle a mile outside the gate. Once water arrived, Will's group cooked rice provided by the camp commander. It was evidently sweepings from a rice mill floor for it turned into a purple mush. Will took a mouthful and made the mistake of swallowing it. It tasted horrible and he coughed up as much as he could. The rest lay noxiously in his stomach.

"We'd better learn how to eat this crap," said a skeletal major whose eyes stared out of deep holes. "Keep it down or starve to death."

Will liked the hard look on the major's face. Here was a survivor and he was going to be one too. Will took another mouthful of the repulsive mush and this time kept it down. He shivered, then forced a smile remembering an old joke Mark had told him. "It tastes like shit," he said, "but I like it."

The others laughed and, in distaste, dipped into the witch's brew.

One, a youthful lieutenant, spit his spoonful out, then stumbled out of the shack.

"He won't make it," said the major and stuffed down another spoonful. "I will."

PART THREE

The Road Back

CHAPTER TEN

1.

Tokyo. April 18, 1942.

Two days after Will arrived at Camp O'Donnell, thirteen twin-engine B-25's appeared over Tokyo and began dropping their bombs. By coincidence a mock raid had been staged minutes before the American arrival and many citizens waved at the Doolittle planes. Although the first belittling reports brought no panic, the more informed citizens went to work the next morning with an uneasy feeling. For centuries they had been brought up to believe that the homeland would always be safe from assault. Now they had private doubts.

The raid itself had been a failure as far as physical damage was concerned but its psychological effect throughout America was tremendous. The leader, Lieutenant Colonel James Doolittle, became an instant hero. The nation had been depressed by the fall of Bataan and this single daring feat was a pledge that America was at last on the offensive. It encouraged allies on every battlefield and brought hope to those prisoners of war in the Philippines who managed to get the news.

President Roosevelt added to the public delight by announcing, with his inimitable flair for the dramatic, that the bombing, launched from a carrier, had come from a secret air base in the Pacific called Shangri-La, the secret paradise of James Hilton's popular novel *Lost Horizon*. It was another tall tale, like the one told after MacArthur escaped the Japanese to land safely in Australia. The general, the President had explained with an infectious grin, had disguised himself as a Japanese fisherman and eluded the entire Imperial Japanese Navy in a leaky rowboat.

Although MacArthur's escape, along with the Doolittle raid, had lifted the spirits of the nation, the denizens of the Munitions and Navy buildings on Constitution Avenue knew there was little to cheer about. The relief of the Philippines would be long in coming. The Japanese navy had practically wiped out Allied opposition in the Battle of Java Sea, and U-boat sinkings along America's East and Gulf coasts were outdistancing the pace of construction. The U.S. Navy, long the pride of the country, seemed helpless. And Hitler was preparing for a massive offensive in Russia.

Late that April a new civilian recruit reported to Op-16-W at the Navy Building. Professor McGlynn had left the peaceful Berkshire Hills for the duration to help win the war against Japan as adviser to a secret naval operational intelligence agency concerned primarily with psychological warfare in the Pacific.

His younger son was on the Kearny Mesa north of San Diego near La Jolla, clambering with full pack up a barren hill dubbed Nellie's Tit. This was Camp Elliott, the West Coast Marine training base. It was a bleak area—hilly, rocky, and sandy with little vegetation, but fine training ground for hiking and running problems from squad to battalion level. And a few miles to the west lay dunes and the lonely beaches of Del Mar, ideal for training in rubber boats.

Mark was a private in one of the three machine-gun platoons in D Company, the weapons company of the 1st Battalion, 6th Marines. This company, which also included an 81 mm. mortar platoon, was larger than the three rifle companies A, B, and C and was therefore commanded by a major. The second in command, the executive officer, was Captain William Joseph Sullivan who was also the battalion machine-gun officer. Consequently the three machine-gun platoons were Sullivan's responsibility and he functioned much like the rifle company commanders. Mark found the veterans of Iceland far more interesting than the recruits at boot camp. They were a rambunctious, spirited, randy group. In Iceland there had been six girls to every male Icelander and even the ugliest Marine could find a girl.

Before the end of Mark's first month at Elliott, he and the recruit replacements had been subjected to numerous lectures on the glory and grandeur of the 6th Marines. In 1918 it had been the keystone of the 2nd Division and had struck fear in the hearts of the Germans with ferocious attacks at Belleau Wood. In twenty-four hours these fabled Marines had stormed machine guns despite losses of 1,087 officers and men, killed or wounded. And when the attack finally faltered, a veteran sergeant had shouted those immortal words, "Come on, you sons of bitches! Do you want to live forever?" The men had surged forward, taken the woods and won the shoulder fourragère from the grateful French government. "Wear it in pride," the lecturer would usually say. "It's prime pogey bait. The girls in Dago will leap at you!"

The purpose of machine-gun drill was to simulate putting the gun in action as quickly as possible under enemy fire, aiming it accurately at one of several preset white stakes a few yards distant and keeping the gun in action while sustaining casualties. As an ammunition carrier, Mark had to tote a forty-pound box of ammunition in each hand in addition to his M-1 rifle. It was a heavy load and Mark's ambition was to become an assistant gunner who wore a pistol and carried only a fifteen-pound tripod.

Having quickly mastered the simple routine of his assignment, Mark became bored with the repetitious exercises. This led to trouble with his first sergeant, a small wiry Irishman named Mahoney who reminded Mark of Jimmy Cagney. Mahoney had a broken nose and despite his size was a formidable sight as, hands on hips, he would bawl out an offender. The Top, as he was called, constantly ragged Mark for his lackadaisical attitude. Once he caught Mark at inspection without cartridge belt or bayonet and he made him wear the belt around his neck for two days, asleep or awake. After several similar infractions Mahoney was in no mood for lenience when Mark was half an hour late for a Monday morning muster. "I'm running you up for company office hours, McGlynn."

As Mark was marched to the office of the company commander he was apprehensive. The major was absent and his executive was in charge. Although Mark had only seen Captain William Joseph Sullivan at a distance, he was already a fearsome character to every replacement. He was addressed as "Captain" by most, and as "Skipper" by his officers and senior NCO's, but he was also known, behind his back, irreverently by all as "Billy J." The Iceland men swore by him. A great officer and the nicest guy you could imagine. Unless you fouled up. Then those baby-blue eyes of his would turn icy and you would wish you were dead.

Captain Sullivan was examining some papers as Mark stood in front of his desk at attention and said, "Private McGlynn reporting as ordered, sir."

Sullivan looked up. "Stand at ease." His voice was quiet. He was not at all formidable. "Why did you miss roll call?" he said evenly.

"I missed the last bus from San Diego last night, sir. My watch stopped." Mark explained that he didn't have enough money for a cab and had only managed to hitchhike as far as La Jolla. "I slept in a park until this morning, sir. I got a ride into camp but a little late for morning roll call."

Only two years older than Mark, Sullivan was already mature. "Private McGlynn, why did your watch stop?"

"I forgot to wind it, sir."

Sullivan looked straight at Mark. "Why didn't you walk from La Jolla to camp instead of sleeping in the park?"

"I didn't think of that, sir."

Billy J.'s eyes were suddenly like steel. "I expect my Marines to fulfill their duties come hell or high water. It's the same as when you say, 'I do,' at the altar. You have a sworn duty. Do you understand that?" His crisp words seemed to bounce off the walls like a .45 ricochet.

"Yes, sir."

"Since this is your first offense, I'm going to let you off with a warning. Don't let me see you at office hours again. Now get out of here."

"About face," snapped Mahoney. "Forward march."

At first Billy J. had seemed like a sucker. Now Mark knew what they'd meant by his icy blue eyes. He looked as if he could be rough as a cob. Mark couldn't quite figure out Billy J. and the NCO's from Iceland. They were rough, no doubt about it, and they would brook no nonsense when it came to Marine Corps matters. They were both elusive and exclusive. And if you weren't one of them, you were nobody. Yet after Mahoney ran him up because he had goofed off once too often, why hadn't Billy J. lowered the boom on him?

It suddenly occurred to him that Billy J. had given him the benefit of the doubt. He had actually trusted him. It bothered Mark that he couldn't figure these people out. But he was determined not to be run up a second time to company office hours.

The training became more demanding with three and four-day field maneuvers and even longer hikes in the hot sun. A fifteen-mile march to Del Mar ended with a total surprise. Instead of bivouacking in their pup tents the men were assigned four to a clean stall at the racetrack. It was a rare morning that Mark wasn't wakened by a comrade whinnying and calling himself Man o' War.

The rubber boat training began the next day on the beach just north of the Hotel Del Mar. Both four- and seven-man boats were used. The men practiced paddling out from shore against the surf and riding the breakers in to the beach. They found neither easy and there was much whooping and hollering as the boats flipped over in the surf. Soon the fun of the early tries became hard work. Arms and shoulders ached. The first two days they wore swim trunks and practice lasted only an hour, but on the third Billy J. put out the word that utility uniforms with pith helmets and web belt must be worn and the practice time increased. On the fourth and fifth days they wore full equipment except for their weapons. Mark enjoyed the brief change in the training routine but considered the time spent practicing with rubber boats useless. Only a damned fool would paddle one of those clumsy things toward an enemy-held shore.

As they got into the long march back to Camp Elliott, their ebullient spirits of the past few days gradually lessened. Mark became lost in his own thoughts. He could sense their training was nearing the end. And now it was obvious that the battalion was not going to Europe. They would soon be bound for the Japanese-held islands of the Pacific.

2.

Maggie had left Mark in San Diego determined to dig up the inside facts of the growing wave of hysteria against the nisei in California. For she saw this as only the first step in becoming a full-fledged foreign correspondent. Secretly Maggie had always resented being a girl, and from childhood had pestered Mark to let her partake in his pranks and adventures. And she despised the horde of upper-middle-class girls whose only ambition was to marry the president of Standard Oil. She vowed never to get married. After all, what man could compare to Papa, Will, or Mark?

Her ambition was equaled by her willingness to work arduously, along with a rare talent for interviewing people. Within minutes she could persuade most people to reveal their most intimate secrets. She radiated trustworthiness and, in fact, had vowed never to reveal a source even if the FBI threatened to put her in jail. Imprisonment would be a welcome experience and make her a better correspondent. So far this zeal had not been tested by reality, but if Mark had been asked to comment he would have replied that, being a born damned fool, she would be the first to volunteer arrest and the last to whine once she got behind bars.

Adding to her driving ambition was indignation at the treatment of the nisei. Not only had she been brought up in Japan but, being half Irish, she was a natural champion of the underdog. She ranged California interviewing top officials and the victims of the unreasoning panic that was sweeping the West Coast. Undeterred by the coldness of officialdom, she persisted in haunting the doors of the mighty until they grudgingly saw her. She also spent endless hours in the sad homes of the bewildered Japanese who were preparing for the inevitable. With the voracity of a prosecutor she unveiled for *Inside* the double-talk of esteemed liberals. Earl Warren, for instance, had declared to the press in early February, "If we start discriminating against people because of their forebears, it will bring about disunity in our war effort." Yet, a few hours later he told members of a leading anti-Japanese group that he believed the military command could move "any or all Japanese out of the combat zone," and that it "should be done" and that the army "has the right to do it." To him the combat zone, of course, meant California. And he warned that if these Japanese-Americans were not evacuated promptly there could be a repetition of Pearl Harbor.

Although most of the Japanese on the West Coast were American citizens, they were now described as "enemy aliens." What particularly incensed Maggie was that all her high-minded liberal and progressive friends were for putting these innocent people in concentration camps when citizens of German descent were rarely even harassed.

Nor was anti-Japanese feeling confined to the Pacific coast. In a national poll four out of five believed that "the Japanese people will always want to go to war to make themselves as powerful as possible." And Roosevelt, being a consummate politician, heeded these voices. With the support of the American Civil Liberties Union and other defenders of democracy, he ordered the War Department to implement a mass nisei evacuation, and it was no surprise that the Supreme Court upheld the legality of the act.

Maggie learned that the first War Relocation Camp would be in a place called Manzanar, California. She was there late that March to watch the first unhappy families enter their miserable new homes. She managed to talk her way into the camp, charming the guards with smiles and the story that she represented the American Red Cross. A smartly dressed, attractive girl had to be believed.

Manzanar in Spanish meant "apple orchard" but to Maggie it looked like a desert. Nearby there were some green acres that produced cantaloupes and vegetables, but the camp itself was already swirling with dust devils. To the west rose Mount Whitney, the highest peak in the United States, but to the southeast lay Death Valley. An area of such violent natural contrasts would bring hot days and cold nights, and the government had not even finished the camp. Carpenters and plumbers were still working on fourteen tar-paper barracks that would contain single-room apartments twenty by twenty-five feet. Two families, usually strangers, were jammed into one room.

Maggie soon learned that only two of the barracks had showers and flush toilets. Occupants of the other barracks had to be satisfied with cold water and outdoor privies with chemical receptacles. Maggie could appreciate why such unsanitary conditions dismayed the scrupulously clean Japanese. One elderly woman, a grandmother, told her how they had been warned a few weeks earlier by a mysterious telephone caller supposedly from the FBI. They were going to be evacuated "sooner than you think." Within an hour, two men arrived offering to buy all their household possessions for ridiculous prices. The beloved piano went for fifty dollars, the car for seventy-five, and the gas stove and all kitchen utensils for twenty-five.

The family sharing the room had had a similar experience. They had trucked their store's merchandise to Los Angeles to be auctioned, receiving only five thousand dollars for goods valued at more than thirty thousand.

Maggie watched as the two families quietly agreed on dividing the room. Then they strung wires across the room, draping it with sheets. Maggie could not help weeping at the humiliating sight yet the ten occupants of the room made no complaints.

"You take this so quietly," she protested.

The father of one family thanked her for her concern. "How can we protest against our own government? We are at war and we all are going to do our best to serve." Every Japanese in the room, young and old, showed agreement. "It is our duty to be loyal and serve. It is our responsibility." But as Maggie was leaving, she noticed that most of the women were stifling tears.

The material turned in by Maggie delighted the porky, untidy editor and owner of *Inside*. Steiner instructed her to turn her attention to revealing those who had fought the government's illegal act as well as those who supported it. An impish devil lurked in both Mark and Maggie, and she was delighted to discover that a prestigious spokesman for democracy, Walter Lippmann, had agreed with Warren that the fifth-column problem in the West was very serious and very special. "The Pacific Coast is in imminent danger of a combined attack from within and without," he said. And therefore those dangerous nisei had to be confined in camps. Conversely, J. Edgar Hoover, the archfoe of democracy, according to progressives, had strongly urged the President not to sign the evacuation bill. The demand for such action was, he wrote, "based primarily on political pressure rather than upon factual data."

Maggie scurried around the capital digging up bits of information from high and low sources, delighting the editor of *Inside* with such tidbits as the report to the President by John Ford, the movie producer in Hawaii making a film on Pearl Harbor. He warned FDR that the majority of Japanese-Americans in Hawaii were "tainted" and deserved to be shown no mercy. Everywhere the film maker looked he found "most of the key positions" being held by "Japs." From the same White House source, Maggie learned that the President had been impressed by a letter from a man in Pennsylvania contending that all Japanese mortally feared bats, and the war could be won by dropping bats on their home islands, thereby "frightening, demoralizing and exciting the prejudices of the Japanese Empire." The President had passed on this letter to "Wild Bill" Donovan, head of OSS, with a note stating: "This man is *not* a nut," and that although the bat project sounded like a perfectly wild idea, it was "worth your looking into." Whereupon Donovan had recruited the curator of the division of mammals at the American Museum of Natural History and enlisted the cooperation of the Army Air Corps. Maggie could not find anyone who had even checked whether it was true that the Japanese were terrified by bats. She could have told the President they were not. In any case, she reported that Air Corps bombardiers were already training for the mission, parachuting bats to earth even though the mammals persisted in freezing to death in high-altitude planes.

Upon reading this report the editor of *Inside* almost tipped over in his chair from laughter. "Too bad we can't use the story," he told Maggie, "but we'd be sent to Leavenworth as traitors." In April he sent her to Hot Springs, Virginia, to get details of the internment of the Japanese officials and civilians. Maggie was delighted, for she had already promised Mark she would do her best to see Floss and her family. Having press credentials, she might be able to arrange a meeting.

But she found the Homestead Hotel a fortress. Neither her press card nor smiles had any effect on the polite FBI guards. She spent several days questioning local residents and two girls who worked at the inn. All she learned was that a kind FBI man had given her nephew, Masao, several toys, and that Ambassador Nomura had set up committees to prepare the returnees for life in Japan. One committee—and she wagered Floss was on it—had opened a school for primary- and middle-school students. The principal task was to correct the Japanese accent of those who had attended American schools.

On her last day Maggie made a final impassioned plea to see her sister for a few minutes. "Just let me kiss her good-bye." The agent was moved but insisted it was against regulations. "Can't she go up to the roof and wave at me?"

"There's no regulation against that."

A few minutes later her heart leaped to see Floss and Tadashi hurry to the edge of the roof with little Masao. They waved. "Don't worry, darling!" called Floss and broke into tears. Masao shouted something Maggie couldn't understand but saw he wasn't crying. Tadashi continued to wave disconsolately.

Maggie controlled her own tears. "Daddy and Mark send their love," she called. "Don't give up!" She too burst into angry tears and the FBI men gently took her arm. She waved a last time.

She didn't reach the little cottage on 143rd Street until midnight. It was like a tomb without Mark. As she was getting wearily, sadly into bed the phone rang. It was Jason Fredericks. She was roused from her lethargy. He was the owner of a string of midwestern papers from Columbus, Ohio, to Kansas City. First he congratulated her on the *Inside* stories.

"I didn't write them, Mr. Fredericks . . ."

"I know that. But you were the one who dug up the material. You have a good sense of story value. How would you like to work for me?"

Almost choked with surprise, she said, "Doing what?"

He wanted her to go at once to Hawaii and follow up stories on the treatment and behavior of the nisei in that key area. She could write as well as research. It was the dream of her life and she stammered an acceptance. Still shaking from excitement, she called her father. It took him several minutes to get to the telephone and bark, "Who the hell is it?" He had been wakened out of a sound sleep, but upon hearing the news he was pleased.

With trepidation she next called Steiner. He paused a moment after hearing of the offer, then belched. "Good luck, honey," he said. "I knew I wouldn't be able to hold on to you very long." She tremulously asked if two weeks' notice was all right. "Two weeks? Hell, baby, get the hell out to Kansas City before that old fart changes his mind." She started to thank him. "Forget it, and stick it to 'em, baby!"

In a week she was in Hawaii, amusing and exhausting her colleagues with incessant questions. She tirelessly pursued every angle of the local nisei and *issei* (those born in Japan). She learned that nisei soldiers at Schofield's tent city, near the center of Oahu, had awakened a few days after Pearl Harbor to find themselves surrounded by a ring of soldiers with machine guns. A handful of Japanese had also been arrested under suspicion of espionage or sabotage. At the same time there was no anti-nisei hysteria, no wholesale arrests. Most important, there was not yet even a threat of evacuation to relocation camps.

The hatred and fear were on another level, and the Japanese population was already living under a cloud of suspicion. Racial feeling, restrained before Pearl Harbor, had become far more open and bitter. Maggie herself had been witness to ugly scenes where servicemen and war workers publicly vented their antagonism toward the Japanese who, for the most part, responded stoically. Several well-to-do American women also complained to Maggie that their Japanese maids and yardmen were unpatriotically demanding higher wages or just quitting. Her investigation revealed that those who had complained were hard to get along with and made unreasonable demands on their help. She was also incensed at the letters in the Honolulu newspapers railing at young American-Japanese for arrogance, lack of civility and indifference to the war.

In her interviews with Japanese families she found a reluctance to complain. The older ones were so eager to show their loyalty that they admitted they no longer went out publicly in kimono or *geta*. They wanted to be as American as possible and were even revolutionizing the old-country wedding and funeral customs. Already placed in discard were three basic Japanese institutions: the Buddhist temples, the Shinto shrines, and the language schools. Further research uncovered that this need to eradicate their past had led to destruction of photographs, family records, passports, and even proof of expatriation from Japan.

These self-restrictions had not been born of paranoia but sad experience. Women who had worn kimono on the main streets of Honolulu before the war without causing comment were jeered at after Pearl Harbor. Speaking Japanese in public had brought insult and threats of violence. Display of the Japanese flag at home was considered dangerous and flags, along with samurai swords and other artifacts of the old country, were secretly buried at night in backyards. Some nisei even changed their names officially to Hawaiian or Portuguese names. An Akira Aoki went so far as to become Angus McDonald.

It became obvious to Maggie that these Japanese were closely attached to Hawaii, yet the great majority had only a faint idea of American history, landmarks, or institutions. Consequently their loyalty was to the Islands rather than to the United States. After two weeks Maggie felt qualified to start her first article. In "The Nisei: A Generation on Trial" she attempted to explain in human terms the plight of those caught between two cultures, now forced to prove sincere fealty to America alone. For some thirty years they had been treated as second-class citizens and now the bombs on Pearl Harbor had forced them to make the heartrending decision concerning the cherished old ways of life lest their Americanism be questioned. Maggie ended with a quotation from Shunzo Sakamaki, chairman of the Oahu Citizens Committee for Home Defense. "There is no turning back now, no compromise with the enemy. Japan has chosen to fight us and we will fight. This is a bitter battle to the end."

She dispatched the article to Fredericks in Kansas City with trepidation, fearing that she might have been too emotional, too sympathetic to the nisei. The telegraphic reply from Kansas City was curt: GOOD STORY STOP KEEP THEM COMING.

Maggie was so elated she decided to branch out into the military field. She met a young naval officer connected with intelligence and let him date her. Encouraging him to boast of the importance of his work, she learned after several drinks that the Japanese were "planning another Pearl Harbor." And so she was not too surprised to learn of the great American victory at Midway on June 4. The Japanese lost the flower of their naval air force along with four Japanese carriers and a heavy carrier at the price of a single U.S. carrier.

She called her navy lieutenant but he was unable to get back to her for two days. She suggested they have dinner downtown at some quiet place. He was bursting with importance and it took little urging to discover details that had not been released officially. He revealed, for instance, the composition of the Japanese ships, giving the names of the four carriers of the Striking Force as well as those of the four light cruisers supporting the invasion force. He expected to score that evening himself and was deeply disappointed when Maggie merely kissed him lightly on the cheek, said she had a deadline, and rushed off.

Within an hour she telegraphed the information to Kansas City. Somehow it passed the censor and on the morning of June 7 the Fredericks chain headlined the story without using Maggie's byline. By coincidence the Chicago *Tribune* came out a few hours later with the same information which had been sent them by their war correspondent, Stanley Johnston. The Navy was enraged, fearing that the release of such accurate information would alert the Japanese to the fact that their most secret code had been broken. The President was equally irate and there was talk of bringing charges against the *Tribune* and Fredericks. But it was finally decided that this might harm the war effort. "Let the historians punish them," Roosevelt reportedly said.

Fredericks sent Maggie a warm letter and promised a modest raise in salary. At first she had felt a bit deflated not to get a byline, but the letter indicated that she might be sent into the war zone before too long. She hugged herself in ecstasy and was awake all that night imagining triumphs in the future that would even outstrip those of Sigrid Schulz.

3.

Tokyo. June 11, 1942.

The fear at the White House that the newspaper stories had jeopardized the secret that had made the victory at Midway possible was groundless. The Japanese navy was convinced that its code was unbreakable and General Tojo, still wearing the hats of both prime and war ministers, had already ordered the truth about Midway withheld from high officials as well as the public. The day after he received the news of the defeat he reported to the Emperor, yet said not a word about Midway. At a restricted session of Imperial Headquarters, Tojo recommended that public attention be diverted from the naval disaster by publicizing their Aleutian operation. Three days after Midway another naval force had seized the small but strategic islands of Attu and Kiska without a casualty.

And so on June 11 the headlines of the *Japan Times and Advertiser* read: NAVY SCORES ANOTHER EPOCHAL VICTORY. Two more enemy "monster warships" had been sunk in a surprise attack on Dutch Harbor in the Aleutians and on Midway Island. "Incidentally, of the seven aircraft carriers America possessed at the onset of the war, only two remain. In the graphic painting above, Ken Matsugae, noted artist, depicts the blasting of a carrier off Midway."

That morning Akira Toda telephoned his friend Yabe that Nippon Steel had just ordered him to take a staff to central China and reorganize a large steel mill and iron ore mine.

"I must see you at once," replied Yabe, the second secretary of Marquis Kido. Akira was puzzled by the concern in his friend's voice. They agreed to meet in Hibiya Park. Half an hour later Yabe was telling Toda that disturbing reports had come to Kido concerning the so-called great victories in Midway and the Aleutians. A naval officer had secretly revealed to the Emperor's chief adviser that four Japanese carriers had been sunk and the naval air force would never be able to replace its critical losses of airmen. The Lord Privy Seal, he added, feared this meant the inevitable turning point in the war had come, and he asked Yabe to inquire cautiously of a few close friends who had connections with the West if peace feelers should be inaugurated while Japan still had bargaining power.

Toda shook his head. He knew several generals and was sure the military would regard any such overture as treason. Even with the cooperation of the Emperor it was far too soon to propose such a thing. "We will have to be on our knees before Prime Minister Tojo will consider peace."

Toda returned to his office, cleared his desk of work and went home to prepare for departure to China. His daughter, Sumiko, was just leaving school. It had been an exciting day. A pompous young army officer had inspected the school and then announced critically to Miss Kuroki, the headmistress, that there was a picture of a Western woman on the top floor. Miss Kuroki, a graduate of Wellesley, could not hide a smile for it was a reproduction of the *Mona Lisa*.

"It is no laughing matter, headmistress. The Emperor's picture is on the floor *below* that of the *gaijin* woman. That cannot be."

"I quite understand," said Miss Kuroki in her stately manner. "I have already instructed that His Majesty's portrait be removed from the building. As you can see our poor building is wooden and an air raid would surely burn up the Emperor's portrait. Thank you for your courtesy, Lieutenant."

As if dismissed by his own school principal, the young man blushed, bowed, and left with apologies. The story soon spread around school, inspiring Christian and non-Christian students alike with even more reverence for their mistress. Sumiko was particularly impressed, silently vowing to stand up for her beliefs with as much courage. On the train home she noticed two fellow students born in America chattering in English. A middle-aged man next to Sumiko suddenly gave a shout of disgust, took off one of his *zori* and slapped the two girls on their cheeks. The girls burst into tears and Sumiko was so shocked she could not move. As the indignant man got off at the next station, Sumiko felt deep shame. Where was her courage when it was needed?

On the short walk home from the subway she worried about Shogo. Where was he now? And Ko, who only wanted to paint pictures. Before long he would graduate from Tokyo University and have to go into the army or navy. She was eager to talk about all this with her mother and as she approached the house could hardly wait to tell her how Miss Kuroki had put down the arrogant officer. Emi opened the door and said, "Father is home early today. He's leaving for China in a few days." Sumiko detected concern in her voice. "He'll be away for a long time. We don't know when he can come home—or anything."

Sumiko found her father busy getting things ready for a long absence. He had been away on short trips many times and wrote postcards and brought back souvenirs. But now he was going far away for months and months. She was going to miss him; she wondered whether her mother, who had lectured her on self-reliance on many occasions, now felt insecure and helpless.

At dinner that night Toda told his son Ko, "You will have to be the man of the family now. I depend on you. Things are going to be very difficult."

"In what respect, Father?"

"The war and all . . ." he said vaguely.

Later that evening Ko went to visit Jun Kato, a close friend who was an English major at Aoyama College. "Did you hear the rumor," said Ko, "that we'll graduate early next fall and be drafted?"

"I hope not!" exclaimed Jun. He dreaded the thought of having to fight against America since he had been born in Honolulu. Ten years earlier he and his baby sister had been brought to Japan by his father, a struggling journalist who felt he could only support his two older sons. And so Jun and his sister had been left with their grandparents, farmers who barely eked out a living.

Feeling unwanted and abandoned, Jun had grown up praying to be freed so he could return to his beloved America. He had secretly attended a Methodist Sunday School and had won a scholarship to Aoyama. Although furious, his stern grandfather had been persuaded by his wife to let the boy take advantage of the opportunity.

Pearl Harbor had come as a terrible shock to Jun. With so many complicated feelings and divided loyalties, he couldn't analyze his own reaction. Later he had felt surprise at the string of victories and couldn't help feeling proud that little Japan had achieved so much. Yet something inside him did not want to accept these victories. He still remembered with a thrill "The Star-Spangled Banner" and the pledge of allegiance to the Stars and Stripes taken with hand over heart every morning in the third grade.

At the same time over the years he had become, without quite realizing it, Japanese. Yet he could not react to the war like the average Japanese. He wanted neither Japan nor America to lose. He wanted them both to win. He felt confused. What could he do? And going into the army or navy would mean he would have to fight a country he still loved.

The two young men left Jun's rooming house to keep a date with a pair of Aoyama co-eds. As they neared the subway they heard shouting and then from around the corner came a lantern procession. The neighborhood was celebrating the great Midway victory. The two students watched the enthusiastic crowd of men, women, and children shouting, "Banzai!" as they headed for their Shinto shrine. The same people had probably marched and shouted after Pearl Harbor and the fall of Singapore and would march and shout after another victory.

"Do you think Japan can possibly win?" asked Ko.

"Of course," said Jun uncertainly and changed the subject. He didn't want to think about it.

They took a subway to Shibuya to meet their dates in front of a coffee shop; if they had been caught walking with them on the street they would have been arrested, for it was decreed that such relationships must cease until victory. Nervous as the two girls were—they were first-year students at Aoyama—they were thrilled to have a date with an upperclassman and a man from Tokyo Imperial University. After more than an hour of coffee Jun suggested they go to his room to listen to his jazz records. The girls wanted to, but being proper young ladies couldn't accept. Besides, listening to such music was also against the law. The young men, who had hoped at the most to hold hands and perhaps get a peck of a kiss, did not press the issue.

The following morning, a Friday, the Tokyo newspapers reported that President Roosevelt, stunned by the new naval loss, had convened a special session of the "Pacific War Council." Japan's "lightning maneuvers" in the Midway-Aleutian defeat were seen as significant. "The unwarranted optimism harbored by the public is causing confusion among the American high officials who have been trying desperately to conceal the latest Japanese success in the Aleutian Islands, according to an international telephone report."

On Saturday Toda made his final farewells, gave a few words of advice and left. The family was used to his absences but Emi now felt as if she were sending him off to war. He wasn't going to Shanghai but into unknown territory, so far away and so dangerous. The young man who used to deliver their rice had died in China and so had the vegetable man. Emi discussed these concerns with Matsu, the only maid who remained.

The next morning Jun showed up to go to church with Ko. They started for the subway with Sumiko and her mother following well behind. The rainy season had not set in yet and the gardens they passed were vivid with camellias and early June flowers.

The little church in Aoyama was almost full. Sumiko did notice in the back row a new face, a young army lieutenant with a cherubic face. He sat sternly erect making notations in a little black book. Another monitor, she figured, come to see whether the Methodists were teaching any sedition. The thought made her bristle. What right had they to enter the house of God with a notebook? But her mother, usually so combatant, had not objected when the first monitor had demanded that henceforth they begin services by facing the Palace, bowing, and singing the national anthem. "Be sensible," she told Sumiko. "We mustn't say anything to hurt the family." Sumiko still felt rebellious and adored Miss Kuroki for openly instructing her girls that there was only one God and that while they should respect the Emperor as their sovereign, he was only a man.

After the service the young lieutenant took Ko and Jun aside. "I presume you young men are determined to die for the Emperor." They were. "Who is more important, the Emperor or God?"

While the two young men were hemming and hawing, Sumiko interrupted, determined to be as courageous as Miss Kuroki. "There is only one Almighty God," she said. "We respect the Emperor as our sovereign. But he is still a man."

The lieutenant was taken aback. "For your own good, I warn you to watch your tongue!" Sumiko's heart palpitated.

Ko and Jun were waiting outside the church. They congratulated Sumiko on her spunk and she was so embarrassed she hurriedly joined her mother who quietly expressed her pride.

"She reminds me of my cousin Hiroko," Jun was telling his friend. The two young men parted and on the way home Jun thought of

Hiroko. She was four years his junior but she meant more to him than any other girl. She and Sumiko had much in common. Both were rebels but Hiroko was even more outspoken. And in a few weeks she would leave Hiroshima. She had been sent there by her father to stay with her aunt and go to school. Now she would have to return to that godforsaken island, Saipan, where her father ran a sugar mill. From birth he had treated her, like so many Japanese fathers, as a sad disappointment because she hadn't been a boy.

Jun's own future looked bleak. Before long he would have to go into the service. It was bad enough having to attend military training classes at Aoyama. Fortunately they only lasted about two hours and came but twice a week. They would be taken through close order drill which was dull but not obnoxious. Then came bayonet practice which *was* exciting but repellent. Even piercing a straw dummy with a bayonet turned his stomach for he could not imagine doing the same thing to an American.

4.
White Sulphur Springs, West Virginia. Spring 1942.

Floss and her family had moved in April from The Homestead to another comfortable hotel, the Greenbrier, located only thirty miles away. Floss was still tormented by her sad farewell to Maggie from the roof of The Homestead. It had only exacerbated her concern for the family now that war had come. Papa, of course, would thrive as would Will, a natural survivor who always came out on top. But the twins were bound to get into trouble. Maggie would have her own way as usual and become a war correspondent. And Mark had already shown his obsession for obeying his first impulse by joining the Marines, the most restrictive of the services. It was a wonder he had even gotten through boot camp without being court-martialed.

Life at the Greenbrier had its advantages. There had still been a little snow in the Appalachians and Masao spent happy hours with other children sliding on a nearby slope. There was also a drawback. Several hundred German internees were there and Floss had to keep a close watch on Tadashi whenever the Germans cried out, "Heil Hitler!" and raised their right hands in salute with every news of any Nazi success. He openly expressed his distaste at such times and it took all of Floss's diplomacy to smooth over matters and get him upstairs. "Most of the

Germans are very nice," she would say, and while he agreed, he argued that some of them were revolting. He would promise to control himself in the future but could not hide his concern for their fate in Tokyo. He feared he would be put into some minor, dull post because of his pro-Western views. "They'll probably stick me in press relations or some insipid clerical job." She reminded him that they had influential friends at the Foreign Office such as Kurusu. "And Terasaki-san will surely put in a good word for you."

"And who will put in a good word for him if they learn we both were involved with the cable Roosevelt sent the Emperor?"

At dinner that evening with a Japanese couple, the observant wife casually asked when Floss would have her baby. Tadashi was startled, and once they were alone learned to his horror that their second child would arrive early in September. She told him there was nothing to worry about. She'd had almost no morning sickness and the doctor promised there would be no repetition of the complications of the first birth.

"Why on earth didn't you tell me when you were in Washington?"

She kissed him. "Because you would have made a big fuss and tried to send me off to Williamstown."

With the end of May came the departure of the Germans for home. By this time many friendships had formed between the two groups and most of the Japanese contingent assembled in the lobby. After tearful personal farewells the Todas and those sharing their views left. The pro-Axis Japanese remained to sing a patriotic march and give three rousing *banzais!* for Germany. The Germans responded with a concerted, *"Heil, Deutschland!"*

Watching from afar, Tadashi clenched his fists. Putting an arm around him, Floss led her indignant husband away. But in the morning, it was she who had to be restrained after reading the latest reports in the New York *Times* of the nisei relocation camps. "They should be called concentration camps!" she fumed. Tadashi was just as outraged but he had accepted the internment as a necessary evil. "They are doing the same to the Americans in Japan," he said.

Floss rarely argued, but today she was too aroused at the bland reports of the mass movements into the camps. "But these are American citizens! The Americans in Japan are all *gaijin*. That's a ridiculous analogy." She stopped abruptly and a few minutes later read him an optimistic report from the State Department that they would soon leave for home on the Swedish ship *Gripsholm*.

A week later jubilation swept the Greenbrier at word that they would all take a night train to New York City on June 10. But their joy was stilled by news of a great American naval victory at Midway. Floss silently rejoiced but little doleful groups discussed the rumors that such a change in American fortunes might make the procurement of ships for repatriation very difficult. Tadashi explained to Floss that Midway meant that their return to Japan would be delayed. She thought this was ridiculous reasoning. And so it proved. The next morning they were instructed by the State Department to pack and be ready for the scheduled departure. Unfortunately pets could not be taken and there was much wailing by adults as well as children who would have to leave behind beloved dogs and cats. Masao, who rarely cried, did so that day in sympathy for families who had animals.

After a muggy overnight train ride, they arrived in Jersey City, and following tiresome processing were escorted aboard the Swedish liner. Officials of the highest rank as well as executive officers of trading firms and associations were placed in cabins on A Deck. The Todas felt lucky to be assigned relatively comfortable quarters on B Deck. Then came a dreary wait of a week and the rumor mill again went into full operation. They were going to be taken back to the Greenbrier. No, they were being sent to far worse quarters. One near-hysterical woman told Floss they were all going to federal prison for the duration of the war.

The children took the wait in better spirits, playing cards and Ping-Pong. Masao was in a constant state of elation for he turned out to be the best player of his age group. At last on June 18 the ship got under way. The three Todas stood on deck watching the tall buildings of Manhattan slowly drop into the sea. Floss tried to hold back her tears. Would she ever see her country again? And what was she heading for? Would she be treated as an enemy? More important, would Masao be accepted by his schoolmates? Within her she could feel the movements of another human caught between two cultures. Was there even a future for such a child in wartime?

The long voyage home seemed endless to most of the passengers. There was too much time to worry. The ship sailed south, taking 380 more Japanese aboard at Rio de Janeiro on July 2. Here the course changed to the east toward Africa, sailing around the Cape of Good Hope before putting in at Lourenço Marques, a Portuguese port on the east coast of Africa. It was July 20 and the passengers' spirits were lifted for it was here they would exchange ships with the Americans arriving from Yokohama. Two days later two ships from Japan did land, one the

145

Conte Verde, chartered from Italy, and the other, the *Asama Maru*. Most of those watching from the deck of the *Gripsholm* cheered to see the Rising Sun fluttering on the Japanese ship. Transferring baggage in the African heat was exhausting and Floss, more than seven months pregnant, had difficulty climbing stairs.

The Todas boarded the *Asama Maru* which crossed the Indian Ocean to Singapore ten days later. This busy port was filled with ships flying the Japanese flag and the harbor was shrill with their welcoming toots and whistles. Reporters rushed aboard. Several converged on Floss and Tadashi but she put them off with a few innocuous remarks and locked the cabin door. The parents stayed in the cabin but let Masao romp on deck with the other children. It was only when Floss felt the ship moving that she came out of the sweltering cabin to go topside. She saw the wreckage of an Allied plane, probably British, and prayed that its occupants had survived. A British prisoner working on the wharf noticed her. He held up two fingers in a V for Victory sign. Even at a distance she could see he was grinning. She waved as Masao ran up to her. The youngster also waved enthusiastically. Several other prisoners made the V sign.

Floss felt herself being drawn back. It was Tadashi; he was petrified. Back in the cabin, he told Floss and Masao that now they should regard themselves as in Japan and warned them not to give any public evidence of their sympathies. Masao was puzzled, and after Floss told him to go out and play she thanked Tadashi for his warning, while suggesting he confine his advice to her. He was only confusing the boy; she would keep him in line.

Just as Tadashi had warned, there was a new spirit aboard ship upon leaving Singapore. Naval officers gave lectures proving that Japan was waging a just war against Western imperialism. Victory was inevitable so long as every Japanese did his duty. Attendance was compulsory and Floss forced herself to keep a straight face despite some of the ridiculous things she heard. The navy men continually harped on the dangerous thoughts the repatriates might have picked up in the United States and lectured that such thoughts must be purged before they could be transmitted to the people back home.

Now it was Tadashi who had to be warned by Floss to be cautious. Indignant at the veiled threats, he almost lost his temper when a naval intelligence officer insisted on interrogating Floss about America. She submitted gracefully, later assuring Tadashi that she had given only information that any tourist could easily pick up.

The *Asama Maru* entered Yokohama Harbor on August 20. Floss anxiously awaited another influx of reporters, but they were allowed to disembark without having to answer a single question. On the pier they were greeted warmly by Tadashi's mother, Ko, and Sumiko. Much was made over Masao. "What a great big boy!" exclaimed Masao's grandmother, and Ko pretended the lad was so big that he couldn't budge him off the floor.

They all boarded the special train for repatriates and in less than an hour were at Tokyo Station. Cars were waiting to bring everyone to the Nijubashi—the double bridge—entrance to the Imperial Palace. Here all, including Floss, bowed respectfully to the Palace. Then Emi and Ko took the newcomers to a small apartment rented for them in a pleasant residential district only a few minutes' walk from the Toda home.

Their apartment house was on top of a hill, and Masao raced from window to window discovering new sights. Just below was a Buddhist cemetery where a small group was reverently burying a relative. Ko pointed out a more famous Buddhist temple where Townsend Harris had opened the first American legation in 1856. Ko promised to show Masao its famous ginkgo tree which was seven hundred years old. A renowned priest, Shinran Shonin, had planted his staff in the ground stating that such was the manner in which the prayer was to be celebrated henceforth. Soon the staff began to put forth buds and grew into a stately ginkgo tree which was now more than thirty feet in girth.

Though completely worn out, Floss made no complaints. But Emi knew what she was going through and assured her that they had already made arrangements at a good hospital. When was she expecting?

"In about five minutes," she said jokingly. "Within two weeks, I believe."

Sumiko, who had remained modestly quiet, finally came forward to present a small package, a present. Tadashi opened it to find three little bars of soap. Ko was amazed. Where on earth had she found such a treasure? Sumiko admitted that it had cost a precious copy of *Life*. Floss was taken aback at this first sign of the deprivations to come. Then she was informed that both gas and electricity were rationed and hot water for baths could only be drawn during two hours in the early evening.

Emi took Tadashi aside and asked why he had insisted on an apartment. An eldest son should live in his parents' house. He told her about the private message President Roosevelt had sent the Emperor. "It

147

would be wise if you all saw us as little as possible. There may be trouble and I don't want you to become involved."

Emi promised to be careful but secretly vowed to do her best to make their life in Tokyo bearable.

The Todas had also brought food for dinner so the newcomers wouldn't have to go down the hill to the shops. Tadashi said little during the meal and, once Masao was put to bed in a small room almost completely taken up by a couch, apologized for having allowed himself to bring his little family to Tokyo. "What have I done!" he said. "Life will be so hard for you in this unfriendly land." He embraced Floss, careful not to press hard against her bulging stomach.

In the morning Ko returned. He assured his brother that he would only take them to Masao's new school and then would follow Tadashi's instructions to stay away. It took half an hour on the subway to reach a private elementary school run by the Methodists. The headmaster assured Floss that Masao would be very welcome in kindergarten. After conversing with Masao, the headmaster exclaimed, "My goodness, what an accent! You must not take offense, Masao, if your classmates laugh at the way you talk." The boy said nothing but scowled.

On the return subway trip he and Floss were the object of curiosity. Riders would glance at them, then hurriedly turn away. Floss overheard one mother telling her little girl that she was sitting next to a *gaijin* and not to get too close. "They are worse than Koreans and have terrible tempers." The girl fearfully pulled as far away from Floss as she could.

One old man across the aisle smiled at Masao until a young woman next to him, probably a granddaughter, vigorously pulled at his sleeve and said loudly, "I think they are Americans."

Other passengers made unfriendly comments assuming the *gaijin* could not understand. Floss noticed Masao bristling and told him not to pay any attention to the remarks. She herself smiled as if all were well but insisted they get off at the next stop and change to a car with fewer passengers.

Ten days later she gave birth to a six-pound girl. They named her Ryuko. When Tadashi first held her he said, "What kind of a world have we brought you into?"

CHAPTER ELEVEN

1.

Camp O'Donnell. April 1942.

Several days after arriving at O'Donnell, Will was persuaded by his bunkmates to have a doctor check his thigh. He hobbled over to the hospital area. A long line of dispirited prisoners stretched from a large shack and wound around the structure. He took his place in the slow-moving line. Those in the rear pushed forward to get to the shady side of the building and avoid the beating sun.

After an hour a doctor emerged from the front door. "Hi, McGlynn, glad to see you made it." Will had met him during the last days of Bataan at Hospital No. 1. The doctor shook his head dolefully. "Our people are dirty, bloated, and damned near lifeless." He lowered his voice. "Look at that poor devil. His extremities are swollen to twice their natural size." He surveyed the line. "It's the saddest sight I've ever seen. What's your problem?"

"I was jabbed in the thigh with a bayonet. It throbs quite a bit and then seems numb."

"You should see Rosen. He knows a lot more about this than I do." They shook hands. "Tell Rosen you're a friend of mine."

At last Will reached the open door. He was shocked to see no cots, no medical equipment, just half a dozen doctors sitting in chairs examining patients. Will could hear a woebegone man tell the first doctor that he defecated five or six times a day. "And nothing comes out, Doc, except this gray-looking stuff and blood."

"Dysentery," said the doctor. "And there isn't any medicine to give you. The Japs have promised to let us have some soon."

"Isn't there nothing you can do?" pleaded the man.

"There is something. Behind the mess hall you can find where they throw out wood ashes. That's charcoal. Chew it up very fine and swallow it. Next."

The next man advanced wobbling and clutched at a small desk to

149

keep from falling. "Last night I shook like hell and then I liked to freeze to death."

"Malaria, son. You're going to stay in the hospital. You rest and eat as much as you can even though it nauseates you. You've got to build up your strength." He motioned to an orderly. "Put him over there." He indicated a corner of the room where a dozen other men were lying on the bare floor. "We're getting cots in a few days, son. Hang in there."

The man directly in front of Will complained that he hadn't had a crap in over a week. "Jesus!" exclaimed the doctor indignantly. "Here's a line of people who have been shitting a dozen times a day in great agony. Get out of here and don't waste our time." He looked up at Will. "Yes?"

"I just talked to Dr. Webster outside. He said I should see Dr. Rosen for a bayonet wound."

"I'm Rosen. Lower your trousers." He examined Will's thigh, then made a clucking noise. "Festering. I don't like the looks of it. But I've seen a lot worse today."

"Is there anything I can do?"

"Yes. You can pray the Japs bring us some sulfa. Several truckloads of medicine and equipment are supposed to come in. Try not to aggravate the wound but don't just sit around all day. Keep active. Next."

Will slowly headed back for his shack through crowds of milling prisoners. It reminded him of the Russian prison in one of Dostoevski's books. A burial detail passed with a dozen corpses. This was an American House of the Dead. Will came upon a block-long line of men standing in the sun at a single water spigot. Each man could fill one canteen. Beneath the spigot was a five-gallon can to catch the few drops that would overflow from one canteen to the next. Will asked a man near the head of the line how long he had waited.

"Five hours, and I'm one of the lucky ones. The guys back there are going to take at least eight hours." The reason was that the Japanese only let the water flow at certain periods, and this one spigot had to serve a couple of thousand men.

Each day at O'Donnell seemed an eternity. By now mess halls were open for three meals a day of the unsavory lugao. Sometimes a few camotes—sweet potatoes—would be added to make a watery soup. Some of the men could not hold this unsalted mess on their stomach and the weaker ones were drifting away into death.

Each meal was contested by huge bluebottle flies. Will had to cover his mess kit with a piece of cardboard and lift only a corner to hurriedly grab a spoonful. Even then the flies avidly followed the food to his mouth and it was no rarity to swallow one or two. The hordes of flies constantly harassed the men, making daytime existence almost unbearable with their menace and eternal buzzing. Bushes overloaded with the pestilent flies would bend to the ground.

Bad as the conditions were for the Americans, those for the Filipinos were far worse. The guards would assemble them in an open field and give them Tsuji-inspired lectures on the "Greater East Asia Prosperity Sphere," and the evil of any oriental's supporting or even submitting to the red barbarians. Attempting to locate Lieutenant Domingo, Will watched one of these lectures from the shade. After the men finally dispersed slowly a score of dead or dying Filipinos dotted the ground. A burial detail soon appeared to carry out the dead on blankets tied to bamboo poles. As this procession plodded toward the cemetery Will recognized Domingo at one end of a litter. He staggered under the weight of the corpse. "We're still dying like flies," he said as he passed Will.

"No talking!" shouted a guard and kicked Domingo, who stumbled, and the corpse rolled into the dust.

2.

Bitter arguments became common among the Americans as men fought over food and water. In the shack next to Will's an argument started over a rat caught in a trap. One man had already cooked the rat and was eating it when his partner, who had helped build the trap, appeared. He leaped at his comrade and started a bloody fistfight that finally had to be stopped by onlookers before someone was killed.

Another time Will was passing the mess hall during delivery of rations from a quartermaster truck. The sight of food attracted a crowd and one of the Japanese lifted up a hindquarter of beef. It was the first sight of meat most of the prisoners had had since Bataan. The soldier tossed the beef to another Japanese who gestured: Want some? Everyone shouted assent as did Will, even though he feared the Japanese was just teasing them. But the soldier leaned over and cut off a piece of meat that must have weighed twenty pounds. He gestured with the meat as if he were feeding dogs in a cage, then lofted it into the midst of the prisoners. It fell next to Will who grabbed it. As he was slicing off a piece with the jackknife he had managed to keep hidden from the Japanese, prisoners swarmed on him like vultures.

"Back off!" he shouted, hugging the beef under one arm while flourishing the knife. The others retreated a few feet as he cut off a few pounds. Leaving the rest of the meat, he stepped back and was almost bowled over in the wild rush. As he surveyed the cursing, shoving, shouting melee he thought, My God, what is happening to us.

Hiding the meat under his shirt, Will hustled back to his shack. There was a burst of cheering at sight of the prize until someone said, "For Christ's sake, shut up! We'll draw a crowd." Secretly they prepared a banquet. Each man contributed something—a hoarded camote, an onion or field weeds. It was unanimously decided to make a stew and the meat and vegetables were cut by a lieutenant with Will's jackknife. They sat in a circle watching the boiling pot. It reminded Will of the witches in *Macbeth*. By dusk several of the men became so impatient they insisted on a testing. The honor went to Will. He took a small bite of meat as if appraising wine at a fancy restaurant. He nodded approval. Each man held out a mess kit and Will began to divide the meat piece by piece. He came to one piece bigger than the rest. As he looked closer in the firelight he saw it was a frog. "He must have made his last jump into the pot," he said and was about to throw it away.

"Give it to me," said the lieutenant, who promptly did away with the frog.

After the meal the men chatted in the dark about memorable meals at home. The talk went on and on until the last ember of the fire was dead. Then they all crawled into their hard beds. To his surprise, Will felt depressed rather than triumphant. The food did not sit well in his stomach and several times he thought he was going to throw up. They had acted like animals. Hunger had sunk them all to the lowest depths. What would it be like in a month, in a year, in two years? If they survived, would they be worth it?

In the morning he volunteered for tomorrow's burial detail. That night there was a long torrential rain. The grass roof leaked in a dozen places and the men huddled together for warmth. At dawn Will was roused. His burial group was ordered to pick up the dead at Zero Ward which was just behind the hospital. It looked like a small warehouse and even from a hundred yards gave off a sickening stench. The man in charge, Sergeant Dix, tied a handkerchief over his nose and entered the building. Will thought he would faint from the overpowering stink. The

sun on the corrugated roof had already turned the place into an oven.
Men were lying on the filthy floor in their own feces. Skin seemed to be
holding their bones in place. They were all skeletal. Luckier ones were
on bamboo window shutters. One man was standing. He slowly shuffled
toward Will.

"What are you doing here, soldier?" asked Will.

"Just waiting to die. That's why they put me here." He grinned
horribly. "But I got news for them. I'm going to make it. I'm getting out
of this morgue, mister!"

He was the only spark of life in the big room. The others had given up
all hope. A man with hollow eyes staggered into a squatting position. He
strained to defecate, moaned in excruciating pain. He pinched his buttocks and tried again without luck. "Hemorrhoids," he said. "I haven't
crapped in two weeks."

"Why don't you go to the medics?"

The man looked up hopelessly. "I am a medic."

Others in the detail were already carrying corpses out on their own
bamboo shutters. Will took the shoulders of a man who had died on the
floor. To his horror skin came off in his hand. The putrid body was finally
placed on a litter. It took four men to carry it, each himself a walking
skeleton with pop eyes, sunken cheeks, and ribs showing. Will's litter
was too short and the legs of the naked corpse hung over one end, bent
at the knees. The arms and head hung down over the other end, causing
the dead eyelids to open, the mouth to gape, and the tongue to hang
out. As the procession of a dozen corpses started off it was met by
another procession from the hospital.

"Replacements for Zero Ward," said Sergeant Dix with mordant humor.

The burial column passed through the camp. In the first days those
who watched used to stand at attention and salute. Now death had
become so normal that no one gave the column a second look. No one
seems to care, thought Will. Perhaps this was nature's way to keep men
from going mad.

They were stopped at a barracks. Someone pointed under the building. Another poor devil had crawled underneath to die. Here it was that
Father O'Malley joined the group. He recognized Will and asked how
his wound was.

"Better, Father," he said though every step was painful.

"They won't let me conduct any services," he said. "But every so
often I pretend I'm on the detail." He took Will's place at the rear of the

litter. Will protested but the priest said, "Do you want me to get into trouble? You take over in a few minutes."

As they approached the gate, Sergeant Dix was handed a Japanese flag. They passed through and headed up the rocky slopes to the burying ground, a long, half-filled mass grave. Because of the rain bodies had risen. Legs and arms were sticking up. Buzzards were eating them. Dix waved off the birds and indicated where the corpses should be placed. Will shivered at the thought of touching the bodies. But the sergeant, an old hand, showed the others how to make ropes from the tall cogon grass. "That way you can lift the bodies off the litters without getting flesh on you."

Will and his partner carefully laid their corpse into the watery grave. Father O'Malley said something in Latin and threw in a handful of dirt on top of the corpse. Then as Will began shoveling dirt over the body he said, "The Lord is my Shepherd, I shall not want. He maketh me to lie down in green pastures; He leadeth me beside the still waters . . ." The body kept popping to the surface and two men had to hold it down with poles.

A pugnacious-looking Irish private named Kelly recognized the next corpse to be buried. "Lieutenant Murphy!" he cried in triumph. "I told the son of a bitch I'd piss on his dead body even if I had to dig him up!" He unbuttoned his fly and urinated on the body before anyone could stop him.

As the detail marched back to camp, Kelly couldn't stop detailing his grievances against Murphy but his nervous energy abruptly ended once he reached his own barracks. He crawled underneath like an old dog.

"Ten to one we have to drag him out of there tomorrow morning," said Sergeant Dix. "He and Murphy hated each other's guts. Now that he's pissed on him there's nothing left to keep him going."

Will thought he would never get back to his shack. He flopped onto his pallet. His bunkmate, a baby-faced lieutenant named Benny Williams, brought him a cup of water. He drank it in a few gulps and asked for more. Then he felt as if his stomach was going to explode. His thigh was burning. Someone suggested he go on sick call but he couldn't face returning to the hospital area. He wouldn't even go to the mess hall. What was the use of fighting to live?

That night the stench of the burial grounds seemed to be with him. He could still smell the rotting flesh and the stink of feces, puke, and decaying bodies in Zero Ward. The quiet of the night was broken by a scream from a barracks. This was followed by angry voices, moans and groans. At last came blessed silence again. But a moment later he could hear the howling of wild dogs in the distance. He knew why they were howling. They were digging up bodies at the cemetery and having a feast. The awful sight of buzzards eating arms and legs returned to him. He took a deep breath and choked. The stink of death was not an illusion but right here. The taste of death was in his mouth and it was real. He was dying.

He fell asleep from exhaustion and was awakened by Williams. Benny was a lanky youngster, a recent college graduate but with the look of a teenager. He had endured the march and O'Donnell without a word of complaint and always volunteered for more than his share of details. He good-naturedly ignored the jibes of the others for constantly reading *Science and Health* by Mary Baker Eddy.

"I'm taking you to sick call," he said.

Will managed to grin. "I thought you were a Christian Scientist."

"I still am," said Benny, "but you aren't." He forced Will to his feet and helped him make it to the hospital. As they approached a detail was pulling out several corpses from underneath the hospital. Conditions were far worse than Will had seen the first time. Some naked patients were lying outside the building on the bare ground without any covering.

Dr. Rosen seemed surprised to find Will still alive. He shook his head dolefully. "My colleagues at Presbyterian will never believe what I tell them," he said. "Provided I get back. Look at these poor devils. They've got dysentery, malaria, beri-beri and something we call wet beri-beri. See that man. He's got what the orderlies call 'rice belly.' Malnutrition. Malnutrition, hell. It's plain starvation. Those fellows with swollen feet and legs? Edema." He told Will to lower his trousers. He tenderly touched the area around the festering wound. "Swelling. Must be painful."

"Yes, sir. Lately streaks seem to be shooting up my leg."

Rosen examined the leg cautiously. It seemed an eternity to Will before he spoke. "I hate to say this, Captain," he said, "but you must have sulfa tablets. Otherwise your leg will have to come off."

"Jesus Christ!" exclaimed Will. It was rumored they had to operate without any anesthetics at all and those who heard the screams of such a patient would never forget it. Worse still was going through life with only one leg. No more tennis, no more climbing. And what chance would a one-legged man have of surviving this hellhole? God, he wished

155

he had died last night. He heard a buzzing and realized it was the doctor talking to him.

"There may be a few sulfa tablets I can scrounge, Captain. But don't count on it." Rosen left the building.

Will felt a hand on his shoulder. "Don't give up," said Benny quietly and Will felt a surge of hope. Then Rosen came back, head bowed. His eyes were soft and sad. "I'm sorry, Captain. There's not a sulfa pill left." He leaned forward. "I've got to operate. Otherwise you will certainly die." He took Will's arm.

Will pulled free. "I'd rather die." The doctor tried to restrain Will but he limped to the door as fast as he could. An orderly tried to stop him but Benny pushed the man aside and helped Will down the steps. "You won't die, Will," he said. "You don't have to die."

They almost bumped into Father O'Malley who insisted Will come to his bamboo shack where they could talk in private. "I've been watching you, son," he said once they were alone. He was incredibly thin and looked as if a breeze could blow him over. But his thin, ascetic face was peaceful.

"I want to die," said Will.

"No," said O'Malley, "it is not God's will."

"You still think there's a God with all this hell around us?"

"All this is only comprehensible if there *is* a God," he said.

How could anyone be so stupid, thought Will.

"I believe I can get you sulfa tablets," said the priest.

Will felt a surge of hope. "Where?"

"Do you have any money, son?"

Will had two American twenty-dollar bills he'd kept hidden in a shoe.

"I have a contact at Fort McKinley, a Filipino who was a clerk for General Brereton. He's already sent me some quinine." He explained that a large group of Signal Corps men had been transferred to Fort McKinley where quantities of telephone line from Bataan were stored. The detail was now busy transferring this material from McKinley to the Manila port area. Every few days replacements were sent to McKinley. "Would you be willing to go there?" asked Father O'Malley.

"Yes, Father!"

Two days later Will was awakened just before dawn by a scrawny private. "I'm Mike. Father O'Malley sent me," was all he said. Other men were already assembling for various details as the two men made for the officer's mess hall. Half a dozen other prisoners were standing in the back of a ramshackle little truck. Will and Mike crawled aboard and a few minutes later the truck headed out the gate.

"Who's the American sitting up front with the driver and the Jap guard?" Will asked.

"Private Popov," said Mike, "the biggest bastard at O'Donnell, bar none."

Will had heard of him. He had been a professional club boxer when drafted and he ran his barracks as if he were MacArthur. He had a vicious temper and could floor anyone who protested with a single punch. The guards tolerated him because he kept order. He operated the biggest black market in the camp and managed, with bribes, to make at least one trip a week to McKinley or Manila to pick up food, cigarettes, and assorted articles. The story was that the ubiquitous Popov had bought into a disreputable night club upon arrival in Manila and still did business with the local racketeers.

"I was in his company on Bataan," said Mike. "He dogged every tough job and gained weight while the rest of us were starving."

The air was still cool and Will luxuriated in the rare freedom. As they passed through a barrio, people watched stoically but a few would make surreptitious V-for-victory signs. They came to burned-out buildings but most of the suburbs of Manila were untouched. The civilians here were more careful and seemed to ignore them. At the gate of Fort McKinley, Will recalled the last time he had been there—the panic, the bitterness of those who had been left behind. The truck stopped near a warehouse and Will disembarked with the others. Mike nudged him and indicated a Filipino standing near a pile of telephone line making notations on a clipboard. "That's the one."

Will's heart thumped so hard he was sure it could be heard. He approached the Filipino casually. "Father O'Malley said you might be able to get me some sulfa pills."

"Maybe," said the other, barely moving his lips.

"How much?"

"How much you got?"

"Forty American dollars."

"Okay." With practiced furtiveness the Filipino took the money. "Be here at six o'clock when the truck goes back to O'Donnell."

"It means a lot . . ." started Will but the Filipino turned and walked away as a Japanese guard came over and poked Will in the back with a rifle butt.

By noon Will was exhausted from loading wire into trucks and he limped to the shade of the warehouse to rest. A guard started forward menacingly just as Private Popov and a bleary-eyed Japanese lieutenant came out of the warehouse. Popov said something to the lieutenant who, somewhat tipsily, waved the guard aside.

"Come on, Captain," said Popov and jerked Will to his feet. He led the confused Will into a nearby barracks. "This is where the permanent detail is billeted." Will longingly eyed the rows of cots. "Get yourself some decent clothes," he said, pointing to the lines of footlockers. "Most of the Air Corps guys bugged outa here without taking their gear." Will finally found a corporal's khakis that fitted. Popov had put on a colorful Filipino shirt. He tossed another one to Will. "Put this on now. I and you and that Jap lieutenant are going into town for some fun." He explained that he had been feeding the lieutenant liquor confiscated from the officers' club.

Popov helped the lieutenant into the front of a car flying little Rising Sun flags from the fenders, then got into the back with Will. As a Japanese driver maneuvered the car out the gate, the sentries saluted. The lieutenant turned around and mumbled, *"Onna."*

"Hai, hai!" said Popov and told the driver to get onto the boulevard running along the bay. "He wants girls," said Popov and directed the driver to a run-down cabaret. Popov helped the lieutenant out of the car with Will behind feeling foolish and frightened. Once inside, the lieutenant flopped into a seat and began shouting for Will to dance with one of the girls on duty. He picked out the tallest. "You German?" she said in English.

"Yah," he said and hoped that was the end of the conversation.

"You speak English?"

He gestured with thumb and forefinger. "A leetle."

The girl laughed, then whispered, "American?"

He nodded. A Japanese captain whirled by with his partner. "I'm a POW—don't give me away." The girl hugged him. "I like Yanks," she whispered.

No sooner had he sat down next to the lieutenant, who was getting drunker by the minute, than another girl came up and claimed him. As soon as they were on the dance floor she asked if he had seen Private Guillermo Peralta at O'Donnell. Another girl cut in and wanted news of her brother. He was kept so busy that he finally had to explain that he was wounded and couldn't dance another step. This girl suggested he walk to the back door with her and simply disappear in the depths of

Manila. It was tempting but he declined. If he escaped, the other men in his group might be punished.

By this time the lieutenant was shouting for a girl. He wanted one now and he didn't want to dance with her. "Get the driver," said Popov. Will with his help managed to half-carry the lieutenant to the car. They shoved him into the back seat where he lolled back and went to sleep.

Just before 6 P.M. the Filipino returned to the warehouse where Will and Popov were waiting near the empty truck.

"You got it?" asked Will.

The Filipino nodded. He took out a small package. "But it cost me twenty dollars more."

Will was in despair. "I have no more."

The Filipino shrugged. "Come back again."

"Bullshit," said Popov and sank his fist in the Filipino's stomach. Popov tossed the package to Will, then went through the moaning Filipino's pocket. He found two twenty-dollar bills and extended them to Will.

"Let him keep them."

"He's a cheater. If you don't want them, I do." He put them in his pocket and stepped into the truck cab. "C'mon," he beckoned Will. "Sit up front." Their driver emerged from the barracks with a bagful of food contributed by men just returned from the permanent detail. As the truck started off, Popov leaned out and pointed a finger at the Filipino he had hit. "Try that again, Flip, and I'll feed you to the Japs."

Will was counting the sulfa pills. There were twelve. He swallowed one with a swig from his canteen. He knew it was an illusion but his thigh already felt better. He closed his eyes and thanked God. By the end of the week it was no illusion that his wound was drying up. He no longer felt the searing stabs followed by deep throbs of pain. He showed Father O'Malley the mending thigh. "It's a miracle, my boy," he said. Was it a miracle or the drugs or both? Will didn't care and thanked the priest for all he was doing for the men.

"They are closer to God than I am," said the priest. "They are near death and will soon be with Him. What I do for them is so little."

"How could you possibly do any more?" said Will.

O'Malley grinned. "I must confess, Will, that sometimes I can't sleep nights for dreaming of the smell of a good tenderloin steak with mashed potatoes and fresh carrots and a glass of beer."

Early in June a rumor swept the camp. They were being transferred to another camp and the first detachment was leaving in the morning. The men in Will's shack didn't take it any more seriously than a recent rumor that Hitler had been assassinated. But late that night they were moved with several hundred others to the hospital area and packed into the already crowded hospital barracks. It began to rain heavily but it was pleasant hearing the heavy drops slam harmlessly against the sturdy roof. The rain stopped just before dawn. In the dim light the men were jammed into open trucks like cattle.

"We're going north," someone observed as they turned onto the highway at Capas. Less than an hour later they reached the outskirts of a town. Someone said it was Cabanatuan. They stopped and civilians surrounded the trucks. Some tossed rice balls and other food into the trucks. The guards acted as if they were bored and didn't even make a threatening gesture.

A pretty girl with a very low-cut dress began blowing kisses to the men in Will's truck. "Christ, get a load of those knockers!" said a skinny private. "I could pole-vault outa the truck!" Will had no reaction at all and felt somehow humiliated. "That jerk would screw a monkey if you held it," someone said disgustedly. "Yeah," added another. "I'd rather have a big juicy hamburger!" The universal enthusiastic response to this alternative made Will feel better.

As the convoy turned onto a dirt road someone remarked that today was an anniversary. Exactly six months earlier the Japs had hit Pearl Harbor. Will had gone through more in those six months than in his previous life. It was incredible what he and the others in the truck had suffered in that short period of time. And they were the lucky ones, the survivors. It was a miracle that anyone was alive after the battles, the starvation and disease on Bataan, the march, and O'Donnell. He had seen more death and pain, more meanness and cowardice and heroism than any fictional character he'd ever read about. Yet here it was a common experience. How much had it affected him? For the first time he wondered if he had become hardened, corrupted by the repetition of horror. Had he been dehumanized? He conjured up the thin, ascetic face of Father O'Malley. In his previous life he had never met men as noble as this. Then he thought of the feral fight for the piece of steak; of the selfishness of those officers who hoarded food for themselves; of the angry Irishman urinating on his enemy.

Of one thing he was sure. He was no longer the assured Will McGlynn who had succeeded at everything he ever tried. The importance of impressing General Marshall and making his way to the top seemed petty. Now he was driven by only one thing—to survive without doing so at anyone else's expense. He felt stirring within him something more than hope. Perhaps a third of those in the truck would survive; he knew he was going to be one of them. Perhaps many of those who survived would do so by cheating, hoarding, and informing and he vowed he would not be among those.

"Hey, Captain!" called someone in the back of the truck. He looked up at an unbelievably thin face. "Remember me?" Will was incredulous. It was the man he had seen staggering around Zero Ward, given up for dead. "I told you I'd fool those bastards."

CHAPTER TWELVE

1.

Guadalcanal. August 1942.

The first Allied step on the road to Tokyo came at a peaceful-looking island in the Solomons ten degrees below the equator. This was Guadalcanal, Japan's southernmost outpost. From the air it looked like a tropical paradise. On the ground it was a hell on earth of steaming jungles, fierce white ants, crocodiles, leeches, scorpions, beating sun and torrential rains.

The overconfidence of the Japanese navy that had led to Midway was not diminished by that crushing defeat. The Japanese high command never expected a counterattack so soon and the Americans landed on Guadalcanal without a casualty. As they drove deeper into the Japanese positions, it became obvious in Tokyo that something drastic had to be done. Colonel Tsuji and Shogo had recently returned to Tokyo and the "God of Operations" persuaded his superiors to send him south to find out what was really going on at Guadalcanal. After studying the problems of the grim fighting at the headquarters of the 17th Army in Rabaul, he persuaded its commander, General Hyakutake, to let him draw up a new operation to retake the only airfield on Guadalcanal, which had become American headquarters. Final plans for the attack on Henderson Field, as it was now called, were made by Tsuji and Shogo together with the senior staff officer of the 17th Army. Tsuji then volunteered to go to Guadalcanal as unofficial adviser to help put his own plan into operation.

On the eve of their departure from Rabaul, Tsuji held a press conference. He told Shogo not to bother accompanying him since he did not want the young idealist to hear what he intended to say. He trusted Shogo but realized he was not yet ready to accept the necessity for harsh medicine. The young man had renounced Christianity but was still too squeamish to understand that the ends do justify the means. But Shogo in all innocence did follow his chief unobtrusively and heard him shout, "Oi, you newsmen! You know the expression *gashin-shotan?*"

They did, for the people recently had been called on by their leaders to face years of *gashin-shotan*. Literally it meant "to sleep on kindling and lick liver," but in this context the people were being asked to endure a life of hardship and austerity in order to win the war. To Tsuji, however, *gashin-shotan* was a call for vengeance. He dramatically held up what looked like a lump of black sugar. "This is the enemy's liver. I lick it every day." He did so.

Shogo was horrified. But what was even worse was the cruel smile on Tsuji's face. What had driven this great man to such terrible extremes?

On October 9, the transports carrying reinforcements for Guadalcanal along with the destroyer transporting 17th Army headquarters landed safely at Tassafaronga Point. Hyakutake and his staff as well as Tsuji and Shogo waded ashore. The latter felt a chill run through him as he touched dry land. What lay ahead? As bags of rice and other supplies were piled on the shore, he saw ragged figures creep out of the brush. They timidly came closer to the supplies. Were these walking skeletons really soldiers? Their hair was long, filthy; their tattered, grimy rags no longer resembled uniforms. One man staggered up to Tsuji explaining they were survivors of a bloody battle with American Marines at a ridge near the airfield. "We have come to help unload the supplies."

The newcomers were led down the beach to the field headquarters of the 17th Army. It was dawn when they reached their destination near a little river. While they breakfasted, a runner brought bad news. Most of the rice unloaded the night before had been stolen by the volunteer coolies. Instead of responding angrily, Hyakutake sighed. "It is my fault for having brought such loyal soldiers to such a miserable pass. May they fill their stomachs with our food and be remade into good soldiers."

Shogo had difficulty swallowing the food in his own mouth. What a noble man the general was. During the day the last survivors of the ridge battle with the Marines were stumbling out of the jungle. Their ribs protruded. Their black hair had turned a dirty brown, and Shogo saw one man pull out a handful. Their eyebrows and eyelashes were dropping off. One took a bite of food and spit out several teeth.

Shogo noticed an enlisted man eagerly drinking sea water and asked how he could do it. He explained that his body was so starved for salt that the sea water tasted sweet. The water brought on a painful urge to evacuate but the man was too weak. Several others were also writhing in agony. They helped each other with fingers. Their relief was indescribable. Tsuji shook his head in despair as Shogo related all this. Dismay deepened when he learned that the Marines had just scored another victory five miles away at the Mataniko River. Almost a third of the entire effective force they had come to relieve now lay dead along the Mataniko.

Hyakutake radioed Rabaul: SITUATION OF GUADALCANAL IS FAR MORE SERIOUS THAN ESTIMATED. He requested immediate reinforcements and supplies. The latest Marine victory also made it necessary for Tsuji to draw up an entirely different battle plan, to start in ten days. Instead of an attack down the coast across the Mataniko River, they would launch a surprise night attack on Henderson Field from the rear. The fresh reinforcements, the 2nd Division, would push through the jungle at the foot of Mount Austen, a rugged 1,500-foot hill behind the airfield, and launch a two-pronged attack.

A semicircular trail leading behind Mount Austen, started a month earlier, was almost finished. It ran some fifteen miles through jungle so dense a man could not walk upright for more than a few paces. The army engineers had only hand tools to cut down huge trees and hack through tough vines as thick as a man's arm. Log roads spanned marshes while camouflage netting hid those stretches across grassy plains. Wide ravines were bridged with the larger vines while smaller ones served as handrails up steep inclines. The success of Tsuji's plan depended on traversing this trail on schedule so the double attack could be coordinated.

2.

Camp Elliott, California. October 1942.

The 6th Marines were preparing to embark, destination unknown. The general feeling was that they were heading for Guadalcanal where the 5th Marines were having a rough time with the Nips and suffering heavy casualties. It would take the 6th, as usual, to come to the rescue. Mark was as excited as the others but secretly worried. How would he act when the shells started flying overhead?

Late that day the 1st Battalion began boarding a Matson luxury liner by companies. An enlisted man guided Company D to its quarters below. Mark laid out his blankets, hung his pack at the foot of his bunk, and tied his rifle on the bar of the bunk overhead. Half a dozen men of Company D had smuggled musical instruments aboard knowing that their executive officer, Captain Sullivan, would be in charge of loading.

And Billy J. encouraged singing. There was excited horsing around until their platoon sergeant quieted them down and took the roll. "It's prep time to leave," he said. "If you don't act like a bunch of spooked steer, I'll let you go topside." The men scrambled up to the deck. A navy band was playing; family, friends and sweethearts were waving, calling out. The Marines, jammed tight, shouted back. Mark just looked.

The return to quarters was relatively quiet. Men were assigned to mess and guard duty with Mark getting the fantail watch. After abandon ship and fire drills, the men were noticeably subdued. Until then most of them hadn't thought of the possibility of getting sunk by a Jap sub even before getting to Guadalcanal.

The days passed slowly, relieved almost every night by a movie—usually one already seen. The ship's captain claimed the Marines were using too much water and so each man was rationed to a single canteen a day for drinking and bathing. By the end of a week the hold was stinking with cigarette smoke, B.O., and sweat. Word was passed that they were heading for Auckland, New Zealand, and not Guadalcanal. Thank God, thought Mark, they would get more training first.

On the twelfth day they steamed into Auckland. The harbor was beautiful and the city, which held a third of the population of the two main islands of New Zealand, was a welcome sight. A New Zealand band serenaded the newcomers as the ferries and tugboats clustered around the liner. But the festivities ended once word came that they were in the wrong port. They were supposed to be in Wellington, some 500 miles to the south.

They approached Wellington next day. The rolling hills were a lush green with Victorian buildings and snug homes that reminded some of the men of San Francisco. It was the beginning of November, summer down under, but the men disembarked in a cold drizzle. The people greeted the Americans as saviors and the young Marines strutted as they set foot on foreign soil, most of them for the first time in their lives. The old-timers, those from Iceland, already felt at home. They knew they were in for a good time.

Their campsite was some thirty-five miles to the northeast near the village of Paekakariki. Here they would spend six weeks building camp, training, and trekking up and down the green, grassy mountains surrounding them to get back into shape. The steep, rugged climb to the top (soon nicknamed the "Burma Road") with full field pack was miserable in the midsummer heat, but to Mark the four- or five-mile descent down cliffs and gorges was far worse, with a heavy pack banging into your back at every step. By the time he reached the bottom his knees would be wobbly, his legs numb.

He was also at odds with half his tentmates. Declining to go into Wellington on the grounds that it was "just a hick city," he instead would read voraciously the treasured books he had bought at San Diego. One day a big PFC nicknamed Goldie, whom he had detested since Elliott, grabbed his *War and Peace* and tossed it to another man. At first Mark tried to get the book back by persuasion but the two tormentors kept it away with reckless throws. Losing his temper, Mark began dumping Goldie's gear on the floor. Only the entrance of Mahoney prevented a brawl.

Mark was already in bad with the top sergeant for wearing his hat on the back of his head and for twice flipping cigarettes on the ground. The next day Mark fell out with his rifle for muster. But he saw no reason for toting his cartridge belt and bayonet, since the day was scheduled for snapping-in exercises. He was the only one in the platoon who had done this; the others were too dumb to have seen the obvious. It was Mark's misfortune that Mahoney passed by as the platoon was drilling.

"McGlynn," he called out. "Get your cartridge belt and bayonet and report back here on the double." Mark took off trying to think what excuse he could give but Mahoney didn't give him a chance. "Put the cartridge belt around your neck," he said crisply. "Wear it while you eat, while you sleep, during your free time. Wear it until I tell you to take it off." Before Mark could protest, the sergeant said, "Shove off."

That afternoon Billy J. noticed the belt hanging around the sheepish Mark's neck. "What's up?" he asked and after Mahoney explained said, "When you figure McGlynn has learned his lesson, schedule him again for office hours."

Two days later Mark appeared before Billy J. since the company commander was in sick bay. Mark felt like the Ancient Mariner with the belt around his neck. The humiliation and discomfort were beginning to make him realize he couldn't beat the system. "Private McGlynn reporting as ordered, sir," he said.

"At ease." Sullivan had taken the trouble to thoroughly examine Mark's records and was curious why a college graduate and honor student should act like such a damn fool. He should make a good Marine and perhaps become an officer. Mark spread his feet smartly and clasped hands in the small of his back.

"McGlynn, you are rapidly establishing a reputation as a malcontent in this outfit. Maybe you thought I was a patsy because I accepted your explanation the last time you were standing before me. I let you off with a warning that I expected my Marines to fulfill their duties at all times. I also told you I didn't want to see you at office hours again." His blue eyes took on that cool icy look that had chilled Mark the first time. "This is your final warning to start acting like a Marine—not a punk spoiled mama's boy. Do you read me?"

Mark flushed in embarrassment. "Yes, sir," he said.

"Better men than you have tried to pull my chain, McGlynn, and they landed in the brig on bread and water." He stared at Mark, then said quietly, "You're feeling sorry for yourself for having to wear that cartridge belt. Some wise man said, and it's been proven, 'The more you sweat in training, the less you'll bleed in war.' My job is to see that I get you back to your mother and father. They expect us to take care of you. I can't hope to bring all of you through safely. But I'll bring back as many as humanly possible. What if you didn't take your bayonet up front someday because you didn't think it was necessary? You might die. More important, you might get some other Marine killed. We don't stand for this stuff. You're expected to do your part. If you don't give a damn about your own tail, you'd better worry about your buddy's tail. In the Marines we count on each other—like brothers." His eyes seemed to pierce Mark. They were not icy this time but filled with concern. "Dismissed," he said quietly.

"About face, march out," said Mahoney.

As Mark left he vowed he would never again subject himself to the disdain of a man he so admired. He would show Billy J. that he was no punk mama's boy.

The next morning Mahoney allowed him to remove the cartridge belt and, after a hike up and down the Burma Road, he joined those heading for Wellington. Unlike Auckland, Wellington was not a barracks town and therefore was an excellent place for liberty. The 2nd Marine Division was the first major American unit to arrive and the doors of the best homes in town were open, with the town girls friendly to enlisted men and officers alike. He followed the crowd to the Cecil Club. All the girls here were extremely affable but the good-looking ones had already been taken and he wandered out to the street. Several times he was stopped by citizens who invited him to their homes. He politely declined; he was looking for a girl. He finally stepped into a public bar, the Triple X, only to find out that women were not admitted. A chubby bar girl welcomed him boisterously. "Hey, Yank, roll out your piss and roll up to the bar." He thanked her but was about to leave when a PFC from his platoon shouted to come to his table. It was a rowdy group and Mark hesitated, then decided he'd better learn how to get along with his platoon. He ordered a beer which he nursed while the others boisterously sang lewd songs they had picked up from those who had served in Iceland. They went from "One Ball Reilly" (Rack 'em up, stack 'em up, ball and all, Jig-a-jig-a boom, shag on), to one which began:

> Well, it was on the good ship Venus,
> My God, you should have seen us,
> The figurehead was a whore in bed,
> And the mast was a bloated penis.
> The cabin boy was chipper, the dirty little nipper,
> He shoved ground glass up his ass,
> And circumcised the skipper.

There were innumerable verses, each one dirtier than the last and Mark, excusing himself to go to the head, kept walking to the street. He sauntered to the railroad station to return to camp only to learn that the next train, the last, wouldn't leave for an hour. He stepped into a diner.

"What'll you have, Yank?" said the waitress.

"Coffee," he said.

"That all?" She suggested a homemade pie.

"No thanks." She had a pleasant face and a trim figure. She also had dark red hair and was apparently the first pretty girl in town who wasn't hog-tied. "I suppose you people get bored seeing so many Americans."

"Why should we? Our boys are all off in North Africa and we're counting on you to keep off the Japs. They're getting closer all the time."

He noticed her wedding ring. "Your husband there?"

"He was killed in Greece."

"I'm sorry."

She left to wait on another Marine, a private who had obviously been drinking heavily. He was a small youngster, probably from a farm.

"Hey, beautiful," he said, "Gimme a cup of Joe." She handed the private the coffee. "How about something to sweeten it, honey?" She passed him a sugar bowl. "Nah, I mean a kiss."

"Not on the menu, Yank," she said with a nice smile.

"You only go for officers and noncoms? Didn't you know most of them have V.D.? That's why their blue trousers have big red stripes up them." He reached for her arm.

Mark walked over and tapped the private on the shoulder. "Hey,

168

Mac," he said, "I know you don't want to have any trouble. Sheila and I are getting married next week." He slapped the boy on the shoulder. "How about if you let me pay for your coffee and you get the hell out of here?" He grasped the private's collar.

"Hell, I didn't mean no harm," said the private and staggered out.

"Thanks," said the waitress, "but my name's Molly and my daughter doesn't want me to marry a Yank."

"Why?"

"Because they all want to take you to bed on the first date."

"Smart girl. How old is she?"

"Four."

"I'd like to meet her someday. You live nearby?"

"Not far. We have a little apartment."

He began asking about New Zealand and was surprised to learn there were no snakes. "Like in Ireland," said Mark. "It took a saint to drive them out of there."

"I don't think we ever had them. I mean snakes, not saints. Or maybe the Maori drove them out."

He was fascinated by the Maori. "Is there much discrimination?" She didn't understand. "You know, like the Negroes in America." She admitted that intermarriage was shunned but most people were proud of the Maoris. Their battalion was famous.

Mark abruptly changed the subject. "Next Thursday is Thanksgiving and I have liberty until Monday. Perhaps we could get together sometime? You know, for a movie or dinner?"

She hesitated. He suddenly noticed it was after midnight. "My God, I've missed the last train!" He cursed his stupidity.

"You can hire a taxi," she said. "You can usually find a few other Marines outside who also missed the train." Mark started for the door. "Why don't you drop by next Thursday?" she said. "Perhaps I'll have some free time."

Mark turned around, grinned. "I'll see you. By the way, my name is Mark."

Outside he found three privates dickering with a cab driver. He asked if he could join them. They were only too glad to share the fare. As they were scrambling aboard, Sergeant Mahoney appeared. Mark blanched at the thought of another session with Billy J. It was not as though he had been having a wild night on the town.

"Got room for me?" said the top sergeant and pushed into the seat. With him along they now wouldn't be able to sneak into camp through a hole in the fence. They'd all have to pass through the main gate and end up on report. This time Mark was sure he'd be court-martialed, and knew he would head Billy J.'s shit list. As they neared the camp, Mark felt doomed. The three privates were equally grim.

"Stop the cab," ordered Mahoney just before they were in sight of the main gate. "Get out and pay the man." They did. "Follow me," he said and led them through the hole in the fence. The Top, thought Mark, was either AWOL or compassionate. Mahoney silently headed for Company D's area as if unaware that Mark was at his heels, turning off at his own tent without a word.

As Mark quietly crept into his cot he was more than ever determined to make good. He would stop wearing his hat on the back of his head, quit smoking, be alert during all drills and become the first to get to the top of the Burma Road and the first downhill. He would get along with his tentmates. Why was it, he reasoned, that he never had any such trouble on the road? With the road kids he had never been a snob. Why now? It was stupid. Soon these men would be facing death with him and his life would depend on them. He realized that he had become so bored with the training that he had taken it out on his tentmates. He hadn't even bothered to find out what they were like, what they wanted out of life.

3.

On Guadalcanal the desperate Japanese counterattack on Henderson Field had ended in disaster. Tsuji's plan had depended on prompt arrival of all forces at the various lines of departure. But some units had been slowed on the rugged trail. The result was annihilation by the Americans.

Tsuji and Shogo were among the survivors who faced the seemingly impossible trek back to the coast. Many dropped in exhaustion, praying for death. To Shogo's surprise his chief seemed to gather strength with every mile. His spirits rose. Finding a battalion commander lying at the side of the trail, the lower half of his body soaked in blood, Tsuji said, "Hold on. We'll have someone come back for you."

"I haven't eaten since the day before yesterday," was the weak reply.

Tsuji opened his *hango* and from it put a chopstickful of rice into the wounded officer's mouth. He ate it, and another chopstickful, then pointed feebly to several enlisted men lying nearby. Shogo felt choked with emotion to see these men open their mouths like baby sparrows as the God of Operations tenderly fed each one of them. Could this be the same man who'd made such a cruel mockery of *gashin-shotan?*

Tsuji pressed on relentlessly, urging others to eat roots, buds, anything to survive. By the third day the trail was littered with rotting bodies. Late in the day a torrent of rain drove them into a rude hut for shelter. Three men lay on the floor dying from malaria. A fourth was dead. Beside his head was a piece of hard biscuit, left by a friend, to eat on his way to Nirvana. All those who had passed through had not touched the precious food.

That night Tsuji and Shogo slept beside the dead and dying, wakened often by voracious mosquito attacks. In the morning the march continued. Noncoms had to lash the younger soldiers with switches to keep them moving. Shogo could hardly put one foot in front of the other. Late in the afternoon he emerged from the dark jungle into a palm grove. Ahead was an endless expanse of green sea. They had come out at Point Cruz, seven miles west of the airfield.

"Oi! The sea!" a soldier shouted and rushed into the surf. He gulped down sea water. Tsuji had already showed Shogo how to recover some of their lost salt content by wiping sweat from the face and body with a handkerchief and sucking it. But the pain from loss of salt was unbearable and Shogo eagerly gulped down seawater until Tsuji warned him to stop.

As soon as they reached 17th Army headquarters Tsuji ordered rice sent to the front, then dispatched a radiogram to Army Chief of Staff Sugiyama:

> I MUST BEAR THE WHOLE RESPONSIBILITY FOR THE FAILURE OF THE 2ND DIVISION WHICH COURAGEOUSLY FOUGHT FOR DAYS AND LOST MORE THAN HALF THEIR MEN IN DESPERATE ATTACKS. THEY FAILED BECAUSE I UNDERESTIMATED THE ENEMY'S FIGHTING POWER AND INSISTED ON MY OWN OPERATIONS PLAN WHICH WAS ERRONEOUS.

Adding that he deserved "a sentence of ten thousand deaths," he requested permission to stay on Guadalcanal with the 17th Army. Any doubts that Shogo may have had concerning Tsuji's nobility were set to rest by this message.

But Tokyo ordered Tsuji to return at once and several days later he and Shogo bade farewell to their friends.

4.

New Zealand. December 1942.

Mark, now a private first class, was no longer having trouble either with Sergeant Mahoney or his tentmates. He was promoted to assistant machine gunner and was privileged not only to wear a World War I .45 caliber pistol but to carry a relatively light tripod. It pleased him more than making Phi Beta Kappa. And when his tentmates started talking about themselves or their families he listened and began to understand them. He would even join in singing their bawdy songs. One in particular, "The Dog Song," so tickled him he copied it down for Will. It would do him good to see how the other half lived. He was off on some high-level secret mission for FDR. Trust old Will, who knew all the right people, to make the most of a war.

> Oh, the dogs they had a meeting,
> They came from near and far.
> And some dogs came by motor bus
> And some by motor car.
> On entering the meeting hall
> Each dog could take a look
> Where he had to hang his asshole
> Up high upon a hook.
> Now when they were assembled,
> Each canine son and sire,
> Some dirty bulldog son of a bitch
> Jumped up and hollered, "Fire!"
> Now all was in a panic,
> T'was hell upon to look,
> Each doggie grabbed at random
> An asshole from a hook.
> The assholes were all mixed up
> Which made each doggie sore
> To have to wear another dog's ass
> He'd never worn before.
> And that is why until this day
> A dog will leave a bone

To run and smell another dog's ass
To see if it is his own.

Mark had also progressed with Molly. On Thanksgiving they went to the cinema and during the next two weekends he took her dancing at the Cecil Club and to dinner. A week before Christmas she got off early and brought him to her apartment. Her four-year-old, Betsy, was delighted with Mark who let her climb on his back to play bucking bronco. After she was put to bed Molly and Mark made love on the sofa.

Later neither spoke. Molly snuggled up to Mark. "It's been so long," she finally whispered. She kissed his neck and reached for a pillow. "Light one for me, love," she said. She had grown accustomed to having him light a cigarette for her. He reached for her pack, lit a cigarette. It tasted stale and he marveled how he had ever started smoking at Elliott. She took several puffs, gave a sigh of pleasure. He turned away from the smoke, surreptitiously glancing at his watch. The last train wouldn't leave for an hour and a half and in all decency he couldn't leave for an hour.

Molly snuffed out the cigarette and again snuggled up to Mark. She was a sweet girl but he didn't want to make love to her again. She reminded him of Miriam, red hair and all, and he silently cursed himself.

"You're so quiet, Mark. Is something the matter? Was I . . ."

He kissed her forehead. "You were wonderful."

"Next week is Christmas. You'll be getting another long weekend liberty, won't you, love?"

He hesitated, searching for an excuse.

She sat upright in alarm. "You're leaving! I know you're leaving!"

He detested himself for being too cowardly to tell the truth. "Well, there's the usual scuttlebutt about going to Guadalcanal."

She held him tightly. "Love me again, honey."

He forced himself to make love again. They were quiet for a long time and then she said, "I love you."

He couldn't say the lying words and kissed her.

"Dearie, I'll pray for you," she said. There was another silence.

At last it was time to leave and Mark began dressing. "I don't want to lose you too," she said, then quickly added, "She'll be all right." He was puzzled. "That's New Zealand for 'everything's going to be fine.' "

"Don't get up," he said and kissed her.

She clung to him. "Think of me over there in that rotten jungle."
"I will," he said truthfully and hurried away filled with shame.

Molly's fears were soon confirmed. On December 24 the Marines
began marching down the docks of Wellington to board four large
transports. These ships had been nicknamed "The Unholy Four" by the
previous batch of Marines who had taken them to Guadalcanal. Mark's
company was assigned to the *President Hayes* and they had to climb up
cargo nets. As he clambered over the rail Mark heard one gunnery
sergeant say to another, "They're tough. They're ready." But he felt
neither tough nor ready. It was stifling in the hold and the men groused
that this was a helluva way to spend Christmas. The long wait until
everyone was aboard increased the queasiness in Mark's stomach and
when the big ship began to move out slowly he felt sure he was going to
die on Guadalcanal. And his mind kept returning to Molly and her last
words.

The next nine days were spent on mess duty and other details such as
swabbing the decks, as well as practice landings with full pack. At night
there was group singing, letter writing and an interminable poker game
at which Mark confounded the other players by systematic play interspersed with daring gambles. As they grew nearer to the equator the
heat and stench in the hold were almost intolerable. There was little
singing but the poker continued without pause and Mark's winnings
grew to more than a thousand dollars.

On the ninth night they were some 500 miles below the equator.
Mark was on watch duty with another man. Several hours after midnight they sighted a black pyramid in the distance. "Savo!" said his
partner. This was a small volcanic island just off the western end of
Guadalcanal, which was hidden by a heavy mist. The *President Hayes*
slipped into calm waters. The stillness gave Mark a creepy feeling. A
few minutes later a breeze from Guadalcanal was rank with the stink of
swamp and jungle. The haze abruptly lifted and Mark could see a range
of mountains etched black against the clearing sky. He felt a lump in his
throat. Where would he die?

In the morning, the 'Canal, as the island was now referred to, did not
look at all ominous but like a poster of a South Seas paradise. The
landing was uneventful. The long beach, lined with graceful palm trees,
was calm as a vacation resort. They marched inland past a coconut
plantation. As they started toward Henderson Field, natives surrounded them. They were blacker than any Negroes Mark had ever

seen. In pidgin English they began bartering for supplies with coconuts. But Mark's fear of the island returned once night fell. Then the quiet, interspersed by jungle noises, began getting on his nerves. No one else in the platoon seemed to share his apprehension. They joked and chatted as if on maneuvers. In the next few days they slowly moved forward, following orders of the overall commander of the island forces, an army general. The Marines groused at the snail's pace. They wanted action and cursed the army.

The Americans were unaware that on Christmas Day the Japanese high command had decided to withdraw from Guadalcanal. Their hapless troops were retreating in good order, leaving behind a rear guard with orders to make the enemy pay for every yard of advance. The Japanese soldiers had left home to die for country and the Emperor. The battles were over but the stubborn Japanese rearguard action was taking its toll. Mark couldn't imagine a worse place to have to fight. It was steaming, hot, muddy, rainy. The stink of death and rotting undergrowth was nauseating and in some places the jungle was so thick they had to hack a pathway.

The 6th Marines moved up the coast to relieve the 2nd Marines, who looked like ghosts as they passed to the rear. Most of them had malaria or jaundice. They had been fighting for five months without letup. There was only enough daily water ration for drinking and washing their teeth. They ate their C rations, usually cold, from the can.

"Well, if it ain't the pogey-bait 6th," Mark heard a bearded 2nd Marine sergeant remark. "What finally drug you darlins into this nasty horrible war?"

"Well, you can bet your sweet ass it's none too soon," retorted Mahoney. "If they'd left you monkey-fuckers in here much longer this whole fuckin' island would look like a New York garbage scow. You sure you're still Marines? Looks to me you've gone native."

The line of the 6th Marines followed the top of a ridge that dropped sharply into heavy jungle. On the slope to the front, mounds indicated where Japanese had fallen and had been so hastily buried that here and there a hand or a foot was still exposed. The sight sickened Mark, but he was the only one in the platoon who didn't hate Japs and he had to hide his feelings. He was stupid not to have enlisted on the east coast. Then he surely would have been sent to fight the Nazis instead.

Only the Iceland veterans slept that first night on the line. Toward midnight the word was passed to the battalion that the Japanese could be seen smoking cigarettes down in the jungle-matted ravine. A heavy concentration of artillery was called in to destroy the careless enemy troops who had lit up after dark. The whistling of shells overhead and the explosions in the ravine awakened both Billy J. and Sergeant Mahoney, who moved forward together to see what was going on. An excited lookout pointed out the Japs still smoking in the midst of the artillery barrage. Billy J. just shook his head while Mahoney bawled out in a voice that could be heard along the entire line, "For Christ sake! Haven't you numb-nuts ever seen fireflies? Cease firing! Post the watch! Get some sleep!"

In the next few days there were no casualties in Mark's platoon. But his terror grew. The nights were the worst, especially when someone out front would begin moaning. Their platoon leader, Lieutenant Tufts, derogatorily nicknamed "Caspar Milquetoast," assured them this was a Jap trick to lure them into attempting a rescue.

By the end of the first week Mark's socks had rotted off and he was so filthy he vowed that if he ever got back home he'd only wear white shirts. It rained every night and sleep in a muddy foxhole was impossible. He had become used to the scratching, crawling noise of land crabs but they still sounded like Japanese trying to infiltrate the lines and he had to control himself from firing his pistol.

It was a relief to learn that he wasn't the only one in Company D living in almost constant terror. On the ninth day Sergeant "Tiger" Rogers, a Golden Gloves heavyweight champion, the very picture of the rugged Marine, was sent to the rear after refusing to budge from his foxhole. This was the man they all had expected would win the first medal. Their platoon leader, the insignificant-looking little Lieutenant Tufts, acted as calmly as if he were back in New Zealand. The former accountant led the men forward quietly but with authority through the coconut groves. Men in each squad were designated to watch for snipers in the tops of trees while others scanned the underbrush for additional enemy. When a sniper was spotted, the fire of the entire squad concentrated on the palm fronds. Sometimes a body would fall to the ground, other times only a foot or a head would appear since the Japanese had tied himself to the tree.

When the battalion reached the Kokumbona River in early January security was set up across the river and they were allowed to shave, bathe, and wash their filthy clothes. Corpsmen walked the banks treating the worst of the jungle rot cases. The foot inspection ritual by platoon commanders that Mark had thought so ridiculous at Elliott now made sense.

It was pure bliss, Mark thought, as he cavorted in the river with Ski, a streetwise youngster from Los Angeles nicknamed Peewee, and Goldie, the bully. "My God," he thought, "I'm beginning to tolerate Goldie!" That night they set up lines on the far side of the river and the next day continued their advance up the coast toward Tassafaronga Point. Before they had advanced fifty yards the patrol to their front came under heavy fire. Tufts calmly pointed at one of his squad leaders, then indicated a grove of trees where snipers were pouring out lead. After the meticulous drills on New Zealand, the squad leader knew what he meant and in seconds the squad was falling out in pairs. Soon Japanese began tumbling down from the coconut trees. Tufts now pointed to another squad leader and then at a clump of heavy bushes. This squad began blasting the bushes. The lieutenant didn't even have to point at Mark's squad; they started moving on a course that would envelop the bushes. The machine gunners were right behind him. While setting up the machine gun the gunner, Ski, was hit in the stomach. Mark was petrified at the flow of blood. "Take over," mumbled the wounded man and passed out. After futilely trying to stem the gushing blood, Mark frantically dragged the man to the rear.

"Where do you think you're going with that man?"

Startled, Mark turned around. It was Captain Billy J. Sullivan, who was now company commander.

"I'm taking him to a doctor, sir! He's been shot!"

"Put him down." Sullivan summoned a corpsman. "You're to be praised for thinking of your fellow Marine, McGlynn. I admire that, but by taking him out you jeopardize your whole machine squad who are responsible for covering this advance."

"He's dead," said the corpsman.

"All right," said Billy J. quietly. "McGlynn, if everyone did what you just did, where do you think we'd be? You lost your head and I don't want you to do it again. Do you understand?"

"Yes, sir." Mark didn't move.

"Hop to it. Return to your squad."

Mark started back. I was chicken, he thought. That was why he had dragged back the sergeant. And Billy J. knew it. Why hadn't he called me yellow? To give me a second chance? He hurried back to find the fight was over and other platoon leaders were complimenting Tufts on his performance.

The next day they ran into heavier concentrations of Japanese. Mark was appalled by the ferocity of some of his comrades who seemed to revel in killing Japanese, stripping them of souvenirs and even knocking out their gold teeth with rifle butts. Skulls were mounted on jeeps. The few Japanese captured never survived the trip to the rear.

The slow advance continued and during the periods of inaction Mark tried to write Molly. But he could neither use false words of love nor tell the truth. If he got killed that would solve the problem.

They crossed another river, bringing another chance to clean up. It was the usual scene. Security across the river and on the flank away from the beaches; stacked rifles in uneven rows with packs and helmets in front; nude Marines bathing, washing clothes, splashing water at each other. With Ski dead, Mark was now the squad leader, and to his surprise he was enjoying the new responsibility. Even Goldie took orders from him without protest.

Lieutenant Tufts had just fallen into step beside Mark to ask him how his squad was holding up when he heard a gasp of surprise and saw the lieutenant fall. While Mark was still staring in a stupor, Tufts grabbed his arm. "Sniper!" he said. "Take cover!" Mark sprang into action, dragging Tufts behind a bush.

"It's my arm," the lieutenant said between clenched teeth. "Feels like a clean wound. Not too much bleeding."

Mark ripped open the jacket over which blood was seeping, took out his first aid packet and bandaged the wound as gently as possible. He ordered two men to turn the lieutenant over to a corpsman. "The rest of you see if you can spot the sniper."

A minute later Goldie saw the sniper and with one shot brought him to the ground. Peewee was leaning over the body, prodding it with his foot. "Skinny bastard!" he said. "Bandages on one leg, mud all over his body. Hell, he was already dying. They must be using their sick in the trees as sharpshooters."

"O.K. Saddle up and move out," Mark ordered. Christ, he thought sheepishly, he was beginning to sound like Billy J.

Contact with the enemy continued to be sporadic, but if the wind was right Mark could smell them. Denied water for bathing, the Japanese were dousing themselves with perfumed cologne.

"Fuckin' foo-foo water! Them bastards stinkin' up the jungle," Goldie complained. "Smells like a fuckin' cat house in Frisco."

By now the numbing experience of rotting corpses was affecting everyone. The smell of man was more awful than that of any other rotting animal.

It was toward the middle of January that forty Zeros approached. But army and Marine planes were waiting and poured down on them. Violent dogfights covered the sky and the Marines stood up to watch. Suddenly there was a roar as seven Mitsubishi 97 bombers swept overhead at treetop level, scattering bombs along the beach and inland. They were gone in seconds but Goldie's body had been blown ten yards and lay in a bloody heap.

The 1st Battalion had advanced over five thousand yards since relieving the 2nd Marines but in those few days Mark's platoon had lost Lieutenant Tufts, wounded, and two dead, Ski and Goldie. The sight of blood no longer sickened Mark and he could distinguish between normal and extraordinary night noises. He stank and must have lost twenty pounds. But he was still alive.

On the night of February 1, 1943, ten Japanese destroyers evacuated 5,424 men from northern Guadalcanal. The rescued men were sullen, embittered by defeat and humiliated for having to leave behind comrades who had not been given proper burial rites. During the next week another eight thousand were brought back through the dangerous channel up through the Solomons the Americans had nicknamed The Slot. But twenty-five thousand others, dead or within hours of death, had been left behind. At last Guadalcanal was cleared by the Marines and G.I.'s but most of the Americans were racked by malaria, dysentery, jaundice, and jungle rot, better known as the crud.

Gradually moving back to their assigned bivouac area near Lunga Point, Mark's battalion paused at each river to bathe and wash clothes. Although they were assigned the job of coast defense, they knew their battle was over. But every day someone would begin shaking uncontrollably and report for sick call. Almost everyone in Mark's company had malaria.

Finally, in early February, gray transports appeared on the horizon. A week later the 1st Battalion began climbing up the cargo nets of the *President Adams*, each man loaded with his bulky transport pack. Mark was one of the few not suffering from malaria, thanks to Lieutenant Tufts's motherly treatments of Atabrine, although his face was yellow from the dosage. He climbed the cargo net without difficulty but noticed that Billy J., just behind, was laboring.

The captain had jaundice but didn't know it, and halfway up the net had to force himself to continue. If he fell with the eighty-pound pack, it would take him to the bottom of the harbor. Every rung was torture. At last he could see the rail. He reached out but had used his last strength. As he started to topple over, Mark grabbed his pack and hauled him over the gunwale. Billy J. tumbled onto the deck wondering, before he passed out, who had saved his life.

Mark joined those at the rail taking a final look at the miserable island. From afar it looked inviting. But what a hellhole! "Now hear this!" came a raspy voice over the loudspeaker. "Our destination is Wellington, New Zealand." The men cheered and cavorted. Mark too was elated. Back to cool weather and paradise! Then he remembered Molly. What would he tell her?

CHAPTER THIRTEEN

1.

Camp Cabanatuan. June 1942.

The afternoon sun came out just as the truck convoy from Camp O'Donnell approached the new camp. There was a kind of beauty in the gently rolling countryside. The roiling storm clouds had cleared as if by magic and some twenty miles to the east Will could see the dramatic cone of Mount Arayat. And to the west a range of mountains, the Zambales, loomed up like giant sentries. Someone explained that this was Camp Cabanatuan and had been a U.S. Agricultural station before being turned into a training camp for the 91st Philippine Division.

Even from a distance it was obvious the buildings were sturdier and more uniform than the ramshackle huts of O'Donnell. A rainbow stretched across the sky. Could it be an omen, Will thought, of better days to come? As they drove into the compound, prisoners gazed at them as if they were freaks.

"Helluva welcome," said the man next to Will. "Guess more coming in means less food for them."

The trucks drew to a halt and as Will painfully disembarked he recognized a Marine major he had met on Corregidor. "Harry!" he called but the Marine ignored him. He called again and the major looked at him quizzically.

"Who the hell are you?"

"McGlynn."

The major's jaw dropped. "My God, what happened to you! You must have lost seventy-five pounds."

"You think so?" Will surveyed the skinny frame which he had become used to and realized that standing next to the husky Marine he must look like a skeleton. But the sight of the men from Corregidor enheartened him. They all looked in fairly good shape and that spoke well for Cabanatuan.

The newcomers were formed in columns of fours. The man next to Will was weak from dysentery and had to be helped along. "I got to crap again," he said. Will waved to a guard and pantomimed permission to take the sick man to the side. The guard nodded and Will helped the man to the ditch. He grunted and grimaced but could only pass blood.

It took an hour before Will's group of a hundred was led into a barracks about sixty feet long made of bamboo, nipa, and sawali. An alley ran down its length; along each side were double-decked bays, each about eight feet long. One bay was intended for two but had to be shared by five. The beds were bamboo slats. But to everyone's delight there was a blanket for each man. A warrant officer shouted for attention. "You guys are lucky," he said. "This is the last barracks with blankets."

Rain began pelting on the nipa roof. To Will's wonder there were no leaks. Another sign of better days. "You new guys got to learn to stay away from the barbed-wire fences. If you have to crap at night, walk straight to the latrine and back. No wandering around or one of the guards patrolling the fence will shoot you. Understand? Just do as the rest of the old-timers are doing. The Japs are trigger-happy."

By now it was pouring. "Okay," continued the warrant officer. "It's chow time. You'll be fed here." There was a clang of metal as a hundred men eagerly prepared mess kits for their first meal at Cabanatuan. Two prisoners staggered in, each carrying a five-gallon can of food. The one coming up Will's aisle hollered, "Soup with rice today, boys!" There were several whistles of appreciation.

Will held out his mess kit and got a full portion of rice. Then soup made out of boiled greens was plopped into his cup. The rice was not bad and he didn't even bother to pick out the few weevils he saw. "Blowgun soup," said the server. "You'll get to love it."

The greens were tender and quite tasty and Will gulped everything down. Water was running off the eaves and Will stepped outside to wash his gear. Others followed suit. "Room with running water," someone said and there was laughter. It was an unaccustomed sound. Another good augury, thought Will. But by the time he returned to his cubicle he and several other newcomers were seized with severe stomach cramps. The pain was excruciating.

Will writhed in agony. He felt a cold wet cloth on his forehead and heard someone say consolingly, "Take it easy." The cramps stopped but his relief was only momentary. He felt a terrible urge to defecate. Since it was still pouring, he hastily stripped off pants and shirt and headed for the latrine in his shorts. The earth around the straddle trench was already mud and he almost fell into the mess. He seemed to explode and felt relief. He staggered back in the pelting rain, dried himself with his blanket, then put on his trousers and shirt.

The rain had slackened, its soft patter similar to that on the roof over his little room in Williamstown. He shivered under the damp blanket, huddling into as small a ball as possible. He tried to use his breath to warm himself and at last fell into an uneasy sleep. He was awakened by stomach cramps, more severe than the first time. He could feel the blowgun soup boiling inside him and realized he'd better hurry for the latrine. But no sooner had he stepped into the aisle than his bowels let loose. The wet excrement dripped down his legs. He knew if he stood up he would leave a nasty trail, and so crawled outside. It was raining lightly but there wasn't enough water dripping off the eaves for a wash. He looked around. A Japanese guard on the other side of the fence was standing nearby but he finally moved away. Will looked for a large puddle and found one a hundred yards away. He took off his clothes. They stank from the blowgun soup. First he washed himself with his shorts. Then he wrung them out and put them on. The Japanese guard reappeared and he froze. The guard looked around and passed out of sight. By the time Will washed the rest of his clothes he was so tired he had to crawl toward the barracks. Halfway there the guard returned and Will flattened in the mud. A minute later he resumed his painful trip and had just enough strength to crawl under the barracks. He was dirty again but this was clean dirt and soon he fell asleep.

He felt a nudging kick in the side. It was the warrant officer and it was morning. "Get out of there."

Will crawled out.

"What the hell are you doing under there?"

Will explained.

"Where did you wash?" Will told him. "You damned fool, that guard would have shot you if he'd seen you."

"I couldn't go back into the barracks stinking the way I did."

The warrant officer shook his head as if saying, "Now I've heard everything." Big drops of rain began falling. The tempo increased. "Well, get the hell back into the barracks. Breakfast is coming in a few minutes."

Will grabbed his stomach and began jogging toward the latrine. He made it just in time and this time was careful not to slip in the mud. On the way back, rain washed over his face. He saw the two men carrying chow cans into his barracks and to his amazement discovered he was hungry. He got into line just in time to get a ladling of lugao. "No blowgun soup today," said the server with a grin.

The first two weeks at Cabanatuan passed quickly for Will and he could feel himself growing stronger from the larger quantities of food. With strength came the determination to survive so he could inform Marshall of the foul-ups committed by the brass. His unit was moved to the east side of the prison compound to a small barracks occupied solely by forty officers. It had been designed for a dozen men and there was only a two-foot-wide space in the bays for each man. Will slept between two young army lieutenants on a level of bunks reached by shinnying up a pole. They were now permitted to visit with friends from Corregidor and at last learned what had happened there in the final days. The navy liaison officer who had told him of the half-million-dollar gift to MacArthur greeted him warmly. "I heard you made it!" he said and wrung his hand. "Did you hear our buddy, Mac, got to Australia?" he said with a malicious grin. "He's the big hero back home now."

Two majors from Wainwright's staff joined them and began cursing MacArthur. "He sold us down the river," said one.

"He made a big speech down in Australia," said the navy lieutenant. "He said, 'I came through and I shall return.'"

This brought a chorus of obscenities.

The lieutenant nudged Will. "Yeah, he'll return. So would I for half a million bucks and the Manila Hotel." He drew Will aside and told him about the last terrible hours on Corregidor. His face was grim. "I never thought I'd see our flag lowered and stomped on. Sons of bitches!" He slammed a fist into the palm of the other hand. "I don't mean the lousy Japs. I mean MacArthur and his cronies!" He nodded toward the two majors. "Skinny's staff. They make no bones about what they think of MacArthur. If he walked into camp today they'd probably beat the hell out of him."

Will's barracks was run by a heartily detested Marine captain nicknamed Captain Bligh. He was constantly lecturing his charges on cleanliness, military courtesy, and patriotism. One of Will's bay mates, Wilkins, was constantly harassed by Bligh. "He thinks we're at boot camp," said Wilkins, who was having trouble keeping his food down. He was weak and despondent. "You eat the rest," he said, handing Will his mess kit. Will encouraged Wilkins to eat a few more mouthfuls. He dropped his spoon. "I can't eat any more. I promise I'll eat everything tonight."

One of Captain Bligh's orders was that every man must serve himself.

Even so, at dinner Will slid down the pole to the floor with his and Wilkins's mess kits.

Bligh was standing spraddled over the five-gallon can, arms folded. "Only one mess kit," he said.

"It's for Wilkins. He's too weak to come down."

Bligh seized Wilkins's mess kit. "He'll damned well have to come down himself. No exceptions." Will started to protest. "Move on. You're holding up the line." Then the captain began berating the others in line. "Stand up straight like soldiers! You look like a bunch of bums at a soup kitchen."

Will returned with the bad news. "Oh, the hell with the lousy rice," said Wilkins. He rolled over. Will felt his forehead. He had a fever.

"You've got to try," said Will. "Don't give up."

Wilkins struggled to his knees and started down the pole. He grunted and moaned from the effort and by a superhuman effort made it to the floor. The others stopped eating to watch him slowly crawl toward the five-gallon can, mess kit in one hand, cup in the other. It was only twenty feet away but it must have looked like a mile to Wilkins, thought Will. His progress was like a slow-motion film and his comrades silently rooted him on. At last he held out his mess kit, touching the food can.

"Okay," said Bligh. "Let's put him back." It took four men to take Wilkins back to his upper bunk. Bligh handed up the filled mess kit and cup.

Will helped Wilkins sit up. Bleary-eyed, the latter said, "Why did he do that to me? Why did he make me crawl to the rice can and then carry me back?"

"Men are dying here because they give up," said the third man in their bay, Lieutenant Bliss, who had always stood up for Bligh. "The captain is trying to save your life. If you can't help yourself, you might just as well dig a hole and bury yourself." Bliss, a graduate of Swarthmore who hoped to be an English instructor, stuck a spoon into Wilkins's hand. "Now eat, goddammit!"

Wilkins began spooning rice into his mouth. Exhausted, he lay back and fell asleep. It was past midnight when Will heard him mumbling prayers, then exclaim, "Dear God!"

"What's the matter?" whispered Will.

"The cross!" said Wilkins in an awed voice. "Can't you see the cross? It's a foot high and bright as can be!" He struggled to a sitting position. "Didn't you see it?"

"No."

"It was right there in front of me. And I don't feel sick at all now. I don't feel sick at all." He dropped back and slept as if drugged. But in the morning he was moaning painfully. Will climbed down with two mess kits. This time Bligh let him have both portions. But neither Bliss nor Will could persuade Wilkins to eat a thing.

"Give it a try!" urged Will. "Come on."

"I'll take it if your friend doesn't want it," said someone from the bay below.

Bliss put a foot in the intruder's face and pushed. "Get the hell out of here. You'd eat the eyeballs of a dead man if you had the chance. Stinking vulture!" Bliss was breathing heavily as if trying to calm himself. "They can't help it," he finally said. "It's not the Japs who are our greatest enemy. It's hunger." He gently brought Wilkins to a sitting position with Will's help. "Okay, sport, now let's try a spoonful for Mother." Wilkins's parched lips came to a little grin and he managed to force a spoonful of rice into himself. Will helped him take a gulp of water. Wilkins took another spoonful of rice but couldn't hold it down. Bliss mopped his lap. Will cleaned his mouth. "Okay," said Bliss, holding out another spoonful. "Now let's have one for your third-grade teacher." Wilkins forced it down.

2.

By this time the prisoners had been formed into ten-man squads. If one escaped, the remaining nine would be shot. Fortunately Will was in a group with Bliss, Wilkins, and seven other men all of whom pledged as blood brothers never to attempt to escape unless all could go together. Bliss trusted his two bay mates but he privately distrusted the other seven, and in an ominously quiet voice and with a flexing of muscles promised to break the neck of anyone who even contemplated escape.

The food rations grew worse and smaller as more men from O'Donnell crowded in. The most resourceful organized themselves into a "quan." Each quan would set up a homemade oven and cook up scrounged food ranging from weeds to rats. The search for food was called quanning and Will wondered what his father would think to see him trapping a rat in a drainage ditch. The ditch, a foot wide and about two feet deep, was a communication trench for the growing rat population. The hunters would squat for hours staring fixedly into the fringe of grass sprouting along the edge of a ditch. When a rat started running down the ditch, the hunters would shout war cries and swing clubs at the rat. The lucky man brought home the carcass to be boiled. If it was a good rat it tasted like a young squirrel, according to those who had eaten squirrel in civilian life.

The quality of the rice grew worse every day, containing so many weevils that every portion looked as if it had been heavily peppered. In addition there were little white worms with brown heads and huge eyes. There was no salt or seasoning to make the mess more palatable but Will ate everything, weevils and worms included, on the assumption that they contained protein. Even Wilkins was eating the poor food and was now able to clamber down the pole for his rations.

Almost every night before dropping off to sleep Will would try to visualize food that he loved: roast chicken smothered in gravy, a charcoal-broiled steak, medium rare and a fat inch thick. He could smell the steak as he mentally cut off piece after piece. Then he would dream up all the food he disliked: broccoli, Brussels sprouts, liver, blood pudding. How he would relish a taste of luscious Brussels sprouts! One night he recalled Mark's story of eating Ken-L-Ration on toast on the dark, endless plains of eastern Colorado. That would be a treat at Cabanatuan. In the past week Will had gratefully downed boiled rat, the leg of a cat, lizards and locusts. He guessed some of his mates would even revert to cannibalism if they had the chance. Would he? Of course not! Of course not? He wasn't sure.

Food became an obsession and Will could no longer sleep because of the constant gnawing of his stomach. He had to get more food or he would die. The next morning he did what he had never dreamed he could do. He hung around the kitchen after breakfast and held out his mess kit for more food like Oliver Twist. Like Oliver he was turned down. Then he noticed two men carrying five-gallon cans to one of the other barracks. He slowly followed and when he saw the men finally turn into a large enlisted men's barracks, he hurried to the other door and surreptitiously joined one of the lines. The wait seemed interminable. He was sweating from shame and fear of being discovered. The men in this barracks were so apathetic no one noticed he was a stranger. At last it was his turn. He held out his mess kit and received a big blob of lugao.

"Soup?" asked the server.

He had forgotten to bring his cup and he hastily said, "Not today, thanks."

"Don't blame you."

Will slithered outside expecting to be tapped on the shoulder any moment. He sneaked around to the side of the barracks as if looking for a place to eat and once the coast was clear scuttled off to his own barracks. He got up to his bunk without anyone noticing he had another helping of food. The bay, thank God, was empty. He started to eat the lugao, telling himself that someone from the other barracks probably had sneaked into his barracks to get an extra portion. A head appeared. It was Bliss. Will hastily hid the mess kit behind him, his face flushed with shame.

"Don't sit in your mess kit," said Bliss casually.

Will guiltily retrieved the mess kit. "I went to another barracks," he confessed.

"You're not the first. Nor the last. We all steal—one way or another. Even you. And me." Bliss climbed down to the floor, leaving Will alone. Dirt had fallen into the kit but Will gobbled down every bit of the mess. He was still sick with humiliation and vowed he would never again stoop to such a mean trick. Nor would he ever again be critical of anyone else's selfishness.

That night the terrible gnawing in his stomach returned and he decided to do something about it that wouldn't be shameful. In the morning he walked to the other end of the area where, he had been told, an enlisted man ran a thriving black market. He finally found the place. It was an enlisted barracks guarded by two husky privates holding clubs. Two of the bays were piled up with canned goods, fruit, cigarettes, and used clothing. It was a little store! Lolling back in an easy chair was Private Popov. He smiled when he recognized Will. He rubbed his hands, exuding a benign aura of power. He explained that he had stayed in business by bribing Japanese guards with a percentage of the goods smuggled in from Manila through his peacetime sources in the capital.

"I don't have any money," said Will. "Could I work it off some way?"

Popov shook his head. "I've found it's too much trouble trusting officers, Captain."

"Well, thanks anyway." Will turned and started shuffling away.

"Hold it. I think we can work something out."

Will swung around eagerly. His heart beat fast. "I'll do anything," he said, then hastily added, "within reason."

"I'm not a frigging fruit, Captain," said Popov, coming out of his chair aggressively. He looked like a bull.

"I didn't mean that," said Will.

Popov subsided and grinned evilly. "I had to beat hell out of a major the other day who wanted to bugger me." Then he became the affable storekeeper. "I hear you're okay, Captain. I'll give you credit up to two hundred dollars. You just sign this blank check and pay me after the war."

Will couldn't believe what he heard. It was generosity looming on idiocy. The chances of collecting were minimal. He quickly scrawled his name on the check and wrote in the name of his bank in Washington. Popov blew the check dry and put it in an enormously fat wallet. "You never high-hatted me like other officers, Captain. Now pick what you want."

Will took half an hour going over the entire stock and left with a can of tuna fish and a can of corned beef. "Twenty-five dollars," said Popov, making a notation in a worn notebook.

Weak as he was, Will hustled back to the barracks, his treasures hidden under his shirt. Wilkins and Bliss were hovering over their quan "stove," an ancient iron pot hanging from a tripod. Will covertly slipped the two cans to Bliss. "For the pot," he said. That night Bliss opened the cans with a borrowed jackknife and they had a feast.

In two weeks Will had used up all his two hundred dollars and made no protest when Popov said he couldn't issue any more credit. The supply of rats had also been exhausted and the three comrades were back to starvation rations.

Near the end of June a rumor swept the camp. This was more important than the stories of approaching American carriers or the death of Hitler and had more validity. That evening they were to get a special meal, liver soup!

All afternoon the men talked excitedly of the possibility of getting meat in their soup and not the usual blowgun variety. For most of them it would be their first taste of real meat in months. One man came into Will's barracks with tangible evidence. He had smelled liver as he passed the kitchen. Several men headed directly for the kitchen to enjoy the odor. Will sat outside the barracks on a bench. He watched as men converged near the kitchen. They would raise their heads and sniff like dogs who had located something interesting. Will saw men nodding and smiling. It must be liver soup!

At last a five-gallon can arrived at the barracks. The men clustered around like children waiting to open presents on Christmas morning.

Prisoners who had never spoken to each other began gossiping like old friends. Spirits were high and grudges temporarily forgotten. Captain Bligh took charge of the ladling to give everyone a fair share. As he stirred the liver soup with a long wooden spoon the men intently watched the hunks of meat floating around.

The hollow-eyed Wilkins was eager. He held out his cup, his eyes glistening as a particularly large piece of meat plopped into his cup. Will also got a good-sized piece. The soup was dark brown and murky but smelled delicious. The men sat around eating and talking as if it were Thanksgiving.

While Will was washing his cup Bliss came over. "Some meal, hey?" Will agreed enthusiastically.

"But it wasn't liver," said Bliss. "The Japs butchered a carabao and what we got was *congealed blood.*"

"Keep your voice down," said Will. "If this gets out most of the guys will puke." Will just made it to the latrine before he did.

The liver soup was a rare occasion and because of the dwindling food rations, dysentery, malaria, and beri-beri, almost 750 of the men from O'Donnell were already dead. A pall of gloom spread over the camp. Then came another rumor, this one a "straight from hole number one" story. The Americans were about to launch a huge bombing raid on their area followed by a land rescue party on the Fourth of July. This information, written on an egg, had been smuggled into camp by a friendly Filipino boy.

Will and Bliss were convinced this was a harebrained tale but many believed it was a fact, and on the evening of July 3 Captain Bligh summoned the men into a large huddle. "It's probably a lot of crap," he said. "But if American planes do fly over, you people will quietly return to the barracks wherever you are. Don't talk, don't hurry." He glowered. "One more thing. You will not, repeat not, leave this camp under any circumstances unless it is seized by U.S. troops. If you want to get killed, join up with a Filipino raiding party. Any questions?"

The Fourth of July dawned and nothing happened except another few helpings of blowgun soup and maggoty rice. The prisoners became even more morose and apathetic. Among the higher-ranking officers criticisms of MacArthur grew more bitter. "He knew damned well he was sentencing all of us to death," said Brigadier General William Brougher. "He and his staff knew we'd be rotting in a lousy prison camp. And now they're eating steak and eggs in Australia. God damn them!" Brougher proposed they form a veterans' organization after the war with membership limited to those senior officers who had stayed in the Philippines after April 1, 1942. "That will keep out the lousy MacArthur gang!"

But Skinny Wainwright quashed such feelings. "We must keep our grievances to ourselves, not spread them around to the world at large." To make matters worse, quarrels began to break out among the colonels over unfair distribution of food and bunks. After several feeble fistfights broke out, Wainwright finally convened the field-grade officers. "You gentlemen have had an easy life for years. Now you taste some hardship and it is apparent that some of you cannot take it well. I want no more behavior of the sort that has occurred recently."

The squabbling stopped and senior officers began issuing orders as though they were in full command. But this well-intentioned attempt to bring order soon collapsed. Few obeyed, for here the law of the jungle prevailed and it was the fittest who would survive.

As respect for rank deteriorated, some senior officers still did their utmost for their men. They fought for their rights at work and in the barracks. But others thought only of their own comfort. Will had to restrain himself from striking one who said, "It has always been the custom for officers in this man's army to be the privileged class and I see no reason to change that procedure."

Will wrote this down in his precious little notebook.

3.

In Washington the intended recipient of this notebook, George Marshall, had just sent a radiogram to MacArthur in Australia recommending Wainwright for the Medal of Honor. This highest award had been presented to MacArthur after his escape to Australia with the approval of almost all Americans, but he didn't believe Wainwright deserved it. He replied indignantly that the citation written up by Marshall "does not repeat not represent the truth." Giving the Medal of Honor to Wainwright would be a grave injustice to other generals on Bataan who had "exhibited powers of leadership and inspiration to a degree greatly superior to that of General Wainwright thereby contributing much more to the stability of the command and to the successful conduct of the campaign. It would be a grave mistake which later on might well lead to embarrassing repercussions to make this award."

It was a damning indictment. Marshall was deeply distressed but the threat of "embarrassing repercussions" raised questions. Had Skinny done something reprehensible they weren't aware of? Would this be made public later if the medal were awarded and bring embarrassment to the army?

Marshall asked his deputy chief of staff to study the matter. General McNarney reported next day: "Personally, I question General MacArthur's motives and my emotional reaction is to award the decoration." At the same time McNarney agreed that both Skinny and the army would suffer from a public hearing of the case. His recommendation of no further action was reluctantly endorsed by Marshall. He regretfully shelved the proposal, promising himself to see to it that someday Skinny would get the medal. MacArthur's derogatory remarks were stamped "Super Secret" and filed in a safe.

4.

As summer turned into early fall, life dragged on at Cabanatuan. With the passage of time the Japanese allowed the prisoners to organize entertainments and lectures to help keep the men from deteriorating. Those with special training gave talks on gardening, beekeeping, handicrafts, and cultural subjects. One lecture eagerly awaited was by Major Spring whose daughter Molly was a Hollywood starlet. Her photograph had graced many foxholes and Spring promised to give a "behind the scene" view of the many stars he had met. As if in celebration of the event, the Japanese provided another super supper just before the lecture: a heaping cup of beans to go along with the daily meal.

Like everyone else Will mixed the beans with the rice to make the bean taste linger longer. First he poured water into the emptied cup, swirled it around to get every particle of bean, and drank it as if it were nectar of the gods. That was the first course. Then came the bean-rice concoction and like all the men he ate it slowly with relish and much lip-smacking.

After the meal those who wished to attend the lecture were marched by Captain Bligh to a nearby barracks. Soon it was jam-packed. As Major Spring began to talk about the stars someone shouted, "How about a behind the scene squint at Betty Grable?" Another wanted a "front view." The major good-naturedly continued his fascinating tour of Hollywood until a man in the rear row made wind. It passed unnoticed. Then came a far louder fart. The crowd roared. "Hey, guys!" shouted the perpetrator triumphantly, "I farted without shitting in my pants!" This brought another roar of laughter.

Major Spring smiled and started to talk about Gary Cooper when another fart came, followed by the comment, "Let's hear it for Gary Pooper!" Hollywood was forgotten as four men farted simultaneously. It took a minute for the crowd to quiet but Major Spring was in no mood to continue. Stern-faced, he rose and strode out of the barracks carrying his chair. His exit was the signal for a chorus of farts. This went on, to shouts of laughter, until big raindrops began pelting the roof. The men scuttled back to their barracks.

Will's group reached theirs just before the torrent came. After they told those who had stayed in the barracks about the lecture, Bliss, who had not bothered to attend, leaned over from his bunk. "Flatulence," he said in his professorial manner, "was regarded by Chaucer as an accepted part of daily life. And Shakespeare used it as a legitimate piece of theater." He explained that in his studies he had discovered that a very dramatic episode involving farts had been deleted from "Hamlet" by later puritanical censors. He climbed down to the floor. "I'll demonstrate." It was now dark, but everyone could see him take off his trousers and shorts and bend over. There was a flash of a match, a loud fart and then a foot-long blue flame shot out of his rear. It was so startling that there was awed silence. Then Wilkins exploded in a high-pitched infectious laugh. Everyone laughed and there were pleas for a repeat performance.

Bliss bowed solemnly. "One encore only," he said. The clamor ceased and there was an expectant hush. Another match, an even louder fart, and a longer bluish flame. There was such a roar that a Japanese guard banged on the side of the barracks, shouting, "Quiet in there! What's going on?"

Someone tried to explain in broken Japanese. The guard didn't understand and it was obvious he was angry. Then Will said in Japanese, "Honorable guard, a man lit his fart with a match."

There was a short silence. "Why?" asked the guard in bewilderment.

"The long blue flame," said Will, "is quite an extraordinary sight."

"Crazy Americans!" said the guard, touching his head.

A few days later guards went from barracks to barracks searching for prisoners with fairly decent shirts. Will and Bliss were among those chosen. Several hundred were loaded into trucks and driven into a deserted hilly area. Here they were issued new trousers, steel helmets, and rifles. Then they were marched to a field where a Japanese civilian stood on a bamboo platform. He began shouting through a megaphone in good English. "We are making a movie. You are American soldiers and will come out of those woods with your rifles in a charge. There will be a few explosions but they are harmless." Guards passed out pieces of coconut as if the prisoners were performing dogs and then began positioning the Americans in the woods. The prisoners hefted their Japanese rifles appreciatively.

The Japanese director began shouting through his megaphone, first in Japanese, then in English. "Attention! Attention, please. You will please not pull triggers." The prisoners were puzzled. "There has been some mistake," continued the director. "The guards passed out their own rifles and they are loaded. Sorry." It was a ridiculous situation. Outnumbered and unarmed guards were faced by several hundred armed prisoners.

Lieutenant Bliss was the first to move. He walked up to a guard and handed over his piece. The Japanese bowed in thanks and Bliss bowed. Will handed over his weapon and was thanked. Soon everyone followed suit.

An American major standing next to the director now took over the megaphone. "You men assemble at the bottom of that hill." He indicated a spot fifty yards away where another American officer stood with two white flags. Upon reaching that point, this officer explained, two men would carry the white flags and walk toward a cameraman. "Everyone will follow until we are told by the director to stop. Then we straggle past the cameraman for a close-up."

The director came forward and shouted, "Action! Camera!"

"That's our cue!" said the American officer. "Get moving." He held out the two flags but no one would take them.

There were angry Japanese shouts. The American officer pleaded. "For God's sake, take the flags! We'll all be in trouble."

"Oh, hell," said Bliss. "I surrendered once. May as well do it again." He picked up one flag. Will took the other and the prisoners started climbing the hill. As he neared the top Will saw flaming G.I. trucks and smoke erupting from bombs. But the men straggled past the camera as nonchalantly as if they were walking down their own Main Street. They were chatting and many were chewing on the coconut.

An assistant director at the top of the hill screamed, "No talkee! No eatee!" The prisoners were sent down the hill. This time most of the men walked glumly past the camera. But one youngster couldn't resist putting thumbs on his ears and wiggling his fingers while looking cross-eyed. A guard slammed him in the back with his rifle butt. The young soldier would have fallen if two comrades hadn't caught him and dragged him away.

That evening Will could not get to sleep. He felt as if he were burning and bathed in sweat. He was nauseous and hastily climbed to the floor but before getting outside threw up. As he got to his knees to clean up the mess, Bliss pulled him erect. "We'll take care of that," he said and helped him outside. Despite the stink of the camp the air was pleasant.

"You must have malaria," said Bliss. He and Wilkins managed to get Will back to the upper bay. They bathed his face with wet rags. His teeth began chattering. He was freezing. Bliss and Wilkins threw their own blankets over Will. Soon he was sweating again and the blankets were oppressive.

The next morning Bliss and Wilkins half-carried Will to the hospital. "Malaria," said the examining doctor. "If we had quinine it would fix you up. Perhaps we'll get some next week." He pointed to an empty place on the floor. "Put him over there."

Will's friends put a blanket on the bare floor and tenderly laid Will on it. "We'll get you some quinine somehow," said Bliss. "Don't give up."

Will managed to nod. He knew the best medicine was spirit and he was determined to live. For three days he sweated. He vomited a dozen times a day but almost nothing came up. Twice Wilkins brought in a cup of milk which he had bought with four cigarettes. Even though Will couldn't hold the mixture of rice and milk, it seemed to give him strength.

The urge to live was sharpened by the steady decline of the man next to him, an infantry captain renowned for his courage in battle. His men adored him and although they brought extra portions of food every day the captain surreptitiously dumped the food down a hole in the floor and day by day seemed to shrink. Within a week he was dead.

At last Bliss returned with four quinine tablets. He refused to say how he got them but Will noticed he no longer wore his cherished wrist-watch. Will's protests only brought a grin from Bliss. "Hell, the guy who has it will have it stolen or confiscated by tomorrow."

All the people lying near Will were newcomers. His former neighbors had either died or been transferred to Zero Ward, the next step to the cemetery. Will knew he had to keep moving to stay alive and busied himself crawling to the water spigot with his neighbors' empty canteens. It would take an hour to fill each one and he was so industrious that the days seemed to fly by. He became the favorite of the medics and one would occasionally slip him a quinine tablet. This particular medic was hated by most of the patients. He would patrol the lines of inert men slapping those with closed eyes on the soles of their feet with a club.

"If a guy don't want to live, we've got to clear him out of here," the medic explained to Will. "We need the space for the men who will fight to live." He nodded toward a man who was glaring at him from across the room. "He hates my guts and he's going to make it." He strode over to this man and made a threatening motion with his club, then looked back at Will with a crooked smile.

The man next to Will died and his replacement was a young soldier with a tropical disease somewhat similar to elephantiasis. He was eighteen with innocent round blue eyes and corn-colored hair. "My name is Scotty Adams and I'm from Iowa," he said. The medics set up a special bed for him with a backboard so he could sleep in a sitting position. Next to him was placed a wooden tub which a doctor had wheedled from the Japanese.

"What's that?" asked Will.

"A portable toilet," said a medic. "He can't get to the latrine. When I'm not here would you give him a hand?"

"Of course." That evening Scotty told of life on the farm and the girl he had left behind. Tears streamed down his cheeks. Will tried to comfort him. "I have to take a crap," he said. "Can you get me onto that thing?"

Will unpinned the huge skirt Scotty wore and couldn't believe what he saw in the dim light. His testicles were almost as big as volley balls. Will got the toilet into position and started to move Scotty. He yelled in pain. Will stopped and tried to be more gentle. Finally, after half a dozen tries, Will with great difficulty got Scotty seated. When he was finished he said, "I can't wipe myself. Will you please do it for me?"

Will gritted his teeth at the disgusting thought but he did it, then tried his best to get the youngster back into bed without hurting him too much. It was terrible for both of them, and by the time Scotty was finally back in a sitting position Will could hardly move.

"Thanks, Captain," said Scotty. "You're a swell guy."

Will felt a surge of affection for the poor devil and knew he would never again find wiping him repugnant. He couldn't sleep for thinking of the grotesque testicles. Why had God or Nature or whatever done this cruel thing to the boy? Finally he fell asleep but almost immediately was awakened by a choking sound. Scotty had fallen to one side and was gasping for air. Will found strength to set him straight.

Will's feeling for Scotty increased with every day. The youngster never complained and whenever he cried out in pain as Will helped him to the toilet he would apologize. After a particularly agonizing trip to the wooden tub one night Scotty gasped, "I think I'm going, Captain."

Will misunderstood him. "Don't worry, I'll clean you up."

"No, Cap-tain . . . dy-ing." He gasped for breath. Will hurried to his feet and straightened Scotty.

"No use," said the youngster. "Can't breathe. Can't . . . I'm glad, Captain." He frantically grabbed toward Will. "Hold hand!" Will clutched Scotty's hand. Scotty's nails bit into Will's palm but he didn't feel anything. "M-mother!" Scotty struggled like a fish out of water, then suddenly subsided. He was dead. Will wept.

By the end of three weeks Will was strong enough to walk without any help and he was sent back to his barracks. He knew he would never be the same again. Lying sleepless in his bunk that night he thought how lucky he was to have friends such as Bliss and Wilkins; how lucky he was to have known Scotty. He thought of his family. How dear they all were to him. And their peculiarities and quirks only made them dearer. When he got back, he vowed, he would do his best to understand rather than judge them. He could see the ugly old house in Williamstown. Every room was clear in his mind. He remembered how the wind used to howl around the gable near his bed and how the telephone lines would hum musically. He could hear the rain dashing against his window. It was all so cozy. And he could smell the sweet aromas coming up the back stairs from the kitchen in those wonderful days when Floss was acting as mother to all of them. They had all taken her for granted. And when she had gone off to have her own life with Tadashi, all of them, himself included, had felt she was deserting them. We were all so unfair, he thought. Rain beat on the roof overhead, bringing him back to Cabanatuan, and it reminded him of the great storm in Tokyo when a tree crashed through the roof. He had screamed in terror. And Mama had hurried in to comfort him. Was he three or four? Her words still came to his ears. "Whenever you feel frightened and think you don't have a friend and think the whole world is against you, just say a little prayer." Funny, he couldn't even remember what his mother looked like but her words were with him. He had not prayed in many years but he did now. He fell into a deep sleep and began to dream a lovely dream. He was at home but it didn't look like the place in Williamstown and he was sitting at the head of a long table and everyone was there: the whole family, Mama and all, and the table was piled with the most delicious and aromatic foods he had ever seen. And there was more than enough for everyone. There was a huge turkey and mashed potatoes and steaming gravy. There was a big dish of homemade cranberry sauce and muffins and milk. There were pumpkin pies and lemon meringue pies and nuts and candies. And everyone was laughing. There were no arguments, no sullenness, no wrangling debates.

He awakened fresh and full of hope. He knew now that he would surely survive. He had faith and good friends and all he had to do was keep busy. After breakfast he told his two friends that he was going to volunteer as an overseer at the camp farm. Officers didn't have to work but those who wanted activity could take charge of a group.

5.

That morning Will lined up with the farm detail. He was wearing Wilkins's precious battered wide-brimmed hat. The prisoners were marched out the gate and down a dusty road to the farm. This was a large clearing of some 300 acres where rice, corn, and vegetables were grown.

"Nice to get out here," said Will.

A tall, skinny man looked at him as if he were crazy. "This must be your first day," he said out of the corner of his mouth. "Pipe down, here comes the Angel."

A squat, powerful three-star Japanese private descended on Will with a four-foot-long hoe handle. "Bend over!"

Will pretended he didn't understand and the guard roughly pushed his head down and walloped him on the rear half a dozen times. "That's for talking," whispered the skinny man.

Will staggered and the skinny man had to help him keep up with the group. "Just keep moving and keep your mouth shut." Fortunately it was only a few more yards to the camp. Groups began to peel off for various duties. Some carried water; some hoed; some were weeding.

The American major in charge of the detail took Will aside and explained that he would supervise a weeding section.

"Keep the men working at a good pace but not too fast. The two meanest guards are the Angel and a little bastard we call Air Raid. He's really mean. Remember, the object is to look busy." He introduced Will to his section. "This is McGlynn's first day here so don't try any tricks. Air Raid is in an ugly mood. He wants you to pull every weed in that camote patch over there. He says you're not to kneel or squat. You must bend at the hips and keep your legs straight."

There were several groans.

"All Air Raid wants to see today over here are asses and elbows. Now hop to it."

Will noticed that most of the men wore homemade wooden shoes called go-aheads, cut out of a two-by-four. The sun soon became oppressive and one man stopped working. Will warned him to keep active and was told to blow it out his ass. Just then a husky three-star Japanese private appeared and shouted, "Speedo! Speedo!" He waved a stick energetically, repeated the same word half a dozen times, and moved on.

"That's Big Speedo," someone explained to Will. "That's the only English he knows. He waves that stick around but he never hits anyone. Uh-oh, here comes Little Speedo." The men made a big show of work as a small, mean-faced guard approached. He also chanted "Speedo, speedo!" but accented his words with cruel jabs at the prisoners with a long bamboo pole.

Within an hour Will had met a dozen more guards and learned there were three types: regular army men in their mid-thirties who were stern but military, young recruits who had seen no fighting and wanted to show how tough they were, and conscripts from Formosa who were ill-treated and took out their misery on the prisoners.

At eleven the men were marched back to camp for the midday meal. Will's group was in agony from the tedious weeding and he felt guilty for only having to oversee. The two-hour recess revived the men and they returned to the camote patch with some spirit.

By the time they were marched back to camp even Will was fatigued. No sooner had he flopped on his pallet for a rest before dinner than someone rushed into the barracks shouting, "The colonel is making an inspection!" There were groans of disgust. The assistant camp commander, Colonel Bartlett, a supply officer on Corregidor, had been making life miserable with his frequent tours of inspection. Will took down the mosquito nets in the bay and hid all the extra clothes he and his two mates had collected. Outside, Bliss and Wilkins were hurriedly storing extra quan cans, bottles, and cooking equipment under the barracks.

"Here comes the son of a bitch!" someone shouted and the men lackadaisically formed up raggedly in front of their bays. Colonel Bartlett, who hadn't seen combat, strode in, the picture of a commando, jaw jutting out like the prow of a ship. He looked around. "Fine, men! All shipshape!" He did a smart about-face. As he walked out someone belched, but Bartlett was oblivious and didn't miss a stride.

"Americans," said Bliss, "have the supreme knack of making a wretched existence even more wretched for each other."

"The bastard just does it so he can walk in and look important," said the usually meek Wilkins.

While the men were forming up to depart for the farm the following morning, something unusual happened. A big PFC known as Gloomy Gus was chattering away cheerfully. "He hasn't smiled since he got kicked in the nuts on the march," explained someone. "The only time he talked was to ask how the hell he could tell his wife that he would never be able to get it up anymore."

Gloomy Gus was triumphant. The night before, he had had a wet dream. Now he was a man again.

Today Will's group was assigned to tote water from a nearby stream for the camote patch. Each man had to carry two five-gallon buckets. The men only half-filled each bucket since it was physically impossible to carry such a load two hundred yards. The Angel and the three other guards were stationed along the route to see that no one covertly dumped out any water on the way.

It was back-breaking work made intolerable by the Angel, who used his hoe handle on anyone who spilled water.

After the midday break the prisoners were taken off water duty and returned to weeding. All was peaceful. The Angel patrolled as if eager to find someone loafing but the men worked diligently. Gloomy Gus was still in high spirits and he began singing contentedly as he pulled weeds. Suddenly the Angel came up from behind and clubbed him in the groin. Gloomy Gus staggered to his feet and turned. The Angel was glaring at him like an angry cat. He raised the hoe handle and Gus flung up his right arm to defend himself. The club struck with a frightening crack. Gus was dazed with pain. The Angel struck again and again until Gus collapsed.

The American major in charge ran up. Instead of protesting he began shouting to the prisoners, "Get back to work! Mind your own business!"

When the men got back to the camp that night there were threats of retaliation—not against the Angel but their own major. Will did his best to cool them off but he feared that some of the hotheads meant it when they vowed to waylay the bastard some night. But fellow officers took care of him in their own way. He was removed from the detail and restricted to the officers' area. A week later Gloomy Gus died.

By the beginning of December more than two thousand men from O'Donnell had died but life on the whole had become more bearable at Cabanatuan. There were fewer beatings and the camp commander now allowed the men to entertain themselves with shows put on at an outdoor theater they had constructed; an arts and crafts shop had been set up by the chaplains and at Christmas there was an art festival of the men's work and a songwriting contest. The winning entry was a sentimental love song. So was the second prize. The third was a rollicking, obscene satire on life at Cabanatuan which Will and others thought deserved to win.

Wilkins was director of the camp orchestra that accompanied all the shows. He could play four instruments including the violin and at one show he brought down the house with his rendition of a one-armed fiddler. He came out on stage with his left sleeve empty and dolefully played a tune one-handed. There was applause and then, in acknowledgment, he bowed slightly. The middle finger of his invisible left arm suddenly appeared from his fly like a little penis and grasped the bow. The crowd roared with delight. Men pounded each other on the back. The Japanese guards couldn't understand what was going on and explanations only further mystified them.

The Christmas celebration was capped by the arrival of the first Red Cross packages. Cigarettes were prized above all and they soon became the equivalent of money. Those who didn't smoke, like Will, could trade a pack for considerable food. This, together with the Red Cross supplies, was enabling him to build his strength.

Most of the prisoners doled out the food to themselves slowly, but some stuffed themselves the first day. At least five men died from overeating and scores of others were deathly sick. Some of the packages were pillaged by the guards; fortunately they didn't like corned beef or processed cheese.

The early days of 1943 gave further indication that things were going to improve. First came the rumor that they would be able to send mail home and receive word in return. A few of the men still had letters received in Bataan. These cherished, worn pages had been reread many times. At last the men were called together in Will's barracks. They were handed out cards with certain phrases printed on them. The men were instructed to underline certain words but to write nothing of their own. There were moans and protests but as usual Bliss was philosophical. "The most important thing is to let our folks know we're alive and haven't lost our spirit."

Wilkins was almost in tears. "I had so much to tell her," he said and then reverted to silence.

The next week came another treat for those in Will's barracks. They were among the lucky ones chosen to see a movie. It was the Marx Brothers in "Room Service." The men laughed at the clowns but their eyes were mainly for Lucille Ball and Ann Miller. "It sure is *good* to see an American girl again," said someone, echoing the thoughts of the audience. "They sure look delicious!" There was a chorus of enthusiastic lip-smacks. The movie was followed by a film showing the Japanese advances in southeast Asia. Then came pictures of the Pearl Harbor raid. The scenes of burning ships were shocking. The man next to Will nudged him. "Makes you want to get back in the swing, doesn't it?"

Early in February came another break in the monotony of camp life for Will and his two baymates. All three were selected to go on a detail to the town of Cabanatuan. They were roused at 5:30 A.M. one Sunday and after breakfast were loaded into a truck with other officers. It was a thrill just to see people walking about. The air smelled fresh and sweet. As they entered the town, church was letting out. Hundreds of girls were on parade in gay colored dresses. All wore flowers in their dark hair.

Will noticed that the town park had gone to seed and the playground was deserted. The once well-tended yard in front of the capitol building was now tall with weeds. The truck let them out at the local dump. It was foul but they were used to far worse smells. Their job was to load garbage into the trucks. It was hot, exhausting work but the guards let them spell each other in fifteen-minute shifts. During the rest periods the prisoners would loll in the shade of a tree near a stream.

It was market day and streams of Filipinos walked by with great loads of corn, eggplant and other vegetables. The civilians were afraid even to look at the Americans and would speak to the guards only when addressed. Bliss bribed one guard with a pack of cigarettes to buy corn for them and then allow a boy to boil the ears. Even without salt or butter it was delicious. Later that afternoon Wilkins maneuvered himself near the street and, under his breath, asked a Filipino to get some ice cream.

Fifteen minutes later another Filipino arrived with a small cart. The guard, after some persuasion, let the prisoners buy ice cream. Will handed over five cigarettes and got a cup filled with coconut ice cream. He gulped the cold treat down so fast he thought his eyes would pop out. Other prisoners lined up and the guards joined in. Will tried to get another portion but the supply was sold out. He could have eaten two quarts. The prisoners were festive on the trip back. Will and his two friends were still in high spirits as they entered the barracks. A somber Captain Bligh was surrounded by a large group.

"This concerns you," he said to the newcomers. "Four men of your shooting group tried to escape from the farm this afternoon." But they were caught and brought to the guardhouse. "They're probably being interrogated now. My guess is they'll be shot."

Will's heart was beating like a trip-hammer. This meant the other six men in the blood brother group would also be executed. He looked at Bliss, who suggested they wander over to the guardhouse and see what was going on. Wilkins started to join them but Bligh said, "Three's a crowd."

They watched a Japanese sergeant rush out of the headquarters building and into the guardhouse. Moments later three American officers were pushed out the door by guards. Behind was the Japanese sergeant, a small man whose right hand was permanently bandaged. It was said he had lost three fingers on Bataan.

The sergeant began beating the three Americans with a club. Will was staring in dumb horror and Bliss pulled him behind a small building where they could watch without being observed. They wondered what had happened to the fourth prisoner.

After five minutes the Americans were bleeding and helpless. Then the little sergeant, a jujitsu expert, lifted a captain and slammed him down. The American hit the hard earth like a sack of potatoes. He groaned and was picked up again. Will could not bear to look but he heard a heavy thud and a cry of anguish. The same punishment was meted out to the other two Americans. When it was finally over each prisoner was forced to kneel with a two-foot piece of bamboo behind his legs. His hands were then tied behind his back with a rope tied from neck to hands and down to feet. It was obvious to Will that the bamboo would cut off blood circulation, and if the victim fell asleep the rope would choke him.

After the three were lined up, guards passed by. Some spat at the prisoners, some slapped them. The headquarters door opened and the fourth American, a major, head bleeding, hopped out on one foot. He grabbed at a railing to keep from pitching off the steps. A guard jabbed him in the side and he tumbled clumsily to the ground. He tried to get up but needed help from the guard who then pushed him forward. He hobbled painfully toward the little sergeant who grasped him as if to give him the jujitsu treatment. Instead he disdainfully pushed him to the ground where he was trussed up.

That night it rained and Will wondered if it came as relief to the four victims or became an additional pain. It was chilly in the barracks and he huddled in his own precious blanket. It must be terrible out there for those poor devils.

The next morning it was announced that all prisoners except those on work details would be restricted to their areas for thirty days. Rations would be reduced to one meal a day. As the farm detail trudged out of the gate Will saw the four prisoners tied to poles outside the barbed wire on the main highway. Three wore shorts; the limping captain was naked.

When the detail returned for midday rest Will could see that the four men were in obvious agony from the blazing sun. Guards were forcing Filipino passersby to beat the Americans with bamboo poles. One guard shouted to a Filipino that he wasn't beating his man hard enough, hit the Filipino with a club and ordered him to try harder. The Filipino obeyed, tears streaming down his cheeks.

The following morning as the farm detail was passing through the gate, Will was alarmed to see the four Americans being loaded into a truck. They stood erect without expression although it was obvious they were being driven to their execution. As the truck slowly started off, prisoners on the other side of the fence stood at attention and saluted.

The truck stopped only a hundred yards from the squash patch being tended that day by Will's group and he could see the four victims, standing with backs to freshly dug graves. Their hands were tied behind their backs. Cigarettes were put in their cracked, bleeding lips and lit. After a few deep puffs the cigarettes were taken away. A firing squad, a dozen men, marched onto the field and lined up unevenly in front of the doomed men. They kept their chins high; no one whimpered or begged for mercy.

A Japanese officer raised his saber and the firing squad raised rifles. The saber fell and a volley of shots crackled. One man fell into his grave, a second dropped to his knees, a third pitched forward. But the fourth, a big redheaded second lieutenant, was still erect, staring forward, chin jutted. The officer raised saber again and shots rang out. The young American staggered and tumbled into his grave, but then Will saw two hands emerge and then a crop of red hair. The American crawled out. The officer kicked him back, pulled out a pistol, and ended his agony with a shot in the head. The officer went along the graves, firing into each body. Then he shouted an order. The firing squad did an about-face and marched off in ragged formation. They passed so close by that Will could see their troubled faces; one young soldier had tears in his eyes. They were followed by four farm guards who were laughing and joking.

The next day there were several beatings within the camp and a soldier marched around with the severed head of a Filipino stuck on a pole. Beneath the head was a crude sign in English: "He Help American."

That evening a guard appeared at Will's barrack. He read out the names of the six who had been in the shooting squad with the four executed escapees. Will, Wilkins, Bliss and three other men came forward and were marched in the fading light to the main guardhouse. They were locked in with no explanation but during the night they noticed that extra guards were patrolling around the building.

Every day they expected to be interrogated but two weeks passed without a word from their sullen guard who shoved a helping of rotten rice at them twice a day. A captain with a wife and two children could stand it no longer. He shouted at the guard that the Japs were violating the Geneva Convention. Bliss tried to quiet him but he kept up his tirade until the guard beat him over the head with his own mess kit.

"They won't shoot us, will they?" said the captain. "They won't really shoot us?"

No one answered. Finally Bliss said, as if he had long considered the question, "Haven't shot any other groups, have they?"

"But why are they keeping us here?"

Someone else argued that the Geneva Convention would protect them.

"Ever read it?" said Bliss. No one had. "Neither have the Japs," he said with a wry smile. That day a Japanese major, smartly dressed, arrived to announce in copybook English that he would return in the morning and read out their sentences.

No one slept that night. They talked of their homes and sweethearts and parents. One man read aloud the letter from his wife he had hitherto refused, for any price, to share with his mates. They listened to a long description of his six-year-old son's first day at school; of the dancing classes of his daughter; and the problems with the mother-in-law who insisted on spoiling the children. The best was the simple heartfelt closing: "Goodnight, my darling Harry, until I once again hold you in my arms. Your loving Glenda."

Wilkins told about the last Christmas dinner he had had in Wisconsin with details of how each dish looked, smelled, and tasted. "Tell us again," said a young lieutenant when he finished. "It would be worth being shot to get a meal like that."

"Hell," said another, "I'd settle for a dozen scrambled eggs and a half pound of sizzling bacon and a pot of real coffee."

Just before nine o'clock someone saw the Japanese major coming toward the guardhouse followed by a dozen men with rifles. A friend of Will's who had been policing the area peered into their window. "Take it like a man, Will," he said huskily.

The six men shook hands. They agreed not to give the Japs the satisfaction of seeing them plead or break down. The six were led outside and lined up. The major solemnly stood in front of them and read off their names. "Now you hear your punishment."

Will remembered how Dostoevski had waited for his sentence of execution—and his miraculous reprieve. Dostoevski had hated those who made him suffer so terribly for a brief moment. Will prayed he would have the same fate.

The Japanese major announced that they would be restricted for two weeks in their barracks. They would meditate about the men who had escaped and realize that they had been justly executed. One of the Americans burst out crying. The others were silent. Will thanked God for saving him.

The major held up a warning hand. One of the six, he said, must be punished more severely as a lesson to the rest of the camp. He would be tied to a pole just outside the barbed wire for a week. He pointed to an area feared for its red ants.

The major asked for a volunteer. No one stepped forward. The major looked along the line. Will sighed with relief when the cold eyes passed him. But the major's eyes began a return trip and stopped at Will. The major nodded.

No sooner had Will been stripped naked and tied to the post than a line of red ants started crawling up his leg. At first they seemed harmless and merely annoying. Then one bit him. It was like a hot pinprick. Another bit, then half a dozen at once. Will shouted in pain. A guard walked out and lightly clubbed him on the back of the head. "Only a coward cries," he said.

After an hour Will felt that he could endure no more pain and tried to analyze what pain was. It didn't help. He prayed. It was no use. Just when he thought he was at the end of his endurance the ants, after a few farewell bites, left. He thanked God. He was aware of throbbing all over his body. The bites seemed to be swelling. A new pain traveled all over his naked body. It was a throbbing pain that was followed by an itch. He tried to rub against the pole but could reach only a few parts of his body. He thought he was going to scream from inability to scratch the myriad itches.

Sweat was pouring down his face. He closed his eyes but the sun burned through the lids. Finally a shadow fell over his face from the pole. What exquisite relief. Minutes later a guard stood over him. The guard changed his position so his head was again in full sunlight.

At last the sun sank behind the Zambales Mountains and there came blessed coolness. He was facing the camp and could see a line of prisoners staring at him through the fence. One looked like Bliss but Will's eyes still ached from the sun and he wasn't sure. Guards were watching the prisoners inside the barbed wire but did nothing to shoo them away. Apparently the camp commander wanted Will's comrades to see his misery as an object lesson.

With darkness came a cool breeze. He shivered. Then rain fell in soft soothing drops which felt wonderful on his riddled body. Then it came faster and harder. A breeze turned into a strong wind. He longed for his blanket, certain he would freeze to death before welcome heat came from the sun.

The next morning its rays soon became the enemy. They also brought out the ants, which seemed to attack him with even more vehemence. His lips were swollen and he could feel himself dehydrating. Thirst became worse than the ants. His head began ringing; he saw the landscape whirling around. Upon regaining consciousness it was midafternoon and his face was in shadow. But this relief was brief. He kept his eyes closed as a guard shifted him back to the sun.

He opened his eyes to see a private staring at him. He did not have a cruel face and Will said in Japanese, "Please, water!"

The guard looked furtively over at a tower where another guard sat with a rifle. He shook his head sadly.

"Then kill me. I can't stand it any longer."

The guard furtively put his canteen to Will's lips but before he could swallow a drop, there was an angry shout. An officer ran out brandishing his sword. The guard pulled the canteen away. The guard stood at rigid attention while the officer berated him, then marched off to receive his own punishment.

A few drops of water had spilled over Will and these only made his thirst worse. There was a final attack from the ants, then again a gorgeous sunset, followed by dusk and darkness. Despite his suffering the night before, Will prayed for another rainstorm to bring some relief to his baked body. But tonight the stars came out and he could have read a newspaper in the midnight moonlight. Knowing he could not stand another day, he banged his head against the pole but was too weak to hurt himself seriously. He tried again and again. He prayed for death and this time meant it.

A long cloud slid over the moon and all at once it was dark. He heard a rustling near the barbed-wire fence, then saw something crawling toward him. Some animal? Maybe it was one of the wild dogs that pulled out bodies from the graveyard and ate them. The thing came closer but he wasn't afraid. The moon reappeared briefly, long enough for Will to see it was a man, now lying face down, motionless. In seconds a long cloud brought dark again.

It was Popov. He wet Will's lips and face, then slowly fed him water. He wanted more but Popov restrained him. The black market king rubbed his body with a lotion that stung sharply but then brought exquisite relief. Popov fed him corned beef as if he were a baby, then evaporated milk.

"You're the only one who didn't treat me like scum," he said. The long cloud was nearing its end. "I'll be back tomorrow night." He softly scuttered away, making it under the fence just before the moon peeked into sight.

Will felt strength and hope flow back. He begged forgiveness for praying to die. He was going to live—thanks to a man everyone despised. In the past year Will had learned that the most incongruous traits could exist in the same man. The most selfish prisoner in camp had risked his life for another.

Will was going to live and he vowed that somehow he would escape and bring back proof of the atrocities committed by the Japanese.

PART FOUR

Band of Brothers

CHAPTER FOURTEEN

1.

New Zealand. February 1943.

It was late summer by the time the convoy from Guadalcanal approached Wellington. The 6th Marines rushed to the rail. There were the lush green hills many had feared they would never see again. The pleasant warm breeze humming in the rigging was a welcome relief after the steaming jungles of the 'Canal. As the ships neared the docks Mark could see honor guards from the other regiments along with the division band. All at once the musicians broke into "Semper Fidelis." Mark felt gooseflesh and a lump in his throat. He could imagine his father's scoffing grin.

There were cheers on deck at the sight of a crowd of women on the docks but Mark only felt guilt. He would have to tell Molly. But how?

The camp was not yet completed since so many of the able-bodied New Zealand men were overseas. Many of the construction trucks were driven by women, who were given rowdy greetings by Marines unloading their gear. Mark helped pitch tents and bring in cots, pads, and blankets. Several men collapsed from "the bug" and were carried off to the hospital.

In the first days duty was light and liberty to Wellington was dispensed liberally. The men rushed to the milk bars, swilling down milk, ice cream sodas, and milk shakes. Then began the search for girls and the consumption of the local warm beer and whatever hard liquor was left.

Mark wouldn't accompany his squad to town and he finally had to admit why. There was no lack of suggestions. "Tell her the fuck's off," said one. "The Japs shot off your balls," said another and a third, "Tell her you fell in love with Tuffy." This was the nickname won by their platoon leader, the former Caspar Milquetoast, after his exploits in Guadalcanal. The laughter ended abruptly when the lieutenant himself, recovered from his wound, walked in. He made no comment, only grinned slightly and asked Mark to come to his office.

"I haven't had the opportunity to talk to you in private, McGlynn, about your behavior during the ambush." Mark sheepishly explained that he had been stopped by Captain Sullivan, eaten out and sent back. "In that case," said Tufts, "I have nothing to add. Dismissed." After Mark did an about-face, the lieutenant said, "I couldn't help overhearing about your problem. Would you like some advice?"

Mark turned around. "Yes, sir."

"Tell her the truth—in person."

"In person, sir? Not a letter?"

"It's the manly thing," said Tufts.

Tuffy looked more than ever like a scoutmaster, thought Mark as he slowly returned to his tent. But that afternoon he did go to Wellington on the crowded train. He headed reluctantly for the restaurant. Another girl was behind the counter. He felt reprieved.

"Where's Molly?" he asked.

"She's home—sick."

Mark walked the streets for an hour, then bought a Maori doll and resolutely marched to Molly's apartment. Betsy answered the door. She shrieked in delight and jumped into his arms. He gave her the doll which she hugged. Then he saw Molly. Her face was sallow. She looked older. "I thought you were dead!" She came toward him tearfully. He put his arms around her. Betsy was pulling at him, insisting he play "bucking bronco." Finally she allowed herself to be put to bed after Mark told her a story about a talking cat named Blackie.

"What's the matter?" asked Molly. "You're acting so strange. Why didn't you come before?"

His throat felt dry. "I—I got hit by the bug. You know, malaria, and was in the hospital."

She hugged him. "Oh, Mark."

He freed himself. "No." He told her the truth. Each word was painful. Molly did not cry or say a word. She seemed to draw herself together. "I see," she finally said.

Mark tried to think of something to add that would soften the blow. He tried but she stopped him. "There's nothing more to say." She led him to the door, opened it. She looked at him without rancor. "She'll be all right," she said, meaning "everything's going to be fine."

More and more men were put out of action by recurring malaria. The regimental hospital unit was soon overcrowded and only severe cases were sent to the base hospital at Silverstream. The rest stayed in the tents, tended by friends and corpsmen who fed them as much quinine as they could take. More than 80 percent of the battalion had been stricken. For those still able to get around a movie theater had been set up.

Mark tired of such diversion and spent his free time in Wellington wandering around by himself. He often thought of Will, for Maggie had written that he was a prisoner of war in the Philippines. All Will's life had run smoothly and he wouldn't know how to survive. Mark couldn't even picture him scrounging food and longed to be with him. The two of them together could make it.

Once Mark took the cable car up the hill at Kelburn for the breathtaking view but the sight of scores of Marines and their dates picnicking and necking sent him down on the next car. He took to walking around the residential sections where he would be less likely to run into other Marines. Several times he would be invited into homes for dinner or high tea and he was cheered by the warm hospitality.

In late March Mahoney died of malaria. Mark was summoned by the new first sergeant. Tullio Rossi was short, weighed only 135 pounds, but those who challenged his authority soon found themselves on the deck. He had won scores of amateur bouts and had a deadly right. Just twenty-two, he seemed mature to Mark. "Major Sullivan wants to see you out at Silverstream." He handed Mark a packet of letters. "Give him his mail."

Mark was concerned. "What does he want to see me for?"

"Why don't you ask him? Take the company jeep but don't go cruising."

The hospital was located inland about halfway to Wellington and during the trip Mark worried. Was Billy J. going to send him back to the mainland for bugging out at the 'Canal? This had already happened to several enlisted men. The humiliation would be too much. At the hospital the major's room was empty. Mark found him standing in line to buy chocolate-covered cherries.

"The top sergeant said you wanted to see me, sir." He handed over the letters and waited for the ax to fall.

"I've seen you someplace before in the company."

Mark hesitated. "I was in that ambush, sir."

Sullivan recognized him. "Oh, yeah. What I wanted to talk to you about is, I understand you saved my life on the *Adams*. I wanted to thank you."

"Yes, sir."

Sullivan grinned. "Now I remember. You also came up before me at office hours. Cartridge belt, wasn't it?"

"Yes, sir."

"We all make mistakes, McGlynn." They talked about Guadalcanal—its stink and swamp. "If there's a hell it will be modeled after that miserable place," he said, then changed the subject. "I'm now the battalion exec."

"I heard that, sir."

"Mark, I'm transferring you over to Headquarters Company." Mark was so stunned he didn't answer. Sullivan thought he was reluctant. "Not a bad deal. You'll have better quarters. Not so much noise. You might even find someone who knows how to play chess."

2.

Within a week Major Sullivan had reported for duty with the 1st Battalion. His superior, already destined for another assignment, was spending so much time at regiment and division headquarters that Billy J. was the de facto battalion commander. The task facing him was colossal. Strength was so low that it was impossible to start serious training for the next campaign. Replacements from stateside were pouring into the entire division and the first arrivals, young and raw, were not at all promising.

Despite the drudgery of the new work, Mark was enjoying himself. Headquarters Company was composed of specialists who knew what they were doing. They were better educated, less boisterous, and more inclined to mind their own business. From the beginning Tullio Rossi respected Mark for his efficiency in any kind of paperwork. He was also impressed by Mark's education and background and never tired of hearing about life on a college campus. Mark found Tullio's stories about life in a dingy Pennsylvania coal mine town just as fascinating. Tullio's ailing father, his strong-minded mother, and older brother Tony, now fighting in Italy, became familiar characters.

Mark saw a different Rossi the day they accompanied a group of replacements on a ten-mile hike to see how they were shaping up. Tullio counted cadence the last five miles and then called the men to attention. They looked cocky, pleased with themselves, and expected praise from the spruce Rossi. He looked as if he had just stepped from a

216

shower. His rifle was at sling and the stock as shiny as his shoes. His belt and holster, bleached from many washings in salt water, were as neat as the rest of him. He began speaking quietly as if he were going to sing in the Sunday choir at the local chapel.

"Ladies," he began, "don't you look pretty. Now you think you're one big bunch of hairy Marines. My, didn't we finish boot camp, and didn't the C.O. pin on us our expert and sharpshooter badges? And today you've had such a rough time. Don't we think that the good corporal standing back there should get you warm showers? I think so. And wasn't that last mile terrible? You even managed to double it. Now let me tell you a short story."

The recruits shifted uneasily.

"I have an old mother sitting back in Pennsylvania, for nine whole months she carried this ugly monster in her belly, but she also did all of the washing by hand, hung it out to dry, and then pressed every inch of clothing that she washed. But she didn't stop there; she also made all the bread before going to bed and tucked all nine of us in and had enough time to tell each of us a story. She did this because my old man was too drunk or out on the town. Now this little old lady weighed only ninety-five pounds and was almost five feet tall. And here in front of us we have a group of the best-educated, best-fed, best-dressed men in the world. Don't tell me that I must write this little old lady in Pennsylvania and ask her to come out here and carry that little old pack and seven-pound rifle for you." He suggested they repeat the march, this time with heavier packs.

The men did an about-face, loaded each other's packs with stones and, paced by Tullio and Mark, hiked where they had come from. Mark was amazed that they did this without groaning or any protest.

"They don't want to let a little old lady be stronger and harder than they are," said Tullio.

That night Mark dropped into his bunk exhausted. The bugle awakening him reminded him that today was liberty. The prospect was boring. Another dull day in Wellington. But it was better than lolling around camp. After a breakfast of steak, eggs, cereal and a quart of milk, he helped police the area before donning his greens: green overseas cap, full green uniform with fair leather belt, dress shoes. He followed the rest of his squad to the first sergeant's office to pick up his liberty pass. Rossi was also in his greens. "Going anyplace special, Mark?" he asked.

"No."

217

"Why don't you come along with me to the Home of Compassion?"

"Home of Compassion? No thanks. I never paid for it yet."

Tullio was upset. "What the hell do you think I'm talking about? The Home of Compassion is a Catholic orphanage run by nuns. 'The Beast' and some other NCO's are going too."

The Beast! Mark couldn't believe it. This was a huge man of over thirty with a face bearing the marks of a hundred street and bar brawls and long powerful arms that hung, gorilla-like, below his knees.

"I think you'll enjoy spending the day with the kids. You'll also meet some nice girl volunteers from Wellington."

Mark, Tullio, and four hardened staff NCO's walked the two miles to McKay's Crossing. All the sergeants were carrying wooden machine-gun belt boxes painted battle green and filled with candy bars and cookies.

It was an afternoon that Mark would never forget. First came the shock of seeing the roughest, meanest, most filthy-mouthed animals he had ever known playing with children. One was teaching hopscotch to a six-year-old, another was giving a crippled boy a piggyback ride, and a third—The Beast himself—was holding a three-year-old girl as if she were a treasure, not minding that she was tearing off his ribbons and twisting his lapel ornaments.

There were more than a dozen Marines at the orphanage, including a major and lieutenant colonel. Also present was Father O'Brian, better known as Big Joe, the regimental Catholic chaplain. He welcomed Mark with a hearty handshake that numbed his fingers.

"I haven't seen you at Mass, son."

"I'm not a Catholic, Father."

"With a name like McGlynn?" He laughed. "Half of the others aren't Catholic either, Mark. Glad to have you with us." He noticed that Mark was staring at one of the civilian volunteers, the most exotic girl Mark had ever seen. "Hinemoa," called Big Joe to the girl, "I want you to meet one of our new Marines."

She was tall, slender, and moved like a dancer. Her skin was light brown, her long hair jet black. She was the most beautiful girl Mark had ever seen and he found it difficult to speak. Her voice was soft and her gentle smile made his heart thump. They talked for several minutes but later Mark could not remember a word he said, except to mutter on parting that he hoped he would see her next week.

On the train home Mark only spoke in monosyllables. Tullio, who had clambered into the baggage net as if it were a hammock, leaned over and said, "That was a nice-looking girl you were talking to."

"What is a Maori girl doing in a Catholic orphanage?"

"She's Catholic. Didn't you notice her cross? Her father must be Irish. Her last name is Flynn or something like that. She's a half-caste."

Mark flared. "That's a stupid thing to say."

"What are you heated up about? I just mean she's got a white father."

"It's an offensive phrase."

"I didn't mean to be offensive," he said, trying to be conciliatory. "But what the hell should I call her?"

Mark tried to come up with a proper phrase and couldn't. He laughed. "Lovely," he said. "That's the best description." That night he dreamed about her. Usually he dreamed in black and white. This time was like a technicolor movie. Her eyes were a strange brown that turned violet and she was saying something in a language he couldn't understand.

The next six days seemed endless to Mark. He mooned at his type-writer, writing over and over on the muster roll, "Hinemoa." Tullio, a born romantic, was careful to say nothing to Mark about the girl. When they left on the next liberty, Mark also carried a green box filled with sweets. As soon as the battalion contingent walked into the orphanage, they were surrounded by eager children.

"What have you brought today?" one little boy asked The Beast. He held up his box. "Can I carry it, please?" asked the boy.

"Sure thing, little one," said the burly Marine. "What have you got for me in return?" The boy hugged him.

Mark gave his box to two little girls who looked like twins. They stared at the contents in wonder but wouldn't even touch anything. A soft voice said, "These girls just arrived a few days ago and don't know what's in the wrappers." It was Hinemoa.

Mark set the box down before he dropped it, then opened up a Milky Way and took a little bite. He handed the bar to one of the girls, who tentatively took a nibble. Her face lit up. She handed the bar to her sister. They shared it bite for bite with such relish that Mark guessed this was their first candy bar.

Throughout the afternoon Mark assisted Hinemoa in organizing games and passing out ice cream and cake. As the volunteers were preparing to leave, he asked if he could take her home. She said she didn't date. She was engaged to a boy in the Maori battalion. He said he was interested in Maori culture and only wanted to ask some questions.

For instance, did her name have a special meaning? She started telling him that her father had named her after the heroine of one of their best-loved legends. Hinemoa had fallen in love with Tutanekai, a handsome but poor warrior who lived on an island in Lake Rotorua. Her people had forbidden a marriage but one cold night the courageous Hinemoa had swum to her lover's island guided by music from his flute, and married him.

By the time the story was finished, they were on a tram.

"To give you such a name," said Mark, "your father must have the touch of the poet."

She laughed softly. "He's a carpenter. But he does like to spout after a few drinks." His name was Jack Finn and his father had come from County Cork.

"So did my great grandfather," said Mark.

When they reached Wellington, despite Hinemoa's protests Mark took her home on another tram. It was a small, neat house on the side of a hill overlooking Oriental Bay.

Mark escorted her to the door. It was opened by a big man with touseled black hair and a broad grin. He insisted that Mark have a friendly drink. Her mother was short, plump, with the same soft voice as her daughter's. Finn was delighted to learn that Mark was Irish, and impressed that his father was a history professor who wrote books. He himself was going to write a book and he already had the title, "An Irishman in Paradise." It was his own story and would, of course, be a grand success. Did Mark write too?

Mark said he had no talent except listening to people more interesting than himself. Finn invited Mark to stay for dinner but he was wise enough to decline. But the father, despite secret signs of protest from Hinemoa, insisted that he come stay with them when he got his next three-day pass, and then drove him to the railroad station in his charcoal-burning car.

That night Mark wrote Maggie that he had fallen in love, and that this time it was the real thing.

The next morning word came that Billy J. had been given the battalion. The men cheered as if they all had been promoted. They were proud that their Billy, at twenty-six, was the youngest field battalion commander in the Marines. After breakfast he took the entire battalion on a ten-mile hike to get them back in shape after liberty. And the following day he ordered resumption of the old grind, starting with a rough climb up the "Burma Road" and back. Unlike most commanders, he didn't accompany them in a jeep but led the way on foot. Nor did he need a cheering squad to make the men move. Now that they were back in good physical condition they reveled in the rigorous training. The secret was Billy J. Mark, like everyone else in the battalion, did his best to emulate him. By now the weather was brisk and 1/6 went up the Burma Road with full equipment without losing a step. At the crest they would run company problems, have a hot lunch, then hustle down the mountain as if the Japs were trying to beat them to McKay's Crossing for mail call. At the foot of the mountain they would double-time or jog the last mile to camp.

Later in the week Mark was called to Sullivan's office. "How would you like to be my runner, Mark?" he asked.

Mark was so surprised he hesitated.

"Here's the job. You'll have to be with me at all times. And you'll be doing things that, with your education and background, might seem demeaning. I'm supposed to spend all my time taking care of the other Marines here and looking out to see they get food and water, that they are safe and doing the right things. You have to draw my rations and fill my canteen. You have to dig my foxhole. And we are *always* together. Where I go, you go."

"I'd like that, sir. And I wouldn't find it at all demeaning to do those things."

"Mark, you'll be my companion, closer than anyone else in the battalion. In a sense you'll also be my bodyguard, riding shotgun for me. While the battalion commander is doing his job of commanding, the runner must keep his eye open for snipers or any danger."

"Yes, sir," said Mark enthusiastically, "I'll do my best." Then he added reluctantly, "I was scared as hell at that ambush. I think that's why I escorted my buddy to the rear."

"Yes," said Sullivan. "I recognized that you were afraid, but that's nothing to be ashamed of. All of us are afraid at one time or another."

"You, sir?"

"Yes, Mark. Only damn fools claim they're never afraid. Fire a shot across their bow and they'd have to change their skivvies. The important thing is that you didn't succumb to that fear. If you had you wouldn't have helped that wounded Marine. You would have just bugged out."

Mark was thinking: Billy J. is only twenty-six but he's already a man. "Why didn't you say anything to me at the time about being afraid?"

"I would have embarrassed you in front of your buddies. If I'd done that, you'd be of no further use to this outfit. I don't want a Marine who doesn't believe in himself and in his buddies." He grinned. "You can bet your hat and ass that if you'd pulled out again I'd have sounded off loud and clear."

"Would you have transferred me to another outfit?"

"I wash my own dirty linen." He came from behind his desk and put a hand on Mark's shoulder. "Don't have any more doubts about yourself. If I had any do you think I'd put my life in your hands?"

3.

Mark decided not to return to the orphanage for fear that Hinemoa might cancel the invitation. Two weeks later he appeared at the Finn doorstep with his bag. Hinemoa had not yet returned from part-time work at a small variety store and Jack Finn was on a job. But Mark spent an interesting afternoon with the mother, who told him about the first Maoris who had arrived at New Zealand in 1050 in seven canoes. They had come from Hawaiki, an island west of Tahiti, after many months at sea, and landed north of Wellington along the east coast of North Island.

The mother told of the bloody battles with the white men and the fight of the Maoris for an honorable treaty. Since then relations between the *pakeha* and the Maori had gradually improved. When she was young, she said with a little smile, a *pakeha* boy had to meet a Maori girl secretly. Otherwise he'd be ridiculed. "Today it is not so bad."

At dinner Jack dominated the conversation, then insisted on taking Mark to a nearby pub, the Shamrock, where the newcomer was shown off. The others had gone to bed by the time they returned and Mark's little bedroom was bitter cold. Even a hot brick wrapped in a towel failed to warm up the bottom of the bed. At last dawn came and with it a hearty breakfast that finally thawed him out. It was one of Hinemoa's days off and Jack insisted she spend it guiding Mark around the city. It was obvious to Mark that she was reluctant; once they were outside he suggested they go to the orphanage. They spent the entire day with the children.

The next morning Jack suggested they borrow his little car for sightseeing. They got back early enough for Hinemoa to dress up and they had dinner at the Majestic Cabaret. When they said good night in the living room she pecked him on the cheek and ran upstairs. Next day they drove into the country to visit Grandfather Finn's sheep ranch. That evening they went to the cinema and Hinemoa let Mark hold her hand.

As Mark was leaving for camp, the parents asked him to come again soon. Jack started to accompany him to the tram stop but his wife led him into the kitchen. At last alone with Hinemoa, Mark asked if he could kiss her.

"Please don't," she said, backing away slightly.

He released her without protest, only looked at her gently. She felt a surge of warmth toward him and impulsively kissed him. He returned the kiss lightly.

"May I see you next week?"

She nodded.

At first Mark had feared that he would become bored at being Billy J.'s dog robber but he found that every day presented new and fascinating problems. It was almost like being an aide, and he found himself sharing the major's concerns and triumphs. This morning the problem was finding a replacement for the commander of Headquarters Company. Captain Barker, the current commander, had been unable to deal with the individualists of the unit, riding roughshod over the specialists who regarded such things as inspections as a waste of time.

Mark suggested Lieutenant "Moon" Mullins, the executive officer of Company B, known as the playboy of the battalion. When he took his company on a hike he would wear nonregulation cowboy boots and a nonregulation belt. He'd also take along a football and every so often would stop the march and play touch football with his men. Yet somehow he managed to get them to the top of the Burma Road ahead of other units. Nor did he ever have to exhort his company when they lagged on the trip home. A master of the ocarina, he would simply pull his "sweet potato" out of his hip pocket and play a lively tune.

While Sullivan appreciated Moon, he was concerned about such fraternization. Even so, he decided to bring him up to Headquarters Company. Besides, here he could keep a closer watch on him. The rise of morale among the prima donnas was noticeable at once.

By now it was so cold that the stoves in the tents were kept going continuously. The tempo of training increased with more field problems that left Mark exhausted, since the major insisted on observing on foot. They traveled from unit to unit until he, like Billy J., got to know every man in the battalion.

In July the routine was enlivened by the appearance of Eleanor Roosevelt at McKay's Crossing. She had been touring New Zealand, visiting hospitals and talking to the wounded as if she were their aunt. She also delighted the civilians by such unorthodox acts as rubbing noses with Maori women. The battalion, dressed in greens for her visit, were pleased by her simplicity and friendliness. Mark was one of those chosen to speak to her and he was tempted to ask how he could find out more about Will in prison camp. But when it was his turn and she held out a hand, all he could do was thank her for coming way out, down under, to see them.

He wrote Maggie about his meeting with Mrs. Roosevelt and urged her to get their father to use his influence with the President to check on Will. In his own short letters to the professor, he briefly told of the training and how well they were treated by the New Zealanders, and that he had finally made corporal. But to Maggie he wrote at length about characters such as The Beast, Moon Mullins, Tullio Rossi, and Billy J. He told in detail about his dates with Hinemoa. They would go dancing at the Cecil Club to the music of the 2nd Division band. Believe it or not, he had learned to jitterbug and was teaching Hinemoa. He tried to show enthusiasm for Maggie's high hopes of covering the war in the Pacific, but hated to think of her being quartered near a bunch of filthy-mouthed Marines and G.I.'s. Secretly he hoped they would keep her in Hawaii. That was bad enough.

His courtship proceeded slowly but surely during the next weeks. Hinemoa felt almost hypnotized in his presence. He seemed to exert some incomprehensible force over her. He was like a creature from another planet, so different from the boys she'd grown up with, but his intense love for her was overcoming her own doubts. Early in September on a bright spring day she admitted to him that she had written Tara, her Maori fiancé, that she could not marry him, then buried her head as if in shame. But her feeling of guilt gradually wore off and it was obvious to her parents that she was falling in love with Mark.

The next time Mark went to Wellington the two of them took five children from the orphanage on a picnic to the top of Kelburn and then to an ice-cream parlor downtown. Time had never passed so slowly for Mark. At last they were alone in a tram. He put his arm around her and kissed her. "You know how much I love you," he said and before she could reply said, "Will you marry me?"

Although this came as no surprise, she looked at him in wonder. After a brief pause she said, "Yes."

He began to tell her all his faults: his impatience, his stubbornness, his immaturity . . .

"A fine time to tell me," she said but smiled happily.

He promised to be more patient, less stubborn, more mature. When they arrived at the Finn home, Jack was ecstatic and Mrs. Finn kissed both Hinemoa and Mark. He explained that he had to get his commanding officer's approval but that would be no problem since they were good friends. Mark had a three-day pass the next week, and Jack insisted the couple take the family car and tour the northern part of the island. Mrs. Finn suggested they spend at least a day in Rotorua where her relatives lived.

As soon as Mark reached the camp he had to tell someone. He woke up Tullio. "I'm not surprised," he said feeling more flattered than annoyed at being rousted out of bed. "She is a very nice girl and you both will be very happy." He explained that there would be some red tape. Mark would have to get approval first from a chaplain and then from Billy J. He assumed that Mark would see the Protestant chaplain, Little Joe, but Mark balked. "He's a cold fish. Couldn't I go to Big Joe? He's more understanding." Rossi said it made no difference that Mark wasn't Catholic.

Late that afternoon Mark arrived at Father O'Brian's tent. On the bulletin board outside was a large centerfold from *Esquire* of a beautiful woman in a negligee on a chaise lounge. Above it, the chaplain had written: "Unless the girl you want to marry is as pretty as this, don't bother."

Mark knocked on the tent frame and was told to enter. He said he wanted to get married. "I presume you saw the picture outside?"

"Yes, Father."

"I guess she's just as pretty, isn't she?"

"Far prettier, sir."

"Well, tell me about her."

"You know her, I believe, Hinemoa Finn. I met her at the House of Compassion."

"Yes, she's a lovely girl from a good family." He sighed. "But there are problems."

Mark bridled. "Because her mother is Maori?"

"Of course not, son. That's of little importance. I mean that you two come from different worlds."

"You mean because she's Catholic and I'm Protestant?"

"No, that is not the problem. We'd never hold that against you even if you do have a good Irish name."

Mark refused to smile. "We love each other. That's what's important."

"Everyone who comes in here thinks that. I will assume you are both in love. It's that you've been out of the States too long. There are more pretty girls waiting for you back there than you can dream of."

"I'm not some eighteen-year-old, Father. Don't treat me like one," said Mark.

"All right. I'll just try to talk facts. I know something about you from Major Sullivan. Your father is a famous professor and hers is a plumber."

"He's a carpenter."

"You know what I mean. You come from a cultured family and Hinemoa would find it painful to be suddenly flung into your background. And how do you think your people will welcome a Maori girl, beautiful as she is?"

"My family has no stupid prejudices," Mark bristled.

"She's never been out of New Zealand. Nor have her parents. You must seem like a Martian."

"They have already consented to our marriage, sir. I get along fine with them."

"But how can you be so sure that Hinemoa will like America? She is a very sensitive girl, a lovely girl. Is it fair of you to take her out of the place she loves and throw her into a strange culture? She would be miserable and you would be miserable. And that would mean your marriage wouldn't really have a chance from the start."

"Father, that's only a supposition. I will appreciate it, sir, if you will just sign this application."

"Oh, I'll sign it." He scribbled on it, "Disapproved."

"Father," said Mark, "do you think it's fair of you to make up her mind?"

The chaplain tore up the slip. "You have a point. Bring me another slip in a week. In the meantime I'll talk with Hinemoa."

That Friday Hinemoa and Mark started north in the little charcoal-burning car. It was a bright spring morning with a breeze touched with warmth. They took many pictures of the lush rolling green hills dotted with white sheep and cattle, and by late afternoon reached New Plymouth, its homes and buildings clustering about the foreshore of the sea. They got single rooms at a little, neat hotel with a spectacular view of the snow-covered cone of Mount Egmont. That evening Mark came to

226

her room. He told her about his former girl friends, including Molly. She listened, then said, "I too have a confession."

"About Tara?"

"Yes."

"You two made love?"

She blushed furiously. "No. We almost did."

He laughed, kissed her, and returned to his room.

Early next morning they drove inland and by late morning could see several fuming volcanoes. They passed through a great chain of steaming lakes and hot pools of bubbling mud. The lakes were so rich in minerals that some were teal blue and others a beautiful translucent green. Early in the afternoon they reached the resort town of Rotorua, famous for its hot sulfur and mineral baths. They drove to a nearby village, Whakarewarewa, to see her grandparents who lived in a *whare*, a traditional Maori house. They were much darker than Hinemoa and greeted Mark with simple dignity. The village was dotted with scores of boiling mud pools which spluttered and bubbled.

That evening they watched, with tourists, a fierce war dance, the *peruperu*, performed by warriors brandishing long clubs. When their leader would shout out commands the others replied in chorus, stamping their feet in unison, gesturing with their hands, rolling their eyes and contorting their faces ferociously.

"That's scary," Mark said.

"You should see it done by the young men."

Then the maidens and women began the graceful, gentle *poi* dance. Clad in silvery flaxen skirts with greenstone ornaments in their black hair, they began swinging the *poi* balls made of bulrushes in time with a rhythmic chant.

Mark wanted to go to a hotel in Rotorua but Hinemoa said the grandparents would be offended if they didn't spend the night in their *whare*.

On the way home they lunched in a field at the foot of a little mountain. Afterward they lay on their backs watching the clouds pass, and kissed until Hinemoa realized it was getting late. As they were packing Mark felt the ground rolling under him. Earthquake! He grabbed Hinemoa and pulled her toward the road. "Stand still," she said calmly.

He grasped her tightly. There was a strange rumbling noise and a stretch of ground more than fifty yards in length miraculously opened up just ahead of them. Hinemoa said it was all over but Mark was so stunned he couldn't move for several moments. Never had he been so terrified—not even at Guadalcanal. Hinemoa walked up calmly to the long crevass and looked down. Mark cautiously joined her, peered down. He could see no bottom. He dropped a good-sized rock into the narrow chasm. There was no sound.

The first thing he heard on his return to camp was that the Maori battalion was back and there had been a classic brawl the previous night at the cinema. There had been some trouble a day earlier since many of the Maori, having lost their women to the Marines, were in an ugly mood. As usual before the movie started everyone stood for the British national anthem. Then "The Star-Spangled Banner" was played and the Maoris as one man sat down. This insult was too much for the Marines, who began throwing punches. The Maori, longing for the opportunity to let off steam, piled out of their seats and converged on the Americans. Although outnumbered, the Marines were old hands at brawls. They ripped off their belts and pounded the Maori over the heads with the buckle ends. New Zealand and Marine M.P.'s arrived and broke up the fight but the word had already come that the entire Maori battalion was going to drive the Marines out of Wellington the next weekend. Even so, Mark was determined to see Hinemoa on Saturday. By that time she would have had her talk with Big Joe and the marriage would surely be approved.

On Friday Father O'Brian did meet Hinemoa at the House of Compassion. "I realize you two young people love each other," he said. "But I can't see it ending in a good marriage. I would not be doing you a favor to approve it." He repeated the arguments he had used with Mark.

She said she was willing to live in America since she was so much in love with Mark but admitted she was somewhat nervous about meeting Mark's family. It might be difficult at first, she argued, but they loved each other and could work things out.

"My dear," he said, "it is not good sense to marry a man who is going off to battle in a short time and could be killed."

She could not hold back the tears.

He held her hand. "You know I am only thinking of your own welfare, don't you."

"Yes, Father."

"I know that Mark is a good man and that he sincerely loves you. But these are terrible times and we must think of the future. Now I'm going to have to ask you something very personal and you must not be offended." She nodded. "Have you and Mark had sexual relations?"

"Oh, no, Father!"

He was relieved. "I would have been very disappointed. Now please take to heart what I'm going to ask you, beg you, to do. Be patient. Let Mark go off to battle without the responsibility of leaving behind the girl he loves. There is very small chance that he will ever get back here until the war is over. When that time comes I will bless your marriage. Try to talk some sense into that young man of yours."

Sadly she relayed all this to Mark on Saturday. He was defiant. "Billy J. will back me up." Almost five hundred men had already had permission to marry New Zealand girls. "I should have gone to the Protestant chaplain. We're not going to be stopped by one damned fool priest."

"Mark! How can you talk that way about Father O'Brian?"

"He's not infallible. He's not God."

She was shocked. "He's only asking us to be patient."

"What's all this I hear about being patient?" It was Jack Finn, home from the bar after several drinks. When Mark told him he began cursing Father O'Brian. "I'll tell off that black Irish bastard!"

Mark couldn't help laughing.

"He's been drinking," apologized Hinemoa.

"He reminds me somewhat of my father," said Mark. He kissed her softly. "I'll never let you go, my darling."

There was a sharp rapping on the door. There stood an angry man in a Kiwi uniform. "Tara!" Hinemoa exclaimed.

He stepped in, glaring at Mark. "So you're the Yank."

"Yes."

Hinemoa came between them.

"I got your letter," Tara said, clenching his fists.

"I'm sorry," said the distressed girl.

"I just wanted to tell you—"

Finn reeled in, a bottle of beer in one hand. "What the Bejeezus Christ are you doing here?" he said, ready to do battle.

Tara went up to Hinemoa. "I just wanted you to know I wish you well."

Finn was instantly the good host. "Well, stay and lift a few with us."

Tara declined and hastily left.

Mark could see how upset Hinemoa was and said he also had to leave. He kissed her briefly and left. On the way back he thought about Tara. He had acted like a man.

In the morning Mark asked Major Sullivan if he could have a few minutes on a personal matter. "I can understand why Big Joe refused to okay the marriage of the younger fellows. But I've been around and am old enough to know what I'm doing."

Billy J. began asking almost the same questions as Big Joe had, and Mark wondered whether there had been some collusion. "Have you already discussed this with Father O'Brian?"

"No, these are the questions I always ask in such a case. I think you'd be making a big mistake."

"Major, this is the finest girl I've ever met and I'm deeply in love with her."

"I don't doubt that, Mark. I still think that she would be a fish out of water in the United States."

"I know at least five hundred other Marines got permission to get married. Why is such a big deal made about my case? If you'll permit me to be frank, sir . . ."

"Go ahead."

"I don't think it's any damn business of the Marines to try and run my personal life."

"Just a minute. You're way out of line there. You are my Marine and you're my responsibility. I'm responsible to see that you don't mess up your life. Because if you do you'll be a worthless Marine."

Mark told about Big Joe's meeting with Hinemoa. "He scared her to death. What right had he to do that?"

"If you really loved that girl you wouldn't think of inflicting this on her. You can write letters to each other. And if, after the war, you're still in love, go back to New Zealand and marry the girl."

Mark saw there was no use in arguing. Angry at being rejected by a man he counted on, he stood stiffly at attention.

"Mark . . ." began Billy J. "Oh hell, dismissed."

4.

At 2nd Division headquarters in the Windsor Hotel in downtown Wellington, operations officers and representatives of the Navy and the Army Air Force were mulling over the plans for the next offensive. The target was the atoll of Tarawa in the Gilbert Islands. The plans called for the initial landing on little Betio Island, code-named Helen, which from the air resembled the tip of an anchor. Here was the site of the main enemy installations. Many of the Marines protested. Initial landings, they argued, should be made on adjoining islands so land-based artillery support could be given to the main landings on Betio.

During a break a group of Marine officers who would have to lead the assault exchanged bitter comments. They feared much heavier resistance because of the interview General MacArthur had granted the Hearst newspapers that September. "The son of a bitch was griping because he's going to play second fiddle," said a full colonel, "and revealed that the navy was going to carry the main attack by island-hopping. Now the Nips will be all prepared for us when we hit the beaches."

Word leaked from regiment that a move was coming soon, and Mark persuaded Tullio to give him liberty that weekend so he could see his girl. He brought with him a fat packet of pound notes, most of his winnings from poker. He told her to put it in her name in a savings bank. By the end of the war, he said, there'd be enough to buy a home and get a good start in some business. She paled. "You're leaving?"

"Pretty soon." He told her there was nothing to worry about. He was the battalion commander's runner and would be at his side at all times. They would remain in the rear where it was safe. She couldn't say anything, only hold him closer.

He told her that Major Sullivan refused to interfere with Father O'Brian's decision. But he had an idea. Why didn't she tell Big Joe that she was afraid she was pregnant?

"That's not funny," she said, and when he assured her he was serious she was shocked. "I couldn't tell a lie to a priest! What kind of a Catholic do you think I am?"

"Then I'll tell him."

"No, you won't." She was so indignant that Mark promptly retreated. She forgave him and they spent an hour saying good-bye.

In the morning word came to break up camp and prepare for departure. Three days later they boarded a transport. Instead of heading for Tarawa, the ship turned north at Hawke Bay in rehearsal for the landings on Betio. The maneuvers were a fiasco, with many rubber boats capsizing in the heavy surf.

To the surprise and delight of the New Zealanders, the 2nd Division returned to Wellington and were transported back to their empty camps. Training resumed but the men, impatient for action, became increasingly restless. At last, near the end of October, Oriental Bay was crowded with transports. And on the twenty-eighth the battalion began loading onto the *Feland*. Liberty boats were run in from the transport every night. Mark was allowed to go the first and third nights and he spent all his time at the Finns'.

Being at Billy J.'s elbow, Mark learned on the fourth day that they were to embark the following morning. He asked for liberty, but Tullio said he was not on the list since he had already had two liberties. Swallowing his pride, Mark appealed to Major Sullivan.

"Are you on the list, Mark?"

"No, sir."

"How many liberties have you had since we boarded?"

"Two."

"That's plenty for a corporal." He had discussed the matter with Tullio and both felt it would not be wise to give Mark liberty on the last night. He might go AWOL.

"But, Major—"

"No, Mark. Have you checked all my equipment?"

After checking Sullivan's gear, Mark bought a pass from the bugler for a pound and went over the side without being seen by Tullio. At the dock a group of tearful girls was awaiting the Marines. They welcomed their men and, silent for the most part, walked off sadly, hand in hand.

Dinner at the Finns' was subdued. Even Jack had little to say except to make disparaging remarks about Father O'Brian. Afterward Mark and Hinemoa quietly discussed their plans. He suggested she take some of their money and go to secretarial school so she could get a better job. It would also, he said, keep her busy. She dutifully agreed. The parents, after a fond farewell to Mark, went upstairs early to leave the young people alone.

Hinemoa held him close to her while he tried to assure her that he'd be safe with Billy J. She kissed him ardently and then, for the first time, they made love. When it was over Mark was exultant. He kissed her tenderly, then noticed her cheeks were damp. "What's the matter?" he asked although he knew. She whispered that she was ashamed. She had sinned. "We're as good as married," he said.

She could not be consoled. "It's all my fault," she said. She stroked his head. "I love you so much."

They talked quietly for a long time, pledging eternal love.

On the tram he realized to his consternation it was past ten and the last liberty boat had gone. For the first time, Mark was scared. At the dock he came upon a bizarre sight. Moon Mullins, now promoted to captain, was playing a merry tune on his sweet potato like the Pied Piper as he led half a dozen wayward Marines.

A special boat arrived to transport the latecomers. On boarding the *Feland* Tullio grabbed his arm. "Where the hell have you been? We've been sweating you out all night." He was angry but relieved. "Damn it, Mark, you didn't have a pass. You were AWOL."

Mark said nothing, only cursed himself for getting into such unnecessary trouble.

Tullio escorted him and the six other battalion latecomers to a cabin. "The sergeant major will see you when he has time," said Rossi. An hour passed. The long wait was unnerving to everyone. Would they be put in the brig on bread and water or busted and fined? They discussed the possibilities. The first alternative would be disastrous since they'd be in bad shape for a battle. Someone thought they'd just get a blasting from the sergeant major and then a lecture from Billy J. But Mark knew Sullivan was too smart for this. If so, half the battalion would go AWOL when they loaded up for the next battle.

At last the door opened and the sergeant major motioned them to come in. He surveyed them with gimlet eyes, then read them off loudly and blasphemously, calling them the foulest names he had learned in twenty years of service. "Well," he finally said, "the major will see you now. You wait in the passageway." Finally they were brought to Sullivan's cabin. One man was told to enter. He left five minutes later, face pale. "Work in the engine room," he muttered and hurried off. Mark was the last to enter. He stood at attention.

"Corporal McGlynn," he said, "Reporting as ordered, sir."

Billy J. looked with disgust from behind a little desk. "I'm disappointed in you," he said quietly. Mark quavered at the major's icy words. "What are you? A coward? Are you afraid?"

"I wasn't going to miss the ship," protested Mark. "I just wanted to get ashore a last time."

"You didn't even have a pass. What would happen if the whole damn battalion did that?"

"I don't know."

"They're Marines. That's why they don't. And you have the gall to wear our uniform. I once had hopes for you. But I don't think you really are a Marine." Sullivan gave him a scathing look. "Well, we'll just put you ashore and let you stay back with the rear troops. I think I can get you a job with one of those service battalions."

Mark was stricken. "You couldn't do that!"

"I damn well could. You have been acting like a crybaby the past

233

month. Do you think I want to go into a battle with a crybaby at my side?"

Mark tried to apologize.

"It was bad enough going out tonight without a pass. But to come back late was unforgivable." He shook his head. "You don't have to tell me what you were doing tonight. You were back with—what's her name —weren't you?"

"Yes, sir. I felt I had the right. You people wouldn't let me marry her and I felt the least I could do was see her till the last minute and—"

Sullivan cut him off curtly. "You took an oath to be a Marine and knew we expected obedience. But what concerns me most, McGlynn, is that I had selected you to the closest position of trust as my runner. And you have betrayed that trust."

"Sir, it had nothing to do with that," protested Mark.

"What kind of crap is 'it had nothing to do with that'? You had your orders, didn't you? Your obligation is to the United States Marine Corps and your fellow Marines." He made a notation. "I must have absolute faith in my runner. I must know he'll be where I expect him to be when he's supposed to be there. My life depends on it." His eyes seemed to drill into Mark. "You have shaken my faith in you, McGlynn. Get out of here."

"Yes, sir." Mark did a smart about-face and left in despair.

The ships, traveling at a lively pace for transports, disappeared. Those aboard who believed the rumor that they were merely going back to Hawke Bay for maneuvers realized by the following dawn that they were wrong. And it became obvious they were bound for battle when cruisers and destroyers pulled up over the horizon. But even Billy J. did not know their destination, and the zigzag course, meant to confuse the enemy, made it impossible to guess what the target would be.

CHAPTER FIFTEEN

1.

At sea. November 1943.

By the end of the second day after leaving New Zealand for battle, the excitement of the men of 1/6 had turned into boredom. There was little to do but exercise topside, and when forced to return to quarters grown increasingly foul, they could only play poker, read, write letters, or clean equipment already spotless. But their life would have been considered paradise by Mark and his six fellow inmates in the engine room. They had been ordered to take off their uniforms and select ragtag discarded sailor clothing from the Lucky Bag. Their hair had been clipped to the bone "for sanitary reasons" as if they were entering boot camp. During the times they were allowed to leave the sweltering engine room—half an hour in the morning and half an hour in the afternoon as well as for all mess formations—their buddies ragged them mercilessly with cries of "Smart-ass yardbirds!"

Mark could endure the hard work below but these occasions were humiliating and, figuring that Billy J. had done this primarily to teach them a lesson, he was determined to become the best damned runner Billy J. ever had even if he now hated the major's guts. On the fourth day he chanced to meet him on deck. He had learned a lot down below, said Mark, and he would be glad to get back to real work.

Sullivan surveyed him coolly. "I haven't yet decided whether I want you back, McGlynn, or if I should find someone I can trust more than you. The sergeant major will tell you what's going to happen to you."

Mark was crushed. He returned to the engine room realizing how bleak life would be if he had to return to the routine of a snuffy. He might even get sent back to the States—a chilling prospect.

The next night the old hands aboard the *Feland* could smell land. In the morning those on deck could make out a large, lush island. This was Efate in the New Hebrides. They passed a harbor crowded with a formidable congeries of gray warships—destroyers, cruisers, and battleships down from Pearl Harbor. The *Maryland*, its huge sixteen-inch guns polished for battle, steamed toward the newcomers who were heading for Mele Bay. "Old Mary" would be the flag and command ship for the battle.

During the next six days the combat teams were busy and practice landings were made on the hot beaches, but the men in the engine room did little but sneak topside as often as possible to gather the latest scuttlebutt. On the afternoon of November 12 Mark and his fellow outcasts were ordered to report to the sergeant major's cabin. "We're sailing at 0600," he said, and told them to get back in their uniforms. While Mark was dressing, Tullio Rossi greeted him warmly. "The major wants to see you."

"Am I staying in Headquarters Company?" he asked uneasily.

"I hope so. Billy J. hasn't said a word about you."

Fearing the worst, Mark knocked at Sullivan's office and was told to enter. "Corporal McGlynn reporting as ordered, sir."

Sullivan looked at him without expression and Mark's heart fell. Then Billy J. said, "Still want to be my runner?"

"Yes, sir!"

"All right. Get out of here. We'll talk later about what you have to do."

"Yes, sir! Thank you, sir!"

Mark found two letters waiting for him. A brief one from his father revealed that Floss and Tad were back in Tokyo and she was going to have a baby, and that Will was still a prisoner in Luzon. The second letter, from Maggie, was long and chatty; she told about her big story on Midway (which appalled Mark), and her articles about the nisei in Hawaii (which pleased him). He had hoped to hear from Hinemoa even though he knew it would have taken a miracle for a letter from New Zealand to get to Efate so quickly.

Next morning the transports began moving out of Mele Bay. From adjoining Savannah Harbor came the *Maryland* and two other old battleships, a heavy cruiser, three light cruisers, nine destroyers, two tiny minesweepers and a strange ship, a landing ship dock, which carried fourteen General Sherman medium tanks and a company from the V Amphibious Corps.

Mark watched in awe as the transports and warships formed up off Efate. Even before the impressive volcanic peaks of the island disappeared, dull roars could be heard far off the port beam. The three battleships were firing practice salvos. The exhilarating sounds were accompanied by word that spread by some mysterious means from transport to transport almost simultaneously: their destination was

Wake Island. They were going to avenge the Marines that had put up such a gallant fight in the early days of the war! Each battalion hoped it would have the honor of landing first. The next day these high hopes were dashed by a message from the *Maryland*. "Give all hands the general picture of the projected operation and further details to all who should have this in execution of duties." And so on every transport it was revealed that their target was a long, skinny little island called Betio on an unknown atoll called Tarawa. There was further disappointment for the men of 1/6. They would not make the initial landing, only be in reserve. Billy J. hid his own disappointment. "You'll get all the action you want," he assured them.

The landing would come in six days and those battalions making the initial landing lorded it over those which were in reserve. The navy personnel on the transports could not understand the glee of those who had been selected to do the hardest fighting, or that their only fear was that the naval bombardment and bombings would kill too many Japs before they got there.

As the convoy grew closer to Tarawa, Mark, realizing he had acted like an arrogant ass, became so diligent and efficient that Tullio nick-named him Gunga Din. The hours passed slowly for the troops since there was little to do and the heat belowdecks, as they neared the equator, was stifling. What little there was to read was passed around, except for those books Mark had brought along. He had bought second-hand volumes of Trollope and Shakespeare in New Zealand but no one else was interested in reading the Bard's plays or dumb stories about ministers. Mark had already read *Barchester Towers* and was presently engrossed in Prince Hal's misadventures, which reminded him some-what of his own inanities.

At a press conference on the flagship, the commander of the 2nd Division, General Julian Smith, was listening impatiently as a naval commander announced that he would bring his ships a mere 1,000 yards from the beach for saturation gunfire. His armor, he said, would make him invulnerable. Another ship's commander boasted that his armor was even better and he'd get in even closer. Smith could take no more. He stood up. "Gentlemen, when the Marines meet the enemy at bayonet point, the only armor a Marine will have is his khaki shirt."

On D-Day minus three, cruisers of the Fifth Fleet began bombarding Betio. The following day conflicting reports came from the Air Force bombers: first that they were receiving no antiaircraft fire, then that they were. Some experts belowdecks in the transports held that Betio

237

would be another Kiska and all they'd find there would be a single dog. Then came the chilling word that the reef over which they would have to attack had been barricaded by coral boulders linked by steel cables.

By the afternoon before D-Day they had come three thousand miles from Wellington and were just about to cross the equator. In a few hours they would reach their destination. Conditions in the hold of the *Feland* had become far worse than anything Mark had encountered on the road. It was, he thought, like living in a city dump with fresh garbage arriving every few hours. The temperature was never below 100 degrees; the air was foul; and to add to the misery, this group of animals would think up the worst ways to make hell even more miserable, such as farting in the dark. In addition, you had to take a bath in your helmet, and share a sleeping space with almost no room between you and the man above or below or to your right or left.

By now the enlisted men were a pack of wild dogs ready to chew their way into hell. Even a beach loaded with Japs would be more welcome than another day in the hold. Perhaps, concluded Mark, some smart sadist had figured all this out.

Late in the afternoon Big Joe held a final Mass on deck.

Mark accompanied Billy J. He was welcome; many wouldn't be Catholics. Mark was moved by the simple ceremony and then imagined how aghast his father would be to know he had attended such superstitious rites.

After dark the men wrote their last letters home. "Dear Mom: In a few hours we'll be landing on a little island you never heard of . . ." Mark wrote to Hinemoa, Maggie, and his father; then checked his field marching pack: a poncho, blanket, his razor-sharp Ka-Bar (short for "Killed a B'ar") knife, a change of underwear and sox. Oh, yes, and bullets, plenty of those. Everything else, like his precious novels, were to be left behind as useless in battle. There was one exception. He did keep a slender, tattered copy of Shakespeare's *Henry V*.

2.

At dawn on November 20 those not yet awake on the *Feland* were wakened by earsplitting crashes as the Fifth Fleet methodically began leveling the palm and coconut trees of Betio. Mark was already topside with Moon Mullins watching the bombardment pockmark the island's surface. It was awesome to see flat little Betio turn into one huge fire.

"Poor bastards," said Moon. "It must be hell over there."

On nearby transports they could see Marines dropping into Higgins boats. "There won't be anyone alive on that island by the time they hit the beaches," said Mark.

Moon shook his head. "Can't you see those big fourteen- and sixteen-inch shells ricocheting off the coral? Those battle wagons are in too close. They should have moved farther out for a higher trajectory. Then they'd lob directly down and do real damage." He clucked like a mother hen. "It's going to be another damn screwup."

Major Sullivan joined them. Mark could see he too was concerned despite the volume of shells being poured into the island. Where in hell was the Army Air Force? They were supposed to be covering the island with bombs that would explode on contact and spray deadly shrapnel. Nor were dive bombers and strafing planes from the carriers doing much good since the island by now was completely shrouded by smoke. And the wind from the southeast was blowing smoke over the shore defenses and the reef.

It was obvious that the first wave of Marines was being clobbered with heavy enemy fire. There were still a lot of live Japs. But the onlookers could only guess what was happening beyond that pall of swirling smoke. As the hours went on there was an eerie feeling aboard *Feland*. When would they go in? First tangible evidence of the tragic cost came with returning amtracs. Through his glasses Sullivan could see casualties hauled up to their transports on stretchers. Such sights only briefly dampened the enthusiasm of 1/6; then some of the enlisted men began boasting that it was going to take the 6th Marines as usual to clean up! And the junior officers were making bets on who would get the first Jap. These people, Mark noted, hadn't been at Guadalcanal.

He couldn't sleep that night from fear of what would happen the next day when they would probably be sent into that hellhole. At dawn he again checked all of Billy J.'s equipment and his own. He only picked at breakfast and lunch. Then came a message for Sullivan to report to the regimental commander's ship, a troop transport. He, Mark, and the staff made the trip in an LCVP, a regular landing craft with a ramp. The cargo net hanging over the side of the troop transport was hooked fore and aft and pulled into the landing craft. After six Marines held out the net at an angle, Billy J. started up. Mark couldn't help thinking of the last trip up a cargo net at the 'Canal. But this time Sullivan was going up like a monkey.

"Follow me, Major," said a waiting Marine orderly on deck and led Sullivan to the commander's cabin. Mark waited outside. He unslung his rifle, took off his helmet, and stood ready to snap to attention in case an officer appeared.

Inside, Sullivan was told that 1/6 would land next day on the narrow neck at the northeast point of Betio. Just as Sullivan and Mark were descending the net, they were called back. Good news had just been received that Major Mike Ryan had secured about a hundred yards inland on the west section of the beach. Therefore 1/6 would embark in a few hours for Green Beach on the western end of the island.

It was midafternoon by the time 1/6 began loading into landing craft, each of which towed six empty rubber boats. As Mark, sitting next to Billy J., saw the dim outline of Betio through the haze, his heart beat faster. He hoped he wouldn't throw up. But there was no fire. At a coral reef a thousand yards from shore the men scrambled into the rubber boats, cast off, and began paddling toward land. The sea was calm but there was a swell. The boats seemed to stretch from horizon to horizon. "God," Sullivan muttered to Mark, "how am I ever going to get control of these guys again?" Over the radio he kept calling each of his company commanders for progress reports. So far no one had hit any of the mines planted along the reef. Mark had already seen two mines slowly pass underneath, almost grazing the bottom of their boat.

Still no fire came from the beach, and Mark wondered if the Japs were just waiting until they were closer. On their left came an explosion. One of their two supply amtracs flipped over. Six men were killed.

Nearby, the boat carrying Moon Mullins and Tullio Rossi became snagged by sharp coral and sank. Tullio disappeared from sight but Moon pulled him up and put him on his shoulders. He handed the top sergeant a box of cigars and a flask of whiskey. "Guard these with your life," said Moon and, chin just above the water, slowly started for shore.

Now Mark could hear small-arms fire from the island. "Major Ryan's people must be laying down covering fire to protect us," said Sullivan. Daylight turned quickly to dusk as they scrambled onto the beach. Ryan was sitting there to welcome them. As he was starting to fill in Sullivan, the radio operator said, "Sir, Colonel Shoup wants to talk to you." Sullivan took the speaker. "Bill, this is Shoup. You know I'm in command here?"

"Yes, sir."

"Now here's the plan." The next morning 1/6 was to pass through Ryan and head up the south side of the island along the right side of the airstrip. "You'll be attacking up to Kyle." His battalion, the first of the 2nd Marines, was pinned down halfway up the airstrip between the runway and the beach.

Sullivan summoned his company commanders and ordered everyone to stay low since stray rounds were coming overhead. While Mark held a poncho over him, he studied a map in the glow of a flashlight. Then he beckoned Major Ryan. "Mike, those two tanks of yours would come in handy tomorrow."

Ryan grunted.

"You probably won't need them." Ryan was noncommittal, for these tanks had already saved his bacon. Sullivan argued so persuasively that Ryan finally agreed, but he made the other solemnly promise—as one good Irish Catholic to another—that Sullivan would return them after the attack.

Mark tried to dig foxholes for himself and the major but for every shovelful of sand he took out, another slid back in. Finally he found a better place higher up on the beach and managed to dig shallow holes. Just after midnight Mark heard the approaching rumble of planes. "Japs!" shouted someone and Mark huddled as deeply as he could. There was a whistle of a falling bomb and a dull explosion several hundred yards away. There had been a few bombs dropped on them at Guadalcanal but this was the first real air raid the battalion had experienced. There was nothing to do but pray. Bombs fell closer and there were cries from those hit.

But no one was killed and 1/6 was practically at full strength when it jumped off at first light. Since there was only a narrow space between the edge of the airstrip and the beach, it was an attack in a column of companies with the two tanks leading the way. These vehicles were followed by B Company in a column of platoons. The going was painfully slow since every ten yards or so they were held up by a pillbox or dugout made out of bamboo logs covered with sand and concrete. These had to be blasted out with satchel charges and then cleared with flamethrowers. Sullivan kept pressing those in the lead to move faster and let succeeding units clean out what had been missed. Within an hour the pace quickened and by noon they had reached the beleaguered men of the 2nd Regiment. Sullivan's men had come six hundred yards through the heaviest fortifications of the island but they kept moving. So far there had been few casualties, but one made Billy J.

clench his teeth and say a silent prayer. The commander of B Company was paralyzed from a shot in the neck. Sullivan ordered A Company to pass through B and lead the attack. The men were exhausted and the heat from the sun and burning dugouts was almost unbearable. The sheer effort to dash from one trench or revetment to the next became such that the men slowed down, indifferent to their own peril. And the toll mounted.

Sullivan himself was moving up as far front as possible with Mark at his side. They ran in a crouch from one shell hole to the next. The space between lagoon and airfield widened and the pace slowed. Reports of heavier casualties up ahead came in but Shoup, the regimental commander, ordered the attack to continue. He also said, "I think you can get your two tanks across the airfield, Bill. Send 'em over."

"I can't do that."

"Why the hell not?"

"I promised Mike I'd return them to him."

"Tough shit."

"Yes, sir," said Billy J. and regretfully ordered the tanks to take off. Then he told Mark to fetch the Top, who was just ahead. Mark loped forward. Tullio and two men were walking upright, as if on parade, toward a bunker. He saw Tullio casually lob a grenade into the machine-gun aperture and head for a second bunker made of coconut logs and sandbags. The ground was covered with Japanese bodies and gear: rifles, helmets, small bundles of clothing. Mark felt sick. Would one of these corpses turn out to be an old friend?

As he approached, still in a crouch, Tullio said, "No sweat," and strolled up to the second bunker. As he started to pull the pin of a grenade, machine-gun bullets began spitting at them. Grenades came raining out of the bunker. A round from a knee mortar exploded, ripping off the head of young Jenks next to Tullio. Head and helmet rolled like a bowling ball down the alley. Tullio dived into the third bunker followed by Mark who landed on top of him. Both were dazed. They were in a small room some twelve feet wide and six feet deep. Light came from the entrance and a shell hole made by the bombardment. Mark's hands were wet and it took only a moment to realize this wasn't water but a mixture of blood and urine. Tullio was spitting it out. Both could hear strange mumblings, and as their eyes became adjusted they could see they had leaped into a roomful of dead and wounded Japanese.

The survivors were so groggy they didn't realize the newcomers were the enemy. Tullio signaled Mark to keep quiet and both slowly, cautiously crept out. Mark was stunned. His dungarees were covered with water, blood, and urine. Tullio was in a worse state. He kept spitting to get the taste out of his mouth. The smell and sight of his dungarees was nauseating and although his uniform soon dried in the equatorial sun it felt as if it had been starched.

After cleaning his hands with sand, Mark reported to the major that Tullio was recovering from a bad shock. At the Headquarters Company command post, five Japanese prisoners were approaching, hands in the air.

"What the hell do you expect me to do with them?" exploded Tullio when two of his Marines turned them in. The chances of getting them back to the ship before dark were slight. It wasn't his problem and he didn't give a damn what happened to them.

Tullio said none of this but a buck sergeant in the mortar platoon got the message and raised his rifle. He was about to fire when Captain Mullins came out of a foxhole. Moon's face was red. "It's against the Geneva Convention to kill these prisoners!" he said. The buck sergeant thought it was just one of Moon's jokes and again raised his rifle. Moon pushed it down. No one had ever seen him so serious before. He really meant what he said.

"Okay, Moon," said the sergeant. "But what the hell shall we do with the bastards?"

Moon indicated four men. "You, you, you and you—take them to the beach on the double. And if I hear any firing on the way I'll have all your asses."

The men hustled the prisoners away. This was a Moon the men had never seen before but none of them held it against him. As for Tullio, he was deeply impressed. All those Japs would have been dead because of his own stupid reaction if Moon hadn't brought them all to their senses.

It was getting dark and the battalion, which had advanced sixteen hundred yards since morning to reach the end of the airfield, was ordered by Regiment to dig in for the night. The lines of 1/6 were stretched out with C Company between the lagoon and the north side of the runway. On the left A Company was tied into B Company. Now the 1st Battalion alone manned the front lines. Sullivan told Moon to set up their command post behind B Company with his headquarters and a mortar platoon. They were only fifty yards behind the front lines.

The companies began feeding their men for the first time since early morning. Ammunition was issued but the water they had brought from

New Zealand in five-gallon cans had become unpalatable because the heat in the ships' holds had dissolved some of the cans' enamel lining. Consequently it could only be used to fill the water jackets of the water-cooled machine guns. The only water for drinking was in the two canteens each man had filled before leaving the transport. Yet Mark recalled seeing, during the day's attack, several Marines give wounded buddies the last drops of their precious water.

Final protective lines were set up for the night defense with their interlacing stream of .30 caliber and tracer bullets a foot above the ground making it seemingly impossible for the enemy to infiltrate. The flamethrowers were placed near each gun to protect the gunner from the possible breakthrough of a wild Japanese banzai attack. Psychologically it also kept the gunner on his assigned final protective line. By dark the guns were sited, foxholes dug, and the men on the ready.

There was no sound. No animal, bird, or human noises. Then came the distant crack of a rifle, followed by a machine-gun burst. Again silence settled over the little island.

In the battalion C.P. Mark was straining to hear any furtive noises ahead. Again came the lone crack of a rifle and silence. Tullio slipped in beside him.

"For Christ's sake! Give me some warning."

Tullio's voice was soothing. "Don't start shooting your friends." He wanted to know if Billy J. had had any orders for the night and the next morning.

"The 3rd Battalion has just landed and will pass through us early, about 0700, and sweep out the rest of the island," whispered Mark. "You okay?"

"I still stink." He had washed his stained dungarees as best he could. "I know I stink but I can't smell anything. Can't taste anything." A moment later he said, "I'm going back to that bunker after we secure the island."

"What for?"

"To see if it was as bad as I thought it was."

Sullivan himself was almost exhilarated. He was proud of his men. They had come more than a thousand yards through a complicated system of defenses and had suffered relatively few casualties. He felt confident they could hold back any counterattack during the night. He wanted to talk and relived the day with such enthusiasm that Mark, caught up in the exuberance of victory, almost forgot the harrowing experience inside the bunker. There were closer bursts of fire. Sullivan called the commanders of A and B companies. Both were being probed by the enemy. Both were confident they were "cocked and ready." Sullivan told them not to fire their automatic weapons until the actual attack began. He instructed the destroyer off his right flank to bring in illuminating gunfire and high explosives five hundred yards in front of A and B. Then he registered the line of supporting artillery, .75 mm. pack howitzers, the only artillery they were able to bring ashore. He called for more illumination and soon Mark, peering over the edge of the hole, could see, as bright as day, palm stumps, shattered coconut log emplacements. Several figures creeping toward him were caught in the light and scurried away.

"They were just looking," said Sullivan. "Trying to find exactly where our front lines are. They're going to hit us." Something nagged him. He had no reserve. During the day he had been ordered to send C Company across the airfield. He told Mark to fetch the exec and operations officers; he himself called for Moon Mullins and the mortar platoon commander. Once they were assembled he ordered them to form a composite reserve consisting of the mortar platoon ammunition carriers and those headquarters people who could be spared: clerks, typists, runners, communicators, cooks, and bakers.

"Fix bayonets," Sullivan quietly told this group. "I don't know when I'll use you, but if they attack and they split our lines, your job is to go in and eject them." Mark had expected that some of these odds and sods would be scared out of their wits, but all, including the perpetual complainers, had been inspired by the major's few words. A pep talk would only have scared them. Billy J. just assumed they would do their duty.

Several hours passed. Another illumination shell disclosed several more Japanese observers. Bursts of small-arms fire dispersed them. About 3 A.M. Sullivan said, "I think they'll be coming pretty soon." Within ten minutes the silence was broken by chanting that terrified Mark. "It's a banzai!" said Billy J. and ordered the destroyer to start lobbing in five-inch shells a hundred and fifty yards beyond the front lines. "And keep up the flares."

In the light Mark could see figures approaching. Sullivan ordered the artillery moved back to a hundred yards. The Japanese kept coming and Mark could hear the Japanese shouting, "Marine, you die!" and "Japanese drink Marine blood!"

The machine guns opened up all at once. Interlacing bands of tracer ammunition, like so many intertwining fingers of light, showed where the .30 caliber heavy machine guns were spitting out almost four hundred rounds a minute in short bursts. Screams pierced the air mingled with the shouts of the Marines.

"Corpsman, here!"

"More ammo! More ammo!"

"Christ! look at them fall!"

"Yeah, but the dumb bastards keep coming!"

The pungent odor of gunpowder drifted waist high like a misty ground fog in the illumination.

It looked as if the enemy was breaking through at the junction of A and B Companies. "They're all through us!" reported B. "I can't stop them."

"You will stop them," said Sullivan. "That's an order."

"I told you I can't stop them! I need reinforcements!"

"I told you, and I repeat, You will stop 'em *and that's an order*. Do you understand?"

"Yes, sir."

Now the commander of A Company, Captain Murphy, was on the line. "They're in our lines, Major," he said as if announcing the arrival of welcome guests.

"Are you holding them?"

"We'll hold," he said. "I think they've split us from B Company. It looks to me as if they're going through a gap down the middle."

In spite of having to attack through a rain of high explosives, the Japanese kept coming.

Sullivan turned to Moon Mullins, explained the situation and ordered him to move out with his hastily formed reserve company. Moon scuttled away to give his orders. However, some of the Japanese now were approaching the battalion command post. One, an officer shouting and brandishing a sword, was about to leap into their hole. Mark speared him with his bayonet. He jerked the blade loose and scrambled out of the command post.

"Get the hell back here!" shouted Billy J., unaware that another Japanese was about to fire his rifle at him. Mark fired first and the Japanese tumbled down. A third Japanese fired close range at Mark, knocking his helmet awry. His head buzzing, Mark tried to return the fire but his rifle jammed. Not having time to use his bayonet, he brought the butt of his rifle up savagely into the attacker's face.

Sullivan was shouting for him to get back into the foxhole since bullets were flying around. But he stood erect, dazed. "McGlynn, get your ass in this hole! Now!"

Mark jumped into the foxhole. "I got him!" he said. "I killed a damned Jap!"

A man from the rear dove in, one hand grasping a gallon can.

"What are you doing here?" asked Sullivan. "What do you want?"

"Major, the chief engineer sent this to you."

"The engineer. What the hell is it?"

"Alcohol, sir."

"All right, son," said the major. "Thank you. And give our thanks to the chief engineer. Now you turn around and get the hell out of here. Understand?"

"Yes, sir!" he said and gratefully crawled off.

At first light Sullivan shook Mark. "Let's take a look. Both A and B sent out patrols this morning so I told them I was coming up."

Feeling gutted, Mark clumsily climbed out of the large foxhole. The exultation of battle had been succeeded by a surge of conscience. There were a dozen dead Japanese nearby. He and Sullivan started toward B Company. Here the ground was littered with bodies, most of them Japanese. Men were stirring out of their foxholes. Sullivan patted the head of a short youngster whose face was filthy. "Son, you people made me proud last night."

The boy grinned. "You told us we had to hold, sir. And by God, we held."

Ahead were two dead Marines sprawled out as if groping for two dead Japanese. There were tears in Sullivan's eyes but he kept his voice steady.

At the next squad Sullivan patted everyone on the shoulder. "Thanks," he said.

"We did it, Major," said a corporal cockily.

One of those who had done it was staring up at them with dead eyes. Billy J. turned and wiped away his tears. Then he spotted a man who had been up at office hours half a dozen times. "Shilstone, I've been trying to get rid of you ever since we left Elliott. And here you are."

Shilstone laughed. "I'm too tough, Major."

After they went down Company A's lines, Sullivan said, "Murph, give me a squad. I want to walk out in front of the lines."

"Can I go with you?" he asked eagerly.

"Sure."

The squad was delighted to go out front too. Everyone wanted to see how close the shells had come in last night. Mark noticed the holes were not big since the shells were antipersonnel. Japanese bodies were riddled with shrapnel; heads and limbs were blown off.

Murphy was counting. "I count two hundred Japs killed in our lines, Major. But look, you can see where the artillery started and how close they came to our lines. Last night it sounded like it was on top of us."

"My orders," said Sullivan with a grin. "It saved your hat and ass, friend."

"Yeah!" Murphy said. "But it was my hat and my ass, not yours. Next time be more concerned about my ass at least."

After progressing about seventy-five yards in front of the lines they stopped.

"God," muttered someone, "look at that mess!" The area worked over by artillery and naval gunfire was thick with bodies, many of which had literally been shredded.

"Hard to be sure," Murphy said calmly shading his eyes with his hand and looking around, "but I'd guess an additional hundred and twenty-five Japs here who never reached our line. Amazing so many did!"

There was no sign of life. No sniper fire. Mark could see across the airfield to the bay on the other side of the island. All was quiet. An hour later the 3rd Battalion, led by two sturdy tanks, passed through to clean out the Japanese dug in at the far end of the island. The battle was over for 1/6. Overnight they had lost fifty-five killed and one hundred and forty-four wounded. Sullivan and Mark visited with every wounded man before he was evacuated by amtrac. One was Moon Mullins, who had taken a bullet in the shoulder. As usual he was in high spirits and his only request was for someone to fetch his beloved sweet potato out of his pack.

Clean water from the transports was brought up and the battalion started shaving and washing their teeth. Then they were fed again, and by this time the men were building up their war stories, out-lying one another. The walking wounded were proud of their bandages and refused to take them off even when they became filthy.

Billy J. established a new command post in a large Japanese tank trap and told Mark to get some rest. But the latter couldn't sleep in the daylight and looked for some solace in Shakespeare. He came upon a passage in *Henry V* that struck home. "Major," he said, "listen to this." And he read:

> We few, we happy few, we band of brothers:
> For he today that sheds his blood with me

Shall be my brother; be he ne'er so vile,
This day shall gentle his condition.

Sullivan was impressed. "He was writing about the Marines."

At dusk Tullio arrived with sad news. Just as Moon's litter was being carried to the amtrac for evacuation it came under sniper fire. Moon had been hit in the head and was either dead or dying. Within minutes there was a pall throughout the battalion. What irked the men was that they couldn't get out and shoot up some more Japs in revenge.

3.

In the morning Mark was overwhelmed by the ghastly stink of death. It permeated everything—his dungarees, his food, his comrades. Everything and everyone smelled of death. He had noticed the smell before but had been so stunned and exhausted it was only a passing unpleasantness. Now it was appalling. He automatically accomplished his duties. He saw that the major had water for washing; he got his food, cleaned his equipment, and stood by for any orders.

Billy J. noticed he was troubled and told him to find Major Bemis in charge of division logistics. He was someplace on the beach supervising the off-loading of supplies to those Marines who had not been evacuated or sent to clean out other islands of the atoll. "Give him this note. We need some grapefruit juice for the alcohol." He put a hand on Mark's shoulder. "I was thinking about that quotation from Shakespeare—the band of brothers. When you get back, write it out for me. No rush, grabass around awhile down on the beach."

Mark set off down the airfield. It was only eight and the sun was already brutal. The beach to his left was lined with rows of land mines and double fences of barbed wire. He climbed the remains of a large bunker. From the top he could see Betio from one end to the other. All that remained were stripped coconut trees standing like skeletal sentinels over a vast charnel house. In the distance a burial detail was flinging bodies into a large mass grave.

Straight ahead he could see where 1/6 had come, yard by yard, blasting a path of death. Burial parties had not yet completely cleared this area and there were bodies in and around every pillbox. There was a big Marine, crouching forward, rifle in hand—charging in death. Mark jumped down and over another bunker. Was this the one he and Tullio had dived into? He passed it quickly, almost stumbling over a body so mangled he couldn't tell if it was a Marine or a Jap. Then he saw laced leggings around its remaining leg. It was a Marine. A live Marine was standing staring down at the body from a pile of rubble. His face was gaunt. "He didn't make it," he said. "I did."

Mark turned toward the north shore and soon could see the lagoon where so many comrades had died the first day. He climbed the sea wall and was horrified to find several bobbing bodies. They were bloated balloons. Why the hell hadn't they been picked up? It was indecent.

It took only a few minutes to locate Major Bemis who read the note and grinned. "Your boss wants me to liberate a case of grapefruit juice." It was a bulky load and Mark's face was streaming with sweat by the time he was back on the airstrip. Near the lagoon men were lying around in small solemn groups. This morning there was none of the bravado seen after the banzai attack. He sat down with several friends from Company B. They were talking of buddies who had died, those who were missing.

"Well, they got most of what's left of your old squad, Mark," someone remarked. "I saw Tuffy laying over his gun, hand still on the trigger, all rounds gone; the Chief was face down next to him and Tex Boyle was laying on his back with most of his face gone. Looked like one Jap grenade got all of them."

"How about Peewee and Pancho?" Mark asked. God, he thought, Ski and Goldie on Guadalcanal and now these three.

"Didn't see Peewee," the Marine answered, "but Pancho was walking around with a silly grin on his face." Then, almost in whispers, they began talking of Moon. There never would be another officer like old Moon. It was, thought Mark, like a wake. They all shared the common tragedy.

He found Billy J. sitting under a tent fly attached to bamboo stumps. He was being interviewed by three reporters who had just landed. Unlike *Time-Life* correspondent Bob Sherrod, who had come in on the first day, they had seen no action and were prodding Billy J. for some colorful copy. Welcoming the distraction, Sullivan got up to mix cocktails with the grapefruit juice. Mark asked if it was all right to go back to Dog Company and see the fellows.

"Sure. Just be back before dark," he said and asked the reporters if they'd like some gin and grapefruit juice.

They were having lunch at D Company—a treat, since supplemental rations had just been brought to shore. They too were talking of those who had died. Then Tullio arrived and ordered a burial party. He, Mark, and a dozen others trudged off carrying ponchos. At their former battleground they put bodies in the ponchos and carried them to the battle cemetery that had been started near Division C.P. even before the shooting stopped. Here each Marine was wrapped in his poncho and reverently placed in a shallow grave scooped out of the sand. A simple stake marked the location of the body with one of his two dog tags, the other one staying with the body. Mark could see other burial parties laying enemy bodies in a mass grave, a long tank trap dug by the Japanese.

Returning to the bunker area, Mark and Tullio came upon a young Indian private whose hair was cut like an Apache's. He was pulling out the gold teeth of a Japanese with pliers. He was twisting, yanking, grunting. Mark couldn't believe what he was seeing. Red with fury, Tullio seized him by the throat. Mark and another man pulled Tullio off. "Hell," said the Indian, "he can't feel a thing and won't need teeth where he's going."

Mark and the others assured Tullio that there would be no more dental work. The top sergeant threatened to send the youngster back to the States to be court-martialed, then cooled down and told him to get back to work.

On the next trip Tullio confided to Mark that he was very troubled about just putting the bodies side by side in the sand. "I was taught that the body is sacred and has to be buried in a cemetery that is holy ground and blessed." They carefully laid the body into the sand grave. "I can go to hell for doing this," said Tullio.

"Well, where the hell is Big Joe?" said Mark. "Isn't he supposed to give the last rites and all that?"

"He's on the beach helping them evacuate the wounded. He's been working forty-eight hours without sleep."

On the third trip they came to the trio of bunkers where poor Jenks had had his head blown off. They found his torso but not the head. Correspondent Sherrod was stunned. "What a hell of a way to die!"

"You can't pick a better way," said Tullio. In the blazing sun Tullio scratched with his pocketknife on a mess-gear cover:

> Lt. Frank Jenks
> 1st Lt. U S M C

KIA 21 Nov 43
Tarawa

"These other poor bastards may be buried without a gravestone," he said, "but not Jenks."

A delegation of high-ranking Marine and naval officers strode up to the grave. With their clean-shaven faces and spotless uniforms, they were a striking contrast to the men on the burial squad. They watched as Mark and Tullio placed, as gently as possible, the corpse of Jenks into his grave. Tullio was furious. "Those bastards are ignoring us as if we had leprosy."

A navy captain came over. "Sergeant," he said, "have you searched all those bodies for documents?"

Mark saw his friend clench fists. "No, sir," Tullio said tersely. "Don't ask my men to do that. They're already puking."

The captain's face reddened. He was about to say something, evidently thought better of it and strode off.

"We're a raggedy-ass group but the least they could do is acknowledge us," said Tullio. "I think I'll go over and tell the bastards what I think of them," he said with mounting anger as Mark held his arm. "These poor devils we're burying are paying the price for the brass's errors."

The officers were now starting toward the bunkers. "Let's plant a few booby traps in the bunkers," said Mark. "That'll scare the piss out of them."

They went back for another body, and near a gun emplacement saw an emaciated dog wandering drunkenly. Mark whistled and Tullio called out. The dog, trembling, started to run toward them but fell in a heap—dead.

Just before dusk, while Mark was trying to make some sense out of the sad experiences of the day he heard "The Good Ship Venus" from an ocarina. He got to his feet. "Major, do you hear that?"

Billy J. was on his feet.

Only Moon could play like that. There were jubilant shouts. Up to the command post walked Moon with his arm in a sling and a bandage carelessly tied over his forehead like the famous Revolutionary War soldier. He was surrounded by a joyous group of enlisted men pummeling him affectionately.

"Fortunately," he explained above the uproar, "I got hit in the head.

It merely bounced off. The shoulder is a clean hole." He announced that in the hospital he had written a dozen more verses to "The Good Ship Venus" and presented to Billy J. a plaque, supposedly from General Smith, for his great feat of successfully landing 150 rubber boats. It was addressed to "The Admiral of the Condom Navy."

4.

In the morning Tullio took Mark's arm. "Let's look at the fucking bunker. I've got to see if I was dreaming." It was a distasteful idea but Mark could not refuse. All the bodies around the bunker were gone but the stink was even worse. The two stood outside for several minutes. Finally Tullio entered with a flashlight with Mark close behind. The little room was alive with buzzing flies. In the dim light they could see four or five rotting bodies. The smell of blood was stomach-wrenching. Mark rushed out. Tullio was pale. "I had to see for myself," he said. On the way back Tullio confessed he couldn't smell a thing in the bunker. "I don't think I'll ever be able to smell anything again." Mark didn't know how to console him. "It has its advantages," said Tullio and fell silent.

The next week dragged on. There were more burial details, endless cruising back and forth from island to ships, loading and unloading. Mark at last found time to think of home and Hinemoa. He had deliberately kept both from his thoughts during the battle and the terrible days of aftermath. Now he felt free to write letters to her and Maggie, and notes to his father. He told them of the battle but not the things that civilians should not know of. How could they possibly understand the bunker or the burials? It was easy to write of Moon's triumphant resurrection and the battle for souvenirs that was now raging. He told of the swords and pistols they found, of the Japanese documents and flags and how they were traded for food and liquor. Each company would take inventory of its loot and price it. Then their best agent would be sent to the ships to bargain with naval personnel. Mark had been selected for this duty by Headquarters Company and was excused by Billy J. He would go over in a Higgins boat, returning with large quantities of money and good food.

At last orders came to leave and by December 4 the battalion was loaded onto an old Pacific liner. It was large, clean, and quite comfortable. Most wonderful of all there was no stink below. On the deck as they started off Mark imagined he could still smell Betio. At last the little island dropped from sight as if swallowed by the sea. But the stench remained and Mark guessed it must be his own dungarees, which he had already washed a dozen times. Or perhaps the stink would always remain with him. Even so he was luckier than Tullio, who had been robbed of one of his senses.

Mark prayed they were heading back for New Zealand and Hinemoa. But by evening word came that they were going to the big island of Hawaii. There they would train for their next operation. What would that be? Another little unknown flat island? He hoped there would at least be green mountains and some respite from the damnable sun. He wrote another letter to Hinemoa. The 1/6 was not returning to New Zealand, he said, but his heart was there. He hoped she was making progress at secretarial school.

CHAPTER SIXTEEN

1.

Camp Cabanatuan. February 1943.

The morning after Popov's night visit, Will was cut down from the pole. He wondered why he had been released ahead of schedule and found out as soon as he was escorted back to his barracks. Some 250 officers were being shipped to a special camp at Davao in the most southern of the main Philippine Islands, Mindanao, and Will was on the list. Unfortunately his two best friends, Bliss and Wilkins, were not.

A week later Will's group was marched to the town of Cabanatuan. By this time he had been stuffed with extra rations by his friends and was in relatively good condition. The prisoners reached Cabanatuan before the sun was oppressive and spirits ran high as they were loaded into a freight train. This time the cars were not too crowded and guards left the doors open. The train stopped at the next station and Will could hear chattering voices. He peered out at women and children holding up pieces of fried chicken, bananas, and rice balls.

Will got a piece of chicken and a banana. He tore into the chicken. It was delicious. Just as the train began to move slowly he heard singing. They passed a dozen small boys humming "God Bless America." His flesh tingled. The Filipinos had not lost their courage or their feeling for America. He was sure they would help him to escape. Anything was better than going into another hell camp. At each succeeding stop there were growing crowds. Food was showered on them: chico, boiled eggs, and rice wrapped in banana leaves. A few men openly made the V sign before ducking out of sight. The women looked at the Americans with compassion and the children threw kisses. No one in Will's car seemed to notice the heat and the time passed quickly. They were unloaded at the freight yards in Manila before noon and, in the beating sun, were marched down a street toward Bilibid Prison. Thousands lined the sidewalks. The Filipinos were somber and silent but Will could see tears in their soft brown eyes. Many made little secret signs of recognition to him. One woman called softly to Will, "Victory, Joe. *Mabuhay!*" Yes, they would help him if he ever got free.

The prisoners spent three days in the two-storied Spanish-built prison, which was surrounded by a high brick wall. There were no beds or pallets for the newcomers, only a concrete floor. The food was no better than that at Cabanatuan but there was one luxury: for the first time since Bataan, Will had his fill of drinking water and could bathe himself every morning.

He felt almost at full strength by the time his group was marched out of the prison gates. It was a muggy, oppressive day and the sights of destruction were depressing. Many buildings were scarred hulks and entire blocks of the residential sections were mere heaps of ashes. The saddest sight of all was the once beautiful Dewey Boulevard, which ran along the bay. Formerly it had reminded Americans of a prosperous Southern California avenue with its Western hotels, banks, stores, and apartment houses. Now it was a succession of ugly ruins with notable exceptions. The luxurious Manila Hotel was intact as were the Army-Navy Club and the American High Commissioner's home. But these symbols of American and Filipino prosperity and cooperation only made the great gaps of wreckage more tragic.

At the dock area Will lurched up the swaying gangplank of an inter-island steamer and down a vertical ladder to a hold. Here there was enough space for every man to have room to stretch without bumping into anyone. It was hot, but fresh air came through the open hatches. Late in the afternoon Will heard the throb of motors and felt the ship come alive. She was moving out to sea. Someone remarked that pretty soon they should be passing Corregidor. Everybody wanted to take a last look at it. Will started up the ladder. A Japanese soldier on deck poked his rifle menacingly at Will. "Get down there!" Will pretended he didn't understand Japanese. He pantomimed that he had to go to the bathroom and kept climbing up. *"Benjo!"* he said, atrociously pronouncing the Japanese word for toilet.

The guard must have been a recruit for he hesitated. Will repeated *"Benjo!"* twice and the guard reluctantly let him climb on deck. Will looked around. The guard gestured at a crude toilet constructed over the side of the ship. Will sat down. Ahead was a sight of beauty. The sun was setting behind Corregidor. The golden waters of the China Sea shimmered. For a moment he forgot Cabanatuan which lay behind him as well as the unknown hell ahead.

"Hurry up!" shouted the guard banging on the side of the toilet with his rifle butt.

Will stepped onto the deck, took a last look at Corregidor. For a moment its scarred summit seemed to burn with a golden glow, then a dark cloud obscured the sun. Will bowed to the guard and said, "Thank you." The young guard was puzzled. He began to bow in return but stopped himself. He smiled in embarrassment and then halfheartedly jabbed his rifle at Will.

The next few days were pleasant. The guards serving meals were almost civil and the food was good. Each prisoner got a large helping of fresh rice and a canteen of soup. Sometimes it was made of cabbage with tasty slivers of pork. On two grand occasions the prisoners were fed large hunks of corned beef.

They all agreed that no prisoners of the Japanese had ever before been served such banquets. Perhaps Davao would be nothing like O'Donnell and Cabanatuan. Such optimism did not deter Will from his plan to escape. He was more than ever determined to get back to America and tell about the atrocities. On the night of the second corned beef feast, Will overheard a guard remark to a comrade that they were approaching the island of Cebu and would land at Cebu City before dawn. That meant they were already in the Visayan Sea and passing between the islands of Leyte and Cebu. And the latter had a strong guerrilla force headed by a legendary figure, Jim Cushing. He and his two brothers had been miners in Luzon and were supposed to be half Mexican, half Irish.

Will waited until he judged it was about four in the morning, then started up the ladder clad only in a pair of old shorts held together by a single button. The guard at the top was bent over his rifle. Will softly said, *"Benjo."* The guard wakened so startled that he made no protest as Will leisurely headed for the outrigger toilet. He paused as if to enjoy the fresh air and the sharp outline of hills to the west. Farther ahead were mountains. This had to be Cebu. The shore was probably three miles distant. The moon was so bright he almost gave up his plan. He would be an easy target for at least a minute. Suddenly he leaped over the side. It was a fifty-foot drop but he hit the water feet first, quicker than he expected. The fall knocked his breath out and he thought he would never get to the surface. The water was cooler than he had anticipated and he felt as if he had gone through a roof. As he gasped for air he heard the crackle of rifles. Bullets were hitting nearby. Perhaps his struggles had caused a phosphorescent glitter. He took a deep breath, dived, and wormed his way underwater like a porpoise. When he came up, as slowly as possible, he heard shots but they were farther away. He floated motionless. There were several more shots, then silence.

The sea was choppy. He made out the silhouette of hills and struck out in that direction. At first he made good progress despite the rough water. Then he felt resistance. The tide evidently was running against him.

He kept on doggedly and was near the end of his endurance when he saw a palm tree. He had made it! He put down his feet but sank over his head. He broke through the surface and gasped for air. A gentle wave pushed him forward into calm water. With his last reserves he flailed his arms. He touched sand, stumbled onto a beach and fell asleep.

He awakened shivering. His right foot ached. He must have hit it on a reef. He felt the first rays of the rising sun and again slept.

2.

Something poked him in the ribs. He woke startled to see a face staring at him. It was a dark-skinned boy. "Jap patrol!" he whispered and pulled Will toward a large bush. His heart pounded as he watched the boy dart to the beach and brush out traces of footprints, then back up wiping out his own prints.

Will could hear Japanese voices, rough and frightening. They were searching for someone. The boy disappeared just as three soldiers appeared. One shouted, "Look over here! Someone's been here." Will saw them examine the place he had slept and start toward him. As he was about to make a run for it the boy jumped from behind a palm tree, cried out, and dashed inland. The three soldiers gave chase.

The next hour was torture for Will. He couldn't decide what to do. Had the boy been caught? Would the patrol come back? Should he try to go farther inland? But he decided this would be too dangerous in daylight. Suddenly a face appeared and he almost cried out in alarm. Without making the slightest noise the boy was back. He grinned. "Okay, Joe." He said he had led the Japanese into a swamp a mile away and they were having trouble getting out. He motioned Will to follow and they went several hundred yards into deep undergrowth. "Stay

here," he said. "Dark I come back. No sweat, Joe." The boy grinned
again, said his name was Hipolito, and was gone.

The hours passed slowly. It was sweltering and the mosquitoes were
ferocious. At least there were no red ants. He was dying for a drink of
water. It wasn't much better than Cabanatuan except that he was free.
Free! That was a ridiculous concept. Any moment he could be caught
and beaten, put on exhibition, and killed. Then he remembered the
terrible hours on the ant hill and his prayer to die. This was nothing in
comparison. The fact was that he was just scared to death. Now he was
afraid to die. At last came dusk and sudden darkness. There was a slight
rustling followed by a bird whistle. It was Hipolito.

Will stumbled after him in the dark. Finally they came to a grove of
palm trees and Will could make his way easily in the bright moonlight.
Here there was a pleasant, balmy breeze. The scent of flowers was
strong and sweet, then was mingled with the pungent smell of a barrio.
Food was cooking and he heard the lilting laughter of women. They
passed several nipa huts on stilts.

"Here," said the boy and clambered up into the next hut. Inside were
three women—one was old with deep wrinkles. The other two were
young. Will had heard of the good-looking Cebuan women but never
imagined they had such beauty. Their skin was like satin, the dark
coloring exquisite, and their features were delicate. They were both
slender but full-breasted. The girls smiled shyly. "Sisters," said Hipolito.
Will was amazed to learn they were only thirteen and fourteen years
old and that the third woman was not the grandmother but their
mother.

During a meal of fried bananas and rice Hipolito explained that
someone was coming the next night to escort him to a guerrilla camp in
the mountains. It was obvious that the mother was very worried; she
was polite to Will, but she kept eyeing him uneasily. Although Will had
already learned to speak a little Tagalog, the language of the northern
Philippines, he could understand little of the language the family used.
Guessing that the mother wanted to get him out of the house, he offered
to leave. The children would not hear of it and he was given a pallet in
one corner for his bed.

The day passed quickly. The sisters knew little English but taught him
to play several card games. Their brother returned at dusk with a shirt,
trousers, and a worn pair of shoes. The trousers were impossible and the
shirt was so small he couldn't button it. Fortunately Will had small feet
for his size and could squeeze into the shoes.

While they were eating the evening meal there was a pounding on the door. Will was hurriedly hidden in a small closet. He heard a man talk excitedly and then rush away. Hipolito said the Japanese were searching the nearby village of Maslog and were heading toward this barrio. He put Will in the woodbin under the house and piled faggots on top of him. A few minutes later Will could hear heavy footsteps and talking in Japanese about an escaped prisoner. Then the voices faded away and he could breathe again.

After midnight there was a soft knocking at the door. In the darkness Will saw a small figure in a white nun's habit. Hipolito whispered that his guide had come. Will tried to express his thanks but the boy told him to hurry. They shook hands. One of Hipolito's sisters pressed a holy medal into his hand. The other said something in Cebuano and kissed his cheek.

The guide was a small nun. He followed her into the jungle. She made no noise but he kept stumbling. After two hours she finally stopped. "Is safe here," she said in a rasping voice. It sounded as if she had a permanent cold. He wondered what she looked like. All he could tell in the darkness was that she was small. "We sleep," she said curtly and curled up on the ground. He was too keyed up to sleep. The sounds of the night were frightening. There were moans, screeches, scrambling noises. Then came a silence that was equally ominous. Why were all the birds and animals so abruptly quiet? Were Japanese coming? The steady breathing of the nun was reassuring. What wonderful people these Filipinos were, he thought, and fell asleep.

He woke damp with dew and shivering in his worn shorts. Just before the first rays of sun the nun uncurled as if awakened by an alarm clock. Will closed his eyes but he sensed she was staring at him. He pretended to come awake. She was now dressed like any other village woman. She was slight, plain, and very solemn. "Let's move out," she said and briskly headed up a narrow path. After an hour they began to climb but the nun kept such a steady pace that Will asked for a rest. She kept going for another hundred yards until they came to a small, swiftly running stream. She flattened herself, drank sparingly. He did the same. From her small pack she took dried fish and pieces of bread.

They approached a clearing and ahead Will could see a cluster of nipa huts. She headed off into the brush, explaining they had to circle the village to avoid detection. It was sweltering in the underbrush. At last they reached a grove of large teak trees with leaves like elephants' ears. He begged for rest under their welcome shade. She reluctantly agreed and for the first time began to show interest in Will. She eyed him as if he were a horse for sale and seemed to approve. She asked about O'Donnell and Cabanatuan. When she heard of the particularly cruel treatment of Filipinos her dark eyes burned angrily, and she said something in Cebuano that sounded like cursing. He was shocked to hear such sounds from a nun.

He asked if they were going to Cushing's camp. She silently got to her feet and resumed the punishing pace. They had to bypass two more villages and by dusk Will was exhausted. She was fresh and energetically began preparing a meal of mixed edible wild greens, fern tops, sliced green papaya and leftover bread. All this was wrapped in several layers of banana leaves and cooked over embers.

The next morning they started up the steep slopes of a small mountain. The first mile was torture to Will but the nun showed no mercy and pressed upward without pause. Will grumbled, moaned, and finally sat down in protest. The nun ignored him, and when she disappeared he forced himself to his feet and stumbled after her. Finally he caught sight of her where the trail, now denuded of brush and trees, made a horse-shoe curve. He swore angrily. She laughed and kept moving. This made him angrier and he increased his pace. He longed to curse but was too tired to waste his breath. He doggedly climbed upward and soon saw her sitting on a rock. She smiled at him approvingly. "I knew you make it," she said. Five minutes later she got to her feet and started off without consulting him. He was about to berate her when he realized he was no longer tired and his muscles didn't ache. She turned. Her solemn face was now mischievous. "I Socorro. Mean She Who Help." She looked more imp than nun and the liveliness in her face made her attractive.

It was late afternoon by the time they reached an imposing mountain ridge. Will turned back to behold a spectacular view all the way to the dark blue sea where he had jumped ship. She squatted behind a bush. "Rest here till dark," she said. It was too dangerous to walk along the ridge in daylight since there was no cover at all. Ahead the trail narrowed to two feet. On the left was a rock wall and on the right a precipitous drop of several hundred feet. Will paled.

"Better rest," she said and soon was snoring.

What kept Will awake was thought of the narrow mountain trail in darkness. There was no moon when they resumed the trek. Clouds obscured most of the stars. He followed the dim figure of the nun, keeping his eyes glued straight ahead. He loosened a rock which tumbled noisily down the ravine. He looked to the right at black oblivion.

"No look down," said Socorro calmly. "Put hand my shoulder." They edged around a sharp curve with him pressing toward the rock wall. He shuffled.

"Pick up feet," she said.

At last they plunged into a large stand of trees. "Balamban Forest," she said. They would make camp here for the night.

In the morning Will was surprised at the monstrous size of the trees, which rose up like cathedrals. From each tree dropped long vines. With a knife Socorro slashed a particularly bulbous one. Liquid flowed out and they filled their canteens.

They started off in high spirits, soon coming to the end of the forest. The trail narrowed again but by now Will was so confident he strode along without thought of danger. No sooner had she called out to be careful than he slipped over the side. As he rolled down the steep incline he grabbed frantically at stumps of shrubbery. He slid forty feet before he could come to a stop—just at the edge of a cliff. Socorro directed him up to sturdier bushes. At last he heaved himself to safety. His hands were bleeding. Socorro scolded him like a mother as she gently bathed his lacerations.

They pushed on until they could look down upon a peaceful valley replete with coconut and banana trees. Little figures were laboring in a large clearing for corn. Socorro waved and the figures waved back. "Friends."

They climbed again and late in the afternoon came upon a swiftly moving mountain stream. Upstream was a large pool with a sandy bottom. She told him to take a bath; she would go behind a heavy growth of bushes to another pool. Will plunged headfirst into water so icy he came up shouting. As he flailed around, his wet back was warmed by sunlight pouring through an opening of the trees. He could hear Socorro laughing behind the bushes.

He went in and out of the pool a dozen times before Socorro shouted to get dressed. Upon emerging he looked in vain for her.

"I am at your backwards," she said.

He turned to see her peering from a bush.

They headed up an extremely steep trail for half an hour. Will felt full of energy. Even the cuts on his hands no longer bothered him. They scrambled up a huge rock that reminded him of those near the summit of Mount Chocorua in New Hampshire. Close to the top was a cave, a wide shelf with a rock overhang. After they collected brush for beds Will sat on his to enjoy the view across a canyon to dense woods on the other side.

It was a paradise. After dinner Socorro took out two cigars. She stuck one in her mouth and lit it with practiced ease. She offered the other to Will. He said he had given up smoking but she insisted he at least try hers. He took only two puffs and his head swam. She was delighted at the sight and took back the cigar. Only then did it occur to him how odd it was to see a nun smoking.

With the darkness came sharp cold for they were now 3,000 feet high. They built a fire in front of the cave. She told him they would reach Cushing's camp the next day. "Jeem great man," she said. Jim and his brothers, she explained, were American miners. Walter was still in Luzon organizing his own group of guerrillas. Both brothers were resourceful and daring. There was a third brother and she thought he lived near Manila. They got along well with Filipinos. But Jim had a partner, Harry Fenton, who distrusted most of the Filipinos in the group even though he had taken a Filipino wife. Fenton—his real name was Aaron Feinstein—had come to the Philippines as an enlisted man for duty at Sternberg Hospital in Manila. He had managed to get a discharge to become a radio announcer at KZRC, Cebu City. Before the surrender he was known for his violent denunciations of the Japanese on his programs. He had brought radio equipment to the mountains and now delighted in continuing his tirades against the occupiers. His hatred against the Japanese extended to all spies and collaborators and he hung, without trial, any captured suspects. Fenton's men, said Socorro, feared him while Cushing's loved him. The latter openly opposed Fenton's rash actions but had found it necessary to join forces with him. Their headquarters were divided into two sections. Fenton, in charge of administration, had a camp seven miles from Cushing who was in charge of combat. On paper it was a good arrangement, admitted Socorro, for Fenton had a flair for administrative detail as well as propaganda, and Jim, a born leader of men, had built a formidable fighting unit. Unfortunately, in reality Fenton had already executed so many suspects that the entire guerrilla movement on Cebu was in danger. Moreover, Cushing was suffering from malaria and was in no condition to bring Fenton under control.

She proudly informed him that Cushing trusted her so much he had made her an officer. "I was lieutenanted!"

Socorro put enough wood on the fire to last until dawn and then curled up like a cat in her bed. Will fell asleep in a few minutes. He dreamed he was making love to a beautiful young woman. He wakened to find Socorro embracing him. She kissed him and clung closer to him. My God, he thought, I'm being seduced by a nun! And he had his first erection in over a year.

She whispered something he could not understand.

All he could say was, "No!" and try to pry her off him.

She laughed softly. "No worry, Weel," she said. "Not really nun." The habit was a disguise.

He tried to get her off him as affably as possible but she was amazingly strong.

"Japs died Socorro's husband."

"It's not that." To his embarrassment the last button of his shorts popped off and since somehow her skirt had hiked above her waist, he felt her firm warm flesh.

"Think Socorro ugly?"

"Oh, no!"

"You got wife home?"

"No."

"Ah, Socorro still barking in wrong tree. You like boys?"

"Of course not!"

She was puzzled. "Then you got to like girls, no?" She wriggled sensuously.

"Yes, I like girls, but . . ."

"Long, long ago for Socorro. Too long." She kissed him.

"And I think you're attractive . . ."

"No talk, Weel," she whispered as she guided him into herself.

For a slender woman she was surprisingly voluptuous and Will found himself cooperating willingly but once they were finished he gently put her to one side. Then an awful thought occurred to him. What if General Marshall found out! He was notoriously straitlaced and Will recalled vividly the time he tossed aside a report from Claire Chennault on how to fight the Zeros muttering, "How can you trust such a dissolute man?" The head of the Flying Tigers was reported to have had affairs with Chinese women including Madame Chiang Kai-shek. As a result his report, which told in detail how the Flying Tigers had successfully downed Zeros, had not been relayed to the fighter pilots in the Philippines, who were knocked out of the sky.

Socorro saw he was worried and tried to console him.

"Is natural these days. Jim and Fenton both have Filipino wives."

Kissing him on the cheek, Socorro snuggled up to him. In a few minutes she was asleep while he fretted for hours before finally dropping off. She was not at his side when he woke at dawn. Then he smelled food and turned over. Socorro was hunkering down before a fire. She brought him food on a leaf.

"Here," she said as if nothing had happened during the night, "something to appetite you."

Will fastened his shorts with his last safety pin and they climbed out of a valley to open terrain. Still not a word was spoken about the night before. They reached a sitio where the houses were made of cogon grass. The people, puffing away contentedly on homemade cigars and cigarettes, were friendly and welcomed Socorro. Soon they began another steep climb and in the afternoon came to a rugged ridge covered with large trees.

Socorro pointed. "Tabunan," she said. This was guerrilla headquarters. Will could see nothing. They plunged into dense jungle growth. Socorro whistled and a small Filipino appeared. He beckoned them. They followed into deeper undergrowth and finally came to an outpost. A guard nodded as they passed. Ahead were lean-tos and small grass huts connected by trails through the underbrush. Will was surprised to see many women and children. The few Americans were friendly but some of the Filipinos eyed Will suspiciously. Most of the men had long hair and beards.

The settlement was completely hidden from above by a green canopy of trees. Socorro led Will to the main building which, she explained, served as headquarters, chapel, and social hall. He would find Cushing inside, she said.

"I'm—sorry," stammered Will.

"No worry. Socorro no spill the bean. Maybe never see again," she added and left.

He entered an anteroom. In the corner a man lay on an army cot. He was in his thirties and wore glasses. His skin was like mahogany; his head was shaved. He opened one eye to survey Will. He looked neither Filipino nor American.

"I'm looking for Major Cushing," said Will.

The man jerked a thumb at the inner room. Angry voices could be heard inside. "Conference," said the man with a grimace.

"You been with Cushing long?"

The man lit a black cigarette and lay back nonchalantly, smoking it in the Humphrey Bogart style. "Too long," he said in a slow Southern drawl. "Strange duck."

"In what way?" Will was beginning to feel uneasy about linking up with such a man.

"He runs scared but none of these fools know it. He never wanted to run this crummy outfit. Only wanted to live out the war in the mountains with his wife and kid." He blew a smoke ring, then coughed. "Jim would rather drink than fight." He flicked the butt into an empty gallon can. "Used to be a wrestler and a boxer but he never could hit his way out of a paper bag." He wiped sweat from his face with a filthy handkerchief. He leaned on an elbow. "Did you know there are a dozen different guerrilla mobs on this island? And no two get along. They're like a pack of snarling dogs. Old Jim was the only one who could bring them all together." His chuckle made him look like Mephistopheles. "Damn fool. A saint couldn't bring them together." The voices in the other room became louder.

Will squatted down, held out his hand and introduced himself. "You're Major Cushing, aren't you?"

"I thought you'd never guess." Cushing's grin was shy, winning and deceitful. He wiped his face, then began to shiver. He pulled up a blanket made of burlap bags.

Three men burst in from the other room, two Filipinos and one American. The last was shaking his fist violently at the others. His eyes blazed with fury. "They were traitors!" he shouted. "They had to be shot!" His long yellowish hair and handsome face reminded Will of pictures of Jesus. But his eyes were cold, distrustful. This had to be Harry Fenton.

One of the Filipinos turned to Cushing. "This son of a bitch killed my brother!"

"He was working with the Japs! I have proof."

"All Fenton has is the word of a stinking mayor who's kissing Jap ass."

"He was a collaborator, Paraguya!" shouted Fenton. "I don't give a damn if he was your brother."

The other Filipino had another grievance. "Jim, he still refuses to print money and pay the men. I already lost half a dozen good fighters. They got to have money for their families."

"Good point," said Cushing. "We're losing ten percent of our people every month." He turned to the two Filipinos. "But Harry also has a good point. If we printed money it would probably lose its value before long. Perhaps we should rely on the real money that Governor Abellana is raising for us."

The mention of the pre-war governor of Cebu roused Fenton to new fury. "His escape from the Japs was a trick! He's still working for them. I wouldn't trust him as far as I could throw him."

Cushing grinned sardonically. "Harry, sometimes I think you don't even trust me." He forced himself to a sitting position. "If you three don't work things out I'm going back to my family. You can fight the Japs without me. Argue outside. I'm trying to get some rest." The three left, quiet but sulky.

Cushing hugged himself with burlap bags for warmth. "Sorry you jumped ship, McGlynn?"

3.

In the next few weeks Will became adjusted to his new life as a guerrilla. At first he had spent sleepless nights on the floor of a small hut keeping a wary lookout for the vermin that inhabited the bark walls—millipedes as big as his thumb whose bite could cause blindness and giant centipedes ten inches long whose bite brought high fever and sometimes death. It had also taken time to become accustomed to the unusual food, but by now his body responded to the chicken, wild pig, carabao, and vegetables. He no longer tired during the hunt for food and could tramp through the rough, steep terrain for hours without rest. Already he had become the confidant of Cushing who was apparently training him to be his chief of staff.

Every day reports from neighboring villages indicated that Fenton's nightly broadcasts had become so vituperous that the Japanese were responding with reprisals against the civilians. Although some of Fenton's own men deserted, this only inspired him to launch night raids on Japanese installations. This resulted in counterattacks throughout the island which caused Cushing to send out orders to lie low until they could regroup. Supplies and ammunition now were almost exhausted and it seemed as if the guerrilla cause was hopeless. Then word came that a party from MacArthur's headquarters had been landed by submarine at Negros, the island just west of Cebu. The group had come to coordinate guerrilla activities. The leader, a Major Villamor, was sending an envoy to consult with Cushing and Fenton.

Will was surprised that Cushing was not enthusiastic. "Harry probably won't listen," he explained. And he himself didn't trust MacArthur.

Will asked if this Villamor was the pilot he had met on Bataan. Cushing wearily nodded. "I'm sure you can trust him," said Will.

"But Harry trusts nobody."

A week later Fenton arrived at Tabunan with a prisoner named Martin, an American professor of chemistry at Silliman University. With a gun at his back Martin explained that Villamor had sent him with a proposition from MacArthur. "General Headquarters is anxious to appoint a single island commander. Which of you two will take over the assignment?"

Fenton's eyes blazed. "Things are going to continue as they are—joint command." Fenton glanced malevolently at Will, having heard how impressed Cushing was with the newcomer. "I'll handle the paper and organization work. Jim will do the fighting. What makes you think we want recognition from MacArthur? What can he do for us?"

"Well, Harry, this isn't a bad proposition," said Cushing. "And why don't you put the pistol away?"

"The hell with that stuff!" exclaimed Fenton, gesturing with the weapon. "We don't want *recognition*"—he made the last word an epithet—"or anything like that from MacArthur or anybody else until the American flag is flying over here once again."

Will was dismayed. So was Martin; unable to believe what he was hearing, he turned desperately to Cushing who made a slight warning shake of his head. Martin would not take the hint. "If your people don't get the recognition they deserve," he said, "they may lay down their arms and surrender to the Japs."

Fenton jumped to his feet. "Let them try it!" he cried.

"Take it easy, Harry," said Cushing. "Let's have another drink."

But Fenton was out of control. "Tell Villamor the next time not to expect the return of anyone he decides to send! If he is going to be crazy enough to do so." When Martin started to protest, Fenton made a move toward him and Cushing struggled to his feet. "Harry, be a good fellow and help me to my cot." As Fenton assisted Cushing, the latter gave a knowing look to Will who quietly escorted Martin out of the room to a lean-to shelter far from Fenton's quarters.

Will was wakened before dawn by Cushing. "We've got to get Martin out of here before Fenton wakes up." He was shivering violently and pulled a ragged blanket around him. Just before first light the three of them and four guides started down the narrow trail. Cushing insisted on going the first half mile. Then he stopped and told the guides to wait a hundred yards down the trail. He stared at Martin with a look of despair on his face. He hesitated a moment. "I hope your report to Villamor about Cebu won't be all negative. Harry was in one of his bad moods last night. He's really a good man. Try to understand." His voice suddenly became anguished. "But I can't go on like this much longer." He shook Martin's hand and slowly turned, trudging back toward the camp, each step painful. Will followed.

On May 7, the first anniversary of the fall of Corregidor, Cushing confided to Will as he lolled on his cot that it was a day of shame he would never forget. He told how General Chynoweth had arrived on the island in mid-March, 1942, to find apathy. No sensible defense plans had been made by his predecessor whose concept of guerrilla warfare was to dig a series of trenches. Morale was low, there was little ammunition, and those who wanted to fight were in the minority. Chynoweth had done his best, said Cushing, but it was too late. He grimaced. "I was one of the damned fools that itched to fight." He sighed. "You should have seen me before I got malaria—the Errol Flynn of Cebu!" He chuckled. "In those days Harry Fenton was really the one who built up our group. Then something happened that drove him berserk." One of Fenton's officers, a Filipino, was captured and to save himself revealed the whereabouts of Fenton's mestizo wife and child. The Japanese sent word that they would be freed if Fenton surrendered. "He didn't, of course," said Cushing, "and then we heard the wife and kid were killed. Since then Harry has been suspicious of everyone, particularly the Filipinos."

There was little activity in the next weeks since Cushing was still recovering from malaria and had to be half carried to a new retreat farther in the mountains. Without Cushing on hand to restrain him, Fenton's broadcasts became even more abusive and Japanese patrols in the region increased. Growing numbers of men deserted Fenton's ranks. Those he caught were executed and this ended whatever loyalty the villagers felt.

Despite Will's protests, Cushing got out of his cot and returned to his main camp where he sent word to Fenton that things were so desperate they should seek outside aid. The next day Fenton arrived. Will had never seen a human being so livid. No outside aid! insisted Fenton and when Major Paraguya, the brother of a man he had executed, protested, it took all of Cushing's powers of persuasion to prevent a gunfight.

Cushing put an arm around Fenton. "Harry," he said quietly, "You've convinced me. You're right. No outside aid. Just take it easy for a while. Things are too stirred up." He walked Fenton down the trail a few hundred yards. By the time he returned to the hut he was exhausted. He flopped on his bed. Will bathed his sweaty forehead. "Will," he said finally, "I'm going over to Negros to see Villamor. I want you and a few men we can trust to go along." He scribbled on a sheet of paper, then showed Will what he had written. Addressed to Major Paraguya, it ordered him to take command of all the combat units if he, Cushing, should be captured. He signed it, sealed it in an envelope and sent for Paraguya.

"Here are written orders." He handed over the envelope to Paraguya. "If you find it absolutely necessary you are to arrest Fenton. But only if he goes off the deep end."

"Yes, sir!" said the other and left.

Will was unhappy and Cushing knew it. "I had to do it," the latter said. "God knows what Harry will do next. Half of our people have already left for other islands. Food is running low and the organization could break up."

"I didn't like the look on Paraguya's face."

"Neither did I. Do you have a better idea?" There was no answer. "In that case, let's get ready. It'll take us over a month to reach Villamor."

Besides Will, Cushing took four trustworthy regimental commanders, all Filipinos. Socorro would accompany them to the southern part of the island. At that point the five men would paddle two outrigger canoes across the narrow channel to Negros. Their progress down the mountain range was slow and painful. Cushing had to take frequent rests. On the second day they were drenched by a thunder shower. In the morning they slithered along on the wet trail. Leeches brought out by the rain fell from the tall bushes onto their faces and arms and soon began fattening on human blood. Will at first pulled them off but found this left the leeches' jaws embedded, causing a painful itch. There were only two ways to kill them—with the lighted end of a cigarette or by sliding a sliver of bamboo under the leech and flipping it off.

As soon as they reached the road connecting Cebu City on the east coast with Toledo on the west, Cushing insisted that he and Will wear the white robes of a priest. Will was reluctant until Cushing, in a rare display of anger, told him to obey orders and shut up.

They safely reached one of the upper barrios of Toledo and spent the night in a friendly house. In the morning they were awakened by a horde of women with children to be baptized. Will saved the situation by saying they had no more holy water.

They continued south with Socorro going ahead in her nun's disguise to check every barrio and village. After ten days they left her at the port town of Alegria and crossed the strait to the island of Negros in two small boats.

On the way Cushing asked if Will knew Socorro's background. "She's a very remarkable woman."

"She told me about her husband."

"She tells no one about the time she was captured by the Japs. I heard about it from her mother-in-law. Socorro was visiting her village last year when someone betrayed her. The Japs beat her for two days— that's how she got that voice—but she refused to tell them where I was. On the second night her guard raped her. He dozed off and she took the bastard's bayonet, stuck him in the throat and escaped. A remarkable woman!"

Will wondered if Cushing knew that he and Socorro had made love, but when the subject was dropped he felt sure she had kept her word.

Soon after arrival in Negros they were delayed by the infection of an old shrapnel wound in Cushing's leg and it was not until a week later that the party was finally met in southern Negros by an escort sent out by Major Villamor. He had ordered the escort to bring Cushing to the far side of a stream while he observed him from hiding on the other side to make sure he was genuine. Villamor was surprised to see a smallish man emerge from a thick tangle of growth and stop at the edge of the stream. He was curiously dressed as a priest. Behind was another priest, this one very tall, and behind were four Filipinos in khaki carrying carbines.

Villamor realized that the little priest must be Cushing. Was this mild figure really the great Cushing, the one who had all Cebu behind him and every Japanese after him? He looked frail, unlike any of the guerrilla chieftains he had already met. Villamor stepped out of the underbrush, crossed the stream with outstretched arms. "Welcome to Negros, Cushing. I'm Villamor."

Cushing's eyes widened. He said nothing for a moment. Then his face lit up with his engaging smile. "I'm so glad!" he said. The two men embraced.

Cushing introduced Will whom Villamor had not recognized, and the three sat on the ground. Cushing's hands trembled as he emotionally told about the problems his guerrillas faced in Cebu. "I am the last of the major guerrilla leaders not yet recognized," he said. Tears came to his eyes. "Unless I get recognition from MacArthur the entire guerrilla movement of Cebu will collapse." What they needed most of all was immediate financial aid. And they needed authority from MacArthur to issue their own scrip money to keep the unit together.

Villamor led the way to the housing area of his headquarters and while his guests were being quartered he radioed MacArthur of Cushing's arrival and his requests. The answer from Australia was a curt note: the issuance of currency was a function of the Philippine Commonwealth Government. Villamor was surprised and disappointed. Cushing was crushed and Will thought he was going to weep. The four regimental commanders were glum and speechless.

Two weeks passed without further clarification from Australia and Villamor radioed another plea to give Cushing money. The answer was that Cushing was henceforth to take orders and money from guerrilla leaders in Negros and Mindanao. Cushing was incensed and Will sought out Villamor. "Don't they know Jim has probably done more against the Japanese than any other guerrilla leader in the islands?"

Villamor sighed. "Keep this to yourself, but Jim has powerful enemies down there. You and I know that he deserves recognition and money." He didn't mention the name but a certain well-respected Philippine expert had persuaded MacArthur and General Courtney Whitney, who was head of the Allied Intelligence Bureau, that Jim couldn't be trusted since he was little more than a beachcomber in pre-war days.

Matters were aggravated by a message from MacArthur ordering Cushing to report at once to his superior, the guerrilla leader in Mindanao. Cushing was enraged. Why should he make the dangerous trip to Mindanao? What good would it do? After sulking for three days he wrote a message to MacArthur stating he was proceeding to Mindanao but would have to go via Cebu to pick up essential papers. "I'll tell him I'm suffering from the effects of malaria and so he won't be surprised when I find myself unable to leave Cebu."

Both Will and Villamor felt Cushing was playing with fire, yet he was so impatient for action that the major reluctantly transmitted Cushing's message with no changes.

Two days later the Cushing party was ready to leave. Villamor went up to Cushing holding out both hands. Villamor had seen the torment boil in him and had grown fond of this much misunderstood, much maligned man. "Take care," he said grasping Cushing's hands.

"I sure damn well will try," he said huskily. Then he abruptly turned and walked away.

A few hours after they landed on Cebu they were met by Socorro. Her face was grim. "They died Harry," she said.

"Who killed who?" said Cushing, his face paling.

"Paraguya died him." There had been a trial and he was found guilty of treason and murder.

"Oh, God!"

She told how Paraguya had called a conference of battalion leaders and convinced them they had to eliminate Fenton. He claimed that Harry had executed Father Patrick Drum, a Cebu missionary, for collaboration with the Japanese.

"Harry did that?"

"Maybe," said Socorro. Father Drum had been executed but there was no proof Fenton had done it.

Cushing swore. "Paraguya was just looking for an excuse."

Paraguya, she said, had also started to reorganize the entire guerrilla organization. "In your name, Jim," she said. "He tell us everything he does is in your best interest."

That night while Will was on guard duty Socorro crept out to him. Without a word they made love and this time Will took the lead.

In the morning Cushing insisted they march north with as little rest as possible. Will did his best to slow the pace but Cushing was a driven man. He refused to wear his priest's disguise and ignored safety precautions on the trip north. Just before they reached the cross-island highway they were met by a runner with the latest news. Paraguya had not only commandeered all of Fenton's hoarded treasury but had already squandered it.

It was evident to Will that Cushing was nearing the end of his physical resources. Even so, he pressed for more speed. Several times he almost fell over the precipitous edge of the narrow mountain trail leading to the White Horse Inn. These narrow escapes only seemed to give him more energy. A day's march from home headquarters they were met by several battalion commanders Cushing had always trusted. Sitting around a small campfire in the early November chill the newcomers told how Paraguya was trying to take full control of all units before Cushing's return. More alarming, there was strong evidence that

Paraguya had agreed to turn over Cushing to the Japanese for sixty thousand pesos.

Cushing wanted to know if the men in the combat headquarters camp were still loyal to him. The four battalion commanders were indignant. Of course! These men were just waiting for Cushing's return to turn on Paraguya. It was decided to delay arrival at the camp next day until after dark so they could take Paraguya by surprise.

All was quiet in the camp as the Cushing party approached. The guards had been alerted to let them pass without challenge. Will wondered if it was a trap, an elaborate plan by Paraguya to take Cushing by surprise? They were met by a dozen silent guerrillas. Cushing shook hands with each one. After a few whispered instructions, the men fanned out to surround the headquarters hut. An owl hooted mournfully and several canjons began yapping like hyenas. Will could make out the figures of two men sitting inside—guards. Barely visible were dim forms at the side of the hut. The forms—Cushing's men—crept up to the guards. There was a slight scuffling noise, then a bird called.

"Okay," said Cushing and walked boldly into the hut, Will at his heels. The two guards were meekly silent. A bewildered, bleary-eyed Paraguya came to the door followed by a girl with long straggly hair.

"I'm back," was all Cushing said to Paraguya. "Tie him up."

The next morning Cushing left camp with Will and a small party to visit outlying units and restore order. They returned three weeks later to learn that Paraguya had been tried, found guilty of treason, and executed. Cushing pretended consternation but Will was sure it was an act. "My God, Jim," Will said, "when will the killing of our own people stop?"

"Soon, Will, soon," said Cushing with an endearing smile. "But first we've got to get back to killing Japs." He laid an affectionate hand on Will's shoulder. "You're a good influence on me."

Cushing was slyly eyeing him with his unrepentant Mephistophelian smile and Will couldn't help laughing.

CHAPTER SEVENTEEN

1.

1943 had been the Year of the Sheep in Japan. It was also the year of the conference for the Allies with sites ranging from Casablanca to Cairo and from Quebec to Teheran. Roosevelt and Churchill had planned to meet their partner, Stalin, at the first of these conferences. Casablanca seemed the ideal setting for such a momentous convocation, the name itself synonymous with mystery and intrigue, but the suspicious Stalin begged off on the grounds that he must give all his time and effort to holding back Hitler's legions.

The American military leaders—the Joint Chiefs of Staff—held preliminary discussions in mid-January at the Anfa Hotel, four miles outside of Casablanca, to take a deeper look at global strategy after the unexpected Allied triumphs of the preceding two months on both sides of the world. Now was the time to make long-range plans for victory in both Europe and the Far East. The Joint Chiefs felt that their British counterparts, who wanted a limited war in the Pacific until after Hitler was defeated, far underestimated the Japanese.

Once the conference started, the eloquent demand of the Americans for the prompt capture of Truk and the Marianas had little effect on the British, who insisted that nothing should be done to weaken the attack on Germany. Crusty Admiral King retorted icily, "It is up to the Americans alone to decide when and where to attack in the Pacific." By the third evening, after some acrimony, the British had backed down from their original stand, realizing that the names Pearl Harbor, Bataan, and Guadalcanal meant more to the American public than Rome, Paris, and Berlin. And it was agreed that for the Year of the Sheep "operations in the Pacific shall continue with the object of maintaining pressure on Japan," but that such operations should not excessively drain resources from Europe.

Of more far-reaching importance, however, was a startling announcement Roosevelt made to the press during a chat in generalities about the course of the war. "The elimination of German, Japanese, and

Italian war power," he said deliberately, "means the unconditional surrender of Germany, Italy, and Japan."

It was a shock to everyone present except Churchill, who had heard the President recently utter the phrase at a private luncheon. Churchill frowned but quickly said with a grin, "Perfect! And I can just see how Goebbels and the rest of 'em will squeal!"

Professor McGlynn was at breakfast when he read the phrase. He was tempted to smash his coffee cup as so many of his Irish forebears had done under similar circumstances. But he restrained himself to a string of epithets. How could Franklin have been so overbearing! He himself could be overbearing, if unconsciously, but he found this same trait in others exasperating. That was what came of Roosevelt's having a neighbor like Morgenthau, whose views on the subject were well known. McGlynn had already counseled the President that a public announcement of unconditional surrender would mean handing both Tojo and Hitler an invaluable piece of propaganda to incite their people to bitter resistance to the end. Now the Allies would have to destroy the enemy by military force. The weapon of diplomacy had been abandoned and they were now irrevocably set upon the rigid course of unlimited war. Not only would many thousands more lives be lost but the devastation of both Germany and Japan would undoubtedly bring chaos after victory.

McGlynn vowed never again to give Roosevelt advice, but that autumn events in Asia impelled him to write the President a long paper with the approval of Captain Ellis Zacharias, head of Op-16-W, indicating that the central instrument of Japan's political aims, the Greater East Asia Co-prosperity Sphere, was not the farce Western analysts pictured. This policy, which envisaged an Asia united "in the spirit of universal brotherhood" under the leadership of Japan, had been created by Japanese idealists who wanted to free Asia from exploitation by the white man. "As with many dreams," wrote McGlynn, "it has been taken over and exploited by realists, but its call for Pan-Asianism remains relatively undiminished in its appeal to the masses throughout Asia."

The fall of Singapore in 1942, cautioned McGlynn, had marked the emergence of mainland Asia from Western domination and gave all Orientals a sense of pride. "Japanese victory was heady to most Asians and today much of the continent is ready to actively ally itself with the victors. And so," he continued, "even before defeating Japan, the Allies

276

must plan for the hearts of Asians. We must and will win on the battle-field, yet let us do so with as much humanity and foresight as possible."

McGlynn sent this paper to the White House on November 27, the day Roosevelt and Churchill left the Cairo Conference for the first meeting of the Big Three at Teheran. In Cairo, America, China, and Britain had disagreed not only on military priorities for China but on the political future of Asia. Each had been waging a separate war for separate reasons. Churchill would not even consider dismembering the British colonies; Chiang Kai-shek was primarily interested in eliminating communists and setting himself up as the sole leader of his country; and Roosevelt was intent exclusively on bringing about the surrender of Japan as soon as possible with the fewest American casualties.

Upon reading the reports of the Cairo Conference, McGlynn was glum. His Harvard classmate was not taking seriously his admonitions and those of Pearl Buck that the Asians were determined to free themselves from Western domination no matter who won the war. Mc-Glynn's fears were heightened by reports of the historic meeting in Teheran where Stalin, after applauding the successes in the Pacific, promised to send reinforcements to eastern Siberia once Germany had been defeated. "Then," he said, "by our common front, we shall win." Roosevelt was so pleased that during an informal lunch the next day he suggested that Russia be granted use of the warm-water port of Dairen in Manchuria.

All day McGlynn brooded about the conferences of the Year of the Sheep. He could see no good coming from them. At any rate the time for talk had ended and men on the battlefield, like Mark, would make the next decisions.

2.

Tokyo. 1943.

With Akira Toda in China running a steel mill and ore mine for the duration of the war, Emi felt she had to be responsible for various family decisions so she wouldn't have to bother her husband. She made no outward show of the deep concern instilled in her by a family friend named Obata, who had warned her that things would soon get much worse and that she should invest her money in material and clothing such as kimonos and obis, suits, and coats, to barter when money lost its value. As yet, Obata cautioned, there was little shortage of food and commodities but if the war lasted another year—and he was sure it would—she could not keep the family afloat unless she had plenty to barter. Obata said, "We can't hope to win this war, and the Americans will fight until Japan capitulates. It is a very serious situation." Unfortunately he had recently been sent to Korea by the army to help procure raw material and she had no one to turn to for advice. Who would help her shoulder the burden? Such a decision should certainly call for consultation with Akira, as considerable amounts of money would be required to obtain goods enough to last the family for years of difficult times. Many items were already getting scarce and their prices were going up. She couldn't help feeling a sense of distaste at the thought of resorting to such means, when others were giving up so much for the war, not only their possessions but their lives. Akira and Emi had willingly donated their gold wedding rings and other precious metals to the government. But now Emi had to plan for the survival of the family.

Emi feared that Akira, being a man of honor and integrity, might not approve of her engaging herself in dealings he might call unpatriotic and selfish. It would be difficult for her to discuss such matters with her husband in letters. He wouldn't understand the situation at home, which had drastically changed. Akira would only worry if she brought up the problem. So the pragmatic Emi decided to act on her own initiative and tell her husband later. Ko would soon be in the army or navy and Tadashi was already burdened with enough responsibility providing for his own little family. Emi had opposed his marriage but Floss had turned out to be a treasure. She was strong, levelheaded, and blessed with good humor. In the critical times to come she would be a staunch mate. She welcomed her mother-in-law's constant and courageous support as well as her advice on how to save fuel, how to shop, how to cook, and how to cope with insults in public.

It had been a hard year. Little Ryuko was thin, sickly, and a constant cause for concern. And Masao, who had entered elementary school in April, was having trouble. His teachers attempted in vain to correct his pronunciation and his classmates laughed aloud at his mistakes. What also caused Floss distress was the cool attitude of most of her old school friends. Long ago they had all pledged eternal friendship but now most of them avoided her in public. A few did have the courage to remain loyal and their regular visits kept up her spirits. Two women in the apartment house were also friendly but the others were openly hostile to see an "enemy" walk freely through the corridors. With so many women in munitions plants it was difficult to get a maid. And whenever Emi found one the girl soon left because of the stares and insults heaped on one who stooped so low as to serve an American.

The first winter had come as a shock to someone accustomed to pre-war standards of comfort. The only heat came from portable gas heaters. Like the other women she now wore *monpei,* the work clothing of farmers. The trousers were like baggy bloomers. Underneath she wore heavy woolen underwear, a wool skirt and woolen stockings. It hurt Tadashi to see her in such unflattering attire but Floss reveled in its warmth.

Early in 1943 the gas company announced that they had used so much gas their supply was being cut off. Floss bought a portable charcoal stove. When she first lighted it clouds of smoke filled the apartment. The solution was to kindle it outside on their little porch and bring it inside once the smoke subsided. She never had been much of a cook, but a friendly neighbor gave her lessons and by spring she could even bake a cake on her little charcoal stove.

Masao could no longer stand the taunts of his schoolmates who, during recess, shouted at him, "Half-breed!" and "American devil!" He challenged the biggest boy, who was half a head taller. Masao was knocked down twice but doggedly returned to the fray, flailing his arms so furiously that the big boy ran off.

"Why do they call me names, Mama? I haven't been mean to them."

His concern and confusion stabbed Floss. "You haven't done anything wrong, dear. It's—just because of the war. The women at the markets insult me too," she said. "I just ignore their talk, but if one of them tries to push ahead of me in line, I stand up for my rights. The other women seem to respect me for it."

"You want me to do that too?"

"Yes," she said wondering if this really was good advice.

By summer, rationing had become the major problem. The latest information of available goods would come from the city ration center to the *kumicho,* chairman of her neighborhood organization. She in turn would send runners around to the fifteen houses of the group shouting, *"Haikyu ga mairimashita!"* and Floss would join the other women in the long queue.

The summer of 1943 passed uneventfully except for Masao's long bout with whooping cough which the Japanese called "the hundred days' cough." The war had wrought a drastic change in the traditional Japanese family structure. Mutual hardship had forced families to depend more on their neighbors than on relatives, who might live far away. Women of all classes now took part in community air-raid drills. Side by side the well-to-do and the poor would relay water pails and carry stretchers, lumber, and sand.

It was Floss's duty to dig the family shelter behind the apartment house and see that it contained a knapsack filled with first-aid supplies, rice, cooking pan, and cotton-padded hoods to protect the wearer against burns. Floss caused a stir at one neighborhood meeting by warning that the padding would probably catch fire and do more harm than good. Several women grumbled that the *gaijin* could be a spy but others agreed that they should investigate.

Floss's main concern was Tadashi, who had become frustrated at being kept at such a minor post. Every attempt to get a better assignment was met with the excuse that there was nothing suitable as yet. To make matters worse, he detested wearing the leggings of the men's national uniform. It was required that this uniform be worn on the eighth of every month in honor of the raid on Pearl Harbor and when Tadashi appeared at the office one day in civilian clothes he was sharply informed by his superior that any repetition of his "carelessness" would have serious consequences.

Since this reprimand he had been more withdrawn than ever and she could imagine how worried he'd be if she revealed that a man—probably from the *Kempeitai*, the military police organization—was following her. Then it came to her that she was wrong to keep hiding problems from Tadashi. She had become so used to being a mother to the twins that she was treating her husband like a son.

"I must talk to you," she said and told him about the *kempei*.

"My God! Why did I ever agree to bring you here!"

For a moment she regretted what she had done, then burst out with exasperation, "I'm tired of hearing you apologize! We both agreed the family must stay together. How do you think it makes me feel? I need your support, not your apologies! I'm a foreigner in an unfriendly land and ever since we arrived I've had to keep *your* spirits up!"

"I didn't realize." He embraced her. "I'm so sorry!"

She pushed him away. "Damn it! Don't ever say you're sorry again!"

He was startled. "That's the first time I've ever heard you swear."

"It won't be the last unless you stop feeling sorry for yourself." She hugged him. "Oh, darling, it's really my fault. I haven't been treating you like a man."

He kissed her. "It's time I acted like one. I'll raise the devil with the *Kempeitai!*"

"That's the worst thing you could do. We should just ignore the man following me. It's only because I'm an American and he has every right to watch me. I'll keep him so busy he'll get tired of it."

For the first time in a month Tadashi laughed.

And for the first time since they arrived in Japan Floss felt secure.

Emi had come to rely mainly on Sumiko. The two had a rare relationship for Sumiko, besides being the only daughter, had a strong sense of independence and silently bore the difficulties of wartime without a father. She thought for herself yet knew how to take reprimand and not repeat a mistake. Important too was the influence of her school headmistress, Miss Kuroki, who had served on a peace mission to the United States and somehow managed to suppress the nationalistic spirit that was rampant in other schools. Yes, Sumiko was a plucky child, an extension of herself, and Emi wished the boys had more of her qualities. As for Sumiko, she dearly loved her mother but sometimes wished she were more like other mothers—softer, not quite so rigid.

In August 1943 middle-school students were ordered to wear uniforms. Sumiko was issued hers at school. It was a navy blue outfit made of synthetic fabric, *sufu*. Regular schooling continued until October when the older students were ordered to work part time for the government in small factories near school, sewing buttons on naval uniforms or working with Bakelite products. Sumiko's class was assigned to a laundry located near Yoyogi Army Training Grounds in Tokyo to help clean military uniforms and bedding. It was a large three-story wooden structure managed by a Christian who knew Miss Kuroki. Here, unlike the practice in other factories where students were sent, Sumiko's classmates were allowed to have morning religious services and one hour every other day to study English with their homeroom teacher, Miss Narahashi. The girls were divided into groups that rotated in different tasks—washing, drying, ironing, shipping, and the repairing of irons. Sumiko found scrubbing sleeves and collars of civilian suits with washing soda a cold, wet job, and brushing lint off dusty clothing onerous and unpleasant. Eventually she was placed in the ironing room and found it so much more to her liking that she soon became an expert.

As soon as the students learned the routine, life at the laundry became boring and tiring. With no entertainment available, many of the girls read voraciously during their breaks and while commuting. Miss

Narahashi had studied in America and returned home a modern woman. Like the principal, she was outspoken and liberated. She openly wore a badge reading PAX. Sumiko looked up this word and discovered it was Latin for peace. How courageous! thought the girls, who were also intrigued by the way she dressed. She would come to the laundry wearing a short-sleeved cardigan over a long-sleeved blouse. Nobody else dared dress like that! And once Sumiko noticed her reading a book in English on the train. An old man shouted, *"Hikokumin!"* (traitor) but she continued reading calmly. And when the man began shaking his finger at her she stared at him so coolly that he walked away talking to himself. Someday, vowed Sumiko, I will be like Miss Narahashi.

By October the war situation had become so desperate that the exemption of college students was also suspended and the graduation of Ko's class at Tokyo University took place at once rather than the following March. Ko and his best friend at school, Hideo Maeda, openly deplored the oppression by the military authorities. "They are poisoning the culture," asserted Maeda who dreamed of being a poet and novelist. At the same time he felt they had to do their bit for Japan.

Ko agreed that they must defend their country at the front even if it meant abandoning his painting. "And," said Maeda, "I probably will never finish my novel about Don Juan."

Ko's other close friend, Jun Kato, also graduated ahead of schedule from Aoyama. He confessed to Ko that he was thankful a slight heart murmur would postpone his army physical examination for two months. He felt loyal to Japan, he said, but how could he fight against America where he had been born? In the meantime, he had found an interesting position as a reporter in the foreign department of the Tokyo *Shimbun*.

He had become close to an older man in the economics department, Fujita, who had counseled him to make sure he did not pass his army physical. "Never die for a lost cause," he said. Fujita never mentioned Marxism, but it was evident he was a member of the secret left-wing movement.

Although Fujita could read all the foreign economic news, he was not privy to those dispatches dealing with foreign policy. And since Jun was one of the few privileged to read these, the older man regularly pumped his junior on the latest developments. Then he would add his own information and give a summary of the subject. It was, thought Jun, like taking a course in political science. Fujita would openly explain the military and political mistakes being perpetrated by the government, making it plain that Japan's only hope was an early peace. In the office Fujita was cautious and reticent and their private conversations always took place while strolling through Hibiya Park or during their night shifts.

Ko and Maeda had decided to go into the army rather than the navy. "We'll probably be squashed to death on some miserable little island," said the latter. But it was the unspoken duty of dedicated scholars to bind themselves to common troops.

The night before Ko was to leave for basic training was sad, silent. His mother was distressed, knowing her youngest son was unfit for the maelstrom into which he was about to plunge, but she hid her concern. Sumiko did her best too not to make Ko's last night at home a gloomy one.

Sleeping fitfully, he rose an hour before dawn to check his rucksack. He realized he had packed too many books and it took an hour to winnow out all but poems by Rimbaud and a sketch pad. At first light he went to the little back room where his mother allowed him to paint. On the easel was a painting of the great rock at Nagatoro he had just finished. Would it be his last painting? After breakfast he made his farewells to mother and sister as brief as possible for fear he might break down, and so their parting was almost formal. Maeda was waiting at the railroad station. There too was Jun Kato. They talked self-consciously, hiding their true feelings, and it was a relief to everyone when the train finally arrived.

Throughout Japan some 130,000 other recent college graduates who had majored in law, literature, economics, or agriculture were also setting out for the rugged training programs of the Imperial Japanese Army and Navy.

Jun returned to his office across the street from Hibiya Hall, feeling compassion for his two friends who had just departed for a life that was bound to be distasteful, arduous, and almost certainly end in death. In the days that followed, Jun's relationship with Fujita added excitement and enlightenment to his life. Never before had he known a man with such wide experience. He always talked logically, quietly; he never argued or used exaggerated language. And Jun was an eager student, soaking in all the astounding data and insights without question.

Besides translating foreign dispatches and Japanese reports from the paper's correspondents in Singapore, Manila, Peking, and Hong Kong, Jun covered two agencies: the Foreign Ministry and the Government Information Bureau. Both of these offices were within a fifteen-minute walk and Fujita introduced him to key officials in both places. These officials all belonged to the pro-British, pro-American faction whose secret function was to bring about peace before Japan was destroyed. One, a diplomat, had just returned from Shanghai and gave Jun a pirated edition of Edgar Snow's *Red Star Over China*. Jun devoured the book in two nights. He was shocked by Snow's revelations but, thanks to his indoctrination by Fujita, believed every word he read. Another friend he made on his own was Ko's older brother, Tadashi Toda. They had much in common and would often lunch together after press briefings.

Early in November Jun got a white slip ordering him to report in two days for his physical examination. His regiment was located in Yamaguchi, a city near the southern end of Honshu. His office friends gave him a party and loaded him with presents. Fujita's gift was a long walk in the park with a final admonition—"Make sure you come back to Tokyo alive"—and advice on how to make sure he would fail his exam. Jun locked up his desk and took the train to Iwakuni to say farewell to his grandparents. The old man greeted him in his usual stern manner but it was obvious he was at last proud that his grandson would soon serve his country like a man. He even gathered together Jun's friends for a sake party which lasted far into the night. The next day Jun completed the trip to Yamaguchi. It was a cold, drizzly day and, as instructed by Fujita, he purposely did not wear his overcoat. At Yamaguchi he took the bus to the camp of the 42nd Infantry Regiment and by the time he reported he was sneezing and his forehead was hot.

During the next ten days he was issued uniform, shoes, and leggings and given a long series of tests. X rays revealed foggy spots on his right lung and the doctors were unhappy with his coughing and high temperature. On the tenth day a doctor informed him with regret that he was not acceptable. "Make sure you come back well for your test next year." Hiding his delight, Jun said he would do his best. He put on a sad face and walked back to the bus. Only on boarding the train for Tokyo did he permit himself to smile. He had done it! He was a free man. He did not stop at Iwakuni since he knew his grandfather would feel disgraced. Some parents, he heard, had committed suicide upon learning their sons had been turned down. In Tokyo he was welcomed warmly by his colleagues, and Fujita took him out to dinner in celebration.

The Todas had just received another letter from the head of the family. As usual it was a brief message merely saying that all was well at the steel mill in central China and that he hoped the family was getting along without too much privation. He did add a postscript asking if they had heard from Shogo. Was he still in China where he and Colonel Tsuji had been sent after the Guadalcanal fiasco?

A few days later a letter from their middle son did arrive, the first in six months. This was no more informative than his father's. All was going well in Nanking despite some differences between Tsuji and the commander of the Japanese Expeditionary Forces in China. Shogo was vague about their duties, only mentioning that he and the colonel traveled a lot on inspection tours. He didn't mention that many of these trips had been on the initiative of Tsuji who was, as usual, covertly rousing young officers to join his radical Asia-for-Asians crusade. Nor did Shogo mention that his own enthusiasm for this crusade was fast ebbing. He feared his idol was half mad.

CHAPTER EIGHTEEN

1.

Australia. November 1943.

About the time Will and Cushing returned to their mountain camp in Cebu, Major Jess Villamor arrived in Perth by submarine. He was brimming with information and plans for better coordination of guerrillas. Upon arrival at MacArthur's headquarters in Brisbane he expected a warm welcome. General Willoughby, head of Intelligence, was as friendly and enthusiastic as ever but Courtney Whitney, who had become one of the commanding general's closest advisers, was cool. And Sutherland, the chief of staff, was as distant as ever.

In the days to follow Villamor felt an undefined uneasiness. Had he been caught in a struggle for favor, a contest for power? Finally one night a friend warned Villamor over dinner that he should be careful—he was indeed caught in the middle of the Willoughby and Whitney-Sutherland differences.

Villamor devoted all his energies to writing a long report on his findings. One section reviewed the disposition of the various guerrilla units and ended with a plea to give Cushing immediate recognition and material help. Willoughby, as expected, was impressed by the entire report and perhaps for this reason MacArthur approved sending Villamor to the United States to take his report in person to President Quezon. It was cold and raw when Jess arrived in Washington to find a very sick President of the Philippines. "I honestly cannot say that things are going well," Villamor told Quezon who was in bed.

Quezon's face hardened. "You're telling me that there doesn't seem to be any hope for an immediate solution to the problems at hand?"

"That's right. But fortunately the people are behind the guerrillas."

With a frail hand Quezon motioned Jess to sit next to him. "I think GHQ could be doing more," the President said, shaking his head dolefully. "There are some people in headquarters who are trying to make it hard for Filipinos and I don't think they have permitted this kind of information to reach MacArthur." After leafing through the seventy pages of Villamor's report, Quezon stroked his forehead. "Did MacArthur read this report?"

"I don't know, Mr. President," said the disheartened Villamor.

"It's not your fault. I know who in MacArthur's headquarters can make it hard for you. You could be a stumbling block to their postwar aims."

A few days before Christmas Jess was summoned to Quezon's bedside. "I want to tell you something now, Villamor." His dark eyes blazed. "And I don't want you ever to forget. Tell our people when you get back to the Philippines that those in MacArthur's headquarters, those *hijos de putas*"—he struggled to compose himself—"that those sons of whores will not get away with making fools of our people." He dropped back, spent, and began coughing until his body shook. "I will not let anyone wreck the future of our country! *Puñeta!* They think we're their *little brown brothers*. The condescending bastards!"

Quezon's fighting words ignited Villamor's lagging hopes and he was impatient to get back to Australia and then on to the Philippines to tell the people what the President had just said.

Quezon clasped Villamor's right hand with both of his own. "I swear to you, Villamor, I won't let our people down."

2.

Cebu. January 1944.

Cushing, with the help of Will, was rebuilding the shaky structure of his organization. Although recovered from his long siege of malaria, he was now stricken with arthritis and walked with difficulty. Even so he drove himself and Will mercilessly. Morale among the units improved and the people's confidence in Cushing was restored. In retaliation the Japanese launched heavy attacks in mid-January. Three drives were directed against Cushing's headquarters, the last one turned back only after a desperate counterattack. But the Japanese increased their pressure, on the night of January 27 attacking Cushing's forces at six different points.

Cushing radioed Planet Party camp on Negros for desperately needed ammunition but none was available. "God damn it, Will," he raged, "why doesn't MacArthur allow me to communicate directly with him instead of having to go through Negros? Why is he sending ammo to Bohol and none to us? My men can't understand why MacArthur won't recognize me." He grabbed a pencil and began writing. "I'm radioing Negros to tell MacArthur he can stick his recognition up his ass."

"Let me write the message," said Will calmly.

Cushing irritably tossed Will the pencil. "Just spell it right—ASS!"

Will laughed and Cushing couldn't help grinning. In a few minutes Will handed over a draft.

> NIPS DRIVING LINES OF 27 JANUARY IN SIX POINTS. ENEMY CAPTURE ONE DUMMY TRANSMITTING STATION. WILL DO MY UTMOST TO CARRY OUT ALL ORDERS TO FULFILL THE CONFIDENCE YOU HAVE ENTRUSTED IN ME. ALL PAST ATTEMPTS IN LIEU OF POLICIES HAVE PROVED DISASTROUS . . .

Cushing burst out laughing. "Will, you sly son of a bitch! I wish I had gone to Harvard!" He resumed reading.

> . . . OUR INTELLIGENCE REPORTS BOHOL AS HAVING RECEIVED SOME ARMS AND 160 BOXES OF AMMO. WE WOULD APPRECIATE 80 BOXES OF 30 CALIBER AMMO TRANSSHIPPED TO US. GOOD LUCK AND KEEP 'EM FLYING.

"I love that last line," said Cushing, then sobered. "Do you think we'll get anything except another sermon?"

"As your lawyer," said Will, "I advise you to send it. We'll get nothing by blowing off steam."

The message was radioed to Planet Party camp on Negros which passed it on to Australia. Within a month supplies, arms, equipment and other supplies began trickling into Cebu. Then, to the amazement of everyone but Will, a powerful shortwave radio and special codes were received from GHQ. And by the end of March word arrived that MacArthur now recognized Lieutenant Colonel Cushing as commanding officer of the Cebu Area Command.

This brought a celebration lasting two days. Although Cushing drank heavily, it didn't seem to affect him at all. He was elated. Now he could plead directly to MacArthur for arms, ammo, medicines, signal equipment, money, and clothing. He didn't know it but Courtney Whitney, once an opponent, had become one of his staunchest supporters upon studying action reports and it was he who had persuaded MacArthur to meet Cushing's supply requirements. In a memorandum to MacArthur,

Whitney praised Cushing's fighting spirit and leadership. "I believe he and his followers merit all assistance reasonably possible."

The resultant rise of morale among Cushing's men had an instant effect on their fighting spirit and efficiency. Not only was the Japanese offensive repelled but an effective intelligence net was put in operation throughout the island. This turned out to be a godsend to the Allied cause on the first day of April. At 2 A.M. a four-engine Kawanishi flying boat was running out of fuel just short of Cebu. It had taken off from Palau and was transporting Admiral Shigeru Fukudome, chief of staff of the Combined Fleet. Fukudome could see the long, narrow island in the moonlight but as the plane descended the sea became lost in blackness. The pilot, disoriented, lost control. Fukudome, an expert aviator, groped forward, clutching a briefcase. Yanking back on the controls to bring the bulky ship out of its dive, he pulled too far. The Kawanishi stalled, then cartwheeled sickeningly into the sea.

As the plane was sinking Fukudome fought his way to the surface, still gripping the briefcase. It contained "Operation Z," the plan for a decisive naval battle off Leyte that was Japan's last hope of winning the war.

On the shore at the barrio of Bahed, fishermen saw a great flash of light offshore. It could not have been lightning since it was red and yellow. Figuring it must be an explosion, the fishermen set out in bancas in hopes of finding something of value. They caught sight of Fukudome hanging desperately with one arm onto a seat cushion. Fukudome feared the approaching banca might be manned by guerrillas and released his hold on the valuable briefcase. One fisherman saw it sinking and seized it.

The fishermen rescued the admiral along with nine other Japanese and turned them over to guerrillas stationed nearby. Their leader, who had spent a year at Tokyo Imperial University, noticed that Fukudome was treated with the respect of a high-ranking officer; perhaps he was a general. The guerrilla leader also was so impressed by the red TOP SECRET markings on the papers in Fukudome's briefcase that he wrote down this information and dispatched it by runner to Cushing. Without waiting for an answer he and his men set out for Cushing's mountain headquarters. Nine of the prisoners had regained enough strength to walk but Fukudome, with a leg badly injured in the crash, had to be carried upland in a litter. It was grueling not only for him but for his bearers in the trek through the tangled vines and creepers. Going up twisting steep inclines was even more arduous and often it took an hour to go a hundred yards. After a week they were still a mile from their destination.

That night Cushing radioed MacArthur that ten Japanese prisoners were now en route to his headquarters.

> PLEASE ADVISE ACTION TO BE TAKEN. CONSTANT EN-
> EMY PRESSURE MAKES THIS SITUATION VERY PRECARI-
> OUS. FURTHER INFORMATION FROM PRISONERS FOL-
> LOWS.

Early the following afternoon the safari arrived. "You're safe as long as you stay in my hands," Cushing told Fukudome who bowed his head in thanks. Cushing let him rest for several hours. After a good meal Will interrogated him in Japanese. Fukudome, worn from the long, painful trip, pleaded that he was in no shape to answer questions and would only admit his name was General Furumei, commander of land and sea forces in Macassar.

Will took Cushing aside. "I think he's lying. My guess is he's a high-ranking naval officer." They let Fukudome sleep while Will studied the documents. Certain pages were obliterated and Will, confused by some of the ideographs, still knew these were very important papers. "Jim, this could be the plan for a great naval counteroffensive!" Another set of documents appeared to be an entire cipher system. "You'd better alert MacArthur."

No sooner had a message with this information gone out to Australia than Socorro arrived, exhausted, with bad news. Two survivors of the plane crash had managed to escape to Cebu City and Japanese patrols were just a mile behind. Will noticed a bloodstain on the back of her shirt, but she waved aside any attempt to bandage her and said it was only "a cresh," which Cushing interpreted as a crease. He gave orders to break camp.

Fukudome was loaded into a litter with an advance party which headed farther into the mountains while Cushing hastily wrote orders to his regiments for a fighting withdrawal absorbing as few casualties as possible. He sent a dozen men west to hold off the oncoming Japanese, then ordered the big radio to be destroyed. They would take the little ATR4A set so they could keep MacArthur informed by way of Negros.

Rifle fire crackled. "Mount up!" said Cushing and preceded by his Great Dane, Senta, led the way up the face of a steep slope. Despite arthritis he traveled so fast that Will had difficulty keeping up with him. Before dusk they found a safe refuge for the night and the men who had delayed the Japanese had caught up with the group. Cushing had twenty-five soldiers, Socorro and another female lieutenant, several nurses, and ten captives. It would be impossible to get help in time from any of the regiments and there appeared to be at least five hundred Japanese closing in.

Cushing summoned Will and three officers and in the darkness they discussed their predicament. The main task was to get the secret papers to Australia by submarine. It was also obvious, said Cushing, that MacArthur would want the ten prisoners. Someone suggested they head for the submarine rendezvous on the southeast coast of Cebu but Cushing decided they'd never make it with so many prisoners. The northeast coast was the best possibility. At the same time they had to fool the Japanese into thinking they were trying to escape to Negros or Bohol. In the dim light of a small campfire, Cushing and Will composed a message:

> JAP CAPTIVES FROM PALAU. ENEMY AWARE THEIR
> PRESENCE HERE. WE ARE CATCHING HELL. WE ARE
> STAGING A FAKE WITHDRAWAL FROM THIS ISLAND TO
> WITHDRAW PRESSURE WHILE AWAITING YOUR FUR-
> THER ORDERS. SOUTHEAST CEBU IMPOSSIBLE NOW.
> WILL MAKE EVERY ATTEMPT TO HOLD THE JAPANESE
> GENERAL AND NEXT RANKING OFFICER. PLEASE RUSH
> ADVICE. NORTHEAST COAST STILL CLEAR FOR SUBMA-
> RINE.

While this message was being transmitted to Negros, Socorro was telling Cushing and Will something she didn't want the others to know. The island Japanese commander, Lieutenant Colonel Seito Onishi, was posting bulletins all over Cebu threatening to burn down villages and execute civilians if the prisoners were not released immediately.

After a grim silence Cushing asked for Will's opinion. He was reluctant. As a U.S. Army officer he should advise Cushing to hang onto the "general" at all costs. But he finally said, "I think we should hand over all the prisoners."

Cushing was relieved. "If we didn't we'd never again have the support of the people." He told Socorro to locate the advance party and bring back the Japanese general. A day later she returned with Fukudome, carried by four guards.

"General," said Cushing, "I am thinking of releasing you and your

291

men. But you must first send a note to your army ordering them not to harm any civilians in retaliation for your capture."

Fukudome agreed. The note was written in Japanese and he signed it as Admiral Koga, Commanding Officer, Combined Fleet. Will smiled. "Thank you, Admiral."

"Admiral?" said Cushing. "Not General?"

"Admiral, Colonel Kooshing," said Fukudome in English.

At dawn Socorro cautiously set out with Fukudome's note. An hour passed. The prisoners were openly nervous, except for the admiral. He lay on his litter petting Cushing's fierce Great Dane, who bristled at the other Japanese. Will sat beside Fukudome and they talked about the beauties of Hakone. Cushing joined them. From the first he had admired the admiral's stoic acceptance of pain and admiration had ripened, despite Cushing's natural dislike of all Japanese, into friendship. He questioned Fukudome about his family.

After four hours there was a rustling noise. Senta barked once before Cushing could quiet him. A bird whistled. It was Socorro. She handed a note to Cushing who passed it on to Will. He smiled. "Colonel Onishi promises to abide by the proposal."

Late in the afternoon Cushing warmly shook Fukudome's hand. Four guerrillas hoisted his litter and started down the mountain path followed by the other prisoners. The group, led by a Filipino carrying a flag of truce, was escorted by an unarmed platoon of guerrillas. Will and Socorro followed at a distance. Within an hour the little party approached a huge banyan tree under which more than a hundred Japanese soldiers were waiting.

The guerrilla party halted. From the top of a small gully Will and Socorro watched engrossed as the two groups silently faced each other. Apparently at an order from Fukudome, the Japanese prisoners moved forward followed by the litter and the unarmed guerrillas. No one spoke as the two groups slowly neared each other. Then a Japanese soldier held out a pack of cigarettes to a guerrilla who tentatively took it. Other Japanese offered cigarettes which were accepted. The ragged, spare guerrillas and the well-fed Japanese lit up, sending up puffs of smoke. Once the litter carrying Fukudome changed hands, the guerrillas slowly turned and headed back up the gully. The admiral sat up in his litter waving an arm. This, thought Will, had to be about the most bizarre scene of the bloody war.

By dusk the Cushing party was back at Tabunan. Cushing and Will argued until midnight over what to tell MacArthur, the latter insisting they should stick to the facts and not make too many excuses. They settled on this:

> JAP PRISONERS TOO HOT FOR US TO HOLD. DUE TO NUMBER OF CIVILIANS BEING KILLED, I MADE TERMS THAT CIVILIANS ARE NOT TO BE MOLESTED IN THE FUTURE IN EXCHANGE FOR THE PRISONERS. ALTHOUGH THE ENEMY DID NOT KNOW IT, WE HAD ONLY 25 SOLDIERS BETWEEN THE ATTACKING FORCE OF APPROXIMATELY FIVE HUNDRED AND OUR POSITION. ALSO, WE WERE UNABLE TO MANEUVER OUT OF OUR POSITION. ENEMY NOW WITHDRAWING TOWARD CITY.

This message was picked up by guerrillas in Mindanao and passed on to the GHQ. Enraged, General Sutherland replied:

> YOUR ACTION IN RELEASING IMPORTANT PRISONERS AFTER NEGOTIATION WITH THE ENEMY IS MOST REPREHENSIBLE AND LEADS ME TO DOUBT YOUR JUDGMENT AND EFFICIENCY. YOU ARE HEREBY DISCHARGED FROM YOUR FUNCTIONS AS COMMANDER OF THE 7TH MILITARY DISTRICT.

Cushing's anger turned to tears. "The son of a bitch has busted me to private! He'll throw me in the brig when he comes back to the Philippines!"

Will advised him to send the general a message apologizing for being forced by circumstances to turn over the prisoners. "And remind him how eager you are to turn over the captured documents." While Cushing was simultaneously writing this message and blasphemously berating MacArthur a guerrilla scout arrived with a pamphlet dropped by a Japanese fighter plane. It was addressed to Mr. James Cushing and signed by the Commander of the Imperial Japanese Naval Garrison of Cebu. It demanded that Cushing return to the mayor of San Fernando within a week "all documents, bags and clothing either picked up from the crashed seaplane or robbed of the passengers and the crew."

Cushing had no more time for anger. He was all for action. He said they had to get the Japanese documents over to Negros where there was an alternate submarine rendezvous point near Planet Party camp. He added this information to his apologetic message with the suggestion that the meeting take place in ten days.

"Do you think you're in shape to take the papers to Negros?" he asked Will.

"Yes."

"I'll have two of my best men go along with you. The Japs have given us a week to return the documents. Then they'll give us hell. The sooner you get started the better."

Will could scarcely restrain his enthusiasm. After turning the papers over to the sub commander he could demand passage to Australia so he could bring Marshall evidence of Japanese atrocities. If Cushing knew he planned to do this he would undoubtedly send someone else and so he said nothing.

"Get a move on," said Cushing impatiently.

Will started toward his hut, then impulsively turned around. "Jim, I want permission to go back on the sub."

Cushing was indignant. "I need you here!"

"My first responsibility is to General Marshall."

"Damn it, Will. You'll do a lot more good here. I'm going to send someone else."

"I could tell Marshall how MacArthur has been screwing you up."

Cushing swore in Tagalog. "You crafty son of a bitch!" He sighed. "Oh, hell, go ahead."

In an hour the exultant Will was packed. Then he hurried to Socorro's hut. She took the news stoically. He kissed her but she did not respond.

She smiled sadly and gave him a Catholic medal. "Don't get died." They kissed and he left, guilty at his own elation.

Will shook hands with Cushing.

"Damn you, Will. Who's going to keep me straight now?" Then he said soberly, *"Vaya con Dios."*

"I didn't know you were a religious man, Jim."

The two shook hands as if they would never see each other again. The documents were wrapped in oilskin and stuffed into two empty mortar shell cases which were packed in a knapsack along with emergency rations. Will volunteered to carry this and suggested his two companions tote rifles and water. Unlike Will's first trip to Negros this one was rapid with short rests. All three men were in good condition. On the mountain trails the two smaller men had the advantage of agility but on flatter surface they had difficulty keeping pace with Will's long strides. In a week they had reached southern Cebu despite half a dozen narrow escapes.

The trip across the channel to Negros in the dark almost ended disastrously when the lights of a Japanese patrol boat picked up their banca moments after they shoved off. As Will lay inert the two Filipinos changed course twice, then paddled at top speed toward two tiny islands. The patrol boat, engine roaring, sharply swerved in their wake. As the banca skimmed between the islets it was caught by the searchlight's rays. Bullets whistled just over the paddlers' heads. The next machine-gun burst would kill them all. Instead, from close behind came a shrill ripping, crunching noise and sudden darkness. The Filipinos laughed. They had lured their pursuers into a large jagged rock lying a foot below the surface.

They reached Negros an hour before dawn but were still a day's march from Planet Party camp. It was dark by the time they reached Villamor's old site. His replacement welcomed them anxiously. The submarine was ahead of schedule, he said. It would surface at the rendezvous at midnight and they would have to rush to get there on time. In his haste, an hour later, Will tripped over a root. He struggled to his feet. The pain in his right ankle was excruciating but he hobbled forward as fast as he could.

As they neared the beach they ran into a Japanese patrol. Will knew he could never make a run for it. Cursing his luck, he removed his knapsack. "I'll draw the Japs away," he whispered. "You two stay put."

He limped noisily through the brush away from the beach followed by rifle shots and shouts. For half an hour he scrambled painfully through the jungle. Then he stumbled over a log. Momentarily stunned, he got to his feet to be blinded by the rays of a flashlight.

Slowly, he raised his hands in surrender, consoled that he had given the Filipinos time to get Operation Z to the submarine.

CHAPTER NINETEEN

1.

Washington, D.C. December 1943.

Professor McGlynn's duties as one of the civilian assistants to Captain Ellis Zacharias, head of Op-16-W, were interesting, if exasperating. McGlynn had already made himself either revered or detested since his acid wit was unrestrained in his attacks on those "benighted creatures" whose goal was to bring Japan to terms by threats of unconditional surrender.

He was also free with his advice on all matters concerning the war in the Pacific. The President had not sought his counsel for several months after an open letter he sent to the Washington *Post* comparing the treatment of Japanese on the West Coast to that of Jews by Hitler. His harried superior, a Jew, although personally agreeing, begged him to stop baiting the White House since it could impede their own hopes to bring about a more reasonable settlement.

He compromised by writing cautionary letters to the President which were never mailed. But he was so entranced by their brilliance that he sent them on to Maggie in Honolulu. He also wrote her at length of his growing concern over Will. Through a friend in Marshall's office he learned that Will had been sent with other officers on a ship bound for Mindanao. He never arrived and apparently had tried to escape. McGlynn had been warned to expect the worst but it was impossible to imagine Will dead. Somehow he would manage to survive. In a brief postscript McGlynn reported that there had been no news about Floss and Tadashi since the report of their arrival in Japan a year earlier.

He also wrote Mark but these letters were shorter and more impersonal. He tried to be less stiff but found it impossible. There was something about Mark that inhibited him, some barrier which he had never been able to cross despite many attempts. It seemed that every time either of them had tried to break through, the other one had bristled. Perhaps it was a question of chemistry.

Mark was halfway to Hawaii. The ship reeked of the smell of death. There were no clean uniforms and attempts to wash out the stink of blood and slime in salt water were fruitless. Like so many others, Mark had lost his gear but he had managed to save several hundred dollars from the sale of souvenirs to sailors. This, with his poker winnings, brought his "Hinemoa Fund" to over two thousand dollars.

Mark was helping Tullio write and revise casualty reports. They would hunt through the ship for buddies of those missing in action in an effort to find out how, where, and when a man was hit or first missed. There was no system for keeping reports, no forms or account books. Tullio had to use toilet paper and a pencil stub; his field desk was his helmet. Billy J. left most of the details to Tullio. His time was taken up with the painful task of writing letters to parents of the dead and seriously wounded.

The most harrowing day was November 22 when all Marines who could walk were asked to come topside to act as honor guard for those to be buried at sea. They were a motley lot still clad in dirty, sweaty dungarees, some wearing bandages, some unshaven, some so weak they had to hang onto a mate. After Father O'Brian and the ship's captain gave the last rites, a sailor cut the line for the first man to slide into the ocean. Mark watched as he hit the water to disappear forever. Body after body made the plunge. It chilled Mark to remember that not long ago some of these dead were crawling over the side with him into a Higgins boat. But they hadn't made it and now they were sinking to the bottom of the Pacific with no tombstone as a marker. As the bugler played taps there were tears in the eyes of the toughest Marine.

At last they could see the outlines of two peaks and lush green terrain. It was the big island of Hawaii. Their ship anchored in Hilo Bay and the men were off-loaded in landing craft. The town of Hilo was dotted with palm trees. There were girls and they all looked pretty, but to Mark none could compare with Hinemoa. It was pleasantly warm, a paradise, and the men envisaged comfort at last in a dream camp. Everything about the island was relaxing and the men climbed into six-by-six trucks, eager to get to Camp Tarawa which, they were told, was on the other side of a great volcano. It was a sixty-five-mile trip and the first stage, along the coast, was dusty but fairly pleasant for those who rode in the cab. Mark and Tullio sat on the tailgate end, however, and the vibrations were brutal.

"I feel as if my ass is coming up out of my mouth," complained Tullio.

Having had experience riding freight trains, Mark advised him how to soften the blows but Tullio could only say, "I think I'm going to die." He coughed and there was blood on his handkerchief.

"I'm going to get you into the cab where it doesn't bounce so hard," said Mark.

Tullio pulled him down. "If I went up front everybody would start bitching about the ride."

The desert dust stirred up by the trucks ahead swirled over them. To this was added heavy exhaust fumes. Eyes, noses, and mouths were filled with the dust. Then they started climbing and could see snow on top of a volcano. It began to get chilly and by the time they reached Camp Tarawa it felt like December in Alaska. The camp, located on the vast Parker Ranch, lay in a saddle between two volcanoes, Mauna Loa and Mauna Kea, but no one enjoyed the impressive sight. Mark started to help Tullio descend but he jumped down agilely, hiding his pain.

"Get your asses off!" he shouted loudly. "Fall in and let's get this show on the road." What they saw was enough to make the toughest Marine wonder what the hell they had done to deserve this fate. It was bitterly cold, a shock to those who had just fought near the equator and still wore light clothing. The wind swirled like a Kansas dust storm. And this was the dream camp? Rows of stacked platforms, the pyramidals not even unfurled. They were orphans in a cold land that called itself a paradise.

"Same old garbage," said Tullio and set men to work putting up tents. There was no hot food waiting for them and dinner was the usual cold C rations. Afterward Mark took a short walk as the sun was setting. The wind had died down and he could appreciate the magnificent view. They were on a plateau with rolling plains extending for miles between the two volcanoes.

Even under blankets it was freezing so he put newspapers between the blankets—an old trick of the road—and managed to sleep soundly until awakened by a sadistic bugler. The first thing he heard was someone returning from a look outside: "Hell, we might as well be in New Mexico. Cactus, dust, century plants, and wind!"

Billy J. issued the men face masks to protect them from the dust, then explained that this place had not been selected out of spite or ignorance but because the cold climate would help those still suffering from recurring malaria. And the terrain was perfect for training since both beaches and mountains were nearby.

Although there was good food, real American beer, and a USO camp show troupe which gave a rousing performance, Christmas was glum for most of the men. The mist and chill cast a pall among those who had not yet recovered from the physical or psychological wounds of battle and were haunted by thoughts of home. Realizing something had to be done, Billy J.—in command of the battalion—summoned Tullio and the mess sergeant and turned over a case of liquor. He was sure, he said, they would know what to do with it. These two mixed up a huge vat of liquor, grapefruit juice, and oranges. The word went out that there would be free drinks in the first sergeant's tent from ten to midnight.

By ten there was a mob waiting with cups. Mark took only one swallow of the potent mixture. It brought fire to his eyes and burned his stomach like an ulcer. Tullio refused even a taste since he was going to midnight Mass and was not supposed to drink hard liquor or eat any food. Within an hour the battalion area took on the appearance of a rowdy barroom. There wasn't an officer in sight to inhibit the men. By some miracle there were no fights. By eleven-thirty scores of men had passed out along the company streets.

After Tullio and Mark supervised removal of the bodies, the former took off for Mass. Mark returned to his tent but it reeked so badly of liquor fumes that he retreated to the mess hall with his writing materials. He wrote a long letter to Hinemoa in answer to two from her that had just arrived. While her letters were not as impassioned as he had hoped, she did call him "My Dearest" and ended with "All my love." He told her something of Tarawa but without the gruesome details, adding that he was sending his winnings on the big poker games as soon as he could find a way to do so. "Now, at least we have enough for down payment on a house." He wrote a letter to his father giving him more details of the battle but mentioning nothing of poker. He finally told Maggie about all the funny things that had happened on Tarawa, adding that he had learned Major Sullivan was putting him in for the Bronze Star. He urged her to come to the Big Island for the award ceremonies. Being a reporter she should have no trouble covering the story. Much of his letter spoke of the wonders of Hinemoa and how lucky he was to have found and won her. He only hoped Maggie too would finally find someone to love.

She replied with an amusing account of her adventures tracking down stories. She was bored writing articles about the training of troops and how noble the population was acting so close to the front lines. She was anxious to see the war. She wanted action, not a lot of ____ and she shocked Mark by using a word that was common around 1/6. Life as a correspondent was changing her—for the worse, he thought.

The entire 2nd Division faced a seemingly hopeless task. Every company had been riddled by casualties and many of the wounded and sick would never return to front-line duty. The gaps were filled mainly by seventeen-year-old replacements who had seen no action.

Planeloads of officers of various ranks were also being flown in from the States, including lieutenant colonels because six of the division's infantry battalion commanders were majors. Since Billy J. was far too junior it looked as if he would lose his temporary command of 1/6, but he was given a field promotion to lieutenant colonel to the relief and elation of the battalion. Mark accompanied Billy J. to division headquarters for the promotion ceremony and proudly watched Billy J.'s gold major's leaves being changed to silver ones.

By this time the close relationship between Mark and the colonel had resumed, and the latter again brought up the problem of fear in battle as they were driving back from mortar platoon practice with live shells. "Some men who did okay on Tarawa might fall apart next time," he observed. "I hope not, but you never know. Just one or two boys can start a domino reaction, and if some man isn't there to kick their ass or shame them by his example, they'll freeze—become stationary targets for the enemy. A lot of lives can be lost."

Upon entering Sullivan's office, both were startled to see Captain Mullins. His arm was still in a sling. "What the hell are you doing out of the hospital?" asked Billy J. "You're not supposed to be released for two weeks."

"Well, Colonel," drawled Moon, "it seems I made a mistake to fool around with a nurse that happened to be the favorite dolly of the chief surgeon. She was beginning to really like me." He grinned like the Cheshire cat.

"Glad to have you back, you rascal." They shook hands. "Here's something about discipline I've written to all the new officers. Point this out to your officers."

Moon read: "This is not a YMCA Camp, a Boy Scout troop or a football team. Do not interpret the team to mean that you should be a coach or a personal friend of your men by becoming familiar with them."

"Yes, sir," said Moon, knowing the paper had been written for people like himself. "I'll pass this on." He saluted with his left hand, spun around smartly and walked out.

"I'd hate to lose him," muttered the colonel. "He's a crazy bastard but he knows how to get results."

2.

The next morning when Mark reported for duty Billy J. handed him a paper. "You were recommended for the Bronze Star but it's been knocked down to a Letter of Commendation. Sorry." Mark didn't show his disappointment. "Tomorrow Admiral Nimitz is flying in from Pearl with a lot of brass to give out medals to the division."

Mark grimaced. "I'll bet my sister talks her way onto the plane," he said, then added in embarrassment, "I told her I was getting the Bronze Star."

"Who tipped you off?" Sullivan was upset.

"Sir, would you really want me to tell you?"

"Forget it."

The next day was rainy, cold, and windy. The awards ceremony on a flat, barren field was simple. There was no parade, no band. Only those getting awards were present. From a distance Mark watched staff cars debouch an imposing delegation of officers, several photographers and reporters, one of whom was Maggie in a trench coat and cap. Admiral Nimitz first honored those getting Navy Crosses. Then officers and men who were to receive the Silver Star. The admiral went down the line, finally coming to Billy J. He pinned on the Silver Star, shook his hand. Nimitz now came to a longer line, those getting the Bronze Star. Mark saw Maggie straining in vain to pick him out.

Later he brought her to Billy J.'s office at his request. After a few complimentary remarks about Mark the colonel told them to use his office as long as they liked and left them alone. Her face was shining, her hair wild. She embraced Mark. "What happened?"

He explained about the Letter of Commendation. She was indignant and said she'd complain to Admiral Nimitz on the flight back to Pearl Harbor. "He's an old sweetie!"

"For God's sake, Maggie, no!"

After hastily reading the Commendation she was even more indignant. "My God, you should have got the Medal of Honor!"

"Don't be ridiculous. What I did was nothing compared to almost everyone else in the outfit." He begged her to lower her voice and stop waving the letter around. By now curious passersby were peering through the screened open sides of the office.

"Oh, Mark, I'm really so proud of you. Can I have a copy of this?"

"Take it. I don't need it."

"I'll send Papa a copy. He'll really be puffed up."

Mark made no comment but had his doubts. After Mark gave Maggie his poker winnings to deposit in his bank in New York, she urged him to get a leave and come to Honolulu. Then she kissed him and rushed off to get a ride to the airfield in "Old Sweetie's" car.

"We've got to take the boredom out of training," Billy J. announced to the exec in Mark's presence later the following day. "The old-timers have been through too much hell already to accept ordinary drills." He had a plan to mix work and play. "At the same time we must keep them blind to what our next target will be." He began by personally directing the rubber boat training on an excellent beach not far from camp as though it were a sport. At first the men would only ride the rubber boats back to shore like surfboards. In a few days, after they all had the feel of the boats and the heavy surf, they returned in formation so that communications among fire teams, squads, and platoons could be maintained. In the afternoons Billy J. and the officers swam, surfed, and played softball and volleyball with the men.

Long hikes in the mountains were interspersed with occasional tours of the cane fields of the Parker Ranch. To the men these educational tours were like a holiday. They did not realize that Sullivan was getting them prepared for the cane fields of Saipan. There followed training in taking bunkers erected by the engineers. Every man had to become expert not only with a bazooka but a flamethrower.

3.

Early that March, Mark received another letter from New Zealand. As usual he waited until he was in the office to read it. Every letter from Hinemoa was a treat he wanted to enjoy in private. He was so unprepared that he didn't realize at first that he had received one of those letters servicemen had a name for. And when he finally read the words, "It hurts me so much to have to tell you that I can't marry you," it came as an unexpected blow in the stomach. He was so dazed it took some

time before he could read that she would always love him but could not
be happy in his new world. Father O'Brian had been right. She would
be a fish out of water in America. "When you talked about your New
England you made it sound so wonderful, but now that you're away I
think I would wither in your land." The letter ended with the bitterest
sentence. "I'm going to marry one of my own kind, Tara. Please don't
hate me. I shall pray for you every day of my life." She enclosed a bank
draft for all the money in her account.

His first impulse was to tear up the check, then to send it back to her.
Tears flowed down his cheeks and he didn't know it. He swore as he
drove his fist into a post. It hurt and he was glad. He rushed to his tent,
pulled all her letters and precious little gifts from his footlocker. He
stuffed everything, including a lock of black hair and the check, into a
large manila envelope and mailed it to New Zealand. That night as he
lay in the dark he could recollect Hinemoa's letter word by word. He
could clearly see her writing it—so neat and clear, so regimented and
sensible, so without guile. The pain in his chest was not imagination and
he could feel hot tears well in his eyes.

He told no one he had received a "Dear John" letter but it was
obvious something was the matter. Tullio hesitated to question him and
went to the colonel. "I'll talk to him," promised Billy J.

He asked Mark what was eating him.

Mark dug out the letter which he had tried to tear up a dozen times.
Sullivan read it carefully. He was sympathetic. "That's rough." Mark
was silent.

After a long pause Billy J. said, "Why don't you talk to Big Joe?"

"He'll just say, 'I told you so.'" Mark took back the letter. "May I be
excused, sir?"

Mark slept only briefly in the next week. He ate little, did his work
mechanically. Finally Billy J. could take it no longer.

"I've had enough of your crap, Mark. You're acting like a baby again.
There are probably a hundred guys in this division who got a Dear John
letter this week and you don't see them sulking around." He put a hand
on Mark's shoulder. "I'm going to tell you something that no one else in
this outfit knows. Before the war the Marine Corps had a rule that a
regular officer could not marry for the first two years. If he did his
commission was revoked. The Marine Corps didn't want any of its
junior officers marrying until they were in a financial position where
they could at least support a wife decently. Well, Mark, I was dating this

girl in college. I told her about the two-year restriction and she understood we'd have to wait even though we were in love."

Mark, who had been listening impatiently, became interested.

"When I was in Iceland we wrote back and forth many times. After recall from Iceland half the battalion was given two weeks' leave traveling cross-country to Elliott. I was one of the lucky ones. First thing I did in New York was telephone my girl. She said something about getting engaged to some Air Corps colonel. I told her not to do anything until I got home. I knew I could talk her out of it. So I left New York with three friends and we drove to Kansas City. The night we arrived I phoned an old friend and told him I was seeing my girl the next day. And he said, 'Bill, Mary is getting married tomorrow morning to an Air Corps colonel. I know because I have an invitation.' Mark, I never felt so stupid in my life. My two friends never kidded me but I was getting madder and madder. I thought of the wedding and honeymoon and got so damned mad I wanted to tell her off. Then something inside of me said, 'All that's hurt is your ego—your false pride. You want to be proud of yourself— yes, proud of being a Marine.' I told myself that I was going to find a girl, the right girl, and marry her when the right time came along." They sat silently looking at Mauna Loa. "Remember what I've told you. I want you to go over and see Big Joe. I'm telling you this as a friend—and your commanding officer."

Billy J. began to chuckle. "Damn, but I was mad at the crummy Air Corps colonel. And at Mary too. At least your girl played it aboveboard. My girl did not. Your girl will always love you, Mark. She's using her head instead of her emotions."

Mark said nothing.

"Big Joe knows more about these things than I do. He's a wise old boy and he'll be thinking of what's best for both of you. Will you see him?"

"All right," said Mark reluctantly.

As he rose to leave Sullivan said, "We've got a tough campaign coming up, Mark, and if you want to save your ass you'd better concentrate on that and forget this."

"Yes, sir."

The next day Mark showed Father O'Brian the letter. "She's a fine girl, Mark. She made the right decision for both of you. You two will be true friends for the rest of your lives. You're going to be interested in her and her family. And she will be interested in you and yours. You are lucky to have such a girl feeling such pure love for you and praying for you."

"Lucky?" said Mark bitterly.

"You're just feeling sorry for yourself. Can't you see how painful this has been for Hinemoa? She truly loved you but the marriage would probably not have worked out."

Mark got to his feet. "Thanks, Father."

"Why don't you come over again and we can talk some more."

"Sure," said Mark disconsolately and left.

Hinemoa was reading Mark's reply. She wept to see all her letters and the lock of hair which she hoped he would keep. She had been miserable for weeks and tomorrow would marry Tara. It was not that her love for Mark had diminished but she had come to realize that living in an unfriendly, strange land would have been too much for her. She would have pined and made Mark miserable. What had been fascinating at first in his actions, even his words, made her fear she would never be able to keep pace with him. She had told Tara everything and he had been torn to learn she was pregnant but she knew he would never hold this against her. His love for her was strong and she would grow to love him dearly.

When she showed the endorsed check to her mother, she advised Hinemoa to put it in an account for the child and to say nothing to Tara about it, and she was sure Tara would eventually accept the money for the child's education.

Mark never intended going back to Big Joe but a week later he found himself drawn to the chaplain's tent; this time he told about his inability to get close to his father.

"No matter how hard I try to please him, he brushes me off."

"Perhaps your efforts to please him aren't the right ones. Perhaps he is one of those people who have difficulty showing affection."

"He shows it with no trouble to Will and Maggie."

"And you resented it and probably showed it."

"Wasn't it his fault?"

"Of course it was. What does that have to do with it? I'm talking to you, not your father."

"What in hell should I have done?"

"You should have loved him."

"I did!"

"Not enough."

GODS OF WAR

Mark was thoughtful, then said, "Did you know my father was born a Catholic?"

"I'm not surprised."

Mark told about the nun beating him with an iron ruler. "I was brought up to hate Catholics. I was scared to walk past the Catholic church. But one day a Catholic friend of mine took me inside. It was eerie with all those statues and altars and the smell of candles and incense. It made my flesh crawl." He laughed in embarrassment. "A few years later I secretly began to read the Bible. I was ashamed for I knew my father would make fun of me. But I became fascinated with Jesus. As a character, you know. I loved the way he stood up to the fat cats in the temple."

Big Joe laughed. "I think I'll give a talk on Jesus and the Fat Cats at the next Mass." He invited Mark to chat with him whenever he felt the urge.

As Mark was leaving his eye was caught by a poem on Big Joe's desk. "That's an intriguing title, Father, 'The Hound of Heaven.'"

"A strange work by an Englishman named Thompson. He became hooked on drugs when he was a young man and ended in the gutter. A prostitute took him to her place and nursed him back to health. During this period he recovered his faith. He describes the whole experience in this poem. The Hound is Christ pursuing him. He uses very fanciful language. It might appeal to you."

"Could I borrow it?"

"Certainly. It contains some very important concepts. It may have some meaning for you."

That evening Mark read the poem. It fascinated and repelled him. How his father would ridicule the extravagant language and images.

Naked I wait Thy love's uplifted stroke!
My harness piece by piece Thou hast hewn from me,
    And smitten me to my knee;
    I am defenseless utterly.
    I slept, methinks, and woke,
And, slowly gazing, find me stripped in sleep.
In the rash lustihead of my young powers,
    I shook the pillaring hours
And pulled my life upon me; grimed with smears
I stand amid the dust o' the mounded years—
My mangled youth lies dead beneath the heap.

My days have crackled and gone up in smoke,
Have puffed and burst as sun-starts on a stream.

Mark was moved and ridiculed himself for being moved. The words
kept him awake almost till dawn. A week later he returned the poem to
Big Joe. "It's weird, Father. I don't understand it. Too much for me." He
was nervous. Finally he said, "I wouldn't want you to tell anyone about
this but how do you become a Catholic?"

The padre was not enthusiastic. "You'd better not be jumping into
anything as important as this, young fellow."

"I've been thinking over what you told me. Perhaps the gap in my life
will be filled by . . ."

"Slow down. I'm not at all sure that you're ready for conversion. You
shouldn't think of becoming a Catholic for some emotional reason, as a
sort of rebound from your pain at losing Hinemoa or as some way of
getting back at your father."

"It may have started like that," admitted Mark, "but the past few days
I've been trying to analyze what's wrong with me. You didn't know that
I bugged out at the 'Canal. Panicked."

"That could happen to any of us. How did you do at Tarawa?"

"I was all right but I was still scared as hell."

"We're all scared. Anyone with sense is scared."

"But people like Colonel Sullivan and Tullio always manage to carry
on. They seem to know how to handle—" he struggled for a word—
"death."

"Okay," said the priest. "So you think your C.O. and Tullio are great
guys. Maybe you even think I may be a great guy. And all three of us
happen to be Catholic. You may think your pattern of values has a lot to
do with your actions on life, death, on everything; but there are all kinds
among Catholics as there are in any group. The name itself translates
from the Greek, 'universal.' As a Catholic, if you should choose to become one, you will probably grow to a broad acceptance of people as
they are, as God seems to do—to love them all, with all their imperfec-
tions, because they are trying. Grace builds a nature: do the best you can
now with the equipment God gave you, and He will take it from there.
As a matter of fact, when your life is all mixed up it may be that 'God
writes straight with crooked lines.' "

Mark grinned. "That sounds more Chinese than Irish."

"Well, I think it's an old Belgian proverb. God may be forming you for
some plan of His. About being a Catholic, think it over a bit and come

back in a week or so if you're still serious." He gave Mark a pat on the shoulder. "Come back even if you're not serious."

Mark never mentioned his meetings to Billy J. but he did confide in Tullio. After warning Mark about jumping into conversion, Tullio did agree to take him to Mass.

4.

With the advent of spring the tempo of training accelerated. The teamwork of tank, infantry, and engineer units which had proven so effective on Tarawa was sharpened. Adding realism, carrier planes swooped down in close support, spraying live ammunition. By late April the division was ready for battle.

Mark was now seeing Big Joe regularly. In the first few sessions the chaplain quizzed Mark on what he already knew about God, the universe and creation, then he had Mark study the Catholic explanation. He gave Mark a book, a catechism. "Study the questions and answers. Absorb everything; be very critical." When Mark returned with many questions Big Joe encouraged argument, which sometimes became heated. "I can't accept some of this ritualistic stuff," he said. "But I still want to be a Catholic."

"I don't think you're ready. You intellectualize everything."

On the first of May it became known that at dusk there would be plenty of beer in back of the camp. The veterans of New Zealand knew what this meant, for the same thing had happened just before loading for Tarawa. Officers and noncoms would strip their collars and sleeves of insignia and mix with the men as equals. Liquor and rations had been saved for several weeks and at dusk the men of the 1st Battalion began drifting to a field that was fairly level. At first they just ate and drank and chatted. Then the sipping of beer advanced to the chugalug stage. By then most of the battalion was on hand and sporting competition began: "Can you drink that whole bottle without stopping?" or "I bet your boots the lieutenant can put your shoulders to the deck." Challenges were accepted and soon company commanders were wrestling with PFCs and staff noncoms with riflemen. Others were singing all kinds of songs, off color, off tune, without accompaniment. There were songs about the army and the navy, none complimentary, with new verses ad-libbed.

For the first time officers learned the nicknames they had been given by the enlisted men. With one exception. It was an unwritten law in the battalion that Colonel Sullivan was never to know he was called Billy J. The carousing went on and on and although there were many tough wrestling matches there were no fistfights. Not a single belt was used. It was just good-natured hell raising with all men equal. It gave the officers and noncoms the chance to show the men they were going to lead into battle that they too were human. With all barriers down, it gave the men the chance to blow off steam. A private could deck an officer and both end by respecting each other. By some miracle, perhaps the be-nevolent presence of Billy J., the rowdyism never got out of hand and by midnight a comradeship had been established that would last for life.

The enlisted men and junior officers had no idea the 2nd Division was bound for Saipan in the Marianas. First the transports headed for the neighboring island of Maui whose long beaches were suitable for a practice landing. Those who thought the landing at Hawke Bay in New Zealand had been the fiasco to end all fiascos were chagrined by the ensuing foul-up on Maalaea Bay. Everything seemed to go wrong. Add-ing to the confusion was a submarine alarm; destroyers rushed in to depth-bomb the whole area, causing minor tidal waves that tangled up a number of landing craft. The subs turned out to be two whales.

"Poor rehearsal, good show," muttered General Holland "Howlin' Mad" Smith after the critique when everyone expected him to lose his fabled temper. The ships were ordered to Pearl Harbor for staging and rehabilitation before proceeding to Saipan. On the day of arrival Colo-nel Sullivan gave Mark, Tullio, and several other noncoms shore liberty. Mark wanted to go directly to Maggie's hotel but Tullio persuaded him to have a drink with the noncoms. "The Beast thinks you're a fruit," explained Tullio, "since you never go with us to bars."

"I don't like to drink or brawl."

"You may need one of these guys in our next fight. Show them you're one of the guys." And so six of them went into a brassy, disreputable-looking bar which was occupied by ten soldiers. The Beast swaggered up to the bar, smiled and ordered a bottle of whiskey. "I'm buying for everyone." The soldiers indicated they were willing to accept. "Yeah," said The Beast sweetly, "even you dogfaces." He barked raucously. A big soldier advanced holding a stool in one hand.

"C'mon, fellows," said Mark trying to mediate. "He's only kidding."

"Sure," said The Beast, wagging his battle-scarred head. "Arf, Arf! Back in your kennel, Rover."

The G.I. hit Mark with the stool. As he fell over backward Tullio rushed in. Although a foot shorter than the soldier, he sank a fist into the big man's stomach which caused him to grunt and grab his middle. Tullio then feinted with his left and crossed with a right to the chin. The G.I. flopped to the floor. In the meantime soldiers were coming from two sides. The Beast, his belt out, shouted joyously as he whipped it around with awful effect. While Tullio was holding off one soldier another sneaked behind him and slashed at his head with a broken bottle. Mark seized the man's arm, gave a twist. The soldier, crying out in pain, dropped the bottle. Another G.I. jumped at Mark, brandishing a small baseball bat. Mark let him swing it, ducked and pulled the man off balance. Hearing The Beast shout, "Behind you, Mark!" he turned in time to see a burly sergeant charging him. He pulled aside like a toreador, chopping the man from the rear as he passed.

By this time there was a shout of "Shore patrol!" and Mark felt himself being pulled out the back door by The Beast. After a block they stopped and began boasting of their prowess. The Beast slapped Mark on the back. "You're okay, kid," he said.

Half an hour later Mark was apologizing to Maggie for being late and trying to explain why his uniform was soiled. She told him there was still no news of Will or Floss but she herself had been promised first chance to get to the war zone. "It's no place for a woman," he said wincing at the thought of her being in the rear area with a bunch of Marines who entertained their girls with "The Good Ship Venus." He gave her more money from poker winnings. "I don't care what the hell you do with it," he said and told her about Hinemoa.

She didn't take it seriously. "There's always another trolley car coming along."

He was hurt but said nothing.

"I'm sorry," she said apologetically.

"That's all right."

Her face was anxious. "Are you getting ready to hit another beach?"

He tried to put her off but she guessed. "That's why you're getting rid of all your money. Oh, Mark!" She hugged him.

"We're just making practice landings. There's nothing to worry about." She didn't believe him. "I have the safest job in the battalion as Billy J.'s runner."

He told her about his preparation for conversion.

"You're kidding!" But his serious face told her he was not.

"Daddy will have kittens!"

"It's about time," he said and they both laughed.

By a miracle of efficiency all the LST's, replenished with their preload of water ration, ammunition, and supplies, cleared West Loch on the twenty-fifth of May. The slow, cumbersome ships headed for a target thirty-five hundred miles almost due west. Five days later the faster transports followed.

Tullio wrote his mother in their little Pennsylvania mining town: "We are now only a short time away from D-Day which is the day we land to send some more Nips to their reward. When you get this you'll know the rest of the story—where, when, why and who. Food has been good and I'm living in the CPO quarters with real sheets, showers, and other luxuries. Every so often I let my buddy Mark sneak in here for a shower. Try not to worry, Mom. There will be long gaps in my letters. Just know I'm always thinking of you, the girls and Tony. I wonder where that rascal is. I'll bet he gets another medal over there in Europe before long. Your loving son, Tullio."

On June 11 the men got their last instructions. There were some 19,000 Japs defending an island shaped like a monkey wrench that had an area of seventy-two square miles. In the middle was a 1,500-foot volcanic peak, Mount Tapotchau. They would hit the beaches on the southern shore of Saipan between a village, Charan Kanoa, and Garapan, a town of 20,000 Chamorros who might be friendly. A barrier reef protecting the long beach lay 500 to 1,000 feet offshore.

On June 13, Billy J. wrote his parents that they were on their way to the biggest show yet. "I can assure you it's going to be an interesting one and will make the Japs very unhappy. It won't be easy but we can't fail. Both the men and the officers are confident. I guess we're all getting accustomed to the real thing." Everybody was very happy about the big D-Day landing in France. "It sounds awfully good. And we are going to do our part over on this side of the world. We land in two days and we're ready."

That night the ship was completely darkened. On deck Billy J. ran across youngsters sitting by themselves or in small groups. They were just looking up at the stars or talking quietly. In the hold Mark also noticed a more subdued tone. But all the men were sure of themselves. Each one belonged to the best squad in the best platoon in the best company in the best battalion in the best regiment in the whole damned Marines. At Guadalcanal they had fought with hatred; at Tarawa with desperation. This time they would fight as professionals.

In the morning the last boat drill took place. Every man was at the right place with the right equipment at the right time. Mark went topside after dark and could make out a dim hulk in the distance. It was Saipan. He could see pinpoints of fire and wondered what they were. These were the last traces of three days of naval bombardment and carrier air strikes of Task Force 58.

Mark went below to attend the final Mass. The place was crowded. Many, like him, were not Catholics. It was a simple, moving ceremony. Big Joe spoke Christ's words at the Last Supper: "This is my body and this is my blood. Take it and eat and drink you of this." In the dim light Mark could see Colonel Sullivan take the Host, a thin wafer. Billy J. then glanced over at him with a friendly half smile.

PART FIVE

Decisive Battles

CHAPTER TWENTY

1.

Off Saipan. June 15, 1944.

It was a steaming night. Mark slept fitfully and was awake before the clanging of the ship's bell at four o'clock on the morning of D-Day. At breakfast forty-five minutes later he forced himself to eat the usual steak and eggs. It would be their last hot meal for many days—perhaps his last. "Like being on Death Row at San Quentin," a veteran of Tarawa remarked.

The clatter was as loud as usual but there was a tenseness that made it unique. It was hard to breathe below so Mark and Tullio grabbed their backpacks and came topside with rifles, helmets, pistol belts, and knives. It was not quite dawn and Mark could make out a shadowy, purple mass. Saipan.

Rarely had Mark seen such a beautiful sunrise. The island of Saipan looked peaceful even though, with its mountain range, it reminded him of a prehistoric monster rising out of the sea. After being at sea so long he found the green refreshing. Mark was even tenser than he had been at Tarawa. He knew they were landing that morning behind the first waves and casualties would be high.

The quiet was abruptly shattered as big guns from the battleships and cruisers rumbled. Then came sharp reports from destroyers. This was the final softening up of the beaches. The more the better, thought Mark, remembering Tarawa. He filled his cartridge belt with eighty rounds of ammo, checked his first-aid kit and canteens, and strapped on his pack. He could now see the big LST's. These contained the amphibian tractors called alligators, each of which would carry twenty men over the reef.

A chaplain's voice blasted over the loudspeakers. Tullio couldn't recognize who it was. It certainly wasn't Big Joe. "With the help of God we will succeed and while most of you will return, some will meet the God who made you." There were some irreverent comments. "Repent your sins. Those of the Hebrew faith repeat after me." He read from the

Hebrew manual. "Now, Christian men, Protestants and Catholics, repeat after me . . ."

"I'd like to put a few bullets down his big mouth," said Tullio. Mark was tempted to send a round into the loudspeaker but only replied, "What a send-off."

Billy J. started down the cargo net followed by Mark into an LCVP for transfer to the LST. They descended into the great belly of the LST where the alligators, airplane motors roaring, were parked. They found their vehicle and piled in. It was soon jammed to the gunwales with men, packs, and rifles. With the roar and the fumes the place was an inferno and Mark thought he would suffocate before they reached the discharge point. But at last the big front doors of the LST opened and the alligators began popping out into the sea like water bugs. The crash and jolt almost threw Mark over the side. Billy J. shouted above the roar of the motors to unbuckle heavy cartridge belts in case they had to swim for it. Mark gratefully breathed in the fresh air and welcomed the salt spray slapping into his face. They bobbed around waiting for the first waves to climb over the shore and establish a beachhead; 1/6 was to be sent in whenever and wherever it was needed.

Just after eight o'clock gunboats and amphibian tanks led the way followed by alligators filled with eight battalions of Marines. The four-mile-wide flotilla advanced to within eight hundred yards of shore before being showered by mortar and artillery shells. The first wave of alligators began clambering like crabs over the reef. A few were sunk but those behind pushed forward relentlessly, emerging into the shallow lagoon. High surf pounded the reef, overturning some and causing others to lose their direction. Carried off course, the assault waves landed north of their intended beaches.

As 1/6 maneuvered into position they could see dozens of planes sweeping down to strafe the beaches. Warships pounded the shore defenses for the last time. Mark was awed by the spectacular sight. It was such organized bedlam that he could not see how those in the first wave were faring.

At exactly 8:44 the first Marines hit the beach. But they were met by withering fire that forced most of the alligators behind to dump their loads at the edge of the beach. Those tractors that went farther were getting bogged down in the sand or caught in craters. Even so, by a few minutes after nine o'clock more than eight thousand Marines were on Saipan desperately pushing inland against heavy resistance.

Sullivan finally got word at 10:15 to land and support the other two battalions of the 6th Marines. Now would come the most ticklish part of the operation, maneuvering over the reef. It lay just ahead where surf was breaking. The problem was getting over without broaching—that is, veering to windward and hitting the reef broadside.

The battalion approached the reef in good shape, crawled over head-on to emerge into the calm blue and green waters of the lagoon. But here they came under attack by mortars and artillery. Even more deadly fire came from a hidden tank on the flank. In the confusion the alligators became entangled. On all sides officers popped up their heads to try and direct traffic despite heavy machine-gun fire from the beach. Mark stooped for protection against the increasing small-arms rounds which were bouncing off the alligator. At Mark's side Billy J. stood peering over the edge, then unexpectedly sat on an ammunition box. Mark crouched down to ask what was wrong. There was a flash over their heads. Mark saw that the colonel was covered with blood. Blood was gushing all over Mark. From the colonel, he thought, until he saw Billy J. wiggle his fingers as if to find out whether he was alive. They both turned. The man standing behind them, the operations officer, didn't have a head. The man next to him was also dead but the alligator was so crowded both were still erect. Mark felt nausea but choked it back. "Hail Mary, full of grace; the Lord is with Thee," mumbled Mark and forgot the rest. Another shell set the ammunition of their .50 caliber machine guns on fire.

"Move in as close as you can get!" shouted Billy J. to the driver.

"I can't get in any closer."

Sullivan shouted orders to disembark to the starboard, the side away from the fire. "Go over two and three at a time. Then assemble straight ahead on the beach." The word was passed to those in the back while Sullivan was checking the whereabouts of his companies by radio and giving them orders. Mark was still unable to move. He marveled at the calmness of his commander. What the hell kind of a man was he? "Don't clutter up the beach," he was saying coolly. "Stay put until we get organized." He pushed Mark. "Move it!"

Mark felt as weak as a kitten. Billy J. yanked him to his feet. Mark slouched. Tullio joined them. "Get out before you have two assholes!"

The three of them were the last out of the alligator.

"Are you all right, Colonel?" said Mark dazedly.

"Sure. You should see yourself. You're covered with blood."

Sullivan hastily washed off the blood and brains covering himself as Mark watched in a stupor. "You're a mess, Mark. Damn it, follow me!"

Mark did as he was told almost automatically. The din as he neared the beach was terrifying. Men were pitching to the sand, some silently, others screaming. Sullivan could see his companies were scattered all over the beach. They had to be collected. He sent out company runners to the left. "Mark, go down to the beach there." He pointed to the right. "Look for Captain Belding, Charlie Company. Down toward the 8th Marines. See if you can find him and lead him back here personally." Mark remained in a crouch. "Move your ass out of here."

Sullivan's hard voice was like a glass of cold water in the face. "Yes, sir." He loped away. Soon he came upon a big, hearty priest who reminded him of Friar Tuck. He was leaning over a crumpled Marine, undoubtedly giving the last rites. No. He was reaching into a canvas bag and when his hand came out it was extending a leg of fried chicken to a stunned Marine. "Now, son, you're going to be all right." The priest brought out a bottle of scotch from a bag on his other shoulder as the Marine took a big bite. "How would you like to wash it down?" The scared Marine laughed, took a big gulp and then picked up his rifle and hustled into the brush.

Mark waved at the priest and ran off ignoring the rounds of mortar that were exploding on all sides. A sharp angry burst of machine-gun fire. Sand sputtered to his right. He rolled over, scrambled to his feet and ran off at a crouch. He was still scared but he had control of himself. He wouldn't let Billy J. down. Artillery shells were bursting in the water. Then one round whined overhead, *whew, whew,* and landed twenty yards away, throwing up a cloud of sand as it scattered shrapnel. But Mark had automatically hit the sand and pieces of shrapnel whistled angrily over his helmet.

Wounded were being collected in groups waiting for the enemy fire on the beach and reef to be suppressed so they could be taken out to the hospital ships. Mark found himself staring down at the famous red handlebar mustache of Jim Crowe, the commander of 2/8 and an old friend of Billy J. Mark hurried to the fallen man. Crowe had his thumb stuck in the middle of his blood-soaked chest.

"Hi, Mark!" he said weakly. "Got a hole in my chest. Don't dare take my thumb out before a doc can stick some gauze in or I'll bleed to death."

As Mark reached for his first-aid packet Crowe said, "No, you or Billy J. might need it. Just put my pack on my belly so I don't get some shrapnel in my gut."

After doing this Mark hurried off and soon found Belding, a little

Irishman with jet black hair and blue eyes, and the two started back. The chaplain was still handing out chicken and whisky. Belding was tickled. "My mother will never believe this," he shouted as they hurried past.

Sullivan was just off the beach in the brush. He was motioning to his radioman who crawled to him. "Get me Regiment." He motioned to Belding, dismissed him after a quick order, then said, "This is Billy Red, Six. We're moving out, two companies abreast. One company in reserve." He listened, nodding his head. "Yes, sir. I'll let you know as soon as we reach the first enemy objective."

Word came in of the adjoining battalions. Since both commanders had been wounded their execs were in charge. Even so, both units were slowly moving inland, a fire team at a time. Then Belding of Charlie Company made his first report. He had collected his people and was moving up in good order. He himself was wounded in the hand but refused to be evacuated.

Ten minutes later another report came in from Charlie Company. This time it was the exec. "I'm sorry to have to tell you this, colonel. Captain Belding was shot."

"How badly?"

"Dead, damn it."

"Take over."

"Yes, sir."

Sullivan reported to Regiment and was told to continue the attack and not to dig in until they reached the objective.

Jun Kato's favorite cousin, Hiroko, had been watching the battle from a cave overlooking Garapan. Despite the objections of her father who ran one of the big sugar plantations, she had become a volunteer nurse. During yesterday's appalling bombardment she had run out of the aid station seconds before a naval shell blasted it to bits. She had escaped to the slopes of Mount Tapotchau and now as she watched the horde of Marines slowly approach the beaches in strange boats she thought, "I will never live to be married and have children." American barbarians could seize the whole island and before then she must kill herself rather than be raped.

Dear Garapan was still in flames. Her home was gone. Her parents and little sisters must already be dead and her brother was in one of those tanks moving out to stop the invaders. She exclaimed, "My brother, Tokiji!"

A soldier shouted, "Girl, get back in the cave where it is safe." But she had always been intrepid, and her brother, though two years older, had allowed her to accompany him on adventurous treks in the mountains. She pushed forward for a better look. The Japanese tanks down below were at the pier firing at the alligators swarming ashore. Far out at sea she could see flashes from big warships. Seconds later came a series of deep rumbles and shattering explosions in Garapan. Enemy planes, like angry bees, began strafing the beaches as tiny figures leaped out of the landing craft holding rifles high. They were wading in water chest high across the lagoon toward the pier, toward her beloved brother. She was transfixed. The little figures soon were scrambling up the piers towards the tanks, many erupting smoke. No gunfire came from the tanks. Her brother and all the gallant tankers must be dead. Only two days ago Tokiji had proudly shown her his tank, the "Swallow." He had let her climb inside. It was so fascinating. She had wished she were a boy so she could drive one. Now her brother was dead. And the city of Garapan and all its people were probably dead.

She wondered why she couldn't weep. It all seemed like a nightmare that would soon be over. But it was real and she was alone in the world on an island infested by barbarians. She recalled the wonderful stories her cousin Jun had told her of the Americans in Hawaii. How kind they were, how intelligent. She had believed him until now. But her father had been right. The Americans were barbarians and she must now serve her country. There were few to care for the brave defenders who had been wounded. She made a sudden decision. She would walk across to the other side of the island near Mount Donnay where the main field hospital had been set up. She would volunteer as a nurse.

She bowed toward Garapan where the Americans on the pier were already creeping inland. "Brother, good-bye," she said, then resolutely trudged up the ridge. By early afternoon she was over the ridge. Here it was peaceful as if there were no such thing as war. It was late afternoon by the time she reached the slopes of Mount Donnay and it was beginning to get dark before she finally stumbled onto the hospital. She was aghast. It was only a barren field with a thousand wounded laid out on the ground in rows. She almost retched at the stink and for a moment was tempted to flee. But she gritted her teeth and made her way down a row so narrow she had to sidle sideways.

"What the devil are you doing here, *kimi* [you]?" A young doctor in a filthy white jacket shook a finger at her. "This is no place for a girl. Get out."

A middle-aged doctor, bowed by fatigue, approached. "What's going on, Lieutenant Fukuda?" He held up a flashlight, amazed to see a girl. "My dear young lady. This is not a safe place." He told Hiroko to get down the mountain before it got too dark.

"But I have no place to go. Everyone in my family is dead."

Lieutenant Fukuda brusquely took her by the arm and started leading her away. She shook free and tagged after the older doctor, "You don't understand. I have come to be a nurse." She explained she had taken a course in first aid. He ignored her but she was so persistent he finally sighed. "Against my better judgment I will let you stay."

"But Major Ogawa," protested Fukuda, "a girl doesn't belong here. It's not decent."

"Lieutenant," said Ogawa, "this is no time for decency. She may have the nerve to be of some help." He removed his own Red Cross armband and extended it to Hiroko. "You will now take orders and do everything I say." He took off his helmet and plopped it on her head. "You are in the army now."

Fukuda frowned in disapproval at such joking.

"From now on," Ogawa told her sternly, "you will only think of the wounded. There are ten of us here, three doctors and seven medics. You make the eleventh." He surveyed her and his voice softened. "It will take courage but I think you have it. Do your best, young lady."

She was proudly patting her Red Cross band.

"She thinks it's going to be like a movie," said Fukuda. "When she sees what it's really like, I don't think she'll be able to take it."

Major Ogawa thrust the flashlight into her hand. "Make yourself useful, nurse." She held the light as the two doctors and a medic proceeded down the row hastily handling case after case. The sight of blood made her nauseous and she feared she was going to vomit.

"Keep the light on the wound!" complained Fukuda.

"Steady, nurse," said Ogawa softly and Hiroko managed to control herself.

They came to a man with a badly injured arm. "Take off the bandage, nurse."

It was so blood-soaked it stuck to the wound. Hiroko tugged and the patient groaned. She pulled gently but in vain.

"That's no good," said Fukuda impatiently. He pushed her aside and pulled firmly until the bandage came loose and blood gushed out.

Hiroko paled.

Major Ogawa shook his head. "We're going to have to cut your arm off, soldier. Put back the old bandage, nurse. We'll take care of him later."

When they reached the next patient Ogawa said, "I'm going to let you handle this one by yourself."

Hiroko prayed it would be a simple cut but it was a serious leg wound. The patient smiled up at her and this time she removed the bloody bandage with the firmness of the lieutenant. Ogawa examined the wound, grunted approval and told Hiroko to replace the bandage. She did so skillfully.

By the end of an hour even Fukuda had stopped criticizing her. Then she had the presence of mind to remind the major he had forgotten to operate on the soldier with the damaged arm.

"Thanks, nurse, it slipped my mind. Bring him to the operating table." The bearers placed the stretcher on two boxes. As Ogawa began sawing just above the elbow, Hiroko felt a flash of panic. A lump almost stopped up her throat as the patient sucked his teeth in pain.

Hiroko forced herself to say, "Hang on, soldier! Almost finished." She felt cold sweat under her arms. To her relief at last it was done but then came a new terror. Blood gushed out of the stump. Ogawa reached for the blood vessel but it slipped away. He wiped his glasses and tried again. "I can't find it!" he said. But Hiroko's young eyes were better. She pushed him aside and without a word took the pincers. In one stab she clasped the squirming vessel. Moments later it was tied, stitched and bandaged. Even Fukuda was impressed but he said nothing. But the patient smiled weakly in thanks.

"Yes," said Ogawa, "that was good work, nurse."

Hiroko felt a surge of pride and confidence. At last she was useful.

On the other side of the island 1/6 had reached its objective several hundred yards inland and was dug in for the night. Sullivan and Mark were lying quietly in the new command post, a large shell hole. "I think we'll get a banzai attack tonight," said the colonel, and sent the word out front to expect the Nips to throw everything at them including the kitchen sink.

At eleven Tullio crawled in with them. A moment later there was a scuttling noise nearby. Mark grabbed his rifle, peered out.

"Only land crabs," said Tullio. "The Japs don't make that much noise."

The field phone jangled. Someone from Charlie Company whispered that there was movement out front. Billy J. called in to his supporting

destroyer for illumination. In moments parachute shells exploded lighting up the battlefield. There were no shadows or movements. False
alarm.

Around midnight there was commotion out front. Flares went up and
Mark could see a single Japanese tank in the dim light. Then he heard
chanting and savage cries. Momentarily there was a silence until an
American voice shouted, "Tell the Old Man that the kitchen sink is
here!"

This started a roar of laughter and the battalion yelled insults about
the Emperor of Japan. These apparently infuriated the enemy. From
the tank a bugler sounded the charge. As the tank clanked forward
someone fired a bazooka. By luck it stopped the tank and the Japanese
infantrymen fell back.

Soon the whole front was quiet. "I guess they've had enough for
tonight," said the colonel and went to sleep.

2.

At dawn Billy J. pulled back his outposts. He could see there was good
cover ahead. "Saddle up!" The word was passed to his three companies
and a slow, torturous advance toward the foothills began.

Ahead was gently rolling ground. There were a few farm buildings in
ruins and scattered banana and breadfruit trees. Shallow irrigation
ditches and abandoned Japanese trenches provided good cover. They
ran into numerous machine-gun nests and spider traps and camouflaged snipers and by dusk had advanced only a few hundred yards.
Sullivan gave the order to dig in. He felt almost sure the enemy would
make their big effort tonight. Neither he nor Mark got any sleep but the
hours passed without any sign of action except for a long, noisy artillery
duel. It was difficult to see much out front since the moon lurked behind
the haze of gauzy clouds. Mark finally dozed off to be awakened a few
minutes later by the field telephone. He heard Billy J. talking quietly.
"Keep me informed," he said and hung up. "Baker Company is pulling
in their outposts," he told Mark. "They hear movement out front.
Sounds like track vehicles." He called Able Company. "Do you hear
anything at your front?" They didn't.

"Mark, go tell Lieutenant MacDowell from JASCO to illuminate
heavily over the right flank." Mark crawled out of the hole and headed

for the Joint Assault Signal Company liaison team that called in fire from their destroyer. By the time he returned to the battalion command post star shells were bursting overhead.

Sullivan now called Headquarters Company, alerting Captain Mullins who drawled, "Nobody out here, boss, except us chickens." Moon hung up and beckoned Tullio. "Saddle up the assault platoon and anyone else we can get." He didn't explain, only added he was going over to the battalion C.P. to get a further briefing from Billy J. "Oh, and make sure you have a BAR." He picked up his own Browning Automatic Rifle and grinned happily for he loved a good fight. By the time Moon returned Tullio had the assault platoon and "spare parts"—twenty-five men in all—loaded up. Moon was excited. They were to bring up supplies and support the rifle companies. "Follow me," he said and led the group forward toward Baker Company's foxholes as if they were bound for a picnic. They moved slowly through a tank trap and onto open country. Minutes later Tullio heard grunts and noise of a struggle in the tank trap. One of his men had fallen over a live Japanese. He had a big arm across the enemy's face. "What the hell should I do with him?" he gasped.

"Strangle the bastard," whispered Tullio. "But for God's sake don't make any noise and be quick about it."

Tullio knew something was wrong. They had overrun B Company's lines and were in enemy territory. The patrol carrying ammo and supplies for the two rifle companies was strung out behind. Then he dimly made out a Japanese heavy machine gun manned by three men. "Machine gun!" he shouted. "Hit the deck!"

Tullio saw most of the men fall as fast as drunken G.I.'s but Moon was so busy pushing the man ahead of him down that a burst spun off his helmet. A flare exploded and Tullio could see Moon's face covered with blood. Gunnery Sergeant Kelly, The Beast, swore. He raised his shotgun and loosed both barrels into the nest, silencing it almost immediately. The next moment there was a horrendous noise as a horde of Japanese tanks came at Tullio and the assault platoon from all sides. "Fall back!" he shouted. "Get into the A and B holes!" It suddenly occurred to him that they were between two fires and he shouted to the rear, "We're Marines!" He heard a screech behind him. It was a Japanese officer brandishing a sword. "For God's sake, someone shoot the son of a bitch!" He couldn't get off a shot himself but finally someone from B Company popped out of a foxhole and shot the swordsman in the forehead.

Tullio dashed about getting all his people into the B Company foxholes. Never had he seen such a madhouse. Tanks were ranging among foxholes while Marines stood up with bazookas to bounce shells off their sides. In the midst of the maelstrom was B's commander, Captain Rawlings, directing the battle like an Indian chief. Tullio had never seen a man with more guts. He was oblivious of the flares that lit him up and the bullets flying around his head. On all sides Marines were performing feats. One man crouched in his hole as a tank spun over him. Miraculously he was not crushed. He leaped up onto the tank. Its commander opened the turret to see what was happening. The Marine pulled the pin of a thermite grenade, dropped it inside the tank, then slammed the lid of the turret. He stood atop the tank until the grenade exploded, setting everything inside on fire.

From the Company B C.P., Captain Rawlings was giving Billy J. a running commentary on the battle as if he were broadcasting a football game. "They're coming in from all sides," he said. "They're amongst us." Billy J. could hear an explosion and the walkie-talkie went dead. He turned to Mark. "They've got Rawlings." But a moment later Rawlings was back on the air. "I just fired my rifle grenade," he said calmly. "And I hit the bastard. I'm all right except I can't hear. I can talk and I'm not wounded, Colonel. But I can't hear a damned thing so I'm going to put my X on."

The executive officer took the phone and Sullivan ordered him to take command. He turned to Mark. "Run over to the rear C.P. and get Captain Grogan." The two were back in five minutes. "Get up to Baker Company with a carrying party," he told Grogan. "I think most of the Jap infantry is gone. You send back Rawlings with the carrying party when they bring back the wounded. You take command of Baker Company."

Fifteen minutes later Rawlings's exec was on the phone. "The carrying party is here," he said, but Captain Grogan had been killed on the way up and they had left him where he fell.

"All right. You're in charge. Send Captain Rawlings back with your other wounded and keep me informed."

Out front he and Mark could see tanks burning all over. It was a wild, confusing maelstrom with hundreds of savage little bayonet and fire fights. Most effective were the intrepid bazooka men of B Company whose rockets were deadly.

The tank battle lasted less than an hour but scattered Japanese infantrymen persistently attacked until dawn. Then Billy J. climbed out of his shellhole to survey the battlefield. It was a shambles. More than twenty-five tanks were smoldering wrecks. There was only one operative tank left and he noticed it climbing a winding road up a steep hill. Lieutenant MacDowell of JASCO also saw it and in minutes the naval gunfire officer aboard the destroyer supporting 1/6 fired twenty salvos on the target. Oily smoke rose from the last Japanese tank.

Up in the B Company lines The Beast was bemoaning the death of Moon Mullins. He and Tullio both swore they would take care of Moon's mother and twelve-year-old brother, the ugly kid that Moon was so proud of. Moon was part of their family.

Billy J. and Mark were inspecting the carnage at B Company. Rawlings's exec accompanied them down the line. Near a smoldering tank they came upon the bodies of half a dozen Japanese. They were in a grotesque heap. Mark was amazed to see Billy J. bow his head as if in prayer. Just then there were shouts. Men were clamoring around a figure supported by two medics. It was the irrepressible Moon with a bandage on the side of his forehead. "Just grazed me, Bill," he said. "But I need a new helmet."

"Evacuate him," Sullivan told the medics.

"Aw, hell, I'm just a bit woozy." He looked around at the destroyed tanks. "God damn it, look what I missed! Please, Colonel."

"I think he's okay," said one of the medics.

"All I need is a good shot of booze and a new helmet."

"Okay, get the hell out of here." Billy J. turned to Mark. "I'd rather command this nutty battalion than sleep with Hedy LaMarr."

3.

In the light of day on that morning of June 17 Hiroko Kato saw that the "hospital" lay in a bowl surrounded by steep hills.

She came to a young lieutenant wearing only a loincloth. He covered his face with his hands as if in shame. She took away his hands and almost retched to see his swollen left eye filled with wriggling maggots. The other eye was hollow, eaten out by the larvae. She wanted to run but said evenly, "I think I can help you." With pincers she deftly began picking out the maggots. "My brother was a soldier. He drove a tank. He died fighting for the Emperor."

When she told the lieutenant—his name was Shimada—that she had become a nurse because most of her family was dead, tears began flowing from his left eye. He painfully drew a crumpled picture from his loincloth. It was a pretty, round-faced girl in kimono. His wife.

By noon the sun was so oppressive the patients begged for more water. Hiroko went to the young doctor, Fukuda. "Lieutenant," she said, "may I go to draw water?"

"No," he said curtly. "That's ridiculous." The enemy was not bombing the hospital area but would strafe anyone going to the nearest brook. But she couldn't stand the appeals of the men and, when Fukuda wasn't looking, stealthily gathered their canteens. It was a mile to the stream. First she drank water from her hands. So sweet! She filled the dozen canteens and strung them over a shoulder. They were so heavy she was tempted to lighten her load. Then she remembered the cries for water and struggled on.

When she reappeared in the valley Fukuda went up to her accusingly. "Where did you get the water? From a farmhouse?"

"No, from the stream."

"I ordered you not to do such a stupid thing!" he said angrily. "You must learn to obey your superiors."

That evening while Hiroko was passing among the soldiers doling out the last spoonfuls of water, the lieutenant with the maggoty eye asked if she knew the words to "Ryoshu." This was the Japanese equivalent of "Home Sweet Home." She did.

"Please sing it, nurse," said another soldier.

In a clear, sweet voice Hiroko began singing. Even the moaning stopped as the wounded strained to hear.

> Under skies far away from home, the autumn night grows late,
> And my heart aches in lonely thoughts.
> How I yearn for home and parents,
> In my dream I wend my way home.
>
> Under skies far away from home, the autumn night grows late,
> And my heart aches in lonely thoughts.
> A storm out the window wakes me from my dreams,
> And my thoughts wander far away to home.
>
> How I yearn for home and parents.
> The tops of trees flash across my mind.
> A storm out the window wakes me from my dreams,
> And my thoughts wander far away to home.

At the end someone at the other side of the field shouted, "Little Nightingale, come over here and sing to us."

Fukuda plucked at her sleeve. "Nurse," he said, "I must say you're really great! You see, I have a sister just your age. And it was so awful imagining her here in this terrible place. Please forgive me."

The 1/6 was slowly advancing up the slope late that afternoon. A tank was leading the Able Company advance. Marching beside it was the company commander, Captain Murphy, who had won a Navy Cross on Tarawa. The tank was drawing a hail of small-arms fire from the hill but Murphy was oblivious. He grabbed the telephone on the backside of the tank to direct fire against an enemy machine gun that was holding up the advance. There was a rifle ping and Murphy slumped to the ground, dead.

The exec, Lieutenant Morrow, raised Sullivan on his Walkie-talkie. "Murph is killed!" he said excitedly.

"Okay," said Billy J. calmly. "Take command."

"Don't you understand?" shouted Morrow half hysterically. "Murph has been killed!"

"Yes, I heard you. Captain Murphy is dead. I say again, take command."

There was a pause. "Aye, aye, sir!"

Billy J. walked with Mark up a dirt road toward Able Company. "I'm going to have to watch Morrow. He's emotionally shaky." Morrow was waiting for them at the top of the road. He had a flesh wound and was almost weeping.

"All right, Lieutenant," said Sullivan. "I'm sending you to the rear. I'll put the next senior guy in command."

Morrow protested.

"You're wounded, Lieutenant. Get out of here. That's an order." He called to a medic. "Take charge of him, Doc. Get him back."

They found A Company in good shape, although shaken up by loss of their popular commander. Billy J. walked around complimenting the men on their performance and gave orders to seize the cliff late that night. No, there'd be no artillery preparation. "We want to take them by surprise." After they had crawled back to their own C.P. Mark wanted to ask why the devil the cliff had to be taken that night. It was suicide. While eating their C rations Mark was quiet. "Something eating you, Mark?" asked Billy J.

"No, sir." He put down the can. "You don't seem a damned bit worried after what happened today. You know, losing Captain Murphy and then Morrow—and that lousy cliff."

"We're in good shape."

What kind of a man was this? "You know, Colonel," said Mark, "I figure we've had some pretty close calls ourselves since we came ashore."

"I have a feeling that God has his hand on my shoulder," said Sullivan. They were silent. There was a burst of machine-gun fire ahead. Billy J. phoned Company B and was told it must have come from a nervous Jap. "I say a prayer of thanks before sleeping and a prayer asking His help when awaking before an attack."

This reminded Mark of the prayer Billy J. had seemed to be making over the dead Japs. "Were you praying for them?"

"Yes. We believe we're right. They believe they're right. And a lot of us end up dead. We're fighting a brutal war and it's my job to see that we kill Japs and save as many of our men as possible." He was silent for a long time, then said, "That damned Murph had no business being up with that tank. He should have been back at his C.P. directing things and not playing cowboy. Murph just wanted to look around. And he got a bullet right between the horns."

After midnight there was a flurry of fire, then the field phone rang. Billy J. listened. "Took them by surprise. Good. How many casualties? Only three slightly wounded. Very good." He hung up.

"They took the cliff okay?" asked Mark as the colonel huddled in his poncho.

"Yeah. No sweat. We should be at the next phase by dusk tomorrow."

Mark woke him just before dawn. "Father O'Brian is having early morning Mass," he said. Billy J. wet his stubble-covered, haggard face and the two joined a score of men a hundred yards to the rear. The first light broke as they reached a little grove amid shattered trees. A small group was crowded around Big Joe who looked equally spent. Before the service was over Billy J. looked at his watch and nudged Mark. "We'd better get back to the C.P. and start things moving." As they walked off Big Joe was saying, *"Dominus vobiscum."* A shrill whistle came and the chaplain yelled, "HIT THE DECK!"

One of the artillery pieces the Japanese had hidden in the innumerable caves of Mount Tapotchau was registering in on the grove. Billy J. leaped into a depression. Mark was a second behind and as he hit the hard ground he heard an explosion and felt shrapnel whistling overhead. Then he heard shouting and shrieks of pain. Where Big Joe had stood was a tangle of humanity. Mark stood stunned while Sullivan was shouting, "Corpsman!" Big Joe was lying atop the pile, blood seeping from his back. A man underneath struggled free. He was crying hysterically. "Big Joe jumped on top of me!" he cried. "He saved my ass!"

Corpsmen ran up and the colonel crisply gave orders to form a carrying party and get the wounded to the beach on the double. Mark turned over the man next to Big Joe. It was a friend, half of his face gone. There but for the grace of God, he thought. "That bomb had our names on it, colonel," he said.

"Bullshit, corporal. You're in charge of the carrying party. Get them down to the beach pronto."

In twenty minutes Mark was helping load Big Joe into an alligator. The priest's eyes fluttered. When he saw Mark he reached out a hand weakly. "God bless you."

"Take good care of this Marine, Doc," Mark told the corpsman.

"Don't worry. Tell Billy J. I'll get him over in time."

Hiroko was awakened by moaning. It was light but the sun was low and it was chilly. She had been up most of the night tending those who cried for water. She staggered to her feet, summoned two medics, and began the morning's routine. By now she felt like a veteran. Nobody had to tell her a thing and the patients all called her Little Nightingale. She was greeted with jokes and those who could, smiled.

She found Shinoda's body clammy. "Lieutenant, are you cold?" He said nothing, made no movement. She felt his pulse. He was not dead. But the man next to him was. She hurried to Lieutenant Fukuda and asked if she could take the clothes off of the dead man and put them on Shinoda who wore only a loincloth.

Fukuda hesitated but a medic said, "The girl has a good idea, sir. The dead have no eyes."

The medic and Hiroko carried the dead soldier into the woods. She hesitated, then, steeling herself, took off his uniform. She dressed Shinoda but felt so guilty for having taken the dead man's clothes that she ran to a nearby abandoned farmhouse, found a dirty pair of work clothes in a closet, and put them on the corpse.

She returned to Shinoda and unfastened the bandage over his eyes. Maggots were creeping over the gauze. They hadn't been killed by the disinfectant. "Lieutenant, where is your native home?" He whispered that he came from Aichi Prefecture and again pulled out the photograph of his wife. "After I die, please send it to my wife."

"Why should you say such a thing! You won't die. I am going to cure you."

PART FIVE

4.

It was a quiet night but during a hasty breakfast carrier planes swept in from the sea to dive over and beyond Mount Tapotchau. The rockets sounded as if a giant in the sky were tearing great silk sheets. That afternoon a runner from the assault platoon reported that a patrol from Headquarters Company had located a cave with someone in it. They wanted the top sergeant to come up pronto. Tullio asked Billy J. to let Mark go along with him. Permission was granted but both were to be back before dusk. The two cautiously went forward to a cave hidden by banana trees. They found The Beast poking at the entrance with his shotgun. Behind him were five men armed with a flamethrower, two bazookas, and satchel charges.

The Beast was calling into the cave with a Southern accent. *"Dataycoyo!"*

"What's that supposed to mean?" asked Mark.

"Come out, you silly bastards!"

Mark went up to the opening and said in Japanese, "We are not going to hurt you. We are soldiers but we don't want to hurt you." He spoke calmly, persuasively. "We have plenty of water and food for you."

Nothing happened.

"Let 'em have it," said The Beast to the flamethrower operator.

"Let me take a look," said Tullio. "Hold my rifle." He kneeled down and looked into the cave. He heard a child crying. Then a moan of pain. He stuck in his head and what he saw made the blood curl up his back. It was a wounded occidental woman. She held a child. He reached in to help her out. The woman angrily shoved his arm away.

"For Christ's sake, lady, I'm not going to hurt you. I want to help you. Now you get yourself out immediately or I'm going to drag you out!" He pulled and a middle-aged nun reluctantly emerged. She was followed by seven children and two young nuns.

Tullio began speaking in Italian but the nun only got angrier. Mark spoke English slowly and she understood. She was from Columbus, Ohio, but had been in the Marianas so many years she had almost lost her mother tongue. She kept pushing Tullio away as if afraid he was going to rape her. It took Mark half an hour to convince her she was in the hands of friends.

That night Billy J. took Mark aside. "I ought to kick your ass. There wasn't anything in your Marine application about speaking Japanese."

"I wanted to fight Hitler, not Japan. I was raised there."

"Why didn't you tell me all this?"

"I didn't want to be sent up to Regiment as an interpreter. I want to stay with 1/6."

"But . . ." started Sullivan, then said, "Aw, to hell with it." It was his own damned fault. With a father like Professor McGlynn, it should have been obvious that Mark would be fluent in Japanese.

Pressed by the relentless advance of the three American divisions, the Japanese commanding general, Yoshitsugu Saito, once more was forced to move his headquarters, this time to a small cave a mile north of Mount Tapotchau. He sat in silence as his operations officer outlined a final line of resistance two thirds of the way up the island. The question was how it could be done with only several thousand able-bodied soldiers and few lines of communication. Officers in the best condition were dispatched to contact all units. A major was sent to Mount Donnay to assemble the remnants of the 36th Regiment. But all he could find in the area were the patients at the field hospital.

That afternoon Hiroko finally had time to visit her favorite patient, Lieutenant Shinoda, and once more pluck the maggots from his eye. He was not in his usual place but to one side, lying motionless. Miraculously there was not a maggot on his face. He looked peaceful.

"Why didn't you come to see him last night?" said a patient. "Poor Lieutenant Shinoda called for you all through the night. He just died."

She had heard so many calls last night. It was like hearing the cicadas sing. How could she possibly have answered everyone? Yet she blamed herself for not hearing Shinoda's special call.

The next morning a group of replacements arrived at 1/6. One of the officers, Captain Kevin McCarthy, had won the Navy Cross on Guadal-canal and was aching to get into action. He showed up in starched khakis with necktie and wore a little fore and aft cap at a cocky angle.

"What in the hell do you think you're doing?" asked Sullivan. "Where's your helmet?"

"I didn't have time to draw any combat gear, sir."

"Well, here we wear utilities. Get into them."

"Yes, sir."

"I'm going to give you A Company," said Sullivan. "You're going to have a bunch of green youngsters."

"Don't worry about that," said McCarthy eagerly. "I'll take care of them and bring them along."

Two days later Billy J. and Mark went out to see how A Company was advancing. There was McCarthy in his starched khakis and necktie, bareheaded, prancing in front of his men, barking like a wild dog. The men were at his heels, happy as if it were a parade.

Billy J. beckoned him and took him beyond a large rock. "What the hell do you think you're doing?"

"Well, it cheers the men to see an officer in khakis. Good for their morale."

"Maybe. But it isn't good for your health. If you're not in utilities the next time I see you, you're going back to Tulagi, buddy. Don't play around with Bill Sullivan, see! I don't give a damn about you but if you don't wear a helmet how can I expect your men to wear their helmets? And I do care about them."

"Yes, sir!"

The next morning while Billy J. was congratulating himself on straightening out McCarthy, Tullio reported that there was a circus out front. The colonel and Mark climbed over a little rise to come upon a fantastic sight. There was McCarthy, spick and span, howling like a dog. Next to him a man was carrying a huge banner on a long bamboo pole. It was a homemade flag of bright red with heavy tassels. Yellow stripes spelled out "A 1/6." It was a ridiculous but thrilling sight with the men charging behind McCarthy as if possessed.

A few minutes later a call came to Sullivan from Regiment. "What's that goddam flag doing flying along your front lines?" A colonel angrily ordered the flag brought to the regimental C.P. within the hour.

Billy J. hustled after McCarthy who again was without helmet, brought him behind a big rock and ordered him to take the flag to Regiment.

"Aw, come on," pleaded McCarthy who had already won the nickname of "Mad Dog." "The men thought it was great. I'm not worried about the Japs hitting anything. They never touched me."

"I don't give a good goddam about you, McCarthy. If they get you they'd probably take a big load off my mind. But you're fooling with my Marines with that damned flag. And where in hell is your helmet?"

McCarthy touched his head. "Gee, must have forgotten it."

"If I see you without your helmet on one more time you're relieved of your command. Do you read me, Captain?"

By June 25 the rugged terrain was about all that stood between the Americans and victory. The Japanese had only three tanks and two thousand or so able-bodied men left. But these remnants fought so doggedly that every advance was costly. During the day three men of 1/6 were killed and seventeen wounded. By now Billy J. had lost most of his NCO's and officers and he was so impressed with Mark's growing maturity that he suggested he go up to Company B and help a new lieutenant run his platoon.

"No, thanks," said Mark.

"It will mean a promotion to sergeant. You'll always be a corporal as my runner. And if you make good at Company B, you could probably get a commission."

"I don't care. You meet more interesting characters here. Besides, I feel a lot safer with you. The Japs will never be able to kill you." He asked permission to go back and talk to the new chaplain. He found Father Joseph Callahan in a foxhole giving confessional absolution to a scared replacement. When it was his turn Mark told about his intention to become a Catholic.

"Is something holding you back?" asked Callahan, a rangy man with an infectious grin who had already won the nickname "Jumping Joe." "Something that troubles you?"

"No," said Mark uncertainly. "Well, yes. I don't feel quite ready." He told of his study with Big Joe and how most of his questions had been answered. "I still have nightmares of the Japs I killed on Tarawa. I can still see their faces staring at me accusingly."

"Weren't you defending your own life?"

"Yes, but . . ."

"Then it is no sin. It is like a policeman forced to kill a criminal to protect himself or to save a victim. If you killed a prisoner in cold blood it would be a sin. Some Japanese will come out of a cave in loincloth with hands up and suddenly pull out a knife. Would it be right to say a man sinned because he feared such a thing and shot a prisoner out of terror? No. It would be a tragedy. But you are defending your country and people. You had to kill and you did your duty." He put a hand on Mark's shoulder. "But I'm pleased that this troubles you."

On the other side of the mountain range that evening the cooks served an unexpected treat at Donnay hospital—rice cakes stuffed with crab meat. The elderly doctor held out one near Hiroko's mouth. "We'll pass them around as soon as the nurse has one." It was as if a father were making his little daughter eat and the young doctor, Lieutenant Fukuda, was delighted. "What a good scene this would be in a movie," he exclaimed.

Hiroko opened her mouth wide and ate the *omusubi*. It was so delicious she felt guilty.

A navy captain was brought in on a stretcher. One leg was badly wounded and his uniform was smeared with blood. "Why didn't I die?" he said over and over. "The only pity is that I didn't die!"

He was treated and they passed on. An hour later she heard a shout, *"Tenno haika! Banzai!"* Then a sharp report.

She ran back to the navy captain. Blood was pouring out of his chin. He still held a pistol. What a brave death, she thought. She was stunned but shed no tears. She thought perhaps her brother had also died shouting, "Long live the Emperor!" A young ensign who had been taking care of the captain was weeping in spite of himself. Major Ogawa and Lieutenant Fukuda looked on with bowed heads.

The next afternoon, the last day of June, the Japanese lines cracked and orders soon came to the hospital from headquarters to "die game." It was growing dark as grenades were distributed: one for eight men. Ogawa climbed wearily to a little rise. "By order of the high command," he shouted, "the field hospital will be transferred to a village four miles from the northern tip of the island."

The vast arena was silent. "All ambulatory patients will join me. To my great sorrow, I must abandon you comrades who cannot walk. Men, do as the gallant navy man did last night. Die an honorable death as Japanese soldiers."

"I am going to stay and kill myself with my patients!" said Hiroko. The captain went up to her. "You will join us. That is an order."

She bowed her head. The patients who could not walk crawled toward her. Each man had a message for loved ones at home. Each tried to tell her something about his family. She promised again and again that she would relate what had happened here at Donnay if she ever got back to Japan.

A man frantically waved for her attention. His jaw had been shattered and he wrote in the dirt: "Kudanzaka," and then, "Song."

"You want me to sing the song of 'Kudanzaka'?"

He nodded vigorously.

It was one of her favorites, a moving song of a mother taking her dead son's medal to Yasukuni Jinja, the shrine of Japanese warriors on Kudan Hill of Tokyo. As she began to sing, the exodus from the field stopped. Everyone listened enthralled in the bright moonlight.

> I was a black hen who gave birth to a hawk.
> And such good fortune is more than I deserve.
> I wanted to show you your Order of the Golden Kite,
> And have come to see you, my son, at Kudanzaka.

There was silence in the natural amphitheater. Then shouts of "To Yasukuni Jinja! To Yasukuni Jinja together!" These were followed by cries of "Farewell, Little Nightingale! Thank you, Little Nightingale!"

Haunted by the calls from those left behind, Hiroko followed the long line of walking wounded in the light of the moon. At midnight they came to a field of sugar cane. Every so often the sky would glare with the light of flare bombs and everyone would drop to the ground. But Hiroko was so dispirited she could only squat. Finally she fainted. When she came to she heard Major Ogawa call out for a stretcher. But there was only one and that carried an old general. Hiroko tried to keep up with the stretcher but faltered.

"Come here," said the general and told her to grab hold of the stretcher for support. "How old are you?" She told him. "I have a daughter your age." He patted her hand. "You are the one who gave me your own blood, aren't you? I caused you all this trouble." He groaned. "It is all my responsibility."

Another flare went off. She looked behind, saw a procession of ghosts. Many figures were staggering as badly as she had. Her own strength returned and she went back to help a man who told her that his baby had been born just before he set sail for Saipan. "Let me fall," he begged. "I have no more strength."

"Courage," she said. "In the morning we will be safe. You must get home to see your wife and baby." He grunted but kept his legs moving automatically.

5.

There was little action next morning, so Billy J. ordered Mark to take a jeep and pick up another replacement, a veteran sergeant who could fill in a big gap at Headquarters Company. This unit was in reserve and Mullins, its commander, offered to drive Mark to the beach. Moon was in a reflective mood as he kept talking of plans for his little brother. Last month he had wanted him to be an architect. Today he was to be a doctor. Mullins parked the jeep under a palm tree, pulled out his sweet potato, extended his long legs over the lowered windshield and began playing a sentimental song. Out on the reef an alligator was having trouble. It had broached and was close to tipping over. An occupant stood up, waving his arms. The boat finally straightened up and eventually climbed up the beach. The passenger, apparently the replacement, was shouting obscenities in a Southern snarl that wakened memories in Mark.

It was Sergeant Redd, who had made life miserable for Mark and his comrades at boot camp. Someone pitched a heavy footlocker onto the beach which brought another tirade.

"If it isn't my old buddy, Sergeant Redd," said Mark.

Redd recognized him. "Oh, Christ, what outfit are you screwing up?"

Mark told him. "I've got a jeep up there. Give me a hand with your footlocker."

"Take it yourself," drawled Redd and started toward the jeep.

Mark followed, carrying a barracks bag. He slung it into the back of the jeep as Moon, who wore no insignia, extended a welcoming hand, then continued his song.

"What the hell kind of security goes on around here?" growled Redd.

Moon paid no attention to him.

"Okay, corporal, get my footlocker."

"Too heavy," said Mark.

"That's an order."

"Kiss my ass, Redd."

"I'm putting you on report, shithead."

"Sonny," drawled Moon, "we don't talk like that to the colonel's runner."

"Both of you get off your asses and get ma footlocker."

Moon looked at Mark. Both smiled.

"I'm putting both of you shitheads on report."

"Gee whiz, Sergeant, don't do that." Moon climbed slowly out of the jeep. "C'mon, Mark, let's pick up that footlocker before we get busted."

At the battalion C.P. Billy J. shook hands with Redd. "Welcome aboard, Sergeant."

"I've got a few things to say, sir," said Redd bringing out his little black notebook.

"Later, Sergeant. I see you've already met your new C.O., Captain Mullins."

Moon smiled benignly at the consternated Redd. "I'll take *good* care of him, Colonel."

"I think you'll find it interesting here, Sergeant," said the colonel. "Tomorrow morning we're scheduled to take Sugar Loaf Hill." He pointed to a little stone mountain. "The Japs hollowed it into a fortress. A nice problem."

"Yes, sir," said Redd but only Mark noticed that he had paled.

They jumped off with another battalion at 0830, July 2. The first hours were easy as they wheeled slightly, reaching the ominous-looking hill with no casualties. Billy J. came forward to direct the assault. At noon the rifle companies of both battalions moved down the slopes to be met by withering fire from caves. A private crawled over a rock and was hit in the left eye. The bullet tore away half his face, spattering a sergeant who leaped up and yelled to the man next to him, "God damn it, Mac, let's go up and get these bastards!" These two got off their bellies and charged up the cliff toward the caves, followed by their comrades. They darted among the rocks, circled and dug their way upward. Hanging onto stony knobs for support, they began flinging grenades into the caves.

Standing below, Mark saw Baker Company's new commander, a young lieutenant, throw his grenade, then tumble to the hard ground, the fourth commander of the company to get wounded or killed on Saipan. Other Marines, when hit, fell onto the rocks to their death. But those behind never hesitated and in a few minutes a horde was at the caves. A score of Japanese, screaming wildly, dashed out of the caves in a desperate charge. The Marines, flopping to their stomachs, wiped them out systematically.

Down below The Beast was leading a charge up the hill. "Out of them foxholes! That's no place to win a Purple Heart!"

338

Moon was fuming. "That new chicken-shit sergeant!" he shouted to Mark. "He's hiding in the purple shrubbery at the bottom of the hill."

In the morning Billy J. ordered Moon to get rid of Redd. He told Mark and The Beast to jeep the sergeant to the landing area. During the trip Redd was silent and on arrival didn't ask anyone to carry his footlocker. He climbed into an alligator. As it crawled into the water The Beast shouted, "Hey, shithead! Here's something to remember us by!" He tossed a grenade into the alligator. The other men in the craft ignored it but Redd leaped overboard with a shriek. He surfaced to a greeting of derisive laughter. A Marine in the alligator tossed the harmless grenade back to The Beast. "Here's your little toy, Sarge."

While 1/6 spent the afternoon clearing out more caves it was Mark and Tullio's job to establish a safer C.P. With them was the JASCO unit setting up communications. Their lieutenant, Ed MacDowell, had been transferred to the 21st Marines and his replacement was a newcomer with almost no field experience. He decided to check the area with his whole team and left without consulting Tullio. Half an hour later a JASCO man came back shouting that the lieutenant's party was under fire and everybody was probably dead. He led Tullio, Mark, a sergeant and a flamethrower private toward two cliffs about fifty feet high. They found the green lieutenant with a hole in his chest the size of a fist. Tullio stooped down. "Dead," he said as savage fire broke out from both cliffs. Tullio and Mark both rolled into the brush. The sergeant was slower. He groaned from a wound in his arm.

"Go back to battalion and get help," said Tullio. "Some more flame-throwers."

They found more Marine bodies—some of Tullio's own assault platoon and two more JASCO men. Tullio moved to the right and drew a burst from a machine gun. He picked up his rifle. He was blazing mad.

"What the hell do you think you're doing?" said Mark.

"Going after those bastards!" Tullio hurriedly collected grenades from the dead bodies, told Mark to stay put until reinforcements arrived, and ordered the flamethrower operator to follow him. He started up the hill followed by the reluctant private. Just ahead Tullio glimpsed a rifle sticking out from the banana trees. He grabbed it by the barrel, flung it away and tossed in two grenades. In seconds he was at the first cave. He threw in a grenade, then another.

Followed by the breathless private, Tullio scrambled up a path to the second cave. He lobbed in a grenade. "Shoot your flame!" he shouted to the operator. But nothing happened. The thing wouldn't work.

"Christ, what the hell now?" he said aloud but to himself, then saw a grenade flying over his head and into the cave.

"Got 'em!" cried Mark.

"I told you to stay behind," scolded Tullio and threw a grenade.

There was a great hissing. The operator had his machine working. He directed the huge orange tongue into the cave. There were shrieks from inside. Mark threw another grenade. The cave mouth belched forth smoke.

"Let's go back and finish the first cave," said Tullio and the three men crawled down the steep path. Mark tossed in the first grenade, Tullio the second. A flame hissed over Mark's left shoulder, slightly scorching him. From inside the cave came agonized cries. Then there was quiet.

After dark Tullio joined Mark and the colonel for a cold dinner of C rations. "I've decided to reenlist, sir," said Tullio. "I get a good bonus. Now my ma can have an indoor privy."

There was no holiday the next day, the Fourth of July. By late morning the area from the slopes to the beach were cleared. There were only a few more caves for 1/6 to clear out and these were occupied almost exclusively by Chamorros and Japanese women and children. Mark asked permission to lend a hand and it was he who was most successful at inducing the terrified civilians out of cave after cave. But even he had trouble at one big cavern where they could hear the crying of children and the moaning of wounded adults. Despite Mark's pleas no one would come forth.

Moon Mullins, who had been taking unauthorized pictures with his little battered Kodak, said he could bring them out. He sat on a rock near the opening and began playing a sweet, plaintive tune on his sweet potato. Mark heard voices and movements and again promised those inside that no one would be hurt.

A gaunt Japanese woman holding a terrified boy tentatively started out. Another woman, carrying a crying baby, joined her. They both reached the opening and Mark slowly went forth to greet them. Suddenly the women were flung to the ground and Mark saw the grim, haggard face of a Japanese soldier. He threw a grenade which landed among the startled Marines.

Propelling himself from his rock, Moon leaped on the grenade seconds before it exploded. Someone shot the Japanese soldier. Mark bent over Moon. He was trying to say something but blood gushed from his mouth and he was dead. Several Marines wept unashamedly. Mark couldn't move. Then Billy J. was there. He kneeled down, his cheeks wet with tears. He tried to say something but there was too big a lump in his throat. In Moon's right hand was still clutched the sweet potato. Billy J. finally got it free. He handed it to Mark and was able to say, "Send it to his family."

Jumping Joe squatted down to give Moon the last rites. He bowed his head and said, "Greater love hath no man . . ."

The walking patients of Donnay had finally arrived at their new location. It was, thought Hiroko, a paradise in hell. Nearby was a swiftly moving stream of cool, fresh water. All the water they would ever need. Here the grass was not scarred by bomb craters and the trees were unshattered by shrapnel. The area was littered with civilian belongings as if their owners had fled in terror at a moment's notice.

The elderly doctor ordered his staff to dig foxholes. Hiroko was told to dig near him but she refused, partly because she was exhausted, partly because it seemed so useless to one preparing for death. But Ogawa insisted gruffly and she did her best to dig in the hard ground with a small branch. He took pity on her. "Come into my hole," he said and made it big enough for the two of them. "Miss Nurse," he said as they rested, "I have given you much trouble. When friendly troops come to rescue us, I will let you go back home."

"My home is rubble and my parents are dead."

The pursuit of the Japanese had become a rabbit hunt. The constant pressure had prevented them from forming their final defense line and they had been herded into the northern quarter of the island. At the Japanese headquarters cave, the three top commanders were listening to a staff officer report that there were no longer any front lines. Men were retreating without orders. After an incredulous silence the commanders agreed to end the battle with one final attack at dawn.

Early in the morning Hiroko was wakened by shouts to assemble. Major Ogawa was atop a huge rock. "I have an order from the Supreme Command!" he announced. "Tonight there will be a general attack, combining all forces. We of the field hospital will also take part. Anyone who can walk will fight."

Hiroko was stunned. Only last night Major Ogawa had talked of the arrival of friendly troops. Now she knew they would never come. There were only a few guns and knives and the men began sharpening branches into spears.

After dark Ogawa spoke to the hundred or so men able to walk. "You shall go down the mountain to the shore and join the others. Our nurse will take those patients that can crawl or hobble to the top of the mountain to Supreme Headquarters." He handed Hiroko a grenade. "Use this if you have to."

"Please let me stay here with the patients who cannot move. Let me die here with them."

"No. It is my duty to stay with them. You must go. This is my order."

As the fighters started down the slope, Hiroko led the wounded who could move up the mountain. Their progress was slow, painful. The men panted, groaned. She went to the rear of the line to help those in the worst condition. They walked for two hours. Where were the headquarters? Ogawa had only given a general direction—to the top. Finally she understood. He meant they were to take shelter in the safest place. At midnight they reached a clearing with a full view of the western coast. In the bright moonlight she could see hundreds of ships. What chance would the final assault have?

By the next evening all regimental flags had been burned and the three commanders had committed *seppuku,* the most honorable and dignified form of committing suicide among the samurai class. The bodies were burned and more than three thousand Japanese, including male civilians, clambered down the steep slopes to emerge onto the western coastal plain five miles above the city of Garapan. At zero hour they would charge toward the American positions outside the little town of Tanapag.

From the top of the mountain Hiroko heard the crackle of guns. The general attack had begun. Then from the enemy ships came flashes of light followed by distant thunder and finally the crash of explosions near the beach. She was transfixed. The thunder of big guns ended and from below the noise of battle had diminished. Was the general attack over? Were all her friends dead?

Light was breaking in the east and she could see little figures moving about in the valley she had left. The field hospital was safe! She hurried into the valley and an hour later ran up to Major Ogawa.

"Why have you come back, little fool? You don't understand my soul. We are almost surrounded by the enemy. Go back the way you came!"

"No," she said. "I will die here in the field hospital. I came back to die with you."

Ogawa sighed. "All right, get in the hole with me and Fukuda." He knew it was useless to argue with such a stubborn girl.

She contentedly snuggled into the hole as if it were home. At last she understood the old man's soul and it gave her courage. Before long the red sun appeared and she saw something move on the ridge of the mountain.

"Major," she said, "they're coming."

"Yes."

As the figures grew larger she saw they had black faces. They were stretching themselves and squatting. They looked like gorillas! She heard whistles and the Negroes—they were from the 27th Division—began slowly to surround the field hospital. She had no concept of time, only a strange fear.

The old general called for her. He was lying on his stretcher in the next foxhole. "Thank you, nurse," he said. "It was you who kept me alive. But the last moment is now coming. You are not a soldier, however, and your life begins from now. You must live for all of us. Escape to the West." She was weeping. "I would like to give you a keepsake but I have nothing . . . except this." He held out a pair of small scissors. "I have been using these since my childhood."

She thanked him through tears and scrambled back to her foxhole. Then she was amazed to see the wounded soldiers rising slowly from their foxholes. Some had to be helped by comrades. They stood proudly if weakly and turned to the north toward the Emperor's Palace. After bowing deeply they crouched, ready to attack with wooden spears and clubs.

The Negro G.I.'s were advancing faster now and she could hear weird music. Never had she heard such sounds. Their savage beat was disturbing. The radio music echoed loudly in the valley, striking terror and wonder in her heart.

The soldiers who had so painfully come out to launch their own last attack were just as frightened by the jazz music. In a panic they rushed back to their foxholes. Hiroko heard the report of a gun nearby. The old general must have killed himself. Then came a report from another hole. Hiroko peered over the edge at the approaching figures. Now she could clearly see their black faces. They must be cannibals the Americans had brought from Africa.

She removed the safety pin of a grenade and dashed it onto a rock. "I am dead," she said.

Next she heard strange fuzzy words that grew clearer and clearer. She opened her eyes a slit. She couldn't see well at first, then realized she was surrounded by *gaijin*. A young American sergeant leaned down, and told her softly in Japanese not to move. How amazing to hear

Japanese from the mouth of a barbarian. And his eyes were so kind. But why was she wounded? Then she remembered the grenade. She should be dead. Her throat was parched. *"Mizu,"* she said.

"No. You are wounded. You must not drink water." He gave her tomato juice but it tasted like poison and she spit it out. She wasn't fooled by his kind eyes. She knew he was an enemy and meant her no good.

"What happened at the field hospital?"

"Only you survived."

Being a nurse she wanted to know all about her wound. It was somewhere in the abdomen. She tried to remove the blanket to see but was too weak.

The young American sat beside her. "I studied in a Japanese university," he explained. "But just before the war broke out I returned home and volunteered in the army. But I didn't want to kill any Japanese so became a medic."

She asked what the strange music was she had heard. Was this a new American battle tactic? The medic laughed. "We call it jazz."

She had never heard such a word.

He tried to reassure her. "Although you are the only survivor of the hospital, there are many Japanese civilians alive in a large camp near Charan Kanoa. They are now happy they are alive."

She still didn't quite trust him. "The American devils rape all the women and cut off the testicles of the men they don't murder. And they use black gorilla-like soldiers." Those were the ones she feared the most.

The American laughed. "They were the ones who saved you."

She begged him to let her join her compatriots in Charan Kanoa. She could die in peace with them. He got permission to take her by truck. The driver was a Negro but Hiroko felt safe with the young sergeant. She lay in the back of the truck looking up at the moon thinking of the sad things she had seen. But she held back tears which she refused to shed in front of an enemy.

"Here's Garapan," the sergeant said a little later. "Nothing but wreckage." She burst into tears.

"What's the matter, miss?"

"It's my home." She thought of her dead mother, father, and little sisters . . . and her brother.

"I'm sorry," said the driver.

How strange to hear words of sympathy from this black stranger, she thought, and lost consciousness.

Of the more than three thousand who launched the banzai attack, only a handful survived. Father Callahan was at the battlefield saying Mass for a large group including Billy J., Mark, and Tullio. In the intense heat millions of flies hovered around the Japanese corpses stacked in a ghastly pile. Entrails emerged like balloons blowing back and forth in the breeze. The stink of corruption was overpowering. Jumping Joe noticed that Colonel Sullivan stared at the pile of dead, then bowed his head in prayer. Mark also saw this and though he did not bow his own head, prayed in silence for Moon and everyone else who had died.

On his way back Mark thought of Hinemoa for the first time since landing. He was mortified that he could now think of her without the stabbing pain he had imagined would be permanent. He was beginning to realize why she had chosen Tara even though she loved him more. She was right and he had been too self-centered to see it. From now on the memory of her would be free of bitterness.

On the ninth of July Admiral "Terrible" Turner announced that Saipan was officially secured. But Mark only felt saddened. He knew the fighting was far from over. Moon was gone and who would be the next to fall?

The following few days were dangerous and difficult ones as the Marines tried to inveigle Japanese to come out of caves. Mark and Tullio volunteered for this work and succeeded in saving scores of lives. After a hot, wearing afternoon in the caves on the eastern coast, Mark found Billy J. laboring over letters of condolence to wives and parents. He flung down his pen. "I'm having trouble writing Moon's mother," he said.

"Tullio and I got up a letter to her and his little brother," said Mark. "We told her what the men of Headquarters Company thought of the Moon. Everybody signed it." He handed over the letter and after Billy J. read it carefully, he said in a choked voice, "That's beautiful, Mark. I'll send it along with my letter and the sweet potato." The colonel looked off into space. "I can still see that silly bastard strutting up the beach at Tarawa like a Revolutionary War soldier, playing that damned ocarina." He finished his own letter. "That's that. Now we've got to get ready for Tinian." He pointed at the little flattish island which lay a few miles to the southwest. They needed it as the main base for air raids on Japan. "We've only got two weeks to get ready."

CHAPTER TWENTY-ONE

1.

Saipan. July 1944.

From their bivouac area above Garapan Mark looked across two and a half miles of calm water to the northern tip of Tinian, an island slightly smaller than Saipan, eleven miles long and five miles wide. He could make out Ushi Airdrome, the best airfield in the central Pacific. From here B-29's were scheduled to launch mass air raids on Japan. Shells from battleships and cruisers were tearing up the entire area.

Unlike Saipan, it was a relatively flat island rising to a height of 500 feet with a series of sloping plateaus on the other side of Ushi. It didn't look like too difficult an operation but he remembered what The Beast had remarked after Tarawa. "The roughest deal is the one where you get hit." Would his and Billy J.'s luck run out over there?

Tullio joined him. "Flat damned place," he observed. "From all the shelling and bombing it was taking, there couldn't be much resistance left.

"Tarawa looked that way too," Mark said, "but when we got there it was a different story."

The Marines on Saipan were in an irascible mood. Lieutenant General Robert C. Richardson, commanding officer of all army forces in the Pacific, had recently arrived to pass out decorations to army troops. He hadn't bothered to consult either Admiral Nimitz or "Howlin' Mad" Smith. The feud between the two services was exacerbated by charges in the Hearst newspapers that Marine casualties at Saipan were far greater than any incurred by MacArthur, and therefore "the supreme command in the Pacific should, of course, be logically and efficiently entrusted" to him. Adding fuel to Marine resentment were the stories in the same Hearst papers boasting of the army's triumphant entry into Rome while they were still slugging it out in Saipan. Pictures of the G.I.'s entering the great city on streets strewn with flowers and greeted by cheering Italians were a far cry from their own welcome on Saipan.

Nor had attractive, affectionate girls rushed out to embrace them after they cleared Garapan.

About the only thing the Marines had to cheer about was the erection of cookshacks serving the first hot meals they had in weeks. Tullio wrote his mother what a relief it was to get something besides K rations. Now they were sleeping under canvas and he had managed to liberate a large Japanese mosquito net. "I sure would like to take a bath and smell decent. We all have had to sleep in the same suit of dungarees for a month. But don't worry, Mom. I've been washing my underwear every so often and am not too gamey."

Billy J. was trying to make conditions as pleasant as possible for the men. Their JASCO team had unearthed a vast cache of liquor and was passing it around liberally. The colonel's only instructions were to keep the drinking to their own area and dispose of the empty bottles properly. The next day he passed out certificates to the fifty-five wounded in 1/6. Once they returned stateside, he said, they would receive their Purple Heart medals.

At the Japanese civilian internment camp Hiroko had done little since her arrival except to sleep. When offered large rice balls she couldn't eat them for thinking of the starved soldiers at the mountain hospital. Many people came asking questions about their relatives but she knew none of them since they all came from Charan Kanoa. It also annoyed her that they were unaware of the terrible deprivations suffered by the soldiers. They seemed too easygoing and even flippant. She didn't want to eat or even live; all these people could talk about was the loss of their belongings.

That day word spread that an American lieutenant was touring the internment camp trying to locate Japanese soldiers posing as civilians. Soon this officer reached Hiroko's tent. "You are a nurse, aren't you?" he said in Japanese.

"No."

He handed her a package. "This is yours, isn't it?" She had left it on the mountain and she nodded. The American smiled. "I was asked to bring it to you by my friend, Sergeant Winters, who brought you here."

She took the package, raising it to her forehead and bowing in thanks. The lieutenant explained that Winters had found it at the house where she was first treated. She was grateful since the package contained precious items left in her care by her patients: photographs, hair and fingernail clippings.

The lieutenant asked if she would like to return to the field hospital for treatment of her wound but she insisted that she had recovered. She hurriedly opened the package, stunned to see only American medicine, gauze, bandages. Gone were the precious relics and she wept. At the bottom she did find the little scissors given by the old general. It was some consolation but she was overpowered by guilt that she could not carry out her promise to her dead patients.

The women in her tent insisted on cleaning her wound and putting on a fresh bandage. Ignoring her protests, they also took away her filthy clothes and gave her clean ones. She felt refreshed and, strangely, from that moment she felt that her dead patients were willing her to live.

On the evening of July 24 the men of the 4th Division loaded into LST's. Soon the first wave began landing on the southwestern coast of Tinian. There was little resistance thanks to reconnaissance by a team led by Billy J.'s older brother. Some fire did greet those landing a few hours later in the daylight but there were few casualties.

The 2nd Division was following closely and 1/6 came ashore in midmorning without a single casualty. Sullivan formed his battalion in columns of companies and headed them through the flat fields of sugar-cane toward Ushi airfield. The blazing sun was the worst enemy. Others were complaining of the flies and the stink. "It's a cupcake," said Tullio who would never recover the sense of smell he had lost on Tarawa.

There was not a shot fired the first hour. The only conflict came when several jeeps loaded with loot approached. "Stop!" shouted Major Nelson, the exec, who, as usual, looked as if he had just taken a bath. In the first jeep was a Marine lieutenant colonel hugging a large clock. Though outranked, Nelson said, "I want this column stopped, Colonel. All of this loot is to be returned where you found it. We came over here to fight a war and not to loot the enemy. I want the name of every man who has taken anything. If necessary I will block the road with my guns!"

The colonel sputtered indignantly but the major stood his ground.

Tullio nudged Mark. "There's a featherweight with the guts of a heavyweight."

They continued toward the airfield which was now covered with the smoke of a fire fight. Starting up a rise they came upon a ghastly sight, the remains of almost a hundred Japanese hit by naval gunfire. The road was covered with hunks of human bodies, cut cleanly as if on a mammoth butcher's block. The meat was still red and the blood had not dried in the hot sun.

Tullio was sickened. "You bastards up front pick up the step," he shouted. The replacements, to a man, turned green at their first sight of war. The stink seemed to permeate Mark's nose. He vowed never again to eat red meat. He shoved the man ahead of him. It only took a few minutes to walk through this charnel house but it felt interminable. They pushed through the canebrakes and by dusk were halfway to the airfield. The next day they helped take Ushi, then wheeled and headed straight south toward the far end of the island. There were still so few casualties that Mark no longer feared that he and Billy J. would die. His presentiment had just been imagination.

On July twenty-seventh they were hit by the tail of a typhoon. Rain fell as if poured from huge buckets. The heated earth steamed and within an hour the red soil was ankle-deep mud. The next forty-eight hours were almost constant misery because of the downpour. Advance was slow and sleeping in a foxhole half filled with water was worse than anything Mark had experienced on the road. He and Billy J. would pull ponchos over their heads to keep their weapons and ammo dry. It was like lying in a swimming pool. As long as they stayed immersed up to their necks it was fairly warm. But once they emerged into the cool night air, the wet clothing chilled their bodies. Adding to the discomfort were countless snails which sneaked up their pants legs and attached themselves to the skin. In the morning it took a sharp knife or bayonet to pry them off.

The advance to the south was being slowed by the adjoining battalion. Its commander, "Big Tom" Weston, was a mustang, a former enlisted man, who couldn't read his compass correctly. He was attacking across 1/6's front. Sullivan repeatedly phoned him to head straight. Finally "Big Tom" climbed a little knoll and set up a huge pair of Japanese binoculars mounted on a tall tripod. He searched in vain for 1/6 which, of course, was hidden in the cane and brush. "Where the hell are you, Bill?"

Billy J. patiently gave him the coordinates. "That's where I am, Tom."

"I still can't see you. Wave your map."

"You know better than that, Tom. I'm not going to stand up and wave my damned map and get my head shot off."

"Wave your map. I've got to know where you are."

Billy J. looked at Mark in despair, then took his rifle and tied the map to the barrel. Sullivan waved the rifle above the cane. There was a rat-tat-tat. "All right, Tom, now you've got holes in my map. I just got a machine-gun burst right through it. Are you satisfied?"

"Well, don't get mad about it, Bill. Don't get excited. I know where you are."

It was steady, dull work for the next few days. The sun came out and the men could dry their clothes. Few men were killed and it looked as if the island would be taken cheaply. But as they neared the southern end of Tinian a week after the initial landing, the resistance stiffened and casualties rose.

Early the next morning a landing craft equipped with ten loudspeakers approached the towering cliff on the island's southern shore. "We are American Marines who want to help you," a language officer broadcast in Japanese. "Don't be afraid of us. We are bringing you food and medicine." Those on the landing craft could see crowds of civilians at the foot of the cliff. There were old people, women, children, all hunkering down fearfully, hopelessly. As the landing craft grew closer the language officer could see frightened faces peering out of the numerous caves in the cliff. Then he spotted soldiers in one large cave and directed his telescope on them. There were at least twenty standing and half a dozen, apparently wounded, lying down.

"You soldiers up there. Don't be fools. The battle is over. We will give you water and treat your wounded. We will not shoot if you climb to the top of the cliff and walk north with your hands in the air."

Half a mile away 1/6 was slowly heading for the cliff against intermittent rifle and machine-gun fire. Occasionally a round from a mountain gun or mortar would explode just to the right. "Mad Dog" McCarthy was heading toward Billy J.'s C.P. with Lieutenant Grady, the head of the JASCO team. Another round from the mountain gun flew over their head. Grady hit the ground but Mad Dog laughed. "Pay no attention to it," he said. "They haven't got our range yet." As the two resumed their walk down the road Grady heard the gun's roar and leaped into a shallow hole.

"Screw you, Grady!" said Mad Dog disdainfully. The next moment a shell exploded nearby and Mad Dog was down, his left arm badly wounded. Grady shouted for a corpsman who applied a tourniquet. Mad Dog soon was sitting up and grinning. "Thank God they didn't get my drinking arm." He began laughing when he saw Billy J. and Mark approach. "Hey, Colonel, I got myself a blighty wound. I'm going back to Pearl to see the nurses."

There was another bang from the mountain gun, a shrill shriek. Billy J. and Mark hit the dirt. The colonel got to his feet, surprised that he was not hit by any of the fragments. "Another miss, Mark," he said and then saw his runner on the ground, blood flowing from his chest. His eyes were open but he was in shock.

"Corpsman!" shouted Sullivan and stooped down. "You're O.K., son," he said calmly. "Let's see where they got you."

A corpsman rushed up, cut away Mark's shirt with his knife. "Shrapnel, sir," he said. He covered the wound with powder, stuffed it with gauze. "Are you all right, Colonel?" mumbled Mark.

"You know they can't get me. And you're going to be all right, son."

But Mark knew he was going to die. He also knew it was a myth that you never heard the shell that hit you. He had heard this one. He could feel the life flowing out of him but managed to say, "Father Callahan . . ."

"I understand." He shouted to Tullio who was watching with concern. "Get Jumping Joe. I saw him back there a minute ago."

"He's losing a lot of blood, sir," said the corpsman. "We'd better get him back."

Billy J. shouted for a jeep.

Mark coughed and blood came out of his mouth.

Father Callahan loped up to him and leaned down. Mark tried to say something but the priest couldn't understand.

"Tell my father . . ."

"Yes, Mark . . ."

His eyes glazed and he passed out.

The jeep arrived and The Beast carefully laid him on a stretcher, then helped the corpsman lift the stretcher onto the jeep. Father Callahan was giving the last rites as Mad Dog started getting in the front beside the driver.

"You wait for the next bus," said Billy J. "Tullio, you go along and see that he gets down to the beach in one piece."

The corpsman warned the driver to go slow over bumps.

"Let's get moving," Billy J. said to Jumping Joe, who finished the rites and stepped back.

Billy J. watched as the jeep slowly headed north.

2.

The battle ended officially the next day except for the usual miserable and dangerous job of mopping up the last of the stubborn defenders.

According to those directing operations from the battleships, the island was now "secure," a word that had become obscene to those who had to do the fighting. The 2nd Division had "only" lost 104 men killed and someone mentioned to the correspondents that it was an easy campaign. "There are no easy campaigns," retorted General "Red Mike" Edson. "They are all bad."

On Tinian 1/6 had just cornered a group of Japanese soldiers in the cliffs at the south end. "They are like rats with no way to escape," Billy J. wrote his parents. "We have to dig them out a few at a time. Sometimes the soldiers refuse to let the civilians surrender and these poor people often end up by leaping to their death into the rocks below. It's enough to make you cry to see a mother in kimono with a baby tied to her floating dead in the water below. We have no idea where we go from here and our main job is building a camp out here. For a change we are living quite comfortably in a Jap aviators' quarters. They tell me my runner, Mark, is in good shape after his shrapnel wound. You would love him, Mom. He cooks my meals and makes my comfortable bed every night and sees that I don't go out in the rain without my galoshes." What he didn't tell his mother was that the walls of the aviators' quarters were covered with pornographic Japanese pictures and The Beast was always thinking of excuses to talk to his commander so he could ogle them.

A week later Billy J. wrote that the battalion was going back to Saipan to be in Area Theater Reserve. "Each regiment has been assigned a certain section on the island and provided with engineer support to build what we call 'strongbacks.' These will be a lot better than our old tents. They consist of wooden decks with a wooden railing over which you take a regular squad tent. Instead of having guy lines to hold it up, the flaps go over the wooden deal. This ought to keep us from being blown off the islands in a typhoon. We got hit by one of those during the Tinian battle and it's like nothing you've ever seen in Kansas."

He was back on Saipan on August 13 and, after supervising erection of a bivouac on a cleared area on the eastern side of the island, set off in a jeep with his new runner for the army field hospital. He was directed to Mark's ward. A nurse in seersucker overalls sent him to the middle of the ward. Her face and hands were rough and red from the island's coral dust, the wind and the cruel sun. Another nurse was removing a screen.

Billy J. paled. "What's the matter?"

"I'm sorry, Colonel," said a doctor. "We just lost him."

"He wasn't hit that bad!"

The doctor patiently explained that there had been complications. "Unfortunately he's Type B Negative and—"

"Doctor," said one of the nurses, "I'm getting a weak pulse!"

The doctor issued terse orders, then hovered over Mark as Billy J. watched with hope and fear. At last the doctor turned to him. "I saw this happen out at Denver when I was an intern."

"Will he make it?"

"We're doing our best."

Sullivan saw he was not wanted and left.

He was allowed to talk to Mark three days later. "How are you doing, Marine?" he said.

"Great! Take me back to the outfit with you." They shook hands.

"I'll say, 'Hi,' to our other guys in here and be right back, O.K.?" Upon Billy J.'s return Mark said, "I've been worried the battalion wouldn't get along without me. Must have been rough finishing off the Japs by yourself."

Sullivan sat on his bed, put on a solemn look and said, "You know, it was amazing how smoothly everything began to function. No more screwups, garbled messages, or jeeps running out of gas. I'm convinced you really should become an officer. It sure as hell would make my war simpler." Then he said seriously, "You gave us a scare the other day, Mark."

"The doc told me." Mark lowered his voice. "I had the weirdest dream that day when I passed out." He looked around. "I'll tell you if you won't laugh at me."

"You know I won't."

"I dreamed I was floating above the bed and looking down at myself. It was the strangest feeling. I wasn't frightened. I felt wonderful, so peaceful and secure. Then I saw you standing beside my body. You were very sad and you bowed your head in prayer. I tried to tell you not to worry, that I was okay, but you couldn't hear me. It upset me that you couldn't hear and I shouted louder. That's where the dream suddenly ended . . . You promised not to laugh."

"I *was* standing by your cot. And I did bow my head in prayer. The doctor told me you died."

"Died?" Mark was stunned. "No one told me you had come to see me."

The hours passed slowly for there was little to do but stare up at the ceiling—and think. In the past year Mark had seen extraordinary acts by Billy J., Tullio, and Moon. He began to ask himself in what way they differed from him. The answer was long in coming and was humiliating: his entire life had been self-centered. As a youngster he had convinced himself that his father thought mainly of himself and unless he did the same he'd be nothing. So he had grown self-centered without realizing it. If he had been taxed with this even a few weeks ago he would have been indignant. But now, in bed, the truth had been revealed as if a curtain had risen. He wondered whose life could have been better spared? That of Billy J., Tullio, Moon, or himself? And he had to admit— not himself. He vowed that if he survived he would somehow root out his selfishness.

That afternoon Father Callahan stopped to see Mark on his rounds of the regimental casualties. After talking of those who had been hit on Tinian, Mark abruptly said, "Father, I'd like to become a Catholic."

"What about those matters that held you back?"

"They don't seem to matter a damned bit now, Father."

"We're very happy to have you with us. As soon as you get out of here we'll make arrangements."

A few days later Billy J. brought in an official-looking paper. "As you know we don't have Purple Heart medals yet," he said. "This certificate'll have to do until then." He sat on Mark's cot. "I wasn't kidding the other day about you getting a commission."

"I'm perfectly happy as your runner, Colonel."

"Yes, but I'm not. You have too much ability to remain a corporal."

"Have I done something to piss you off?"

"Don't be an ass. You know how you stand with me. Need anything? Getting your mail?"

"Yes, sir. I can't complain but I want to get out of this lash-up and back to the battalion. How's the camp coming?"

"Great. We're right on a cliff overlooking Magicienne Bay. No way any Japs can get up that side. To the south of us is Regimental Headquarters, to the north is the 2nd Battalion and across the road the 3rd Battalion. They've both got new C.O.'s. Colonel Swift is now regimental exec and a new light colonel named Jonas has the 2nd Battalion. Lieutenant Colonel Haffner, remember him, he's the C.O. of the 3rd Battalion. Because of our location I don't worry about any external security to speak of. After dark I have an internal guard detail in a guard tent and a two-man post watching the road. We're flushing a few stragglers and running across some enemy dead."

The shop talk enlivened Mark. He sat up straighter in bed. "I wonder what the poor bastards do at night, holed up in caves with no lights and probably no food."

Billy J. smiled. "Shit or play poker." He told about the natural amphitheater in a wooded ravine. "In it we built a stage with a movie screen and a projection booth. A generator provides the power. We have movies every night."

"First class. What do you sit on? The ground?"

"Hell, no. We've built rows of sandbags on top of each other for seats. Overlooking the theater Jumping Joe has a tent-fly chapel with sandbags to kneel on. The damndest thing happened at the movies last night. After it was over and we were walking out some guy happens to shine his issue flashlight on the last row of sandbags. At the end near the wooded ravine—" he broke into laughter.

"What's so funny?"

"There was this Jap soldier just sitting there. Well, the Marines started yelling, 'Jap!' and about ten guys grabbed him." Mark broke into laughter. "They bring him to our battalion and he's interrogated. Can you guess what he told us?"

"He'd been holed up in the ravine and came out to surrender?"

"Hell, no. He said he surrendered because he was goddam tired of seeing the same second-rate movies."

Everyone within hearing distance burst out laughing. When it subsided Billy J. said, "Then the bastard started giving the battalion hell for not having better entertainment for the troops!"

Later in the day mail arrived. There was a long, newsy letter from Maggie. She now had an apartment in Honolulu and was preparing to take off for some island in the Pacific as soon as it was cleared of enemy soldiers. She had no idea what island it was and Mark concluded it must be Saipan. It was a repellent idea imagining her mixing with the troops. The Marines were bad enough but the G.I.'s were animals.

She then added a story that intrigued Mark. "A couple of weeks ago we had some famous visitors here. I'll tell you all about it when I see you." The President had come to talk over the next big operation with Nimitz and MacArthur and she had managed to get a picture of the private house on Waikiki Beach where they met. She had also learned from a boastful major that he had heard MacArthur triumphantly tell an aide just before taking off for Brisbane, "We've sold it!"

There was also a long letter from Hinemoa's father together with a picture of a month-old boy. Mr. Finn admitted he had been dead against her marrying Tara but now was bursting with pride over the baby. "The

355

little tyke looks more Irish than Maori. He's a Finn, no doubt about it!" For the first time it occurred to Mark that he himself could be the father. He examined the picture. There seemed to be some resemblance. At first he felt only bitterness, then shame followed by exasperation. If it was his child, why hadn't Hinemoa told him? They could have been married by telephone. Under such circumstances Big Joe and Billy J. could have had no objections. The more he looked at the picture the more the baby looked like a McGlynn. Why in hell had Hinemoa done this? He knew she loved him and that he loved her. After brooding all night he finally concluded that Hinemoa had made the wisest choice. A telephone marriage would have ruined her reputation and given the child a bad start in life. Knowing her, he was sure that she had told her husband the truth. He prayed the proud Tara would not make her suffer for this.

A nurse stopped. "What's the matter, Marine? In pain?"

He looked up startled, only then realizing his cheeks were wet with tears. "A little, nurse."

"Want something for it?"

"No, thanks." He couldn't keep his eyes off the picture. He hoped Hinemoa would forgive him.

By the end of August Mark was out of the hospital. The camp area was completed and he shared a tent with Tullio and several noncoms at the edge of a cliff overlooking beautiful Magicienne Bay. It was peaceful, pastoral, as if there had never been a battle. There was such a constant breeze that they were seldom bothered by mosquitoes or flies. And the food had greatly improved. They now got hot chow and once a week each man got a slice of white bread. There was no beer yet or any prospects of getting any but this was no privation to Mark. He had only used beer and cigarettes to barter.

The mopping up was almost over. In an adjoining regiment they were still talking of the Jap who sat on a hill watching baseball games between the Marines and the Seabees. One day he had got so upset with a bad call from the umpire against the Seabees that he ran down the hill shouting in Japanese, "Kill the umpire!" Some Marine, so the story went, apparently disagreed and shot the Jap.

After Mark felt strong enough to swim, Billy J. took him to a small swimming hole surrounded by coral at the foot of the cliff. Mark expected to find the water uncomfortably warm but to his delight it was refreshingly cool as if fed by a spring.

As they sunned themselves on the beach Billy J. talked about the nicknames given colorful commanders: "Bull" Halsey, "Vinegar Joe" Stilwell, "Howlin' Mad" Smith. Then he said, "Mark, by any chance do the men call me 'Wild Bill'?"

Mark laughed. "Wild Bill! Why would they call you that? You're anything but a 'Wild Bill.' "

Billy J. was a bit hurt and showed it.

"What's wrong with your nickname?"

"What nickname?"

"Don't you know that everybody calls you Billy J.?"

Billy J. sat up straight. He was shocked. "Billy J.! You're kidding."

"Everybody calls you that except for a couple of old gunnies."

"What do they call me?"

"Junior."

Billy J. laughed. "They brought me up."

"The Beast calls you 'The Boy.' "

This also brought a chuckle from Sullivan. "But Billy J. That sounds like a fat little kid from Georgia."

"I think it's a good name, Colonel. Think it over."

"Billy J., Billy J., Billy J." Sullivan wagged his head. "Oh, hell, it could be a lot worse. I guess I'll get used to it. Billy J. Billy J. My mom will love it."

They took another long swim, then lay down on the sand, covering their naked bodies with towels.

"I've been talking to the Division G-2 about your work in the caves, Mark. He says there's a real need for language officers."

"I'd rather stay in the battalion."

"You owe it to the Corps and your country to be a language officer. We're going to need them badly the closer we get to the home islands. You'll be able to save a lot of lives. But it's your decision. You can stay with me for the rest of the war."

Mark said nothing. He couldn't sleep that night remembering the terrified civilians he had persuaded to come out of the caves. He thought of Moon's sad death. In the morning he said to the colonel, "I've been thinking over what you said. If I could still stay in the 6th Marines, I'd jump at it."

"I'm afraid that won't be possible at first. But I will do everything in my power to get you back with us."

"Okay."

"Then with your permission, Mark, I'll start the ball rolling."

"All right."

In the afternoon they jeeped down to Division Headquarters. Sullivan introduced Mark to Colonel Jack Colley, the Intelligence officer. He listened with interest as Mark told of his education in Japan and New England.

"Wait outside a few minutes, Mark," said Billy J., and when he had left said, "I'm writing him up for a Silver Star. That son of a bitch has got guts and brains. He'll make a good officer."

Colley was enthusiastic. "You've sold me. I'm going to Corps G-2 tomorrow and see if we can't grease the skids, get this thing on the line. He'll probably have to go back to Pearl for a short indoctrination."

A week later Colley phoned Billy J. "Corps just heard from Pearl. They've okayed the deal. McGlynn is to get over there as soon as the hospital clears him and his commission comes through. Then I'll put him on the first plane." Billy J. thanked him. "Everyone thanks you. The next big show is Iwo Jima and they just don't have enough language officers. Your boy is a real find."

Several days later at morning Mass Mark and two other men were baptized. All three had to wait a week before a visiting bishop arrived for confirmation. This ceremony was held in the half-destroyed church in Garapan. In the presence of Sullivan, Tullio, and other Catholics in the battalion, the bishop intoned, "I sign you with the sign of the cross. I confirm you with the chrisom of salvation in the name of the Father and of the Son and of the Holy Spirit." He tapped Mark on the cheek symbolizing that he was to wear the cross like the Crusaders of Christ and profess his faith and be ready to accept any suffering in defense of that faith.

Tullio was dejected. "It's going to be dull around here without you," he said. He finally blurted out that he'd just received a letter that his brother Tony had been killed in Normandy. "When I read that letter I felt like I had no stomach. I wanted to kill every damn German. I wanted to take it out on the Japs and what the hell were we doing here? Let's get on with the war. And then I thought about Mom and stopped thinking about myself. How am I going to write her, Mark? What am I going to say? And should I give my sisters holy hell for not writing me about Tony? I had to hear about it from an outsider."

"Maybe you should just write something nice and simple. Tell her not to worry about you and that you are going to live through the war. Don't you think that will lessen her pain?"

"I don't have a brother anymore."

358

They were passing the cemetery of the Marines who had died on Saipan. It was a simple clearing surrounded by a wire fence. They entered and stopped before the cross of Captain Rawlings of B Company who had fought so well during the night tank attack. "I'll never forget him standing up in his foxhole like Geronimo directing the battle as if it was a football game." They found Murphy's cross. "Billy J. kept saying, 'Damn it! He never should have been out front having fun with that tank,' " said Mark. Then they stood before the marker of Moon Mullins. Neither could say anything. As they slowly headed back toward their area Tullio said, "There'll never be anyone like old Moon."

They found an angry group in their tent. Sergeant Major Mills had just passed the word that all the officers who had landed with the division at the 'Canal were getting stateside leaves. But not the enlisted men. There was bitterness on every face and a few were crying. "It's a slap in the face of every enlisted man who came out with the original battalion!" growled The Beast. "It's like finding out your old lady has been shacking up with some swabbie," said another gunny sergeant.

Others chimed in: "Fucking officers get everything, promotions, leaves, medals and you name it." "It figures. Officers first and we get the shit left over." "The only way I'll get home is to get my ass shot off. And then they'll just patch it up and send me back here." "Fucking lousy food, fucking islands, everything stinks."

It was incredibly stupid, thought Mark, who felt guilty because he was going to be an officer and soon would be in Hawaii. These men had watched their buddies from boot camp, Elliott, and Iceland die on Guadalcanal, Tarawa, Saipan, and Tinian. Now all they had to look forward to were more islands and finally Japan itself or death. The food was bad, the recreation was bad, there wasn't a woman in sight except a few army nurses, the quarters were bad, and on top of all that the monsoons had begun. No wonder they were all pissed off at everyone including Company A's dog and the battalion's pet monkey. A few even had harsh words for Billy J. This was so unfair that Mark started to speak up but Tullio gave him a warning look.

That Saturday the medals for Saipan were handed out in the torrid sun. Billy J. received the Navy Cross while Tullio and Mark had the Silver Star pinned on them. All their citations were signed by Howlin' Mad. A week later Mark's commission as second lieutenant came through. At a battalion promotion ceremony, Colonel Sullivan pinned the gold bars on the collar of Mark's khaki shirt. He was razzed unmercifully that night by the enlisted men. But next morning when he left in a jeep the same men saluted him properly before giving him a boisterous farewell. Billy J. and Tullio accompanied him to the large airfield being built for bombings of Japan. Billy J. was beaming like a father sending off his son to boarding school. Tullio hugged him. "So long, Big Brother. Take care of yourself in those caves."

There was a large lump in Mark's throat. "Goodbye, Little Brother. Keep 1/6 in shape." As he boarded the big Marine C-42 it was exciting to think of the new adventures that lay ahead. From his bucket seat he waved at his friends. Would they ever see each other again? The plane lifted off heavily, circled, and swept over the two islands which held so many memories. After landing at Guam to refuel they continued to Johnston Island. The next stop would be Oahu but there was no chance Maggie would be waiting since the weather and mechanical problems made any accurate arrival time impossible. At Hickam Field he was met by an escort officer who drove him to the Joint Intelligence Center, Pacific Ocean Islands. After checking in he was brought to Camp Catlin, the Marine Base. Here he bought new uniforms and all the ribbons he rated. He checked himself in the mirror. Pretty impressive! Then he bought the most expensive perfume he could find at the PX and telephoned Maggie.

She screamed a welcome, wanted to rush out to the Marine base but was persuaded to remain in her apartment. He got directions, hailed a taxi and sat on the edge of the seat until, after what seemed like hours, it pulled up in front of an unimpressive two-story building in Honolulu. She was peering out of a window on the top floor. She shouted and he thought for a moment she was going to jump out.

They met on the stairs. She rushed at him, lassoed him with a lei and hugged him fiercely. Then she stood back to study his lean bronzed face. The last time she had seen him he'd had corporal's stripes. Now he was an officer with shining gold bars. Even more impressive were two rows of ribbons. He looked different despite the same infectious smile. He was older, more sure of himself. When he lifted her off the ground she protested.

"Your wound!"

"Just a scratch."

She towed him up to her apartment babbling about her work. She was going to some island in the Pacific soon. He knew nothing he said could dissuade her so pretended to be enthusiastic. Suddenly she erupted with excitement. "The best news! Papa is here."

Mark was stunned. "How come?"

"I think his old classmate at Harvard pulled some strings."

"The President?"

"After he heard you were coming here, Papa somehow managed to get assigned on temporary duty to your language school. He's giving lectures on Japanese language and culture. I left word for Papa to come from the school as soon as he can." He tried to tell her that he had just registered out there but she was jabbering about her latest stories on the troops training in the islands and how many important correspondents she had recently met. They all were going to help her. And there was this marvelous navy captain in public relations who was going to get her Marine stories.

He finally got a word in that he would love to have some real orange juice. She had anticipated him and in minutes brought in a large ice-cold pitcher. He downed three glasses and had to go to the bathroom. When he returned his father was in the room. Mark's face lit up. "Dad!" He grasped his father's hand.

"Don't shake it off," protested the professor, but he too was smiling. He was taken aback by the sight of his son. He seemed so mature. "You certainly look as if the Marine Corps agrees with you."

"It's a real zoo but I like it. You wouldn't believe some of the characters we have."

During dinner at one of the big hotels all three were absorbed by family news. Nothing was yet known of Floss and her family in Tokyo but the professor had just received a short letter from Will. He was now a guerrilla somewhere in the Philippines. He could give no details, only that he was in good health. It was after midnight by the time they returned to Maggie's apartment. She had to go to bed since she was covering an early morning press conference, but Mark and his father talked until 2 A.M. Mark began relating his experiences on Tarawa. At first he only spoke of the funny experiences, but after downing a jolt of whiskey told of the bloody incident in the Japanese blockhouse. His tongue was loosened and, with the help of another drink, he confessed his fear on landing at Saipan and the close shaves he and Billy J. had in the next two days. Noticing his father's ashen face, he apologized profusely. "I shouldn't have spilled all over you," he said. "I've been keeping it in so long."

"I'm glad you told me, Mark," said the professor. He was appalled yet flattered that his son would confide in him. "I've always wondered how I'd act in such a situation. I got a letter from some priest," he added. "He told me about your wound at Tinian."

Mark was embarrassed. How much had Father Callahan told him? "That must have been from Jumping Joe. He's the regimental chaplain. A great fellow. He's always up front."

"Your commanding officer, Colonel Sullivan, also wrote me. He assured me you were not badly wounded."

"I was lucky to be his runner. He's the best battalion commander in the Marines—and that means the world."

"He certainly thinks a lot of you."

Mark woke next morning with a slight hangover. Never before had he had several consecutive drinks of hard liquor and he hoped he had not been out of line with his father. But he did clearly remember that the professor had been sympathetic and not at all critical.

Mark was greeted with enthusiasm at the language center. "We take about anyone who can sneeze in Japanese," his instructor told him. "I see you went to school in Tokyo. You'll breeze through here. Mainly it's on-the-job training in interrogation. You can skip all the military training, of course. Are you any relation to Dr. McGlynn?"

"He's my father."

The instructor was impressed. "He gave an excellent talk yesterday on the events leading up to Pearl Harbor."

Mark joined a dozen other trainees for a long lecture on interrogation techniques, then each man was required to practice on a Japanese prisoner. When the prisoners went back to their cells, the students listened to their bugged conversations. The prisoners were mimicking the extreme politeness of the American officers and laughing at being treated like honored guests. In midafternoon the entire group of trainees was marched to an auditorium to listen to another talk by Professor McGlynn.

"Many of you people will only have to interrogate prisoners, a relatively simple matter," he said. "Some of you, however, will have to persuade Japanese military personnel who have been trained from childhood to abhor surrender to do so. I address myself to that problem. If you listen carefully it may save your life and the lives of some Japanese. I can only give you suggestions that may or may not work. You must take these suggestions and then improvise. You will be dealing with desperate men who do not think as you do." He launched into a dissertation on the differences between Western and Japanese thinking. "Your logic is precise, logical; everything makes sense. But the Japanese is a born dialectician who *knows* that his very existence is a contradiction. You know the difference between right and wrong, God and man, black and white. But to him all this is harmonious and one can be good and bad simultaneously. His thinking is far more nebulous. Let me put it this way: your logic is like a suitcase with definite limits. But his is like the *furoshiki*, the cloth he uses to carry all sort of objects. With the same piece of cloth he can carry a small load or a large one and then stow it in his pocket." It gave Mark a tingle of pride to see how engrossed both students and instructors were.

"You regard the Japanese as inscrutable and contradictory since he can be polite at home and rude in a subway station. He can be scrupulously honest and deceive you. He can appear to be lazy one minute and industrious the next. But the Japanese regards all this as sensible—a united whole. And he can't see why you don't understand it. To him a man without contradictions is too simple to be respected, and the man with many contradictions has led a more profound life since he has had to overcome his weaknesses. This is based on Buddhism which I won't go into, only to say that it helps explain Japan's aggression in Manchuria and China. We mistakenly assumed these forays were steps plotted by military leaders who, like Hitler, wished to seize the world for themselves. This tragic misunderstanding led to Pearl Harbor." The professor could sense resistance. "What you have to realize is that the Japanese military man is driven simultaneously by metaphysical intuition and animalistic urges. It was actually idealism that drove the young rebels to resort to assassinations and terrorism before the war. And those soldiers who went to China to drive Western imperialists from the Orient ended by slaughtering masses of fellow Orientals. They were driven by sincere patriotism yet had no concept of sin. They had warmth and sympathy but little humanity; although the rigid Japanese family system gave them security, it robbed them of individuality. The tragedy is that we are now facing an industrious, motivated, self-sacrificing people—a truly noble people—who are being driven in opposite directions simultaneously. And these, gentlemen, are the people you must get out of caves without bloodshed."

He stopped for a moment. "I hope every one of you will come out of this alive. But you have no chance to survive unless you place yourself in the position of the Japanese holed up in the cave. You must *become* him to understand his concept of death. Life to him is expressed in the way he says good-bye: *sayonara*—*sayo* so, *nara* if. That is, 'So be it.' The man in the cave says *sayonara* to everything because his life is a dream. The greatest leaders in the world can die, nations crumble, earthquakes wipe out great cities, disease ravage the land. But Change, which I capitalize, never changes, including Change itself."

He surveyed the group intensely as if willing them to understand. "Get into the skin of this man in the cave. Realize that his recognition of death gives him the strength to accept stoically whatever disaster befalls him and enables him at the same time to intensely appreciate each moment since it might be his very last. He goes to his death without whining, knowing it is ordained. Almost every one of you, I believe, regards this as pessimism. Not so. It is your enemy's resolve to accept whatever happens—joy, pain, success, failure."

He jabbed a finger irascibly at someone in the front row. "Have you taken in anything I've been saying the past half hour? If not you are not qualified to go out there and risk not only your life but that of the Japanese in the cave. Listen carefully. Why is it that to a Japanese the most admirable fish is not the trout or salmon or barracuda, but the miserable carp? But you are wrong, not he. Did you know that this fish, which Americans automatically despise, is a hero in Japan because he swims boldly upstream, leaping the steepest falls like a Marine?" There was a burst of laughter and half the group, including Mark, applauded. The professor smiled, reminding his son of a big cat about to swallow a mouse. "But once caught and put on the cutting board, this piscatorial winner of the Medal of Honor lies quiet, accepting serenely and *gallantly* what must be. So be it. *Sayonara.* And getting such a man out of his cave, convincing him that it is the inevitable and honorable thing to do, is going to be an almost impossible task. How you are going to do it I don't really know. But I think it can be done if you place yourselves in his shoes and then prove to him that you are an honorable enemy come to welcome him as an honorable foe." He gave a short bow. "And *sayonara* to you all."

The applause was so loud and spontaneous that Mark was, in his pride, covered with gooseflesh.

He and his father had dinner alone at a Chinese restaurant where the elder McGlynn was treated with oriental respect. He ordered in Chinese and never had Mark tasted such delicious and varied dishes. "I wish I had heard your lecture before coming to Saipan," said the son. "Old Moon would be alive today if I had." He explained that although he still spoke Japanese fluently he had approached the problem purely as a Westerner. Afterward they went to Maggie's apartment. She was still out on an assignment and Mark had nerved himself up to speaking frankly to his father of matters that had troubled him for years.

He poured the professor a tall drink of bourbon with a dash of water and himself fresh orange juice. For a few minutes he chatted about the language school, urging his father to get an extension of his sixty-day temporary duty. Then he finally said uneasily, "There's something you should know about."

"About what?" The professor was also uneasy.

"A girl."

Oh, God, thought McGlynn, the boy still had developed no immunity to the deadly virus of that strange disease called love. "I never did get around to giving you that talk about the facts of life, did I?"

Mark grinned. "You started several times but never did anything but warn me that if I fooled around with a girl it had better be a nice girl since I might have to marry her."

McGlynn grimaced and took a long drink. "Not even very good advice."

"I was always so relieved when you got put off."

"I should have . . ."

"Hell, Harry Morton told me all about sex in his barn when I was ten." He laughed. "His folks were in show business and he boasted that they even let him watch them in bed."

"Ugh."

"Harry said, 'Mark, it's very simple. Imagine a frankfurter and a split frankfurter.' "

The professor burst into laughter. "That's better than I could have done."

"I've changed a lot since Pearl Harbor," said Mark seriously.

McGlynn nodded.

"I must have been an awful pain in the ass."

"Yes."

"I gave Billy J. a hard time at first."

"Billy J.?"

"Colonel Sullivan. He'll look at you with those icy blue eyes and make you want to crawl into a crack. He can be rough as a cob." He clenched his fists and forced himself to confess about running away at Guadalcanal.

"Your colonel told me that you saved his life there."

"Oh, that. I just grabbed him when he was about to fall into the harbor with a full pack. That didn't take any guts." He then told about Hinemoa and how Big Joe and Billy J. would not give him permission to marry someone he truly loved. "I hated their guts and acted like a damned fool but I later saw they were right. She would not have been happy with me in America." He told about the Dear John letter. "I hated her at first and it took me a long time to realize she had done the right thing." He could not resist pulling out the picture of her baby.

McGlynn took the picture tentatively and his face stiffened.

"You think so too, don't you?"

"Christ! Mark!"

"I really loved her." He brought out a picture of Hinemoa. "She was like no one I had ever met. I would have been happy with her but she probably would have pined away for New Zealand." Tears filled his eyes.

They were silent for a long moment. Mark's throat lumped and he went into the kitchen, ostensibly to get more orange juice. "Can I get you anything, sir?"

"No."

Mark cleared his throat. How could he tell about his conversion to Catholicism without causing hurt? He told how he had squatted in the alligator a split second before a shell passed overhead and splattered him with blood, entrails and brains; the terrors of the night tank attack. "Billy J. and Tullio went through the same things. They were as sickened but never gave in to it and they could handle it. I couldn't. I still dream of the young Japanese I stabbed in the throat with a knife and the middle-aged man I jabbed in the belly with a bayonet and the poor fellow I mashed with my rifle butt. In nightmares I see their faces." He saw that his father's face was gray. "I'm sorry I've had to tell you these things, Dad. But you've got to understand why I did what I did."

McGlynn jerked upright. "Did what?"

"Became a Catholic."

McGlynn gaped. For perhaps the first time in his life he was wordless.

"Billy J. and Tullio are Catholics. So are most of the guys in the battalion. And when I got hit at Tinian I knew I was going to die." He was about to tell of his strange dream at the hospital but could not bring himself to go that far. "When I came to and realized I would live, I felt compelled to convert."

"It's difficult for me to comprehend." McGlynn was perplexed but not angry or sarcastic.

"They taught me how to face death, Dad. I hope you don't hold it against me?"

The professor looked at him. It was one of the few times they had looked at each other searchingly; the first time they had looked into each other's eyes with understanding. McGlynn, without thinking, patted Mark's knee. Mark wanted to embrace his father but did not quite have the nerve.

CHAPTER TWENTY-TWO

1.

Berlin. January 1944.

In the last six months of 1943 the Red Army had advanced in some places as much as 250 miles, throwing the Germans in the south and center back across the Dnieper River. Disaster also threatened the Western Front. The Allies enjoyed such overwhelming air superiority that by the beginning of 1944 the High Command of the Wehrmacht realized that any mass enemy landing in France could not possibly be contained by the present defense force. Every German able to bear arms would have to be mobilized.

Washington. February 1944.

At Op-16-W Professor McGlynn was collating the latest intelligence reports on production and manpower in Japan. It was obvious, he informed Captain Zacharias, that the Japanese were as badly off as their German allies. McGlynn feared that the report he would make to this effect would not be taken seriously enough at the Pentagon. Just as the military had underrated the Japanese before Pearl Harbor, so were they now overrating them.

Tokyo. March 1944.

In Japan production levels were being kept from a disastrous decline at the expense of extraordinary sacrifices by the people. Clothing and household goods were rarely available since so many civilian enterprises had been converted to war production. It had been necessary to buttress the work force by adding more women and teenagers. A seven-day work week was established with Sundays and cherished holidays abolished. The national slogan was "Desire Nothing Until Victory," and the citizens were docilely doing without.

Conditions on trains had become so miserable that the public took out their aggression by stealing seat covers and breaking windows to get in and out of trains. Food had become the major concern for the average Japanese family, with the nutritional level lower than that of the poverty-stricken in the United States. The most wealthy felt the pinch. All high-class restaurants were closed due to bitter opposition by laborers and drafted workers. Why, they complained, should business executives and army officers still be going to *machiai* while they underwent severe food rationing? It was difficult to get anything: gas, charcoal, coffins, clothing. And so many amusement places had been shut down that life had become drab.

French correspondent Robert Guillain was appalled at the countless holes dug in the city for shelters and was annoyed that volunteer diggers in tattered overalls dumped the clayey dirt upon the sidewalks and gutters. Public telephones were ripped out; bicyclists wobbled down the streets on flat tires; old cars were abandoned.

All that was pleasing in Japanese life, observed Guillain, had perished. For half a century the poets and the painters had asked Japan to flatter the taste all men had for niceness, for prettiness. Vanished were the elegant trifles, good manners, feminine graces. He was saddened to see that kimonos had disappeared, not only because they interfered with war work but because the men who ran Japan wanted austerity. Instead they had to don *monpei,* which reminded him of clowns' costumes.

Jun Kato suffered particularly from the rationing of cigarettes. Since six a day were not enough, he bought a cigarette-rolling machine at one of the black markets that were springing up all over the city. For paper he used the thin pages from dictionaries, and to fill out his meager supply of tobacco he resorted to the leaves of eggplant, burdock, and *itadori.*

At the newspaper office, Jun was exchanging information from the European dispatches with reporters assigned to other areas. He took all this information to his adviser from the economics department, the porky Fujita. He in turn would analyze the material, always with a left-wing slant. Early that spring Jun received notice to report for a second physical exam. Fujita advised him to start drinking quantities of sake immediately; and just before reporting to the doctors to down a cup of soy sauce, to raise his temperature. This time he was to report to the 5th Division Headquarters in Hiroshima. By the time he arrived he had a slight fever and was coughing. After a week of tests he was turned down and was again instructed to get well and come back, in 1945.

Soon after returning to Tokyo he was asked to join a small, select group that was receiving informal briefings by Katsuo Okazaki, chief of information for the Foreign Office. Okazaki, a graduate of Tokyo Imperial University, was cultured and intelligent. In 1924 he had represented Japan in the Olympics and had become friendly with Americans and Britons. He belonged to the pro-Western group and every so often would leak secret information to the select group to use as background material for their stories. Everything he said was off the record and had to be used subtly so it could not be traced. For instance, after Okazaki gave them the details of the D-Day landing in France and its political implications, Jun wrote an article entitled, "What Will Happen If France Falls?" There were, he concluded, two possibilities: Germany would either surrender on the spot or wait until the Allies reached Berlin. Jun realized his readers would equate this situation with their own. Would Japan talk peace if America took Okinawa or wait until troops reached Tokyo? It was such a dangerous topic that Jun had to use the most abstract terms, and he submitted his draft to Fujita to check that he hadn't gone too far.

The secret meetings with Okazaki always occurred immediately after one of the information chief's formal briefings for the entire press. The half-dozen members of the inner circle would signal each other secretly and meet in front of Okazaki's office. Once admitted, they would start pumping him and he would answer cautiously with the unspoken understanding that he was not to be quoted.

It was agreed that none of the group would pass on the tidbits of information to his own chief, and Jun would only occasionally give Fujita a hint of what he had learned. A fellow member of the inner circle was not as circumspect as Jun and wrote an article in *Mainichi Shimbun* stating that "the decisive battle in the Pacific will be fought far from the home islands. But once the enemy reaches our coast, it will be the end."

Prime Minister Tojo was furious. He summoned the press and stated, "We will fight to the death until we defeat the enemy even if Tokyo is turned into scorched earth." Half an hour later the Information Bureau prohibited the sale of *Mainichi* and summoned the chief editors of all local newspapers, forbidding them ever to write another such article.

The author was questioned and placed on the blacklist of the *Kempeitai*, for "unwittingly" leaking secret information to the enemy.

Tadashi Toda, being a good friend of Okazaki, knew of the inner circle but kept his distance lest he be involved. He still feared there might be a wide investigation of the Foreign Ministry press staff, and then his connection with Roosevelt's message to the Emperor would come to light. That night, once Masao was sound asleep, he told Floss of Tojo's reaction to the article.

"You had nothing to do with it, did you?" said Floss.

"Of course not. I have been very cautious."

"Then why worry? If you do, they might suspect you of being involved. When you go back tomorrow morning you must act normal."

"Normal?" He laughed. "I have not been normal since leaving the United States."

She kissed him fondly. Her chief concern was the baby, who was still thin and sickly. Although more than a year and a half old, Ryuko had not even attempted to walk and her only words were Mama, Papa, and Sao for Masao. Recently she had caught a cold from her brother and her little racking coughs were heartbreaking.

Shopping had also become more onerous. The few women who had been friendly at first were eyeing her with suspicion. If it had not been for help from Tadashi's mother and old school friends she would have been unable to provide proper food for the family.

As usual they were awakened in the morning by the sound of Japanese planes. Floss groaned. "Here they come again. They sound like someone scraping scorched pots. They must be cheaply made."

Masao was on the little porch watching avidly. Tadashi joined him, putting an arm around the boy. "It's so useless flying over Tokyo every morning," he remarked.

"Why, Daddy?"

"They are supposed to defend the city. How can they do it unless they go out to meet the bombers? The stupidity of the army is beyond belief. They act like our saviors and all they do is wake us up every morning."

After Masao set out for school, Tadashi noticed a rat eating the soap in the kitchen sink. Floss, once terrified at the sight of a mouse, nonchalantly swatted it with a long stick until it slunk off. Tadashi was gazing at the house below. "Stray cats used to sleep on that roof," he said, pointing to a house below. "I haven't seen one for months. Do you think people have eaten them?"

"Papa used to tell us about the cats in Berlin during the First World

War. People called them roof rabbits and they were considered a delicacy."

Tadashi approached Floss, who was cooking a stew. "You are so thin. As if you're starving."

She stirred the stew. "If I were to be born again, I would choose the same husband."

A week later Ryuko died without a cry of complaint. Everyone in the family felt guilty: Floss for not having been able to breast-feed the baby, Masao because she had caught his cold, and Tadashi for having brought them all to Tokyo. But Tadashi was careful to keep his guilt silent.

It was an extremely hot June and work at the laundry was difficult. During the long hours the girls bemoaned their fate. How terrible it was to be washing and ironing in this sweatbox. They longed to be back in school. What was happening around them was far from normal. Young men disappeared one by one. Several students from the church had been drafted. Sumiko had a special feeling for Koji Sugano, a literature major at Keio who had suddenly left and they couldn't even say good-bye. She wished she could write him. Where could he be? Would he ever come home? But now the war was fought at home as well as on faraway battlefields. The government called it the home front defense; the girls at the laundry had to fight the war too, and they wanted to win. They would fight to the end. Unspoken was their fear of the bombings that everyone knew would soon come.

Sumiko felt freer talking to Yasuko, a girl who lent her books by Dostoevski and Gorki, than to any of the other girls. Unlike them she was very friendly to the workers, greeting them cheerfully in the morning and talking to them without any social barrier. Probably what Yasuko had read in Gorki's stories of the lower depths had given her sympathy and understanding of working-class people.

"Don't you wish we could be in school instead of here?" Sumiko said.

"I wonder why we have wars," replied Yasuko thoughtfully. "Something about mankind makes people fight."

"Sometimes I tell myself it's like a law of nature. Even ants have armies and fight other ants. Perhaps all living things on earth are destined to fight."

"Destruction before construction. Maybe it is a necessary process—before real peace comes."

Sumiko lowered her voice, "Only a few of my friends know I have an

American sister-in-law. And those who know don't ever talk about it. If everybody knew it would make things so hard."

"I won't tell."

"My little boy cousin is half American. He's really very nice. So is his mother. We have many American friends. How can I hate Americans just because we are at war with them? I guess there are terrible Americans you can hate, though."

"I hate *war!*" concluded Yasuko.

The resentment of Japanese civilians over the extreme austerity measures forced upon them was aggravated by widespread suspicions that the retreat from Guadalcanal and the fall of Saipan were far more serious than the official communiqués indicated. The unrest of the public centered around Tojo, and the most outrageous rumors were believed. The public was convinced the prime minister was using tobacco, whiskey, and other loot from the occupied areas to bribe members of the Imperial Household Agency, the chamberlains, and privy councilors. It was common gossip that Tojo paid off the Emperor's brothers, Chichibu and Takamatsu, with automobiles. There was no justification for these complaints but Tojo *had* misappropriated power in his use of the *Kempeitai* to control dissidents; many had been jailed and a few tortured to death. This abuse of power caused indignation throughout Japan even though the extent of the repression had been greatly exaggerated.

The public displeasure became so open by mid-July that Tojo went to Marquis Kido for advice. The Lord Privy Seal, disturbed by the fall of Saipan, realized it was time to work covertly for peace. He flatly told Tojo that he held far too much power as both War Minister and Prime Minister. And that Admiral Shimada, who held a similar dual role for the navy, was his creature. "Everyone is concerned about this," said Kido coolly. "The Emperor himself is extremely annoyed."

Tojo was deeply hurt and unsettled, but later cooled off. "If Kido has that attitude," he told a close friend, General Kenryo Sato, "it means the Emperor's confidence in me is lost. Therefore I'm giving up the idea of re-forming the cabinet. Instead I will resign."

"It's out of the question to resign at the most critical time of the war!" exclaimed the fiery Sato. The solution was to replace Admiral Shimada with Admiral Yonai, which would appease not only the navy but liberals like Konoye.

Regretfully Tojo asked Shimada to step down. He was gracious. "I who am leaving can do so with lightened shoulders. You who stay must continue to bear great responsibilities." He wished Tojo a good fight, and the disciplined prime minister was so moved he broke down.

The next day, July 17, Shimada resigned but Konoye and the liberals were not at all appeased. Neither was Kido. It was the Privy Seal's most important function to select a new premier but by tradition he must first convene the *jushin*, the former prime ministers, and seek their opinions before advising the Emperor. By 6:30 P.M. all the elder statesmen had answered Kido's summons. There was conspiracy in the air. After months of ineffectual private complaints they now greeted each other with a sense of purpose. One warned that even if a Tojo cabinet were re-formed, the people would not support it.

The pressure was too much for Tojo. He resigned as prime minister and was succeeded by General Koiso, who had served in Korea and was nicknamed "The Tiger of Korea" for his catlike eyes and flat nose. Kido was pleased with the choice. Koiso would be far easier to handle than someone like Tojo, and the next months would be critical in paving the way for a just peace.

2.

By late summer the food situation was worse. The rice supply had gradually decreased to a point where one month's ration hardly sustained a family for half that time. Substitutes such as barley, cracked corn, and kaoliang were distributed as staple food. Except for farmers, people cooked rationed rice with soybeans, barley, dried sweet potatoes, noodles, or even seaweed to increase the volume.

Practically everything was rationed—soy sauce, *miso*, sugar, flour, cooking oil, vegetables, seafood. There were few eggs, almost no meat or cigarettes, and only occasionally sake and beer. People had to wait in long lines to buy dried food, sausages, ham, and other scarce items. Like so many city dwellers Emi Toda had to make weekly trips to the country with Matsu to barter kimonos for rice, eggs, and vegetables of the season. Shoes were almost impossible to find but Emi had managed to get a few pairs through a friend who had purchased them in Shanghai. Gone also was toilet soap. The crude yellow soap was an efficient cleaner but Sumiko detested its pungent smell. The Toda family could not boil bath water every day but at least they did not have to go to the public bathhouse, where the water was lukewarm and not so clean.

Life at the laundry was as monotonous as ever. Sumiko and the other girls no longer brought lunch and supplies in a handbag. Everyone had a *zatsuno*, a haversack, to keep both hands free in case of an emergency. Air raids were sure to start soon and everyone was urged to carry triangular bandages and ointment for burns, a pocket notebook, a hand towel, a handful of emergency rations such as dried soybeans in a cigarette can, and a few pieces of hardtack.

One day Sumiko used her *zatsuno* to transport her album of clippings from *Life* to show Yasuko and a few close friends. There were photographs of advertisements and life in the United States. During the breaks the girls stole into a small room on the second floor used for repairing clothing and putting on buttons where, free of supervision, they chatted and sometimes played a card game called One Hundred Famous Poems. They devoured with wonder the *Life* photographs of automobiles, machinery, and living conditions in America. The most popular pictures were those of food. Never had they seen such delicious-looking cookies and cake and ice cream. And the roasted turkeys and succulent steaks were beyond belief.

On the first day of autumn Sumiko's boy cousin, Yuji, arrived in a tight-fitting naval officer's uniform. He was so proud of it he kept pulling up his pants legs so they wouldn't bag at the knees. A generous, pleasant young man, he was the only son of her father's younger brother. After graduation from a mining engineering college in 1943, he had been offered a job at Nippon Steel, thanks to her father's introduction.

Yuji was proud of his new insignia, having just been promoted to ensign, and was expected to ship out to some unknown island in the south to run a rocket unit. He had come, he said, to beg a favor. "Mother and Sister have started my thousand-stitch belt and I wonder if you could help finish it." This was a piece of narrow cloth worn around the waist by those setting off for battle. A thousand people would make a knot in red thread on the cloth, thus bringing the bearer good luck in battle. His mother and sister had already made a thousand red dots with the butt end of a *hanko* (seal) on the cloth, and had induced almost seven hundred people to make knots.

Emi, being a Christian, thought this was superstitious nonsense, but it was proper to help a member of the family. She started with a neighbor born in the Year of the Tiger. Such people were allowed to make one knot for every year of their lives. Consequently they were much sought

375

after, and making so many knots had become a tiresome task. For the sake of her nephew, however, Emi imposed on her friend, who made sixty-six knots. Sumiko and her mother then went to the busiest street corner to get one stitch at a time. The next morning Sumiko took the belt to work. And by the time Yuji returned several days later the belt was completed. He bade them farewell and when Sumiko asked why he looked so sad he said, "I am afraid they are sending me to such a tiny, out-of-the-way island that there will be no action. I hoped I would go to the Philippines where they say a great battle will be fought."

A little later Ko arrived in the uniform of an army corporal. He carried a bouquet of gardenias for his mother and a sketchbook filled with drawings of camp life for Sumiko. He laughed when he learned of his cousin's thousand-stitch belt. "How medieval!" he said. "And he probably is going to leave clippings of his fingernails too."

At lunch he was furious at the meager servings. "We are stuffed," he said. "And you should see the meals the officers get!" This set off a tirade against the army. The noncoms were brutal and there was scarcely a soul in his entire company who had ever heard of Shakespeare, let alone read him. "It's like living with a bunch of cattle. We should have gone into the navy."

That afternoon Maeda joined them. He was even more vituperous about the army. "I swear," he said dramatically, "I will live or die for the Fatherland but not for the cursed army."

"Don't talk of dying," said Sumiko, shuddering.

After Mrs. Toda left for shopping, the two young men were even more critical of the army and the government. Sumiko was fascinated by their flights of artistic expression even though she couldn't understand much of what they were talking about.

"I give you my word," said Maeda, placing a hand over his heart, "that from today I shall never compromise with those who are curbing our freedom of thought."

Ko was equally ardent. "I still believe that liberalism is the only answer for Japan's survival."

"Japan has become prosperous through the power structure and totalitarianism," said Maeda, "but that is only temporary."

"Reality is on our side," said Ko. That night Ko wrote in his diary, "I am rather scared since the army is somehow different from what I thought it would be."

At last came the dreaded day for Sumiko and her mother. They accompanied Ko to Tokyo Station where Maeda and his parents were already waiting solemnly. Jun was also there with little presents for his two friends. The platform was filled with families saying farewells to their departing sons.

Nearby a large family group of workers was listening to a man, probably the oldest in the family, address three young soldiers. "Your duty," he said pompously, "is indeed extremely important." As he continued in the same strain several of his young listeners began to giggle which amused both Ko and Maeda. There followed a song of warriors. Then came shouts of, "Banzai! Banzai!" and "One Hundred Million Voices Together!" as half a dozen small children beat out an accompaniment on little tin drums. Sumiko noticed that both Ko and Maeda had tears in their eyes. Despite all their critical talk, they loved their country.

The train pulled into the station and bereaved parents filed out of the cars reverently carrying white boxes containing the ashes of sons who had died in battle. The departing soldiers bowed their heads in respect to their fallen comrades and climbed aboard.

The Maedas and Todas made last farewells.

"Ganbare-yo," said Jun. It meant "good fight," but the two friends knew he was saying, "Come back alive."

"Ganbatte-ne," said Sumiko, giving a girl's version of the same exhortation.

"Kio tsukete"—Be careful—exclaimed Emi, who also wanted to say "Come back!" Her words were swallowed by the shouts of "Banzai! Banzai!" on all sides.

Ko and Maeda climbed aboard and moments later peered out of a window, waving. At last the train slowly started toward their final destination, the port of Moji. There they would board transports bound, though they did not know it, for Manila.

Emi and Sumiko returned home to find a letter containing good news. Shogo was coming home! He was being transferred to the Operations Section at Imperial Headquarters. He could not tell her that Colonel Tsuji and he had been "chased out" of Nanking because of the colonel's open criticism of his commanding general and assigned to the steaming jungles of Burma, arriving just after the disastrous Imphal operation. Three Japanese divisions, augmented by a division of Chandra Bose's Indian National Army, had invaded northeastern India, their target Imphal. They were driven back with horrendous losses. Sixty-five thousand died and the exhausted survivors were in such low spirits that Tsuji had been ordered to restore their morale at all costs. One of Tsuji's methods was to force a selected cadre of young officers to eat the livers of two captured Allied airmen. Ever since Guadalcanal, Shogo had feared that the man he revered was going mad. This cannibalism sickened him and, through friends, he had arranged the transfer. The most difficult task of his life had been to say farewell to Tsuji, who was being transferred to Thailand, without revealing his utter revulsion.

The transports heading south were jammed with men in tiers of bunks and during the first day two ships in the convoy were sunk by mines planted by American submarines. Another was sunk by a submarine as the convoy approached Formosa. By this time the air in the holds was foul but fortunately the men were so used to discomfort that there was little complaint. Ko and Maeda spent hours writing letters and discussing their prospects of surviving the war.

"I think my father was a bit embarrassed by my emotion at the train station," Maeda wrote in his diary. "I wanted so much to tell him that I was proud to be a Maeda and that my mind was at peace . . . But I must now confess I am terribly frightened. Some of our transports have already been sunk. Will our time come tomorrow? I am frightened and yet I calmly confront death. Or do I?"

Almost half of the large convoy was sunk before it reached Manila. The men, their filthy uniforms crawling with lice, disentangled themselves and eagerly climbed out of the hold, which was foul with the stench of bodies. Losses were so heavy that the remnants of Ko's regiment were placed aboard ships that would carry the famous Gem Division to the island of Leyte. Both he and Maeda were stricken with the thought of being replacements in a unit where they were utter strangers. They were assigned to the 3rd Squad in Yahiro Company. Their squad leader, Corporal Kiyoshi Kamiko, sympathized with their loneliness and assured them they would be treated as if they had been original members of the division. On the first night out of Manila, Kamiko informed his squad that the Americans had landed on Leyte. "Lieutenant Yahiro has passed down the word that Gem Division is to stop the enemy. He said we have long been preparing for this day, and the hour has come when we must use all our training and skills."

Kamiko did not know that a few days earlier the U.S. Navy had dealt a disastrous blow to Japan's Combined Fleet in a three-day battle in Leyte Gulf. Four carriers, three battleships, six heavy cruisers, three light cruisers, and ten destroyers had been sunk. Once the Gem Division landed, the Japanese troops on Leyte would be cut off from all supplies and reinforcements. They were already doomed.

But Kamiko's calmness was reassuring to Ko and Maeda, who felt he was one of them. He had been a primary-school teacher before being conscripted just after Pearl Harbor and shared their love of literature. They listened without protest when he urged them to control their feelings of disgust with the army. "I felt the same at first," he confessed. "But after the years of training in Manchuria I learned to accept the brutalities of noncoms. Their cruelty will save us in battle." With some embarrassment Kamiko confided that he had grown to like the comradeship of the army, the feeling that they all depended on each other. "We're all eager to prove our worthiness in battle and die if we must for the Emperor." Such naïveté was appealing to the two young cynics.

"It is reassuring," admitted Ko, "to know that when we go into battle our comrades won't let us down."

At dusk the throbbing noise of the transport's engines stopped. Then came the loud clatter of chains as anchors plunged down. Above they could hear the shouting of orders. They had arrived in Leyte! Ko started up the steep ladders to the upper decks out of the stifling hold. He savored the fresh air of the tropics. Above, the brilliant night sky was pinpointed with bright stars. The sea was calm . . . but he could hear the distant rumble of big guns. He glanced at his watch. It was a moment to remember all his life. *All his life,* he thought, as the rumble of guns accelerated. How long would that be? Those ahead were starting down rope ladders tumbled over the side of the ship. Weighed down by ninety pounds of gear, Ko began the torturous descent. "Jump," said a voice below and he plunged toward a pitching boat. As he landed on his back, Maeda dropped on top of him.

Yahiro Company marched to a nearby coconut grove where they began digging *takotsubo*, octopus traps, the Japanese version of foxholes, while waiting for the rest of the 57th Regiment to come ashore. Sweat stung Ko's eyes and his shirt was plastered to his back but he reveled in the tropical heat. He settled down in his *takotsubo*. The smell was exotic. His thoughts wandered and before he knew it a faint pinkish light came from the east. He crawled out of his hole and stretched himself luxuriously. How peaceful and quiet. Then he heard a distant buzzing.

"Enemy planes!" shouted someone and Ko leaped into his deep foxhole.

The buzzing became a roar. American B-24's approached, oblivious of the balls of ack-ack fire that swallowed up the planes. Ko saw tiny bombs plunging erratically toward the transports where men were still disembarking. There was a cheer from the *takotsubo* as Zero fighters began to dive in hordes at the bombers, which seemed to ignore them as they sedately continued their run. Ko was horrified to see two Zeros suddenly explode into flame and descend like meteors. Another wave of bombers approached. Ko watched transfixed as a string of bombs tumbled toward the transport that had carried them to Leyte. Two smashed into the deck. Flames soon enveloped the ship. Ko could see the commander of the 57th Regiment watching as if in a trance. The colonel headed dazedly toward Ko, muttering, "How can we stop the Americans now?" Trucks, horses, and most of their ammunition were on the blazing ship.

Soon after dawn the 57th Regiment began straggling north along a narrow road, Highway 2. All morning the men were harassed by American bombing and strafing attacks. Ko was in a state of almost constant terror. He saw a dozen comrades blown to pulp or riddled with bullets. By noon he was exhausted from the heat and fell to the roadside. Maeda tried in vain to raise him. Kamiko peered down. "If you stay there you will soon be killed," he said and walked off.

Ko forced himself upright and with the help of Maeda staggered down the road. On that third of November more than two hundred men of the regiment died, and when darkness finally came there was little relief. As the men fell out exhausted on both sides of the highway they were attacked by swarms of vicious mosquitoes. Kamiko kept warning his squad not to fall asleep or they would wake with eyes swollen shut by bites.

The regiment resumed the march soon after midnight. There were no complaints or even grumbles from the men. Some even joked and Ko himself found new strength from their surging animal enthusiasm. By dusk of the following day the 57th Regiment had climbed the winding highway to the crest of a ridge. A jagged hill mass on the right was covered with shoulder-high cogon grass. It was a natural fortress with numerous ravines and dense woods.

Here is where they could stop the advancing Americans, decided their colonel, who ordered a halt. Word was whispered from man to man to dump all but battle equipment and pack their small battle haversacks with hardtack and grenades. Yahiro Company was given the honor of taking the lead and Kamiko's squad had the additional honor of leading the company. "Some honor," muttered Maeda to Ko, but said nothing to Kamiko whose face was beaming with pride.

With dawn the slight chill vanished and soon sweat was soaking their uniforms. The acrid smell of powder smoke assailed Ko's nostrils. His heart beat faster. The battlefield must be near, but it was silent as a grave. The moment he had wondered about was approaching. Would he turn and run at the first shot? A rifle cracked. Silence again. He heard the cheerful chirp of birds. He turned and saw Kamiko, eyes glistening with eagerness. The other squad members, except for Maeda, were just as excited.

As Kamiko pushed through the brush and started up toward the crest, the platoon sergeant yelled, "Wrong direction!" Grenades began exploding. Debris showered Ko. The man next to him groaned. Blinded momentarily, Ko panicked but realized he must control himself or die. He forced himself to wait motionless until he could dimly see geysers springing up on both sides. And a grenade was tumbling down toward him. The Americans must be tossing them over the crest! He rolled into a hollow just as the grenade exploded.

American soldiers were charging down the hill toward him. He frantically squirmed toward Kamiko, who was firing his rifle relentlessly. On the right Maeda was also firing. Ko realized he was clutching his own rifle and blindly fired round after round.

Then came the hollow thump of mortars, the deep *chunk-chunk* of a machine gun that sounded more ominous than their own. Bullets were whistling past and he heard one bang into a man just behind him. The man shouted in surprise as blood spilled out of his mouth in a gush. They were being wiped out and Ko knew he would soon die. Angry at himself, he reloaded and continued firing. There was a blinding flash, a thunderous roar, and darkness as earth and pebbles rained on him. To his wonder he was unhurt. He leaped into a smoking crater.

Somebody fell on top of him. It was Kamiko. Then two other men scrambled in with their light machine gun, but as they were assembling their weapon two rounds of mortar fire bracketed the foxhole. "Get out!" shouted Kamiko and scrambled to the right followed by Ko.

They hastily dug a *takotsubo* among the roots of a shattered palm tree. Abruptly the mortar barrage ceased and Ko raised his head. Kamiko yanked him down and put a helmet on his bayonet. "I saw this in a movie," he said. When nothing happened the squad leader slowly peered up. The slope was empty. "The Americans have gone," he said in wonder. "Let's eat before they come back."

Ko looked about anxiously for Maeda and started out of the foxhole. Kamiko said, "Where do you think you're going?"

"I'm afraid Maeda was hit."

He crawled cautiously to the left and finally saw his friend crouching in a smoking crater, bayonetted rifle at the ready. Maeda swung around in terror and lunged at Ko, who fell back just in time. "Thank God it's you!" said Maeda and began laughing nervously.

They wriggled back to Kamiko's *takotsubo* only to find it empty. A few minutes later he quietly slid down. "The other two squads are almost wiped out. Only three alive." There were six men to hold the entire hill.

When darkness fell Kamiko brought back the other three men and ordered them to dig adjoining holes. Then he, Ko, and Maeda crept up the hill to collect ammunition, arms, and water from dead comrades. Now they were ready for the dawn attack.

The hours dragged on. It was impossible to sleep. After a long silence Ko asked Kamiko if he agreed that it was the destiny of their generation to die in the war. Kamiko said he only thought of the good days when he could return to his classroom. "We students were deprived of our independence and studies and were sent to the front," said Ko. "I feel that everything is going away and everything will vanish. It may be good. It may be a very natural process, in one sense."

Kamiko was puzzled. They were all Japanese and had to fight for their country, he said. You hoped you would survive and experience a better world when peace came.

"Foolish Japan," said Ko. "But you are right, Squad Leader. No matter how foolish, it *is* our country and we must rise up and defend it."

"We'll certainly get the chance tomorrow morning."

During the night they were joined by the 4th Squad. Kamiko spread the good news. Now they had nineteen men to hold back the enemy. Dawn came but no Americans. Two hours passed. Where were the G.I.'s? Still sleeping? What was wrong with them? Yesterday they had no sooner pinned down Yahiro Company than they retreated. Were they cowardly as some pamphlets claimed? Finally at nine o'clock Ko heard a faint command in English. "Their officer is ordering them to hurry up the hill," he translated. A few minutes later bullets began pounding into the earth along Kamiko's *takotsubo* line. When the fire let up briefly, Kamiko called out the names of each of his men. All answered, *"Hai!"*

"If they close in, throw grenades!" he shouted.

Enemy fire resumed, augmented by the deep chunking of heavy machine guns. Someone from the next hole shouted that the brush up front was burning. Ko could see smoke rise on a wide front and hear the angry crackle of burning cogon grass. Wind swept the smoke aside briefly and he could make out figures erupting over the ridge. Americans! His heart beat like a hammer. He could hardly keep from fleeing to the rear.

"Third Squad!" shouted Kamiko. "Fix bayonets and prepare grenades!"

Ko fumbled with his bayonet, finally snapped it into place. With trembling hands he armed three grenades. He feared he was going to choke on the lump in his throat upon hearing someone shout, *"Totsugeki!"* It was little Lieutenant Hakoda, the platoon leader, ordering them to charge. Ko reluctantly started to climb out of the hole but Kamiko held him back and called out, "Third Squad, hold!" He explained to the grateful Ko that a charge should always be preceded by some sort of barrage. Despite his fear, Ko was impelled to peer out. The enemy was screened by flaming brush. Then to his horror they leaped into sight on his right only a hundred yards away.

"Target, right oblique!" ordered Kamiko. "Fire!"

Rifle and machine-gun fire broke out.

"Totsugeki!" shouted Lieutenant Hakoda, angrily repeating his order to charge into the deadly fire. Ko saw Hakoda tumble to the ground. Hakoda shouted back in a boyish high-pitched voice, "Kamiko, take command!"

The Americans looked huge and Ko was sure everything was over. But Kamiko stood up and threw a grenade. It exploded and two men fell. But this only momentarily stopped the advance. Ko heard a screech, then saw an explosion throw up earth only a few yards ahead. It came so suddenly that both American and Japanese infantrymen stopped firing. A second shell landed, wiping out a group of G.I.'s; another smashed farther back into the American heavy-machine-gun positions.

"Ours!" exclaimed Kamiko excitedly.

No sooner had several enemy machine guns resumed their chattering than a fourth Japanese shell whistled overhead and exploded. All at once there was silence. It was eerie. Ko felt heat. Driven by the wind, the grass fire was racing down the hill.

"We must find Hakoda," said Kamiko. Maeda pretended he didn't hear and only Ko followed the squad leader in search of their fallen platoon leader. All they could locate was Hakoda's belt and saber.

"The Americans must have taken him prisoner," said Ko.

A machine gun rattled, throwing up dirt just to their right. They leaped left into a hole. Ko's curiosity got the better of him again and he peeked out. "They're coming again!" he said and was about to toss a grenade.

"Too far away!" said Kamiko, restraining him. He himself started forward with a grenade in each hand. Ko couldn't move. He hugged the ground. Then from behind he heard the voice of their company commander, Lieutenant Yahiro! The main force had finally arrived. Ko hurried after Kamiko who was shouting exultantly, tears of joy running down his cheeks. He slammed a grenade on his helmet, counted one-two and heaved the activated missile up the hill. Ko and the others did the same. There were five quick explosions.

"Totsugeki!" cried Kamiko as he clambered recklessly toward the heavy-machine-gun position. Ko felt a strange surge of power and found himself yelling as he plunged forward. Maeda was racing at his side. His eyes too were wild with excitement. On both sides Ko could see dead Americans in grotesque positions. The little squad leaped into the machine-gun nest. Ko gaped at the swollen bodies of the gunners. The cartridge belt of one G.I. was crackling like a string of fire crackers. One of those set off a grenade which flung Ko and Maeda backward. Neither was hurt but for a few moments Ko could not move. Why was he still alive? This must be a nightmare. Ahead Kamiko was also stunned, then crouched as if returning to reality. With Ko and Maeda at his heels, Kamiko raced toward the crest of the hill which the G.I.'s had already nicknamed Breakneck Ridge. As Ko burst over the top he saw the enemy fleeing pell-mell down the other side of the ridge. It was like a scene from a comedy until a dozen G.I.'s fell head over heels, victims of the withering fusillade his squad was pouring on them from the crest. Ko could not bring himself to press the trigger. It seemed so inhuman. Next to him Maeda was firing as rapidly as possible, his eyes gleaming from the excitement of the kill.

Although his own blood lust had waned, Ko felt a surge of pride. His little platoon, with the help of a few artillery shells, had thrown back a gallant enemy attack and this would give the entire 57th Regiment time to come forward and turn the ridge into a fortress.

Maeda, too excited to talk, was grinning like a cat. He held up in triumph an American officer's helmet, and finally found his tongue. "The samurai used to take the head of an enemy," he said. "Is it proper for a modern man, a liberal, to take booty?"

Kamiko was being congratulated by Lieutenant Yahiro, one arm in a sling. "Thank you for enduring such hardships," he said.

Captain Sato, their battalion commander, unexpectedly appeared and wrote their names on the merits list, an incredible honor for infantrymen. Sato took the American helmet from Maeda and clapped it on. He praised its lightness. "Have you got one without a bullet hole?" Kamiko said they could find one.

That evening Sato sent word that Kamiko would replace the missing Hakoda as platoon leader. "I can't sleep," he confided to Ko and Maeda. He was quiet for several minutes, then said guiltily, "The corpses of our comrades lying out front unattended haunt me."

"I was not scared today," said Maeda. "Yesterday I wanted to run after the first shot. But today I felt thrilled and if I do happen to die I feel confident I'll see my dear elder brother, Tatsu. What could be better than such a reunion in heaven?" Ko could hardly keep from smiling and nudged Kamiko, who understood. "Death means nothing to me now," went on Maeda, "since I take it as a process which will lead me to heaven. You see, even an intellectual, if he has faith, can find death meaningful and enhance its value. People only fear death if they have an unclear understanding of what it means."

In the morning the Americans resumed their attack on strategic Breakneck Ridge, this time assaulting on a broader front with the 1st Cavalry Division. The main target was the hill where the eighty men of Ko's company were waiting with orders to hold their fire. Not until the G.I.'s were within seventy-five yards did Lieutenant Yahiro shout, "Fire!"

Ko's jaw dropped as he saw a long line of Americans crumple over. But others leaped over the inert bodies, throwing grenades long distances as if they were baseballs. The toll was frightful along the defense line and Ko did not see how they could hold out much longer. But no one panicked and such steady fire was maintained that finally two Americans fled. This turned the tide. Others wavered and then began scrambling down the other side of the hill.

They had held but there were only twenty-five alive in the entire company. Maeda and Ko were in the first group sent back to rest in the other side of Highway 2. They gratefully washed their faces in the cool water of a stream, filled their canteens, ate hardtack and lolled on the ground. This, thought Ko, is the pleasure of nothingness. Maeda was too tired to philosophize.

On November 8 the skies darkened as a typhoon swept over Breakneck Ridge, flailing the cogon grass. Soon another storm began, this a heavy artillery barrage from the enemy. Then mortar shells began accurately ripping up the *takotsubo* on the crest of the ridge. The effect was so devastating, Yahiro ordered the company to return to their original *takotsubo* nearer the highway for their final stand. Ko and the others slipped and stumbled their way down to the old holes and found them almost filled with water. Ko dived into one as a refuge from the rounds that pursued them.

Ko could see only ten yards up the fog-covered hill. Kamiko joined him. "We have underrated the enemy," he said. "He is no coward and he can throw grenades twice as far as we can. And he always seems rested."

Ko, miserable and soaked, said nothing, only wished they had as much artillery and food as the enemy.

An enemy tank joined the assault but two of Yahiro's men flung a satchel charge under its tracks. After it exploded the American infantrymen started falling back. Kamiko jumped out of their hole, shouting, "Charge!" Ko readily followed for it was a relief getting out of their watery refuge. As they reached the top of the hill, Kamiko began throwing grenades after the fleeing Americans. The others followed suit, then all skidded back to get more grenades. Soon the obverse side of Breakneck Ridge was free of enemy. A few of the men cheered but Kamiko was not triumphant. "It is no victory," he told Ko. "The Americans make retreat a tactic and will come back again and again until we have nothing to stop them." He ordered the men to return to their holes at the bottom of their side of the hill. The storm intensified and the few remaining palm trees were uprooted. To Kamiko's surprise the enemy did not return that afternoon. "I guess they don't like the rain," he said.

In the morning there came another heavy enemy artillery preparation. Then two soaked American battalions of the 24th Division resumed the attack in the driving rain but their slogging advance was thrown back. Rain had become an ally of the defenders. The American supply route was a swamp and the skin was peeling away from the infantrymen's feet.

Kamiko's men were trying in vain to bail out their *takotsubo*. By the end of the day they were drenched to the skin and so cold they set fire to the rubber tubes of their gas masks. "What a stink!" protested the fastidious Ko, but Maeda huddled over the smoldering mess.

The next day was greeted by another dark dawn. The rain increased as enemy shells plowed into the crest above them. Under the constant trembling of the earth the sides of the *takotsubo* began to crumble and he wondered if this was to be his deathday. There was only one consolation—the rain had at last stopped.

Once the barrage lifted he led his men up the hill, now pockmarked with shell holes reminding him of pictures of the Great War in Europe. At the top Ko looked down on a swarm of G.I.'s climbing toward him. At least two battalions! Ko was convinced he would never survive the day. Only about twelve were left in the company to stop this onrushing horde.

Kamiko hurried along the line frantically gesturing to return to the *takotsubo* at the bottom of the slope. Ko needed no second warning. He dashed down the hill, diving out of sight into a hole like a submarine as bullets swept down. He could see grenades skittering down toward him. Luckily they all exploded before reaching the last line of defense.

On all sides men were shouting that they were out of ammunition. Kamiko leaped out of his foxhole. Ko could see he was driven more by anger than fear. He started up the hill followed by one man. Maeda set out after him and Ko found himself bringing up the rear. As Kamiko neared the crest he lobbed a grenade and impulsively shouted in English, "Charge! Charge!"

An American, thinking it was an order, rushed over the crest with fixed bayonet. He and Kamiko gaped at each other, both unable to move. Finally the G.I. yelled and somersaulted down his own side of the hill. Then came another surprise. Both Ko and Kamiko heard Lieutenant Yahiro shout from the rear, "Company, *tenshin!*" This meant turn around and advance. They had never heard such an order, since they had always been forbidden to retreat, and were unaware that it had recently been created in imitation of American tactics to cut down on unnecessary casualties.

Instead the urgency of Yahiro's repeated command brought all his men out of their holes ready to launch a final attack while he was frantically running around shouting, *"Tenshin!"* in an effort to make them run down the hill to safety.

Ko looked to Kamiko for guidance but he was standing paralyzed. Yahiro was firing a captured American carbine from the hip. He dropped one G.I., and another, then was himself sent spinning to the ground. Kamiko and Ko dragged him to a shell hole, where Ko held a canteen to the lieutenant's mouth. After taking a single gulp his head flopped to one side. This left the fate of Yahiro Company in Kamiko's hands. He had been so thoroughly trained that he could not order a disgraceful retreat. What else to do but make the enemy pay dearly before dying gloriously?

"Charge!" he yelled, this time in Japanese, and plunged up the muddy slope with Ko, Maeda, and three others. Shouting wildly they threw all their remaining grenades. The Americans were so startled they broke. If only we had one machine gun, thought Kamiko. But it was such a ridiculous idea he recovered his senses and realized the battle was lost. He must save his men for another day.

"Follow me!" he shouted and fled toward Highway 2 with ten survivors. At the bottom he looked back. Enemy figures were already at the top. Kamiko hustled his men down the highway toward Ormoc, silently cursing himself for his cowardice. Ko and Maeda could see that the shame of retreat gnawed his conscience.

"Lieutenant Yahiro ordered the retreat first," said Maeda.

"It is my own responsibility," muttered Kamiko. "I abandoned the body of my commander. I valued my own life above honor."

"And you saved the rest of us," said Maeda. "Why die so needlessly?" Kamiko cheered up.

"How would it have helped the nation if all of us had died on the ridge?" said Ko.

"That's true," said Kamiko and began to feel almost light of heart.

They came to a culvert with a stream running underneath. "The only thing," said Maeda, "is to do one's best and not worry about the future. We are still alive." He began stripping off his foul uniform. The others did the same. Their bare legs were as colorless as bean curd but their spirits rose as they washed their clothes in the stream, and several even began playfully snapping wet clothing at each other like schoolboys. Then, in loincloths, they all stretched out along the bank and soon were fast asleep.

By mid-November American tanks ranged the winding trail of Highway 2, while G.I. infantrymen finally overran all but the southern end of Breakneck Ridge. Here were Kamiko and his small group, this time as replacements to Yasuda Company. For two days they huddled in the holes, their food ration a single rice ball for eight men. On the third day Kamiko was wounded on the arm and foot. They were minor wounds. Even so, under protest, he was ordered to the rear. Ko and Maeda were detailed to help him return to Ormoc. A few days later their regiment, reduced to fewer than four hundred men, was overrun by G.I.'s of the 32nd Division. The Battle of Breakneck Ridge was over.

Kamiko, Ko, and Maeda were slowly heading south along the highway. As they approached a ravine they were assailed by an overpowering stink. Then they came upon thousands of swollen, decomposed bodies covered with what looked like snakes. Maeda's eyes seemed to pop out. "What a way to die!"

A haggard soldier sitting on a rock laughed mirthlessly. "Those are tubes from gas masks. We call this Death Valley." His division, he said, had been wiped out by American artillery while marching up to Breakneck Ridge.

The three men headed into the jungle and kept passing wounded men sprawled along the trail just waiting patiently to die. Ko, Kamiko, and Maeda pressed on even though they too were tempted to give up. As they were working their way painfully over a mountain, they came upon seven other stragglers and learned that the Americans had driven below Breakneck Ridge and were threatening to break through the entire Japanese line. They trudged on until, out of hunger, they attacked the next American position. Grabbing armloads of G.I. rations, they escaped despite a fusillade. After wolfing down a piece of chocolate Maeda said, "If we had as much to eat as the Americans we'd still be up on the ridge."

Kamiko had to admit that victory in battle was simply a case of supply, and asked, "How can we win against such a rich foe?"

CHAPTER TWENTY-THREE

1.

Cebu City. October 1944.

After his capture Will was held on Negros more than four months before transportation to Cebu City where he was to wait for a ship from Davao bound for Manila. On the outskirts he joined a group of twenty other prisoners and they were marched in the blazing sun to a church-yard. Since it was covered with concrete cobbles, the prisoners scraped shallow spots for beds. Despite the discomfort, Will and the others were so exhausted they slept around the clock. For three days they lolled in the hot, airless yard of stones. It was boring but Will regained his strength and spirits. For hours he stared out at the island of Mactan. A Filipino prisoner had told him that it was here Magellan was killed by natives who resented his efforts to convert them to Christianity and Portugal.

At last they were led through the streets to the dock area. No sooner had they sighted a ship than they knew it was theirs from the stench of humanity coming from its holds. They found prisoners from Davao in a miserable condition. The congestion and salty water had felled many with dysentery. Others suffered from malaria and beriberi. After his months with Cushing in the open, Will was not prepared for the stink and confinement he had become accustomed to at O'Donnell and Ca-banatuan. Although the trip to Manila took only a few days, he thought they never would arrive. And when he learned they would have to remain in the hold for some time after arrival he had to restrain his anguish. Two men died the first night and another the second. At last they were allowed to disembark. Will sucked in the tepid air of the Manila dock area. He even enjoyed the march to Bilibid Prison despite the beating sun. His stay there was short and within a week he was back in Cabanatuan. As he approached the familiar scene he felt depressed. There was the post where he had suffered for three days and nights. Would he be able to survive another sentence out in the brutal heat of day and chill of night, a constant meal for red ants? He vowed to stay out of trouble.

Inside he saw many new faces and some of the old ones were almost unrecognizable. A few men called out to him. They seemed so much older, so much thinner. Then he saw a smiling face. It was Lieutenant Bliss. He was unchanged, still composed, unruffled. He felt his own courage returning.

But there was no chance for talk as the new arrivals were taken to a distant part of the camp and kept in isolation. After a week they were finally moved to the main camp. Will was amazed to see there were only several thousand prisoners left. Bliss revealed that two details had left for Bilibid and were later shipped out to Japan.

"The Japs," he said, "are getting as many workers up there as they can before MacArthur lands here." A friendly guard had told him the Americans were already at Leyte. "Our bombers are already hitting Clark Field."

A week later they were loaded into trucks. "Through the gates of hell," said Bliss as they swung out of the camp, throwing up clouds of dust. Will had mixed feelings. Thank God they were leaving this place. But what lay ahead of them? In the same truck Popov hunched in a corner, downcast. He seemed to have shrunk. All that remained of his possessions was in a burlap bag.

Will, Bliss, and Popov and another enlisted man were locked into a single cell in the old federal prison of Bilibid. It was on the upper floor and by pulling themselves up on the bars they could see American planes diving on ships in the harbor. These attacks brought the only cheer to the despondent Popov. "Now they'll never be able to take us out of Manila!" But the air raids stopped and Popov lapsed into despair.

There was little to do but sit and wait. Occasionally a single man would be brought out of his cell to carry rice buckets and water, which was plentiful, or to join a cleanup detail. After two weeks the planes returned. When it was safe Will asked their guard in Japanese what was going on. The guard, who was growing friendlier every day, revealed that the Americans had taken most of Leyte and would soon head north.

Will passed the news to the others. "No wonder they want to send us to Japan," said Bliss. "We'll be hostages." All four watched the next diving attacks and could hardly restrain their cheers. Will felt as if his chest would burst. The Americans were coming! The news swept from cell to cell. Men cheered. Some shouted with joy and danced about. Others sat hugging themselves, thinking of freedom and home.

Popov refused to join the celebration. "Just another lousy rumor," he mumbled. The contents of the burlap bag had been ransacked by guards and all he had left was a precious waterproof bag which held a packet of I.O.U.s from comrades in Cabanatuan. Will tried to encourage him but he merely shook his head dolefully.

High spirits were dampened the next morning. The American medical officers, in the presence of a Japanese doctor, began inspection of all those from Cabanatuan to determine which were sufficiently healthy to endure the arduous journey to Japan. Popov pleaded that he was dying, and when an American doctor shook his head sadly accused him of being a collaborator.

On the evening of December 12 the men were fed half a cup of steamed rice and a quarter of a cup of soup. "The last supper," predicted Bliss and advised everyone to fill up canteens with water in the morning. "If MacArthur gets this close and then lets us go, we'll really be pissed off," he wrote in his diary.

Long before dawn the great gong of the prison guardhouse tolled. They all knew now that this was the day they had been dreading and it was too late to be freed by MacArthur. Will painfully rose from the concrete floor. He showered and shaved in the dark not knowing when he would have such luxuries again. He stowed a jacket, a change of clothes and a few toilet articles in his pack. Popov was furtively counting his I.O.U.s in a corner as if fearing his cellmates would rob him. Each ate a half cup of watery rice gruel.

At the first light of day the guards let the prisoners out of their cell and they were lined up with their baggage. It took hours for their own commanding officer, a Marine colonel, and a Japanese guard to get a head count. There were 1,619. All were Americans except for thirty Allied prisoners of war. Some 1,100 were officers and many of these were field grade.

The Japanese doctor attempted to calm the prisoners. In good English he explained that a liner had reached port and would take them to Japan. "You will be safe. Aboard will be our own women and children and the ship will be marked so it will not be bombed. You have nothing to fear." Apparently he did not realize that what the prisoners feared most was being sent to Japan just as freedom seemed so near.

At eight o'clock the long line slowly started through the gate and down Rizal Avenue. The sick and wounded, left behind, shouted and waved from doors and windows. But the line was only halfway out the gate when the air-raid alarm shrieked. The guards frantically reversed the line, shouting, "Back into the prison!"

The prisoners restrained their cheers.

"Speedo! Speedo!" shouted the guards.

No planes appeared despite a thousand prayers. An hour passed. The sweat rolled off the prisoners. Guards rushed along the ranks snatching mosquito nets and tropical helmets from the prisoners and throwing them in a pile. No need for these in Japan.

At last, near eleven o'clock, an officer called out a command and the line began to move again. The prisoners passed through lines of sober Filipinos. On all their faces was pity. Before the war Rizal Avenue had been filled with festive crowds and heavy traffic. Today the Filipinos were haggard, ragged. No longer were there any small ponies or carts. Many stores were boarded up and homes showed signs of looting. There was little metal. Manhole covers and iron bars from windows had been sent to Japan as scrap.

The men looked to the skies hoping the clouds would disperse so the planes could resume their bombing. Most of the prisoners were barefoot and the hot pavement was painful. Despite warnings to conserve water, some were guzzling it from canteens, empty ketchup bottles, and other containers.

On all sides was debris from the bombings, and from still smoldering buildings live sparks shot out into the street. They crossed Quezon Bridge which, to Will's surprise, was still undamaged.

As they trudged past Luneta Park Will was surprised to see it crammed with hastily erected barracks; here and there were artillery and antiaircraft positions. A Filipino tossed Will a piece of candy; a guard seized the Filipino and flung him to the pavement. They came to the walled city section that had been built long before the advent of the white man. It was surrounded by huge flame trees with their brilliant red blossoms, an incongruous touch of beauty amid destruction.

At last they crossed the open compound of Santo Domingo Church, now a pile of rubble, and approached Pier 7, the Million Dollar Pier, reputedly the longest in the world. Its famed white marble columns were in ruins. Beyond Will could see a large luxury liner, the *Oryoku-Maru*. A large crowd of Japanese women and children was getting aboard. They were eager to return to the homeland before the battle for Luzon began. The women, in kimono and laden with large cloth or straw bundles, were good-naturedly herding their excited children, ignoring the prisoners. A group of sailors, apparently survivors of sinkings, followed along with soldiers who were to man the antiaircraft guns.

Once the fifteen hundred passengers were aboard, the prisoners were herded like cattle up three gangplanks. Bliss pointed to winches hastily raising American-made cars and appliances to the deck. "MacArthur's Packard," he said and laughed when the shiny vehicle careened against the side of the hold, smashing its fenders. A man behind said, "I wish the bastard was inside."

Bliss, looking as if he were leading a group of students on a field trip, started to climb down through the hatch. Just behind was a reluctant Popov. He turned to Will. "We'll never get out of there alive."

Will pushed him.

There were seven hundred men in Will's hold. The only air came from a hatch twenty feet square. A man next to Bliss fainted but the crowd held him up. Will found it difficult to breathe even though he was not far from the open hatchway.

The men were too stunned to do much talking. Suddenly from the darkness came a shriek. "Oh, my God! This man is drinking his own urine!"

Then came Bliss's casual voice. "Did you know I'm a member of the *Faerie Queene* club?" Someone muttered, "We've got a frigging fruit here." But Bliss ignored him and explained that anyone who had read the complete chivalric romance in verse by Spenser could join this select group. "Just thought you'd like to know."

Will couldn't help chuckling as did several others. There was quiet despite the stifling air. Most of the men had thoughtlessly emptied their canteens and water bottles during the march. They began fanning the air in unison with mess kits but it made no difference.

"When are we going to shove off?" complained someone. Then they would get some sea breeze.

Men shouted for water but the guards ignored them. Hadn't their own comrades come to the Philippines in the same holds? They had not whined. The Americans were weaklings. The prisoners' exertions slowly exhausted the oxygen from the air. A major nearby, suffocating, toppled over silently. What admirable restraint, thought Will and tried to calm himself. Hundreds, gasping for breath, thrashed about calling for water.

It was not until three o'clock in the morning that the ship began to move slowly and a faint breeze brought some relief. They were moving north at about twenty knots along the coast of Zambales and were in a convoy including a cruiser, destroyers, and troop transports. A big silver amphibious Jap plane was hovering overhead. They were being protected and it looked as if they now had a good chance of getting through without being sunk by U.S. planes.

No sooner had this welcome information been passed around than there came the terrifying whine of the air-raid alarm. Then Will could hear the rumble of approaching planes and the barking of the antiaircraft guns on deck. Bullets and shrapnel began ricocheting around the hold.

Everyone near the open hatch pushed to a safer place. The tension was broken by a Southern drawl: "Who wants to buy my watch?" With motors going full speed, the ship bounced from a near miss. Dozens were bleeding profusely and their neighbors were doing their utmost to staunch the flow of blood. The hold was clogged with bomb dust and chips of rust. Those who had not prayed for months called upon God to save them.

The shriek of diving planes and the rattle of machine guns increased, then died down. Will and his friends moved back to their old place for fresh air. The medical personnel and volunteers bandaged the wounded as best they could and moved them to the safest places.

Again came the roar of planes and the chatter of guns, the explosion of bombs. This time there was no joking. Throughout the day came intermittent raids. On the last raid fragments of rocks burst into the hold—the ship had been beached, apparently to prevent its sinking.

2.

As the sun was setting, Will felt the ship move ponderously. It was probably backing off the beach. At last it was free and seemed to be heading west out to sea. But was it in any condition for the long trip to Formosa? A food carrier climbed up the ladder, soon returning with a bloody head. No food, no medicine, no water. After all the damage done by American planes, why should the prisoners get anything?

As the ship moved out to sea in the dark, Will could occasionally hear muffled explosions. "Depth charges," said Bliss. "Our subs must be trying to attack." Men prayed the Americans would give up the chase. Then the engines stopped. The anchor dropped and Will could hear small boats coming alongside. Bliss guessed they were taking off the Japanese civilian passengers and the wounded.

A guard shouted down for all doctors to get topside "speedo." They climbed up to find the deck in shambles. Five times the gallant gun crews had been wiped out only to be replaced by volunteers. The casualties among women and children were appalling. The American doctors and medics found the decks, cabins, and dining rooms littered with dead and dying Japanese. It was a hopeless task since there was only candlelight and no medicine or bandages. In frustration the guards began beating the medical group.

The prisoners near the hull licked the steel plates where a little moisture had condensed. It was even worse than the night before. Those like Will and Bliss who had nursed their supply shared their water with comrades. Now there was not a drop left. As the heat rose to 110 degrees arguments over water turned into riot. In the past months Will had seen intolerable brutality but nothing like this. It reminded him of what he had read as a child of the Black Hole of Calcutta. He felt a sharp pain on his neck, then a sucking noise. My God, someone was sucking his blood like Dracula. He swung around, grabbed a man who shrieked wildly. Bliss hammered at the man who slumped lifelessly. A dozen others were slashing at the throats and wrists of comrades to suck blood. A few were biting arms, legs, throats in the quest.

The sick and wounded were trampled by the frenzied. Wild, deadly fights erupted. One man was swinging two canteens filled with urine, knocking down everyone who came within range. A colonel climbed halfway up the ladder and shouted for order. He threatened, then in a momentary calm began to talk soothingly. But someone grabbed his leg and pulled him back into the melee.

Will felt he would go out of his own mind if the madness kept on. Who could ever have imagined anything so horrible? It was the end of civilization. Then came a commanding voice from the center of the hold. It was Father Cummings, the Maryknoll priest Will had met in a Bataan hospital. He was one of fourteen chaplains on board the ship. "Our Father who art in heaven, hallowed be Thy name!" He spoke with such authority that the frenzy lessened. "Thy kingdom come. Thy will be done on earth as it is in heaven." He continued praying, forcing the men to listen by his own confidence. Then he told them—no, thought Will, he ordered them—to have faith. "Believe in yourselves and in the goodness of one another." How can he talk of man's goodness, thought Will, after the unspeakable things men had done that night? But he noticed prisoners were looking at each other shamefacedly. "Know that in yourselves and those that stand near you, you see the image of God. For mankind is in the image of God."

Will could not believe in a God that could permit such indecencies but found himself wanting to. The priest continued, undaunted by a new chorus of whimpers and shrieks; most of the men had been brought back to sanity by the chaplain and the faint light of day from the hatch. Gradually the mad were brought under control. It was like the end of an unspeakable battle.

At dawn they approached a port at the western base of the Bataan peninsula. A civilian interpreter named Wada, a hunchback, climbed down. "You are going ashore pretty soon and can take along pants, shirts, canteens and mess kits. You must carry your shoes." Will crammed as much as possible into his pockets. In the near darkness he pawed through his battered musette bag for his toilet articles, extra shirts and shorts. He tied everything in a bundle as Mark would have done. Around him men were gobbling down their last emergency food.

"All right," shouted Wada through the hatch. "Send up your first twenty-five men." This group, including five wounded, slowly started up the ladder. Mr. Wada was back a few minutes later calling for another group of twenty-five. But as they started up Wada frantically warned them back. "Many planes! Many planes!" he yelled.

"Men," called out another Maryknoll priest, Father Duffy, "Thank God for protecting us yesterday. Ask him to deliver us today if it be his Holy Will. If not, to take us to heaven." He prayed, recited an Act of Contrition and gave everyone General Absolution.

Seconds later a bomb crashed into the hold, scattering shrapnel. Someone grabbed Father Duffy, who was still standing, and yanked him by his feet under protective shelving. Superstructure tumbled down the hatchway, narrowly missing Will and Bliss. Planked flooring fell into the bilge, dumping scores of men into the bottom of the ship. Others near Will were hopelessly pinned down. Flames swept through the wreckage. Explosions shook the ship as bombs plunged into other holds.

Bliss started up the ladder followed by Will, bindle on his shoulder. The iron rungs were painful on his bare feet but he kept moving up. At the top of the ladder Bliss was trying to push up the debris that covered the hatch. Will helped and they forced their way onto the deck. Nearby they discovered sacks of raw sugar. They dropped several to those below, then wolfed down a handful of the sweet. Will thought he had used his last strength to get up the ladder and push aside the debris but the sugar gave him a surge of power.

He saw Japanese killed by last night's strafing and bombing shrouded in straw rice sacks and piled in a long row five bodies high. Beyond, prisoners were leaping out of another hold like freed animals. Will's throat was raw from the pungent stink of burning phosphorus. Black smoke was belching from portholes as flames enveloped the ship's stern. He heard the crackle of rifles. Guards were shooting at Americans who had salvaged food and medicine. Will looked around for Bliss. He was waiting, ready to jump overboard. "Jump," called Will. "I'm coming!" He followed his friend in a wild leap. The cool water was invigorating and the exercise of a dozen strokes after two cramped days abruptly loosed his bowels. Then he realized he had left the bindle containing his precious notes on the deck. He shouted to Bliss to keep going and headed back toward the burning *Oryoku-Maru*. It looked like a scrap heap. He started up a dangling rope ladder, not realizing how weak he was until he was halfway up. By will power he kept going and flopped onto the deck. He retrieved his bindle and was about to leap again when he noticed Father Cummings standing indecisively at the rail.

"The ship is going down, Father!" he called. "Get the hell off."

Cummings smiled sheepishly. "I can't swim a stroke." He took off his glasses, carefully stowed them in a pocket. "Well, here goes anyway," he said and leaped into space.

Will jumped. When he surfaced he looked for the chaplain. He was dog-paddling vigorously, his head lifted above water like a drenched cat.

"I thought you couldn't swim, Father."

"I—seem to be doing all right so far," he gasped.

"Don't talk. If you can't make it, roll onto your back and let me pull you in."

The priest nodded vigorously.

Then came the shriek of a diving plane and the frightening rattle of a machine gun. Bullets spanked the water nearby. Will dived as far down as he could. His lungs felt like bursting and he shot to the surface. He bumped into a body red with blood. Cummings, he thought. Then he saw the priest, unharmed, scrambling toward shore. There was another roar. A plane started toward them. Will waved frantically. Others in the water were doing the same. With a waggle of wings the plane zoomed off. The men in the water cheered.

As they neared the shore Will noticed prisoners ahead treading water. What was wrong? Then he saw there was a high seawall. Several Japanese soldiers standing atop it were firing into the water to keep them at bay. Will felt his strength ebbing fast. He didn't know how Father Cummings had lasted so long. Will edged forward with breast strokes as a guard hesitantly held his fire. Finally he was able to touch sand.

For more than an hour they stood in water up to their hips begging the soldiers on top of the wall for water. Some of the men tried to drink seawater and vomited. But the guards merely stared down, leveling their guns at anyone who tried to get closer. One frenzied prisoner tried to claw his way up the moss-covered wall. A shot rang out and he tumbled into the water, dead.

At last a guard shouted down in Japanese to climb. Will started up the wall. He thought he would never make it, then felt Bliss pushing him from behind. He helped Bliss over the top and half an hour later more than thirteen hundred men were assembled. After counting off they were marched toward Olongapo. It was only a mile but many of the prisoners had to be prodded with bayonets to keep moving. It was a pleasant little town on the side of a green mountain. They were herded into two adjoining tennis courts surrounded by a high wire fence. There was just room enough for the prisoners to squat down with knees pressed against the man in front.

The sun was blazing and the half-naked men started turning red in the glare. Someone said the Japs were bringing in water but it was only a rumor. Will had put on his extra clothing as protection from the sun and naked ones eyed him enviously as if ready to appropriate something. Will gave Bliss his spare shirt.

Many had broken arms and legs, others had been shot or hit with shrapnel. But their groans were drowned out by the increasing cries for water. At last a guard called for five men. They returned toting five-gallon cans. Water! There was a rush for the water carriers. Everyone wanted to be first. A colonel called to a guard to come in and bring order. A Japanese reluctantly entered the cage of squabbling men and room was at last made in the center of the court so the water could be distributed fairly. Each man got five spoonfuls. The first men protested that this was not enough but they were pushed away. It seemed an eternity before an officer carefully dribbled out five spoonfuls into Will's canteen. He slowly savored every drop. What was more wonderful in life than water?

It was dark by the time he and Bliss settled down. The moon had risen and a slight breeze rustled the palm trees. "Like a travel poster," observed Bliss. Will could not sleep in his cramped position. All through the night the groans and whimpers continued.

3.

At sunrise, a Japanese soldier slipped the nozzle end of a hose into the tennis court. The water was turned on and the men cheered, cavorting in the spray like New York City tenement kids at gushing hydrants. Sated with water, the men turned their thoughts to food and medicine. Then came the ominous rumble of planes. Fright took over. One bomb inside the court would cause a massacre. Planes flew over and Will heard the crump of bombs and the rattle of strafing. Olongapo was getting a pasting. A plane circled overhead, then swooped down and tipped its wings. The men shouted. They had been recognized. Other planes swept down in greeting and flew off.

By this time the cement was like a griddle. Blisters covered their bodies. Will felt like a kettle—as if the water he had guzzled was being steamed out of his body. The hours dragged on. The sun set. Still no food arrived. Then clouds appeared as if by magic and rain pelted down on the thirteen hundred huddled prisoners.

The next afternoon Mr. Wada, the interpreter, appeared holding up sheets of paper. "Here is a list of all Americans who left Manila." Someone was to check those who had died. The reading went on until sunset. Soon the cement was comfortable, then it became cold. They huddled together for another miserable night. In the morning there were another dozen dead bodies. There was plenty of water but no food. The senior officers pleaded with the guard to remove the dead bodies and the prisoners were finally allowed to carry them to the side of a hill.

Will felt dizzy from hunger and heat. "Hang on," said Bliss, as calm as ever.

The following evening two guards brought in a large sack of rice. This time there was no frenzied rush. The men formed an orderly encircling ring around the colonel, who passed out to each man two spoonfuls of the uncooked rice. Will put a single grain in his mouth, chewing it carefully until it dissolved. No restaurant had ever served a more delicious entree. He and Bliss dined until past midnight.

For the next three days they received the same rice ration. The men were growing restless and surly; their constant chatter at night irritated the guards so much they threatened to shoot into the court. Still no medicine or bandages.

On December 20, 681 prisoners were loaded into thirty trucks and driven away. Will and Bliss were in the group left behind. Later in the day they witnessed a harrowing sight: a surgeon trying to amputate the gangrenous arm of a Marine named Dugan with a dull jackknife and no anesthetic.

"Anything we can do for you?" the surgeon had asked. "Would you like to bite on a piece of wood?" Dugan asked for a cigarette and someone lit half of one. Will almost retched to hear the crunching of the bone but young Dugan only spat out the butt and stared up at the stars, gritting his teeth. "I can stand it," he told the surgeon. "We'll soon be out of here and free." At last the arm was severed. Now came the task of cauterizing the wound. The Japanese would not allow a fire to be built inside the enclosure but finally did pass over a burning piece of wood. Will smelled the noxious odor when the flame touched the wound. Dugan uttered not a sound. Two hours later he died.

The next morning Wada announced that the rest were to be trucked out. Those who couldn't walk the half mile to the loading point would have to be done away with. Will wondered if he could make it. Bliss helped him to his feet. "Put your arm around my shoulder," he said.

Will thought of Dugan who had died a hero's death. "I can make it," he said and staggered toward the gate. He passed a dozen men stretched out on the cement. Several were moving feebly. Guards were kicking the inert forms to get them moving. Several made futile attempts. A youngster was trying to drag his friend upright. "Jack, you can do it!" he pleaded. Bliss came to his aid and together they dragged the helpless man away. Will wished he had strength to help those who couldn't walk but knew he would be lucky to make it himself. He winced to see a rifle butt crush into the head of one inert victim. Father Cummings brushed past a guard who tried to stop him and made the sign of the cross over the dead man. As Will passed through the gate he turned to see the chaplain, ignoring the shouts of the guards, administer the last rites to others who had died.

It was a long, slow, hot trip over a rough mountain road. Again planes flew by and Will feared that the clouds of dust raised by the truck convoy would draw bombing and strafing. But luck held and they reached San Fernando, Pampanga, safely. Here they were marched into an empty movie theater. This time there was plenty of water waiting for them. Will hoped they would get their daily ration of un-cooked rice and his heart leaped when two men piled steaming rice on two corrugated sheets. Their first hot meal since leaving Bilibid! He felt strength surging back. Now he knew he would make it.

By the morning of December 24 he and the other prisoners had regained their spirits. That morning they were routed out of the theater and marched down the street to the railroad station. Lines of openly sympathetic Filipinos watched silently as the guards goaded the bare-foot, ragged prisoners. The station was badly damaged and Will noticed that the locomotive heading ten freight cars was riddled with bullet holes. About 130 men had to be loaded into each boxcar and Mr. Wada called out for volunteers to ride on top. If the planes saw Americans they would not bomb the train. Few men volunteered, since it would obviously be a rugged ride in the burning sun. Father Cummings, spry as a boy, clambered up the ladder to the top of one car. A score fol-lowed. Will started and Bliss held him back. "Don't be a damned fool. You'd fall off after an hour." They climbed into a car that used to haul rice. In minutes the place was stifling and it was difficult to breathe. The wounded and sick moaned as the train jerked to a start.

Hour after hour passed. They knew they were not going to Manila for they were heading north. Near midnight they stopped at a town and heard, from a nearby church, Filipinos singing Christmas carols, then the indistinct voice of a priest celebrating midnight Mass.

"Jesus Christ," exclaimed someone, "it must be Christmas Eve."

There were a few feeble attempts to joke. Will felt his head spin and passed out. Upon waking he was lying on the floor of the boxcar, his face toward a large crack in the flooring. Bliss must have put him in this position; otherwise he would have suffocated. He felt sorry for himself until he realized what Father Cummings and the others atop the cars were suffering. It must be bitter cold up there with the train in motion.

It was almost three in the morning by the time the train reached its destination. This was the town of San Fernando, La Union, at the head of Lingayen Gulf not far from where General Homma's troops had first landed. The men hobbled out of the cars. Although Father Cummings climbed wearily down from his perch, he was as aggressively optimistic as ever.

After bedding down on the gravel of the railroad yards, they were rousted in the early morning light and driven up the main street. Peo-ple peered sympathetically from windows at the slow procession. They passed through a gate into a schoolyard surrounded by a high stone wall.

It was a shady spot brightened by a garden of hibiscus bushes and tiger lilies. The hungry men began stripping the leaves of the plants and bushes. Will chewed on the sweet red and salmon hibiscus blossoms. Within an hour it was as though locusts had swooped onto the garden. Then the men devoured the bark from trees and the grass along the paths. Someone uprooted one of the lily plants. The bulb looked delicious. Will tasted one. It was like a raw sweet potato. "Better leave it alone," warned Bliss but Will gulped it down. It felt as if his stomach would explode. He fell to his knees. His head spun. Some fifty others were writhing on the ground in pain.

That evening for Christmas dinner they were given half a cup of cooked rice. Despite his bout with the lily bulb Will had no trouble getting down his rice. As they were settling down on the grass for the night, Wada announced that they were moving out. Those who complained were quieted by angry gestures from the guards, who were becoming exasperated with their charges. They marched for several miles. The sky was brilliant with stars and it was not as chilly as the previous night. Will could smell the sea. Soon they passed a line of palm trees and were directed onto a beach. The sand felt good on his bare feet. It was still warm. He and Bliss dug holes, covered themselves with sand and went to sleep, lulled by the gently lapping waves.

At 5 A.M. they were rudely awakened, divided into groups of one hundred, and issued rice balls. As usual there were not enough to go around and Will shared his with Bliss. Then their group was led to the water and instructed to bathe. This did more to liven the men than food. Will luxuriated in the warmish, clean water. This was followed by a torturous wait on the beach with no shade from the sun. Each man got three teaspoonfuls of water during the day. Two died.

The following morning they were again counted and marched out. They crossed a peninsula to a pier where six large transports were anchored in Lingayen Gulf which was littered with half-sunken vessels. They watched as landing barges from the transports brought in soldiers and ammunition. The first group of prisoners was loaded into the empty barges which were bouncing from the heavy waves. It was an eight-foot jump into a barge and many of the prisoners hesitated. Guards pushed the reluctant and some landed awkwardly, breaking arms and legs. One of these hit his head on the side of the barge and plunged into the water. His body was dragged out and carried off.

These barges headed for an old freighter of 10,000 tons, the *Brazil-Maru*. At last it was time for Will's group to board an empty barge.

Knowing what happened to those who hesitated, Will gauged the rise and fall of the barge and jumped. He toppled over but was not hurt. Bliss landed awkwardly but only grunted. As the barge was about to leave, the air-raid alarm sounded. In the confusion the barge headed for another transport, one with the number 1 on its stack. This was the *Enoura-Maru*. Will clambered up the long ladder into the ship and followed the line into a hold which had brought horses from Japan. Manure covered the deck. Worse was the horde of large horseflies that began attacking the prisoners. They did their best to sweep the manure to one side and at last lay down to rest.

Hours passed. Since they were now covered with manure, the flies descended on their bodies and no one talked for fear of swallowing one. At last they could hear the anchor being hauled up. The ship vibrated and the long journey to the north began. What new hardships would they face in the enemy's homeland? Could they possibly be worse, thought Will, than those endured since capture on Bataan?

4.

Leyte. December 15, 1944.

Organized resistance was at the point of collapse and Kamiko, Ko, and Maeda had fought their way through the American lines to reach a crossroad ten miles from Ormoc. Here they met a small group of paratroopers sent forward to stem the relentless American advance. They were young, well-equipped, and eager for battle.

"You'll be outnumbered ten to one," cautioned Kamiko.

"My goal is to kill ten before I die!" said one baby-faced private, and blushed to see the looks of pity on the faces of the three stragglers. Once out of hearing, Kamiko began berating Imperial Headquarters. "How dare they send such children on suicide missions!" He made a sudden decision that would have appalled him a few weeks earlier. "We must escape to another island. Why should we too die uselessly?"

Neither Maeda nor Ko needed any persuasion and they decided to try to work their way to the nearest coast, steal a native boat, and make for Borneo. And so they headed due west toward the coastal town of Palompon, battling native guerrillas, slogging through swamps, scaling steep ravines and threading their way through areas of quicksand, pushing on despite the temptation to give up the quixotic plan to escape their island of death. Near the coast they encountered two other stragglers who joined them. One, a fisherman, claimed he could navigate them to some safe island. The other was wounded but with help made it to a beach only a few miles from the temporary headquarters of the commander of the dwindling Japanese forces. Upon learning that there was a great battle at nearby Palompon, they became conscious-stricken at the thought of desertion. They abandoned the wounded man and started up the beach to join the fight but half an hour later a retreating Japanese officer ordered them to follow his unit. They did so reluctantly until they reached the coconut grove where their wounded comrade, Tokoro, lay. After exchanging significant glances the three stragglers furtively dropped behind and hid in the grove. They agreed to attempt the escape and began looking for a boat.

It was late Christmas afternoon but they did not know it.

General MacArthur had just announced that the Leyte campaign was over except for minor mopping-up operations. He was preparing for the invasion of Luzon. Soon after dark the sounds of battle at Palompon subsided. Ko could hear in the distance a familiar song he had learned in Sunday school:

> Silent night! Holy night!
> All is calm, all is bright . . .

Ko realized the G.I.'s up on the hills above the beach were playing recordings of Christmas carols, and the yearnings he had been repressing for home and family almost overwhelmed him. It took an hour for the stragglers to find a banca. After fitting the little outrigger with a sail made from a tent, they loaded it with their meager possessions and rifles. As they were embarking, Ko said, "Tokoro?"

Nakamura, the fisherman, warned that five would probably swamp the boat but Kamiko protested. "He's right. We can't abandon a comrade."

Maeda sided with the fisherman. "He knows best."

A voice came from the dark. "Group Leader, I am staying here. It is my fate."

Startled, the others turned to see Tokoro squatting nearby. Nakamura stepped out of the banca. "Group Leader," he said, "I am staying too." Ko followed him.

Kamiko and Maeda dragged the boat onto the beach and joined the other two who were sitting silently with Tokoro. After a long pause

Tokoro said, "I apologize for the trouble I'm causing." He struggled to his feet and painfully limped into the dark.

"It's hopeless anyway," said the fisherman. "Even four of us will swamp the boat."

Kamiko stood up angrily. "Why didn't you say so in the first place?" he shouted. "First you're afraid to die on land and now you're afraid of dying at sea!"

"Who cares where we die," argued Maeda the realist. "Which choice offers the best chance of survival—land or sea?"

There was no reply and they all huddled together, staring at one another. The silence was broken by a pistol shot.

"Tokoro," said Kamiko.

"Poor devil," said Ko.

"It's better he did that than drown us all," said Maeda.

This was too much for Kamiko. "Let's follow Tokoro! Let's end it all on land with honor!" He ordered them to huddle closer and banged a grenade on a rock. They all knew it would explode in five or six seconds. Maeda immediately flung himself backward. Nakamura, the fisherman, shouted, "I'll go!" and Kamiko flung the grenade toward the sea seconds before it exploded.

They pushed the banca through the first waves, clambered aboard. As the boat sailed slowly out in the moonlight, Nakamura became a new man. With authority he headed the outrigger toward Cebu. The moonlight suddenly was cut off by a cloud and Ko felt rain sharply slap his cheeks. The rain increased and they were soon immersed in an ominous dark cloud.

Nakamura's confidence evaporated. He looked around with concern. "I think we should turn back."

"We're at sea, Nakamura," said Kamiko. "We're going to die anyway so let's do it here!"

The frail craft was already pitching and tossing in the lively sea. Nakamura gripped the tiller determinedly while his passengers bailed energetically with their mess gear. The rain stopped as abruptly as it had started and they heard the roar of a motor. Dimly ahead a dark shape was approaching. Kamiko was sure it was a speedboat transporting 35th Army Headquarters to Cebu. They all shouted, hoping to get aboard. But the craft droned past and when the moon briefly peered out from a cloud, Ko could see it was an American PT boat.

Hours later the rising sun revealed they were surrounded by small,

406

bare rock islands. And to the west Ko could distinguish through the dawn light a large island.

"Cebu," guessed Nakamura and changed course. As a good omen the wind picked up, driving the loaded banca briskly through the calm waters.

"Here is a song I taught my pupils," said Kamiko. "It is my favorite," he added in embarrassment and began to sing softly:

> From a far-off island whose name I don't know
> A coconut comes floating.
> How many months have you been tossing on the waves
> Far from the shores of your native land?
> I think about tides far away
> And wonder when I will return to my native land.

Ko tried to hide the tears that flooded his eyes until he saw that the others were also weeping silently.

CHAPTER TWENTY-FOUR

1.

Guam. November 1944.

Mark had completed his training. It was an enjoyable tour for he found his fellow language officers compatible. Most of them were quiet, introspective, and far more interested in chess, reading, and listening to classical music than haunting bars, whoring, and brawling. Few would have passed Marine physical qualifications. At first, awed by his decorations, they regarded Mark as an outsider because of his combat experience. But upon learning that he, like most of them, was a BIJ—born in Japan—and had spent years at Japanese schools, he was not only accepted but admired for his exploits.

He arrived in Guam, still on Temporary Additional Duty orders from the 2nd Division, the week before Thanksgiving to get further training with his new regiment, the 21st Marines of the 3rd Division. A number of 3rd Division people from Saipan and Tinian had been sent on to help liberate Guam in a bloody engagement in which four Marine combat photographers and a combat correspondent had been killed. Now they were preparing—but didn't know it—to hit the beaches of a tiny, unknown island halfway to Tokyo. It was to be used for emergency landings of B-29's and fighter escorts returning from raids on Japan.

By the time Mark arrived, Guam had developed into a major naval base for further operations. The living conditions seemed luxurious to someone used to Saipan. The Island Command officers' club, for instance, was erratically furnished with contrasting items: native mats, island souvenirs, and relics of battle. Parachutes were draped from the ceiling like a canopy to provide insulation and decoration. The bar, embellished by camouflaged ponchos, was presided over by a former Pullman car attendant who could mix any drink known to man. More important, there was an abundance of nurses and Red Cross girls. Enlisted men were not allowed to take them out, however, and Mark was advised to stay in officer country on a date. A number of officers taking girls to isolated places had been attacked by resentful enlisted men.

Mark had first dated an army nurse with a pleasant personality but thick ankles. The advent of a large group of more attractive navy nurses ended that relationship and he was presently going with a nubile redhead from Boston named Eloise.

On the first of December Mark was amazed to bump into Billy J. at the officers' club. "What are you doing here, Colonel?"

"Duke Jorgensen and I are going home for Christmas," said Billy J. Mark brought them to the bar. "Duke and I stopped here to refuel and there's something wrong with one of the motors."

"You won't believe it," said Duke, a lieutenant colonel, "but one of the damn motors started groaning right after takeoff. And the copilot comes out of the cockpit telling us not to worry."

"The kid must have been all of nineteen and he only had fuzz on his chin," said Sullivan. " 'Could you possibly be the copilot?' I asked. He said he was and I said, 'What do you think of this plane?' "

Duke interrupted. "And the kid says, 'Oh, it's all right, except for the port motor.' And I says, 'Whatya mean?' And he says, 'Well, sometimes it just quits. Just goes out.' 'What happens then?' I ask. And the kid just gives a Bronx cheer and does like this." He made downward circles with a forefinger.

Billy J. laughed. "Here's the kid blasting out with his mouth and Duke says, 'You son of a bitch, you didn't have to tell me that.' "

Mark escorted them around the island and took them to dinner. Sullivan was as proud of his former runner as if he were his young brother and couldn't help telling Duke of several of Mark's trips into caves. Mark blushed, embarrassed but pleased. In the morning he drove them in a regimental jeep to the airport.

"There's the kid we were telling about," said Billy J. He walked over to the copilot, who was instructing a ground crewman to take the wooden blocks out of the stabilizers and rudders. "What're those in there for?" asked Billy J.

"Just a precaution after we land. In case a wind comes up."

"Do you ever forget to have those things taken out?" asked Duke.

"Oh, yeah, but not often. Once in a while. As a matter of fact, we had one plane take off just three weeks ago with the blocks still in."

"What happened?"

The youngster grinned and gave a raucous Bronx cheer with downward gestures.

Duke grabbed Billy J.'s arm. "Our next stop is Johnston Island. Now before we take off from there I'm going to check the blocks, and I'm going to check before every damn takeoff until we get to California. You take the starboard side, Bill, and I'll take the port side."

Billy J. pushed Duke up the gangway, then shook hands with Mark. "Did you see your sister in Hawaii?" After Mark gave him a brief rundown of his reunion with Maggie and their father, Sullivan put a hand on his shoulder. "Glad to hear you're tidying up your personal battlefield. I'll be thinking of you. Maybe I'll see you on the way back through."

Mark felt a lump in his throat as he watched Sullivan climb into the plane. What if, after surviving the 'Canal, Tarawa, Saipan and Tinian, Billy J. ended up in the Pacific?

During the next three weeks Mark and the other language officers taught the combat Marines a dozen or so phrases in Japanese such as "Come out and surrender." They also interviewed the Japanese taken prisoner during the Guam battle. Mark was amazed to find that almost all of them were contented. They seemed to have overcome their first shame and depression at having surrendered. Mark would play cards with them and they would exchange stories about pre-war Japan. He was regarded as their friend. He brought them cigarettes and candy and made sure their wounds were treated regularly.

There was one exception, an army captain who sat by himself and could only glare at Mark every time he tried to engage him in conversation. One day Mark noticed that he had settled himself near the barbed-wire enclosure. A fellow prisoner suddenly shouted, "Hara-kiri! He's cutting himself on the barbed wire!"

Mark ordered a guard to keep the other prisoners back and walked slowly toward the captain. Mark bowed, mentioned what a good day it was, and asked permission to speak.

The captain stopped slashing his wrists and bowed. "I must kill myself," he said. "I am disgraced. I can never go home."

"It is a sad fact," said Mark and sat next to him cross-legged.

The Japanese grasped the barbed-wire to continue.

"Do you think that Japan will win the war?" asked Mark calmly.

"No. America is too strong. We Japanese have much *bushido* but you have more guns. We shall lose."

"If Japan is going to lose the war then why shouldn't you go home after the war?"

The Japanese laughed without humor. "You know Japan better than that, Lieutenant. A man who surrenders has his name crossed off the town roll. He no longer exists. My family would not greet me. I must kill myself."

"But if Japan loses the war the generals and admirals will be disgraced. The government officials will be disgraced. So will the Emperor. And if the entire nation is disgraced, why shouldn't you go home?"

"No, I cannot go home. Their disgrace is not the disgrace of a man who surrenders."

"You were wounded when you were captured. I understand you tried to kill the man who captured you."

"I failed and allowed myself to be captured."

Mark bowed. "I understand, but I think you are wrong. Things will be much different in Japan after the war. Because that will mean the whole country has surrendered." He got to his feet and bowed. "I will come back and talk to you in the morning if you allow me."

The captain said nothing but bowed.

Mark gave orders to the guards not to attempt to seize the prisoner. Nor were they to bring him any food and water. In the morning he himself returned, bowed, handed the captain a pack of cigarettes and sat down.

After a long pause the captain said, "I think perhaps that I shall go home." He bowed, lit a cigarette and looked off reflectively. "If someone were to ask you what is the essence of the Japanese spirit, tell them it is the glory of the mountain cherry tree blossoms."

Mark said nothing but bowed.

"I shall go home," said the captain.

On December 20 Maggie McGlynn landed at Agana with a dozen other correspondents and photographers. During the long trip from Hawaii she had been in an almost constant state of excitement. Her dream at last was being realized. For weeks she had hectored her boss in Kansas City for accreditation as a war correspondent. When cajoling failed, she threatened to use her father's influence to find a publisher who would send her to the battle area. "I want to cover what women are doing out there," she said.

"Not a bad idea," was the grudging response.

"And anything else that happens while I'm there."

The publisher growled, then said, "It just happens that we need someone in the Pacific right now. I'll arrange everything at this end. You just be sure you're first someplace!"

Within forty-eight hours the red tape in Washington was cut and her application for accreditation approved. Her war correspondent's uniform was so brand-new that she feared the other correspondents would snub her, but to her relief she was accepted as an equal on the plane. After checking her baggage at her quarters, a tent, she joined several other correspondents in a trip to the Island Command officers' club. Other correspondents were at the bar grumbling about the lack of hard news.

She was awed. Here was the cream of the profession. She recognized famous faces. Late in the afternoon navy and Marine officers appeared and she got a little thrill, which annoyed her, to see Lieutenant Tyrone Power walk in like any other human being. A Marine lieutenant who had cut her out from the correspondents introduced her to the movie star and once he left said, "Nice fellow, Tyrone, but a lousy pilot. He brings in supplies to us. But don't get off the ground with him." Then he pointed out another lieutenant who was drinking with other navy men. "Recognize him?" She did. It was Henry Fonda. "He's with CINCPac," said the Marine.

She heard a familiar voice exclaim her name. It was Mark. After hugging her he introduced her to a slender navy lieutenant with a boyish face. "This is Ed MacDowell. We knew each other on Saipan. He's only navy but quite human. Here's my kid sister."

"Kid sister," she challenged. "You're only ten minutes older."

Mark guided her to a table away from the correspondents and explained that MacDowell was a JASCO leader attached to a battalion in the 21st Marines. "Mac was a promising reporter on the Charleston *Monitor* and the navy in their wisdom assigned him to call down naval gunfire on his own head. A prime example of snafu."

Maggie was not very impressed with MacDowell, who stammered with an accent every time he managed to say a few words to her. Not only was he from South Carolina and undoubtedly archaic regarding Negroes and Jews but he was not much to look at. But Mark insisted that she let Mac guide her around the island in the morning since he had to attend a meeting.

Promptly at eleven in the morning MacDowell, looking neat and nervous, was at her quarters with a jeep. Maggie was in a rebellious mood, for she resented Mark's saddling her with the dullest man on the island. She knew her brother so well; he still considered himself the protector of her virtue and regarded any charming man as a despoiler.

MacDowell did his best to be amusing but it was obvious she was bored with his stories of the historical background of the native Chamorros. He did please her by taking her to a Chamorro restaurant that was little more than a ramshackle hut with a corrugated roof. The food was delicious and the atmosphere unusual. By now she was getting used to his southern accent and had discovered that some of his straight-faced remarks were quite witty. But when she laughed at these it brought blushes to his cheeks and he felt obliged to give her another historical lecture. By midafternoon he turned to a different subject, his experiences on Saipan with Mark. Maggie's interest quickened and she pumped him for every detail of her brother's exploits, particularly his attempts to bring Japanese women and children out from the caves.

As they were driving through the wreckage of the town of Agana they saw a black sailor dart out of a shack followed by half a dozen white Marines. The pursuers were shouting and throwing beer bottles at the terrified sailor who stumbled and fell to the road. As the whites started to beat him, MacDowell brought the jeep to a screeching halt. He angrily shouted at the attackers, who were drunk, to desist. But they ignored him until he seized the biggest one by the scruff of the neck and threatened to shoot him.

The white Marines came to their senses and sheepishly stood in line as he wrote down their names. He delivered a short, sharp lecture, told the black to get into the back of the jeep, and drove off. Maggie began to laugh.

"What is so amusing, Miss McGlynn?" he said.

"You threatening to shoot those men with your finger."

He smiled crookedly. "I forgot I didn't have my side arms."

In spite of herself she was impressed by his actions.

"You off one of the ships, sailor?" MacDowell asked the Negro.

"No, sir, I'm in the 25th Depot Company." He was scared. "I didn't do nothing, sir."

"What were you doing in that shack?"

"Just seeing a girl. She asked me in. Then these white fellows come in and called me a black mother-fu— Excuse me, ma'am. They said all the girls was theirs."

"Do many things like this happen to Negroes?" asked Maggie, who smelled a story.

"I'm not complaining, ma'am. I just learned that that town's no place for me no more."

"There's been a colored-white problem here for the past two months," said MacDowell. "Some of our white Marines give them a hard time. Every so often somebody rolls a grenade into their tent area. Fortunately none of them has gone off."

"Not yet, sir," said the black. "And they call us niggers. And we was all supposed to get leaves at the end of eighteen months and never got a thing."

After MacDowell dropped off the man at the naval supply depot, he pointed out a storage area. "Last week about thirty colored boys were working there without shirts. That was against regulations and when a white M.P. told them to put on their shirts they surrounded him and pulled out knives. He had to draw his pistol to back them off."

"That's a silly regulation, making them work with their shirts on in this hot place."

"Yes," he said patiently. "But it was a regulation and the M.P. was only doing his duty." Neither spoke for a minute. "You think that because I'm from the South I'm for Jim Crow."

She was thinking that but protested it hadn't entered her mind.

"I'm only trying to explain that we have a dangerous situation here that could explode. It started because the colored boys *are* discriminated against here. Some of them know how to take it but others get riled at things not meant to be offensive."

That evening MacDowell told Mark he had reported the beer-bottle-throwing incident but it was decided not to take any action. "They don't realize," said MacDowell, "that one bloody incident, one killing, could set off a real riot."

2.

Just such an incident came three days later, on December 24. In an argument over a Chamorro woman a white sailor shot a black sailor named McMorris. Two hours later a black sailor on sentry duty at the 5th Field Depot was so harassed by a drunken Marine that he fired twice. The second bullet killed the Marine. The shootings were the talk of the officers' club. After dinner Mark said he would drive Maggie to her tent but she refused. This was going to be a big story. MacDowell urged her to consider the consequences. This was the kind of story that would cause embarrassment to the navy and the Marines.

"Then it's just the kind of story I should write."

"And if you did you'd probably get sent home."

"He's right," said Mark. "There's a war on and we have enough trouble fighting the Japs."

"The Japs? That sounds strange coming from you."

"For God's sake, keep your voice down," said Mark. "Do you want to get known as Miss Poison Pen?"

Her spirit was up but she realized they were both right. "Okay," she said reluctantly.

"I'd just like to see you around here longer," said MacDowell and blushed furiously.

What a jerk! she thought, but he really wasn't half bad-looking. In fact, he was rather cute. She allowed herself to be taken to her quarters without further argument.

In the morning most of the talk at the officers' club was of the big Christmas bash to take place that night. The rooms were already gaily decorated with papier-mâché ornaments and an imaginative cardboard replica of a Christmas tree. Maggie was still grumbling about the censorship being imposed on her by Mark and MacDowell, yet secretly was relieved she had not made a public show of her indignation the night before. She was smart enough to know that the only way to succeed as a war correspondent was not to make the wrong enemies. She didn't even protest when her brother brought along MacDowell as her date. Mark was accompanied by the pretty red-haired nurse, Eloise, who hung on every word he uttered.

It was a gay, noisy party with a burly Marine bird colonel, H. A. Evans, notorious for his bad taste, attempting to pat the rear end of every girl present. Since arriving a month ago to take an important job at Island Command, he had earned his nickname, "Heavy Hand Hank." At the same time, he was good-natured and only got mean after three drinks. Unfortunately he started early and by ten o'clock had become irritated at the agile maneuvers of Mark and MacDowell in protecting Maggie and the redhead from his bearish advances. Finally he pushed Mark into a corner and ordered him to get him a drink at the crowded bar. Mark could not refuse and left Maggie in the hands of MacDowell who was not only outranked but far outweighed. The colonel insisted on dancing with Maggie and to prevent trouble she agreed. But after a few clumsy tours of the dance floor he forced her to a porch. Not wanting to offend an important officer, Maggie tried to joke her way free, but he was obviously interested only in one thing. She finally got angry and kicked him in the shins. He was so drunk he never felt the pain. He grabbed her around the waist like a parcel. She hit him several times but he was too big and strong and she had been brought up not to scream in public. As he was manhandling her out the back door Mac-Dowell arrived with a pail full of ice and water. He dumped the contents over the colonel's head. Heavy Hand sputtered in shock and rage.

"I'm sorry, sir," said MacDowell politely. "I spilled my drink."

By this time several Marine officers had arrived and they took charge of Heavy Hand Hank. But Mark was still so furious he lunged toward him. Evans, shocked to a degree of sobriety, grabbed Mark by the shirtfront. "I won't forget this, you bastard!" He drew back a fist but two Marine captains deftly intervened and escorted him back to his quarters.

Fortunately there was a hubbub at the other end of the big room and few had observed the scene. Someone had arrived with news that two truckloads of "rioting" black sailors from the naval supply depot had been apprehended in Agana. M.P.'s found fourteen automatic pistols, a revolver, nineteen knives, and considerable ammunition.

This information put a damper on the party and most of the women were brought back to their quarters. Maggie, subdued for once in her life, made no protest to Mark's suggestion that he and Ed take her and Eloise home.

"I admire the way you took care of Heavy Hand Hank," said Mark as the two men started back to the regimental area. "I probably would have slugged him and got court-martialed."

"It was just a clumsy accident," said MacDowell wryly.

As they approached the road that passed between the black sailors' tent compound and the naval supply depot storage area, they could see about thirty blacks surrounding a jeep. Mark stopped his vehicle and hurried forward. He could see two white M.P.'s sitting in their jeep. The one in the passenger seat was asking, "What the hell's going on?"

"None of your damn business!" someone yelled. "Who the hell you think you are?"

"I'm an M.P. What's going on around here?"

A black grabbed the M.P. by the throat, then seized the riot gun lying on the seat as the M.P. reached for his pistol. The black put a shot in the chamber of the riot gun. "If you reach for that .45, I'll blow your brains out."

"Hold it," shouted MacDowell. "We're not armed."

The other M.P. had gone to the back of the jeep to restore order. He held up his pistol to put a round in the chamber. A black jammed a carbine in his stomach and yelled, "I'm going to blow your guts out!"

The M.P. pushed aside the carbine, struck the threatening black over the head with the muzzle of his pistol, and scrambled into the driver's seat. As the jeep lunged forward a black slammed the passenger over the head with a stick. There was a volley of shots from pistols and carbines. The jeep swerved but apparently the driver was not hit for the vehicle righted itself and sped off.

It all had happened so fast that Mark was stunned. In battle he had acted automatically, but he was so shocked to see Americans fighting each other that he was paralyzed. MacDowell pulled him toward their jeep. "Let's get the hell out of here!"

Mark expected another volley of shots but no one fired as they careered out of the area.

The next day the Island Commander convened a Court of Inquiry to investigate the circumstances surrounding the unlawful assembly and riot. It would by no means be a trial, merely a board of inquiry to explore the facts and attempt to find ways of keeping down friction between colored and white so as to win the war and get home. By chance, Walter W. White, Executive Secretary of the National Association for the Advancement of Colored People, was on a nearby island as a correspondent for the New York *Post*. He arrived in Guam on December 28 and was allowed to interrogate blacks involved in the incidents.

The inquiry began at the naval supply depot on December 30 with White present as observer and counsel for several of the blacks brought up on charges. He was intelligent and soft-spoken, not at all the firebrand most expected. He was also very shrewd and was determined not only to defend the accused but to bring to the surface the causes of the uprising.

The president of the court, Colonel Samuel Woods, was a distinguished-looking, courtly North Carolinian with a reputation for being fair and even-tempered. "This court," he said, "is interested in the question of whether or not discrimination exists against any race, and if so, why?"

Mark was there as a witness of the Christmas night jeep incident. As he slipped into a vacant seat near the door he glanced at the court. To his consternation, there sitting on the right of Colonel Woods was Heavy Hand Hank Evans. Their eyes met and Evans glared in recognition.

White was politely questioning the quality of leadership among the officers in command of the black units, all of whom were white. A frequent complaint from Negro servicemen, he said, was that they could find no officer who would give a sympathetic hearing to their complaints. Mark thought White had stated the case well and he was impressed by his deep concern unmarred by emotionalism or exaggeration.

In the afternoon session the president asked whether it was not a fact that wherever American citizens lived or worked there would always exist, with certain individuals, racial prejudice which no commanding officer could control.

"Yes," said White. But it was still the obligation of the military authorities to reduce the frictions. "If for no other reason than that they interfere grievously with the successful prosecution of the war effort."

This ended the first day and Mark was informed he need not appear until it was time for his own testimony.

3.

Testimony into the shooting of McMorris, who had died in the hospital on Christmas morning, went on for several days. At last Mark and MacDowell were summoned to appear. As they walked into the naval supply depot toward the hearing room, Mark said, "I'm going to have to tell them that I got a very good look at one of the Negroes surrounding the jeep."

"The one that grabbed the M.P. by the throat?"

"No, the one just behind him. He was sort of a leader and was calling the loudest names. He was waving a knife."

"I didn't see him."

"I'll never forget the fierce look on his face. He had a big, ugly scar running down his right cheek."

"I got a pretty good look at the one who stuck the carbine in the other M.P.'s back but I don't know if I could identify him."

As they entered the inquiry room, Mark noticed White talking with several black sailors. One had a livid scar. This man peered up and saw Mark staring angrily.

Mark nudged MacDowell. "That's the guy. I think I know him. He could be a fellow I had an argument with at an American Peace Mobilization seminar in early '41. A big blowhard."

After lengthy examinations and cross-examination by the judge advocate and White, Colonel Woods called a recess. Mark noticed the black sailor with the scar eyeing him. Mark stared back. There was no doubt: This was the same man who had called him a racist at the APM seminar because he had inadvertently referred to Negroes as blacks. The man had called him a rich college kid who was slumming. Mark had held his temper while the moderator, a Jew, desperately tried to make peace.

When court was convened, the judge advocate began interrogating Mark, who told what he had seen. Asked if he had gotten a good look at any of the colored men surrounding the jeep Mark replied, "Yes, sir. The one behind the man who was choking Sergeant Boltz."

"What was he doing?"

"Waving a knife around. I think it was a Ka-Bar. And shouting."

"Do you remember anything he shouted?"

"He was calling the corporal a mother-fucker."

"Could you describe him?"

"Yes, sir. He had a scar on his right cheek." Mark could see another black restraining the man Mark was describing. "I am pretty sure, sir, that it is the sailor sitting over there." He pointed toward the man with the scar. Then he noticed Heavy Hand Hank Evans whispering to Woods.

Evans leaned forward and, for the first time in the proceedings, spoke. "Lieutenant McGlynn, I've been watching the looks exchanged between you and the sailor you just identified. I have the strong impression that the two of you recall knowing each other prior to the incident you just described. Am I correct?"

"Yes, sir."

"Tell us about it," Evans's mean little eyes glistened.

"I had met him in New York City," Mark answered uncomfortably.

"Under what circumstances," the colonel pressed.

This had no bearing on this case, Mark thought. Evans was just getting back at him for the incident with Maggie.

"Well, answer my question," demanded Evans.

"At a seminar, I believe, in early 1941."

"What kind of a seminar?"

"The APM, that is, the American Peace Mobilization, organized a conference. We were divided into different groups for various seminars. The one I attended was at the Hotel Great Northern and we were to discuss Jim Crow."

The judge advocate was noticeably impatient with the line of questioning. "Colonel Evans, none of this has any bearing on this inquiry. I fail to see what you hope to accomplish, and we're wasting time."

"I got him to admit he hangs around with pinkos, or haven't you ever heard of the American Peace Mobilization?" Colonel Evans retorted angrily.

"Nevertheless," the judge advocate persisted, "that was before the war and has no bearing on this inquiry." He looked expectantly at the president of the court.

Colonel Woods nodded and turned to Evans. "The judge advocate is correct. In the future, please confine yourself to the issues at hand. You may step down, Lieutenant."

The snap of the pencil Evans was clutching in his hand rang out like a pistol shot in the stilled courtroom.

As Mark was leaving the building for lunch a Marine captain accosted him. "Lieutenant McGlynn, I would like to ask you a few questions." He explained he was from an Intelligence unit. "As I understand, APM was a Communist front."

"Yes, sir."

"What in the devil were you doing there?"

"At that time, sir, I believed in the principles of APM. You see, it was the only organization that was for peace as well as against Anti-Semitism and Jim Crow. It was also pro-unions."

"And you were for all those things?"

"Yes, sir. At the time. I did quit APM after Hitler's invasion of Russia. They wanted to turn it into a pro-war outfit."

"Let's get one thing straight, Lieutenant. Were you aware that this APM was a Commie front?"

"Yes, sir."

"And you still stayed in?"

"Yes, sir. In those days I was naïve. I was a communist."

"That's not a laughing matter, Lieutenant. We'll want to talk to you about this in a few days."

At lunch Mark told Maggie and MacDowell what had happened and tried to make light of it. Maggie agreed it was trivial and while Mac-Dowell was far more concerned, he reserved his comments until she had left. Only then did Mark reveal that he had lied in Seattle. "After the recruiting sergeant read my application he advised me to change what I'd written about being in a Communist front organization. He advised me to give a negative answer. I did."

Two weeks passed without hearing from the Intelligence captain but Mark's anxiety increased. By this time the court of inquiry had heard its last witness and the judge advocate asked Walter White if he still felt, as he had stated earlier, that there was a depressingly low morale among the colored troops on Guam. After White reiterated the basic reasons for low morale of Negro troops he said, "It is not that the Negroes are simply trying to get Negro generals and admirals. It is a little more fundamental than that. In a war such as we are now fighting, a war for human liberty, Negroes not only in Guam but in the United States and everywhere else are asking: Is the status which they have been more or less assigned and confined to for a good many years—namely, that of being more or less of a menial class—is that to be continued or are they going to be given the opportunity to advance as far as individual ability, loyalty, and energy will permit them to do?"

The president had one final question. "Is there any doubt in your mind, from your participation in this court of inquiry and your observations on the island of Guam, that justice will be meted out impartially and equally on the island of Guam, in this military establishment, regardless of race, creed, or color?"

"I have no doubt about it now."

That same day Mark was summoned to the division operations office where he was faced by three grim officers. "We have received copies of your personnel file and other papers," said a full colonel named Quinn. "What disturbs us most is that in your enlistment papers you stated that you did not nor ever had belonged to a radical group or party. You answered, No. And you have already admitted under oath that you knew that the American Peace Mobilization was a communist front."

"Yes, sir."

"Were you, in fact, a member of the Communist Party?"

"Yes, sir."

"In other words, you lied."

"Yes, sir."

"Have you anything to say in your defense?"

"I would only like to say that when I became a member of the party, and as far as I know to this date, it was not illegal to be a communist."

"What concerns us is that you lied." Colonel Quinn collected the papers and put them in a folder. "You have a good record at Tarawa, Saipan, and Tinian, McGlynn." He slapped the folder on the table. "But

I don't like this at all. I am not sure what we are going to do about it. Dismissed."

Mark reported the bad news to Maggie, who was close to tears. Mac-Dowell, who had become her companion every available moment, had hopes. "They're really hard up for language officers, Mark."

The following day Mark was surprised to see Colonel Sullivan come out of Colonel Quinn's office. Mark went up to greet him. "When did you get back from the States?"

Billy J. didn't answer. "I just heard over at BOQ about the mess you got yourself into."

"Colonel Quinn is really teed off."

"Why didn't you tell me about the enlistment? I thought you trusted me."

"I didn't want to bother you. It didn't seem important, sir."

"Not important!" Billy J. said icily. "Fraudulent enlistment not important?" With a withering look Sullivan turned and entered the G-1 office.

"Morning, Bill," Quinn said, waving toward a chair. "What can I do for you?"

"It's about Lieutenant McGlynn. I've seen him in action. He's a fine Marine."

Quinn's craggy face grew somber. "Yes, I've talked to Jack Colley. I understand you had a lot to do with his being commissioned. But God damn it, Bill, you know how serious this is. The boy lied. What's just as bad, he doesn't seem to comprehend why we are so upset about it. He justifies his action on the grounds that when he was a member of the Communist Party it wasn't illegal."

"I see." Sullivan shook his head. "Not to admit it to the recruiter is completely out of character for him. The fact that he may have been following some bum advice in no way lessens or changes anything. He did lie. That's what surprises me so much, Colonel. When he first joined my outfit from boot camp I held office hours on him more than any other private. He was always pulling some dumb stunt, but he never once lied or tried to pass the buck."

"Well, what do you suggest we do about it? We can't just ignore it."

"I agree, but he does have an outstanding combat record and we'll continue to need first-class language officers like him for some time to come. Please give him another chance, sir. He can still save a lot of lives."

Colonel Quinn thought this over. Finally he slapped his big hand on the desk. "How do we do that and still get our message across to him?"

"Have someone help him prepare a request to Headquarters Marine Corps stating that at the time he enlisted he was careless in answering the question negatively and desires to have it changed to the affirmative. Then you forward it with a favorable endorsement recommending approval. You could cite his combat record and our continuing need for well-qualified language officers. That will do it."

"Yes, that would do it," Quinn agreed. "But damn it, we've got to get through to him that we don't tolerate lying in this man's Marine Corps. What do we do about that?"

"I would hope that you give him a ration of that famous Quinn ass chewing." Billy J. smiled as he stood up. Then, looking the colonel in the eye, he said grimly, "Remember, after Iwo he'll be coming back to the 2nd Marine Division. I'll take over then."

Quinn smiled and held out his hand. "Yes, I believe you will, Bill. Thanks for dropping by."

Mark was still waiting as Sullivan came out from the G-1 office and looked up.

Billy J. just glanced at him and continued walking. Mark fell in step beside him.

"But," he protested, "you didn't let me finish my explanation."

Billy J. stopped and looked him in the eye. "So?"

"Well, being a communist was not illegal when I was one," Mark said uncertainly.

"So what?" Billy J. said evenly. "Lying on a federal questionnaire was. It not only was illegal, it was immoral and, goddammit, it was un-Marinelike. You got anything else, McGlynn?"

Mark started to tell him that he had just followed the suggestion of the recruiting sergeant. Then he remembered the contempt Billy J. had for passing the buck. As he watched the colonel turn abruptly and stride off, Mark thought, "Oh, to hell with you."

Billy J., in the distance, turned and gazed briefly at him and got into a jeep. Mark clenched his fists and stared at the departing dust cloud.

Many of Mark's acquaintances pointedly avoided him at the officers' club and Eloise, the red-haired nurse, changed allegiance to a newly arrived naval captain. The following Monday Colonel Quinn summoned Mark. "I have been persuaded," he said icily, "somewhat against my better judgment, to let you square away your record. Report to the adjutant and do as he says. It is not often we give an officer a second chance. Learn your lesson and never, never, forget it. Do you read me?"

"Yes, sir."

"Dismissed."

Three days later Mark boarded a transport bound for a little island far away which, from the air, resembled a fat pork chop. Iwo Jima.

PART SIX

The Quick
and the Dead

CHAPTER TWENTY-FIVE

1.

At sea. December 28, 1944.

A thousand prisoners of war were aboard the *Enoura-Maru* bound for Takao, Formosa, the first leg of the long journey to Japan. Will and Bliss were in the afthold with more than seven hundred others. They had found Popov in an apathetic state and were doing their utmost to rouse his will to live. The hold was seventy feet wide, ninety feet long. Halfway up one side of the vast chamber stretched a balcony where the sick were segregated. Human waste dripped down from this balcony of misery onto those below. There was little food or water, a normal state of affairs for these survivors of so much deprivation.

The flies still harried the men. Whenever a tub of rice was lowered, a winged host suddenly appeared like attacking fighter planes. By the time the tub reached the bottom the rice could not be seen for the flies. Undaunted, the men waved away the hornetlike insects and ate voraciously, taking care only to see they swallowed as few as possible. The scanty ration was reinforced by those with enough energy to grovel through the horse troughs for grains of barley.

On the second day at sea rain fell and the men fought to get cups and mess kits under the drippings of the hatch covers. The most successful only saved a few drops. Will could hear men bitterly complaining that their water ration of the day tasted salty. There was weeping and swearing. Then came the strong voice of Father Cummings. He told how the Malays, traveling hundreds of miles in canoes, drank only sea water. They had been trained from childhood to do so and live. "You could, I think, if you tried, if you wanted and had faith." Four of the men did swallow the salty water without ill effects.

At sunset Will was roused from uneasy sleep by the blast of guns topside. He and Bliss dragged Popov off the wooden hatch cover used as a bed onto the steel flooring. The ship rocked from explosions on both sides. "Depth charges," said Bliss. This blasting continued for almost half an hour. Then there was silence and they could hear applause from the Japanese on the upper decks. The hunchbacked interpreter, Mr. Wada, eyes blinking behind his great round glasses, was elated. The Japanese Imperial Navy, he called down, had sunk an American submarine.

It was a cold night, spent in the trading of pens, rings, and mess gear for cigarettes or water. The next day, December 30, was one of unceasing misery for the seas were extremely rough. They received half a cup of rice and several spoonfuls of water. That evening there was another barrage from above and the crumping thuds of depth charges. In the excitement a Japanese soldier fell into their hold and died from his injuries.

The seas were just as rough in the morning. Since they were about halfway to Formosa the nights had turned very cold. The threadbare remnants of summer uniforms worn during the swim from the sinking *Oryoku-Maru* or the thin cotton shirts and trousers issued to many who had reached shore naked that day gave little protection. The chill seeped into the hold and the men huddled together for warmth. The tattered jacket Will had doggedly hung onto despite stifling heat was now a lifesaver. The death toll had risen to ten a day and on this last day of 1944 the prisoners raised such a disturbance that Wada finally got permission to have the corpses hauled up and thrown into the sea.

A whimpering man begged Father Cummings to baptize him. He was going to die soon. Cummings crawled over to Will. "Could you spare . . ." he started. Will had no water nor did Bliss. The priest went back to the dying man, spat on two of his fingers and ran them over the man's forehead. "I baptize thee in the Name of the Father, and of the Son, and of the Holy Ghost." He held the man's hand and the whimpering stopped.

They were given a treat on New Year's Day—five moldy hardtack biscuits and three quarters of a cup of water. It was like a banquet but even so some crawled around begging slavishly for a cigarette. Others were cajoling and threatening for a scrap of food.

"They're getting like animals in a cage," whispered Will.

"The wonder," said Bliss, "is that we don't all claw each other to death."

It had grown even colder and rest was impossible. Two days later Wada called for volunteers to clean up quarters topside. Will and Bliss volunteered and were surprised to see they were in a large harbor surrounded by steep, snow-covered mountains. It was Takao in southernmost Formosa. Sick and wounded Japanese had already been brought ashore and the volunteers were called upon to fumigate the abandoned areas. They all worked industriously, hoping to be rewarded with a little extra food. But when one man held out his hand a guard slammed it with his scabbarded sword.

The American colonel in command of the prisoners made another request to Wada for larger food rations. United States submarines, he replied, had sunk all Japanese food ships. "Blame them, not us."

During the next few days there was little food or water. It had become so cold that guards bundled in heavy overcoats were shivering. Several hundred prisoners from the other ship, the *Brazil-Maru*, were transferred to the *Enoura-Maru*. And on the afternoon of January 8 all men in the lower level of the hold were moved into the forward hold to make room for the storage of sugar.

The next morning while they were eating a scanty breakfast, Will heard the drone of planes. From the pitch Will knew these were American. Air-raid sirens screeched. Bursts of antiaircraft fire came from many ships in the harbor. Thoughts of water and food vanished. Some prisoners cried out in terror. Panic swept the hold as men scattered from the wooden hatch covers to the steel decks.

"Everybody stay put!" shouted a young captain. "You are as safe in one place as another."

Then came the whistle of falling bombs. As the ship rocked violently from a near miss, another bomb crashed into the deck. There was a great orange flash and a deafening explosion. Hatch covers fell into the bilge, dropping men thirty or forty feet below. Loose timbers crashed into crowds of men. Will felt as if he were falling through space. The ship leaped and bucked. Slugs of metal whistled past him and holes miraculously appeared in the side of the ship. It was like a sieve. There were screams, cries, groans and obscene oaths, and dead all over. Will coughed from the cloud of dust and dirt. Where was Bliss? He searched frantically, finally found him under a pile of debris. The dust cleared and Will hefted a huge beam with strength he didn't know he had. Bliss slowly crawled out. His hair was white with dust. He tried to say something but nothing came out of his mouth. He staggered to his feet. "Popov," he finally said. They found him pinned across the legs. He stared out, eyes wide open. Will and Bliss struggled with a twisted iron girder, lifting it slightly.

"Get out!" shouted Will, but Popov only kept staring blankly.

A major grabbed Popov and pulled him free. "We must help the others," said the major and the three of them worked desperately to do so. Many weak cries came from underneath a mangled eighteen-inch steel beam. Will was horrified. At least fifty or sixty men were trapped. The three men could not even budge the beam. It would take a steam crane. Will sank down exhausted, helpless. More than half of the men in the hold had been killed outright.

In the darkness the shrieks of pain from the wounded heightened the hysteria among the survivors. Several doctors and medics were dragging wounded to one side, binding their wounds with dirty towels, undershirts, or anything else they could get from luckier prisoners.

Will and Bliss found Father Cummings being tended by two enlisted men. He sat up blinking his eyes. "I'm not at all hurt," he insisted. "Just got knocked down by one of the beams." He struggled to his feet and began making the rounds of the wounded. His unruffled presence helped still the panic and when he saw a man was unharmed would peremptorily order him to join those trying to bring order out of the chaos.

Then came the distant whine of planes. The Americans were coming back! Panic returned. Father Cummings shouted for quiet in his vibrant, commanding voice. The cries and moans ceased. He raised his eyes and looked upward. "Lord," he said as if talking on a direct channel, "I do not understand all your ways. You have permitted us to go through a terrible ordeal. We are just hanging on to life, and if you leave us to our own devices we will die in the next air attack. Lord, I ask you to intercede. Guide those pilots to other targets. Spare us from further punishment!"

The planes swept over but no bombs dropped on the *Enoura-Maru*.

The next day, despite cries for food, water, and medical help there was no response from above. Death was so commonplace that it was not unusual to come upon a man perched on a body as he ate his pitiful meal.

A doctor noticed Mr. Wada staring down through the hatch. He begged for help in the name of humanity.

"Those were American planes," Wada shouted back. "We don't care if you die. Your planes killed our men too."

The next day a small Japanese medical party, masked and white-robed, descended into the hold. They painted some of the minor wounds with Mercurochrome but ignored the seriously wounded. On January 13 the sick and wounded were at last hoisted up on ropes. The others climbed a long ladder. Will felt as if he were leaving a charnel house. They were brought to the old freighter, *Brazil-Maru*, which they had last seen in Lingayen Gulf. As they clambered aboard Will thought, would this be the third death ship? Would he ever reach Japan?

Of the 1,619 men who had left Manila there were fewer than nine hundred alive. At dawn the ship slowly moved out of Takao Harbor. The six-foot-deep hold was fitted with two floors and Will found his three-foot space claustrophobic.

Time passed slowly, the once-a-day tiny ration barely keeping the prisoners alive. It began snowing on the third day and the cold increased with their northward progress. For warmth they lay down spoon fashion under straw mats, hugging each other, and when someone had to change position he would say, "Shift!" and everyone rolled as one to the other hip. The preceding night a neighbor of Will's had not turned. He was dead.

By the end of a week it had become bitter cold. Will felt guilty to have the only jacket. Cases of pneumonia mounted. Sometimes a guard could be bribed with a gold ring in trade for an empty rice sack to be used as a blanket. But soon there was nothing with which to barter and at least thirty new dead bodies would be found every morning. The mournful shout of "Roll out your dead!" reminded Will of grim stories of the London plague.

Selfishness was rampant with survival of the fittest the rule of the day. "It seems that prison life either corrupts you or ennobles you," commented Will.

"Both," said Bliss.

The best examples of humanity were set by the chaplains. The most devoted were a Lutheran, a Protestant, and the indomitable Father Cummings. Every night at nine o'clock Cummings would cheerfully announce, "Chaplain calling, boys!" then start with the Lord's Prayer and continue with a special prayer for those who had died and those who were dying. This would be inevitably followed by a short talk urging—demanding, rather—the men to keep up their hope and faith. "Just one more day!" he would plead daily and ask the men to forgive their enemies.

"I won't," Will told Bliss. "I'll curse them with my last words."

"You think so?"

Cummings himself had no shoes. He put out a request for any kind from size nine up. Bliss unlaced his own size tens and handed them over. Cummings protested but Bliss said he knew where he could get another pair in the morning. He took them from a dead man. From the same body he also stripped shorts and a shirt. He gave these to the chaplain who asked where they came from. Bliss grinned. "Heaven, Father." Cummings smiled wanly. It was obvious he would not last much longer unless he got more water.

On the night of January 24 Will fed Cummings several spoonfuls of water but he refused to take any more. "Share them with the boys," he said and passed out. The next day he found it difficult to go on his daily round and at the evening devotional he collapsed. "I'll be all right, boys," he told those who carried him back to his sleeping space. He tried in vain to crawl out the next morning. His lips were parched and cracked and his voice was weak. But that evening he insisted someone hold him erect. He managed to say the Lord's Prayer weakly.

"You are going to make it," said a man named Mosher. "We came this far." Mosher got some water from snow Will had sneaked from the deck at great risk and brought it to the padre.

"I am very cold," said Cummings.

Mosher found a straw mat and with the help of Bliss wrapped it around his own shoulders and then over the priest, hoping his own body heat would warm him.

"I feel all right," said Cummings. Fifteen minutes later Mosher felt his hand. There was no pulse. He called to Will and Bliss. "Father Cummings is dead."

They were silent but Popov, fingering his packet of I.O.U.s, as if they were religious beads, mumbled, "I'm next."

Will helped Mosher wrap the priest in the mat and in the morning they placed him on top of a pile of dead. After ropes were lowered into the hold, a boatswain tied a running bowline around Father Cummings' feet and a half hitch around his neck. "All right, take him away!" he called.

Will and the others saw the emaciated body slowly rise against the winter sky. As Father Cummings emerged from the hold he was illuminated by a ray of sunlight.

"How could he still believe in God after what he had seen?" Will said.

"My father was a minister," said Bliss. "A nice man, well respected if not loved. But I never saw him give up anything for his fellow man. He talked of God and the afterlife but as he lay dying he was scared. I think he feared there really wasn't a God up there."

The following night they reached Moji, an important port in northern Kyushu. A large party of officers, enlisted men, and civilians boarded.

Doctors and medics gave each prisoner a physical test which consisted of inserting a thermometer up his anus. Bliss alone was amused by the painful process. "They're really sticking it up our ass," he said.

At dawn interpreter Wada had a few last words for them. "You will be spending the rest of the war here," he said. "You will be kept safe by the Nipponese Imperial Forces from civilians who would beat or kill you because of the killing and damage done to our homeland by your bombers. So you guys better stay where you are sent. Stay healthy and *sayonara.*"

They were brought topside to receive new clothing. Those like Will and Bliss, near the head of the line, got the complete issue, including long cotton underwear and padded jackets. But they were forced to strip in the icy wind and sleet. One guard, taking a dislike to such a tall, blond man, kept beating Will over the back with a stick to make him hurry. Captured British shoes had been handed out without regard to size and it took great effort for Will to squeeze his freezing feet into the pair he drew.

As Will started off the ship, supporting Popov, both were sprayed with Lysol, which set off coughs that shook Popov's spindly body. It was a cold, foggy day and the buildings rose, grim and frowning, from the bleak streets. On the dock women stevedores in kimono stared at the walking skeletons that tottered down the gangplank. They had not shaved since leaving Bilibid, were infested with lice, and stank. They were marched in driving sleet through the streets. The people watched them go by with incredulity and some held their noses.

The march was only a few blocks but despite the new clothing Will thought he would die of cold before it ended. Bliss was now helping him drag Popov along. At last they filed into an empty warehouse. But the windows were open and icy winds forced them to mass together for warmth. Someone said there was a water faucet and the guards made no effort to prevent them drinking all they wanted. Will took a deep swallow. It was ice cold and he felt his stomach cramp. He warned Bliss and Popov.

Their spirits rose once guards entered with large buckets of steaming rice. It smelled delicious. The rice was ladled out in cardboard containers. Incredibly, other guards brought in more food. Each man got several spoonfuls of salted fish, a large crawfish, a few slices of salted radishes, a piece of something that was peppery, and fruit that tasted like pineapple. Will had not eaten so well since his days as a guerrilla.

In the morning they were divided into groups. The sick and wounded

433

would go to a local hospital and the rest to work camps. Will and Bliss, realizing that Popov had lost his will to live, persuaded him to stay with them. They and ninety-two others were assigned to Camp 13. It was a hundred miles or so to the south and they would work in a coal mine.

Of the 1,619 who had left Manila only 450 were alive and many of these were dying. Will wondered how many of those bound for Camp 13 would live until liberation. He was determined to be one of them, although he feared what lay ahead. They would be slaving in a coal mine, guarded by men whose homeland, they had been told by Mr. Wada, was now being ravaged by American bombs.

2.

It had been a hard, cold winter, the population suffering from lack of heat, insufficient clothing, and a meager diet. Worse than these privations was the fear of bombings. The howling of sirens on the first of November had caused millions of throats to tighten. It was the first genuine alert since the Doolittle raid which had come two and a half years earlier. For months the city had been in a turmoil over fire-fighting drills that often interrupted life in the capital.

At last the dreaded day had come, and Floss joined other women in scanning the skies for the first glimpse of the dreaded B-29's. The air was split with the racket of antiaircraft fire. Then came silence. The all-clear was sounded. The radio reported that one American plane had come over the capital but dropped nothing.

There was another alert the next morning. Again a single plane came over but disappeared without dumping a bomb. In the next few weeks two and three B-29's would appear and the rumor spread that they were merely taking pictures. The newspapers wrote about government plans to evacuate all nonessential civilians but nothing was done. Instead notices were posted in every home instructing the people to stay home during a raid. Tokyo could only be saved if every person prevented his own home from burning. Floss and other women began to believe the raids could not be very serious after all if the government allowed the mass of civilians to remain in the city.

On November 24 the first raid on Tokyo came. The target was the Nakajima aircraft plant at Musashino ten miles northwest of the Imperial Palace. Ninety-four B-29's, unescorted by fighters, roared over the

434

city at almost 450 miles an hour and began dropping their bombs. Only forty-eight bombs hit the plant complex, causing slight damage, the rest blasting dock and crowded urban areas. Three days later sixty-two big bombers headed for the same target. But the engine plant was completely hidden by clouds and they were forced to hit secondary targets.

Slight as the losses were, both the civilians and Imperial Headquarters were chilled for it proved that there was no effective defense against the high-flying B-29's. Already the foundation of Japan's basic industries had been undermined by persistent American submarine and air attacks on shipping. There was little crude oil in the refineries, no coke or iron for the steel mills, and the munitions plants were short of steel and aluminum. A continuation of B-29 attacks would surely mean ruin for the entire economy.

The end of November brought the first night raid. Again, the damage was not serious but the hundreds of small fires that sprang up around Tokyo were terrifying. In early December another bombing set off more fires, leaving blotches of destruction around the city. A rumor spread that the Americans were going to stage a massive raid on December 8, the anniversary of Pearl Harbor, and this instigated a mass exodus from the city by those who had someplace to go.

Tadashi had begged Floss to leave for Karuizawa, the resort refuge for foreigners, but she didn't want to be alone and Masao needed his father. On the anniversary of Pearl Harbor she packed emergency rations and clothing, but despite four alarms that day no bombs fell. Shizuoka to the south turned out to be the target and two hours after the Americans departed the burning city a violent earthquake shook the area with massive tremors that left a long section of railbed in ruin, munitions plants crippled, and a factory producing precision instruments obliterated. By the beginning of 1945 the people of Tokyo had become so accustomed to minor attacks that an air raid alarm meant little more than an inconvenience. On the ninth of January the Superfortresses hit Tokyo for the sixth time and this raid was also ineffectual.

Tadashi was depressed by the drabness of Tokyo. People were clothed in quilted hoods and leggings that made everyone look like a laborer. Floss left Masao with Emi one late afternoon and joined him for a trip to town. There were no streetlights and they sloshed through the dirty snow. They saw a stall where a man was selling food. The steam rising from his stove looked cheerful but as they drew near it smelled revolting. He was toasting garlic for soup. As they turned away the man called out, "Sah, when you drink this soup it'll warm you to your toes. And you won't catch a cold in the shelter tonight. One cup ten sen!"

Others were lining up so Tadashi and Floss joined them. The soup consisted only of boiled water, grated garlic, and a little seaweed. They walked on but found every restaurant besieged by long lines. At last they came to one where there wasn't a soul waiting.

"It's a ration restaurant," explained Tadashi. He had only one coupon.

They passed a poster pasted on a store window with a picture of a fierce-looking American pilot. The slogan read: ANNIHILATE BEASTLY AMERICA AND BRITAIN! Finally they saw a small restaurant with no queue. They entered a narrow door to find a dingy, dirty establishment that looked like a warehouse. Customers crowded four tables eating snacks, drinking seaweed tea, and munching *arare*, rice crackers. Tadashi suggested they get persimmons, *arare*, rice, and tea. He left her at a table since it was self-service. He returned without the persimmon.

"Do you know how much it costs? Three and a half yen!"

Floss had not seen the Todas for a week because of the bad weather and did not know that Shogo had just arrived from Burma and was assigned to the Operations Section at Imperial Headquarters. His behavior worried Emi. Whenever he visited he wandered about the house grimly and would only say that things had been bad in Burma.

Shogo had returned hoping to be revitalized by the homeland. Instead he was dismayed by the changes in Tokyo the past two years. It seemed like a city of the dead. The people were apathetic and moved about like automatons. The fighting spirit of the Japanese seemed to have atrophied. Even at Imperial Headquarters he sensed defeatism.

His depression ended one evening in January when a friend, a dedicated young officer, brought him to a lecture by Kiyoshi Hiraizumi. A former professor at Tokyo Imperial University, Hiraizumi had quit there in disgust at the growth of communism on campus, to establish a patriotic school he called "Green-Green," a name inspired by a quote from a Chinese patriot just before his execution by Mogul raiders: "Evergreens in the snow are even greener." That is, anyone under fire who remains "green" is truly pure.

A mild little man, Hiraizumi nevertheless strode up to the podium with a sword. He laid it aside and began speaking softly, never using his hands or contorting his face for effect. But he electrified every young officer in the room with his burning sincerity. "Japanese society," he said, "is based on complete loyalty and obedience to parents, nation, and Emperor; and Green-Green teaches you that Shinto is its bone, Confucianism is its flesh, and *bushido* is its blood."

He spoke softly but so persuasively of the Imperial Way and their country that Shogo was instantly reimbued with the spirit of self-sacrifice to Emperor and country. After the lecture he was introduced to a fiery young lieutenant colonel named Takeshita who, after several long meetings, urged Shogo to join a special group which was taking Green-Green a step further. The great emergency of the nation required this step but only those with the purest ideals, only those who would not hesitate a moment to sacrifice their lives for the Imperial Way, could be accepted. Within a week he was a devoted member of a group convinced that unconditional surrender would destroy *Yamato damashi*, the spirit of Japan, and *kokutai*, the national essence. At last the gap in Shogo's life left by his complete disillusionment with Tsuji was filled. He had jumped from the frying pan into the fire.

Takeshita and other leaders of this clique had learned of the growing movement among high-ranking citizens to force the military to accept unconditional surrender before Japan was destroyed. On February 12 one of the most important of these men, Prince Konoye, had been summoned to the Palace to discuss the war with His Majesty, the Grand Chamberlain, and Kido. The following evening Konoye secretly visited Shigeru Yoshida, a prominent pro-Western diplomat who also belonged to the group working for peace. Konoye handed over the draft of the private report he would present to the Emperor the following day.

Yoshida read the document titled "Memorial to the Throne." Like almost everything else concerning Konoye, it was an anomaly—objective and subjective, practical and impractical. It began with a courageous pronouncement: "Regrettable though it is, I believe that Japan has already lost the war." Then he charged that the greatest danger to Japan's imperial system came, "not from defeat itself but from the threat of a communist revolution," and that some army leaders were so infused with pro-Soviet sentiment they were urging an alliance with Russia at any cost.

Yoshida realized that Konoye's fear of communism was exaggerated but was impressed by the inescapable logic of his conclusions: peace could be negotiated only if the militarists were circumvented. "Although they know they cannot win the war, I believe they will fight to the death in order to save face. Thus, if the tree is severed at the root, its leaves and branches will wither and die." At the same time, Konoye's recommendation for dealing with the hard-core militarists was unrealistic, however desirable: eliminate them by a coup d'état and negotiate directly with America and Britain.

Since Yoshida basically agreed with Konoye, they worked over the draft until late into the night. Together they made a final draft with some additions. The next day Konoye arrived at the Palace and in the presence of Kido read aloud to His Majesty the eight-page document. All its inconsistencies notwithstanding, the rambling "Memorial" stimulated both the Emperor and his chief adviser. Unlike his fellow *jushin*, Konoye had uncovered the core of the problem, and while his solution was impractical, it could eventually be transformed by the pragmatic Kido into an efficacious plan for peace.

The Foreign Office was soon buzzing with rumors of Konoye's visit to the Emperor, and, as usual, the most accurate information was passed on to Jun's inner circle. He was one of the most concerned recipients of the peace news for he had just received another white slip ordering him to report to Hiroshima for a third examination. He was more convinced than ever that he must fail again. What a waste to die with peace so close! Through his sources he had learned that the army had now caught on to the use of soy sauce to induce high blood pressure. He could not take a chance and repeat this trick. If he were caught, his grandfather would die from shame.

This time there were no farewell parties nor farewell gifts, only another warning from his adviser, Fujita, to avoid military duty at any cost. On the train to Hiroshima he met another young man taking the same exam.

"My cousin recently was examined," he said. "They were taking men who had lost an arm or leg."

"What can they do with a man who's lost an arm?"

"Well, he can use the other arm to polish the regimental commander's boots. Even one leg can be useful to the Emperor these days. We don't have any chance of getting off again."

Depressed, Jun reported the following morning to regimental headquarters. The first examiner, a sergeant, said softly, "Do it well. Our medical officer is a gynecologist. You can fool him with your record." The sergeant coughed suggestively.

A few minutes later the gynecologist asked Jun, "Has your lung condition improved?"

"I regret to say it has not." Jun went into a spasm of coughs.

"We're asked to pass men with a missing arm these days."

"I want to serve my country," said Jun. "But if I should get ill under all

438

that rigorous training, will you take the responsibility for recommending my admission?"

The gynecologist worriedly examined Jun's records. "I see you work for Tokyo *Shimbun?*"

"Yes, sir."

The gynecologist was intimidated. "Well, young man, I'm afraid I must reject you in the interests of the army."

CHAPTER TWENTY-SIX

1.

In Washington, President Roosevelt was preparing to leave for Yalta, a seaside resort in the Crimea where the Big Three would determine the future face not only of Europe but of the Far East. The President had just been advised by his Joint Chiefs of Staff that Russia's entry into the war against Japan was vital. Both Marshall and MacArthur were convinced that defeat of the 700,000-man elite Kwantung Army in Manchuria without Soviet help would cost the lives of hundreds of thousands of Americans.

That afternoon Professor McGlynn was rereading a report he had written several weeks previously on the Kwantung Army when he received a call from the White House to report there as soon as possible. Though greeted informally as an old friend at the Oval Office, he himself always remained formal.

"Frank, what I'm going to tell you must not leave this room," began Roosevelt. He revealed that he was going to Yalta. This was not news to McGlynn but he wisely said nothing. He had not seen the President for several months and was shocked how much he had aged. His skin was sallow, his eyes showed intense fatigue, and his hands trembled. Age and pain were written on his face and McGlynn feared he might not be strong enough to stand up against Stalin at the crucial meeting.

Roosevelt shrewdly read McGlynn's mind. "Frank, I guess I was up too late last night," he said to explain his tremor. "I want to get your thinking on how the Far East matter should be handled."

"I'd rather comment on what you have already been advised to do."

Roosevelt smiled. "You always were a good poker player, Frank."

"A better chess player, Mr. President, if you remember."

"George Marshall and his people are convinced we must persuade Uncle Joe to declare war against Japan as soon as possible. Otherwise we'll suffer frightful casualties."

McGlynn forced himself not to frown. "And what will we have to give Stalin?"

"We will probably be willing to preserve the status quo in Outer Mongolia and let him take the territory seized by Japan after the war in 1904 to 5 such as the southern part of Sakhalin Island."

McGlynn pondered. "What about the Kuriles?"

"If necessary. That shouldn't bother anybody."

"Except the Japanese."

Roosevelt laughed. "Frank, you are delightful."

"I wasn't trying to be delightful, Mr. President. I was thinking of the postwar period. Unless your neighbor, Mr. Morgenthau, plans to plow under the Japanese along with the Germans."

"Frank, I can always count on you to bring up problems of the future before we have solved those of the present."

"It sounds like a very steep price."

"I'm sure I can get Winnie to go along on that."

"At what price?"

"Don't worry, Frank. I'm a pretty good horse trader."

"Unfortunately, Mr. President, you will not be trading horses."

Roosevelt was troubled. "Apparently you disagree with some of this."

"Mr. President," McGlynn said soberly, "I disagree with all of it." He waited for Roosevelt to argue but he said nothing. "Let me explain. In the first place your Joint Chiefs of Staff apparently have not taken seriously the report Captain Zacharias submitted last week."

"George assured me that it was another flight of Zach's imagination. Granted he is a brilliant man, but to believe that the Kwantung Army exists mainly on paper simply does not make sense."

"Mr. President, our findings indicate clearly that the bulk of the Kwantung Army has long since been transferred to Leyte."

Roosevelt shook his head. "Even MacArthur agrees with George."

"He's talking through his hat," said McGlynn.

This tickled Roosevelt. "He usually does. But this time he happens to agree with the Joint Chiefs."

McGlynn knew it was useless to pursue the matter and urged the President to consider the postwar at Yalta. "I strongly recommend that you make no concessions to Stalin. For God's sake, don't bribe him with Japanese territory to do what he is dying to do. He wants to move into Manchuria. He will be running no risk at all and lose few troops."

"What makes you say such a thing?"

"Japan is already defeated, Mr. President. It is just a question of time. Inviting Stalin into the Far East is like opening the chicken coop to the wolf." Roosevelt made some notations and McGlynn wondered whether it was just a doodle. "May I make one final suggestion, Mr. President?"

"Please do, Frank."

"When you get to Yalta, please confine any deals to Europe. I am convinced the fate of the world lies in the East. We must bring Japan back into the orbit of democracy. A weak Japan in that unsettled continent will tip the balance of power to the communists."

Roosevelt leaned over the table extending his right hand. "Thanks, Frank. I can always count on you for a cold shower."

As they shook hands McGlynn thought, "My God, I'm holding the hand of a dying man who imagines he is immortal." He walked thoughtfully out of the White House wishing he had urged cessation of the terror bombing that was devastating every major city in Japan. Roosevelt was the most humane man holding supreme power, and yet he had approved a campaign that would probably kill a million civilians whose only crime was being Japanese. He thought of his own daughter and grandchildren. Would they get through? Would his beloved Will, who he had just learned was a prisoner in Japan, survive? And Mark, who was preparing to storm another Japanese-held island, would he make it? And would he himself ever again see any of his good Japanese friends?

2.

One Toda was on Iwo Jima; Yuji, whose thousand-stitch belt had been prepared by Emi and Sumiko, had just been promoted to lieutenant, junior grade. He had bemoaned being sent to an isolated, out-of-the-way island instead of to a battle area. But once he saw its formidable defenses and the grim faces of those who had preceded him, he realized this would be the site of bitter battle.

The most distinctive feature of Iwo Jima was an extinct volcano at the narrow end. While only 548 feet high, it seemed far more imposing, jutting straight up from the sea. This was Mount Suribachi, a cone-shaped bowl. The island, nearly five miles long and two and a half miles at its widest point, was only a third the area of Manhattan. Its volcano was inactive but the entire island was alive with jets of steam and boiling sulfur pits. From afar Iwo Jima looked like a Rock of Gibraltar but Yuji had the queasy feeling that it might disappear at any minute. A road would vanish overnight. The fat northern part of the island was a plateau 350 feet high with inaccessible rocky shores, but at the narrow end near Suribachi there were broad stretches of beach and Yuji was informed that this was where the Americans would undoubtedly assault. What looked like black sand was really volcanic ash and cinders so light that a heavy man would sink above his knees.

The few civilians had long since been evacuated and the troops—14,000 army and 7,000 navy—were distributed into five sectors with 1,860 men assigned to Mount Suribachi. They would fight independently, delaying the enemy as long as possible. Numerous caves had been dug into the slopes facing the beaches, their entrances angled as protection against blasts and flamethrowers.

The rest of the island was studded with thick-walled pillboxes. The northern section was a rabbit warren of natural and man-made caves; they were labyrinths of chambers and connecting tunnels, vented at the top to allow steam and sulfur fumes to escape. The first main line of defense was a network of dug-in positions for artillery, light machine guns, and buried tanks. This ran along the southern edge of the plateau between two modest airfields. A special defense line lay just beyond the second airfield. Lieutenant Toda was stationed there as commander of the rocket unit. Naval aviation ordnance men had cleverly converted 60- and 250-kilogram bombs into rockets that were launched electrically along slanted wooden ramps. A "rocket" would fly up the 45-degree incline, arch some 2,000 meters in the general direction of enemy positions, and explode on contact. Yuji's battery was zeroed in on the beach area where the Americans were expected to land.

Mark's transport was more than halfway to its destination on February 16. He was fascinated by the relief maps and photographs of their target. What would it be like in reality? And what would he be doing? Before, he had known in general what his duties were. But even his superiors had little idea what was expected of the language officers. Of course, they were to interview prisoners and translate captured documents. But how would they dig out prisoners? Obviously the place was riddled with caves and tunnels.

Throughout the ship men were repacking their gear, fussing over weapons which could save their lives. Many wrote letters to folks and sweethearts. A few read; many just smoked and talked. Most of the men in Mark's division, the 3rd, were veterans and their main complaint was that they had been relegated to floating reserve. Just their luck, they bitched. And the brass was sending in the 5th Division which had never fired a shot in anger.

"It's not fair," said one youngster who had only joined the unit for the last days on Guam.

"Since when did you ever expect anything to be fair in the Marines, sonny?" said a hard-boiled veteran of three landings who himself was barely twenty. Mark had mixed feelings. He wanted to go in but he had an uneasy feeling that this time his number might be up.

On his flagship, Vice Admiral Turner was holding a press conference for about seventy correspondents. Maggie was not present since she had been told it was no place for a lady; she was sulking back in Guam over such discrimination.

3.

"Howlin' Mad" Smith spent the evening in his cabin on his command ship, *Eldorado*, reading the Bible. He knew his Marines could suffer severe casualties in a few hours upon hitting the beach. Several weeks earlier he had written the Commandant of the Marine Corps that he felt storming a fortress like Iwo was not worth the fearful casualties the men would suffer and "would to God that something might happen to cancel the operation altogether."

At 3:30 A.M. the Marines had steak for breakfast. It was February 19, D-Day. By the time Mark moved out on deck it was light. Through the mist he saw, looking lonely and abandoned, the island of Iwo. It reminded him of a half-submerged whale. Mount Suribachi began disappearing ominously in a low cloud.

Lieutenant Yuji Toda was up before dawn. He wrote in his diary. "Today we received an honorable gift of tobacco from the Emperor." He climbed to the top of the hill behind Airfield 2 to behold a mighty armada of ships. It was a thrilling sight. He hurried back to his position and readied his men for the attack. They were to descend into their bomb shelter as soon as the enemy bombardment began. When it ended they were to rush to their positions and propel rockets onto the beach area.

The transports and landing craft jockeyed toward their disembarkation positions. Thank God, thought Mark, the water was fairly calm. And there were no jagged reefs to clamber over. He heard the roar of big guns and glanced at his watch. It was exactly 6:40 A.M. Seven battleships, four heavy and four light cruisers were throwing their shells into the island. Five minutes later nine gunboats showered the plateau with rockets while other gunboats pumped mortar rounds into the slopes of the dead volcano.

At 7:20 came a growing rumble of planes. Then correspondent Sherrod could see the B-24's from Saipan. They circled slowly for their bombing runs, and the bombs walking down the island reminded him of twinkling Christmas lights. At 8:03 by Mark's watch the bombardment let up to allow a horde of carrier planes to approach. There were well over a hundred, he guessed, and they began savaging the island like angry hornets.

The Japanese huddled in pillboxes, blockhouses, and caves. Toda jammed fingers into his ears to endure the concussion. When it subsided he went to the top of his pillbox to see the vast flotilla of enemy ships waddle into place. How systematic and beautiful. Such massed equipment awed him, not the men they carried. He knew all about the American fighting man from propaganda lectures and pamphlets. They were brave only for publicity. Yet they had no desire for the glory of their ancestors or posterity or for the glory of their family name. He knew all about the daredevils who tried to ride over Niagara Falls in barrels. Yet, being individuals, they feared death and didn't think much about what would happen afterward. They were coming into battle with no spiritual incentive and relied only on materiel superiority. All that massive equipment!

By this time the LST's, loaded with the first five assault waves, were moving into final position. Through the smoke Mark could get glimpses of the first wave of amtracs skittering like water bugs then climbing onto the beach where they crawled clumsily forward. A few yards inland they encountered a steep terrace. They churned vigorously, throwing up clouds of the black volcanic ash. A few breasted the terrace but the others were helpless and had to disgorge their occupants, who struggled up the terrace in slow motion. As the first waves heaved themselves over the collapsing terrace of volcanic ash the improvised rockets from Yuji's unit started landing in their midst.

Mark and his companions of the 21st Marines were crowding around the speakers of their transport to listen over the frequencies used by the combat teams and air observers ashore. The younger ones were grumbling that they had to stay afloat while the other two divisions had all the fun. Those like Mark who had fought at Saipan knew the hell that faced them; they were not reluctant to get into action, neither were they eager. As the fog of battle descended over the beaches and reports became vague or conflicting, the men argued. Were casualties higher or lower than expected and would their regiment go in? All through the long day little groups passed along the latest scuttlebutt. Mark tried to read but kept looking toward shore. Others were cleaning their spotless rifles and carbines or trying in vain to catch an hour of sleep.

By dusk thirty thousand Marines were ashore. Almost six hundred had been killed or were dying of wounds while the survivors crowded into a small, narrow beachhead 4,400 yards wide. Unable to reach the first day's objective, they were digging into the yielding ash before the expected counterattack.

Yuji was inspecting his area. A few shells had landed nearby but his launching devices were intact and only a few men were wounded. But by morning the attack became so fierce that it seemed it must change the very shape of the island. At last the shelling let up in the afternoon and each man was issued a bottle of one hundred vitamin pills, twenty Kinshi brand cigarettes, a pair of leggings, and hardtack. Four more were wounded and three were dead. More grievous was destruction of three rocket launchers.

Mark felt like a substitute sitting on the bench in a fiercely fought football game. An old gunnery sergeant muttered, "We're going in," as soon as he heard the first high casualty figures; but by nightfall it was generally agreed that there was little chance now that they would be used. Then at midnight a rumor with authority passed throughout the ship. They *were* going in.

In the morning Mark started over the side with the fifth wave of the 21st Marines. The surf was high and rough and he was soaked by the time he thudded into a small landing craft. It was even more arduous and dangerous transferring to a larger boat, for their own craft was bouncing six feet high and smashing against the larger boat. The seas became so rough they had to remove their gear and hand it up by rope. Mark crawled up first; he poised until the small boat rose on the crest of a wave, then he grasped the ladder of the bigger boat as high as possible and scrambled up before being caught in the collision of the two boats.

"All we need now for supreme misery," said Mark, "is rain." As if in retort, big drops began slowly to fall. Soon they came faster and faster, deluging everyone. Someone shouted, "Why the hell aren't we landing?"

Mark could see the sands of the beach erupting. Heavy mortar fire. For hours the landing craft circled, moved in, moved back, and circled. Late in the afternoon they finally landed on the beach. Mark sank deeply in the volcanic ash. He slogged forward. Fortunately the Japanese bombardment had ceased. But he knew it could break out at any minute. He tried to hurry but sank deeper. He took off his gear, stowed it in a shell hole, keeping only his canteen and carbine. He'd come back after dark to salvage the rest. He scrambled over the high terrace just as he heard a *ker-whi-i-up!* A mortar shell exploded just behind him. He leaped into a shell hole so new it was smoking.

It was a miserable night. The rain poured down interminably as he huddled in cold volcanic ash. Once the rain let up momentarily and he could hear land crabs crawling in the brush and dunes, making the noise of slithering Japs. Every few minutes illumination flares hung in the sky, lighting up the area theatrically with eerie shadows. Mortar shells exploded periodically and missiles flew overhead. Again Yuji Toda's deadly rockets descended, their explosions often followed by shrieks of agony.

The steady cold rain continued all through the next day, D plus three. The Japanese bombardment slackened and Mark finally found the 21st C.P., a former enemy antiaircraft position. There was nothing yet for Mark to do and during a lull in the bombardment he retrieved his gear.

It was another miserable day for Yuji. His position was a mudhole and had been invaded by a horde of lice. "They really have visited us," he wrote in his diary. "The ground is a sea of mud. It is so dark you can't see a thing and the temperature has dropped sharply. It is extremely cold."

In the morning the Marines at the southern end of the island resumed their determined assault on Mount Suribachi. They seized pillbox after pillbox as well as underground galleries, bellying into smaller caves, knives in teeth, to wipe out the enemy in close combat. At about 10:15 an advance party reached the rim of the crater, which was littered with Japanese bodies. After someone found a long piece of pipe, an American flag, 54 by 28 inches, was secured to one end.

From the beach below the small flag was spotted a few minutes later. It was barely visible but men in foxholes cheered and punched each other. Mark's regiment heard the news from the beachmaster who announced over the loudspeaker used to direct unloading operations:

"Mount Suribachi is ours! The American flag has been raised there by the 5th Marine Division. Good work, men."

Mark felt a thrill run up his spine.

The beachmaster continued. "We have only 2,630 yards to go to secure the island."

"Only," said someone near Mark. "We made twenty-five yards yesterday. That means we only have one hundred and five days to go."

4.

Maggie was at the press room on Guam when an unconfirmed report came from the *Eldorado* that a U.S. flag had been sighted on top of Suribachi. Several men jeered. "The teleprinter operator aboard the *Eldorado*," said one, "must be making a bad joke." The others agreed not to relay such an improbable rumor back to their offices in the States. Then the teletype again began to click:

> IT HAS BEEN OFFICIALLY CONFIRMED THAT THE FLAG OF THE UNITED STATES NOW FLIES FROM MOUNT SURIBACHI HIGHEST POINT OF THIS VOLCANIC ISLAND.

The newsmen cheered. Feeling it was all right for a war correspondent to show emotion, Maggie pressed her eyes with her knuckles. She saw the Associated Press man wipe his glasses and continue to type.

As Maggie was hastily banging out her copy, the correspondents' aide, a redheaded navy lieutenant, beckoned her to his office. "Where do you want to go?"

"Iwo Jima!" she exclaimed without hesitation, then added forlornly, knowing there was little chance they would let a woman go to the front, "As far forward as I can."

The lieutenant told her to wait; he came back half an hour later. "You now have orders to the *Samaritan*." This was a naval hospital ship. "It's going to Iwo Jima. Your jeep will be waiting tomorrow morning at five on the road below your tent. It will take you to the ship and she'll be sailing at once." She was dazed. "Maggie, are you listening?"

She hugged him, hurriedly finished her Suribachi dispatch and raced to her tent to prepare for the biggest adventure of her life. When she was ready she looked at her watch. She had sixteen hours to wait.

Time crawled. She got little sleep for fear that she would not wake up in time. At last she boarded the big ship, which was as long as a city block. Painted a gleaming white with red crosses four decks high on both sides, it seemed immune to attack. But during the evening of the second day a single Japanese plane made two passes at the illuminated ship, missing the first time and being scared off the second time by a destroyer. It was an exciting half hour for Maggie and, though nothing really happened, she felt at last she was in the war.

At Iwo Jima a rifleman of the 21st Marines found a Japanese notebook in a cave and brought it back to the regimental C.P. where it was turned over to Mark. He saw that it was the basic plan of defense of the island.

Mark informed the Regimental G2 of the find and was ordered to deliver the notebook to Division at once. Despite heavy mortar fire, Mark set out across a wild, barren stretch of rocky ridges gouged into crags and gullies. It looked like hell with the fire out. The thrill of dread raised hackles on the back of his neck. It took Mark an hour to negotiate several hundred yards safely, and it was with relief that he turned over the valuable notebook to the major in charge of division language officers. Mark hadn't seen a single enemy but he had been scared stiff. On Saipan he had faced almost constant peril, yet there he had not felt this overpowering terror. He wondered why and realized it was because here he felt all alone—on his own. At Saipan he was surrounded by comrades of 1/6 who would never let him down. Here he didn't really belong to a unit. At last he understood what replacements to 1/6 must have felt until they were accepted.

The first thing Maggie saw at dawn was the great rock of Mount Suribachi. The waters were crowded with all kinds of ships. It was a stirring sight. Then she was startled by a roar from three battleships. A cloud of flame hid the *Missouri*—she seemed to stagger; then came explosions on the island with earth shooting up in a dozen places like magical plants. Through the smoke Maggie saw a tiny plane—it was American—diving on Suribachi, perhaps to aid some Marines trapped near the top. To her horror the plane pulled up, but too late, and crashed into the volcano. One wing of the plane seemed to fly away almost in slow motion.

As the *Samaritan* anchored, tiny boats propelled by treads churning at the side approached. She hurried to the flying bridge to get a better look. On the first boat she saw three stretchers lashed across the bow. She climbed cautiously down a long ladder to the after well deck and watched as the ashen-faced wounded were hoisted aboard. She couldn't help examining each new face, praying it would not be Mark or Mac-Dowell. The sight of the inert forms brought a new realization. She loved both of these men. She had ridiculed Mac at first, then came grudging admiration, now love. It was her first such experience, for all her previous affection had been toward the men of her family. And Mac was so unlike either Mark or her father. Comparison with them was ridiculous. And yet she felt something for him that she felt for no one else. Tears came to her eyes and she brushed them off, annoyed at her weakness. She took out her notebook and went to work.

Tirelessly she roamed through the great ship, recording the sights, the smells, the sounds of quiet misery. She found it hard to remain calm and several times had to fight to keep from bawling like a baby. Her attempts to regard the broken men she saw and talked to as objects of cool observation were hopeless. Yet she knew she must keep some distance or her words would be maudlin.

One man wore a tag marked URGENT and a corpsman was transfusing whole blood into his veins. A large M had been written on his forehead; he had been injected with morphine. He moved his blood-foamed lips, trying to say something. The stretcher bearers lowered him to the deck and Maggie kneeled beside him.

"Soldier," she stammered, desperately thinking what she should say, "how are you?" A gun from a nearby ship roared and she couldn't hear his answer.

Then there was silence and he said distinctly, "I'm a fucking Marine."

She saw that he was trying to smile. "Okay, you fucking Marine," she said, using the forbidden word out loud for the first time in her life, "I asked you how you felt."

His face came to life and he smiled. "I—feel—lucky." He saw the look of utter amazement on her face. "Because—I'm here, sister. Off the fucking beach."

She said nothing, hoping he would not waste his strength but he wanted to talk. "I got the—best buddies too." He stopped, grimacing in pain, but continued. "I always knew they liked me." He seemed to gather strength. "But I never knew—the guys cared enough to get me —the hell out of there." The guns roared again. "Those guys carried me three miles. Makes a guy feel lucky."

She heard the words of one man who was receiving the last rites from a chaplain. His foggy eyes caught sight of Maggie. "Who the hell you spying for?"

"The folks back home, Marine."

"The folks back home—huh. Well—fuck the folks back home.' His eyes closed and the doctor told the stretcher bearers to take him away. She was haunted by his bitter final words. Had he received—like Mark —a Dear John letter? Or was he taking a last blast at a despotic father or overbearing mother? She had taken down his name and serial number but this was one family she would not write about. She wandered from ward to ward, making notes, listening over and over to similar stories, yet each man's was indelibly impressed in her memory. The raw emotions of men dying or close to death were unforgettable. And she knew that she would never again be the same or look at life in the same way. What she had read of battle seemed pallid. By the end of the day she was exhausted mentally and physically. As she lay in her bunk she could hear the occasional sound of battle from the deadly little island. And she prayed that her two men were still alive.

The following day the first two prisoners were brought back to the 21st regimental command post and turned over to Mark for interrogation. The first was a lieutenant who refused to say a word. The second, an enlisted man, was still in a state of shock. Mark gave him water and a cigarette, then asked if he came from Tokyo. No, he was from the snow country in the north. Mark told of a trip he had made up there when he was eleven. After they talked of the beauties of northern Honshu, the man said he knew General Kuribayashi, overall commander on Iwo Jima. "He treats us kindly."

After patient questioning the man admitted he was a code clerk for the general. Realizing his importance, Mark got permission to escort him to Division. This time Mark was so concerned in getting the man safely across the danger area that he had no fear. The language officer at Division was equally impressed by the prisoner. Pearl Harbor could dig the code out of him. He ordered Mark to take him farther back to Corps. He did and several hours later the code clerk was on a plane bound for Guam.

At sunset of Maggie's second day off Iwo Jima the *Samaritan* weighed anchor and set sail for Saipan with its load of wounded. Every corridor was a ward and there was such a long line of those who needed surgery that many wounded were packed in ice to prevent infection. Maggie forced herself to watch the surgeons at work. One amputation was performed every thirty minutes day and night and a fifty-gallon oil drum would be filled with arms and legs every three hours.

Upon arrival at Saipan three days later, it was painful for Maggie to watch the transference to waiting ambulances. First off was a man who breathed and took nourishment through tubes, then came a bad burn case, the only survivor of his tank crew; they had been roasted by a new type of land mine and during the previous night the man had raved to Maggie over and over a description of the missile, which had been made from a 200-pound bomb.

After the stretcher cases came the walking wounded. The Officer of the Deck took Maggie aside and said the last to go would be five stretcher cases. These were Japanese and it was forbidden to mention them in her story. "Thank God the wounded Marines didn't know we had them aboard—there would have been a riot!"

More than twenty walking wounded Marines were milling around near the head of the gangway when the Japanese wounded were carried out and laid in a row. The young Officer of the Deck paled as a big Marine with bloodstained jacket, arm in sling, strode toward the nearest Japanese. Maggie saw the O.D. go for his .45 as the Marine reached toward his Ka-Bar. But instead the Marine drew out a torn package of cigarettes. Without saying a word he squatted down, stuck a cigarette in the cracked lips of the Japanese and lit it. Noticing the enemy soldier couldn't move his hands, the Marine removed the cigarette so he could blow out smoke. He let the enemy take several more long drags. At the gangway someone shouted to get a move on and the big Marine stood up, stuck the pack of cigarettes in his pocket, and sauntered off without looking back. Maggie scribbled in her notebook. It was going to make a nice end to her story but she wondered if the editor would delete it out of misplaced patriotism.

That afternoon she flew from Saipan to Guam and slept around the clock in her tent. She wakened obsessed with the need to return to Iwo Jima, this time to the island itself. She complained to a fellow correspondent in the next tent, Barbara Finch of Reuters, that the press office only wanted her to write the woman's side of the war. "There must be other things a woman can write about."

Finch, a veteran correspondent of the South China area, agreed that there certainly were. "I'm flying up to Iwo Jima tonight on an evacuation plane. Why don't you ask for the same flight tomorrow?"

Maggie arrived at the press office breathless, prepared to do battle even if she ruffled feathers. To her surprise, the officer in charge put up

452

no argument and wrote out orders for her. Never had she been more excited as, late the following night, she strode up to the pilot of a bulky-looking C-47 who was anxiously watching the loading of medical supplies.

Maggie held out her orders, smiled brilliantly, and started to follow a group of nurses and corpsmen. But the pilot held her arm. "Sorry, but we're loaded to the gills already."

"But I was told . . ."

"I don't care what you were told. You'll have to write your story from here. Didn't you know we can get no fuel at Iwo and have to take on enough here for the round trip?" She started to protest and he held up a hand. "Please listen. The makers of this plane advised the navy not to take off with more than thirteen gross tons. We are about to take off with fifteen and a half tons."

"Plus 105 pounds," she said, lying a little.

He could not resist the pleading look. "Oh, hell, climb aboard. But don't write your congressman if we never get off the ground."

She scrambled into the plane before he could change his mind. The two motors roared as the clumsy-looking craft rumbled down the runway. As they neared the end of the runway it hoisted itself like a protesting dowager.

Soon after dawn Mount Suribachi hove into sight. Maggie could see blossoms of explosions near the airfield and the pilot had to circle, wasting valuable fuel. After an interminable delay—probably ten minutes—the enemy artillery barrage ended and the plane swooped down. The pilot hastily taxied behind a hill of sand. "Don't walk!" he yelled. "Run!"

She leaped to the ground and found herself sinking into the volcanic ash. She tried to run but it was like a slow-motion nightmare. Just ahead she could make out two tents dug deep into the strange terrain with a sunken road between. It must be sheltering the wounded Marines who hadn't been able to get on the hospital ships.

"Welcome to the unmentionable island," a cultured voice remarked. "You bring us luck."

She saw a distinguished, gray-haired man clad in filthy dungarees. He wore no insignia and was shaving from an upturned helmet half filled with water. He bowed gallantly to the nurses, informing them he was a lieutenant commander from New York, a surgeon. "My field hospital," he said, indicating the two tents.

"You call that a hospital?" said Maggie.

He stroked his face with a razor. "In the sight of God and the authorities it is." He continued shaving. Things were not so bad, he said, and they'd kept working last night by starshells. She peered into one tent, an operating room. There was no furniture, no operating tables. Stretchers rested across upended crates. She took pictures as the bleary-eyed doctors and corpsmen worked. She noticed a patient staring at her. One of his legs, covered with blood, was at an impossible angle. "You don't have a gun," he said.

"Correspondents don't carry guns, Marine."

He serenely informed her that the doctor was going to try to save his leg. "And he's gonna tell me right away if he can. I mean, I won't have to find out. I'm lucky." He was more worried about Maggie than himself. "Take my Ka-Bar," he said, holding out his trench knife.

She hesitated but he insisted. "I feel better about you now."

She took his picture, wrote down his name, serial number, and home town, then went out to the road. Someone shouted, "Hold it, girl!" She came to a halt just as a tank heading for the front brushed past her. Across the road she saw an exasperated Marine captain and guessed it was he who had shouted.

"What the hell's a woman doing here?" he asked.

"I'm Maggie McGlynn, a correspondent. I've come to Iwo to talk to Marines and photograph them."

He dropped his bantering tone. "Where do you want to go, girl?"

"As far forward as you'll let me."

"Okay." He took her arm and guided her to a weapons carrier. "But don't try to talk me any farther out than the front."

What was farther than the front? she wondered as the captain whipped the vehicle back toward Mount Suribachi. After ten minutes he advised her to get some shots of the volcano. She could see smoke and hear distant firing but there wasn't a soul in sight. Then he headed toward the other end of the island. After fifteen minutes the weapons carrier skewed to a halt. "End of the line, girl. No farther."

She got out. She could hear an occasional rifle shot but still could see no one. It was like being abandoned on the moon.

"Where are the Japanese?"

He pointed down. "Under there someplace, I guess. There are a thousand caves here. Our people are farther up, trying to dig them out." She climbed alone up a steep sand ridge. Halfway to the top she stopped for breath. She turned to see the captain lounging nonchalantly against his vehicle, smoking a cigarette. She continued to the summit.

454

Ahead and below was an appalling sight, like a huge waffle. The entire area was honeycombed with ridges. No wonder she had heard no sounds of battle and seen nothing. Several hundred yards away were three tanks. She took a picture as one bounced. Seconds later she heard a roar. Apparently it had fired. She looked around and finally saw three Marines digging in the earth. Soon they disappeared and there was solitude again. Obviously the whole place was alive with hidden humanity. She heard wasps buzzing and waved an arm to brush them away. She took more pictures, brushed more wasps away, then slid down the ridge as if she were slaloming down Mount Washington.

Proud of herself, she smiled at the captain who was still lounging. He flipped away his cigarette and glared at her. "That was the god-damnedest thing I ever saw anybody do in my life. Do you realize all the artillery and half the snipers on both sides of this fucking war had ten full minutes to make up their minds about you?"

She tried to explain.

"Didn't anyone pound into your little head that you *do not stand up* on a skyline, let alone stand up for ten fucking minutes? And do you realize that if you'd gotten yourself shot I'd have had to spend the rest of the war and ten years after that filling out fucking papers?" He stared at her for an explanation.

As they started back she finally worked herself up to say she was sorry. He stopped the carrier. "Girl, are you trying to tell me that you didn't really know any better? You mean you're out here and you don't know what you should have done?"

"You mean I should have made the pictures lying down?"

"Good idea, girl. Do you think you can remember that the next time?"

"I won't forget, Captain. But it was lonesome up there. The only life up there was a couple of wasps."

"Wasps!" he almost exploded. "There are no wasps on this damned island." He held out his right hand like a gun and made popping noises.

"They weren't really wasps?" she said in a small voice.

He said nothing until he handed her out of the vehicle at the hospital area. "Girl," he said, "I just want you to know that you sure made my day." As he was about to drive off she asked if he knew Lieutenant McGlynn. "What outfit is he in?"

"The 21st Marines, 3rd Division."

He shook his head, saying he was in the 4th Division.

"Then you probably wouldn't know a navy lieutenant, Ed MacDowell?"

"Sure. Saw him yesterday." He waved. "Thanks for the entertaining afternoon," he said and roared off spraying volcanic ash.

Maggie learned the C-47 wouldn't be loaded for an hour and she went into the recovery tent. The air was stale with cigarette smoke, sweat, dirt, and blood. Men lay in cots, patiently waiting to be evacuated. It was strangely calm. One youngster was moaning but the rest were either silent or quietly talking to doctors and corpsmen. A man who obviously hadn't shaved since his arrival on the island beckoned her. "Hey, lady, how about taking my picture?" His mother would get a kick out of seeing it in the Asbury Park paper. He asked a corpsman to prop him up and Maggie saw he had only one arm. "Good thing you noticed," he said and pulled a jacket over the stump. She took his name and address and promised to send copies to the paper and his mother.

She glanced at the card of the next patient, a PFC from the 21st Marines. She went up to ask him if he knew her brother but realized he was asleep. She read his ticket: "Multiple fragment wounds left foot, left leg, elbow and buttocks and lumbar area. 40,000 units of penicillin."

"His regiment really got clobbered," said a corpsman. "We got more than a hundred casualties from the 21st yesterday."

Maggie paled and hurriedly went down the aisle, checking tickets. In the last bed she found MacDowell. He looked up in amazement. "What the devil are you doing here?"

His shirt was covered with dried blood; his right arm was in a sling. She felt choked and could only say, "Mac." She knelt beside him and took his left hand. "What happened?"

"Nothing much. Just a busted arm."

She tenderly touched the bloodstained shirt.

"Not mine. The guy next to me." He started to scold her. She had no right to be there. It was no place for a lady. She just nodded and kept holding his hand. Suddenly realizing she was not being professional, she took out her pad and copied down the information on his ticket. Finally she got up her courage to ask about Mark.

"Saw him yesterday, I think, or maybe the day before, at the regimental C.P. He was chatting with a Jap and you'd have thought they were old school buddies."

An officer stuck his head in the doorway and yelled, "Okay, folks, let's start moving them out." Half an hour later the C-47 with Maggie and Mac aboard rumbled down the rough runway. It slowly heaved itself in the air just as a blood-red sun was setting, and circled around the dead volcano before heading home.

In his battered dugout, Yuji Toda was writing his parents of the heroic defense and how the lines of the defenses were being overrun and of his own frustration now that there were no more rockets to fire.

> "I shall acquit myself well. Be assured that the name of Toda will not be disgraced. Please, all of you take good care of yourselves and do your utmost until victory comes. Goodbye. I end this letter expecting to die."

As soon as Toda finished his letter he reported to the commander of the 2nd Mixed Brigade, an impetuous officer who had fought against the Russians in Manchuria. Yuji volunteered to make himself a human bomb and throw himself under the treads of an enemy tank. The commander congratulated him on his spirit and sent him to a nearby tankers' cave. After midnight Toda left the cave with a box of dynamite strapped to his back. He found bodies near the gully through which the three tanks Maggie had seen earlier in the day had erupted. Noting the tank treads he figured this would be the logical route for the enemy tank advance at dawn. He worked his way into the stinking pile of corpses, smearing his uniform and face with blood and draping himself with entrails. Who will be using my guts tomorrow? he wondered.

At last the first light of day came. No tanks emerged. The sun rose and he waited patiently, perspiring, for the welcome clank of treads. The smell was nauseating. Great bluebottle flies hovered overhead like vultures. Why couldn't the end come quickly and cleanly? Scenes from his childhood and treacherous thoughts interrupted his wish for death. Was this what he had been educated and trained for? His mother had sacrificed everything to put him through college. He and his classmates had been taught that the war would keep Japan from degenerating to a third-class nation, and that it was beautiful and glorious to die for the Emperor. He wished the professors who had talked of this beauty could lie among the stinking guts of the dead.

Finally the long day ended and Yuji crept back to his cave in the darkness. He tried to clean himself but the nauseating stench of death clung tenaciously. He slept fitfully, yet something drew him irresistibly back to the battlefield before dawn. He spent another endless day in the tank tracks among the decaying corpses, agonizing over the meaning of life as a Japanese. At first he prayed an American tank would come but late in the afternoon the thought of an iron monster rolling over him was horrifying. Just before dusk he heard an ominous clank and two tanks suddenly appeared in the gulch. The noise increased. He gritted his teeth and closed his eyes. He could feel a tread brushing his right sleeve. It was the end. The insanity of his action seemed so obvious, but it was too late. He could smell the fumes of a tank and to his amazement the sound faded away and soon there was quiet. It was dark enough to return to the cave but he could not move for several minutes. Finally he was able to crawl to safety, robbed of most of his illusions. He was sure of but one thing: never again would he venture out as a human bomb.

The 3rd Marine Division was still making only small gains against stubborn Japanese resistance. Much of Mark's work had been interrogating prisoners. There was no standard set of questions; each language officer had to follow his intuition. Mark first inveigled a prisoner to tell what kind of unit he came from, then his rank and experience. If he was in artillery, Mark concentrated on the types of armament; if infantry, he would check to see if the current information about the Table of Organization was correct, and determine how many men presently composed a platoon and company.

But today he had a more interesting assignment. He was following the advance in a jeep equipped with a P.A. system. Bullets bounced against the jeep. Mark leaped to the lee side of the vehicle, crouched down, microphone in hand. "You have been defeated," he called out in Japanese. "The island is practically conquered. Save yourselves and go back and help build a new Japan. We Marines respect you for your courage in battle. You have fought with honor. Come over and get a lot of tobacco! We have plenty of good food. You will not be harmed."

A small figure crept out of a cave, hands raised. Mark bowed to the Japanese who was so embarrassed he did not bow in return.

"Now, take off all your clothes," said Mark. The man hesitated. "We must see that you have no weapons, no grenades." The man reluctantly stripped. "Now get into the jeep," invited Mark. The man sheepishly climbed aboard. Another Japanese started out of the same cave. He came forth tentatively.

"Join your comrade," urged Mark quietly. "He is safe. You can be safe too."

The man came forward half a step at a time. Mark didn't raise his voice, kept talking in a conversational manner. "Now, please take off your clothes."

The man started to do so, then suddenly made a break back toward the cave. A rifleman behind Mark fired and the Japanese tumbled over, dead.

The advance continued in the morning. Mark got permission to take a prisoner named Isobe up front with him. Isobe, a corpsman, feared that many of his wounded comrades would die if they weren't treated promptly. He had drawn a detailed sketch of the cave, its many passageways and its five different entrances. Mark wore a Brooklyn Dodgers baseball cap won at poker, figuring it would make him look less dangerous. Following Isobe to the main entrance, he pointed a flashlight into the entrance. He stepped over a body blocking the way and came to a steep staircase carved in the soft stone. He cautiously descended about twenty-five steps, then Isobe grabbed his arm. He had noticed the recent remains of a meal in a niche. "Careful," he whispered. "Live Japanese down there!" He motioned Mark to return up the stairs, then called into the darkness below, "Anyone down there?"

"Four of us."

Mark returned and pointed his flashlight toward the foot of the stairs. A Japanese stood defiantly, grenade in hand.

"I myself have surrendered," said Isobe. "I was given food, fresh water, and cigarettes. I have been very well treated. Why don't you also surrender?"

The man with the grenade hesitated.

"No use holding out, comrade," said Isobe. "There are Marines at every entrance. Unless you all give up immediately, they are going to dynamite all the entrances and seal you in like rats. Go back to the others and talk it over. We'll give you exactly half an hour."

The time elapsed.

"Tell them we're going to start dynamiting," said Mark.

Isobe shouted this information.

"Please give us another half hour!" called back the leader.

Just as the second half hour ended a captain appeared, holding a grenade. Isobe said calmly, "Please put down the grenade, Captain."

The captain compromised. He put it in a pocket above his heart to indicate he would commit suicide if there was any trick. Mark slowly edged forward, extending a package of cigarettes. The officer suspiciously took the package. Mark held out a canteen of water. The officer smelled the water, tasted it, and gave Mark the grenade.

"I have sixteen men below," he said. "They are still debating whether to surrender or not."

Mark realized something should be done to convince the ones below. He climbed out of the cave and brought back his portable P.A. system. "I will give you sixteen men exactly one minute to make up your minds," he said in a commanding voice. In half that time seven men scuttled up from below. Each carried a grenade and each, after a bribe of water and cigarettes, gave up his missile.

It was almost dark and Mark knew he must act. "This is my last warning," he announced to those still remaining below. "In one minute we will dynamite each of the five entrances."

They herded the prisoners to the surface. Mark checked his watch. With five seconds to go another prisoner scampered through the opening. Mark waved his arm and there were five explosions.

Isobe shook his head sorrowfully. "The stupidity of men who don't know when it's time to give themselves up."

The Marines advanced all along the front but every yard had to be contested. It was a brutal conflict and by March 25 Kuribayashi estimated he had only fifteen hundred men left, all pressed into a square mile of the most formidable ground on the island. In the northeast end more than a hundred were holed up in a group of caves. For five days they had resisted all attempts by Marines to clean them out. Mark asked for permission to go down and talk to them.

The captain in command of the riflemen couldn't believe what he heard. "Do you mean it, McGlynn?"

"Yes, sir." He knew that Marines would die if they had to assault the caves.

"Well, McGlynn, if you're serious, you're a damned fool."

"Is my request refused, sir?"

The captain surveyed Mark. "McGlynn, you don't win medals for suicide. But I'm not going to stop you. It's your ass, go ahead."

Mark scuttled down the rocks into the valley, holding his carbine above his head. Today he wore a helmet. At the bottom he laid down his piece and slowly walked toward the caves. It was only common sense, he thought, to approach unarmed. He hoped they would consider him under a flag of truce. He stopped at the edge of one camouflaged cave entrance. "I am giving you an opportunity to surrender!" he called out. "Do not be afraid." He peered into the blackness of the cave and took another step. "I have left my weapons behind. I come to you under a white flag of truce." He edged forward. "The attack is starting soon and we are going through. Everyone in this cave is doomed."

He decided to take a chance and go farther. After several steps he could vaguely see men huddled on the cave floor. His eyes became accustomed to the semidarkness and he made out ragged men. They clutched grenades. A few held rifles loosely.

"You have fought honorably and well!" said Mark. "But most of your comrades are dead. Your army and navy forces can't help you. Lay down your arms and come out." He could hear a few of the men mumbling to each other. "I promise you will not be harmed. Your wounds will be treated. We will give you food and water." He waited.

Finally one man said, "Will you give us time? We must talk this over."

"I will return in half an hour," he said and slowly backed away. Once outside, Mark resolutely headed for a second cave. Here he found at least fifty men. He spoke as he had before. "I'll give you time to talk it over," he said. "Then I'll return."

The Marines leaning over the brow of the ridge stared in wonder as Mark moved to a third cave, a fourth, and a fifth. In this cave Mark found four men. They stood shoulder to shoulder almost at attention. As he started telling them how bravely they had fought, one, holding a rifle, stepped forward and said hurriedly, "I must consult my comrades in the other caves." He brushed past Mark whose first impulse was to stop him, but he forced himself to remain motionless. The wait was uncomfortable. The other three Japanese kept staring at him. He said nothing. At last the fourth man, a lieutenant, was back. "Japanese soldiers want more time," he said.

"Ten minutes," said Mark. "I'll give you only ten minutes."

The lieutenant left again. Mark checked his watch. It was 3:13 P.M. He hooked his thumbs in his belt. Ten minutes passed. From outside the lieutenant called, and when Mark backed out of the cave, motioned him to follow.

Mark pointed to the other caves. "What about them?" The Japanese shook his head. "Aren't there soldiers in those caves?"

"They won't come out."

"What about the three men in your cave?"

"They will not come."

Mark was angry. "What in the devil is going on?"

"Come," said the lieutenant and started down toward the other caves.

They passed two caves without anyone emerging, but at the third a single man came limping out. Just when Mark thought he had failed, three men peered out of the first cave, blinking in the sun. He decided to go back into this cave and see if he could entice them all out. If so, the men in the other caves might follow their example. He slowly walked in. The occupants eyed him suspiciously. "I have done the honorable thing," he said. "I have given you the chance to surrender. I give you that chance again. If you do not surrender, the Marines will come down here with flamethrowers and explosives. I warn you that we know the location of every cave and every entrance. I am going to give that information to our troops." He paused. "Will you reconsider?"

No one spoke.

"Surrender or die," said Mark and walked out. "Get moving," he told the five men who had surrendered, motioning them toward the Marine lines. They started off with Mark in the rear. He wondered if the men in the caves would shoot. Would they try to stop their comrades from disgracing themselves and mow him down in the process?

At every step he expected a volley. As he approached the ridge a Marine from above shouted, "They've got grenades!"

The prisoners turned and Mark saw each was holding a grenade against his stomach. "Don't be afraid," he said with assumed calmness. "Keep moving. No one will harm you." The Japanese started up the rise. Mark called to the Marines above. "Move back. Let them come ahead."

At the top Mark told the prisoners to sit down. He passed the first man a cup of water. The man gulped it and placed his grenade on the ground. The other four did the same.

Mark drew a sketch of the caves and the paths leading to the entrances. He showed the Marine captain the safest way to get to each entrance. As they started laying charges, Mark felt he could finally relax. He was drained. He sank on the ground wondering why he was so tired.

"Don't you know you were in those caves more than two hours?" the captain said.

Mark was amazed. It seemed more like half an hour. Explosions erupted from the valley. All five caves were now sealed off. The acrid smell of cordite filled the air. Noticing the look on Mark's face the captain said, "McGlynn, you don't win wars by being nice to the enemy."

Mark grimaced. "Are you sure?"

Twenty-four hours later, D plus twenty-three, a small group of Marine officers and men stood at attention around an incinerated Japanese bunker. A colonel read a proclamation announcing that Iwo Jima was at last secured. Three privates stopped at the bunker, attached a flag to an eighty-foot pole and, as a bugler sounded Colors, raised it.

"Howlin' Mad" Smith turned to his aide. "This was the toughest yet."

Mark was interviewing one of the prisoners he had brought in the day before. The man said that he had been assured by an officer that the left arm bone of a dead Japanese soldier had been removed to make a letter opener for that damned Jew, Roosevelt. While Mark was laughing at this ridiculous story, a call came from Division to report at once. Fifteen minutes later he was told that he was to pack his gear and board a plane leaving for Saipan. He was being reassigned at once to his old division, the 2nd, which was preparing to leave for Okinawa. He said farewell to his friends and then visited the compound where more than 125 prisoners of war were being held. He chatted with those he knew and hoped they could come to terms with themselves in Hawaii.

His plane took off at sunset as Kuribayashi was radioing Tokyo that the battle was approaching its end. Toda was in a deep cave with a dozen comrades. Supplied with water and food, they were determined to remain underground as long as possible.

In Maggie's tent on Guam she and MacDowell were celebrating his assignment that day as a press liaison officer for the Okinawa campaign. His arm was still in a sling, which he could dispense with in a week. He had found some champagne at the officers' club and she now toasted his transference to a job for which he was well qualified and which would give him a longer life expectancy.

"I've had my fill of it," he admitted. "My luck couldn't have held out much longer."

She kissed him. "I now propose a toast to the only man who lost his virginity wearing a sling."

He flushed. "You shouldn't say things like that."

"All right, make it to the only MacDowell who ever did it. My dear Mac, I swear you're blushing like a schoolgirl."

He put an arm around her. "I never thought I'd be so lucky. With my looks."

"Are you going to make an honest woman out of me?"

"I wish you wouldn't talk like that." He was obviously offended.

Her manner was flip but she wanted to tell him how much last night had meant to her. Their union, done in joy and wonder, was inexpressible. Words were poor things and all she could do was smile fondly and say, "Yes, dear."

MacDowell guessed what she was trying to say and kissed her gently.

5.

At Saipan 1/6 was in the last stages of preparations for the next operation. The island itself had been transformed into a little America. It teemed with jeeps, staff cars, and other vehicles. There were half a dozen outdoor theaters where movies were shown and celebrities such as Betty Hutton and Gertrude Lawrence performed. Gertie shocked many of the young Marines with her racy talk. "My God, sir," one seventeen-year-old complained to Billy J., "it's like hearing your mother use four-letter words!"

The food was still not good but there was some beer, and the hospital near Magicienne Bay was clean, well staffed, and as efficient as any stateside installation. It was in full use, not only from wounded but from a mosquito-borne misery called breakbone fever. Few Marines managed to escape it.

Perhaps the greatest physical change was the completed Isley Field. A few miles away an even larger strip had been completed on Tinian and the roar of the monstrous B-29's, which could fly to Tokyo and back, had become as commonplace as the sound of traffic on Fifth Avenue. Many of the Marines were so fascinated by the huge planes that they spent much time at Isley. One of these was Mad Dog McCarthy, now a major, who had returned to duty after a leave in the States that had already become legendary. His most noteworthy prank was the placing of a live shark in the swimming pool of a Marine general living near San Diego. The irrepressible Mad Dog talked an Air Force drinking buddy into taking him on a ride to Tokyo. When the plane returned the following morning, a pale-faced Mad Dog descended and threw up. So sobered by what he had witnessed over Tokyo, McCarthy avoided the officers' club for two days.

It was to this dubious paradise that Mark returned in mid-March. After checking in at 2nd Division headquarters where he was informed he would accompany his old regiment to Okinawa as language officer, he went to the 1/6 area with mixed feelings. It would be wonderful seeing Tullio and his friends, but what would he do when he encountered Colonel Sullivan? He could not forget the scene at Guam when the man he admired most had been so damned cold-blooded.

He approached a new outdoor gym. Lightweights were hitting heavy bags, middleweights were skipping rope, a heavyweight was shadow-boxing. In the corner of a ring, watching two middleweights sparring, were Tullio and Jumping Joe Callahan.

"You old son of a bitch!" shouted Tullio. He embraced Mark. "Welcome home!"

The chaplain held out a hand. "God bless you, Mark. We sure are glad you're back with us."

Others gathered around, pounding Mark on the back and asking if Iwo was as bad as Tarawa. Did he have to go into the caves to flush out the Japs? Had he run into any of their old buddies from the 4th Division? After some time Tullio managed to get Mark aside. "I hear you had a rough time at Guam. It was lucky Billy J. was on hand."

"Lucky? Hell, he shafted me."

"Billy J.? The Old Man loves you. He saved your ass." Tullio had learned through the noncom network that it was Sullivan who had worked on his old friend, Colonel Quinn.

Mark was astounded.

"He placed his head on the block so you could hold onto your commission. He defended you like a mother. You should have leveled with him."

It was with mixed chagrin and relief that Mark made his way up the hill to Billy J.'s tent.

"You took your time in coming to see me." Sullivan extended his hand. "Jack Colley called me the minute you landed from Iwo."

"Good to see you, Colonel." Mark gripped the proffered hand. "Tullio told me how you saved my future in the Corps."

Billy J. pulled a canvas chair out for Mark and gazed silently at him for a moment. "What did you learn from that skirmish, Mark?"

"Well, as The Beast would put it, you can bet your sweet ass I'll never lie again." He grinned.

"Colonel Colley tells me you did a fantastic job on Iwo. Another decoration for sure."

"Everyone on Iwo deserved one, sir. I understand I'm being assigned to 2/6 for Okinawa. How come? Why not 1/6?"

It was Billy J.'s turn to feel self-conscious. "Well, maybe your replacement, Tony, makes better cocoa than you can," he said defensively, then sighed. "O.K., I'll admit it. I don't want to have to watch you do the damn fool things you did on Iwo. Maybe I'm getting old. Besides, Tullio would wet his britches if he saw you going into caves unarmed talking to Japs. You go with 2/6."

Hiroko Kato had fully recovered from her wound and was a nurse at the civilian camp clinic. She worked in the daytime with the sick orphan children, who adored her. At night her principal occupation was emptying chamber pots.

Several days after Mark's arrival a Japanese civilian rushed up to her at the clinic. "Hiroko-chan! A worker thinks he located your brother's tank at the south end of Garapan in the brush."

After work she sought out a new friend, an American M.P. named Chuck. He borrowed a jeep and the two set out for Garapan. She was overwhelmed. The last time she had seen the town it was completely in ruins. Now it was splendid beyond recognition, an American city. But dear old Garapan was gone.

After a futile hour's search they were finally directed by a G.I. to an isolated place at the foot of Mount Tapotchau. There in the deep brush were seven rusted tanks piled up haphazardly by bulldozers. Hiroko clambered over the first toppled-over tank, then a second and third. The fourth lay on its side. In white letters was written, "Swallow." Her brother's tank! She thought her heart would burst. She tried to open the turret. It wouldn't budge. Chuck banged at it with a hammer. But it had rusted tight. The noise drew a crowd of Marines.

"What's going on?" one asked.

"This Japanese girl wants to look inside," said Chuck. "Give us a hand."

"What in hell for?"

"Her brother is in it."

The Marines conferred and returned in a few minutes with hammers and chisels. They climbed up and began working on the turret. After half an hour it creaked open. Hiroko almost fainted from the horrible stench but held her breath and looked inside. There were two bodies. Their faces were unrecognizable, decayed almost to the bones. But on the ragged coveralls of the first man she read, "Kato." Her dear brother. Next to him was a pistol.

Her tears fell on her brother's body. Then she prayed silently and slowly descended from the tank. Chuck and the Marines climbed up, looked inside, and came down somberly. One Marine gently took her arm and tried to lead her away. She resisted. Chuck took the other arm and she finally said, "Brother, farewell." She climbed into the jeep and as it sped off her tears flowed freely and were scattered by the wind.

Mark spent as much time as possible with his old comrades and the day they were to embark he accompanied Billy J. on a final inspection of his fresh-faced replacements, all of them looking, thought Mark, as if they had just left their mothers' apron strings.

A few hours later they all began boarding transports anchored in Tanapag Harbor. Mark accompanied the 2nd Battalion whose commander was an old friend of Billy J.'s. Ahead lay a twelve-hundred-mile trip across the Philippine Sea toward the last major island on the road to Japan, Okinawa. As Mark watched Mount Tapotchau disappear into the sea he wondered how many of the eager youngsters at inspection would survive.

CHAPTER TWENTY-SEVEN

1.

Kyushu, Japan. January 1945.

Camp 13 was located two miles from Omuta, a drab city blessed with little grass and few trees. The camp was enclosed by a black wooden fence ten feet high and topped by a double row of barbed wire. Three strands of electrically charged wire had been placed on the inside wall five feet from the ground. The wooden buildings of the camp were also painted an ugly black. A middle-aged interpreter told Will and Bliss who, as officers, were to share a single room, that they were to place their shoes on the bench before entering. It was, he explained, a Japanese custom, as if they were entering a home. The room, he said proudly as if he were a hotel bellhop, was an eight-tatami section and very spacious for two men. Unfortunately, their men would live in one of the enlisted barracks where eight men had to share a ten-tatami space.

Bliss had never before seen tatami mats and was fascinated by the slight swaying motion as he cautiously walked forward. The interpreter, who asked to be called Inouye-san, was pleased by his delight, explaining that the objects folded on the side were *futon,* the Japanese mattress. "Not as thick as yours, though," he added apologetically. They would please fold each *futon* in the morning and store it away neatly.

In the morning their fellow officers praised the facilities. There was a clean latrine on each end of the barracks with a urinal and three seat-type stools. And they could take a bath daily in a separate building in a large tank fitted with four coal-fired water heaters.

They were led to a large mess hall shared by the enlisted men where they were served rice and a mixture of fish. Their canteens were filled with tea. As they sat at tables wolfing down the food a smartly dressed officer strode in and began speaking in clipped tones. "You are here to mine coal," he said in Japanese. "You will be taught sufficient Japanese to understand the instructions of your overseer. You will be expected to work diligently, and if you do not, you shall be shot." He slapped his thigh with his riding crop and marched out.

Inouye-san, bent with anxiety, waited until he was gone then informed them it was Lieutenant Wakasugi, the commander of the camp. Those enlisted men fit for outside work would work in the mine. "You will work diligently. Please do. Otherwise you will be punished. And you could even be shot, I fear. Now, enlisted personnel, line up outside for permanent barracks assignment."

While the men were going through the slow process of being distributed to their proper rooms, Inouye took the officers aside. According to the Geneva Convention they would not have to work but would be given various assignments such as being in charge of the mess hall or the supply room. Others would oversee work in the mines. "Are there any volunteers for this?" No one responded and Inouye was patently embarrassed. Bliss exchanged looks with Will and both raised their hands. A few others volunteered.

After dinner the officers in Will's barracks were told they could march over to the bathhouse. As they started to climb into the large steaming bath an American corporal who had come to the camp six months earlier shouted, "Wash yourselves first!" It was a Japanese custom, he explained, and a good one. Then they could luxuriate in the water. The water was hot but Will was accustomed to Japanese baths and lowered himself gradually. "Watch each other," cautioned the corporal. "Some of you may pass out in your weakened condition." He then advised them to stay in the bath until thoroughly warmed. After dressing they should put on their overcoats, dash like hell to their barracks, and get into bed while still warm. "You may want to fill a canteen with hot water and take it to bed."

They wakened to a cold, dreary day and were informed they would march to the mines after breakfast. Since they would have the noon meal at the mines, each man was issued a *bento*, a wooden box filled with rice. Their leader, a sergeant named Peterson, warned that the work was rough, particularly when mining in one of the shafts that had been dug under Ariake Bay. Here ice-cold water would come up in places to their knees. With *bento* under arm they were marched, without overcoats, through the gates. After less than a mile they came to a line of empty coal cars. Ahead was a large steel and corrugated tin structure. They were led around a large building and halted at a torii, two upright wooden posts connected at the top by two horizontal crosspieces. "It's the gateway to a Shinto shrine," Will explained to Bliss.

Someone behind said, "Are we expected to pray to those concrete goalposts?"

Peterson called for silence as a Japanese civilian approached. After the two conversed several minutes, Peterson said, "This man is an official of the Mitsui Coal Mining Company. He welcomes you as employees of Mitsui. He hopes you enjoy your stay here. He also says you will stop here every morning and on his command remove your hats and come to attention while there is a ritual." The official bellowed a command and most of the men doffed hats and came to attention. Others had to be nudged. The official checked the ranks and was satisfied.

Peterson marched the group into a large hall with a raised platform on one end faced by rows of benches. Once the prisoners found seats, a large civilian entered. He surveyed the group with a frown, as if unhappy at the sight of such a sorry lot. "You are here," he said in good English, "to learn about coal mining. If you do your work as told, you will be treated well. But only those who work will be paid." Noncoms would receive fifteen sen a day; privates ten sen. "The Mitsui Coal Mining Company, however, is generous to hard workers. You will also be paid a bonus based upon production of from three to fifty sen a day. Those who are industrious can purchase goods in your camp. Those who are not will be unable to buy a thing. That is the Japanese way."

Apprehensively they followed two narrow sets of tracks into a large structure. It must be the mine itself, thought Will. He'd seen mines in the movies and imagined they would be taken down an elevator to the shafts. But Peterson explained that this was a slope mine; they would ride down a steep incline. A string of small cars emerged from the darkness and the prisoners began boarding. Each vehicle also carried an overseer. The one in Will's was short, surly, built like a gorilla. The little train started slowly but picked up speed. It rumbled past occasional incandescent lights that lit up rough rock walls. In a few minutes Will's nostrils were assailed by a damp, musty smell. It had become so warm that he had to shed his jacket.

The jerky, swaying motion of the car kept banging him against one side and by the time the train slowed down his right shoulder was sore. The overseer motioned that they were to disembark and he himself agilely hopped off before it came to a stop. He turned and waved impatiently for his group to follow. Will and three enlisted men followed to a small room where they were issued tools, miners' caps and lamps. After demonstrating how to light the battery-powered lamps, their overseer started down one of the shafts. It became so narrow that Will wondered how a coal car could get through. In the distance he heard a rumbling. The overseer hustled them to a wide part of the shaft just as a car filled with coal emerged from the darkness. It was pushed by three prisoners, eyes peering out of blackened faces.

"You the new Yanks?" asked a scrawny youth.

"Yes."

"Lots of luck, fellows."

All three were thinner than Will and he watched with fascination as they passed. Their bodies were covered with coal dust. Streaks of sweat running down their backs exposed white skin. After a quarter of a mile, the overseer pointed to the ceiling. The men had no idea what he wanted. Three of the prisoners began shoveling loose rock to one side. This infuriated the overseer who slapped the nearest man on the side of the head and shouted, "Wrong side!"

Will translated and offered to pass on instructions. The overseer nodded. He said that they had to build a crib to support the ceiling, but first must clear away the rocks. "And hurry before the ceiling caves in."

Once Will explained this, the prisoners hastily cleared away the rocks and began shoring up the sagging ceiling. It was so hot they all stripped to their underwear. By lunchtime the main supports of the crib were in place and danger of a cave-in was over. While they ate lunch the overseer told Will about his family. He had five children and it was difficult making enough money to support them all. It was good working for Mitsui, he added, because they paid bonuses. After lunch Will ceased doing any manual work himself and merely supervised. This annoyed the overseer, nor was he mollified when Will explained that he was an officer. "Would you like it if the Americans made a Japanese officer work?"

"No Japanese officers surrender," said the overseer but did not press the issue.

By the end of their ten-hour shift the crib was completed. Clutching their clothes they wearily followed the overseer up the shaft. At the surface they turned in their caps, lamps, and tools and followed the overseer into the company bathhouse. Large tanks of warm water five feet deep awaited them. Will sank into the water, soaking for a few minutes until he realized the water was getting colder and dirtier. He dried himself with a towel the size of a washcloth which he had to keep wringing out, then got dressed.

During dinner Will and Bliss learned that prisoners could send one card home every three months. It could be no longer than thirty-five words. No mention could be made of the camp or its location, nor of working conditions or treatment. They were not to write of illnesses or diseases, the conduct of the war, needs for food or clothing, or financial affairs. They also learned that officers' base pay was forty yen a month; non-coms got ten yen; and privates four yen. Afterward they tried to find Popov but he was not in his barracks. Someone thought he had been taken to the hospital.

Will spent the next week in the mines supervising the digging of coal. The conditions were miserable and the men could hardly walk by the end of a day. At first working in the warm mines was a pleasure but soon the prisoners developed sores and the sweat would burn their skin, their eyes, and even their genitals. They would scratch in vain—everything itched and burned. The only solace was Inouye who did his utmost to make their lives more bearable and often spoke up for them, even though it placed his job in jeopardy.

2.

Will learned from a medic that Popov had been put into a special ward.

"It's just a little shack with no heat, nothing," said the medic. "We call it the Death House."

Bliss suggested they try to get Popov back into the hospital.

"If he lasts till morning, it will be a miracle," said the medic.

"If he does, will you see that he gets back to the hospital?" asked Will.

"No one ever gets out of the Death House alive."

Will and Bliss exchanged looks. "We'll give you fifty yen," said Will.

"And ten yen for every day he stays in the hospital," said Bliss.

The medic hesitated. Bliss handed over four cigarettes. The medic squirreled them in a pocket. "What if he's dead in the morning?"

"We'll still give you the fifty yen."

Just before midnight Will crept out of his barracks carrying two blankets, a canteen filled with hot water, and a box containing rice and fish. It was bitter cold. A bright winter moon lit up the compound, which fortunately was deserted. He cautiously opened the door of the shack. In the shaft of moonlight he could see three or four inert forms.

"Popov," he whispered.

There was no answer. He went to the first figure, touched the face. It was stone cold. Dead. He went to the next figure and heard a rasping breath. "Popov!" He shook the man. He groaned. It was a stranger. "Popov!"

From the other side of the room came a faint voice. "Here."

Will was at his side. "We're going to get you out of here."

"You forgot me," he complained. His teeth chattered. Will put the warm canteen on his chest and covered him with the two blankets.

"They wouldn't let us come to the hospital." He fed Popov several spoonfuls of rice flavored with fish particles. "A medic is taking you back to the hospital in the morning."

"Th-thanks, buddy. I was afraid you forgot all about me."

"Hang on till morning. You can do it." He took off his jacket and after considerable struggling put it on Popov. Then he wrapped him again in the blankets.

After breakfast, Inouye-san noticed that Will was shivering. When Bliss revealed he had given away his jacket, the interpreter was so moved he divested himself of his own warm woolen sweater. He insisted that Will take it. "My overcoat is warm enough," he said as he put on that shabby, threadbare item.

The latest news from the British prisoners was passed around that evening. Their allies had managed to smuggle in a radio, piece by piece. MacArthur had taken Manila and soon would occupy all of the Philippines. More important, the B-29 air raids on Japan were being accelerated. Stories of the Superfortresses swept through the camp and for the first time Will saw smiling faces. Optimists were predicting that the war would be over in a month. But the pessimists feared that the guards would take vengeance for the raids on them and they were right. The slightest infraction of rules brought beatings with sledgehammer handles, iron pipes, or two by fours. Guards would sometimes make a man support himself for an hour in a horizontal position on toes and hands. Arms were twisted, hair pulled. Men were kicked in the shins, abdomen, and backbone. If a prisoner fainted he would be resuscitated so the beating could continue.

The two meanest guards were "Billy the Kid" and "the One-Armed Bandit." The latter's left arm was cut off at the elbow. Making up in venom for his small size, he delighted in dealing out punishment with a short club. He had picked up some English and, after beating a prisoner, would rail at him. "You Americans no damn good. You always cause big trouble. You lie to us. You steal from us. You call us monkey people behind backs. When I punish you, you no show proper respect and humiliation. You no willing to do better. You no repent. You no cooper-ate. Why not? We place you in confinement. We slap and beat you. We stare at you. Do you appreciate? Hell, no. You come out of confinement, head up in air with sneer and say, 'Fuck 'em!' You all no damn good!"

But for sheer brutality he could not compare with Billy the Kid. He was big for a Japanese, weighing 175 pounds. Will had seen him cold-bloodedly bayonet a man caught reading the *Nippon Times*. Another time he had found a young sailor smoking while sitting on his bunk. He had shouted, *"Yoku nai!"* (No good!), slammed him in the face with his fist, then stamped on the man's bare feet with hobnailed boots. He ordered two guards to continue the beating until the man was dead. The body was carried to the hospital. He had died of heart failure, asserted Billy the Kid, and forced a Japanese doctor to enter this on the camp record.

Lieutenant Wakasugi condoned this reign of terror and had repeat-edly refused requests by senior American officers to improve the miser-able conditions in the mine and stop the thievery by his own staff of Red Cross supplies. Conditions had grown so bad by the end of February that the American camp commander, Lieutenant Colonel Diggs, called a meeting of officers and proposed they make a special plea to Wakasugi.

Bliss was opposed. "That bastard is as cold as a fish. He hates our guts and he would only make things tougher."

While they were arguing Inouye-san rushed in so excited he could hardly talk. "Lieutenant Wakasugi is leaving! We have a new camp commander! He wants to see Colonel Diggs."

Will suggested he interpret rather than Inouye-san and the latter brought them to the administration building. They passed down an immaculately clean hallway and stopped before the camp command-ant's office. Diggs knocked and there was a polite invitation in Japa-nese to enter. Behind the desk was a man of fifty with graying temples. "Sit down, gentlemen," he said in good English. "I am Major Watanabe." He offered them cigarettes.

"I have been told that morale is low here. There is little or no recre-ation. No laughing, no singing. We must do something about that." He picked up a sheaf of papers. "I have discovered there is considerable material on hand for recreation. There is baseball equipment, enough for several games simultaneously. I see we also have several footballs and, oh, yes, musical instruments—three guitars, two mandolins, two accordions, and a violin. Why don't you people organize your own shows? You can rig up a stage in the mess hall or some other building."

474

He turned a page. "And here we have several chess and checker sets, playing cards."

Will and Diggs were astounded.

"I have my own project." He walked to the window. "Over there! I think we could transform that field into a garden where you can stroll and converse. Do you have any questions?"

"The food, Major?" said Diggs.

"That will be my first priority. I think we can improve things. And perhaps even do something about conditions in the mine. But you must understand that we are operating under wartime restrictions. Our own civilians have very little to eat and the bombings are causing grave hardships. All I can promise is that we will do our best. But don't expect miracles." As he led them to the door he asked if Will were related to the historian, McGlynn.

"He is my father, sir."

"I have read his books and enjoyed them. Unusual for a Westerner to have such insight." He suggested that Will cease supervising in the mine. "I believe you would be more useful staying in the camp so you can help Colonel Diggs look after your men's needs."

Will agreed and asked permission to visit a friend in the hospital. The major nodded. "I also have a few suggestions for better conduct on the part of your men. I understand they are unruly. Even worse than the Australians. I hope you will follow the example of the British and Dutch prisoners."

That afternoon Bliss and Will visited Popov in the 187-bed hospital which had been built for the prisoners by Baron Mutsu, a Dartmouth graduate. They found Popov propped up in a clean bunk, humming as he counted a sheaf of papers. He was smiling broadly as they approached. "One hundred ninety-eight IOUs," he said. "Total of $43,145.65!" All owed from his dealings in Cabanatuan. "I'll have enough to go into business when I get home."

He was still very thin but in good spirits. He mentioned nothing of his rescue from the Death House until Bliss left to talk to another friend. Then Popov took out Will's IOU and tore it to bits. "Thanks, old buddy," he said. He made sure Bliss was still out of hearing. "You never looked down on me like the others did. And I know you won't laugh when I tell you something I never tole anyone else." He cleared his throat nervously. "When I was sixteen I married a girl, a real beaut! Mabel was only fourteen. We lived in a crummy mining town." His face contorted. "My old man annulled the marriage. The sonofabitch! So I run away from home. I become a boxer and learned how to beat the shit out of anyone."

On their way back to their barracks Will said, "What makes us survive? Only one in four or five have made it this far. A lot have survived because they have faith in God. Some like you because you have faith in humanity. I don't have faith in either."

"Maybe you made it because you're a stubborn bastard," said Bliss. "Perhaps because you come from a race of survivors."

"Look at the crumbs that made it. They stole food and water from buddies. The best, like Father Cummings, didn't have the chance the worst had."

"The amazing thing," said Bliss, "is how any one of us is alive. The damned army gave us only one instruction on being captured: give name, rank, and serial number. They didn't tell us the important things."

As they neared their barracks, they came upon Billy the Kid. "At least," said Will, "we don't have to worry about that sonofabitch anymore. The major will keep him on a leash." Both saluted Billy the Kid smartly.

He stared directly at Will. It was a look of dark hatred.

"I think," said Bliss, "that he's telling us he's still top honcho at Camp 13."

3.

Tokyo. February 1945.

It had been an unusually cold winter and the occupants of some homes had to suffer broken water pipes for months before they were repaired. The toilet pipes above Floss's apartment had burst and the family had to use umbrellas for weeks. When the water froze on the floor, Masao delighted in sliding over it. But to Floss the ice was perilous; she was almost four months pregnant.

As the bombings intensified, they became a way of life, almost a natural disaster that had to be suffered. On one food-buying trip into the country, Emi Toda stopped to admire the spectacle of the approaching Bees—the popular name for the Superfortresses. She watched as a flight loomed in the eastern sky. Trailing white streamers of exhaust, they sailed in perfect formation through the blue-gold sky, reminding her of schools of pearly fish riding through the seas of the universe. But such poetic meditation was shattered once the graceful-looking fish dropped their eggs.

She hurried back home, relieved to find that their neighborhood was still intact. "On almost every raid," she noted in her diary that evening, "it seems to me that the Americans bring over new kinds of bombs and shells that behave differently in sound effects from those used the last time. The unaccustomed noises intensify the terrors and thrills of each invasion. And then I pray not only for the family and our neighborhood but for all the people in Tokyo."

Throughout Japan the growing fear of bombings gave birth to new superstitions: if you ate rice balls containing scallions and red beans, you would never be hit by a bomb. Better yet, if you ate only scallions for breakfast, you were sure to be safe, but by late February there was an added fillip: you had to let someone else know about this trick—along the lines of the chain-letter principle—otherwise it wouldn't work. Another superstition was born after a couple who miraculously survived a close bomb hit found two dead goldfish nearby. They figured the goldfish had died for them. Word of their miracle spread and before long it was so difficult to find live goldfish that porcelain goldfish were manufactured in quantities and sold at exorbitant prices. Although Emi ridiculed such superstitions, she served Sumiko scallions for breakfast.

On the last Sunday of February, Sumiko woke to see the blackened streets and drab houses covered with a beautiful blanket of snow. It was deep for Tokyo and she quickly got dressed so she could make angels in the snow. For several hours she enjoyed the transformation of the city into a fairyland. Then came the shriek of the neighborhood alarms. The Bees were coming! Great planes roared overhead harmlessly but sporadically bombs did fall near Tadashi's apartment, and sections of the city were gutted.

Much of the city was paralyzed the next two days not only by the heavy fall of snow but by fires. Trains and streetcars were blocked; entire areas of the city were isolated. Since it was impossible for Sumiko to get to the laundry, she spent the days reading and helping her mother with the shopping and cooking.

Jun was on special assignment, touring the districts hardest hit so he could interview survivors. He tramped through the ruins of Asakusa where people who had lost their homes were digging in the smoldering

477

remnants for possessions. But young and old alike were working industriously. Jun admired them for keeping up their spirits.

"Bon Soir," where he'd had coffee last week, was a heap of ashes. Nearby, the famous "Picasso" coffeehouse was also in ruins. Ahead was a crowd of people queuing up in front of a movie theater. "How stouthearted the people are!" he jotted in his notebook. A few blocks away he came to another theater from which cheerful music emerged.

He took the train to Ueno station. He was shocked by the Kurumazaka and Okachimachi areas. Scorched earth. Then he came to a section that had survived the great Tokyo earthquake of 1923. Many old houses were still there. Lucky again.

He headed for the station to return to his own apartment. Ordinarily a stranger never talked to you on the train but a new type of camaraderie had sprung up in Tokyo. Nowadays people were much more considerate. In crowded cars they moved inside voluntarily without having to be pushed there by other passengers. And people thought nothing of sitting on the laps of strangers so more could be jammed into a car.

On a subway trip a few days later Jun listened to a teacher lecturing a small group of his students. "Churchill and Roosevelt formed what they called the Atlantic Charter and agreed to kill all Japanese. They actually stated they would kill all men and women. Students, shall we let them kill us?" The group gave a resounding, "No!"

Jun wanted to tell them that Roosevelt and Churchill never said any such thing but realized that after the recent bombings, he would probably be physically attacked.

The teacher was now saying, "And if the enemy reach Honshu they are going to remove the testicles of all the men so they won't have children. And the women are going to be raped. And all the children will be sent to isolated islands to work in the cane fields."

The bombing raids had drastically changed the lives and manners of the Japanese, yet their primary purpose—obliteration of all production facilities—had failed. The strategic bombing program, which had devastated Germany, had done little to slow production in Japan where two thirds of the industry was dispersed in homes and factories manned by thirty or fewer workers. Therefore General Curtis LeMay, head of B-29 operations in the Marianas, hit upon a radical scheme. He would send his Superfortresses in low at night, stripped of most armament, to increase the payload. Demolition bombs would not be dropped. Instead, the planes would scatter fire bombs onto the tinderbox buildings over a wide area. Two days later, without consulting Washington, he had field orders cut for a major strike of B-29's on Tokyo.

The crews protested when informed at a briefing the following morning, March 9, that they would hit the capital at low altitudes—from 5,000 to 8,000 feet. Moreover, all guns except tail cannons would be removed to lighten the load. To those who had to make the flight it sounded like suicide. The first B-29 rolled down the runway of North Field on Guam at 5:36 P.M. Less than forty minutes later Mark watched Superfortresses from Saipan and Tinian join the elephantine procession in the air. He had heard their destination was Tokyo, and as the 333 giant bombers thundered northward he prayed that Floss and her family and all the Todas would not come under their attack.

A new moon cast a dim light over Tokyo, but stars shone brightly. LeMay's pathfinders easily located their aiming points at midnight and prepared to mark out the heart of Tokyo with napalm-filled M-47 bombs. They would cover the three-by-four-mile downtown section, not long ago the liveliest entertainment area in the Orient. Now there was little traffic with most of the shops and theaters boarded up. Three quarters of a million low-income workers existed in a congested city-within-a-city that never slept. Thousands of home factories were in constant operation.

Tokyo's profusion of wooden buildings had made it the victim of massive fires from the time it was called Edo. These conflagrations became such an integral part of the city that they were given the poetic name "Flowers of Edo." Despite modern firefighting equipment there was no guard against wide disaster by fire.

4.

The siren howling around midnight on March 9 sounded to Floss no more urgent than a dozen other alerts. There had been no widespread damage as yet and there seemed little cause for alarm. Those on the street, however, were concerned by the strong north wind sweeping over the city. Almost as violent as a spring typhoon, it could spread fires rapidly.

The pathfinders had not yet been discovered in their low sweep toward the unwary city, and the first two bombers, crossing paths over the target, released their strings of bombs in perfect unison at 12:15 A.M.

Those watching from the ground were momentarily paralyzed by the awesome sight of the low-flying planes which blanketed them. Masao was fascinated. The thundering bombers reminded him of great dragons. Floss and Tadashi joined him, fearful of being hit any moment. Emi and Sumiko were also watching from their yard in Azabu as the planes roared by harmlessly. Then they heard a series of distant explosions.

One hundred feet above the ground the M-47 missiles had split apart, scattering two-foot-long napalm sticks which burst into flame on impact, spreading jellied fire. In minutes a blazing X was etched in downtown Tokyo. Ten more pathfinders roared in to drop their napalm on the X. They were followed by the main force, three wings in all, in orderly but random formation, to make a more difficult target. They came in at altitudes varying from 4,900 to 9,200 feet and searchlights poked about trying to pin the raiders. Puffs of antiaircraft fire detonated without effect. No fighter planes appeared.

The fires, whipped by a stiffening wind, spread rapidly as succeeding B-29's fanned out toward the residential areas to unload thousands of sticks of napalm. Flame fed upon flame, creating a fearsome firestorm as at Dresden. Huge balls of fire leaped from building to building with hurricane force, creating an incandescent tidal wave exceeding eighteen hundred degrees Fahrenheit.

The civilians, not allowed to leave the city under the Anti-Air-Raid Law, were terrified. Water was useless in combating the fires and soon the groups of citizen firefighters threw aside their buckets and attempted to smother the flames with clothing and quilts. Nothing worked. The only thought was escape.

When Jun Kato heard the alarm he stayed in his boardinghouse. He knew he would have to cover the story early in the morning and wanted to get as much rest as possible. But as the roar of planes increased he knew it was no usual raid. He didn't have a quilted hood for protection so slapped on his steel helmet, grabbed a bag of emergency supplies, and ran outside. His area overlooked the center of the blaze and Jun watched clusters of bombs flower over the buildings.

Great red flames scorched the black sky on all sides. Above the sound of flames came the earsplitting roars of B-29's. There were explosions. The earth shook. He felt heat, then heard the terrifying sound of wild wind.

From the dull red sky, pieces of flaming debris were floating down all around Jun. A blaze erupted on the roof of a nearby house and he rushed to help the owners. He slapped at the blaze with a "fire swatter," strips of rags dipped in water, attached to the end of a long pole. The next house exploded in flames like a gas-filled oven. Homeowners were now rushing for safety and he followed the crowd. To the right everything was ablaze. How could it have happened so quickly? He ran to the main road on the left where a fire engine stood helpless, its hoses slack, surrounded by flaming buildings. There was no water.

He found himself almost surrounded by flames. The only way to safety was a bridge across the Sumida River but it lay beyond a wall of fire. A group of people huddled in the street, staring at the flames as if hypnotized.

A girl shouted, "Mama, I'm on fire!"

Flames were licking her cotton *monpei*. As Jun reached out to smother the flames on her back a great gust of wind threw him to the ground. He struggled to his feet. Flames were climbing the legs of the girl, who was screaming in agony. Using his bag he beat at the flames, finally putting them out. Her mother, tears streaming down her cheeks, bent over the girl. She was dead.

Charred trees and telephone poles were scattered across the road like matchsticks. Firemen shouted to make for the bridge—or die. Jun grabbed the mother who was cradling her dead daughter. He tore her free and dragged her down the street just ahead of pursuing flames which already licked at the corpse of the girl. The mother jerked free and returned to her daughter. Jun's clothing was smoking. He darted off and began leaping over tree trunks that burned like logs in a mammoth fireplace. He was amazed at his own agility. Blinded by the intense light, he gasped for breath. At the end of his endurance, he stumbled. Then through the roiling smoke he made out a concrete bridge.

People were frantically pushing their way across the bridge to escape the roaring blaze which was pursuing them like a wild animal. He didn't think he could break through the crowd so rushed to the left. A strong wind, sucked into the flames, swept a stinging storm of pebbles into his face. Ahead, oil drums were rocketing through the roof of a factory and exploding into balls of fire a hundred feet in the air.

There was no safety here so he rushed back to the bridge. The railing was almost bent by the huge crowd. Everyone was carrying possessions; some dragged carts, some carried bicycles. Jun realized that people were coming from the other side also looking for safety. But it was too late for him to go back. He was sandwiched in the middle.

The sky was scorching red and the tremendous thermals of heat were buffeting the B-29's overhead, tossing some of them several thousand feet upward in the air.

Jun felt nailed to the railing of the bridge. He thought he was finished when gusts of wind blew sparks onto the terrified crowd. Buildings on both sides of the river were ablaze. Cinders fell on the shoulder of a woman ahead of him. He beat out the fire. Sparks dropped on his own clothing and he frantically extinguished them. A man near him was on fire but Jun was too busy to help. A boy, hair aflame, screamed. His father, also on fire, tried in vain to put out the fire. His mother was holding a baby who suddenly shrieked. Jun saw red in the baby's mouth and tried to reach out. The mother plucked out a burning ember and covered the baby with a jacket. The jacket caught fire.

The father threw his wife and son into the river, grabbed the baby and jumped in after. Jun's eyelashes were gone. His skull was scorched —somewhere he had lost his helmet—and he felt his hair. It was hot. He climbed upon the railing and jumped. The water was ice cold. It felt as if a dagger had been thrust under his nose. He struggled to the surface. He never had been a good swimmer and knew he could last only a few strokes. A raft came drifting by. He hung on desperately. A little man hauled him aboard. It was the one who had jumped with the baby. Somehow he had managed to drag his wife aboard. Jun wondered where anyone so small had found such strength. The man was scooping water and throwing it over his wife. She could only think of their little son who had disappeared.

The current quickened and they passed under another bridge crowded with screaming people. Someone jumped, hitting the side of the raft. It was a girl and Jun reached for her but she sank too quickly. Under the bridge people were covering their heads with a large burned sheet of galvanized steel. They were chanting a prayer to Buddha.

The fires on both sides of the river were even more terrible and Jun could hear a gnawing sound as a building disintegrated. The raft caught on some obstacle and Jun and the little man could not free it.

An old man in a boat rowed by.

"Please help," said the little man. "Take my wife and child."

The old man took the baby and told the couple to come along. As they got aboard Jun looked at them forlornly, too ashamed to ask for a ride.

The old man motioned him to join them. "Don't tip the boat!" he said.

The next bridge was the Kikkabashi. It was wooden and was burning from end to end, the flames reflecting on the water like a ring of fire. The man held his baby tight and hovered protectively over his wife.

"Get down!" the old man shouted to Jun.

He squeezed himself on the bottom of the boat and prayed to God. The little boat, spinning like a cockleshell, swirled under the burning bridge. Jun could hear a chorus of groans. He wondered where they came from. He looked up. They had passed safely under the burning bridge and people were struggling in the water. He extended a hand but couldn't reach anyone.

At last they came to a section where there were no burning buildings. The old man rowed to the shore and they all painfully crawled up a bank. The wife was weeping. Her son was lost and her baby was dead. Her husband tried to console her and put an arm around her. She shrieked in pain from burns. But she seized her dead baby, squatted down and refused to move.

"Nobu, Nobu, cheer up!" said the husband. "Come on. The Bees have gone."

She rocked the baby and would not say a word.

Jun sank onto the riverbank and passed out.

When he woke from a fitful sleep it was dawn. The little man and his wife were gone. He stood up, looked around. The center of Tokyo was flat waste except for stone statues, concrete pillars and walls, steel frames, and a scattering of telephone poles, their ends smoking like tapers. It's gone, he thought.

Heat radiating from the ground made the brisk day seem like summer. It was March 10. He remembered it was Army Day and wondered whether anyone would be celebrating. In the east a clot, the sun, was rising. It seemed to wobble in the heat waves. But the sky was ominously dark.

He walked toward a bridge clogged with bodies of those who had been trapped. The river seemed to be almost evaporated, it was so choked with corpses and household possessions. Men in uniforms were fetching bodies from the river and laying them on the bank like fish in the market.

The ruins of a factory were twisted and deformed like melted candy. There were bodies everywhere. Some were naked, black. A few were upright, crouched as if trying to run. Some clasped hands in prayer. Others were seated in contemplation. One man's head was the size of a grapefruit. Dead covered with straw were already piled high in a schoolyard. The stink of death permeated the air.

He passed a hospital with its emergency pool of water. It was filled, layer upon layer, with sprawling bodies. A man in tattered clothes staggered up to him. "I was in there," he said in toneless disbelief. "Everyone else is dead. It is a miracle. I didn't even get hurt." His eyes were staring blankly.

People were poking at the layers of bodies with long sticks, looking for relatives. Money was spilling out of an old woman's *obi* but no one touched it.

On all sides he saw corpses in agonized positions. Mothers were trying to shield charred babies. Husbands and wives were welded together by the thermal heat in final embrace. Sadder still was to watch survivors looking in vain for loved ones. He wept to see one man scrawling a public message to his wife on the sidewalk.

Jun made his way to the newspaper office, arriving late in the morning. The building was intact. In fact, there was little damage in the area. Ordered to cover the fire bombing, he and a cameraman headed for the Asakusa area in a company car. They were stopped at checkpoints by police but his press card got them through. He left the car and was allowed to pass under the ropes that police had placed to keep civilians from entering. As far as he could see there was total destruction. A dead city. The stink was overpowering. He was in a state of shock at the extent of the catastrophe. He couldn't recognize any part of an area he knew well. There was dead silence except for the clicks of the photographer. Yesterday war had been an abstraction. Now he knew what war was. In a daze, nauseated, he walked back to the car.

Sixteen square miles of Tokyo had been burned and city officials were estimating that 130,000 men, women, and children had died.

5.

Mark returned to Isley Field at dawn to see the B-29's return from Tokyo. There was a cheer from those waiting as the first group appeared in the distance. LeMay's chief of staff had brought back photographs of the conflagration which confirmed that Tokyo was an inferno. For an hour there was a round of congratulations at the extraordinary success and the minimal losses. Then the last waves began to land. A friend of

Mark's, a copilot, shook his head as he approached. His face was ashen. "My God!" was all he could say for a minute. "You could smell the stink of burned flesh," he said. "I think everybody aboard tossed his cookies."

Bombing in Europe had been at high altitude and antiseptic from the air. Here it had become a nauseating reality.

Professor McGlynn was dismayed at the final reports as well as the joyous reaction throughout Washington. That night LeMay sent 313 more bombers to spread napalm over Nagoya, the enemy's third largest city, and bring ghastly death to masses of civilians. There was no doubt, the new methods were a roaring success and universally applauded. McGlynn remembered how revolted these same celebrants had been at the indiscriminate murder of civilians in Spain and China. And how Roosevelt, at the beginning of war in Europe, had dispatched messages to all belligerents urging them to refrain from the barbarism of bombing civilians. He had reflected the humanitarian ethics of all Americans then, and even after Pearl Harbor liberals in particular applauded the decision by leaders of American air power to emphasize daylight precision bombing, aimed at destruction of selected military targets. But despite exaggerated claims by the Air Force it had become obvious that the efficacy of this program was dubious. And so it had been enlarged to include the destruction of anything that sustained the enemy's war effort, even if it meant mass murder of the populace itself.

McGlynn started a memorandum for his friend in the Oval office raising the question of the postwar problems that could arise from a continuation of a policy which had come about largely unspoken and unrecorded. "The alarming civilian casualties at Tokyo and Nagoya," he wrote, "will undoubtedly be followed by similar casualties throughout the major Japanese cities. Will this, in time, brand us as the supreme violators of human rights? Will our success lead to even greater successes that will bring eventual shame to the nation? Will it be necessary, Mr. President, to brutalize the entire Japanese population before their leaders bow to unconditional surrender? Must we be bound to the rigidness of unconditional surrender merely to satisfy a demeaning need for vengeance for Pearl Harbor even as we wave the banner of international democracy? Please forgive my forthrightness but I am nauseated at the thought of so many loved friends being consigned to infernos unimagined a few short years ago."

Two days after the great Tokyo raid, Jun was walking through Tokyo station to change trains. He almost swallowed his breath at the tragic sight of the crowd. Men and women were pale and scorched. Most of them were black with smoke, their eyes puffed red. Some people's eyebrows, like his own, were gone. Many wore *tabi* and some were barefooted.

Soon after getting off at Ueno Station he had to hold his breath again for the stench of smoke and death. The station was jammed with people burned out of their homes. As they waited for trains to take them to the country, they squatted on the floor eating rationed rice balls. Jun tried imagining a similar scene in Honolulu where he had grown up. He walked toward Asakusa. The homes he had seen a few days ago were ashes. As far as he could see there was scorched desolation. Terrible! Terrible! Beyond the wildest imagination. He wished the people of Washington could see this and then think of their own buildings and monuments and avenues in rubble.

Lines of victims were walking, as if seeing nothing, toward Honjo. Others were pouring in from the opposite direction apparently to dig out possessions from burned homes or to locate friends and relatives.

There was the wonderful eel place where he had enjoyed a delicious lunch last week. A pile of scorched rubbish. He walked on as if in a nightmare. Was this the Kannon-sama, the goddess of mercy? But the Nio Gate, beloved by generations, was no longer there. Not a single column had survived. The temple had been burned flat and in the center was a sign surrounded by people. They were praying and throwing good-luck coins at it. Jun sat exhausted on a large stone. But his mind was more tired than his body.

Beloved Asakusa, charming Asakusa. All gone! Kannon had survived the great Tokyo earthquake only to be burned down by the Americans. Corpses of those who had sought refuge here were piled high. There was the body of a little child, red and bloated to huge size. He felt a choking pain in his chest. He wanted to cry but no tears came.

He thought of China and the movies of the bombings there. They made so much noise with far smaller crowds. Here in contrast was the quietness of the Japanese. What bravery, composure, modesty and perseverance. A loud voice woke him from his reverie. An official was haranguing the crowd to clean up the mess. The people put down their burdens of cracked teacups and scorched *futon* and obediently went to work, helped by the smallest children. It was twilight and Jun marveled at the sight. He realized tears were flowing freely down his cheeks. He was overwhelmed with affection. I want to live and die with these people, he said to himself.

In Washington McGlynn was reading *Time*. It described the fire bombings as "a dream come true" which proved that "properly kindled, Japanese cities will burn like autumn leaves." He threw the magazine across the room, although he realized it spoke for almost all Americans. They had little sympathy for an enemy that had attacked Pearl Harbor without warning and perpetrated such atrocities as the Bataan Death March. Only the rare voice spoke out in the name of humanity for the hundreds of thousands of mutilated and cremated Japanese civilians.

He clipped out a letter from a clergyman in the New York *Times* and sent it to the President: "God has given us the weapons; let us use them."

"Here is a typical example of American opinion," he wrote Roosevelt. "The great majority of our citizens sincerely believe that what was criminal in Coventry, Rotterdam, Warsaw, and London has become heroic in Dresden, Nagoya, and Tokyo. You will be applauded for going along with the majority today. What will they say in a hundred years?"

CHAPTER TWENTY-EIGHT

1.

Ulithi. March 1945.

Several days before Mark left Saipan for Okinawa his sister was aboard a plane bound for the atoll of Ulithi where the main force for Operation Iceberg would assemble. With her were a number of correspondents and Lieutenant MacDowell as one of the naval press officers. Maggie was already excited at the thought of covering another campaign even though Mac had warned her that this time the navy was allowing no woman to go ashore. She was confident she would somehow make it.

During the two-hour flight Bob Sherrod, sitting just forward of Maggie, was not at all excited. He could only think, "Here I am going into another landing where a lot of fine young men will die and God knows when it all will end." He did not at all relish going to Okinawa for he had seen enough bloodshed on Iwo to last a lifetime. At the same time, Okinawa looked like the most important operation of all, the logical conclusion to the historic Central Pacific campaign. Okinawa was the last important bastion guarding the homeland. Sixty miles from north to south and a mere two miles wide in the middle, it would be an ideal staging area for the final campaign, the invasion of Japan, with its flat waist for airfields and two deepwater bays suitable for naval bases.

Looking down on Ulithi, Maggie said in amazement, "It's mainly reefs!" The great armada inside Ulithi lagoon seemed to be anchored in mid-ocean. It was a deceptive view. Ulithi, a series of flat little islands strung into a necklace-shaped atoll, was 400 miles southwest of Guam. Its vast anchorage of 112 square miles could hold nearly a thousand ships and had become the main assembly point of the U.S. Pacific Fleet. Even at this late date few knew its real importance, including the Japanese who still held the island of Yap 110 miles to the east.

After landing on the 3,300-foot airstrip which had been carved out of the island of Falalop to protect the massive collection of warships, the correspondents were ferried over to a smaller islet, Asor, the headquarters of the atoll commander. After getting assigned quarters, MacDow-

The man's lips twisted into a snarl and hate filled his eyes. "You free the Mushin and league with the Ronin! I should have killed you the moment I laid eyes on you!" He took two jerky, stiff-legged steps in Edwyr's direction. His hand went to the hilt of the sword he wore at his waist.

For a moment the two stood like statues, their gazes locked. Then Mitsuyama spoke, his voice cold and deadly. "There may be no victory for my army, Seeker. But there will be a personal one for me. And all the Mushin and Ronin in the world can't stop me from seizing it!" With a screaming war cry he ripped his sword from its scabbard and charged Edwyr.

The Seeker still held Nakamura's Sword in his hand. Swifter than sight it flashed from its resting place, meeting and deflecting Mitsuyama's overhead slash. Like a cat, the PlainsLord sprang back out of reach of Edwyr's darting blade.

Edwyr was nothing less than astonished at the sword in the other man's hand. He had never seen one like it in his life. It was shorter, narrower, and not as strongly curved as the one he held. And the PlainsLord held it in one hand!

Mitsuyama circled cautiously, obviously pleased by Edwyr's reaction. "Speed," he hissed. "Speed, Seeker. I'm faster than you are. You have a slight edge in reach. But my blade is lighter, faster, and just as sharp!" To emphasize his point, he launched a swift attack, cutting for the wrists as a feint, then sweeping for the head. Edwyr was barely able to block in time.

Grinning viciously, the PlainsLord moved to the right, trying to open Edwyr from the side for an attack. The Seeker stood his ground, his sword point aimed at Mitsuyama's throat. "Yes," the other man said, "Speed. And another little surprise." Again he attacked, quickly leaping in, blocking Edwyr's thrust, and countering with lightning strokes, one at the head, another that barely missed the Seeker's shoulder.

Edwyr realized he had two choices: either he had to keep the other man away and hope to catch him by virtue of superior reach, or he had to get in close enough to nullify the speed of his opponent's lighter blade. The first course seemed the obvious one, but for that very reason Edwyr doubted it was the best. Mitsuyama was devious. The obvious was most likely a trap.

Yet the alternative was not attractive. Close in he lost maneuverability for his own blade and limited himself to slashing attacks instead of being able to slash or stab. And something bothered him about the idea of being that close to the PlainsLord. He couldn't quite put his finger on it, but it had something to do with the fact that the other man fought one-handed.

His opponent sensed his indecision and moved swiftly to take advantage of it. Darting in he delivered a flurry of attacks, pressing the Seeker hard. Edwyr had no choice in the face of the assault. The shorter sword had the advantage at its own attack length, while his weapon was too slow to block because of its size. Better to close so the disadvantage was equal. As he blocked a head cut, he stepped in, literally locking guards with Mitsuyama.

Mitsuyama's own eagerness gave him away. As the two swords slammed together, a look of triumph flared up in his eyes and they twitched slightly down and to the left toward his empty hand. The meaning of the glance was instantly clear to the Seeker and he threw himself to his own left. The blade of Mitsuyama's dagger barely scratched his right side, slashing his robe instead of his flesh.

As he fell, he twisted forward, holding his sword in his right hand alone, thrusting upward toward his opponent's stomach. The impact as the blade pierced Mitsuyama's gut and smashed into his spine wrenched the weapon from his grasp. He hit the ground and rolled to avoid the PlainsLord's sword which was sweeping down toward him. His roll wasn't quick enough and the steel sunk into his shoulder.

There was no strength behind the blow, since Mitsuyama was already crumpling, a look of dismay on his face. He let go of his sword and dagger and grabbed at the weapon that jutted from his middle. His hands slippery with blood, he jerked it from his body just as he hit the ground on his knees. Without a single sound, he pitched forward on his face, his hands clamped hopelessly across his spilling guts.

Edwyr heard a shriek and looked up just in time to see Miriam flying at him, her own dagger raised high, her face twisted in fury and hatred. From behind him a blade thrust out, meeting the woman in mid-stride and she collapsed in a huddle, her chest a bubbling ruin. Yolan knelt by his side, her bloody weapon forgotten once its work was done, her hands searching and examining his wound.

The Seeker lay back and closed his eyes. A feeling of bonedeep weariness rose up and towered over him. As it broke over his head he sighed. It's over at last, he thought.

No, a tiny voice deep inside reminded him. No. It's only beginning.

EPILOG

Two moons dodged from cloud to tattered cloud across the night sky. A stiff wind was scouring the last signs of rain from the heavens and drying it from the granite planes of the Mountains.

In the middle of First Pass, on a slight rise where only hours before the members of the Free Council had stood, twenty-six hooded figures sat in a circle. The wind caught occasional snatches of their chant and whipped it away eastward down the valley toward the lowlands.

At the top of the south wall of the pass, two more figures stood, gazing down at the seated circle from the depths of their hoods. As the taller one sighed deeply, the other reached out a comforting hand.

"You wish you could be down there, don't you?" Yolan said.

Edwyr nodded, the motion muffled by the hood. "Yes. But now I'm the Way-Farer. Oh, there'll be circles for me in the future. Many of them. But no longer as a Seeker or a Companion." He paused thoughtfully for a moment. "In the future when I join the circle, I come as the Way-Farer. I come alone and stay alone, even while in the center. The name is mine. So is the burden."

He cocked his head suddenly to one side, then looked intently eastward. "Get ready," he muttered, "they're coming."

With a nod, Yolan held out her hands to him. "It'll be easier this way," she explained, a gentle plea in her voice. Edwyr smiled and took her hands in his. The two of them stood facing each other.

The chanting in the valley had ceased. Only the

311

sound of the wind continued to haunt the night. But despite the quiet, a sense of pressure began to grow, and anticipation hung almost palpable in the air.

Suddenly they were there. The Mushin. Thousands of them. Free and swarming through the pass. With one great, silent shout, the Seekers, the Way-Farer, and the Keeper greeted them. The Mind Brothers returned the cry and swept on westward without a pause.

Yolan's eyes were big with wonder. "It's not what I expected," she whispered, her voice tinged with awe.

"No. Things have changed. We have changed."

"But what Andretti said is true, isn't it? A lot of people are going to die?"

"Yes."

A silence grew between them for long minutes. Yolan finally broke it with a tiny question. "Why?"

Edwyr sighed again. "Yolan, we almost destroyed ourselves. The Great Way had become an escape for us, a way of avoiding the painful reality of Kensho. We were splitting apart into separate races. Those who practiced the Way, especially those who followed the Sword, were continuing to develop as Jerome had planned. But the rest, those in the Home Valley and those out on the Plain, were regressing and degenerating. In another few generations, they would have been as helpless against the mind leeches as the original Pilgrims were at First Touch."

"But weren't many of them, at least in the Home Valley, practicing the techniques and disciplines of the Way?"

"Yes, they were. But without the ultimate test of the Mushin, that's an empty gesture. It's the intimate interaction between the Way, and Mushin and our genes that Jerome realized would change us."

An idea struck Yolan. "Then the Ronin . . ." she began.

"The Ronin were exactly the opposite. They had the Mushin, but not the Way. Yet because they were in constant contact with the creatures, they managed to adapt and even develop a symbiotic relationship with them. They aren't the mindless killers of Jerome's time any more. And in another generation or two, they'll be even less so."

Yolan considered thoughtfully. "Then the freeing of the Mushin is meant to put the pressure for change back on everyone and force us to blend and become one people again."

"Precisely."

"Even the Ronin?"

He nodded. "Even the Ronin. Homo Kensho is our goal. And he'll be a mixture of all of us."

"And the Knowledge?" she asked, a slight hesitation in her voice.

"It'll be essential. As our numbers grow, we'll have greater and greater need of a technology to help support our population. And technology will free more and more of us from the drudgery of grubbing a living from the land so we can spend our time following the Way. You Keepers and Artisans will have a full time job developing it for us."

"In keeping with the Way."

"In keeping with the Way and the lessons we learned on the Home World. We'll have to constantly evaluate it in the light of those things."

An unexpected thought: "And the Mushin will act to police those with impure thoughts." Then she continued. "I'm still worried about some of the things we talked about. I guess there just aren't any hard and fast answers, though. Maybe as we change and de-

velop, we'll find a lot of the questions just answer
themselves or go away." She shrugged. "In any case,
we're moving again. And Keepers won't have to hide
in the dark any more."

Her shrug made her suddenly conscious of the fact
that she and Edwyr were still holding hands. She
looked up and found him gazing at her, a curious
expression on his face.

For several minutes the two of them stood that
way, looking at each other without speaking. Finally
Edwyr said, "You're going to be very busy. You
Keepers have a lot of lost ground to make up."

She nodded agreement. "You'll be busy, too,
Way-Farer."

He winced at the name. "Way-Farer," he sighed.
"Yes, but I'm still Edwyr."

"And I'm still Yolan," she answered softly.

With a smile, the Way-Farer raised his eyes to
watch the moons. "And no matter how busy the
Way-Farer and the Keeper are," he said happily,
"there'll always be time for Edwyr and Yolan."

ell escorted Maggie to the officers' club known as the Black Widow. There, perched on a barstool, was a frail little man with graying hair, the center of attraction. His listeners leaned forward in expectation as he neared the climax of a story. All at once everyone burst into laughter.

"C'mon over and meet Ernie Pyle," said MacDowell.

Maggie followed with trepidation. Ernie was her ideal. He had covered most of the European campaign and would land on Okinawa with the 1st Marine Division. Pyle welcomed Maggie warmly and bought her a drink. Instead of asking her what a nice girl was doing there, he treated her as an equal. "I hear you got onto Iwo," he said. "I never even saw the damned place. If we can get a few minutes alone I'd like you to tell me what it was like."

Maggie felt goose pimples of excitement.

"Things are a lot different over here in the Far East," he said. "The distances and the climate and the whole psychological approach. I still haven't got the feel of it. And censorship is much different."

The other correspondents were interested. They had heard of Pyle's battle with the navy. Incensed that he couldn't name names as he had done in Europe, he had threatened to go home or to the Philippines.

"I can't even write about a Seabee who mixes concrete on Asor."

The next few days passed agreeably and the atoll commander, Commodore "Scrappy" Kessing, was a good host. Asor was only a few hundred yards wide and not too much longer. But with its coconut and palm trees and white sand it was pleasant. More important, it was not too hot.

At the Black Widow that evening Maggie met Major General Lemuel Shepherd, commander of the 6th Marine Division. He invited her to visit his unit on Okinawa.

"I don't have orders to go ashore, sir," she said.

"I trust you'll cover my division in combat, Maggie."

She repeated that she didn't have orders but he only smiled enigmatically and began to chuckle.

On March 25 the correspondents were taken in small boats to the *Panamint* for briefing on Operation Iceberg. On the way they passed three carriers which had recently been hard hit by kamikazes off the coast of Japan. MacDowell explained to Maggie that the three ships had suffered more than fifteen hundred casualties. When they drew nearer to the *Franklin* it seemed a miracle to Maggie that the shattered carrier could have made port.

The intelligence officer for Task Force 53, Lieutenant Commander Sutphin, explained that Okinawa was "a foot in the door for the final poke at the Japanese Empire." Iceberg was the biggest thing yet attempted in the Pacific. "All the forces available in the Western Pacific are involved except those in the Philippines and the Aleutians."

The Army Air Force would neutralize Formosa with B-24's and B-25's, knocking out fifty-five airfields and stopping shipping off the China coast. Fast carriers were already protecting minesweepers which were mining the waters around Okinawa as heavily as the North Sea had been mined in the First World War. Submarines were patrolling the outlets to Japan's Inland Sea.

"April 1," said Sutphin, "is 'Love Day'—that is, L-Day, the official designation for the Okinawa landing." The terrain would be rugged for fighting. "It is very mountainous with steep, sharp hills from north to south. It will be the first heavily inhabited enemy island we have invaded. The population is about 450,000 and we have no reason to believe they are any different people from the mainland Japanese. We expect resistance to be most fanatical."

Maggie felt a stab of fear for Mark who, she had learned, was going to land with his old division, the 2nd. It would be his task to go into caves to dig out some of those fanatical civilians.

"We do not know whether the civilians will be armed," added an army colonel. "We suspect there are a police force and a home guard made up of natives. We know there are caves by the thousands and pillboxes, bunkers, and trenches. The defense will be tough—and probably worse than that."

On the trip back to Asor, Maggie was quiet. Knowing her concern, MacDowell assured her the people hitting the beaches would have the most formidable naval and air bombardment imaginable. That night Commodore Kessing gave a farewell party for the correspondents at the Black Widow. Seventy nurses were brought to Asor from the six hospital ships in the anchorage as well as two women radio operators from a Norwegian ship. Present besides generals, admirals, their staffs, and other high-ranking officers were Dennis Day, currently entertaining enlisted men on a nearby island, and Bob Crosby, leader of the 5th Marine Division band.

Ernie Pyle was there, of course, with his special escort, Max Miller, a naval reserve commander and author of *I Cover the Waterfront*. Pyle was in a morbid mood. He had spent sleepless nights on Ulithi worrying about the landing and had repeatedly told Miller he felt certain he would be killed if he hit another beachhead. "When I lie and think about it too clearly I feel afraid that if I am ever in combat again, I'll crack wide open and become a real case of war neurosis," he had recently written his wife. "If I should ever feel that I am getting to the breaking point, I'll quit and come on home." But that night Ernie was the life of the party and signed Short Snorter bills for anyone who asked. These were glued-together banknotes representing the various countries visited, and autographed by friends and notables.

One of Pyle's admirers was Coast Guard Commander Jack Dempsey. They had become close friends, but the liquor flowed freely that night and before midnight Ernie challenged Dempsey to a fistfight. The former heavyweight champion good-naturedly fended off a few futile punches and no blood was spilled.

It was four in the morning by the time MacDowell brought Maggie to her quarters and gave her a good-night kiss. She wanted him to stay longer but he reminded her that in the morning they would sail for Okinawa. It was a bleary group of forty-odd correspondents that came to Asor's dock. Their host of the night before, Scrappy Kessing, was on hand to greet them. He had brought along a black sailors' band which broke out into a boogie-woogie version of sad farewell music. As each correspondent boarded a picket ship, a navy public relations officer passed out a folder of secret material to be opened only on boarding a transport, along with three bottles of Kessing's good whiskey. Maggie was in the picket boat carrying Pyle.

"Keep your head down, Ernie!" a colleague shouted.

"Listen, you bastards," he yelled back, "I'll take a drink over every one of your graves!" Then he turned to Dempsey who was seeing him off and put up his fists. "Want to fight?" Dempsey laughed but Maggie noticed as Pyle was dropped off at his ship there were tears in the boxing champion's eyes.

The 2nd Marine Division, hundreds of miles away, was heading for the same destination.

2.

Late that afternoon three Marine and four army divisions were preparing to go into battle. Some 300,000 troops had been assembled to rout out the estimated 70,000 Japanese on Okinawa. The men packed and repacked their gear, oiled their rifles, and counted the invasion currency of yen and sen they had been issued.

It had turned warmer and the sea was as smooth as glass. "Looks like a typical Hawaiian evening," an officer remarked to Sherrod as they watched the setting sun. "But tomorrow a lot of good men are going to be dead."

"I'm on another invasion," Ernie Pyle wrote his wife, Jerry. "I never intended to. But I feel that I must cover the Marines, and the only way to do it honestly is to go with them. So here I am. But I promised Max Miller, and I've promised myself, and I promise you, that if I come through this one I will never go on another one." After eating a turkey dinner, he packed what he would carry ashore, bathed, and went to bed. But he felt nervous and weak as he tossed and turned.

After dinner MacDowell managed to steal a few minutes from his wrap-up duties to say goodbye to Maggie topside. She had never seen him so nervous. "When we get back to Guam—if we get back—will you marry me?"

"Yes," she said without hesitation.

He glanced around furtively, then hastily kissed her.

The main task force was heading for the wide beach on the west coast of Okinawa near its waist, but the 2nd Division was veering toward the other side of the island near the southern end where they would carry out a fake attack hoping to lure the defenders from the real landing. There was some grumbling among the men, but their officers assured them there was a good chance they would be committed later in reserve. Mark felt none of the uneasiness that had shaken him before and during the landing at Iwo. He had no business, as language officer, going in on the demonstration but had talked Colonel Haffner, commander of 2/6, into it on the grounds that he was bored stiff not having any responsibilities until they joined with the enemy.

They were awakened at 4 A.M. It was Easter Sunday as well as April Fool's Day. After the usual breakfast of steak and eggs, the men picked up the gear laid out on their bunks and mustered on deck to wait.

By now the 2nd Division Marines were resigned to their inaction. Mark for one looked forward to getting into the little gray boats for a quiet morning sail and then a return to the transport and a good bed. It would not be so bad either once they finally did land since they would hit a beachhead already under control. The sun came up and it was going to be a clear, bright day. All at once half a dozen Japanese planes were in among the transports. The navy gun crews threw up flak at the Japanese who waggled wings and flew past unscathed.

Billy J. was leaning on the rail observing preparations for 1/6's part in the demonstration. He hoped the Japs would swallow the bait. A few ships away Mark could see the main force on the other side of Okinawa. It must have stretched out more than fifteen square miles: APA's, AKA's, LST's, rocket ships, destroyers, cruisers, and battleships.

It was an awesome sight. Perhaps as many as fifteen hundred warships in all, undoubtedly the greatest congregation of ships in world history. Would we ever see its like again? The transports were lowering the empty assault boats that would transport the Marines. Once on the water they began circling their mother ships like ducklings. Finally the order to disembark was given and the Marines clambered over the rail into their assigned LCVP's. The sea was bright blue with whitecaps glistening above a clear azure sky. Mark's boat soon was within a few miles of the shore. The coastline reminded him of Southern California: light tan fields and prairies, scrub trees, chaparral, hills.

As the boats approached the line of departure the din was terrific from the bombardment by the destroyers, cruisers, and battleships. But the *schuu-schuu* of shells passing overhead was disconcerting only to those who were hearing it for the first time. In closer they could see the LCI's that had been converted into rocket ships starting to let loose, and their flame and smoke made the racket even more awesome. Once the landing craft neared the Japanese small-arms range Mark could make out the surf breaking on the beach. Enemy mortar and artillery fire started sending up geysers of water in the midst of the flotilla. The boats veered away raggedly to give the appearance that they were being driven off. Navy planes continued to make strafing and bombing runs and the beach and hills were covered with shell bursts.

The boats scooted back to their mother ships and Mark noticed smoke coming from several vessels. The reembarkation was hurried as the APA's had orders to put out to the open sea as rapidly as possible for fear of further kamikaze attacks. Seeking out Haffner, Mark learned that the *Hinsdale* had been hit by a kamikaze.

"Why, that's Duke Jorgensen's battalion," the startled Mark exclaimed, recalling their meeting on Guam.

"Roger that," Haffner nodded, ignoring Mark's familiarity with a senior officer. "I swear I thought I heard Duke bellowing above all the racket, 'Goddam Japs. Haven't even finished shaving. Somebody call a goddam taxi, we're sinking.'"

Ironically the casualties on the *Hinsdale* and two LST's were about the only losses of the entire landing. The main attack on the other side of the island proceeded smoothly and safely. There was almost no opposition as two Marine and two army divisions poured ashore. Upon setting foot on Beach Yellow, Pyle couldn't see or hear a Japanese. There wasn't a single casualty—not one wrecked boat or burning tank. The entire 5th Marine Regiment had only two cases for the medics. One man hurt his foot; the other was prostrated by the heat. "Hell," he heard a Marine say, "this is just like one of MacArthur's landings!" Others regarded Pyle as their luck and one sergeant yelled that he wanted to wear Ernie around his neck as a charm. They hadn't even got their feet wet. Okinawa was a piece of cake.

As Sherrod edged through the shallow water he thought, "What a wonderful sight; no shattered amtracs and broken boats." He could see tanks far up the hills and even the DUKW amphibious trucks were running along the beach delivering supplies as if it were peacetime. Nobody was frantically digging foxholes. Everybody was standing up. He wrote in his notebook, "This is hard to believe."

Maggie had been transferred to the hospital ship, *Comfort,* and spent the frustrating morning merely watching the easy landing. On Guam she had begged Rear Admiral Miller, the ranking navy public relations officer of the Pacific Fleet, to be allowed to follow navy corpsmen ashore with the Marines. But "Skipper Min," as the reporters called him, ordered her to stay aboard the *Comfort* and report how whole human blood was used to save the wounded. It was not fair. All the men correspondents were ashore getting good copy and she didn't even have casualties to interview.

By nightfall more than 30,000 Americans were ashore in a beachhead not quite three miles long and a mile in depth. The cost was twenty-eight dead, twenty-seven missing. The GI's and Marines continued moving swiftly on all fronts and by the end of the second day the Kadena airfield was cleared and repaired for emergency landings. It looked like a runaway. The following morning Maggie's frustration turned into rebellion. She had been ordered to cover the whole-blood story but there were still no casualties coming in. How could she obey Skipper Min's orders yet stay aboard? She decided to seek advice from higher authority and hitchhiked a ride on a passing LCVP to the *El Dorado,* which was anchored a thousand yards away. She was sure she could find a deputy of Skipper Min's here. At the head of the gangway she encountered MacDowell.

"What are you doing here?" he challenged.

"You know I've been ordered to cover whole human blood saving the lives of the wounded." She began wheedling. "The navy needs more donations from civilians. If I could take a few good pictures it may help. It'll make a nice story."

"We certainly aren't getting enough blood from the States," he admitted. What they had was in the army blood stockpile on Brown Beach.

She saluted. "Request permission to photograph the stockpile on Brown Beach, sir," she said.

"You're incorrigible."

"Yes, sir."

"Oh, damn." He took her arm. "We're having lunch in the wardroom. Afterward there's an LCVP leaving for the beach."

She was so excited she only picked at her food. She talked about everything but her trip for fear he might change his mind. He brought her to the LCVP. "It's only a short ride," he said. "It'll bring you back late in the afternoon."

"Yes, sir," she said briskly and surreptitiously winked. She jumped into the boat and as it was about to pull away someone on the *El Dorado* shouted, "That girl can't go ashore!" Maggie said, "Oh, damn," under her breath. Then the voice continued. "She has to have a helmet."

A helmet came flying down. As she caught it, she realized it was her only piece of field equipment. She had come without canteen or even map. The short ride not only took two hours but halfway to the beach she and an Australian correspondent had to transfer to an amphibious tractor.

The two jumped to shore. "This is Orange Beach," explained the driver of the amtrac. "Surf was too high at Brown Beach." As Maggie started down the beach the driver shouted, "I won't be back for you people today. Wind's coming up."

Instead of being distressed, Maggie was delighted. That meant she might be forced to stay overnight. She asked the Australian where Brown Beach was. He didn't even know there was a Brown Beach. "Where's your map?"

"I don't have one," she confessed.

He didn't either. "I just write my stories about the first fighting unit I come to."

That sounded like an excellent idea. But where was the fighting? The sound of battle was far off until there was a swishing noise followed by an explosion. Sand erupted twenty yards away. "Stray round," observed the Australian calmly, then with a straight face added, "Why don't you take a picture of it?"

Replying that her father had always told her to look for a policeman if she got lost, she started up a dirt road. A few minutes later an M.P. jeep drew up alongside.

"Where is Brown Beach?" she asked.

The two M.P.'s had never heard of Brown Beach. "It's an army beach," said Maggie.

"We'll take you to a *real* beach, sister. We'll give you a lift to the 6th Marine Division."

Maggie jumped into the jeep but the Australian preferred to make his own way to another division. Maggie was in an expansive mood. Everything was going her way. The commander of the 6th Division was General Shepherd and she remembered their conversation at Ulithi. He had definitely invited her to visit him and had only chuckled when she reiterated that she didn't have orders to come ashore.

Shepherd was not at all surprised to see her. He had guessed she couldn't resist coming ashore even without orders. "My dear," he said, "you *are* a brave girl." Nobody had ever said anything that pleased her more. He invited her to share a meal and, upon sitting down at a table made of planks, she heard what sounded like freight trains roaring overhead. It was terrifying and she feared she showed it.

"It's all right, Maggie," said Shepherd. "They're ours." He explained it was a round from one of the division's 155 mm. howitzers. Another round came over and again she shuddered. "You'll get used to it," he said.

After the meal the division's ranking combat photographer took her aside. He said her camera glittered and would draw sniper fire. He painted the chromium-plated parts with a black lacquer. "If we draw fire up forward the fighting troops will make us come back." He offered to show her the ropes in the morning but she confessed she wouldn't be there then.

A colonel sitting with Shepherd beckoned her. "You should be starting back for the beach," he said.

She said she didn't have a ride back to her ship but could probably hitch one.

"Perhaps it would be better to stay overnight," said the colonel. There was sniper fire on the road.

Maggie had qualms of conscience. If she didn't get back to the *Com-*

fort that night, Mac would probably get in trouble. She told Shepherd the truth. She was only ashore on vocal orders.

"I won't give a civilian orders. You make up your own mind, Maggie. But you may have what the colonel just said in writing."

Maggie was tempted but repeated that she had better go. Besides, a woman reporter had never stayed out with a Marine combat division.

Shepherd smiled. "I don't believe so either," he said.

Perhaps, she said, it wouldn't be fair to expose a Marine driver to sniper fire just to keep from being chewed out.

"I don't think it would be fair either," said the amused Shepherd.

That night she slept in the general's field office, a tent. Upon waking she was chagrined to find it was bright daylight. After a quick breakfast she learned that there were eight critically wounded Marines up front and a medical jeep was about to take off to bring supplies to a field hospital. Remembering what a veteran photographer had told her about never asking permission to do anything, she hopped into the back seat.

"You coming with us?" a navy commander asked in surprise.

"Unless you throw me out."

"I don't think we will."

And Maggie was off for the front, surrounded by four heavily armed Marines. It was a dream come true. The jeep started to climb a small mountain and around a bend came upon a tank whose barrel blocked the way. The jeep driver didn't bother to slow down, just waved an arm. A hand waved back from the turret. The gun fired and elevated just as the jeep passed safely underneath. Moments later Maggie heard another report behind. The tank crew had not missed a beat in the rhythm of their barrage. There was not much to see except overhanging trees but the thunder of battle grew louder. They hastily ate lunch in the wreckage of a village. Maggie wondered what had become of its inhabitants.

The commander said, "We really plastered this one."

They pushed forward and Maggie readied her camera. There were no people, only dead chickens, dogs, rats. There was such destruction that they could find no place fit for an aid station, let alone a field hospital. It took half an hour's search to locate a building with four huge stone walls intact.

A medic looked inside. "Empty!" he shouted, and they continued the search.

Maggie was impatient. The day was almost gone and she still hadn't seen the front. "Are we going to see it tomorrow?" she asked.

The others were amused. "We're sitting on it right now," said the commander. "You haven't been anywhere behind it since we passed the tank." He cautioned her not to write in her dispatches that she had gone miles out front. "With all that doubling around we did, we probably never got more than a thousand yards across No Man's Land."

"Oh," she said.

It was getting dark when they finally found the field hospital, a wooden building with many windows, each pane crossed with paper tape. The commanding officer, a slim surgeon, gaped at Maggie. "How the hell did you get here?"

"She wants to photograph how you use blood," explained the commander.

After a supper of hot stew she was taken through the hospital, once an Okinawan school. A dozen wounded lay in one classroom. The second room was for the staff. A chief pharmacist's mate showed Maggie her cot. A good place, he said, in case they were infiltrated during the night. "You'll be the last on the list to get your throat cut."

She was awakened by shouting and two rifle shots. It was black outside. Then jeep headlights glared. Seizing her camera she rushed outside to see four casualties carried in on stretchers. She watched as the surgeon worked in the ray of a single flashlight over a Marine with a gaping chest wound. The surgeon ordered the chief pharmacist's mate to wake up two men to hold flashlights.

"You'll only need one," said Maggie who laid down her camera and took a flashlight.

"What makes you think you won't faint?" asked the surgeon, not looking up.

She felt her gorge rise but said, "I won't, Doctor."

For two hours she watched as the doctor from Wisconsin saved a life with painstaking care. By the time the final suture was neatly in place, Maggie's arms were dead. She laid down the heavy flashlight but couldn't stop her hands from shaking.

She marveled that the wounded Marine could endure such surgery. "How could he stand it?" she asked.

The chief pharmacist's mate, in a tired casual voice, said, "Oh, the limit of human endurance has never been reached."

Maggie was irate. "Hogwash, Chief!"

The surgeon, resting on a crate, called out in the darkness, "Girl, sack out and don't try to wake up for early chow." He promised to help her get set up to take pictures.

During the day the Marines had cut the island in two while the two army divisions pushed steadily to the south against desultory resistance. There were still relatively few casualties. What had happened to the Japanese resistance? Had they given up?

In Tokyo Prime Minister Koiso was making frantic but futile attempts to stay in power. He drew up a drastic reorganization of his cabinet but Marquis Kido regarded it so coolly that Koiso declared in a pique that he would resign the next day.

Once more it was Kido's task to recommend a new prime minister. His first step was to sound out each of the four military leaders separately. To each he suggested that it was perhaps time to form an "Imperial Headquarters" or "Conduct of War" cabinet in which the prime minister, necessarily a military man, would control the affairs of state as well as the Supreme Command.

Both Army Chief of Staff Tojo and the war minister protested. "The battle on Okinawa," acknowledged Tojo, "is going badly. But Japan must be prepared to fight to the end." The minister was equally pessimistic. "But after Russia defeats Germany, she may advise her allies to make peace with us."

The navy chief of staff doubted whether even a victory at Okinawa would end the war. "The enemy will simply attack again."

The testimony of these three men convinced Kido that the High Command had finally come to the realization that the war could not be won. As for the fourth military leader, Navy Minister Yonai, he was covertly working for peace, according to Kido's informants. And so when Yonai suggested Admiral Kantaro Suzuki as a suitable candidate for the premiership, Kido approved the choice. He was confident that he could bring the aged Suzuki around to a peaceful solution of Japan's dilemma.

On the afternoon of April 5 the *jushin* assembled in the Imperial Chamber to help Kido select a premier. The first to talk was Tojo. "In his resignation Koiso stated that the affairs of the state as well as the Supreme Command needed revision." He looked around challengingly. "What does that mean?"

"Prime Minister Koiso doesn't give any special explanations," said Kido calmly.

"It is not desirable to have many changes of government during the

499

war," Tojo said belligerently. "The next cabinet must be the last one! Now, there are two schools of thought in this nation: one that we should fight till the end to secure the future of our country; the other to bring peace speedily even at the expense of unconditional surrender. I believe we must settle this point."

Admiral Okada replied that they must also consider a wide variety of subjects. "This is the cabinet on whose shoulders will rest the destiny of our nation till the end and which will marshal the entire strength of the nation. Questions such as war and peace cannot be discussed here."

Two former civilian premiers tried to placate Tojo. Both asserted, tongue in cheek Kido realized, that the war must be fought to the end. After an hour's argument on the requisites of the next premier, one of the civilians proposed Suzuki. The response was enthusiastic except for Tojo. But he was overruled, and Kido persuaded the seventy-eight-year-old Suzuki to accept the post despite his protest that he was hard of hearing. And in his subsequent meeting with His Majesty, having served seven years as his Grand Chamberlain, Suzuki also interpreted correctly the unspoken words of the Emperor: He was to end the terrible conflict as soon as possible.

3.

Maggie was still up front taking pictures, interviewing Marines and learning about battle. These were the most intense, unforgettable hours of her life. She was terrified, disgusted by the realistic face of war, but was rewarded by the depths of courage and sacrifice she witnessed from men she would not have deigned to speak to in civilian life.

Operation Iceberg was still progressing far ahead of schedule against resistance from enemy outposts only. Admiral Turner was so confident he radioed Nimitz at noon on April 8:

> I MAY BE CRAZY BUT IT LOOKS LIKE THE JAPS
> HAVE QUIT THE WAR AT LEAST IN THIS SECTION.

Nimitz replied sardonically:

> DELETE ALL AFTER "CRAZY."

A few hours later the two army divisions finally reached the first formidable Japanese defense positions above the city of Shuri. It was a ridge which didn't look like much of an obstacle for it was neither high nor jagged, merely a squat hump covered with grass, brush, and small trees. The G.I.'s stormed up its crest on the morning of the ninth only to be met by such a spirited defense that they were forced to fall back with heavy casualties. The real battle for Okinawa had begun and for a change it would be the G.I.'s who would have to carry the greatest brunt, not the Marines. As for the 2nd Marine Division, they were still in wait aboard their transports, circling in the East China Sea, ready to be landed when needed.

That morning the jeep that had brought Maggie to the field hospital returned. "You still here?" said the navy commander and told her to pack her camera. "You're on your way out."

"Back?" she said with a sinking feeling.

The commander chuckled. He told her to hop in if she wanted to see the farthest forward medical unit. "This used to be it but not anymore." They were escorted by combat troops and were held up by two sharp fire fights. But before noon she saw the first casualty enter the new hospital. The next forty-eight hours passed in a daze of activity, interviewing numerous wounded.

During the morning of April 11, her jeep was stopped by a Marine M.P. who plaintively said she shouldn't ask them to do it anymore. Maggie had no idea what he was talking about. She didn't know him. "I never asked you to do anything for me."

"You didn't, lady, but they come on the radio two, three times a day to find out if we've seen you." There was, he said, an arrest-on-sight order out for her. "It was shoot-on-sight, but I guess that was a mistaken transmission." He complained that she had passed him three times already that day.

"You want to take me into custody right now?"

"Not me." But would she please see the division P.R.O.?

She was driven several miles down the coast road to a half-wrecked building where she found the division's public relation officer, a harried lieutenant.

"You're under arrest," he said.

"You can't arrest me," said Maggie. "I came in to surrender myself."

After a brief argument, the lieutenant told her she was charged with embarrassing an admiral.

Early the next morning she left Okinawa on an LST carrying wounded. "You can stay on board until I can radio the fleet that you are no longer missing," said the young skipper, a lieutenant, j.g. Ten minutes later he received a top priority reply:

> HOLD MISS MCGLYNN UNDER ARREST IN QUARTERS
> SHE IS NOT REPEAT NOT TO LEAVE SHIP.

After the lieutenant put her in his in-port cabin he said, "What did you do?"

She didn't know and asked how everyone seemed to have heard she was missing on shore. Just then the air-raid alarm screeched and the air seemed filled with dots screaming down out of the sky. It was a massive kamikaze attack. One headed directly toward her. Streams of ack-ack poured up toward the plane from a dozen ships. Maggie was paralyzed. A human being was aiming himself directly at her, determined to kill her and himself. But the plane had a bigger target, a destroyer escort just to the right. It smashed into the ship. There was a tremendous eruption and Maggie expected to see the ship sink immediately. She could see tiny figures scrambling on the deck and half an hour later as it steamed by she saw scorched, naked bodies lying in rows.

On all sides Maggie could see burning ships. A score of vessels must have been sunk or badly damaged. In the afternoon a launch pulled alongside. A Marine M.P. ordered her to board the launch ahead of him. She waved farewell to the men on the LST, hiding her own trepidation. The launch approached the hospital ship, *Comfort*. "Climb aboard, ma'am," said the M.P. gruffly.

On deck she was met by an affable navy flight nurse. A commander was not so friendly. "Miss McGlynn?" he said.

"Yes, sir."

"You will be restricted to quarters until we sail," he said sternly.

"She's all yours, sir," said the Marine. He grinned. "So long, Maggie. Whatever it is, you tell 'em you didn't do it."

Her brother was on the way to Saipan. Just before the kamikaze attack the 2nd Marine Division had been ordered back to Saipan. It was obvious they would not be needed at Okinawa and a few torpedo hits could kill more Marines afloat than a month's campaigning. That evening the men were informed that President Roosevelt had died. Gloom spread through the ship. He was the only President these men had known well and to most of them it was as though a close relative had died. Mark mourned his loss even though there had been a time in his days as a member of APM that he had looked upon Roosevelt as a reactionary.

His father also mourned the loss of an old friend. The professor had concerns beyond his personal grief. Would the President's death affect the conduct of the war? Would his successor, Harry Truman, also demand unconditional surrender? With all his faults, Roosevelt was a humanist and a man of vision, and he occasionally did listen to good advice. McGlynn doubted if Harry Truman even knew who he was, and if he did, he certainly would not seek his counsel.

In Tokyo Japanese propagandists were taking advantage of the situation to promote a story that Roosevelt had died in anguish, altering his last words from, "I have a terrific headache," to "I have made a terrific mistake." But the new prime minister, Admiral Suzuki, broadcast his condolences to the American people. On that same day he also authorized the organization of a voluntary army of men from fifteen to fifty-five and women from seventeen to forty-five for the mainland battle.

A few days later MacDowell managed to see Maggie privately. She feared he would be angry but all he did was embrace her and tell her not to worry.

"I really couldn't help it," she tried to explain.

"You can't help being a damned fool," he said and tenderly kissed her.

To her annoyance this brought a flood of tears. "I hope I didn't get you into any trouble."

He laughed. "Who the hell cares! Do you think I'm making the navy a career?" He advised her to speak to no one. He would try to take care of things when he returned from a little junket he was making with Ernie Pyle. "The army wants to take him to a little offshore island a few miles north called Ie Shima. He asked me to come along to keep him company."

Pyle was on the *Panamint* nursing a cold he had picked up on Okinawa. "I'm getting too old to stay in combat with these kids," he confided to Sherrod. "And I'm going home, too, in about a month." He also wrote his good friend, Commander Max Miller, "I've got almost a spooky feeling that I've been spared once more and that it would be asking for it to tempt fate again. So I'm going to keep my promise to you and to myself that that was the last one."

Keeping this promise, he and MacDowell watched the landing on Ie Shima from their ship. Three airstrips and two thirds of the little island were taken with few casualties. On April 17 Pyle, MacDowell, and other correspondents loaded into a Higgins boat. It was a bit chilly and Ernie put on a jacket so he wouldn't catch another cold. "I'm like the one-hoss shay," he observed. "I'll probably go to pieces all at once."

At the beach they waited for a guide to lead them to the command post of the 305th Regiment for fear of blundering into a mined area. When no guide appeared, they jeeped behind an ammunition train, keeping a lookout for snipers. Just ahead they saw a soldier step on a mine. Ernie blanched at the gruesome sight. "I wish I was in Albuquerque."

During the afternoon Pyle talked to many G.I.'s and officers. "This is my element," he told MacDowell. His cold was gone, his spirits were high, and vanished was the presentiment that he was going to die. The following morning Pyle, MacDowell, and several officers of the 305th Regiment loaded into a jeep and started up the same narrow, one-way road traversed the day before. Ahead towered a 600-foot peak nicknamed the Pinnacle by the G.I.'s. The road had been cleared of all mines and there was no sign of snipers. It was obviously going to be an uneventful trip.

At a road junction near the village of Ie, MacDowell recognized the high chatter of a Japanese machine gun. It was a .31 caliber Nambu raking the area on the left and just ahead. MacDowell saw dust shimmering in the field on their left. The driver braked the jeep and the occupants dashed for shallow roadside ditches. Pyle, MacDowell, and a colonel were safe as long as they hugged the ground. The colonel finally cautiously raised his head to look around for their comrades. So did MacDowell and Pyle. They saw the others and Pyle smiled. "Are you all right?" he called.

There was a burst of fire. Shots chewed up the road and ricocheted over the colonel's head. He turned to ask Ernie how he was. He was lying face up and there was no blood on his face. Then the colonel saw that Ernie had a hole in his left temple. MacDowell was slumped over. His right eye was gone.

The G.I.'s made a coffin from flimsy boards and buried Pyle among the G.I.'s he loved a hundred yards or so from the China Sea. He was buried with his helmet on. "It was the way we thought he would have wanted it," said a chaplain. "A lot of the men thought he looked more natural that way." Nearby they laid MacDowell.

4.

The death of Ernie Pyle was felt throughout Okinawa. Maggie's first thought had been for MacDowell but no one seemed to know what had happened to him. For several hours she swerved from despair to hope. And upon learning the truth she was devastated. She was thankful she was restricted to her cabin; she did not want to share her grief with anyone. In fact, she was unaccustomed to the emotion. Only a few older members of the clan had died and their passing had seemed natural.

But the loss of MacDowell was like a blow in the stomach. Until she met Mac she had thought she would never really fall in love. And she remembered how dull he had seemed at first. He had grown on her as she realized he was that rarity—a quiet and sensitive man of action. Who else would have so readily and calmly dowsed Heavy Hand Hank with ice water?

The days dragged on as the battle on Okinawa intensified. Maggie had nothing to do but sit in her cabin and wait for the ship to leave. At last the *Comfort,* filled with wounded, started on its journey to Guam. The great white ship, fully illuminated, sailed off unharassed by any kamikaze. At last Maggie had freedom of the ship and she tried to forget by interviewing and taking pictures interminably. She sank exhausted on her cot on the evening of April 28 and was deep in the first real sleep since Mac's death when an alarm rudely returned her to reality. She heard shouts, then a thud as something struck the ship. The *Comfort* seemed to rock. There were screams. The general alarm was sounded over the public address system, as the regular signals had been destroyed. Maggie smelled smoke and heard a fierce crackling. She flung open the door to be almost thrown back by a blast of flame. Ahead was a sea of fire. She slammed the door shut, wet two towels, wrapped herself in a blanket, and crawled under her cot. Then she covered her head and shoulders with one wet towel and breathed into the other one.

Half an hour later sailors found her. The mattress above her was burned but she was alive, lying on her stomach. She tried to turn over and felt piercing pain on her back. The next day she learned that a kamikaze had hit the ship and she was one of forty-nine injured. Twenty-nine others were dead.

Despite her burns she was able to walk off the ship in Guam. She was greeted by the press corps lieutenant. He was sympathetic but bore bad news. Her credentials as a war correspondent were canceled. The lieutenant scolded her. She had embarrassed one admiral and caused concern to other admirals as well as a few generals. One Marine general approached as she was boarding an Air Force freight plane bound for San Francisco. After expressing concern over her burns, he congratulated her on her narrow escape and expressed regret that she was being sent home.

Maggie could still smile. "But did you have to send out a shoot-on-sight order on me?"

"That never happened," he protested.

"What about the arrest-on-sight?"

"Neither did that." He gave her a fatherly smile. "We were just trying to save your life, Maggie."

Mark also mourned MacDowell's death but he knew nothing of his sister's fate. He assumed she was still covering Okinawa from an offshore ship. He was back in Saipan training for another battle. There was one rumor they were going to hit the beaches of Kyushu or Honshu, and another that several battalions might have to go back to Okinawa. He enjoyed life, swimming, reading, and horsing around with Tullio and other old friends of 1/6. He and Billy J. were on a new level of friendship. The colonel was as proud as an older brother of his promotion to first lieutenant and the award of another silver star for his exploits on Iwo Jima.

In the meantime the battle on Okinawa was grinding on with the G.I.'s still carrying the burden of battle. They had finally, at great loss of life, broken through the defenses in front of Shuri and were pushing south with help from the Marines. There were now 170,000 Americans on Okinawa which, like Saipan, was being transformed into a little America. Already roads had been widened and improved, supply dumps set up, antiaircraft guns emplaced, and phone service established linking all army and navy installations.

The Japanese launched a desperate counterattack on May 4, but by the next noon the Americans had gained back lost ground and were pushing forward faster than ever. Even the most aggressive young Japanese commanders now saw no hope at all for Okinawa. Defeat was inevitable.

A few days later, on May 8, the Japanese were surprised by three tremendous volleys at high noon of almost every American artillery piece and naval gun. This was an American celebration. Germany had surrendered. But even while admitting that defeat was certain, there was no letup on the part of the Japanese, who were determined to fight to the bitter end and make the Americans pay with blood for every yard.

CHAPTER TWENTY-NINE

1.

Camp 13. April 1945.

Many of the reforms promised by Major Watanabe had been realized. The Americans did play baseball and football, weather permitting, and everyone enjoyed the amateur variety shows and band concerts. Equally popular were sing-alongs with the American favorite, "God Bless America," and the international favorite, "Bless Them All." The food ration had been slightly increased and for a time conditions in the mines were better. But the growing number of fire bombings throughout Japan had brought added authority to Billy the Kid and his followers. He never openly opposed the major but "Gentleman Jim," as Watanabe was now called by the prisoners, could not personally monitor the camp and so the beatings were on the rise.

Moreover, Billy the Kid now had a strong ally, an American lieutenant colonel, Harry Abbot. Although he outranked Diggs, he asked only to be appointed mess officer. He was efficient and diligent. He posted a long set of rules and would punish any violators regardless of rank. He would not tolerate pilfering of food or supplies. His word over food was law and thus he made himself the most powerful prisoner of Camp 13.

At first he was liked by his fellow officers since he got results. But as word filtered to them that he was not only beating violators personally but turning them over to Billy the Kid for harsher punishment, there was a demand that he be replaced. Colonel Diggs first asked him to be more lenient and, this failing, tried to replace him with another officer. But Abbot refused to leave and he was supported by Billy the Kid.

Popov, now fully recovered, was working in the mess hall and kept Will and Bliss informed of Abbot's actions. His latest victim was a corporal named Banning who had bought rice from the Japanese with cigarettes and sold it in the mess hall. The colonel had knocked Banning to the floor and kicked him before turning him over to Billy the Kid who took him to the guardhouse.

"I heard Banning holler back to Abbot, 'If I don't live to see you court-

martialed, Abbot, others will see that you are!' I found out Banning was
on bread and water for two weeks. Then Abbot told me to take him a
half dish of rice. You know, he's a Marine and tough as hell. But I tell you
he's being starved to death."

Will passed along all this to Diggs and the two went to the mess hall.
Abbot was playing a mandolin. His eyes were dreamy. Diggs asked why
he had turned over Banning to the Japs.

"Because he was illegally dealing in rice. He was corrupting his fellow
prisoners. Banning had it coming to him and I'll do the same to any
other black marketeers I catch."

Diggs indignantly demanded that he have Banning brought back
from the guardhouse before he died.

Abbot eyed him evenly. "Colonel Diggs, I have seniority. I will not
take orders from you. I am doing my duty properly. I will run the mess
and you can run the rest of the camp."

Will and Diggs appealed to Major Watanabe. He was embarrassed
and could not bring himself to admit that, because of the bombings,
tough guards like Billy the Kid were gaining more control. "Why can't
you Americans act as properly as the British and Dutch? You and the
Australians are always getting into trouble."

Diggs countered by complaining of Billy the Kid's newest form of
punishment. He would force an offender to face him in jujitsu and
would slam him to the ground over and over. "And, sir," added Will,
"can't you do anything about the American corporal being starved to
death in the guardhouse? His name is Banning."

"I'm sure this must be an exaggeration. But I'll look into the matter."
Watanabe changed the subject. "I must insist that you people cease this
buying and selling among yourselves. It is degrading."

Once outside Diggs said, "I don't think he has the guts to stand up to
Billy the Kid."

A few days later Diggs and Will were summoned to the commandant's office. Watanabe greeted them amiably, almost apologetically. "I
have some sad news for you. Your President died yesterday."

Will was shocked. Roosevelt had been President so long it seemed
permanent.

"Sit down, gentlemen."

Will was assailed by memories. "My father was a good friend of his.
They were at Harvard together."

Watanabe read them the newspaper report of the death. "You know,
it may seem strange to you, but of all leaders of nations I admire Mr.

509

Roosevelt as the greatest. I would like one of your chaplains to conduct a memorial service for him. You do these things in the States, don't you, Colonel Diggs?"

"Yes, Major."

"Would you please instruct one of the chaplains to do so tomorrow. At the parade ground." He hesitated. "I—I am sorry I won't be able to be there myself but I'll send my honor guard to represent me."

The next afternoon most of the available Americans, including the Republicans, met at the parade ground. Eight Japanese soldiers in full uniform were on hand and just before the ceremony was to start Watanabe himself did appear.

A Protestant chaplain asked the prisoners to face the United States and taps were played by an American bugler. Will felt a lump in his throat and tried to hold back tears. There was a long silence. Then the chaplain gave the benediction.

Despite this show of respect to the enemy, Watanabe was unable to prevent cruelties perpetrated by his subordinates. With embarrassment he admitted to Will and Diggs that he could not control Billy the Kid who always had witnesses testifying he had done no wrong. Early in May a sergeant rushed up to Will. A prisoner was being badly beaten outside the guardhouse. Will arrived just as the One-Armed Bandit was raising his club to hit a man whose head already was bloody. From the rear Will took hold of the club. The One-Armed Bandit turned in surprise.

"What is the trouble?" Will asked in Japanese.

"He did not salute me."

Will recognized "Hose Nose" McGee, a feisty Irishman. "Damn it, McGee," he said, "I told you just the other day to salute properly." He turned to the One-Armed Bandit. "This stupid private deserves a good beating. Turn him over to me. I'll give him one he'll never forget."

His show of anger was convincing and he was allowed to march McGee back to his barracks. Will grabbed a broom as if he were going to beat him with it and pushed the youngster inside. "You stupid jerk! Now yell." He slammed the broom handle against a post and McGee howled in feigned pain. After a few minutes Will handed him the broom. "Now sweep out the barracks."

By late April it was no novelty to see B-29's on their way to Honshu. A few bombs were dropped on Omuta and this accelerated the construction of large cement tanks to be filled with water for fire fighting. For the first time women entered the camp, to help in building these tanks. Most were young, and men who had thought only of survival since capture suddenly became aware of sex. One morning while urinating in the barracks latrine Will heard a giggle. He turned to see a girl of about seventeen staring at him.

"Oki chimpo!" she said admiring his penis.

He blushed and hastily buttoned up.

"American man make big strong babies," she said and started to take off her *monpei*. He made a hasty retreat. But others were not reluctant. Usually the Concrete Annies, as they were called, asked for a piece of soap in payment but a few were only interested in getting pregnant.

Spring had arrived early and occasionally a warm breeze would sweep through the camp bringing with it the salty scent of Ariake Bay. Almost every midnight flights of B-29's rumbled overhead bound for Honshu. The men cheered. The end was coming and soon they would be free. These flights would set off the raucous air-raid siren near the guardhouse. The prisoners, grumbling and fumbling in the dark, would straggle to the air-raid shelters which were 120 feet long but only six feet deep and eight feet wide.

Despite the numerous alarms, not a bomb fell into the camp until early May when Will ambled out slowly as usual. Just as he reached the doorway of his shelter he was showered by debris. He dived to safety as another bomb hit near the parade ground. Then came more explosions.

Someone opened the door and Will could see the glare of flames. Colonel Diggs shouted, "The hospital," and scrambled outside followed by Will and a dozen others. The camp was an inferno. The hospital as well as other buildings, including his own barracks, were blazing. The Japanese were trying to put out the fires with old-fashioned water pumps. Some of the prisoners were helping. Others shouted, "Let 'em burn! Let 'em burn!"

Omuta seemed to be covered with orange. The whole city must be on fire. Some of the Americans were cavorting in joy and Will feared that in the morning Billy the Kid would wreak his vengeance.

The beatings did increase, with the slightest infraction bringing dire punishment. It was also the day Banning died in the guardhouse. The senior American doctor, Pruitt, insisted on seeing the body. He was shocked. The man had obviously been starved to death. Normally he weighed about 170 pounds. Now he was down to only a third of that.

That evening Colonel Abbot caught a private named Harris stealing buns from the kitchen. After delivering a lecture to everyone within hearing about the evils of thievery, he sent for Billy the Kid. He arrived with two men, and the three Japanese, in full view of the mess hands, beat Harris with clubs and fists before dragging him off to the guard-house.

During the next week men reported that Harris was being tortured. One corporal saw him forced to kneel on sharp bamboo rods while guards whipped him with their belts. Others saw him suspended by his fingers outside the guardhouse. One testified that after Harris was doused with water after a beating, an electric wire was put around his neck and the power turned on. His food was being cut down to nothing and after nine days of suffering he lay senseless in the mud and rain outside the guardhouse. In the morning a Japanese doctor declared he had died from heart failure.

The overseers at the mines were also becoming more irritable be-cause of the air raids on Omuta and took out their frustration on the prisoners. Billy the Kid was often seen talking to the supervisors and it was assumed he was egging them on to violence. Will and Bliss both volunteered to go back on mine duty to see if they could be of help. On their first day the men in their group refused to take part in the search for undiscovered veins of coal through a new hard rock shaft.

"It's suicide," one man told Will. "Ask Shirasu." He was one of the overseers who sympathized with the prisoners. "Ask him to tell you what happened to the last detail that went up that shaft."

Shirasu was too frightened to talk at first but once Will assured him they would keep quiet he admitted that the last crew miscalculated the timing of the dynamite charge and everyone had been blown to bits. He himself feared for his life but had to obey or lose his job.

Will complained to an official that this was a rank violation of the Geneva Convention. "The war is soon going to be over," he said. "And I promise I'll have you tried for war crimes unless you help us."

The official blanched, then said with the ingratiating smile of the small functionary, "Captain, there has been a misunderstanding. The Mitsui Company has given us strict orders to treat the prisoners prop-erly." He summoned the head overseer, loudly berated him for making such a stupid mistake, then bowed obsequiously.

Even so, most of the overseers continued to treat the prisoners so harshly that some men purposely broke arms and legs to get out of the mines, while the aggressive prisoners retaliated with a campaign of sabotage. They would put fine dust in motors and hide jackhammers and special tools under rubble. It became common practice to pull the

512

cotter pins out of conveyer rollers thus damaging hundreds of feet of rubber. Sugar stolen from the mess hall would be mixed with gasoline used for the various motors.

The sabotage enraged Billy the Kid more than it did the harried mine officials. He and Abbot continued to work together and by early June there was scarcely an officer in camp who would speak to the colonel. Despite the beatings the prisoners were growing more rebellious. They were particularly incensed that the guards were stealing their Red Cross packages. Since January each prisoner had received only half a package, yet guards continually flaunted American cigarettes and chocolates.

Popov had regained not only his health but his spirits and he persuaded two other mess attendants to join him in a foray into their air-raid shelter where hundreds of Red Cross parcels were stored. One man would act as lookout while the second lowered the third through the shelter's air vent. On the next cloudy night, with Popov as lookout, the plan went into effect. But just as the third man started down the vent Abbot appeared.

"Dorobo!" he shouted.

Guards ran toward the shelter to catch the thief. In the darkness all three prisoners ducked into the nearest barracks. Popov and one man got through the latrine and the third man, "Hose Nose" McGee, escaped through the barracks, knocking down a Dutch prisoner who ripped his shirt in retaliation.

In the morning the prisoners were assembled in the compound by Colonel Abbot. His face was purple. "Last night several men attempted to steal food from the air-raid shelter. They were stealing food that belonged to all of us. Some of you men recognized the thieves. I want you to step forward and identify them."

No one moved.

"Step forward!" he commanded. No one moved. As Abbot walked down the line he saw that McGee's shirt was torn. "Were you involved?"

"No, sir."

"Open your shirt."

McGee did, revealing angry scratches.

Abbot seized McGee and shook him. "Where did you get those scratches?"

"In the coal mines," said McGee.

"You're a damned liar. You work in the mess." As he began violently to shake McGee, Colonel Diggs pushed forward.

"Let that man go!"

Abbot ignored him and slapped McGee.

Diggs grabbed Abbot's arm. "Damn it, Colonel, let that man alone."

Will and half a dozen other officers also came forward and were advancing so aggressively that Abbot released McGee.

"If you report this man to Billy the Kid," said Diggs, "I swear you will answer for it."

"I only do what you other officers should be doing. This place is a disgrace," he said righteously. But a feral glare revealed the real Abbot.

Will went at once to the office of Major Watanabe. Still quivering with rage he said, "The situation has become intolerable, Major." He told what had just happened on the parade ground and then spilled out pent-up complaints of the recent cruelties perpetrated by the Japanese guards. "How can you tolerate the things that were done to Banning and Harris? What kind of people are you?" He told of the brutalities suffered by the prisoners on the three death ships. "How can you justify such inhumanity?"

Watanabe had been listening with bowed head. As Will stood sweating from anger, he finally spoke. "There is no justification of inhumanity, Captain McGlynn. I do not deny any of the things you have told me. I am sure they happened." He pointed to a chair. "Please sit down and listen to me." He waited until Will reluctantly did so. "I went to Columbia and my family, although Buddhist, has Christian friends, as well as many Western friends. All of my Christian friends are loyal Japanese, yet they were distressed by the attack on Pearl Harbor. So was I. We all knew America was not our real enemy although you failed to understand some of our problems."

"What has that got to do with your atrocities?"

"Please be patient. I live in a beautiful little city of about fifty thousand souls. We are proud of our beautiful temples and shrines and gardens. Our people are quite cultured and on the whole gentle. We also have a small munitions factory a mile or so out of town. In the past three months our little city has been bombed six times. Our factory was completely destroyed in the first attack but the bombings—directed solely against innocent civilians—continued five more times. One out of every four in our city is dead. That, I believe, is a higher casualty rate than your Marine divisions will suffer during the entire war."

"I'm sorry, Major. But you people asked for it."

"We asked for it? That is debatable. I just received a letter from my once beautiful city. Last Friday my own humble home was hit by fire bombs. And in a few minutes I lost a father, a mother, a dear wife, and two devoted daughters."

Will was abashed.

"Last week I had to go to Tokyo. I was horrified to see our greatest city practically in ruins. Can you imagine New York City with the great buildings hulks and the rest rubble? Can you picture Washington, D.C., with the Capitol Building in ruins and the Lincoln Memorial littered with dead bodies? Now let me ask you a question, Captain. Would you consider the murder of hundreds of thousands of my people any less an atrocity than those perpetrated upon you and others in the death ships?"

Will was unable to answer.

"Granted that your atrocities were antiseptic. No American beat a Japanese woman with a club or speared a Japanese baby with a bayonet. But the Japanese woman and baby were incinerated by your men who sit high above and never hear their last terrified screams." He stood up. "I bow my head in shame at the numerous cruelties perpetrated by my countrymen. I only ask you to look into your own heart. Are your antiseptic murders any the less cruel than our face-to-face atrocities? I have always been impressed by the sayings of Jesus, particularly 'Let him who is without sin cast the first stone.'" He bowed and opened the door.

Will slowly walked toward his barracks. He was impressed by Watanabe's words but not convinced. The bombs falling on Japan were to end a war that had been started by them. All they had to do was surrender and it would be over. America would not make slaves of them or rape their women or beat their men.

Just ahead he saw Billy the Kid and saluted smartly. But Billy the Kid seized one of Will's arms. "They say you are the American jujitsu champion."

Will smiled. "There is no American champion and I am a poor disciple."

"You are good enough to give me some practice."

Will knew what pleasure these bouts gave Billy the Kid. It would be useless to protest. "I will do my best."

The guard grasped Will's shirt and flung him to the ground. Will slowly rose, trying to figure how he could save himself from serious injury without having to throw the guard.

Billy the Kid was triumphant. "Big American," he crowed. "Little Japanese." Again he downed Will who again got up slowly. The next time, Billy the Kid kicked Will's feet from under him and kneed him in the jaw as he fell forward. By this time a crowd of prisoners and guards surrounded the two. The guards were cheering, the prisoners watching with apprehension.

Will limped. Another kick like that would break a bone. He had to protect himself. As Billy the Kid seized his shirt Will twisted, seized his opponent, and spun him to the ground.

The prisoners spontaneously cheered.

Billy the Kid rose slowly. Glaring, the living ideogram of ferocity, he advanced cautiously. They circled each other. The Japanese lunged forward but Will stepped aside agilely and pushed him down. This time the prisoners were wise enough to still their cheers but inwardly they exulted.

The two men once more circled, grasping each other by the shirts. The humiliated guard made a quick move that seemed to put Will at a disadvantage but he feinted and twisted, then tossed the Japanese over his back.

Billy the Kid scrambled to his feet and wildly rushed at Will who easily sent him to the dirt. This time the Japanese snatched up his club as he got to his feet. He ominously approached Will. A commanding voice stopped him.

"Take that prisoner to my office!" said Major Watanabe peremptorily and marched off.

"You won't last another day in this camp," Watanabe told Will a few minutes later in his office. "The commandant of Camp 14 is a friend of mine. You will like him. He speaks good English, plays *shogi*, and runs a model camp. He is blessed with good noncoms."

Bliss arrived with Will's belongings wrapped in a blanket. "See you after the war," said Bliss. "Tonight I shall light a fart in your honor."

What madmen these Americans are, thought Watanabe, and shook hands with Will. "May we meet again under better circumstances."

What strange people these Japanese are, thought Will. He thanked Watanabe for all he had done.

A clerk brought him to the back of the building where a small truck was waiting. He was told to get into the back. He climbed in and a canvas covering was lashed. As the little truck headed toward the main gate, Will hunched down.

A few minutes later Will could smell Ariake Bay. They climbed a small hill and to the left he saw an expanse of choppy water. He was safe and his troubles were over. He tapped the driver on the shoulder. "Where is Camp 14, soldier?"

The driver pointed across the bay. "Over there. In Nagasaki."

2.

Yoshida, the former liberal foreign minister, was still secretly working for peace. The man who had helped Konoye write his "Memorial to the Throne," which had infuriated the military by calling for a quick end to the war, was informed that Vice Admiral Ozawa himself was secretly preparing to negotiate with the British. Yoshida went at once to Imperial Headquarters. Ozawa greeted the diplomat politely, but his jaw dropped upon hearing that the navy was planning to use a submarine to carry a negotiator to the British.

"I know nothing of any such venture," he said stiffly.

Yoshida felt like a fool, for his informant had been a respected elder statesman. He left hastily. A few days later two *kempei* appeared at his home in Oiso. He was asked politely to accompany them to headquarters in Kudan. Yoshida assumed that Ozawa had turned him in and was amazed, when questioned, that his arrest had nothing to do with the submarine incident.

"Please confess all you know of the context of the report to the throne given by Prince Konoye in February."

He guessed correctly that they had discovered that he had helped write the "Memorial." "I have nothing to tell you," he said. Under the constitution the privacy of correspondence was still respected, and surely he should not be required to speak about the contents of a report to the Emperor.

He was pressed and from their searching questions it was obvious that what they really wanted to know were the recommendations Konoye had given to His Majesty. Other interrogators began grilling him about his friendship with the British and American ambassadors. He admitted he had been particularly friendly with Grew and had sent food to him from time to time when he was confined to the American Embassy after Pearl Harbor.

"We have been informed that you promised to meet secretly with Ambassador Grew at that time. Where did you meet? And what was the purpose of the meeting?"

"I never made such a promise!" Yoshida indignantly replied.

"We have evidence you did."

"Then show me your evidence."

One interrogator handed over a letter Yoshida had written Grew just before the ambassador was repatriated.

"I sent that openly and assumed it would be censored. It was merely a farewell message."

Another interrogator pointed to a sentence expressing the hope that they meet again in better days.

"That just means, 'May we meet again in better times.'"

"In other words, it is a promise of a secret meeting."

"Of course not," said the exasperated Yoshida. "In English it may sound like that to you but I was only saying good-bye. There is no such big deal as a secret meeting."

Despite Yoshida's repeated explanations, the interrogators refused to understand. They politely escorted him to a cell. He was resigned to imprisonment. After all, it was almost a family tradition. His father had been in jail for helping the rebels during the Satsuma Revolt.

Yoshida was only the first of a dozen to be arrested in connection with the "Memorial." Others known to have Western sympathies were brought in for questioning, including Prince Saionji's secretary and the chairman of the Japan-America Society. The main purpose was to get enough evidence to imprison Konoye, who protested to Marquis Kido. "Why are the *Kempeitai* so anxiously searching for the contents of my 'Memorial to the Throne'? I simply cannot understand why they should do this. I submitted it in accordance with the imperial wishes and expressed my opinions as requested." He was highly indignant, since he thought his family was as good as His Majesty's. "If things continue like this, I am going to renounce all my court ranks and honors. I cannot carry on my duty as a *jushin* under such demeaning circumstances. I will go directly to War Minister Anami and demand an explanation."

Kido thought for a moment. "Before you talk to Anami, let me see him. I'll get his explanation." Later in the day the Privy Seal was assured by the war minister that the *Kempeitai* were discontinuing all interrogations concerning the "Memorial."

Konoye was mollified but anxiety at the Foreign Ministry was unabated. Tadashi dreaded to hear a knock on his office door for fear he would somehow be connected with the peace group and it would be uncovered that he had been involved in Roosevelt's message to the Emperor.

The only one who seemed completely unconcerned was the debonair Okazaki even though it was well known he was close to Yoshida. But the press chief walked calmly down the corridors, clad as usual in his American-made clothes, exuding confidence. He still filtered information to Jun's inner circle.

The American campaign to destroy Japan's industrial centers continued and the usual greeting between friends in Tokyo was, "Not burned out yet?" Nothing else seemed to matter. Jun recalled the ditty that, until the first great fire bombing, had been broadcast incessantly over Radio Tokyo:

> Why should we be afraid of air raids?
> The big sky is protected with iron defenses.
> For young and old it is time to stand up!
> We bear the honor of defending the homeland.
> Come on, enemy planes! Come on many times!

Jun and his roommate no longer bothered to go to a shelter. Instead they crouched in the closet with their shortwave radio listening to the B-29 crews chattering to each other. Jun was fascinated for it was the first time since the war started that he had heard English spoken by Americans. Even more exciting was the jazz music turned on by the fliers. Both young men were intoxicated by the stimulating music.

Early in May Tadashi and his family were among those burned out when a stray string of incendiaries hit their apartment house. Shogo had found them new lodgings near Imperial Headquarters. Life for the Todas was difficult in their new location. Floss had fewer friends and was surrounded by suspicious neighbors. She could not shop since she was approaching her ninth month but Foreign Minister Togo and others sent food and supplies.

On May 23 two plainclothesmen appeared just as they were finishing dinner. One said they had orders to take Tadashi to headquarters for questioning.

"You must take care of Mother," Tadashi told Masao. "I count on you." The boy glared at the *kempei* and held back his tears. Tadashi wanted to embrace Floss for it might be the last time he would see her. But he wouldn't show such emotion in front of strangers. Floss had no such inhibitions and held him. The *kempei* watched in embarrassment as they made their last good-byes.

"Don't worry about us," she said, but her eyes were more eloquent.

At headquarters Tadashi denied he knew anything about Yoshida or the "Memorial."

"We know that," a major said. "In our investigation we discovered you helped persuade President Roosevelt to send the message to the Emperor."

Tadashi did not deny his involvement. "I only wanted to prevent a disastrous war."

The major asked who else was concerned in the matter but Tadashi refused to answer. "It will go very hard with you, Toda," threatened the major, "unless you help us."

"I alone am responsible," he said.

The major urged him to reconsider, then dismissed him. He was taken to the garrison prison at Yoyogi and put in a cell next to Yoshida. Within an hour the air-raid alarm sounded. Then came the roar of planes and explosions in the Harajuku area. Explosions were followed by shouts. The prison building was on fire. A guard escorted Tadashi and Yoshida to the vegetable storage room. But the heat became so intense that it looked as if they would be roasted to death.

"Let's get out of here!" said the guard and led them across the street to the Meiji Shrine. They ran to the outer garden and safety. For a moment Tadashi thought of escaping, but where would he go?

Two nights later more than five hundred Superfortresses returned to bomb the heart of Tokyo. For the first time flames reached the Imperial Palace. Flying debris leaped the wide moat to set brushwood fires that spread to several buildings, including the Palace itself. Twenty-eight members of the staff died, but the Emperor and Empress now resided in the *Obunko,* the Imperial Library, half a mile from the Palace in the imperial garden. The royal couple was safe in the underground shelter of the *Obunko,* but outside the Palace walls the pavilions of the Dowager Empress, the Crown Prince and other royal personages were completely destroyed as were the Foreign Ministry and the prime minister's official residence. Entire blocks of the financial, commercial, and government districts were soon ablaze including the detention house of Tokyo Army Prison where sixty-two imprisoned Allied airmen were burned to death.

Floss and Masao had rushed from their two-story wooden building as soon as fireballs began raining down on the perimeter of the target. B-29's were buzzing the skyline of Central Tokyo with impunity since antiaircraft guns had been long since bombed out of existence. The thundering boom of the planes was terrifying but Masao showed no fear as he guided his pregnant mother along the street toward the grounds of the Imperial Headquarters. They were following Shogo's instructions to head for the military shelters in case of danger. Other civilians also streamed through the gates.

One plane skimmed low overhead to dump hissing and rattling bundles of incendiaries on the roof of their building. In seconds it burst into flames. Masao, carrying only a fire bucket, thought of all his possessions left behind, then hurried his mother onto the open ground adjacent to the shelters. Hundreds of civilians were clustered at the closed doors.

Large balls of fire were dropping toward them and the people scattered like leaves. Floss felt sharp pains in her stomach and prayed she would not have a premature birth. The doctor had assured her the baby would not come for ten days. Masao was fascinated by the falling fireballs, which reminded him of floating lanterns. It was like watching fireworks. There was no panic, no screaming. Mothers were trying to calm their children and they, though terrified, silently huddled closer to their parents.

An officer shouted a command and enlisted men began opening up the shelters for the people. They did not rush in but waited to be led in by guides. But once they started in, a new burst of fireballs caused a stampede through the doorways. Masao held his mother back since he didn't want her crushed. He watched the "lanterns" silently float down. Just before landing they would burst with a roar, spewing out cylinders. One cylinder flew toward Floss. Masao protected her with his body and the cylinder glanced against his head, which was covered by a quilted hood. Since Floss had refused to wear a hood, Masao clapped his fire bucket over her head just as the cylinder began hissing fire.

He led her to the entrance of the bunker. It was pitch dark inside and the crowd outside pushed those inside farther to the rear. Masao and Floss were so close to the doorway they could see that the entire area was a sea of flames. Children were crying while their mothers tried to soothe them. Smoke from the outside seeped into the bunker and people coughed. The heat grew intense.

Tears from the smoke ran down Floss's cheeks. People farther inside were choking to death and trying to get to the air while those on the fringes were trying to get farther inside to escape the flames. Floss felt dizzy, then fainted. Masao put her on his back as he had seen firemen do in the movies and dragged her toward the door. He hoped the fires outside had abated. In any case it was better to take the chance than stay inside and choke. Near the door his mother's weight crushed him to the ground. He felt her being removed and as he struggled to his feet saw a soldier carrying her outside. He followed them to an open area free of flames. Behind he heard agonized screams. They had escaped just in time, for another fireball had landed at the entrance and flames were erupting.

The soldier was giving Floss a drink from his canteen. Then he apologized and rushed off to help someone else. For hours mother and son huddled together in the narrowing oasis of safety. At last the fires died down.

It was the most devastating raid since the March holocaust; seventeen square miles of the capital were destroyed overnight. Dawn revealed a scorched area but the smoke and dust were so thick that it was impossible to see the rising sun. People were wandering in a daze looking for loved ones. Soldiers organized the survivors in groups, handing out to each person a rice ball. An officer went from group to group. "Never tell what happened here!" he warned.

It was the first white rice Masao had eaten in months. Floss forced herself to eat though she felt nauseated. They heard a cry of relief, "Ah! *Bujide yokatta!*" It was Shogo. He hugged Masao and gently lifted Floss to her feet. "You are all right?" he asked with concern.

"I think so." She stooped down and hugged Masao. "He saved our lives last night. I don't know how he did it but he carried me out of the shelter or I would have suffocated."

Shogo shook the boy's hand. "Good soldier," he said.

A woman, her face black from soot, her clothes scorched, raised a fist at Shogo. "You army officers!" she shouted. "You still wear nice boots. We Japanese people run around barefoot or in worn-out shoes in the inferno of air raids day and night. And we have nothing to eat while you grow fat."

Shogo, head bowed, said nothing.

"How come you, army fellow, swagger around us, your belly full? Why aren't you up in planes shooting down Bees and protecting the homeland? Shame on you!"

Shogo started to say something.

"You think I'm just a cheeky woman." She swung her fire bucket. "You think I'm afraid of you? Just try and knock me down! Shoot me! I'd rather die than live in this world you made."

Shogo dejectedly escorted Floss toward the gate, flinching at the angry words that pursued him. Their building was a pile of smoldering ashes. Even so, two of the tenants were poking through the ruins for possessions. Shogo told Floss to be patient while he left to arrange transportation to the Toda home.

During the wait, Masao noticed a crowd gathering around the wreckage of a B-29. He asked Floss permission to see it and pushed to the front. The charred torso of an American lay beside the fragment of a wing. Some people were praying for his soul. But one woman, carrying a dead baby, pushed through the crowd. "American murderer!" she shouted and started to kick the torso.

A bystander gently restrained her. "He must have a mother," she said. The irate woman turned away, tears streaming down her face.

3.

It was late morning before Shogo was able to take Floss and Masao to the Toda home. Emi and Sumiko were in the midst of evacuating to Nagano, one hundred and twenty air miles north of the capital. They had already made half a dozen trips to their Nagano quarters, a small house rented through a family friend, and so their house was almost stripped except for large pieces of furniture, bedding, and clothing. There were no doctors available but a midwife arrived late that night to examine Floss. She assured the family the baby had not been harmed and that the pains Floss still felt were from the exertions of the previous night. Emi assumed that Floss would join them in Nagano.

"I couldn't leave Tadashi alone here in prison," she protested.

Shogo supported his mother. "You can't go through another air raid in your condition. And there is nothing you can do for him." He promised to try to get Tadashi released. "The complaint against him is not that serious, and he has influential friends."

Floss was finally convinced it would be best for all of the family to leave Tokyo, and at the end of three days the final packing was finished. They would leave the next morning.

That night the air-raid siren sounded, and they crowded into the family shelter. Over an improvised wooden ceiling a foot of soil had been laid. They sat on rude benches, prepared to come out in case any incendiaries fell.

The sound of low-flying planes grew to a penetrating roar. It was obvious they were under attack and they rushed out. The monstrous planes, glaring orange from the fires below, were unworldly and strangely beautiful. Fireballs were falling nearby. The Todas began dousing the walls of their home with water. In minutes two neighboring houses erupted with flames. Theirs would soon catch fire and they rushed indoors to get clothing and a few precious family possessions. Without bothering to remove their shoes they ran across the tatami rooms. What difference did it make since the house would soon be aflame?

They hurriedly headed up the street with their belongings. The safest place would be the open area in a nearby Buddhist temple. Others were streaming toward the same refuge. No one ran; there were no tears or shouting. Masao turned to see flames shooting up behind them.

"Look!" he exclaimed and all turned. Their home must be in flames. Although they had foreseen that the family home might be destroyed eventually, Emi had secretly thought it would never happen. How terrible for her husband to return from China to find only scorched ground!

The Buddhist temple compound was packed with refugees. The Todas huddled on the ground in blankets. No one could sleep but there was little talk. As soon as the sun rose, they headed sadly back toward their home, past the smoldering ruins of other houses. But to their wonder and relief, their home was intact. While still incredulous, Sumiko suddenly exclaimed, "We shouldn't have worn shoes in the house!" Now they would have to clean all the tatami floors with wet rags. It would be unthinkable to leave a dirty house. By the time they were ready to leave, Shogo had arrived on foot to help them carry the last load of possessions to Ueno Station.

The central train terminal was in turmoil with masses of people, carrying huge *furoshiki* filled with household items and clothing, pushing in all directions for various destinations. A chest of drawers appeared to be walking by itself, for all Sumiko could see was a pair of legs underneath. Then a great kimono chest and other furniture joined the parade.

Getting into the train seemed impossible so their *furoshiki* were left with Shogo while they pushed their way into a car jammed with standees. With effort Shogo passed their belongings through a window. There were no vacant seats, of course, but a middle-aged man, seeing that Floss was pregnant, gave her his seat just as the train started. Shogo was running alongside their car trying to find them. There was Floss in a seat! How marvelous! And there were Emi and the children straining to find him. They all waved.

As the train gathered speed Floss felt guilty to see the man who had given up his precious seat pressed on all sides. It was unusual for a Japanese to surrender his seat for a lady, particularly when it meant he would have to stand for hours. Moved by his gesture of kindness, she marveled at how wonderful some people were at the most trying times. Sumiko was thinking, "A man who remains a gentleman in such adverse conditions is a true gentleman. And this man is also courageous to show generosity to a *gaijin* in time of war." It was a sad moment for the family, especially for Floss, but at least they were leaving the perils of the capital.

Two hours out of Tokyo they heard the high-pitched drone of planes. The noise grew louder and passengers looked around uneasily. For the past few weeks planes from American carriers had been strafing trains and other targets. It would be more dangerous for the train to stop than keep going.

The shriek of planes was followed by the terrifying chatter of machine guns. Bullets sprayed into the car ahead. Fearing this was the end, Floss put a protective arm around Masao who was peering out the window as if hypnotized. There was another unworldly shriek as a plane swept down, another burst of fire.

For some reason the planes departed as suddenly as they had appeared. The raid was over and the train was still running.

4.

The Japanese defense on Okinawa seemed to have stiffened and losses from kamikaze attacks continued. And so the 8th Marines, Mark's new regiment, was ordered to seize two small offshore islands that would be suitable sites for radar search facilities. On June 3, after a heavy naval bombardment, twenty-six LST's, carrying the 8th Marines, dropped the hook off Iheya Shima, a pretty little island northwest of Okinawa. There was no answering fire from the island and Mark wondered if this was just another Japanese trick. He watched as two battalions swarmed ashore. Not a shot was fired. Mark went in with the 3rd Battalion and to his relief they were met by silence. There wasn't a Japanese soldier on the island, the only opposition coming from a rain so drenching that Mark and others had to sleep that night in a sea of mud. The next day the Marines pushed to the other end of the island, driving before them terrified Okinawan civilians and a multitude of farm animals.

Six days later Mark's battalion landed without resistance on the second island which was just west of southern Okinawa. It was safer, commented one private, than driving on any freeway in California. The next days were like a resort vacation. A few civilians had to be rounded up and interviewed and several Okinawans had to be treated for wounds incurred in the naval bombardment. The only excitement came with the capture of two Japanese pilots who were posing as civilians. By the third day Mark found them willing to talk freely. The Marines loafed on the beaches, rode the little Okinawa ponies, and attempted to break the bullocks by riding them bareback.

The vacation ended on June 16 when the 8th Marines were ferried to Okinawa and placed under the tactical command of the 1st Marine Division. They were to relieve the exhausted 7th Marines. Soon after dawn on the eighteenth, Mark was again in battle, this time with the 2nd Battalion. Just after noon, an army general came up front to inspect Mark's unit. He was a big man and the word passed that it was Lieutenant General Simon Bolivar Buckner, commander of the Tenth Army.

Someone wanted to know what the hell a G.I. general was doing so far up front. There he sat in a cleft of rock, looking out over the battlefield. "Things are going so well here I think I'll move on to another unit," he was heard to say. Moments later five shells landed directly in the observation post. A fragment shattered a mound of coral and, freakishly, one jagged piece flew up and embedded itself in Buckner's chest. In ten minutes he was dead.

The 8th Marines moved on, driving south toward the town of Makabe. Three days later the island was officially proclaimed secure but it was only the beginning of Mark's task of getting soldiers and civilians out of their caves.

In one cave he persuaded a Japanese soldier to surrender by promising to let him remain with the Okinawan nurse he wanted to marry. The visit to the next cave almost ended in disaster. It was a huge multilevel labyrinth which infantrymen had been trying to clear out with smoke bombs. They were about to dump gasoline into the mouth of the cave and set it afire when Mark asked them to wait half an hour. He lowered himself by rope into the entrance and groped around for several minutes.

A woman shouted, "Hello," in English. "I'm from Hawaii and my older brother, an Okinawan, is with me."

"We've come to save you," said Mark.

A man and woman emerged slowly from the depths and Mark did not have to urge them to follow him to the surface. Outside, Marines greeted the two civilians with water and cigarettes. A lieutenant pumped the man's hand. Upon seeing Marines carry gasoline cans to the cave the Okinawan gestured excitedly. In Japanese he explained to Mark that the burning gasoline would not only kill the soldiers in a higher lateral but some eight hundred civilians in the lower level as well. "Let me go back with you and bring out the civilians."

Mark explained all this to the lieutenant in charge who agreed to wait another half hour. It took almost that long for the Okinawan to bring Mark down to a vast cavern where a mass of humanity was clustered.

The Okinawan explained that Mark, a Marine, would lead them all to safety. "They gave us water and cigarettes," he said. "And one big Marine rubbed cheeks with me."

He and Mark started out and the others followed. Halfway to the opening they came upon half a dozen Japanese who barred their way with rifles. The Okinawan tried to explain but the leader shouted, "You are a spy!"

Mark extended his arms. "I am not armed. I come in peace to save people."

The soldiers conferred and finally grudgingly gave all of them permission to pass.

"Won't you soldiers follow us?" said Mark. "You have fought courageously but the battle is all over. You will not lose your honor."

But the soldiers silently headed back toward the upper level.

After the civilians had been herded outside, Mark told the lieutenant that there were still several hundred soldiers inside and they would not come out. Gasoline was spilled into the cave and a flaming rag thrown after it. Flames erupted.

"You did your best, McGlynn," said the lieutenant.

That night Mark brooded over the soldiers killed by fire. During the week that followed nine thousand other soldiers and civilians who refused to come out of caves were exterminated like rats by flamethrowers or demolitions. By the end of June mop-up operations were finally completed. In three months, at the cost of more than 7,000 American lives, 100,000 enemy troops and 42,000 civilians had been eliminated.

The 8th Marines returned to Saipan to prepare for the final assault on the Japanese mainland. The prospect dismayed Mark. How many more innocent civilians would have to die before peace finally came? The day he arrived in Saipan he found Billy J. packing. He was, he said, heading Stateside to train new officers. "Guess you'll have to tidy up the battle-field yourself, Mark." Billy J. grasped his hand. There was an awkward pause. "Let me know how things go with you." Spontaneously he hugged Mark briefly before resuming his packing.

PART SEVEN

"To Endure
the Unendurable,
to Bear
the Unbearable"

CHAPTER THIRTY

1.

Iwo Jima. July 1945.

The soldiers in the Philippines and the leapfrogged islands of the Pacific were lost to Japan. Few would ever return to the homeland and those who did not commit hara-kiri or die in a last suicidal charge were now abandoned, sick and starving. They lived from day to day escaping from guerrillas or Americans, driven only by the will to survive. More of these stragglers were concentrated per square mile on Iwo Jima than on any other island in the Pacific. At least a thousand still lived in the myriad caves, emerging after dark to prowl for food and safer shelter.

Seabees had already laid down twenty miles of roads, erected extensive housing, and leveled the central plateau to make a 10,000-foot runway, the longest in the Pacific. Japanese scavengers often crossed paths at midnight without exchanging a word. Only when the new moon shone, a time of sentiment to the Japanese, would they stop to reminisce furtively about home, food, and loved ones.

Sumiko's cousin, Lieutenant Yuji Toda, had already tried to kill himself by thrusting a pistol in his mouth. But when he pulled the trigger there was an empty click. Weeks ago he had given his men permission to surrender after reminding them that those who did so would bring eternal disgrace to their families. They would become outcasts, their names erased from the census register of their towns and villages. Legally they would cease to exist and they could earn a living only by assuming a false name and living far from home.

Toda himself was beginning to contemplate surrender even though he knew that, as an officer, he could be punished by death after the war. He and fifty others, already driven from cave to cave, were at last discovered in mid-June. The Americans drove them into the deepest recesses with grenades and smoke bombs. Seawater was pumped into the cave and Toda and seven others were among the few to escape to a slightly higher lateral tunnel. Then Toda heard a *crump;* fire raced across the water. Gasoline had been poured in and ignited. Only those with Toda survived.

The next day a yellowish beam probed the smoke-filled cave. A Japanese sailor was advancing with a flashlight. "The Americans gave us all the cigarettes and food we wanted," he said. "They are treating us very well. There are many prisoners. We even have a major." The sailor bowed. "Make your own decision," he said and left.

"If you want to surrender," Toda told the others, "do so."

One by one the men excused themselves with formal bows and filed out of the cave until Toda was left only with a wounded man. "What do you want to do?" he asked.

"I don't want to die," said the man.

"Neither do I," said Toda. But he had lost his loincloth in the flight and could not surrender naked. He found a bolt of cotton material and, followed by the wounded man, crept out of the cave with pistol in hand. At the mouth of the cave he was met by several Americans. One held out his hand in greeting.

"I am an officer," said Toda, "and must be clothed before I meet you." He turned his back in modesty to fashion a loincloth, then surrendered.

He remained composed until he had showered. Then he broke down and, for the first time in his life, wept. He refused to talk as he donned clean fatigues but watched in fascination as an American doctor dressed an enemy's wounded leg, allowing blood and pus to stain his own uniform. No Japanese doctor would ever do that!

He was repelled by the celebration of his fellow prisoners. In their joy at finding themselves alive, they sang bawdy songs. He was ashamed to be a Japanese and that night bit his tongue to choke on his own blood. With tongue extended he punched his chin again and again. For all the pain there was very little blood. Then he tried to strangle himself with a thick strand of twisted string. A guard rushed in as he was blacking out.

He cursed, then shrugged his shoulders. Perhaps, he told himself, it is my fate to live. But he refused to talk to his fellow prisoners and would not eat for two days. Finally he was persuaded to take nourishment but he still felt degraded for having allowed himself to surrender.

His cousin Ko had escaped capture and death a dozen times since sailing away from Leyte in a banca. Corporal Kamiko's party had now reached Negros, the large island west of Cebu where Will had been captured. They had come across half a dozen other stragglers and persuaded them to join in their quest for freedom. The group, still headed by Kamiko, plunged into the dense jungle and headed toward the southwest coast. They crossed mountain after mountain, finding almost no food and living for weeks on little but snails and crabs.

By late June Maeda was so thin that he could encircle a wrist with thumb and index finger. If he rubbed the dry skin of his arm, white powder scattered. Half his hair had fallen out and he was struck with terror every time he saw his skeletal face in a stream. For relief from poisonous insects there was nothing but urine. And while they slept, leeches crept into their eyeballs, sticking tenaciously until, big as marbles, they fell off and were eaten. Nothing could go to waste.

By now they were so weak they could only travel two kilometers a day. Food had become an obsession. An enlisted man named Ohno recalled hearing how a cook had served his unit soup made from an executed Filipino.

"It's nauseating to think of eating human flesh," said Maeda. "But I've read it's quite tasty."

"As long as you don't know it," added Kamiko, who noticed that Ohno was eyeing Maeda furtively as if considering him as material for soup.

Ohno quickly looked away. "When a man is really starving," he said defensively, "he'll eat anything."

"Have you ever eaten human flesh?" asked Ko.

"No," said Ohno. "But I used to work in a crematorium and before long you don't realize you're handling a human being."

"Ugh!" exclaimed Ko.

"Look," said Ohno defensively, "if you're squeamish you can't be a cremator."

When Ko woke next morning he discovered that both Ohno and Maeda had left their beds of leaves. He found the two men at a nearby stream. Maeda was stretching his skinny body after a bath while Ohno, peeking from behind a bush, sword in hand, was eyeing him like a cat stalking a mouse.

"Look out!" Ko shouted to his friend who looked up in terror.

Ohno's eyes glistened. Then he guiltily dropped his sword, exclaiming, "Forgive me!" Ko beat him until his own hands were raw. Ohno, submitting docilely, finally fell down, his face covered with blood.

While resting late that afternoon Maeda showed Ko a poem. "It is my last," he said and read it in a thin, cracked voice.

By the autumn of this year,
The wind will bluster
Desertedly and coldly,
And nothing will be left.

That night Ko dreamed he was attending a funeral on a bright spring morning. The odor of flowers was pungent and never had he seen such a blue sky. "Shall we bury him or cremate him?" asked Kamiko, who was wearing a *montsuki*, a ceremonial garment.

"Cremate him," said Ohno. "And please let me do it."

"No," said a woman attended by pretty girls as she clapped her hands. "We must first prepare the meal." The girls made soup and handed a bowl to Ko. It tasted like *satsuma-jiru*, a soybean soup with pork and vegetables. "Uhm, very good," said Ko, smacking his lips.

"Yes, of course," said one of the girls. "The meat is Maeda's."

"So? This is Maeda?" said another girl with a merry laugh. "Delicious!"

The dream was so euphoric that Ko waked refreshed. Never had he felt so content since landing on Leyte. Wondering why, he dimly recalled the dream. Strangely, he felt no distaste and his sense of well-being continued. The next day he had to help Maeda on the march, and he was not stricken with guilt when he found himself muttering rhythmically under his breath as he trudged on, "I-want-to-eat-Maeda. I-want-to-eat-Maeda."

After crossing another mountain they descended to a river swirling from recent heavy rains. Kamiko forded the river first and waved that it was safe. Two others came across. Then it was Maeda's turn. His feeble legs collapsed and he was swept away. Ko got a glimpse of his terrified face and rushed after him. Maeda struggled weakly in the heavy current but before Ko could reach him his head disappeared. For an hour Ko tramped downstream without finding a sign of his friend. He retraced his steps but could not locate the others. He was alone in enemy land.

2.

Tokyo. July 1945.

Ko's oldest brother, Tadashi, was still in prison. That afternoon he was brought to the interrogating room and asked once more to reveal his accomplices. Again he refused and again he was beaten, this time with a stout stick. The guards had to carry him back to his cot.

In an adjoining cell, Yoshida was just being released. Returning to his home in Oiso, he was summoned to the Meguro Elementary School where he was brought to the office of a lieutenant general. The general was more than polite; he was effusive: "There is no one who is more patriotic than you, Your Excellency."

The conspirator of yesterday had suddenly become His Excellency and a patriot. "Thank you very much," said Yoshida and started to leave.

"Please wait a moment, Your Excellency, until you hear what I have to say." The general paused as if in embarrassment. "To tell the truth, it was a big issue among the military whether you should be prosecuted or not. I insisted you shouldn't be. It was finally decided by General Anami not to do so." He waited, apparently expecting Yoshida to give thanks to Anami. But Yoshida said nothing.

The reason for Yoshida's release was the recent decision by the military to seek peace secretly, using the Soviet Union as the best go-between possible under the circumstances. But a former prime minister named Hirota who was asked to sound out the Soviet Ambassador found him so noncommittal that Supreme Command enthusiasm cooled.

Until now Marquis Kido, as confidential adviser to the Emperor, had felt required by tradition to remain above politics, but the time had come at last for positive action. The initiative ideally should come from the army, whose power could thwart other peace movements. There was one source alone no one could oppose—the Throne. Kido decided to confront the Emperor with candor. In the crisis such an unprecedented approach was necessary to persuade His Majesty to end the war by personal intervention.

In the morning Kido arranged all his arguments in a paper entitled "Tentative Plan to Cope with the Situation" and presented it that afternoon to the Emperor. It declared that Japan must resolutely seek peace by terminating hostilities and named the minimum terms for an honorable settlement.

Greatly satisfied by what he read, His Majesty suggested dispatching a special envoy to Moscow with a personal message from himself asking the Soviet Union to help bring about an end to the war.

The Emperor chose Konoye for this mission and he was summoned to the Palace on July 12. They met alone at Kido's suggestion, contrary to court protocol. This would encourage frankness, the Privy Seal hoped. After Konoye agreed that it was necessary to end the war as soon as possible, the Emperor said, "Make preparations to leave for Moscow."

Konoye had opposed using Russia as a go-between but felt obliged to take any step that would rectify his past mistakes as Prime Minister. "If it is the imperial command," he said, "I am prepared to risk my life for His Majesty's sake."

"This time," the Emperor told Kido, "he appears to be resolute."

Jun Kato and his roommate were still tuning in to the chat of American fliers as they passed over Tokyo. It was almost an addiction to listen to the jazz and the buoyant American voices and try to fathom their new slang. Strangely, Jun felt no conflict of identity. Although the bombings had drawn him closer to the Japanese people, he did not regard the fliers as enemies. Their talk and their music seemed to have little to do with the terror on the ground. The American voices had become commonplace and he looked forward to hearing them. Even the danger of discovery had given the nightly adventure spice. Besides there was now little risk since the police and *Kempeitai* were kept busy during the bombings, preventing people from looting. And life itself was a daily risk. What made Jun so bold was also the knowledge that the war might end soon. He knew all about the peace maneuvers with the Soviets and spent hours discussing the possibilities with Fujita who, being a communist, was much more enthusiastic than Jun. Most of his influential friends at the Foreign Ministry let it be known covertly that they had suspicions of the Russians and felt that overtures should only be made to the Americans and British.

Despite having initiated the Russian ploy, the military now doggedly completed plans for the suicidal defense of Japan. More than ten thousand planes were collected. Two thirds of these inferior craft—most of them hastily converted trainers—would be thrown into the battle for Kyushu, which would be spearheaded by Mark's division. The rest would repel any landing near Tokyo. After the bloody lessons learned at

Saipan and Iwo Jima, the new plan was to crush the invaders on the beaches with fifty-three infantry divisions and twenty-five brigades comprising 2,350,000 men. In reserve would be almost four million army and navy civilian employees and twenty-eight million civilian militia armed with muzzle-loading rifles, bamboo sticks cut into spears, bows and arrows from feudal times, and modern-day Molotov cocktails.

3.

Washington. July 1945.

Professor McGlynn was meeting with Joseph Grew. Both were convinced that the time had come to initiate peace negotiations with reasonable terms. The former ambassador to Japan had already urged President Truman to inform the Japanese that unconditional surrender did not mean the end of the imperial system. Grew had warned that without such assurance, the Japanese probably would never surrender. Grew was backed not only by McGlynn, whose attempts to arrange a meeting with the new President had so far failed, but by State Department experts such as Eugene Dooman (Grew's assistant in Tokyo), Joseph Ballantine, and Professor George Blakeslee.

"I've already given thought to the matter," Truman had replied to Grew, "and it seems to me a sound idea." He asked Grew to consult the Joint Chiefs and the Secretaries of War and Navy. Forrestal was enthusiastic but Stimson had reservations and Marshall feared that a public proclamation at this time would be premature. The wording of the proclamation, Stimson said, would depend on the successful testing of America's new secret weapon, the atom bomb.

The physicist responsible for the design and testing of the bomb, Dr. J. Robert Oppenheimer, had revealed that a single bomb would probably kill as many as 20,000 people. Stimson was revolted; so was Marshall but he was in favor of using it to end the war quickly and save American lives. The top scientists working on the project agreed that the bomb should be used. But eight other eminent scientists were opposed on the ground that America would precipitate the race for armaments and prejudice the possibility of reaching an international agreement on the future control of such weapons. They recommended that the nuclear bomb be "revealed to the world by demonstration in an appropriately selected uninhabited area."

But such warnings were ignored and it was taken for granted that the bomb would be dropped if necessary. One man would have to push the button and Harry Truman, an artillery captain in the Great War, accepted the responsibility with confidence. After all it was, he thought, purely a military weapon—in fact, just a huge artillery piece, and had to be used to save American lives.

On July 15 Truman arrived in Potsdam to confer with Stalin. Two days later they discussed the war in the Pacific. It was only then that the Soviet leader revealed that the Japanese had been making overtures of peace. "I made no direct reply," he said, "since they are not yet ready to accept unconditional surrender."

Truman knew all this since the message between Tokyo and Moscow in the Purple Code had been intercepted and decoded, but he pretended he was hearing it for the first time. To Truman's secret delight, Stalin said the Red Army would be ready to attack the Japanese in several weeks. But first they had to settle with Chiang Kai-shek little matters such as disposition of Dairen.

Truman had already received word that the atom bomb had been successfully tested at Alamogordo but when he again met Stalin the following afternoon made no mention of the bomb. Stalin did reveal a secret, one which Truman already knew, that the Emperor had requested that Prince Konoye be accepted as an emissary of peace.

"Shouldn't I ignore it?" Stalin asked as if for advice.

"Do what you think is best."

"What if I lull them to sleep? I could tell them that their message about Konoye's visit was so vague that I can't give a concrete answer."

Truman thought that would be a good idea.

Washington. July 17, 1945.

Professor McGlynn guessed what was going on in Potsdam. He and another civilian in the office drafted a letter to be sent to the editor of the Washington *Post.* At first they thought of submitting it to their chief, Captain Zacharias, but McGlynn thought he might hold it up. So on their own initiative they sent it to the *Post,* signing it "An Observer." On July 18 it appeared, proclaiming that American military law, based upon historical precedents, clearly specified that conquest or occupation did not affect the sovereignty of a defeated nation. It suggested that the United States was open to negotiations through regular diplomatic channels.

McGlynn telephoned Maggie, who was in town making final arrangements to fly back to the Pacific. This time she was being sent to MacArthur's headquarters. McGlynn told her to read the letter section of the morning *Post*. A few minutes later she was laughing. "Your brainchild, Papa?" she asked.

"Could be," he said. "It's only a popgun but it may stir up things." His voice became serious. "Maggie, I'm afraid Truman is going to make a hell of a mess of things. They want to rub the noses of the Japanese in Pearl Harbor. There'll be hell to pay when it's all over."

They had dinner that night. He was in an expansive mood since knowledgeable Washingtonians had surmised that the letter in the *Post* was an Administration trial balloon and a minor furor had ensued. She was bubbling over with enthusiasm for her new assignment. "MacArthur's people don't give a damn what a couple of admirals think about me. I'm going to have a much freer hand than in the navy." Her plane, she said, was leaving in the morning.

McGlynn said he had just heard from Mark. "He's back in Saipan getting ready for another landing. This time it must be the mainland itself. Probably Kyushu."

This reminded both of them of Will. Cards had come telling them he was well and was somewhere in Japan. Both were wondering what would happen to him if the Americans landed on the mainland. Maggie feared she might lose not only both her brothers but Floss.

On April 26 President Truman ordered the Office of War Information to beam to Japan the Allies' final warning—the Potsdam Declaration, which threatened the utter destruction of the Japanese homeland unless Japan accepted unconditional surrender. The Japanese military insisted on rejecting the declaration out of hand while Foreign Minister Togo, just as predictably, recommended considering it. Prime Minister Suzuki compromised and told reporters, "We must *mokusatsu* it." This literally meant "kill with silence," but Suzuki intended it to stand for the English phrase "No comment." Truman, however, understandably applied the dictionary meaning: "treat with silent contempt," and so interpreted Suzuki's words as an outright rejection.

Operational orders for use of the atom bomb were drafted instructing

General Carl A. Spaatz, the new commander of the Strategic Air Forces, to drop the bomb "as soon as weather will permit visual bombing after about 3 August 1945 on one of the targets: Hiroshima, Kokura, Niigata and Nagasaki."

CHAPTER THIRTY-ONE

1.

Nagasaki. August 1, 1945.

Will had felt a thrill of expectation upon seeing Nagasaki again. Just before the family left for Williamstown, the professor had taken everyone to that area so he could research an article for *National Geographic* on the gateway through which both Chinese culture and Western civilization had been introduced into Japan.

Their father's almost childlike excitement in his quest for the past had transmitted itself to all of them, even Mark, who at first had pretended to be bored; but he too soon became entranced as the professor had shown them how Nagasaki had become the window to the outside world. As in his books, McGlynn had the gift of making the past come to life when he told his children of the first European explorers in 1543 and the long procession of missionaries and traders from the West who had followed. By the early seventeenth century the Portuguese, Dutch, British, and Russians had established trading firms and settlements on the hills overlooking Nagasaki Harbor. McGlynn walked his children's feet off showing them how the entire area had become so marked long ago by alien dress, food, language, architecture, religions, and customs that it still retained many vestiges of this early contact with foreigners.

Nagasaki was a spectacular port, particularly beautiful on that first day of August. The main part of the city was on hills overlooking the harbor. To the north lay an industrial center along the Urakami River. Here worked most of Nagasaki's labor force. This complex started just north of the Nagasaki railroad station at the site of a former spinning mill. In 1941 the machines had been moved to China along with the factory girls, and the site was purchased by Mitsubishi. They turned it into a machinery manufacturing plant but a section had been set aside for Prisoner of War Camp 14.

The dreary red brick buildings with slate roofs stood between the rails of the Nagasaki Line and the Urakami River, reminding Will of the grim mills in Dickens's "Bleak House," but he found the atmosphere far more friendly than in any camp he had ever seen. There were about two hundred prisoners when Will arrived. Sixteen were English, twenty-four Australian, and the rest Dutch. There had been some Americans but they had been transferred earlier that year along with other Allied prisoners to different camps.

After Camp 13 it seemed a paradise. The quarters were spacious. There was a recreation room with two Ping-Pong tables as well as tables for playing cards and chess. Guitars and violins were available and there was never a lack of musicians to play them. Adjacent was a bathing room with a large tub for the prisoners and a small one for the guards. Will was amazed on his first day to behold the camaraderie between the prisoners, sweaty from work at the Mitsubishi Shipyard, and their guards as they talked loudly to each other during the bathings and even threw soap back and forth.

Only the "other ranks," as the British called their enlisted men, had to work. The officers did little but grow tomatoes, play chess, read, exercise, and try to keep their sanity. And, while arduous, the work at the shipyard where most of the other ranks worked could not compare to the rigors of mining coal. The men would leave the camp at 7:30 A.M. accompanied by a prisoner officer, a noncom, and several guards and march across the Iwasa Bridge to the other side of the Urakami River and then about four miles down to the shipyard, which lay across the bay from the city.

There were no guards as sadistic as the One-Armed Bandit or Billy the Kid although some were strict taskmasters. At first Will had tried to tell his mates how lucky they were but soon learned he was only causing resentment. He also learned they all had experienced hellish conditions before coming to Nagasaki and had arrived in poor physical condition. The past winter had been miserably cold for them and more than a hundred had died of pneumonia. Food supplies had steadily decreased and for months there had been almost no green vegetables. There was little meat and the cooks had to get pig and cow bones from a slaughterhouse to make a stew with potatoes and flour. Sometimes the prisoners were served a mixture of steamed *kaorian*—wheat and soybeans.

On Sundays the prisoners were allowed to attend mass at Urakami Cathedral. Will always went but mainly for the walk. As he listened to the service he could imagine his father's reaction. But it was a historic structure not far from another landmark, the site where twenty-six Christians, most of them Japanese, had been crucified for refusing to renounce their religion.

For Will the time passed quickly. There were few books in English and so he spent many hours trying to learn Dutch. His teachers were very patient and applauded his painful efforts.

On trips to church Will noticed that the people of Nagasaki were not antagonistic like those he had encountered in Moji and Omuta. Perhaps this was because they had become so used to foreigners over the centuries; or perhaps because there had not yet been a serious air raid. A month or so before his arrival a few bombs had fallen, one falling into the Camp 14 compound. But there had been few casualties. Since then shelters had been built near the barracks and although there were subsequently a number of alerts as planes flew overhead, no bombs were dropped.

On the first of August, a sultry day, Will was trying to read a Dutch book in the recreation room when he heard the guard perched in the lookout tower shout, "Air raid!" Will passed on the warning and rushed outside. Prisoners poured out of the buildings pell-mell to leap into the shelters. From his shelter doorway Will scanned the sky.

"Get in quick!" shouted a Dutch officer.

But Will was too fascinated by the specks in the sky that grew larger.

"It's dangerous out there!" yelled a guard just as a plane swept down, its machine gun blazing. Will heard a dull *pusss! pusss!* as the bullets landed behind him.

The guard yelled, "Watch out!" and yanked him into the dugout by his shirt. He heard an explosion. Then another and another. One bomb crashed into the adjoining building and the shelter rocked up and down. The walls started to collapse. Then came a crunching sound as the concrete wall of the bombed building toppled onto the shelter. Will was knocked to the floor and he felt a great weight. This was the end, he thought, until someone pulled him free. He was alive and couldn't believe it. No one spoke. Finally all crawled out and gaped down at a huge hole ten yards in diameter. Remnants of their dugout were tumbling into the great cavity.

Those who had sought safety in the next shelter were less lucky. A bomb had fallen directly on them. Two were dead.

2.

Five days later at 8:15 in the morning an atom bomb was dropped on Hiroshima, the empire's eighth-largest city. Many civilians had been evacuated to the countryside but 245,000 still remained. The city was almost unscarred by war but seconds later some 100,000 human beings were dead and an equal number were dying of burns, injuries, and a new, terrifying disease—radiation poisoning. Twenty-two American prisoners, including several women, were among the dead. A twenty-third American was pulled out of the rubble alive only to be beaten to death by Japanese survivors.

Three days later another American plane, *Bock's Car*, was armed with a spherical plutonium missile ten feet eight inches long and five feet in diameter. The pilot of the plane, Major Charles Sweeney, was told at takeoff that this bomb, nicknamed "Fat Man," would make the first atom bomb obsolete.

As *Bock's Car* was heading for its primary target, Kokura, it seemed to be jinxed. First it was discovered that the fuel selector to the bomb-bay gas tank was inoperative, restricting the plane's range, but Sweeney refused to turn back. One minute ahead of schedule, *Bock's Car* reached the southern coast of Kyushu where it was to rendezvous with two escort planes. Several minutes later the instrument plane arrived. After a forty-five-minute wait for the photograph plane, Sweeney headed for Kokura. Learning it was covered by smoke and haze, he asked the officer in charge of "Fat Man" if he'd agree to bomb the secondary target. When the weaponeer approved, Sweeney announced to his crew, "Proceeding to Nagasaki," and turned southwest.

Some of the prisoners of Camp 14 were working as usual at the shipyard, but most were still at the compound clearing rubble from the recent bombing or repairing damaged shelters. Will was supervising a group pumping water out of an inundated shelter.

Just before eleven o'clock a man in Will's group with excellent hearing thought he heard a plane. Will crawled out of the shelter to listen. He thought he could hear a faint rumble but put it down to nerves. There was nothing in sight.

Misfortune continued to dog *Bock's Car.* As it neared the target the weather deteriorated. The cloud cover over Nagasaki would probably be nine-tenths. With the reduced fuel they could only make one pass. Sweeney suggested dropping the bomb by radar and the weaponeer in charge of "Fat Man" agreed if they couldn't do it visually. The drop point, chosen for maximum devastation, was on high ground in the center of Nagasaki. An explosion above it should wipe out the main part of the beautiful city, the port area, and even reach up into the factories of the Urakami Valley.

At exactly eleven o'clock Nagasaki appeared on the radarscope. The bombardier shouted, "I've got it. I can see the city." He wouldn't have to bomb by radar. He could do it visually after all. Through a break in the cloud cover he made out the oval rim of an outdoor stadium on the banks of the Urakami River. It was almost two miles northwest of the scheduled hypocenter but would have to do. The bomb would now explode only a thousand yards from Camp 14. At one minute past eleven the bomb dropped and the plane lurched upward.

Will still could see nothing. Then a man working on a roof shouted that there *was* a plane. Will noticed three parachutes blossoming almost overhead. What in hell could they be? He ran excitedly into the barracks to tell the Dutch officer who was writing out the morning report.

As Will was climbing the stairs to the second floor he saw through a window an intense bluish flash. Seconds later came a weird whooshing noise. His lungs seemed to collapse and something struck a hammer blow at the back of his head. He felt a burning sensation as if his body was being seared by a sheet of red-hot iron. Then he lost consciousness.

Mrs. Michiko Goto was getting ready to leave for an air-raid meeting at the Iwasa Elementary School where she taught the second grade. Their school was not in session but the principal wanted to organize his staff for any emergency. She looked at her watch. Mrs. Ohto had promised to come at eleven to watch the two children. She opened the window to call to them in their tiny backyard. Tamiko, five years old, was playing with two dolls; Hajime, three years older, was pointing to the sky. "The plane!" he shouted. "A wonderful silver plane is coming, Mama!" He shouted in glee to see three parachutes burst open. "Tamiko, see the parachutes!"

"Come in, children," called Mrs. Goto. "Get ready for Mrs. Ohto." There was a tremendous flash and a great explosion. Michiko saw hundreds of thousands of yellow balls suddenly appear. Some were as big as baseballs, a few as big as basketballs. The whole atmosphere was pink and a series of golden circles were shooting into the sky. She thought, "How beautiful!" A split second later she felt herself driven to the back of the room; then she blacked out.

Those directly under the explosion heard nothing but a sound like *Saaaa!* Nor could the survivors later agree what color the lightning flash, the *pika*, was. Some thought it was pink, others blue, reddish, dark brown, yellow, or purple. The heat emanating from the fireball was so intense it melted the surface of granite within a thousand yards of the hypocenter—ground zero—directly under the burst. All over the Urakami Valley numerous silhouettes were imprinted on walls and bridges.

Seconds after the *pika* came an unearthly concussion that obliterated all but solid buildings within two miles. If there had been no clouds that day, the center of one of the most lovely cities in the world would have been wiped out. And if the bomb had dropped where aimed, on the outdoor stadium, most of the prisoners at Camp 14 would have died instantly. Fortunately for Will and the others they were now almost fifteen hundred yards from ground zero, and those inside the buildings or working in shelters were protected from the direct flash.

One minute before the bomb fell Prime Minister Suzuki had called an emergency meeting of the military leaders. The Soviet Union had declared war against Japan.

"Under the present circumstances," he said, "I have concluded that our only alternative is to accept the Potsdam Proclamation and terminate the war. I would like to hear your opinions on this."

There was utter quiet.

"Why are you so silent?" asked Admiral Yonai. "We won't accomplish anything unless we speak frankly."

The other three military leaders felt betrayed that one of their number was willing to discuss surrender. Yet the Russian invasion of Manchuria had shaken the trio more than the bombing of Hiroshima.

The meeting was interrupted by an officer who revealed that a second atomic bomb had just been dropped. This news infuriated the three stubborn military men. One by one they refused to accept the Potsdam Proclamation even if the Emperor were allowed to reign. They also demanded that Japanese war criminals be tried only by the Japanese themselves, that they themselves demobilize the army, and that the occupation forces be limited.

Stemming his impatience, Togo tried to explain how ridiculous these conditions were. "Can you offer any hope of victory?" he asked.

"No," admitted War Minister Anami. "But we must fight one more great battle on the mainland."

"Can you keep the enemy from landing?"

"With luck we will be able to repulse the invaders before they land," said General Umezu, the army chief of staff. "At any rate, I can say that we will be able to destroy the major part of an invading force. That is, we will be able to inflict extremely heavy damage on the enemy."

"What difference will that make?" said Togo. "The enemy will simply launch a second or third assault."

But the three military recalcitrants refused to budge and the argument went on inconclusively.

3.

When Will came to, water was pouring over him from a broken pipe. In the pitch dark it took some time before he could remember what had happened. Although his head was dull, heavy, he realized he had to escape. The place could burst into flames any minute. But a beam pinned him down and he could not move. He tried to turn his body sideways. This only caused a heavier gush of water from the pipe. He carefully twisted again and again until he finally could move a little. Exhausted as he was, he knew if he rested he would die. He made a final effort and squirmed out from under the beam.

After kneeling down to get his breath, he began probing for a way out of the darkness. He writhed and turned until he finally saw a ray of light through the debris. It was like coming out of a nightmare. He fought his way to the shattered roof. His shirt and trousers were black and tattered. He stood up to behold mounds of debris for as far as he could see. Yellow smoke swirled everywhere. The cathedral was on fire. So was the vocational high school. The sky was turning to red and murky yellow. Everything was in a turmoil.

There were countless fires. Many housewives had been preparing lunch and charcoal braziers full of hot coals had ignited the tinderbox rubble. These thousands of small fires were being whipped into fury by a blast of wind that was sucked in toward the hypocenter with such force that large trees were uprooted. Blasts of flame, as if from monster blowtorches, were erratically ripping off corrugated roofs as if they were cardboard, blasting houses apart and twisting metal bridges.

Will saw a nearby telephone pole ignite explosively. And the gas tanks of a factory flew into the air like rockets in slow motion. He clambered to the ground to look for more survivors. Most of the prisoners working outside had been sheltered by the buildings and the water tower from a yellow glow that had hissed like water being poured on fire. Not exposed to the direct rays of the *pika,* they showed no primary effects of radiation such as peeling skin, but the unsheltered ones lay on the ground moaning. One man was burning like a torch and the trousers of another were on fire. A third, horribly burned, called out to Will, "Help me!" His ribs were sticking out. He keeled over dead.

There were explosions from a gas-producing plant and debris fell around him in slow motion. The poisonous black clouds of smoke from the gas plant were asphyxiating. His throat burned, his tongue felt swollen. He ran toward the railroad. Long files of people were walking dazedly along the tracks. They were burned, half-naked, but moved in spite of everything. Some were so charred Will could not make out whether they were male or female.

A railroad worker shouted out that a rescue train was coming soon and they should wait. But no one paid any attention to him. A woman ran up to Will screaming. Her *monpei* was gone and all she had around her waist was a white cloth belt. It was on fire. Will started to beat out the flames with one hand but to his horror found strips of her skin dangling from his fingers. She fell and mercifully died.

Nearby was a dead baby. Its mother, badly injured, was trying to crawl to the child's side. She cried out so piteously that Will picked up the baby and brought it to the mother who hugged it and then died. Maggots were wriggling in the dead woman's wounds. My God, where had they come from?

Then he caught sight of Kitano, one of the guards who had been kind to the men. He had rounded up twenty prisoners and was trying to lead them to safety. He told Will they couldn't get across Iwasa Bridge and would try the next one. But that one was destroyed too. They heard a boy shouting. His shirt and trousers had been blown off and he was in his underwear. Skin hung from his head and body. It was Hajime Goto. "Mama!" he shouted. "She's under the house!"

The prisoners hurried to the Goto home, which had collapsed, and began digging. It seemed hopeless but the boy and his sobbing sister urged the men to further efforts. Then Will saw a hand sticking out of the rubble. He called out for help and in a few minutes they had dug out Michiko. Her face was black, her *monpei* ripped, but she was apparently uninjured. The two children hugged her. The mother was horrified to see how badly Tamiko had been burned. The little girl's eyebrows were gone and her face was so swollen that her nose seemed to have disappeared.

"Can't you help her?" Michiko asked Will.

What could he do? He carried the girl in his arms and followed the others. The boy was helping his mother, who staggered at first but soon regained strength.

Ahead, Kitano had stopped to rescue an old lady caught in a house. A few minutes later the group came upon a woman desperately trying to free her son wedged under a fallen wall. Five prisoners managed to pry up the wall so Kitano and the mother could pull him out. Twenty meters farther on they dragged out an elderly man. To Will's horror, his skin came off like a glove.

At a street corner they found another old man lying as if dead. He began to have convulsions. Flames were approaching and Kitano told the prisoners to carry him. "We've got to take him or he'll burn to death." He hoisted the old man onto the shoulders of a husky Australian.

Seeing it was impossible to move farther north because of the intense fires, Kitano found a way to the right and led them across a canal to a steep hill which rose east of the Urakami River. At last they came to a road that was not blocked by burning buildings and started up the slope. Many others were trudging with them. One women with disheveled hair wore only a tattered blouse. Dark red skin hung from her face, breasts, and hands. Her eyes were shining unnaturally. She was obviously in great pain but said nothing.

A man next to her was bleating like a sheep. "What pain! What pain!" The others looked at him in disdain.

Ahead was a burning two-story wooden school where older students had been trained in first aid. A student shouted to the prisoners, "Some are inside!"

Will heard a muffled cry for help, a student trapped by a falling beam. Will put down the girl and rushed forward with other prisoners. They lifted the beam and dragged out the youngster. His stomach had burst open with the organs spilling out. Next to him lay a dead teacher. Students, their clothes on fire, were leaping into a pond. Others staggering from the building were so badly burned that their raw, bleeding

549

flesh was exposed. A burst of flames set the entire structure ablaze, trapping the remaining students who cried out piteously.

The prisoners continued the trek up the hill, carrying a dozen wounded with them. Tamiko, at first a light burden, was as heavy as lead. A woman next to Will collapsed. Kitano examined her.

"How could she have walked at all?" he said. All her leg ligaments and muscles had been severed by sharp shards of glass. Two Dutchmen carried her on a door. By now all were so tired their feet dragged and they breathed with difficulty. As soon as they came to a terraced field with good visibility Kitano called for a break. The men sank gratefully onto the field.

Will tried to soothe Tamiko who was holding back tears of pain. "She's such a brave girl," he said to Mrs. Goto.

"Papa is far away from home in a dangerous place," said Tamiko. "He wants me to be brave and help Mama."

Michiko took the girl in her lap and sang a lullaby. The girl fell asleep. Hajime nudged Will. "She's a baby," he whispered. "She thinks Papa is alive. He died in China a year ago but she loves him so much we don't tell her."

It was the first time Will had had a close look at the mother. Despite her filthy face and tattered clothing, he could see she was an attractive young woman. Noticing his examination, Michiko modestly bowed her head.

"It is strange you understand Japanese," she said.

"I was brought up in Tokyo," he said and told her about his schooling.

"You are English?"

"No, American." They were silent.

"It was terrible at the school," she said with a shudder. "I thought of my own students."

They noticed the other prisoners hurrying into another field for food, returning with eggplants and other vegetables. Will went to the field and brought back a pumpkin and several eggplants for the Gotos. Tamiko was awake but she could not eat a thing. The boy and his mother tried to eat the raw eggplant. Will saw they were only being polite and said he would finish the vegetables himself.

As the sun was about to set Kitano asked the prisoners whether they should stay overnight here on the summit or go back on another trail and look for other prisoners.

"No use just staying here," said an Australian, and the Dutch agreed.

Kitano pointed to a group of houses near the bottom of the slope. "Let's go to the village," he suggested and they started off silently.

As they approached the village Will noticed that most of the houses were tilted with their wooden and paper sliding doors blown off. He was finding it hard to drag his feet and the burden on his back had become painful. At a bridge leading into the village an officer ran toward them brandishing his sword. "Stop! If you try to escape I'll cut you down!"

Kitano came forward and the officer held his sword at the guard's throat.

"What on earth is the matter?" asked Kitano indignantly.

"You're a soldier?" asked the officer. He eyed Kitano closely. "I thought you were an escaped prisoner." He sheathed his sword.

Will and the other prisoners approached. "Everything all right?" asked Will in Japanese. "Everything settled?"

Seeing that the prisoners were not aggressive, the officer relaxed. He patted Kitano on the back. "I've got to go now. Take care of yourselves."

They proceeded to a crossroad near Katsuyama Elementary School and Will finally realized where they were. Just to the left was the Shinto shrine of Suwa, the patron deity of Nagasaki. This was where the famous Okunchi festival was held every fall. Just as they turned into the Nishiyama Road they heard someone cry, "Air raid!" Others picked up the cry and Kitano shouted to look for shelter.

The prisoners crowded into a dugout near a house as a plane swept over. No bombs dropped and they continued to a military police barracks.

"This looks like a good place for us," Kitano said and called out, "We have a favor to ask!" No one answered and he repeated the request. All was quiet. As they entered the barracks, an M.P. appeared. "Do us a favor, please," said Kitano. "We came from the prisoner of war camp. May we rest awhile here?"

The M.P. was suspicious until Kitano explained that he was a guard. "Ah, so," he said and escorted the prisoners down a corridor. The walls were intact but the windows had been blown out and debris was scattered around.

"Could we have something to eat?" asked Kitano.

The rice for dinner had just been blown up and was mixed with glass but Kitano said they would take it anyway. An Australian suggested they soak the rice in water. The glass bits would sink to the bottom. Water was brought from a well and the prisoners wolfed down the rinsed remains, the first cooked rice they had had since the August 1 bombing. Will felt one small piece of glass go down his gullet but took another mouthful of rice to push it farther down.

After the meal Kitano informed the M.P.'s that he was going to take his prisoners back to Camp 14. They looked at him as if he were crazy. "That whole area is a sea of fire!" said one. "You'll never get through."

"We'll make it somehow," said Kitano. "We must report back there."

In half an hour the prisoners came to a wall of fire. As Kitano looked around for a place to break through, M.P.'s began rounding up the prisoners.

"Tamiko is dying," Mrs. Goto said. "We must take her to a hospital." She desperately pulled Will behind a pile of rubble to escape the M.P.'s.

"Where could we possibly find one? We'd better stay with the others." All the hospitals in the Urakami Valley must have been demolished.

"There is a good hospital in Omura," she said and explained this was a town only an hour away by train. They could catch one at the northern outskirts of Nagasaki.

In the dusk they climbed partway up the slope before heading north, skirting the roaring flames below them. Just ahead a badly wounded Japanese soldier fell to the ground. His comrades tried to pull him to his feet but he screamed out.

"A servant of the Emperor should not show pain!" shouted an indignant noncom and kicked him. The other soldiers joined in the beating.

Seeing the look of indignation on Will's face, Michiko pulled him away. "It is their way," she said in English.

In the glare of flames a woman noticed that Will was a *gaijin*. "Murderer!" she shouted and spat in his face.

"He saved our lives," said Michiko, coming between them.

Pouring out insults, the woman tried to hit him then dropped exhausted to the ground. As Will stood helplessly, Michiko took his arm and hurried him away. They crossed a field where at least fifty teenage girls lay sprawled. Long strips of skin hung like ribbons from their faces, legs, and arms. They reached out to the prisoners in supplication for water.

Several village women were laying sliced cucumbers on the burns of the girls. One woman had heard the cries for water and warned Will not to give them any. "It will kill them. That's what everyone says." Flames shot up nearby and Will could see that enormous blisters deformed the girls' faces.

Will and Michiko continued their trek and soon began to pass a long line of slowly moving survivors also bound for the train station. They drifted along expressionless, silent like sleepwalkers, in tattered, smoldering clothing. Will was mesmerized until Michiko, grasping his hand, pulled him away. He was stricken by the sight of this solid stream of silent humanity, half naked and bleeding but without hysteria, not even tears. The unreality of it was terrifying. It was a procession of the damned.

Just then he heard a rattling as a horse slowly dragged a scorched wagon across the field. The horse was pink. The blast had seared off its skin. It followed Will for a few faltering steps.

Michiko stopped before a large pumpkin to cool her bare feet, she said. Will marveled she could walk this far without complaint. She plunged her right foot into the pumpkin, assuming the inside would be wet and cool. She cried out—it was still hot from the blast.

Ignoring the pain, she hobbled down the path. They came to a scene of further desolation. There were no fires, only smoking rubble. Far ahead a crowd was climbing into a train. Will prayed they would get there in time and helped the limping Michiko. The train engine puffed and started off. Will swore as he lowered Tamiko to the ground. She called for her mother.

"Please stay alive, Mama," said the girl in a weak voice.

A plane swept overhead and Will shook his fist at it. Again no bomb was dropped. Then he shouted with relief. "The train has stopped!" The passengers were scrambling out for fear of another air raid.

Finally a conductor shouted to get back on the train. Will and the Gotos crowded into a double seat and the train started off again. The injured and burned endured their pain quietly but at every stop they would call out the windows for water. Those on the platform shook their heads. It was forbidden.

At one stop Will ran out to soak his shirt in a fire bucket filled with water. The two children and Michiko eagerly sucked the wet shirt, all three looking up gratefully. He got a few drops which soothed his swollen tongue.

It was after nine by the time the train pulled into the Omura station. Will remembered being taken here by his father during their Nagasaki trip; the city had been a center of Christianity in the seventeenth century. At the station they were informed there were too many patients at the hospital and they would have to return in the morning.

"We will go to the family home," said Michiko. She had been born in a village ten miles to the north. Luckily they caught the last bus; it was almost eleven by the time they trudged up the long hill from the bus stop to reach a large two-story farmhouse. Michiko pounded on the front door but there was no response. The front door was locked but Michiko knew how to get in by a small window in the rear. First they bathed the two children in cold water and put them to bed. Then Michiko took care of her own bleeding feet while Will sponged himself.

As she was making tea, Hajime came in. "Tamiko is calling for you, Mama."

Tamiko reached up her arms for her mother. Again she said, "Please stay alive, Mama. If both of us die Daddy will be very lonely." She mentioned the names of all her friends and relatives. When she came to her grandparents she said, "They were so good to me, Mama." Then she cried, "Papa, Papa!" and died.

For the first time Michiko broke down.

"Don't cry, Mama," said Hajime. "I will take care of you."

She kissed him and made him go back to bed.

In the kitchen she tried to pour tea for Will and herself but burst into tears. Will put an arm around her. "I will take care of you too," he said.

Sounds of vomiting came from Hajime's room. He had a fever and all the symptoms of his sister. "We will take you to the hospital in the morning," Michiko promised and made him as comfortable as possible.

It was only when he lay on his *futon* bedding that Will realized how many bruises and cuts he had. The day had been so shattering that such minor pains were nothing. He could find no comfortable position. He couldn't get to sleep for several hours and then he had a nightmare about a pink horse with a skeleton rider. He woke to a reality worse than the nightmare. Vague feelings of guilt and shame swept over him. The anguished voices of those who had died haunted him. In the next room Michiko was blaming herself for the death of Tamiko.

Back in Nagasaki thousands of Japanese were experiencing similar feelings of guilt as survivors. And what would happen tomorrow?

CHAPTER THIRTY-TWO

1.

That evening in Tokyo the cabinet continued its fruitless debate. In frustration Prime Minister Suzuki adjourned the meeting just before eleven, instructing the cabinet secretary to arrange for an emergency imperial conference. Within an hour the puzzled conferees were assembled in the imperial underground complex in the *Obunko* annex. The conference room was spare and gloomy, poorly ventilated and sweltering.

Just before midnight the Emperor entered and sank into his chair on the dais. He looked tired, concerned. Despite the oppressive heat Foreign Minister Togo was self-possessed as he declared that the Potsdam Declaration, the Allied demand for unconditional surrender, should be accepted at once so long as *kokutai,* the national essence, was maintained.

Admiral Yonai agreed, his ready concurrence enraging Anami who exclaimed, "I oppose the opinions of the foreign minister!" He stubbornly insisted on the army's terms. "If not we must continue fighting with courage and find life in death." Tears flowed down his cheeks and his voice became strident. "I am quite sure we could inflict great casualties on the enemy, and even if we fail in the attempt, one hundred million people are ready to die for honor, glorifying the deeds of the Japanese race in recorded history!"

Army Chief of Staff Umezu, his shaven head glistening with sweat, sprang to his feet. "It would be unthinkable to surrender unconditionally after so many brave men have died for the Emperor!"

As Baron Hiranuma slowly rose, Anami and Umezu eyed the former prime minister suspiciously. Despite his ultranationalist reputation, they feared he was a Badoglio like the other *jushin* and was just looking for an excuse to surrender. The baron asked a number of questions, all calling for a direct answer from the military: "Can you continue the war?"

Umezu was confident they could stop further atomic attacks by antiaircraft measures. "We have been preserving our strength for future operations," he added, "and we expect to counterattack in time."

Unimpressed, Hiranuma backed up Togo with one proviso. "First we should negotiate with the Allies for the army's demands." The crusty old man turned to the Emperor. "In accordance with the legacy of His Imperial Forefathers, His Imperial Majesty is also responsible for preventing unrest in the nation. I should like to ask His Majesty to make his decision with this in mind."

The old arguments continued for two hours, repeated almost word for word. At last the prime minister deliberately got to his feet. "The situation is indeed serious," he said. "But not a moment has been spent in vain discussing this crucial matter. We have no precedent—and I find it difficult to do—but with the greatest reverence I must now ask the Emperor to express his wishes." He faced his ruler directly. "Will His Majesty decide whether Japan should accept the Potsdam Proclamation outright or demand the conditions the army wants?" To the amazement of all, he started walking toward the Emperor.

"Mr. Prime Minister!" exclaimed Anami in protest.

But the aged Suzuki advanced to the foot of the Emperor's small podium. He bowed very low. The Emperor, unruffled, asked Suzuki to return to his seat. Not quite hearing, the old man cupped a hand to his left ear. After motioning him to sit down, His Majesty stood up. "I have given serious thought to the situation prevailing at home and abroad and have concluded that continuation of the war means destruction for the nation and a prolongation of bloodshed and cruelty in the world." Usually his voice was expressionless but now it was palpably strained. "I cannot bear to see my innocent people suffer. Ending the war is the only way to restore world peace and to relieve the nation from the terrible distress with which it is burdened." His voice choked with emotion and he had to stop. His counselors, listening with bowed heads, could not control themselves at hearing such words. They flung themselves forward, some sobbing unashamedly.

The Emperor resumed speaking but had to stop again. "It pains me," he finally managed to say, "to think of those who served me so faithfully, the soldiers and sailors who have been wounded or killed in far-off battles, the families who have lost all their worldly goods—and often their lives as well—in the air raids at home. It goes without saying that it is unbearable for me to see the brave and loyal fighting men of Japan disarmed. It is equally unbearable that others who have rendered me devoted service should now be punished as instigators of the war. Nevertheless, the time has come when we must bear the unbearable." He recalled the feelings of his grandfather, the Emperor Meiji, at the time of the triple intervention by Russia, Germany, and France in 1895. "I swallow my own tears to recall this and give my sanction to accept the Allied proclamation on the basis outlined by the foreign minister."

The others stood. "I have respectfully listened to His Majesty's gracious words," said Suzuki.

The Emperor nodded, then, as if burdened with some intolerable weight, he slowly left the room.

The cabinet convened at Suzuki's home and drafted identical notes to each of the Allies, accepting the Potsdam Proclamation "with the understanding that the said declaration does not compromise any demand which prejudices the prerogatives of His Majesty as a Sovereign Ruler."

The next morning, August 10, dawned hot and muggy. At Ichigaya Heights more than fifty officers of the War Ministry waited in an air-raid shelter for General Anami. Hastily summoned to an emergency meeting, they wondered if he was going to announce the merger of the army and navy. Or was it about the atomic bomb? Or last night's imperial conference?

The general mounted a little platform at 9:30. "Last night at the imperial conference," he said quietly, "it was decided to accept the Potsdam Declaration."

Several shouted incredulously, "No!"

Anami held up his hands for quiet. "I do not know what excuse I can offer but since it is the wish of His Majesty there is nothing that can be done." He did promise to make an attempt to get the Allies to accept the army's minimum conditions. "Whatever happens," he said, "I ask your help to keep the army in order. Your individual feelings and those of the men under you must be disregarded."

Shogo Toda could not control himself. "What about the duty of the military to protect the nation?" he called out.

Anami brandished his riding crop at Shogo. "If anyone disobeys Anami's orders, he will have to cut Anami down!"

After the meeting Shogo and a score of other dissidents met secretly in another room of the War Ministry. All disciples of Professor Hiraizumi's Green-Green School, they agreed not to accept unconditional surrender.

"It will destroy *Yamato damashi* and *kokutai!*" exclaimed a captain.

557

"And so it is perfectly proper for us to defy the Emperor's decision for peace. It was a mistaken and ill-advised judgment!"

"True faithfulness to the Throne," said Shogo, "makes our temporary disobedience to His Majesty imperative!"

But it took a lieutenant to put words into action. "We must plan a coup!" he said, and there was excited approval.

"Let me warn you," said Lieutenant Colonel Masahiko Takeshita, Anami's brother-in-law. "What we plan to do is punishable by death." They couldn't act rashly or hotheadedly. "First we must isolate His Majesty from the pacifists. Then we can persuade General Anami to advise the Emperor to continue the war." They could wage a decisive battle on the mainland that would cause such casualties that the Americans might agree to an honorable peace. "If not, we can carry on the war as guerrillas in the mountains."

They all recalled the aborted military coup on February 26, 1936— the 2/26 Incident—and vowed to avoid its mistakes. This time they would use the troops stationed in Tokyo to surround the Palace grounds. Lines of communication would be cut; broadcasting stations, newspapers, and key government buildings seized. Then they would arrest Suzuki, Togo, Kido and others who were betraying the country.

Will awakened at dawn. He quietly washed and went outside. From the hill he could look across the bay toward Nagasaki. Smoke was still rising and he shuddered at the memories of yesterday. He noticed Michiko beckoning insistently from the doorway. She pulled him inside, scolding him for going out where their neighbors might see him and report to the police. She had dressed Hajime, whose face was swollen. Will wanted to help her take the boy to the hospital but she was adamant. He would be arrested and she would be disgraced. She did let him put Hajime in a wheelbarrow she had brought to the back door, and he watched with concern as she wheeled her son down the hill toward the bus stop.

After a long wait the bus arrived. With the help of a woman passenger Michiko lifted the boy into the bus, and she was fortunate to find other helpers in Omura. Since there was a long line of patients at Kyosai Hospital, it was not Hajime's turn until noon. A woman doctor examined the boy, then took Michiko aside. "He has the atomic disease," she said.

"Isn't there anything you can do?"

"I can make no promises." Then she added, almost angrily, "But I have no intention of remaining idle while youngsters like your son are suffering from this horrible disease." She explained that no one at the hospital really knew what should be done. "From what I have seen the Nagasaki victims are dying because their stomachs and intestines are filled with poisonous gas." She made sure the door was closed. "My mother is Chinese and has told me of many Chinese cures that are not recognized by medical doctors." She wrote down an address. "Three blocks away there is a drugstore specializing in Chinese remedies. Ask for Tentokosan." She wrote this down. "If your son's stool is bloody after taking this medicine, he may survive. If not, there is no hope for him."

Michiko bowed half a dozen times in thanks.

Once more she found willing helpers to carry Hajime to the drugstore and back to the bus station. Hardest for her was pushing the wheelbarrow up the steep hill and she discouraged a nosy neighbor who offered to help. It was late afternoon by the time Will, who had been keeping cautious vigil, let her in the back door.

"He was such a brave boy," she said. "Not a word of complaint all day."

Hajime smiled wanly. After swallowing the Chinese medicine he seemed to fall asleep and the adults quietly left his room. But moments later he manfully struggled to his feet. "I have to go to the toilet, Mama!" he called out.

He fell down in a faint. Will rushed in to help and was awed by the rush of fecal matter.

"It's bloody!" cried Michiko joyfully.

They cleaned Hajime and put him back to bed. Both watched with concern and after an hour he opened his eyes. They were glazed. He held out his arms to Will. "Papa!" he said. "You've come back!"

Will kneeled down to embrace the boy.

"You told me to be a brave boy and protect Mama and Tamiko."

"You were a very brave boy, Hajime," said Will huskily.

The boy was sweating profusely and his mother kept bathing him with a damp cloth. "Am I going to die, Papa?"

"No, son."

"I'm glad," he said drowsily and dropped off to sleep.

Michiko left for several hours to make arrangements for the cremation of Tamiko. Soon after her return Hajime awoke. He ate a little *miso* soup and fell asleep again. The swelling of his face had gone down considerably and the blisters did not look as angry.

"It is a miracle," said Michiko and crossed herself.

"Are you Catholic?"

"Oh, yes. For generations our family have been what we call Hidden Christians." Will had learned about them during the trip to Nagasaki years ago but he let Michiko explain. "My ancestors went underground rather than apostatize." During more than two hundred years of secret ceremonies they had developed their own form of worship. When Christianity became legal they had refused to join any Christian church, clinging to the rites passed down from generation to generation.

She took Will upstairs to a small room where there was a fake Buddhist altar. She picked up a small wooden image of Kannon, the Buddhist god of mercy who has no sex. This image depicted a woman in kimono holding a baby. Michiko turned over the image so Will could see a cross carved in its back. To the Hidden Christian such statues represented Mary and the Christ Child.

During tea Hajime called weakly. They both knelt by his bed. He looked up at his mother. "I dreamed Papa came home. It was just a dream, wasn't it, Mama?"

"Yes, Hajime," she said and stroked his head.

The boy smiled. "Good night."

As they closed the sliding door, Will thought of all the horrors of the past two days. What a wonderful woman she was! How could she have stood the pain of bare feet without complaint? She was so thoughtful of others, so full of compassion. "How beautiful you are!" he said and kissed her cheek softly.

"You are so tender," she said. "Not like our men."

He embraced her and kissed her cheek again.

She freed herself. "Good night" she said and went into her room.

As Will was lying down on his *futon,* he heard Michiko scream and rushed into her room. Her hair had come off in her hand like a wig. She burst into hysterical tears. He tried to comfort her but she pushed him away to cover her head with a towel.

She was so distraught that Will kneeled beside her, took her face in his hands, and kissed her on the lips. "You are still beautiful," he said. They had shared more grief and pain in a few hours than most married couples did in a lifetime, thought Will. And then he said what he had never said or heard any other McGlynn except Floss say: "I love you." Now it came naturally and it also seemed natural to kiss her again and again. And Michiko let the big, gentle man do so as they began, tentatively, to make love.

2.

The plot of the dissident army officers was gaining support. Takeshita assured his followers that his brother-in-law, Anami, would eventually join them and influence Umezu to do likewise. With the war minister and the army chief of staff supporting the coup, the two local commanders of the Konoye Division and the Eastern District Army would surely have to follow suit. It would be, in the truest sense, an army operation. For they would be acting lawfully under its highest commanders for the good of the nation.

By this time the Allied reply to the Japanese qualified acceptance of the Potsdam Declaration had been received. Although it did not reject outright the Japanese demand to retain the Emperor, his fate was not indicated. The form of the Japanese government, insisted the Allies, would be established by the freely expressed will of their people.

At the *Obunko* Kido explained to His Majesty the problems this would present. But the latter said unconcernedly, "That's all beside the point. It would be useless if the people didn't want an emperor. I think it's perfectly right to leave the matter up to the people."

But the army and navy chiefs of staff saw in the reply ample excuse to continue the war. During the discussion by the cabinet that afternoon, Togo argued there was no reason not to accept the Allied terms. "It is impossible to conceive that the overwhelming loyal majority of our people would not wish to preserve our traditional system."

Just before Anami had left for this meeting Shogo and several other army dissidents had burst into his office demanding that the Allied proposal be rejected. "If you cannot bring that about," said Shogo, "you should commit hara-kiri!" This may have induced Anami's strong opposition to Togo. He was supported by three civilians who were so vociferous that Suzuki went over to their side. Infuriated, Togo informed Kido of Suzuki's "betrayal," and the Privy Seal summoned the prime minister to the Imperial Household Ministry. Something had to be done to bring him back in line with the Emperor's desire for peace.

"I intend no belittling of the argument of those who are anxious to jealously guard the national essence," Kido told Suzuki, "but on the basis of careful study Foreign Minister Togo assures us that there is nothing objectionable in the paragraph in question. If we should turn

561

down the Potsdam Proclamation at this stage and should the war be
continued, a million innocent Japanese could die from bombings and
starvation." Kido could see that his words were having an effect on the
old man. "If we bring about peace now, four or five of us may be
assassinated but it will be worth it. Without wavering or hesitation let us
carry out the policy to accept the Potsdam Proclamation!"

"Let us do it!" exclaimed the prime minister.

At a meeting the next afternoon most of the cabinet members favored acceptance of the Allied demands but four still opposed it and
others were reluctant to take a positive stand. But the old prime minister bullied them until all but one approved surrender. "I have finally
made up my mind," said Suzuki, "to end the war at this critical moment
in compliance with the wishes of the Emperor. And so I will fully report
to the Throne what we have discussed here and ask for his final decision."

Although General Anami's brother-in-law, Takeshita, was the high-
est-ranking officer among the key conspirators, the de facto leader was a
major, Kenji Hatanaka, a quiet, studious, modest man, the antithesis of
the revolutionary. Shogo and the others had been impressed by his
unshakable dedication to *kokutai* and his unwillingness to compromise.
Takeshita had been reluctant to use his privileged position as relative to
persuade Anami to join them. Now Hatanaka insisted on a face-to-face
confrontation with the war minister.

The night was still and muggy as Hatanaka and the inner circle of
conspirators, including Shogo, crowded into Anami's modest one-story
wooden house which now served as official residence after the fire
bombings.

The general greeted the conspirators quietly. "What do you want?"

Hatanaka stepped forward. "War Minister, you must alienate yourself
from those who want to surrender. After imprisoning Kido, Suzuki,
Togo, and Yonai, martial law will be declared. Then we shall isolate the
Palace grounds."

"How do you intend to do this?" asked Anami politely.

"By getting your cooperation, sir. And that of Generals Umezu, Tanaka, and Mori." Tanaka was commander of Eastern District Army and
Mori commanded the Konoye Division, which guarded the Palace
grounds.

"How are you going to handle communications?" asked Anami, and pointed out faults in their staff work.

"We must carry out the plan!" said his brother-in-law, Takeshita, and there was a murmur of assent from Shogo and the other conspirators. "And it has to be done before the imperial conference formally accepting the Allied note."

"But there are so many complications," said Anami. His noncommittal manner weakened the resolve of one colonel, but Takeshita, Hatanaka, Shogo and the others remained determined.

"We must have immediate action," said Hatanaka.

"Give me some time to think things over," said Anami. He escorted them to the porch. "Be careful!" he cautioned solicitously. "You may be under surveillance."

Takeshita stayed behind, presuming on their relationship. "Are you going to join us?" he asked.

"One cannot reveal one's thoughts in the presence of such a large group," answered his brother-in-law. Anami said no more but Takeshita took this as a positive sign and left with renewed optimism. There was still a good chance they could stop the Emperor from surrendering the nation.

3.

It had been an eventful day for Will. He woke at dawn to see Michiko's quiet form next to him. Her head was still wrapped in a towel and he smiled upon remembering how upset she had been when it had come undone last night during their lovemaking. He was still astounded that such a woman could love him. He was fascinated by a face so serene after what she had experienced the past two days.

She opened her eyes, smiled to find him staring at her. She pulled him toward her and kissed him. The moment was shattered by a commotion at the front door. It sounded as if half a dozen people were coming into the house. Michiko hastily donned a *yukata* and left the room. Will could hear her talking to the intruders but the words were indistinct. Apparently the family had at last come home.

After putting on the work clothes he had borrowed, Will emerged. Three women and an old man surveyed him coldly. Michiko was in tears for she had just told them how Tamiko had died. Embarrassed, she introduced him to her grandfather, her mother, her sister, and her sister-in-law. They had all been in Omura where an aunt had been injured in a bombing. They had stayed until she died.

Michiko told how Will had saved her and the children from the wrecked home and brought them to the village. They did not seem at all impressed and her husband's sister criticized her for not bringing Lieutenant Goto's samurai sword from the wreckage.

The unspoken contempt expressed by the relatives toward Will, the enemy, was humiliating but what hurt him most was that they treated Michiko with cold scorn, as if she had disgraced the family forever. And it was almost a relief when the sister-in-law, looking triumphant, appeared half an hour later with two *kempei*. They were scrupulously polite.

"I'll be back," Will told Michiko in English. He bowed to her and to the family and left. On the trip to Nagasaki one of his captors remarked that Will had gone farther than any of the other prisoners—as if it were an honor. It was midafternoon by the time their rickety truck reached the outskirts of Nagasaki.

In broad daylight it was an expanse of wreckage, unbelievable to behold. Could a single bomb have done all this? People were wandering in the smoldering ruins looking for missing members of the family and friends or poking in the rubble for possessions. The ghastly sweet stench of rotting and burned flesh almost made Will retch. They passed the remains of a factory on the banks of the Urakami River where men and women were bringing out the bodies and parts of bodies of more than two hundred girls who had worked on the second floor.

As they approached the ruins of Nagasaki Station, Will noticed a long line of men with bundles on their shoulders. Some were carrying the ashes of dead comrades, recently cremated by the Japanese, and others toted wounded on stretchers or wooden doors. At close range Will realized these were the survivors of Camp 14, and the *kempei* let him join their procession. After crossing a bridge, the guards allowed the exhausted prisoners to rest. During the break Will found Kitano who told him they were heading for a Mitsubishi dormitory a few miles south of the shipyards. This would be their new home.

Will was in better condition than most of the others and volunteered to be a stretcher-bearer. It was backbreaking labor and he was grateful they stopped again after several hundred yards. At last they came to Hirakaido and everyone stopped even though there was no order to do so. On the left was the sea; just to the right rose a steep hill. Nearby was the Taihei temple of Namino-dairo. One of the guards suggested asking permission to deposit the ashes of the prisoners in the temple. The chief priest agreed.

By the time they passed through the tunnel leading to the town of Tomachi it was dusk. Silently they trudged through the quiet streets until they reached the dormitory, a spacious two-story wooden structure.

Will slept fitfully, haunted by a nightmare. Again he dreamed of the grinning skeleton astride the pink horse, which was now hauling a wagonload of corpses, arms and legs sticking out askew. Then he was haunted by the burning school and the piteous cries of the young students trapped inside. Their screams awakened him. It was dark and he could hear only heavy breathing, snoring, and the mumbling of those talking in their sleep. Will could not get back to sleep for worries over Hajime and Michiko. Why had her hair fallen out? She had been inside her home and protected, as he had, from the *pika* flash. But she had not told him that she had seen from the window thousands of mysterious yellow balls.

4.

The next morning an emergency imperial conference was called. As the members hastily convened at the *Obunko* annex, they expressed resentment at having been maneuvered into a confrontation for which they were unprepared and poured out their resentment on the aged prime minister. He brushed aside their complaints and when the Emperor entered the conference room just before eleven, clad in his army uniform, Suzuki said, "I apologize to His Majesty that my cabinet has still not unanimously approved acceptance of the Allied note." He turned to the three military leaders who had been the principal dissenters. "Please present your arguments to His Majesty."

"I must advise His Majesty that continuation of the war is necessary," said Umezu. "If surrender means the end of *kokutai*, then the entire nation must be sacrificed in a final decisive battle."

Anami was so choked with emotion that he could hardly speak. "I too advise continuation of the war unless the Allies definitely promise to guarantee His Majesty's safety." He coughed to clear his throat. "There

565

is still a chance to win. Even so our resistance would at least end the war on better terms."

The Emperor surveyed the other members of the cabinet but no one else got to his feet. He nodded. "If there are no more opinions, I will express mine. I want all of you to agree with my conclusions." There was a tense hush in the room. "I have listened carefully to all of the arguments opposing Japan's acceptance of the Allied reply as it stands, but my own views have not changed. I have studied internal as well as international conditions and have come to the conclusion that we cannot continue the war any longer."

With gloved hand he brushed away tears from his cheek. The sight unnerved several conferees who could not stifle sobs.

"I realize full well how difficult it will be for the loyal officers and men of the army and navy to surrender their arms to the enemy and see their country occupied and perhaps stand accused of being war criminals." He looked directly at the war minister. "Anami, I understand it is particularly difficult for you, but you must bear it."

His voice broke and he had to stop.

"So many died in battle and their families still suffer." Again he had to wipe tears away. "All these feelings are so hard to bear but I cannot let my subjects suffer any longer. I wish to save the people at the risk of my own life."

He stopped, for two ministers had collapsed to the floor.

"The people know nothing about this situation and will be surprised to hear of my sudden decision. I am ready to do anything. If it is for the good of the people I am willing to make a broadcast." He asked the cabinet to draw up at once an imperial rescript to end the war.

The ministers clung to one another in their anguish. Suzuki managed to struggle to his feet. Once more he apologized and walked unsteadily to the front of the dais. He bowed.

The Emperor rose, then wearily headed for the door.

Word of the decision to surrender swept throughout Imperial Headquarters. Discipline began to disintegrate on all levels. *Kempei* noncoms assigned to the building were deserting, taking with them clothing and food. Junior officers were insulting their superiors and some senior officers had locked themselves in their offices with whiskey and sake.

Hatanaka and his key cohorts were meeting to carry out an emergency plan. "There is still a good chance of seizing the Palace," he told

Shogo and half a dozen others. "Two majors of the Konoye Division are still with us." And there was now a new objective, to intercept the recording of the Emperor's message to the people before it was delivered to NHK. Shogo was charged with this assignment.

During the hot afternoon, while Hatanaka was bicycling around Tokyo attempting to revitalize the coup, Shogo learned that the broadcast recording would be made in a room on the second floor of the Imperial Household Agency. He strode into this room as if he were in charge and asked the four-man crew from NHK if everything was in order. It was.

"Who is bringing the record to the recording room?" he said. No one knew but Shogo guessed it would be someone connected with Privy Seal Kido and decided to check his office.

His brother, Tadashi, was being interrogated once more at a *Kempeitai* prison. But the questioners did not have the heart to beat him again and only perfunctorily asked him to reveal the names of any coconspirators. A shake of the head ended the questioning. When he was seized with a fit of coughing the two interrogators were so concerned they asked guards to take him back to his cell and give him water. The guards had grown to respect Tadashi for his refusal to talk, and for more than a week had been sneaking tidbits of food to him. Tadashi felt the end was near. Each breath was difficult. He shut his eyes as he lay on his cot and thought of Floss and Masao. He did not know he was the father of another daughter, born two weeks ago.

In a suburb of Nagano Floss was feeding the baby from a bottle for again she was unable to give sufficient milk. Floss could hear Masao playing outside with their two egg-producers, Chicken A and Chicken B; and she could smell the stew Emi was cooking over a wood fire in the little kitchen. Sumiko had come home from work the day before with some meat bones given her at the Nagano radio station where she had been working the past month, since all young people of her age and older had to participate in the labor mobilization. The men in her office were friendly. The section chief was a mild, kind man in his fifties and there were three radio announcers who took turns broadcasting local news and weather forecasts. Her job was to write down all the scheduled programs transmitted from NHK in Tokyo and pass them on to the local newspapers. The announcers also asked Sumiko to roll their cigarettes, taking it for granted that such a menial job should belong to a subordinate. She had felt obliged to do so since she was the only girl in the section.

The air-raid siren shrieked. A moment later Masao burst into the room. "Mama, a plane is coming!"

Now Floss could hear a motor. It wasn't a B-29 but a much smaller plane. She looked out the window as a U.S. Navy plane swooped down. There was a chatter of machine-gun fire.

"Strafers!" shouted Masao as he saw the plane turn and start back toward them. He burst out the door to save the chickens.

"Masao!" screamed Floss.

But he ignored the growing noise of the plane and picked up Chicken B. The American plane came so low that Floss could see the pilot's face. Then came the terrifying noise of the machine gun as dust flicked up in a line toward the boy.

Another plane came shrieking down. In a daze Masao looked up. His left arm was numb. For some reason he couldn't fathom he waved with his good arm. The American pilot waved back and zoomed up without firing a round.

Thrusting the baby at Emi, Floss rushed outside. Blood was flowing from Masao's left arm. It looked shattered. With his right arm he was still clutching the frantic Chicken B.

"Is Chicken A all right?" he mumbled and fainted.

5.

At 8:30 P.M. the Emperor signed the imperial rescript ending the war, and after his seal was affixed the cabinet members began adding their signatures, making the surrender official.

The plans of the conspirators were developing and by midnight a thousand men had cordoned the Palace grounds. Most of the soldiers thought this was emergency reinforcement of the permanent guard posts, and had no idea they were acting as insurgents. Soon all the great gates clanged shut and the Emperor was isolated from the outside.

Half an hour earlier, Shogo had watched as the Emperor was escorted to the microphone on the second floor of the Household Agency. He heard the Emperor ask, "How loudly should I speak?" An NHK official replied that his ordinary voice would be adequate. But as he spoke into the microphone, the Emperor unconsciously lowered his voice and failed to finish some words.

"After pondering deeply the general trends of the world and the actual conditions obtaining in Our Empire today," he began, "We have decided to effect a settlement of the present situation by resorting to an extraordinary measure."

Shogo, himself awed, could not understand all the words but knew it meant surrender. Earlier Hatanaka had ordered him to report to the nearest exit, the Sakashitamon Gate, as soon as he was sure the recording was being made, so he quietly left the room.

At the Sakashitamon Gate he was stopped by soldiers with fixed bayonets. They were from the Konoye Division and Shogo was elated. The Palace grounds were sealed off. But none of the officers in command knew where Hatanaka was. They only knew they were to allow no one to leave the grounds without his permission.

Then Shogo saw cars coming from the Imperial Household Agency. They were halted by the soldiers and Shogo recognized that they contained members of the NHK crew. As soon as he heard someone reveal that the recording had been turned over to a chamberlain for safekeeping, Shogo picked a dozen men and led them back to the Imperial Household Agency, cursing himself for not staying to see who had taken the recording. Finding the recording room empty, he returned to Sakashitamon Gate to learn that everything had gone wrong. The commanders of Eastern District Army and the Konoye Division had both refused to join them. Hatanaka himself had admitted that the coup had failed and promised to withdraw all the troops from the Palace grounds by dawn. What Shogo did not know was that although Hatanaka had verbally capitulated, he privately had not yet given up. He was on his way to the NHK Building determined to prevent the Emperor's broadcast since his own troops still occupied the building. Instead he would make a personal plea to the nation.

It took Shogo so long to learn that Hatanaka had gone to the NHK Building that it was an hour past dawn, August 15, before he managed to talk his way past the guards at the studio. He found Hatanaka holding a pistol to the head of Morio Tateno who was about to broadcast the early morning news.

"I must talk to the nation," said Hatanaka, pushing Tateno away from the microphone.

While the announcer was protesting, the phone rang. It was Eastern

District Army and they wanted to talk to the rebel officer at the studio. Hatanaka took the phone. "End the uprising at once!" said a high-ranking officer.

"I must make a final explanation to the public!" said Hatanaka, but the request was denied. Hatanaka put down the receiver. It was all over. Secretly Shogo was relieved but he said nothing. He silently gave thanks that not a hand had been laid on the Emperor. It had all been so useless. And now the whole nation would have to endure the utter humility of defeat. But he had no tears left.

Soon after he and the dejected Hatanaka left the studio Tateno announced that the Emperor would broadcast his rescript at noon. "Let us all respectfully listen to the voice of the Emperor."

At exactly noon Shinken Wada, Japan's most popular announcer, sitting pale and tense behind a microphone, said, "This will be a broadcast of the gravest importance. Will all listeners please rise. His Majesty the Emperor will now read his imperial rescript to the people of Japan. We respectfully transmit his voice."

After the reverent, moving strains of "Kimigayo," the national anthem, there was a pause of a few seconds. Finally came the voice that few Japanese had heard: "To our Good and Loyal Subjects: After pondering deeply the general trends of the world and actual conditions obtaining in our Empire today, We have decided to effect a settlement of the present situation by resorting to an extraordinary measure . . ."

CHAPTER THIRTY-THREE

1.

Jun Kato was listening to the speech at the auditorium of the Information Bureau. Finally it has come! he thought. The full meaning of the Emperor's words was not easy to grasp, but to Jun and everyone else in the auditorium it was clearly unconditional surrender. Most of those around him were in tears. He rejoiced but kept his face sober.

"Cultivate the ways of rectitude," concluded His Majesty. "Foster nobility of spirit, and work with resolution so as ye may enhance the innate glory of the Imperial State and keep pace with the progress of the world."

There was awed silence. Those with contorted faces could no longer contain their emotions. They sobbed openly, without restraint. And throughout the empire millions wept in concert—perhaps more people simultaneously than at any other moment in the world's history. Yet underlying the humiliation and sorrow was an undeniable sense of relief, even among those in the army and navy. The terrible burden of years of war, death, and destruction was at last over.

Those at the Information Bureau began slowly drifting outside. Jun and four others headed for the Foreign Ministry soberly discussing what unconditional surrender would entail. How would America occupy Japan? What kind of administration would be set up?

"And how is it going to effect us newsmen?" asked Jun. Would they be imprisoned for writing government propaganda?

As they neared their destination a man from *Mainichi Shimbun* said, "I think they'll arrest His Majesty and hold him responsible for the war."

"As a war criminal?" asked Jun.

"Why not? Who deserves it more?"

Another said, "It's time anyway for the Emperor to step down."

Everyone agreed and there was no sympathy for His Majesty.

At the Foreign Ministry, Okazaki, looking as dapper and self-assured as ever, explained to them the meaning of the Emperor's words. "We don't know what is going to happen. We have no idea how we civilians will be treated or what the occupation regulations will be. But I assure you that under the Potsdam Declaration we all will be treated according to international law."

Jun was impressed by his cool analysis yet was worried about his own status. Would a nisei face charges as a traitor to his country? His articles about the U.S. atrocity bombing campaign would make him a marked man. He would have to stay very quiet.

The entire nation had listened attentively to the Emperor's words, awed by his high-pitched, almost ethereal voice. His failure to complete some words, coupled with poor reception, permitted few to understand exactly what he was saying. Yet everyone knew it was surrender or something equally catastrophic since he was speaking to the people for the first time ever.

His voice had reached troops and civilian workers thousands of miles from the homeland. In China the head of the Toda family did not weep. He knew it was best for the nation. While he was collecting his valuable formulas and papers, a staff officer burst into his office.

"Good!" he exclaimed upon glimpsing the pile of papers. "Everything must be burned that can be of any help to the enemy. Warn your staff that anyone who disobeys this order will be punished."

As soon as the officer left, Toda carefully wrapped the papers and placed them in his safe. How could he possibly burn formulas and valuable scientific data the loss of which would hold up production for months, perhaps years? As a man of peace, he must turn this material over intact to the proper authorities of the Chinese people.

On the island of Negros, Ko knew nothing of the surrender. When he had been unable to locate Kamiko, he had joined another group. Now, a week later, they were suddenly attacked by a band of Filipino guerrillas. The leader of the Japanese group, a lieutenant, called for a fight to the end but the others, including Ko, wanted to surrender at once. A musician named Sen Tanabe was their spokesman. "Why on earth do we have to die this way? For Japan? The country we are supposed to defend is going to be defeated."

The lieutenant angrily raised his sword but Ko restrained him.

"Japan will surrender sooner or later," continued Tanabe. "I'm sure of it. My father, mother, and brothers and sisters will not be pleased if I die this useless way." He appealed to the lieutenant. "Who will reconstruct Japan after the surrender? The homeland will be burned to the ground and we young soldiers will have to rebuild her." Tanabe stood up, waved a white cloth. "I'm going down there, Lieutenant. Who will follow me?" He smiled at Ko. "Remember the song I taught my mother just before I left home?" As he started down the hill, he began singing, *"Tsu, tsu, rero, rero . . ."*

The lieutenant raised his rifle and fired. Tanabe spun around. He looked back at Ko, perplexed, before he died.

"You see," said the lieutenant, "we must never surrender. Never!" He told them of a small island nearby that was uninhabited. "Tonight we can find a few bancas and escape. We can hold out forever!"

How long is forever? thought Ko, but made no protest. He now had one goal in life, to survive and get back to Japan. His greatest regret was going home without Maeda.

In a suburb of Tokyo, Sen Tanabe's mother had just heard the Emperor at a station platform and was still in a state of shock. As she climbed down the steps to the street she saw just ahead a tall, slim soldier. He was singing, *"Tsu, tsu, rero, rero . . ."* She called, "Sen!" and gave chase but the crowd was too thick. She hurried to her temple and told the Buddhist priest what had happened.

"A phantom," he said. "And perhaps the phantom has come to help you."

She nodded. Tanabe must have died and his soul had come to bid her farewell.

Floss, Sumiko, and Emi Toda heard the Voice of the Crane at the waiting room of the Nagano Hospital. All of them silently rejoiced. A doctor in a soiled white gown came up to Floss. The operation on Masao, he said, had been successful.

"His arm?" she said.

The doctor lowered his voice sympathetically. "We could not save it." Floss fought to control herself. She thanked the doctor.

"He's still groggy but he wants to see you."

Masao was sitting up in bed. At the sight of the bandage around the stump of his left arm, Floss burst into tears. So did Emi and Sumiko.

Masao put his right arm around Floss, and looked up at his grandmother and Sumiko. "It doesn't hurt," he said.

An official and a guard were approaching his father's cell with good news. "You may go home now," the official said.

Tadashi, lying on his back on his cot, made a feeble effort to get up.
"We apologize for what we had to do," said the official.

Tadashi mumbled something but the official could not understand.
"He's talking in English," said the guard.

The official leaned down to hear better. "What does 'Floss' mean in English?"

It was the last word Tadashi spoke.

2.

In Washington, Frank McGlynn was lying awake in his bed mulling over a proposal that had come from the Administration. Would he accept a position in Japan as a political adviser to General MacArthur who would head the Occupation? His first reaction was resentment that his advice hadn't been sought earlier. Then he thought what a rare opportunity it would be to see history in the making, and perhaps exert some influence on the future of Japan. And it would give him a chance to be with Floss and the Todas. At the same time he had grown tired of bureaucracy and longed for the peace of Williamstown. He promised to think the matter over.

Training for *Operation Olympic,* the landing on Japan, had ceased and the rumor swept Saipan that the 2nd Division would be sent to Kyushu as occupation troops. Mark longed to see Will who was in some camp there. So much had happened since last they had met. Old Will must have gone through hell.

At the Saipan camp for civilians, Jun's cousin Hiroko had joined others to hear the special radio broadcast from Tokyo. They all listened in silence as their Emperor spoke. By now most of them felt it had been wrong to fight America. Hiroko thought, Oh, my native country has collapsed! And was moved to tears.

Treatment by the conquerors improved. The Japanese were given better food and allowed to take a bath in the sea once a week. Hiroko figured the Americans were trying to get them to forget their sorrow at such a humiliating defeat. She headed for the mountain to arrange the bodies of dead Japanese soldiers for burial. How pitiful the fate of these men compared to the American dead who had neat graves marked by neat crosses.

Maggie was in Manila where MacArthur's staff was preparing to receive a Japanese mission from Tokyo to arrange the surrender of their troops in the field. MacArthur's press officer assured Maggie she would be allowed to accompany the general on the trip to Japan, tentatively set for the end of the month. She had been in the Philippines for only a week but she had already made influential friends and was brimming with thoughts of the stories she would write in Japan. What an opportunity, to witness and report the first days of occupation! And at last she could see dear Floss. How much she must have suffered. And Will. He must be alive. He had always been a survivor. But would Mark get to Kyushu now that *Olympic* was no longer necessary?

Will and the other prisoners at the Tomachi dormitory had not been informed of the Emperor's speech of surrender. Those in fair condition like Will were kept busy helping civilians clear the rubble of the Urakami Valley. That day they walked, as usual, from their new quarters to the bay and took a ferry to Urakami station. They quit early and it was late afternoon when they took roll call at Tomachi. Just then came a clap of thunder. The Dutch officer in charge leaped headlong into a nearby pond. For a few moments Will and the others were in a state of panic. Was it another atomic bomb? A guard shouted it was only thunder and they all laughed to see the Dutchman crawling out of the pond dripping wet.

In the morning they again set out for Urakami but the following three days they were allowed to rest. The guards were still debating whether they should inform the prisoners of the surrender. Some, like Kitano, were for liberating them at once but the majority were shocked at such an idea. As no details had come from headquarters, they should carry on normally.

At Camp 13 the guards had disappeared. Popov found a Japanese rifle and set off for Omuta with Bliss. At the first village Popov caught sight of a mine overseer who had treated them harshly. The man started to run. Popov raised his rifle, shouting, *"Chotto matte!"* The man stopped in his tracks, eyes filled with fear. He came slowly toward Popov as a woman and three ragged children emerged from a nearby house.

"Why the hell am I doing this?" said Popov, lowering the rifle. "Is this your wife and kids?" The man nodded. "Do you live in that crummy house?"

"Hai!"

"Do you remember how mean you were to us in the mine?"

"Hai!"

"You can thank your wife and kids I don't shoot your head off."

The overseer bowed in thanks.

"Did you ever see such skinny kids?" said Bliss. "Don't you have enough rice to feed them?"

"Little food," said the man in English.

"Oh, hell," said Popov. "Let's go back to the warehouse and get them some rice." He turned to the overseer. "Wait here." As they walked back to camp Popov said, "I guess they didn't get much more to eat than we did. And I almost shot the bastard!"

On the afternoon of the nineteenth Will heard a droning. A guard shouted, "Air raid!" A plane was sighted coming in low. There were shouts of alarm as it dived on the dormitory area and dropped something black. A parachute burst open and landed nearby. The guards found it carried emergency supplies. The prison commander decided they would now have to tell the prisoners about the surrender and the three ranking Allied officers were summoned.

"The reason I asked you gentlemen to come here," said the prison commander, "is to tell you that Japan has been defeated in the war." The words had come out painfully. "I imagine you have had a very hard life until today. I think the Allies will come to get you people and it is my wish that you all stay at Tomachi Dormitory until that time."

The prisoners showed little emotion on hearing the news. Perhaps, thought Will, their long ordeal had made them apathetic and they could raise no enthusiasm although they did cheer at the announcement that henceforth there would be no work parties.

That night Will read portions of the Bible, one of the few books in English. What struck home most were two verses from the 90th Psalm:

> For all our days are passed away in thy wrath: we spend
> our years as a tale that is told. The days of our years are
> threescore years and ten; and if by reason of strength they
> be fourscore years, yet is their strength labor and sorrow;
> for it is soon cut off, and we fly away.

Almost four of his threescore years and ten had been spent in hell. How many of the men in the dormitory would even reach threescore after all their deprivations and diseases? He himself was beginning to feel vaguely sick and he wondered if it had anything to do with the bomb. He thought of Michiko and how her hair had come off like a wig. Was that only the beginning of her suffering? Would she die horribly like her little girl?

In the morning he went to Kitano and asked if it was possible to go to the village near Omura. The guard begged him to stay in the area. It might be dangerous to take such a trip. Some of the people might attack him because of the bombings. "Please wait a few more days."

Will was ashamed to find relief in such counsel. He could picture himself entering that farmhouse filled with Michiko's relatives who detested him. He blanched at the thought of the embarrassment.

3.

The die-hard spirit to resist capitulation did not end with the crushing of the Palace revolt. In a wave of self-destruction, ten young men calling themselves the Righteous Group for Upholding Imperial Rule and Driving Out Foreigners blew themselves up with grenades on Atago Hill within sight of the American embassy. Then eleven transport officers belonging to a Buddhist sect killed themselves outside the gates of the Imperial Palace, and fourteen students committed mass hara-kiri at the Yoyogi parade grounds.

There were sporadic attacks on communications centers. The NHK station at Kawaguchi was briefly occupied by a major and sixty-six soldiers, and some forty civilians, including ten women, after seizing the broadcasting station in Matsui attacked the post office, a power station, the local newspaper, and the government office for the prefecture.

There were also incidents of public misbehavior. Some began fleeing wildly in commandeered vehicles or on foot, their possessions strapped to their backs. Some made off with government gasoline stored in mountain depots. Order in many places collapsed, with people willing to do anything to survive. Such un-Japanese acts were set off by the announcement that the American forces would shortly occupy the country. Wild rumors spread panic: the Chinese, full of vengeance, were landing at Osaka; thousands of American soldiers were already raping and looting in Yokohama. Girls and family treasures were evacuated.

Newspapers ran columns of advice on how to get along with the
enemy troops. Women were told: "Don't go out at all in the evening.
Keep watches and valuables at home. When in danger of being raped,
show the most dignified attitude. Don't yield. Cry for help." Young
women should avoid provocative acts such as smoking or going without
sox. All girls should don the bulkiest *monpei* or cut their hair and
pretend to be boys. Some factories issued poison capsules for women
workers.

Prince Konoye, now deputy prime minister, was so concerned that he
ordered the head of the Metropolitan Police to protect the chastity of
the Japanese women. "Under the peaceful occupation," he said, "lives
of the Japanese people are guaranteed. But we do not know what sex-
hungry American soldiers, after their long stay in battlefields, will do to
Japanese women."

The police chief summoned leaders of business associations from the
entertainment districts. They were told, "We must build breakwaters to
keep Japanese women from anticipated sexual attacks by the Occupation forces. You must recruit prostitutes, both licensed and unlicensed,
geishas, bar girls and waitresses to set up facilities to entertain the U.S.
soldiers with sexual services." The government, said the chief, would
provide fifty million yen for the facilities and the Metropolitan Police
would not only supply the recruiters but support their activities. Thus
was born the RAA, the Recreation and Amusement Association. And a
large signboard was placed outside its headquarters: "Attention to new
women of Japan! New women required for recreation projects for the
Occupation forces. An emergency establishment set up by the government to cope with the postwar situation. You must have spirit of positive
cooperation."

At 2 P.M. on August 30 a silver C-54 transport named *Bataan* approached Atsugi air base near Yokohama. Aboard, General Douglas
MacArthur was discussing the fate of Japan with his military secretary,
Brigadier General Bonner Fellers, who had often visited Japan. "It's
very simple," said MacArthur with supreme confidence. "We'll use the
instrumentality of the Japanese government to implement the Occupation." He was, for instance, going to give Japanese women the right to
vote.

Maggie would have been delighted but she was sitting too far back to
hear a word.

"The Japanese men won't like it," said Fellers.

"I don't care. I want to discredit the military. Women don't want war."

The plane landed and at exactly 2:19 P.M. MacArthur, long-bowled corncob pipe tightly clenched between his teeth, paused at the top of the ladder. "This is the payoff," he said. He lighted his pipe and descended. Maggie pushed forward and so was close at hand when MacArthur was greeted by General Robert Eichelberger. As they shook hands MacArthur grinned broadly. "Bob, from Melbourne to Tokyo is a long way, but this seems to be the end of the road."

Jun Kato, who had come in a company truck with several other reporters to cover the story, watched the ceremonies from afar. He was mightily impressed. These were the first Americans he had seen for five years. While eager to get the story, he was apprehensive lest anyone discover he had been born in the United States.

A line of dilapidated cars was waiting to take the MacArthur group to temporary headquarters in Yokohama. At the head was a red fire engine which lunged forward with a startling explosion, and the motorcade began crawling noisily on its fifteen-mile trip to Yokohama. Several cars behind MacArthur, Maggie thrilled to see the entire length of the road lined with thousands of Japanese soldiers. They stood on guard, backs to MacArthur as if, she thought, he were the Emperor himself.

Excited and apprehensive, Jun watched the cavalcade leave. An American journalist approached.

"Is the Imperial Hotel still okay or not?" asked Russell Brines, the Associated Press correspondent.

Jun was the only one of the reporters who could speak English. "Yes, sir," he said. "It was hardly hit at all."

"Take me down there, will you?"

After hopping into the truck Brines passed out Lucky Strike cigarettes. Jun took a deep puff. He could hardly remember what a real cigarette tasted like. His head swam and he almost fainted. Delicious!

September 2 dawned cool and gray. Maggie wondered whether this was a bad omen, for today the formal surrender ceremonies were to take place on the battleship *Missouri* in Tokyo Bay. Along with correspondents from all over the world, she boarded a destroyer and at about 7:30 climbed aboard the big battleship which had been christened by President Truman's daughter. Maggie thought of the long road from Pearl Harbor and her own part in the savage war in the Pacific. She wished both Mark and Will could be present; also her father, who had often warned the family that an unnecessary and cruel war with Japan was inevitable because of the blindness of both nations. She smiled to think how he would fume to see the rows of faces on the battleship as joyous as if confidently celebrating the beginning of a brave new world. She was sure he would tell them in a few thousand words how naïve such hopes were. And her own excitement was suddenly embittered by memories of dear Mac who had died so uselessly on an island no one would ever remember except for Ernie Pyle.

She watched as destroyers pulled alongside to discharge a brilliant array of Allied generals and admirals. Then at 8:05 she recognized Admiral Nimitz coming spryly aboard and had to keep from winking at him when he gave her a brief smile of recognition. He must have remembered their trip to the Big Island where they had come to bestow medals on the 2nd Marine Division for Tarawa.

Another destroyer was approaching. It was the *Lansdowne*, named after the commander of the dirigible *Shenandoah*, and it carried the twelve Japanese delegates. She was one of the few onlookers who felt sympathy for their leader, Mamoru Shigemitsu, who had replaced Togo as foreign minister when the entire cabinet resigned. He was limping, for his new artificial limb obviously caused him excruciating pain. Maggie remembered meeting him years ago before his left leg had been blown off by an assassin's bomb. How pained her father would be to see a man he admired so much for his progressive ideas forced to endure such ignominy.

Several of the correspondents near Maggie were watching Shigemitsu's painful progress with such savage satisfaction that she wanted to punch them. And she was so proud of the courageous old man when he shook off an American naval officer's thoughtful offer of assistance. He mounted the ladder leading to the ceremony deck, his face a mask.

There followed the invocation by a chaplain and a recording of "The Star-Spangled Banner" that drove shivers up her back. MacArthur, followed by Admirals Halsey and Nimitz, briskly walked to a table covered with documents. "We are gathered here," he said in his dramatic manner, "representatives of the major warring powers to conclude a solemn agreement whereby peace may be restored." As he continued, Maggie could feel the mass emotion of the convocation. Each, she guessed, was thinking of his own part in the tragic war as well as that of his country.

MacArthur's final words would have pleased her father. "It is my earnest hope—indeed the hope of all mankind—that from this solemn occasion a better world shall emerge out of the blood and carnage of the past, a world founded upon faith and understanding, a world dedicated to the dignity of man and the fulfillment of the most cherished wish for freedom, tolerance and justice."

She closed her eyes as she briefly prayed that the fine words would beget fine deeds. Just then the clouds parted and Mount Fuji appeared, sparkling in the sun. How appropriate, she thought—and then was disgusted to see a drunken Allied delegate making faces at the Japanese. Thank God, it was not an American. Shigemitsu stonily stared down the drunk; his face still a mask, he slowly, deliberately put on his top hat. The other Japanese civilians followed suit. How delighted Papa would be to see such an exhibition of Japanese subtlety.

MacArthur uttered a few final words. "Let us pray that peace now be restored to the world and that God will preserve it always. These procedings are now closed." He walked over to Halsey, put an arm around his shoulder to say, so Maggie later learned, "Bill, where in the hell are those airplanes?" Then there was a rumble in the distance and hundreds of carrier planes and B-29's began sweeping over the *Missouri.* It was an inspiring exclamation point to the proceedings.

Maggie spent the next day trying to find out what had happened at Hiroshima and Nagasaki and finally wired her publisher that she was making a trip to the latter, "the forgotten atomic city."

The long train ride was an incredible adventure. Passengers were packed on the roofs of many of the cars. There were interminable stops. At some stations groups of unarmed Japanese soldiers obeyed the orders of their officers who had been stripped of their braid but still retained their swords. In other stations enlisted men shouted insults at their superiors.

It was September 7 by the time she gazed in horror out the window at the incredible heap of rubble that used to be the Urakami Valley. It seemed that only smokestacks remained of most of the big buildings. An Australian correspondent joined her at the window. He was aghast. He had come to Nagasaki, he said, to visit a camp of Australian and Dutch prisoners of war. The Australian could speak no Japanese but Maggie learned that the prisoners had been transferred. She decided there was a story in it and managed to get them a ride in an ancient truck to Tomachi Dormitory.

"Are there any Americans here?" was her first question.

An Australian said all Yanks had been shipped out months ago but a Dutch officer revealed there was one American captain. Moments later she was hugging an astounded Will. She was shocked to find him as thin as a skeleton. His face was gaunt, his skin pallid. "Will, Will!" she exclaimed, clasping him tightly.

Finally he held her at arm's length. "You've changed so much!" he said. He touched the scar on her neck gently.

"A kamikaze hit the hospital ship I was on," she said offhandedly. She was concerned by what she had seen of the ravaged city, but he was only hungry for news of Mark and Floss. As Maggie started to tell him, she was besieged by other prisoners who wanted to know what was going on. They'd only been told there was a surrender but the guards were still armed and insisted they stay in the area.

"Our planes have dropped food and supplies," explained Will. "Three Red Cross men were just here, two Swiss and a Swede, I think. They promised to get help here soon."

The Australian correspondent was surrounded by his countrymen. The Yanks, he said, were lengthening the runway at a city in the southern end of Kyushu. "I think you can get a flight to Okinawa from there."

It was an hour before Will and Maggie could find a quiet place at one end of the dormitory to talk about the family. Then she expressed her horror at the destruction of Nagasaki and listened, in shock, at his brief recital of what had happened to him after the *pika* flash. She could get even better information for her story, he said, from the guards and other prisoners. He introduced her to Kitano who told about the trip up the hill and down again. She was fascinated by the rescue of civilians by the prisoners and made copious notes. At dusk Kitano suggested she stay at the home of his sister who lived across the bay.

In the next three days Kitano and Will showed her around the devastated Urakami Valley where the stink of death still lingered. She was sickened by the desolation. Only then did Will tell her about his trip to Michiko's village.

"I promised to go back and see them," he said and suggested she go along. Kitano could arrange it.

They met Kitano as he was leaving an emergency meeting called by the camp commander who ordered the prisoners to be assembled. "We have just been ordered to hand over all arms and ammunition to you prisoners," Kitano told them. Other camps had been given this order immediately after the signing of the surrender papers but because of the atom bomb and Nagasaki's isolation, there had been this delay. "We have also been ordered to leave. You are on your own now and can go where you please."

"What is the best way to get to a village on the other side of Omura?" Will asked Kitano.

They could take the train, he said, but suggested they borrow the charcoal-burner-fueled Toyota used by the guards; train schedules were too erratic. As Will and Maggie headed north past the Urakami Valley, he told about Michiko's trek through the hills with bare feet, the death of her daughter, and the miraculous recovery of Hajime. Upon hearing how Michiko's hair had come off, Maggie gasped audibly. She could read between the lines and wondered how serious Will was about the woman. Before, he had always managed to keep from any serious romantic involvement, but he was clearly changed by his wartime experiences.

It was early afternoon by the time they drove up the steep hill to the large farmhouse. As they got out of the car, Will pointed across the bay where Nagasaki lay behind hills. It was a beautiful sight, for today there was no sign of war. He knocked at the door and was admitted by Michiko's mother. She bowed several times, led them inside. A crowd of women, relatives and neighbors, surrounded Michiko who was lying on a *futon*.

Harpies! Will thought. These same relatives who had heaped scorn on him before now bowed and scraped in apology. Two hurried into the kitchen to make tea while others brought pillows for Maggie and Will. He kneeled beside Michiko who smiled weakly at him. He held her hand and she squeezed his. Then she had to rinse her mouth. Her infected gums bled. There were purple spots on her skin and festering sores on her neck. The towel around her head slipped off and Maggie could barely restrain tears at the sight of her bald head.

"They are coming to take her to the hospital," said Michiko's mother as she wiped her daughter's sweating forehead with a damp cloth. "She won't eat a thing and sometimes is delirious."

"I brought someone to meet you," said Will, motioning Maggie to approach.

Maggie, moved by Michiko's stoicism, kneeled down. "I am Will's sister," she said in Japanese. This caused an audible stir among the women.

Will wished he could drive all of them out with a broom so he could have privacy. He had so much to say and how could he speak in front of these strangers? He gritted his teeth and tried to ignore the staring women.

"I'll be going home soon," he said. "Please let me know how you and

Hajime are getting along. If there is ever anything I can do let me know."

He wrote down his Williamstown address, then took her hand. "Sayonara."

She lowered her head.

On the way back to Nagasaki, Will and Maggie spoke little. As they neared the city, Maggie noticed his eyes were troubled and hoped he wasn't thinking of returning to the village to make some noble gesture he'd later regret. Maggie admired Michiko but knew she and Will had little in common except suffering.

As they approached the shipyard, Will was startled to see American vessels in the harbor. There was a large tanker which looked as if it had been converted into a carrier, several Liberty ships, and a white hospital ship. Thank God, help had come at last.

When Maggie returned to Tomachi Dormitory the next morning she found her brother deathly sick. Fearing it was from the radiation, she suggested he board the hospital ship for treatment. Despite his protests, Maggie and Kitano helped him into the Toyota, and they drove to the other side of the bay where tents and sheds had been erected on Dejima pier. Will was registered and disinfected. Then a corpsman helped him shower in hot and cold water and don new clothing. Only then did Will realize he was being sent on the first leg of the journey home.

"But I must see Michiko again," he protested. "I don't feel right leaving so abruptly."

"I'll see her and explain," said Maggie.

"You must tell her I want to do something for her and Hajime."

She promised and then the corpsman brought him into a room for a thorough physical examination. An Australian ahead of Will was being asked questions about his diet the past few months. When he tried to tell what he'd eaten since his capture, the doctor broke in impatiently. "I'm not interested in any war stories. Just give me facts. No one could have survived with what you say you were given to eat."

"Well, *I did*, dammit, and so did all these other fellows. You had better not sit over there like God and tell us we're liars or we'll beat your bloody head in."

The doctor bristled. "I'm an American officer, corporal, and that kind of talk can get you court-martialed!"

The Australian laughed bitterly. "What the hell can you or your whole damned army do that hasn't been done to me by the Japs the last four years?"

"Get him out of here," said the doctor and examined Will.

After receiving new clothing, a Bible, tobacco, towels, and soap, he and a score of other prisoners were taken by landing craft to the white ship. A loudspeaker was playing, "Don't Sit Under the Apple Tree with Anyone Else But Me." Will never could remember how he got into bed but upon waking he felt the movement of the ship. And he heard someone say, "Okinawa, here we come!"

4.

The 2nd Marine Division was on its way to Nagasaki. As usual there was no air conditioning on Mark's transport and the air in the holds was hot, humid, and foul. Fortunately there was a refrigerated water fountain in his area since he was in officers' country; when he noticed two enlisted men hurriedly sneaking water for their canteens, he walked by without comment.

He wondered what faced them in Nagasaki. They were combat-loaded, prepared for any kind of reception. If this had been a victorious Jap transport bound for San Francisco which had recently been ravaged by an atom bomb, he knew how they would have been treated by the conquered Americans. He couldn't sleep that night for worrying about Will. Had he made it?

His brother was impatiently waiting with the other Nagasaki prisoners in Okinawa for a plane to the Philippines. What the hell was holding them up? There was nothing to do but eat, wait, and gripe. The other prisoners had perked up at the sight of the Red Cross girls, but Will's mind was on Michiko. Was she still in the hospital or had it been too late?

Will was examined by another doctor who assured him he was not suffering from any radiation, only exhaustion and malnutrition. When he reached the West Coast he'd be sent to Letterman General Hospital. "They'll fatten you up." The next morning the former prisoners were bused to the airfield. Spirits rose and Will caught the excitement of his comrades. At last they were really on the way home!

Bliss and Popov were just taking off from Kyushu in a B-24 bomber. Popov had asked the pilot to fly over Camp 13 so he could drop a dirty sock. He shouted in glee when the plane skimmed over their old camp. The B-24 headed across the bay, swooping down on Nagasaki for the benefit of the passengers. The unbelievable destruction sickened Bliss. They were so low he could clearly see women and children. What the hell were they doing there? Where could they live? He watched in wonder as a little girl disappeared down a hole under a corrugated sheet of metal.

On the long flight to the Philippines Will was haunted by the memories of the hell trip from Manila to Moji. How could he ever forget the ghastly scene in the hold of the first ship where thirst and heat had driven men to sucking their mates' blood? Or the courage of those who went against human nature to help others survive? No one who got out of there alive would ever forget Father Bill Cummings, inspiring, haranguing, and persuading the men to keep up their courage and live.

At last there was Mount Arayat, a signpost that he could never forget. Moments later Clark Field hove into sight. And now his thoughts were for other comrades in the islands—gallant Socorro and the inimitable Cushing. Had they lived to greet MacArthur? He smiled, remembering Jim's curses aimed at the great general who had busted him to private. Was he still a private or had all been forgiven in the jubilation of victory? It would be many months before Will learned that Colonel Cushing, restored to MacArthur's good graces thanks to General Whitney, had also been awarded a substantial cash bonus for his contributions to victory.

Will's first request on landing at Clark was to make a call to his father. The insistent ringing roused his housekeeper, Mrs. Quimby, from bed and she was so flustered to hear Will's voice that it took a minute to comprehend he was calling from the Philippines. Then she spent another minute in wonder at such a miracle of communication. Finally he got the telephone number of his father's apartment in Washington. Frank McGlynn's "hello" was alert, for he had been unable to sleep. Upon hearing Will's voice he could only repeat his name several times. Huskily he finally asked whether he was all right. Will himself was so moved that he could only say, "Yes, Dad!"

"When will you be back?" asked McGlynn.

"They think a C-54 is leaving for Travis in the morning. I should be there in three or four days if I'm lucky." He was going to a general hospital to recuperate.

"I'll come out and see you," said McGlynn and revealed that he had just accepted a position as one of MacArthur's advisers. "But I won't be leaving for at least a month. Do you have any plans for the immediate future?"

"I don't know, Dad." He laughed nervously. "It's still hard to believe I'm free."

"Old Adams at Adams and Snow of Boston has been pestering me for information about you. Isn't that the outfit that you turned down to join Marshall's staff?"

"Yes, Dad." It was the best law firm in New England and it made him feel good that they apparently still wanted him.

5.

As soon as they neared the coast of Japan Mark could feel a pleasant balmy breath of air. Then the tiny offshore islands peered through the lifting fog and soon were silhouetted against the sky. A sense of excitement mixed with apprehension swept the ship. At last Mark sighted the entrance to Nagasaki Bay. The sea was calm with small whitecaps stirred by a slight breeze. He could see floating objects and to his horror realized they were swollen corpses, spread-eagled, bellies distended with gas, and colored like jack-o'-lanterns. On the right rose the fabled city which he had seen as a youngster. It reminded him somewhat of San Francisco and he thought he could see Glover House where Cio-cio-san, babe in arms, waited on the veranda for that miserable Pinkerton. There were no Pinkertons returning to betray women, he thought, but plenty of Marines ready to repopulate the ravaged city. He could see no real damage. The bomb must have hit farther up the river.

A Japanese pilot was guiding them past floating mines while expert marksmen shot at their horns to explode them. On a dock Mark saw a group of nuns waving handkerchiefs. The Marines returned the greeting and there was a sense of relief. It looked as if they would land without a single casualty. Their ship headed cautiously for the opposite side of the bay toward a complex of large buildings. Someone said it was the Mitsubishi Shipyard. They were to bunk in a warehouse.

The next day Mark and Tullio jeeped through the Urakami Valley. They couldn't believe their eyes. How could a single bomb have caused such complete destruction? The center was reduced to dust and rubble. Farther out Mark could see only parts of buildings with the sides torn off and the frameworks leaning away from the center of the area. Here and there he made out a curious spot that looked like white ash or soda.

"All that's left of some poor devil," said Tullio.

"Makes you feel guilty for being alive," said Mark. "The best ones died."

Tullio nodded. "Like old Moon. I feel somehow as if I let him and the others down."

"So do I. The only medals belong to the dead."

On their tour of the Urakami Valley the following day Mark was relieved to find signs being erected: "KEEP OUT"; "RADIOACTIVE"; "DANGER" in both English and Japanese. On his return to the shipyard, he could see Tullio gabbing with a woman correspondent. They both waved and the woman ran so recklessly toward the jeep that she was almost knocked over in her enthusiasm. It was Maggie. She practically pulled him out of the jeep so she could embrace him. Then she spilled out information so fast he couldn't understand half of what was said.

"Calm down," he said, embarrassed to be the object of numerous envious eyes. Marines crowded around as if it were a show.

"Break it up," said Tullio, clearing away the curious.

Two days later Mark and Maggie headed toward Omura in the regimental jeep. They found Michiko at home. She was wan, exhausted, but the blisters had disappeared and she no longer had a fever. Mark was an instant hero to Hajime, who was allowed to crawl all over the jeep and examine his side arms. He had brought a large supply of food, including candy bars which made Hajime's eyes bulge. The two brought the supplies into the kitchen while in the main room Maggie was explaining in Japanese to Michiko that Will had returned to America to get treatment for possible radiation effects.

"He was very concerned about you and Hajime. He wants to do what he can for you both."

"Thank you," Michiko said, looking up at Maggie. After a pause, she added slowly, "Will-san was very kind to me. We would not have been able to make it here to my parents' house without his help." Her eyes slowly shifted to Mark and looked away into emptiness. "Will-san is an American but went through a lot of suffering . . . even the atomic bomb . . ."

What had happened to her was just as surprising as it had been unexpected for Will. She had been told how terrible the barbaric American and British soldiers were, and that she was to kill at least one enemy before dying.

The enemy had turned out to be totally different from what she had been told. This big American stranger who helped her during the nightmare of Nagasaki had shown her a gentleness and kindness she had never known before. And it wasn't strange at all that she responded when he kissed her and embraced her with such tenderness. She now felt the warm feeling of gratitude as well as something else—a desire to abandon herself for the real man she had come to trust. This man lifted her spirit in her distress and comforted her in the hour of grief when the world had seemed to come to an end.

It was hard to her to grasp the meaning of all that happened with so much death and destruction all around her. She was probably still in a state of shock, yet there was an undeniable feeling of longing for Will. But now she had to get well, take care of Hajime and think of a future without Will. The presence of Maggie and Mark also brought her down to reality.

"Please tell Will-san that I am all right now. I was lucky I could come to my parents'. Many people had no other place to go. I shall never forget how kind he was. I pray he will get well soon."

Maggie was moved to tears. On their way back she couldn't help feeling guilty as an American for what had been done to so many innocent people. Human beings shouldn't be subjected to such cruelty, ever! That night she lay in bed thinking about Michiko, lovely in so many ways, and what her future would be. Mark was also thinking of Michiko. He too felt sympathy but was relieved that Will was on his way home.

"I've finished my research," Maggie told Mark in the morning. "Why don't you go back to Tokyo with me and see Floss and the Todas?" She had found the Toda home empty. They had evacuated to the country but were expected back soon.

Mark was already planning such a trip and, with Tullio's help, got ten days' leave. They went by train, a trip he would never forget, passing city after city flattened from one end to another by ordinary bombs. They were heaps of ashes like bonfires that had burned themselves completely out. Here and there he could see a lone figure searching for something of value.

He marveled that the railroads were in such good condition with rails and rights-of-way intact. Upon reaching Honshu they changed to a train that was already packed with Japanese soldiers and civilians who not only made way for them but offered seats. Maggie sat but Mark stood all the way to Tokyo, much to the bewilderment of the Japanese.

Teenage boys finally got up their courage to talk to Mark and once he replied politely, he was deluged. One wanted to know the cost of taking an electrical engineering course in the United States. Another wondered if he knew his brother who was in the U.S. Army. Others wanted to try out their English but not one asked for a cigarette, food, or money.

Because of Maggie's credentials, they had no trouble getting rooms at the Imperial Hotel. After unpacking, she took him across the street to the Domei News Agency building at the edge of Hibiya Park. She led the way to the large room which corresponded to the city room of an American newspaper. It was an old story to Maggie but Mark was impressed by the hectic sight of a crowd of reporters working on stories, talking on phones, and handing copy to messengers.

After making arrangements for office space to write her article, Maggie requested and was granted transportation as if she were Walter Lippmann. It took the twins an hour to get to the Todas' because of the detours necessitated by bomb damage. Floss rushed to them, trying to hug both simultaneously. She was momentarily unable to speak, then spilled out the tragic news about Tadashi and their daughter.

Emi brought out the baby, who had survived. "We call her Maggie," she said.

While Maggie was admiring her namesake, Masao came in. At sight of his bandaged stump Maggie had to restrain a gasp, and when Floss told how it had happened Mark felt a strange guilt.

"I saved Chicken B," said Masao proudly. He was fascinated by Mark's ribbons and automatic, and when his uncle extended a package of gum Masao didn't know what to do with it. Mark demonstrated and Masao imitated him enthusiastically.

Floss had been so taken aback by the great change in him that at first he seemed like a stranger. But this was the Mark she knew. "You're still a good-for-nothing bindle stiff," she said fondly, and scolded him for corrupting her son. She was hungry for news of the family.

"Will's gone through hell," said Maggie and told briefly of Nagasaki.

It was hard for Floss to believe he had managed to survive such hardships.

"You would be proud of him," said Maggie, then told of Mark's exploits and how he had saved many Japanese in caves.

Floss kissed him. "That doesn't surprise me at all. But I don't see how you ever behaved yourself enough to become an officer."

Maggie asked where the other Todas were. Sumiko was taking care of a sick neighbor. Shogo had just been arrested by the Allies. "We're afraid he's going to be tried for war crimes," said Emi, explaining that he had been on the staff of the notorious Colonel Tsuji, a born survivor who, upon hearing the words of the Emperor, had felt "as if my very bowels were being torn into shreds," and was now underground in a Burmese jungle working in secret "for the reconstruction of Japan."

There was distress in Emi's voice when she told about Ko being sent to Leyte. She looked questioningly toward Mark.

"I wasn't there," he said. But he had heard of the heavy Japanese casualties and didn't want to give her too much hope.

Sumiko came into the room, wearing a *monpei*. At the sight of an American soldier she became breathless and stared at everyone in amazement.

"Sumiko," said Emi, "This is Floss's Marine brother." Sumiko felt flustered and bowed shyly, then smiled. Mark thought, So this is little Sumiko! Almost grown up, and pretty.

On their way back to the Domei Building Maggie asked Mark what his immediate plans were. "You've certainly got enough points to get out of the Marines."

"I haven't made up my mind yet. If I just took off it would be like leaving the scene of a bad accident." He craned his neck at the vast expanse of damage. "Some of the language people are staying on until next spring with the Navy Technical Mission or the U.S. Strategic Bombing Survey. Could be interesting. What about you?"

"The big story is over here," she said and explained that her boss wanted her to cover the Occupation until something broke in Europe. She asked him to wait while she filed a story at Domei but he insisted on taking a walk before returning to the hotel.

He wandered through the Marunouchi business district and finally crossed over to the outer gardens of the Imperial Palace. He was drawn to the Nijubashi Bridge, symbol of the Emperor. Several civilian men were bowing and a Japanese captain stood at attention reading aloud from a prayer scroll. "I offer my deep apology to His Majesty and the nation for losing the war."

Mark wandered back toward Yurakucho station. What curious people the Japanese were. Throughout his long walk Japanese soldiers and officers had bowed to him. He wished they weren't so damned subservient. No, the Japanese were not really subservient. The soldiers who had bowed did so, he realized, in acknowledgment that their nation had been defeated in battle. It was very proper to accept defeat without ado.

As he came back to the stately Daiichi Seimei Building, MacArthur's new headquarters, he noticed an old man, his back loaded with a towering bundle of kindling. He was bowing to MacArthur's standard. Then he turned and bowed equally low to the Imperial Palace. An American major grinned at Mark. "The inscrutable oriental!" he said with amusement.

Mark said nothing. The major was a "smooth bar," with no stars on his campaign ribbons, which meant he had never been in battle. The major was really the inscrutable one. The old man was merely acknowledging without reservation the temporal power of today's *shogun* while revering what was eternal across the avenue. Mark thought of the letter from Billy J. which had finally caught up to him. Written on V-J Day, it had started with one of his favorite phrases: "All that remains is to tidy up the battlefield which will take years." That, concluded Mark, was the answer. He would help tidy up the battlefield. He would stay in Japan with the Marines.

On a transport plane bound for San Francisco, his brother was also pondering his future. Was he ready yet to accept the tempting offer of Adams and Snow? He was not the Will McGlynn who had left Washington in 1941 any more than Maggie was the same Maggie or Mark the same Mark. God knows what Floss had undergone but she would probably keep her own steady character. And the professor was also a known and steadfast equation.

Despite Major Watanabe's words at Camp 13, Will had carried his bitter hatred of Japanese to Camp 14. His experiences in Nagasaki had burned out this hatred. Watanabe was right. Both sides were at fault. And his hatred would eventually have destroyed him. But he could never forget the past or even fully forgive those who had dealt cruelty to him and his comrades.

He heard someone say, "Hey, there's the Golden Gate!"

In the distance stretched the magnificent bridge. Now he could see a city of peace and order with no sign of destruction. At last he felt truly free. His incredible ordeal was over and, though he still felt confused

592

and somewhat dazed, he realized that life would go on—even if nothing would ever be simple again. But tonight he would experience the exquisite ecstasy of cool, clean sheets, and tomorrow return to the good things he had dreamed about in prison camps . . . and feared he would never see again.

He was home.

(The saga of the McGlynns and the Todas will be continued in *Occupation.*)

Sources and Notes

Gods of War is based on numerous interviews conducted for *But Not in Shame* in 1959–60, for *The Rising Sun* in 1966–67, and specifically for this book in 1980–83. Information on the 1st Battalion, 6th Marines was collected by Lieutenant General William K. Jones and First Sergeant Lewis J. Michelony, Jr. Material on the prisoners of war came from numerous documents at the National Archives, books (notably *Death March* by Donald Knox and *Give Us This Day* by Sidney Stewart), and interviews with members of the Survivors of Bataan and Corregidor, including Charles Balaza, Manny Lawton, Wayne Carringer, and Tony Bilek. Of the numerous Japanese who contributed, I am particularly indebted to Katsuhiko Ohtake, Tetsuo Shinjo, and my wife, Toshiko. I am also grateful to Archbishop John J. O'Connor, Monsignor Joseph Gallagher, and Father Robert Emmett Sheridan for not only helping me understand the role of chaplains in battle but advising me on the process of conversion.

Among those Marines who contributed their experiences are:

1st Battalion, 6th Marines (rank as of 1944)

George Arms, Private First Class. A Co.
George Azud, First Lieutenant. Hq. Co.
Froman Barrett, Corporal. D Co.
Bernard F. Berger, Sergeant. A Co.
Thomas R. Bormann, Platoon Sergeant. Hq. Co.
William J. Brown, Corporal. A Co.
Joseph Cado, Gunnery Sergeant. A Co.
B. E. Campbell, Corporal. A Co.
Clyde F. Carrington, Gunnery Sergeant. Hq. Co.
William Cheney, Sergeant Major. Hq. Co.
Peter Costello, Sergeant. A Co.
Kenneth Crone, First Lieutenant. A Co.
Raymond Dabler, Corporal. Hq. Co.

Pancho Dela Cruz, Corporal. C Co.
James A. Donovan, Major. Battalion Executive Officer
Robert Dyer, Platoon Sergeant. Hq. Co.
Jet Fore, Corporal. A Co.
Merrill Frescola, First Lieutenant. A Co.
Norman P. Haber, Corporal. Hq. Co.
James Hale, Sergeant. Hq. Co.
Leo Halverson, Sergeant. Hq. Co.
A. D. Duayne Henss, Sergeant. Hq. Co.
William T. Homer, Gunnery Sergeant. D Co.
John E. Hough, Corporal. D Co.
Marcie James (widow of Platoon Sergeant George James, C Co.)
William Jeffries, Corporal. A Co.
Herbert E. Johnson, Sergeant. A Co.
James C. Johnson, Sergeant. A Co.
William K. Jones, Lieutenant Colonel. Battalion C.O.
Paul Kennedy, Private First Class. D Co.
Baines Kerr, First Lieutenant. A Co.
Ervine E. La Plante, First Sergeant. D Co.
P. F. Lake, First Lieutenant. C Co.
Howard M. Leggett, First Lieutenant. Hq. Co.
Madge Lyons (widow of Howard Lyons, Battalion Sergeant Major)
John Martini, Sergeant. A Co.
Ellis McGee, Platoon Sergeant. A Co.
Lewis J. Michelony, First Sergeant. Hq. Co.
W. D. Miears, First Lieutenant. Hq. Co.
Francis Modde, Platoon Sergeant. A Co.
Paul Moore, Corporal. Hq. Co.
James Richardson, Platoon Sergeant. A Co.
Charlton B. Rogers, Captain. Hq. Co.
Frank Roh, Sergeant. B Co.
Harold Rusk, First Sergeant. A Co.
Samuel P. Shaw, First Lieutenant. A Co.
Lyle E. Specht, First Lieutenant. D Co.
R. J. Vroegindewey, First Lieutenant. Hq. Co.
W. L. Wallace, Chief Pharmacist's Mate USN. Hq. Co.
E. L. Walsh, First Lieutenant, JASCO Detachment.
William Wilson, Private First Class. A Co.
Albert Woods, First Lieutenant. A Co.

Others

Father Joseph Gallagher, Lieutenant, USN. Hq. Co., 6th Marines.
Loren E. Haffner, Lieutenant Colonel. Operations Officer, 6th Marines.

Chapter Nine. The experiences of Third Lieutenant Mateo Domingo are based on those of Third Lieutenant Antonio Aquino, older brother of Benigno Aquino, former Vice-President of the Philippines.

Material on Father William Cummings in this and following chapters comes from the files of the Maryknoll Library, from Father Robert Sheridan, Lieutenant Hattie Brantley, and *Give Us This Day* by Sidhey Stewart.

Chapter Nine. The half-million-dollar payment to General MacArthur is confirmed by documents released under the Freedom of Information Act to the National Archives. After General Marshall received the radiogram from MacArthur telling of President Quezon's desire to give MacArthur and three of his subordinates $640,000, the Army Chief of Staff passed on this information to President Roosevelt. On February 15, 1942, Marshall then sent this memorandum to the Adjutant General: "The Secretary of War directs that the attached radiogram from General MacArthur be paraphrased and sent to the Chase National Bank of New York City. The letter to the bank should indicate that the report of execution is desired and inform them that such report will be forwarded by the War Department when submitted by them. The letter should be authenticated in such a manner as to require no further verification by the Chase National Bank. This action should be expedited." It was signed G. C. Marshall.

Chapter Sixteen. The story of the guerrillas of Cebu comes from interviews with James Cushing, Admiral Fukudome, and Jess Villamor, author of *They Never Surrendered; Tabunan,* a history of the Cebu guerrillas by Colonel Manuel F. Segura; the recollections of Father Robert Sheridan; and research by Aurelio Repato, my guide in the Philippines in 1960.

Regarding the rejection by General Marshall of the report from Chennault on how to fight the Zeros, this story was told me by General Emmett "Rosie" O'Donnell in 1959. I referred to the incident in *But Not in Shame* without revealing Marshall's name. I had promised not to reveal his identity until after the deaths of both Marshall and O'Donnell.

Chapter Twenty. The experiences of Hiroko Sato are based on those of Shizuko Sugano, author of *The End at Saipan.*

Chapter Twenty-two. The battle scenes on Leyte come from interviews with Kiyoshi Kamiko, author of *I Didn't Die on Leyte.*

Chapter Twenty-four. The chronicle of the black uprising on Guam is corroborated by the official records of the Court of Inquiry, which concluded that there was no evidence of organized racial prejudice and recommended that more than forty black sailors be tried by general court-martial for unlawful assembly and rioting. It also recommended that several white Marines also be court-martialed for harassing blacks. It further recommended that two Naval Supply Depot officers be reprimanded for negligence. More serious judgments were leveled against the three black sailors accused of stealing weapons from the Naval Supply Depot, and four others for buying or possession of the stolen weapons.

The fates of the white man who had killed the black sailor and the black sentry who had killed a white Marine were decided by general court-martial. In his court-martial the white was convicted of voluntary manslaughter and sentenced to confinement for five years and a bad-conduct discharge. The confinement was reduced to three years and further reduced to eighteen months and probation for eighteen months as to the remainder of the confinement if his conduct during the confinement was satisfactory. The black was convicted of voluntary manslaughter and sentenced to confinement for three years. "No mitigating action" (according to a "Memorandum for the Judge Advocate General," July 14, 1945) appears to have been taken in the case of the black.

Chapter Twenty-six. Maggie's exploits on Iwo Jima and later on Okinawa are based on those of Dickey Chapelle, author of *What's a Woman Doing Here?* After I told her of my intent to write a novel someday in which a leading character would be inspired by her deeds she said, "Be sure and mention my book." A few days later she left for Vietnam where she was killed in action.

Mark's trips into caves are based on the actions of Major Don Redlin, nicknamed "The Incredible Redhead." He was decorated for his hero-ism.

Chapter Thirty. The experiences of the Japanese guard, Kitano, are similar to those of Jidayu Tajima, author of *Renga no Kabe (Brick Walls)*.

THE
SNOWBLIND
MOON
JOHN BYRNE COOKE

"An epic canvas created with sure, masterful strokes. Bravo!"
—John Jakes

"*The Snowblind Moon* is an intensely readable story."
—The Washington Post

"An epic tale . . . lyrically beautiful."
—Los Angeles Times Book Review

☐ 58150-4   PART ONE: BETWEEN THE WORLDS $3.95
    58151-2   Canada $4.95

☐ 58152-0   PART TWO: THE PIPE CARRIERS $3.95
    58153-9   Canada $4.95

☐ 58154-7   PART THREE: HOOP OF THE NATION $3.95
    58155-5   Canada $4.95